Here Comes Civilization

THE COMPLETE SCIENCE FICTION OF
WILLIAM TENN

VOLUME II

Introduction by Robert Silverberg
Afterword by George Zebrowski

edited by James A. Mann and Mary C. Tabasko

The NESFA Press
Post Office Box 809
Framingham, MA 01701
2001

DEDICATION

This volume is dedicated
To the memory of my parents:
Millie and Aaron-David Klass—
She who gave me my sense of humor,
He who gave me a reason to use it

ACKNOWLEDGEMENTS

This book, like all NESFA Press books, was put together through the efforts of many volunteers. Bill Shawcross of Rotten Apple Press and Rick Katze did most of the scanning. Bill also did a lot of proofreading. Mark Olson helped get the contract approved, unearthed stories, dealt with the printer, and in general provided a lot of support. Eileen Dougherty, Janice Gelb, Leslie Mann, Scot Taylor, and Roz Treger proofed most of the book. George Flynn, copyeditor extraordinaire, thoroughly examined all the stories. Kevin Riley designed and produced the dust jacket. Dennis Lien and Richard Horton helped us track down stories we were missing. Fruma Klass provided significant editorial assistance, and Adina Klass provided technical assistance. Teresa Nielsen Hayden and Terry McGarry provided valuable editorial advice. Laurie Mann and Christina Schulman also pitched in. Finally, a number of colleagues in NESFA, IBM, and elsewhere looked over many sample page layouts, providing us with a user test of the book design.

James A. Mann
Mary C. Tabasko
Pittsburgh, PA
June 2001

CONTENTS

Here Comes Civilization: Introduction iii

HERE COMES CIVILIZATION 1
Bernie the Faust 3
Betelgeuse Bridge 25
"Will You Walk a Little Faster" 39
The House Dutiful 49
There Were People on Bikini, There Were People on Attu 63

THE SOMEWHAT HEAVY FANTASTIC 73
She Only Goes Out at Night... 75
Mistress Sary 81
The Malted Milk Monster 91
The Human Angle 107
Everybody Loves Irving Bommer 113

FOR THE RENT 129
A Matter of Frequency 131
The Ionian Cycle 137
Hallock's Madness 157
Ricardo's Virus 175
The Puzzle of Priipiirii 187
Dud 197
Confusion Cargo 211
Afterword: For the Rent 225

BEATING TIME 229
The Discovery of Morniel Mathaway 231
Sanctuary 243
Me, Myself, and I 255

It Ends with a Flicker   267

The Girl with Some Kind of Past. And George.   279

Flirgleflip   289

Errand Boy   309

A LAMP FOR MEDUSA   323

ESSAY   377

On the Fiction in Science Fiction   379

OF MEN AND MONSTERS   389

Part I: Priests for Their Learning   391

Part II: Soldiers for Their Valor   448

Part III: Counselors for Their Wisdom   487

AFTERWORD TO THE TWO VOLUMES   539

William Tenn: The Swiftest Tortoise   541

Here Comes Civilization

HERE COMES CIVILIZATION: INTRODUCTION
Robert Silverberg

The lone lamentable thing about this two-volume collection of William Tenn's science fiction (of which this is Volume Two, and if you don't already own Volume One, *Immodest Proposals*, you should run right out and buy it) is its subtitle: *The Complete Science Fiction of William Tenn*. In a properly ordered world, the complete science fiction of William Tenn would fill many more volumes than these mere piddling two. You could not get the complete science fiction of Robert A. Heinlein or Philip K. Dick or Isaac Asimov into just two volumes, be they the size of the Manhattan telephone directory. Even Ray Bradbury, who like William Tenn has primarily been a short-story writer, would need half a dozen or more omnibus-sized books. As for the complete science fiction of Robert Silverberg—well, you get the idea.

But here we have the complete William Tenn—the *gesammelte Werke* of a man who has been writing the stuff for more than half a century—and the whole megillah takes only these two volumes. This is truly lamentable, and I lament it herewith. There should be eight volumes this size. There should be eighteen. If you believe that the stories in these two books are brilliant, intricately inventive, and tremendously funny, which I assure you they are, then you ought to read the stories he *didn't* get around to writing.

They are, let me confidently assert, absolutely terrific. The least of them would burn a hole in your memory bank forever. When I think of all the magnificent unwritten William Tenn stories languishing out there in the limbo of nonexistence, I want to weep. The great trilogy set in the parallel universe where Horace Gold and John Campbell are the rival emperors of a decadent Byzantine Empire—the dozen mordant tales of the Solomonic decisions of the Chief Rabbi of Mars—the intricate reverse deconstruction of Heinlein's "By His Bootstraps"—you'd love them. I guarantee it. But where are they? Nowhere, that's where. Phil—that's what I call "William Tenn," *Phil*, because that happens to be his real name, Philip Klass—never got around to writing them. And though he's only in his ninth decade and still posing as an active writer, the same pose that he has hidden behind for the past fifty years, I don't think he ever will.

I'll tell you why, too.

It's this Scheherezade business. In her introduction to Volume One, Connie Willis lets us know that Charles Brown of *Locus* magazine once referred to Phil as "the

Scheherezade of science fiction." I confess I have some issues with that tag—it is very hard for me to envision Scheherezade as a diminutive male Jewish octogenarian with a grizzled beard, and I bet you that Sultan Shahryar would have had an even tougher time with it—but I do see Charles' point. Scheherezade had the gift of gab. She was one of the world's great storytellers, right up there with Homer and Dickens and the Ancient Mariner, a spellbinder whose tales everybody still knows and loves a thousand years later. When she spoke, you had no choice but to listen. Of course, Scheherezade was telling you about Sinbad the Sailor and Ali Baba and Aladdin, irresistible, imperishable stories. But she must also have been quite a talker, because she had to get the Sultan's attention first, so that he would let her tell the stories that would distract him from cutting off her head.

Phil Klass—I remind you, that is the natal name of the man who wrote the Complete Science Fiction of William Tenn—is quite a talker too. And it is my belief that he let the other eight, or ten, or sixteen volumes of the Complete Science Fiction evaporate into the smoky air of ten million cocktail parties instead of writing the damn stuff down.

My image of Phil, a man whom I've known since 1956 or thereabouts, is that of a small man with constantly moving jaws. He was talking a mile a minute when I met him at some gathering of our colleagues in New York in the 1950s, he has talked at the same dizzyingly rapid rate all through the succeeding decades, and, though it's a few years since I've seen him, since we live on opposite coasts of North America these days, I'm quite certain that he is talking right now, back there in far-off Pennsylvania. Now, of course, this being the twenty-first century long fabled in song and story by the members of our little guild, his verbal velocity really ought to be measured metrically, and so we can consider that nowadays he talks at 1.6 kilometers a minute, but the effect is just the same, which is that of a man bubbling over with immensely interesting ideas, all of which he wants to share with you in a single outpouring of breath.

Among those ideas, I'm afraid, were some of his best stories. We professional writers are all taught, back in the days when we were would-be writers who read *Writer's Digest* and studied books on how to double-space manuscripts, that writers must never talk about work in progress, because there is a real risk of talking the work away. Phil knew all about that rule long before I had ever heard the name of John W. Campbell, Jr. He didn't care, or else he is just such a compulsive talker that he can't stop himself. I can remember his talking about a long story that he was writing called "Winthrop Was Stubborn" for something like a year, back in the vicinity of 1956 and the early months of 1957. I got to know the story very well in that time, to the point where I began to think I was writing it myself. I also came to believe that the story wasn't being written at all, merely talked, and great was my surprise when it actually appeared in the August, 1957 issue of *Galaxy* (I remember the date very well, because I had a story in the same issue) under editor Horace Gold's title of "Time Waits for Winthrop." You will find that story—Phil's, not mine—in the first volume of this set, under his original, and preferred, title of "Winthrop Was Stubborn."

"Winthrop Was Stubborn" is the exception that proves the rule. Phil *almost* talked that one away, but somehow he wrote it, anyway. It's a sly, splendidly mordant story, almost as good as the ones you can't read because Phil never bothered to write them. He did the same thing with the novel contained in this volume, *Of Men and Monsters*, talked and talked and talked about writing an actual novel, which he had never done before, and which none of us expected to live long enough to see, even after a piece of it appeared in *Galaxy* in 1963. By that time it had been at least a thousand and one nights in the making, perhaps more; yet it was five years more before the complete opus was offered to an incredulous world by Ballantine Books.

Of Men and Monsters is, unless I've lost count, the only novel Phil Klass has managed to finish. (His other long story, "A Lamp for Medusa," is just a novella.) He's talked the rest away at parties. Some went into thin air and were never heard of again. Others did get written, but not by Phil. You've heard of *Stranger in a Strange Land* by Robert A. Heinlein? *Rendezvous with Rama* by Arthur C. Clarke? *Battlefield Earth* by L. Ron Hubbard? *The Great Gatsby* by F. Scott Fitzgerald? All of these should have borne the William Tenn byline. But he talked about them and talked about them and talked about them at party after party ("my Long Island story," is what he called *Gatsby*, and "my definitive space-opera novel," is how he described *Battlefield Earth*) and the ideas for them sounded terrific. And finally, when they realized he was never actually going to write them, those other guys went ahead and did the job for him. It's a crying shame, one of the great scandals of twentieth-century literature.

Well, now and then he did, over the past five decades plus, actually sit down and write something, and I suppose we should be grateful for the small fraction of the Complete Works of William Tenn that NESFA Press was able to publish in these two slender volumes. Let us rejoice that we do, because, as I said somewhere or other once, he is a writer of witty, cynical, and often darkly comic science fiction—I know I said it, because I'm quoted to that effect on the back cover of these books—and, moreover, he is a *superb* writer of witty, cynical, and often darkly comic science fiction. I will cherish these two books forever, and so should you. And we all should hope that Phil, as he continues to live long and prosper, will perhaps do a little writing once in a while, and give us a few down payments against the magnificent third volume of the Collected Works that he owes us all.

ॐ

Here Comes Civilization

BERNIE THE FAUST

That's what Ricardo calls me. I don't know what I am.

Here I am, I'm sitting in my little nine-by-six office. I'm reading notices of government surplus sales. I'm trying to decide where lies a possible buck and where lies nothing but more headaches.

So the office door opens. This little guy with a dirty face, wearing a very dirty, very wrinkled Palm Beach suit, he walks into my office, and he coughs a bit and he says:

"Would you be interested in buying a twenty for a five?"

That was it. I mean, that's all I had to go on.

I looked him over and I said, "*Wha-at?*"

He shuffled his feet and coughed some more. "A twenty," he mumbled. "A twenty for a five."

I made him drop his eyes and stare at his shoes. They were lousy, cracked shoes, lousy and dirty like the rest of him. Every once in a while, his left shoulder hitched up in a kind of tic. "I give you twenty," he explained to his shoes, "and I buy a five from you with it. I wind up with five, you wind up with twenty."

"How did you get into the building?"

"I just came in," he said, a little mixed up.

"You just *came in*," I put a nasty, mimicking note in my voice. "Now you just go right back downstairs and come the hell out. There's a sign in the lobby—NO BEGGARS ALLOWED."

"I'm not begging." He tugged at the bottom of his jacket. It was like a guy trying to straighten out his slept-in pajamas. "I want to sell you something. A twenty for a five. I give you…"

"You want me to call a cop?"

He looked very scared. "No. Why should you call a cop? I haven't done anything to make you call a cop!"

"I'll call a cop in just a second. I'm giving you fair warning. I just phone down to the lobby and they'll have a cop up here fast. They don't want beggars in this building. This is a building for business."

He rubbed his hand against his face, taking a little dirt off, then he rubbed the hand against the lapel of his jacket and left the dirt there. "No deal?" he asked. "A twenty for a five? You buy and sell things. What's the matter with my deal?"

I picked up the phone.

3

"All right," he said, holding up the streaky palm of his hand. "I'll go. I'll go."

"You better. And shut the door behind you."

"Just in case you change your mind." He reached into his dirty, wrinkled pants pocket and pulled out a card. "You can get in touch with me here. Almost any time during the day."

"Blow," I told him.

He reached over, dropped the card on my desk, on top of all the surplus notices, coughed once or twice, looked at me to see if maybe I was biting. No? No. He trudged out.

I picked the card up between the nails of my thumb and forefinger and started to drop it into the wastebasket.

Then I stopped. A card. It was just so damned out of the ordinary—a slob like that with a card. A card, yet.

For that matter, the whole play was out of the ordinary. I began to be a little sorry I hadn't let him run through the whole thing. Listening to a panhandler isn't going to kill me. After all, what was he trying to do but give me an off-beat sales pitch? I can always use an off-beat sales pitch. I work out of a small office, I buy and sell, but half my stock is good ideas. I'll use ideas, even from a bum.

The card was clean and white, except where the smudge from his fingers made a brown blot. Written across it in a kind of ornate handwriting were the words *Mr. Ogo Eksar*. Under that was the name and the telephone number of a hotel in the Times Square area, not far from my office. I knew that hotel: not expensive, but not a fleabag either—somewhere just under the middle line.

There was a room number in one corner of the card. I stared at it and I felt kind of funny. I really didn't know.

Although come to think of it, why couldn't a panhandler be registered at a hotel? "Don't be a snob, Bernie," I told myself.

A twenty for a five, he'd offered. Man, I'd love to have seen his face if I'd said: Okay, give me the twenty, you take the five, and now get the hell out of here.

The government surplus notices caught my eye. I flipped the card into the waste-basket and tried to go back to business.

Twenty for five. What kind of panhandling pitch would follow it? I couldn't get it out of my mind!

There was only one thing to do. Ask somebody about it. Ricardo? A big college professor, after all. One of my best contacts.

He'd thrown a lot my way—a tip on the college building program that was worth a painless fifteen hundred, an office equipment disposal from the United Nations, stuff like that. And any time I had any questions that needed a college education, he was on tap. All for the couple, three hundred, he got out of me in commissions.

I looked at my watch. Ricardo would be in his office now, marking papers or whatever it is he does there. I dialed his number.

"Ogo Eksar?" he repeated after me. "Sounds like a Finnish name. Or maybe Estonian. From the eastern Baltic, I'd say."

"Forget that part," I said. "This is all I care about." And I told him about the twenty-for-five offer.

He laughed. "That thing again!"

"Some old hustle that the Greeks pulled on the Egyptians?"

"No. Something the Americans pulled. And not a con game. During the depression, a New York newspaper sent a reporter around the city with a twenty-dollar bill which he offered to sell for exactly one dollar. There were no takers. The point being, that even with people out of work and on the verge of starvation, they were so intent on not being suckers that they turned down an easy profit of nineteen hundred percent."

"Twenty for one? This was twenty for five."

"Oh, well, you know, Bernie, inflation," he said, laughing again. "And these days it's more likely to be a television show."

"Television? You should have seen the way the guy was dressed!"

"Just an extra, logical touch to make people refuse to take the offer seriously. University research people operate much the same way. A few years back, a group of sociologists began an investigation of the public's reaction to sidewalk solicitors in charity drives. You know, those people who jingle little boxes on street corners: *Help the Two-Headed Children, Relief for Flood-Ravaged Atlantis?* Well, they dressed up some of their students..."

"You think he was on the level, then, this guy?"

"I think there is a good chance that he was. I don't see why he would have left his card with you, though."

"That I can figure—now. If it's a TV stunt, there must be a lot of other angles wrapped up in it. A giveaway show with cars, refrigerators, a castle in Scotland, all kinds of loot."

"A giveaway show? Well, yes—it could be."

I hung up, took a deep breath, and called Eksar's hotel. He was registered there all right. And he'd just come in.

I went downstairs fast and took a cab. Who knew what other connections he'd made by now?

Going up in the elevator, I kept wondering. How did I go from the twenty-dollar bill to the real big stuff, the TV giveaway stuff, without letting Eksar know that I was on to what it was all about? Well, maybe I'd be lucky. Maybe he'd give me an opening.

I knocked on the door. When he said, "Come in," I came in. But for a second or two I couldn't see a thing.

It was a little room, like all the rooms in that hotel, little and smelly and stuffy. But he didn't have the lights on, any electric lights. The window shade was pulled all the way down.

When my eyes got used to the dark, I was able to pick out this Ogo Eksar character. He was sitting on the bed, on the side nearest me. He was still wearing that crazy rumpled Palm Beach suit.

And you know what? He was watching a program on a funny little portable TV set that he had on the bureau. Color TV. Only it wasn't working right. There were no faces, no pictures, nothing but colors chasing around. A big blob of red, a big blob of orange, and a wiggly border of blue and green and black. A voice was talking from it, but all the words were fouled up. "*Wah-wah, de-wah, de-wah.*"

Just as I came in, he turned it off. "Times Square is a bad neighborhood for TV," I told him. "Too much interference."

"Yes," he said. "Too much interference." He closed up the set and put it away. I wished I'd seen it when it was working right.

Funny thing, you know? I would have expected a smell of liquor in the room, I would have expected to see a couple of empties in the tin trash basket near the bureau. Not a sign.

The only smell in the room was a smell I couldn't recognize. I guess it was the smell of Eksar himself, concentrated.

"Hi," I said, feeling a little uncomfortable because of the way I'd been with him back in the office. So rough I'd been.

He stayed on the bed. "I've got the twenty," he said. "You've got the five?"

"Oh, I guess I've got the five, all right," I said, looking in my wallet hard and trying to be funny. He didn't say a word, didn't even invite me to sit down. I pulled out a bill. "Okay?"

He leaned forward and stared, as if he could see—in all that dimness—what kind of a bill it was. "Okay," he said. "But I'll want a receipt. A notarized receipt."

Well, what the hell, I thought, a notarized receipt. "Then we'll have to go down. There's a druggist on Forty-fifth."

"Okay," he said, getting to his feet with a couple of small coughs that came one, two, three, four, right after one another. "The bathroom's out in the hall. Let me wash up and we'll go down."

I waited for him outside the bathroom, thinking that he'd grown a whole hell of a lot more sanitary all of a sudden.

I could have saved my worries. I don't know what he did in the bathroom, but one thing I knew for sure when he came out: soap and water had nothing to do with it. His face, his neck, his clothes, his hands—they were all as dirty as ever. He still looked like he'd been crawling over a garbage dump all night long.

On the way to the druggist, I stopped in a stationery store and bought a book of blank receipts. I filled out most of it right there. *New York, N.Y.* and the date. *Received from Mr. Ogo Eksar the sum of twenty dollars for a five-dollar bill bearing the serial number .... "That okay?" I asked him. "I'm putting in the serial number to make it look as if you want that particular bill, you know, what the lawyers call the value-received angle."

He screwed his head around and read the receipt. Then he checked the serial number of the bill I was holding. He nodded.

We had to wait for the druggist to get through with a couple of customers. When I signed the receipt, he read it to himself, shrugged and went ahead and stamped it with his seal.

I paid him the two bits: I was the one making the profit.

Eksar slid a crisp new twenty to me along the glass of the counter. He watched while I held it up to the light, first one side, then the other.

"Good bill?" he asked.

"Yes. You understand: I don't know you, I don't know your money."

"Sure. I'd do it myself with a stranger." He put the receipt and my five-dollar bill in his pocket and started to walk away.

"Hey," I said. "You in a hurry?"

"No." He stopped, looking puzzled. "No hurry. But you've got the twenty for a five. We made the deal. It's all over."

"All right, so we made the deal. How about a cup of coffee?"

He hesitated.

"It's on me," I told him. "I'll be a big shot for a dime. Come on, let's have a cup of coffee."

Now he looked worried. "You don't want to back out? I've got the receipt. It's all notarized. I gave you a twenty, you gave me a five. We made a deal."

"It's a deal, it's a deal," I said, shoving him into an empty booth. "It's a deal, it's all signed, sealed and delivered. Nobody's backing out. I just want to buy you a cup of coffee."

His face cleared up, all the way through that dirt. "No coffee. Soup. I'll have some mushroom soup."

"Fine, fine. Soup, coffee, I don't care. I'll have coffee."

I sat there and studied him. He hunched over the soup and dragged it into his mouth, spoonful after spoonful, the living picture of a bum who hadn't eaten all day. But pure essence of bum, triple-distilled, the label of a fine old firm.

A guy like this should be lying in a doorway trying to say no to a cop's nightstick, he should be coughing his alcoholic guts out. He shouldn't be living in a real honest-to-God hotel, or giving me a twenty for a five, or swallowing anything as respectable as mushroom soup.

But it made sense. A TV giveaway show, they want to do this, they hire a damn good actor, the best money can buy, to toss their dough away. A guy who'll be so good a bum that people'll just laugh in his face when he tries to give them a deal with a profit.

"You don't want to buy anything else?" I asked him.

He held the spoon halfway to his mouth and stared at me suspiciously. "Like what?"

"Oh, I don't know. Like maybe you want to buy a ten for a fifty. Or a twenty for a hundred dollars?"

He thought about it, Eksar did. Then he went back to his soup, shoveling away. "That's no deal," he said contemptuously. "What kind of a deal is that?"

"Excuse me for living. I just thought I'd ask. I wasn't trying to take advantage of you." I lit a cigarette and waited.

My friend with the dirty face finished the soup and reached for a paper napkin. He wiped his lips. I watched him: he didn't smudge a spot of the grime around his mouth. He just blotted the drops of soup up. He was dainty in his own special way.

"Nothing else you want to buy? I'm here, I've got time right now. Anything else on your mind, we might as well look into it."

He balled up the paper napkin and dropped it into the soup plate. It got wet. He'd eaten all the mushrooms and left the soup.

"The Golden Gate Bridge," he said all of a sudden.

I dropped the cigarette. "What?"

"The Golden Gate Bridge. The one in San Francisco. I'll buy that. I'll buy it for…" he lifted his eyes to the fluorescent fixtures in the ceiling and thought for a couple of seconds "…say a hundred and twenty-five dollars. Cash on the barrel."

"Why the Golden Gate Bridge?" I asked him like an idiot.

"That's the one I want. You asked me what else I want to buy—well, that's what else. The Golden Gate Bridge."

"What's the matter with the George Washington Bridge? It's right here in New York, it's across the Hudson River. It's a newer bridge. Why buy something all the way out on the coast?"

He grinned at me as if he admired my cleverness. "Oh, no," he said, twitching his left shoulder hard. Up, down, up, down. "I know what I want. The Golden Gate Bridge in San Francisco. A hundred and a quarter. Take it or leave it."

"The *George Washington* Bridge," I argued, talking my head off just so I'd have a chance to think, "has a nice toll set-up, fifty cents a throw, and lots of traffic, plenty of traffic. I don't know what the tolls are on the Golden Gate, but I'm damn sure you don't have anywhere near the kind of traffic that New York can draw. And then there's maintenance. The Golden Gate's one of the longest bridges in the world, you'll go broke trying to keep it in shape. Dollar for dollar, location for location, I'd say the George Washington's a better deal for a man who's buying a bridge."

"The Golden Gate," he said, slamming the table with his open hand and letting a whole series of tics tumble through his face. "I want the Golden Gate and nothing but the Golden Gate. Don't give me a hard time again. Do you want to sell or don't you?"

I'd had a chance to think it through. And I knew that Ricardo's angle had been the angle. I was in.

"Sure I'll sell. If that's what you want, you're the doctor. But look—all I can sell you is my share of the Golden Gate Bridge, whatever equity in it I may happen to own."

He nodded. "I want a receipt. Put that down on the receipt."

I put it down on the receipt. And back we went. The druggist notarized the receipt, shoved the stamping outfit in the drawer under the counter and turned his back on us. Eksar counted out six twenties and one five from a big roll of bills, all of them starchy new. He put the roll back into his pants pocket and started away again.

"More coffee?" I said, catching up. "A refill on the soup?"

He turned a very puzzled look at me and kind of twitched all over. "Why? What do you want to sell now?"

I shrugged. "What do you want to buy? You name it. Let's see what other deals we can work out."

This was all taking one hell of a lot of time, but I had no complaints. I'd made a hundred and forty dollars in fifteen minutes. Say a hundred and thirty-eight fifty, if you deducted expenses like notary fees, coffee, soup—all legitimate expenses, all low. I had no complaints.

But I was waiting for the big one. There had to be a big one.

Of course, it could maybe wait until the TV program itself. They'd be asking me what was on my mind when I was selling Eksar all that crap, and I'd be explaining, and they'd start handing out refrigerators and gift certificates at Tiffany's and...

Eksar had said something while I was away in cloud-land. Something damn unfamiliar. I asked him to say it again.

"The Sea of Azov," he told me. "In Russia. I'll give you three hundred and eighty dollars for it."

I'd never heard of the place. I pursed my lips and thought for a second. A funny amount—three hundred and eighty. And for a whole damn sea. I tried an angle.

"Make it four hundred and you've got a deal."

He began coughing his head off, and he looked mad. "What's the matter," he said between coughs, "three hundred and eighty is a bad price? It's a small sea, one of the smallest. It's only 14,000 square miles. And do you know what the maximum depth is?"

I looked wise. "It's deep enough."

"Forty-nine feet," Eksar shouted. "That's all, forty-nine feet! Where are you going to do better than three hundred and eighty dollars for a sea like that?"

"Take it easy," I said, patting his dirty shoulder. "Let's split the difference. You say three eighty, I want four hundred. How about leaving it at three ninety?" I didn't really care: ten bucks more, ten bucks less. But I wanted to see what would happen.

He calmed down. "Three hundred and ninety dollars for the Sea of Azov," he muttered to himself, a little sore at being a sucker, at being taken. "All I want is the sea itself; it's not as if I'm asking you to throw in the Kerch Strait, or maybe a port like Taganrog or Osipenko..."

"Tell you what." I held up my hands. "I don't want to be hard. Give me my three ninety and I'll throw in the Kerch Strait as a bonus. Now how about that?"

He studied the idea. He sniffled. He wiped his nose with the back of his hand. "All right," he said, finally. "It's a deal. Azov *and* the Kerch Strait for three hundred ninety."

Bang! went the druggist's stamp. The bangs were getting louder.

Eksar paid me with six fifties, four twenties and a ten, all new-looking bills from that thick roll in his pants pocket.

I thought about the fifties still on the roll, and I felt the spit start to ball up in my mouth.

"Okay," I said. "Now what?"

"You still selling?"

"For the right price, sure. You name it."

"There's lots of stuff I could use," he sighed. "But do I need it right now? That's what I have to ask myself."

"Right now is when you've got a chance to buy it. Later—who knows? I may not be around, there may be other guys bidding against you, all kinds of things can happen." I waited a while, but he just kept scowling and coughing. "How about Australia?" I suggested. "Could you use Australia for, say, five hundred bucks? Or Antarctica? I could give you a real nice deal on Antarctica."

He looked interested. "Antarctica? What would you want for it? No—I'm not getting anywhere. A little piece here, a little piece there. It all costs so much."

"You're getting damn favorable prices, buddy, and you know it. You couldn't do better buying at wholesale."

"Then how about wholesale? How much for the whole thing?"

I shook my head. "I don't know what you're talking about. What whole thing?"

He looked impatient. "The whole thing. The world. Earth."

"Hey," I said. "That's a lot."

"Well, I'm tired of buying a piece at a time. Will you give me a wholesale price if I buy it all?"

I shook my head, kind of in and out, not yes, not no. Money was coming up, the big money. This was where I was supposed to laugh in his face and walk away. I didn't even crack a smile. "For the whole planet—sure, you're entitled to a wholesale price. But what is it, I mean, exactly *what* do you want to buy?"

"Earth," he said, moving close to me so that I could smell his stinking breath. "I want to buy Earth. Lock, stock and barrel."

"It's got to be a good price. I'll be selling out completely."

"I'll make it a good price. But this is the deal. I pay two thousand dollars, cash. I get Earth, the whole planet, and you have to throw in some stuff on the Moon. Fishing rights, mineral rights and rights to Moon buried treasure. How about it?"

"It's a hell of a lot."

"I know it's a lot," he agreed. "But I'm paying a lot."

"Not for what you're asking. Let me think about it."

This was the big deal, the big giveaway. I didn't know how much money the TV people had given him to fool around with, but I was pretty sure two thousand was just a starting point. Only what was a sensible, businesslike price for the whole world?

I mustn't be made to look like a penny-ante chiseler on TV. There was a top figure Eksar had been given by the program director.

"You really want the whole thing," I said, turning back to him, "the Earth and the Moon?"

He held up a dirty hand. "Not all the Moon. Just those rights on it. The rest of the Moon you can keep."

"It's still a lot. You've got to go a hell of a lot higher than two thousand dollars for any hunk of real estate that big."

Eksar began wrinkling and twitching. "How—how much higher?"

"Well, let's not kid each other. This is the big time now! We're not talking about bridges or rivers or seas. This is a whole world and part of another that you're buying. It takes dough. You've got to be prepared to spend dough."

"How much?" He looked as if he were jumping up and down inside his dirty Palm

Beach suit. People going in and out of the store kept staring at us. "How *much?*" he whispered.

"Fifty thousand. It's a damn low price. And you know it."

Eksar went limp all over. Even his weird eyes seemed to sag. "You're crazy," he said in a low, hopeless voice. "You're out of your head."

He turned and started for the revolving door, walking in a kind of used-up way that told me I'd really gone over the line. He didn't look back once. He just wanted to get far, far away.

I went through the door after him. I grabbed the bottom of his filthy jacket and held on tight.

"Look, Eksar," I said, fast, as he pulled. "I went over your budget, way over, I can see that. But you know you can do better than two thousand. I want as much as I can get. What the hell, I'm taking time out to bother with you. How many other guys would?"

That got him. He cocked his head, then began nodding. I let go of his jacket as he came around. We were connecting again!

"Good. You level with me, and I'll level with you. Go up a little higher. What's your best price? What's the best you can do?"

He stared down the street, thinking, and his tongue came out and licked at the side of his dirty mouth. His tongue was dirty, too. I mean that! Some kind of black stuff, grease or grime, was all over his tongue.

"How about," he said, after a while, "how about twenty-five hundred? That's as high as I can go. I don't have another cent."

I didn't think so. I've got a feeling when a guy says this is as high as he can go that actually he's prepared to go a little higher. Eksar wanted to make the deal real bad, but he couldn't resist pulling back just a little. He was the kind of guy, he could be absolutely dying of thirst, ready to kick off in a second if he didn't get something to drink. You offer him a glass of water, and you say you want a buck for it. He looks at it with his eyes popping and his tongue all swollen, and he asks will you take ninety-five cents?

He was like me: he was a natural bargainer.

"You can go to three thousand," I urged. "How much is three thousand? Only another five hundred. Look what you get for it. Earth, the whole planet, and fishing and mineral rights and buried treasure, all that stuff on the Moon. How's about it?"

"I can't. I just can't. I wish I could." He shook his head as if to shake loose all those tics and twitches. "Maybe this way. I'll go as high as twenty-six hundred. For that, will you give me Earth and just fishing rights and buried treasure rights on the Moon? You keep the mineral rights. I'll do without them."

"Make it twenty-eight hundred, and you can have the mineral rights, too. You want them, I can tell you do. Treat yourself. Just two hundred bucks more, and you can have them."

"I can't have everything. Some things cost too much. How about twenty-six fifty, without the mineral rights and without the buried treasure rights?"

We were both really swinging now. I could feel it.

"This is my absolutely last offer," I told him. "I can't spend all day on this. I'll go down to twenty-seven hundred and fifty, and not a penny less. For that, I'll give you Earth, and just fishing rights on the Moon. Or just buried treasure rights. You pick whichever one you want."

"All right," he said. "You're a hard man: we'll do it your way."

"Twenty-seven fifty for the Earth, and either fishing or buried treasure rights on the Moon?"

"No, twenty-seven even, and no rights on the Moon. I'll forget about that. Twenty-seven even, and all I get is the Earth."

"Deal!" I sang out, and we struck hands. We shook on it.

Then, with my arm around his shoulders—what did I care about the dirt on his clothes when the guy was worth twenty-seven hundred dollars to me?—we marched back to the drug store.

"I want a receipt," he reminded me.

"Right," I said. "But I put the same stuff on it: that I'm selling you whatever equity I own or have a right to sell. You're getting a lot for your money."

"You're getting a lot of money for what you're selling," he came right back. I liked him. Twitches and dirt or not, he was my kind of guy.

We got back to the druggist for notarization, and, honest, I've never seen a man look more disgusted in my life. "Business is good, huh?" he said. "You two are sure hotting it up."

"Listen, you," I told him. "You just notarize." I showed the receipt to Eksar. "This the way you want it?"

He studied it, coughing. "Whatever equity you own or have a right to sell. All right. And put in, you know, in your capacity as sales agent, your professional capacity."

I changed the receipt and signed it. The druggist notarized.

Eksar brought that lump of money out of his pants pocket. He counted out fifty-four crisp new fifties and laid them on the glass counter. Then he picked up the receipt, folded it and put it away. He started for the door.

I grabbed the money up and went with him. "Anything else?"

"Nothing else," he said. "It's all over. We made our deal."

"I know, but we might find something else, another item."

"There's nothing else to find. We made our deal." And his voice told me he really meant it. It didn't have a trace of the tell-me-more whine that you've got to hear before there's business.

I came to a stop and watched him push out through the revolving door. He went right out into the street and turned left and kept moving, all fast, as if he was in a hell of a hurry.

There was no more business. Okay. I had thirty-two hundred and thirty dollars in my wallet that I'd made in one morning.

But how good had I really been? I mean, what was the top figure in the show's budget? How close had I come to it?

I had a contact who maybe could find out—Morris Burlap.

Morris Burlap is in business like me, only he's a theatrical agent, sharp, real sharp. Instead of selling a load of used copper wire, say, or an option on a corner lot in Brooklyn, he sells talent. He sells a bunch of dancers to a hotel in the mountains, a piano player to a bar, a disc jockey or a comic to late-night radio. The reason he's called Morris Burlap is because of these heavy Harris tweed suits he wears winter and summer, every day in the year. They reinforce the image, he says.

I called him from a telephone booth near the entrance and filled him in on the giveaway show. "Now, what I want to find out—"

"Nothing to find out," he cut in. "There's no such show, Bernie."

"There sure as hell is, Morris. One you haven't heard of."

"There's no such show. Not in the works, not being rehearsed, not anywhere. Look: before a show gets to where it's handing out this kind of dough, it's got to have a slot, it's got to have air time all bought. And before it even buys air time, a packager has prepared a pilot. By then I'd have gotten a casting call—I'd have heard about it a dozen different ways. Don't try to tell me my business, Bernie: when I say there's no such show, there's no such show."

So damn positive he was. I had a crazy idea all of a sudden and turned it off. No. Not that. No.

"Then it's a newspaper or college research thing, like Ricardo said?"

He thought it over. I was willing to sit in that stuffy telephone booth and wait: Morris Burlap has a good head. "Those damn documents, those receipts, newspapers and colleges doing research don't operate that way. And nuts don't either. I think you're being taken, Bernie. How you're being taken, I don't know, but you're being taken."

That was enough for me. Morris Burlap can smell a hustle through sixteen feet of rockwool insulation. He's never wrong. Never.

I hung up, sat, thought. The crazy idea came back and exploded.

A bunch of characters from outer space, say they want Earth. They want it for a colony, for a vacation resort, who the hell knows what they want it for? They got their reasons. They're strong enough and advanced enough to come right down and take over. But they don't want to do it cold.

You know, a big country wants to invade a small country, it doesn't start until there's at least a riot on the border. It gives them a legal leg. Even a big country needs a legal leg.

All right. These characters from outer space, maybe all they had to have was a piece of paper from just one genuine, accredited human being, signing the Earth over to them. No, that couldn't be right. *Any* piece of paper? Signed by *any* Joe Jerk?

I jammed a dime into the telephone and called Ricardo's college. He wasn't in. I told the switchboard girl it was very important: she said, all right, she'd ring around and try to spot him.

All that stuff, I kept thinking, the Golden Gate Bridge, the Sea of Azov—they were as much a part of the hook as the twenty-for-a-five routine. There's one sure test of what an operator is really after: when he stops talking, closes up shop and goes away.

With Eksar, it had been the Earth. All that baloney about extra rights on the Moon! They were put in to cover up the real thing he was after, for extra bargaining power.

I go out to buy a shipment of small travel alarm clocks that I've heard a jobber is stuck with. Do I start arguing about the price of clocks? I do not. I tell the jobber I want to buy a truckload of folding ladies' umbrellas, maybe a couple of gross of alarm clocks, say travel alarms if he's got a nice buy in them, and can he do me any good in the men's wallet line?

That's what Eksar had worked on me. It was like he'd made a special study of how I operate. From me alone, he had to buy.

But why me?

All that stuff on the receipt, about my equity, about my professional capacity, what the hell did it mean? I don't own Earth; I'm not in the planet-selling business. You have to own a planet before you can sell it. That's law.

So what could I have sold Eksar? I don't own any real estate. Are they going to take over my office, claim the piece of sidewalk I walk on, attach the stool in the diner where I have my coffee?

That brought me back to my first question. Who was this "they"? Who the holy hell were "they"?

The switchboard girl finally dug up Ricardo. He was irritated. "I'm in the middle of a faculty meeting, Bernie. Call you back?"

"Just listen a second," I begged. "I'm in something, I don't know whether I'm coming or going. I've got to have some advice."

Talking fast—I could hear a lot of big-shot voices in the background—I ran through the story from the time I'd called him in the morning. What Eksar looked like and smelled like, the funny portable color TV he had, the way he'd dropped all those Moon rights and gone charging off once he'd been sure of the Earth. What Morris Burlap had said, the suspicions I'd been building up, everything. "Only thing is," I laughed a little to show that maybe I wasn't really serious about it, "who am I to make such a deal, huh?"

He seemed to be thinking hard for a while. "I don't know, Bernie, it's possible. It does fit together. There's the U.N. aspect."

"U.N. aspect? Which U.N. aspect?"

"The U.N. aspect of the situation. The—uh—study of the U.N. on which we collaborated two years ago." He was using double-talk because of the college people around him. But I got it. I got it.

Eksar must have known all along about the deal that Ricardo had thrown my way, getting rid of old, used-up office equipment for the United Nations here in New York. They'd given me what they called an authorizing document. In a file somewhere there was a piece of paper, United Nations stationery, saying that I was their authorized sales agent for surplus, second-hand equipment and installations.

Talk about a legal leg!

"You think it'll stand up?" I asked Ricardo. "I can see how the Earth is second-hand equipment and installations. But surplus?"

"International law is a tangled field, Bernie. And this might be even more complex. You'd be wise to do something about it."

"But what? What should I do, Ricardo?"

"Bernie," he said, sounding sore as hell, "I told you I'm in a faculty meeting, damn it! A *faculty* meeting!" And he hung up.

I ran out of the drug store like a wild man and grabbed a cab back to Eksar's hotel.

What was I most afraid of? I didn't know, I was so hysterical. This thing was too big-time for a little guy like me, too damn dangerously big-time. It would put my name up in lights as the biggest sellout sucker in history. Who could ever trust me again to make a deal? I had the feeling like somebody had asked me to sell him a snapshot, and I'd said sure, and it turned out to be a picture of the Nike Zeus, you know, one of those top-secret atomic missiles. Only this was worse: I'd sold out my whole goddamn world. I had to buy it back—I had to!

When I got to Eksar's room, I knew he was about ready to check out. He was shoving his funny portable TV in one of those cheap leather grips they sell in chain stores. I left the door open, for the light.

"We made our deal," he said. "It's over. No more deals."

I stood there, blocking his way. "Eksar," I told him, "listen to what I figured out. First, you're not human. Like me, I mean."

"I'm a hell of a lot more human than you, buddy boy."

"Oh, sure. You're a custom-built Cadillac and I'm a four-cylinder factory job. But you're not from Earth—that's my point. My point is why you want Earth. You can't personally need a—"

"I *don't* need it. I'm an agent. I represent someone."

And there it was, straight out, you are right, Morris Burlap! I stared into his fish eyes, practically pushing into my face. I wouldn't budge an inch if he killed me. "You're an agent for someone," I repeated slowly. "Who? What do they want Earth for?"

"That's their business. I'm an agent. I just buy for them."

"You work on a commission?"

"I'm not in business for my health."

You sure as hell aren't in it for your health, I thought. *That cough, those tics and twitches—* Then I realized what they meant. This wasn't the kind of air he was used to. Like if I go up to Canada, right away I'm down with diarrhea. It's the water or something.

The dirt on his face was a kind of suntan oil! A protection against our sunlight. Blinds pulled down, face smeared over—and dirt all over his clothes so they'd fit in with his face.

Eksar was no bum. He was anything but. I was the bum. Think, Bernie, I said to myself. Think and hustle and operate like you never did before in your whole life. This guy took you, and big!

"How much you work on—ten percent?" No answer: he leaned his chest against mine, and he breathed and he twitched, he breathed and he twitched. "I'll top any deal you have, Eksar. You know what I'll give you? Fifteen percent! I'm the kind of a guy, I hate to see someone running back and forth for a lousy ten percent."

"What about ethics?" he said hoarsely. "I got a client."

"Look who's bringing up ethics! A guy goes out to buy the whole damn Earth for twenty-seven hundred! You call that ethics?"

Now he got sore. He set down the grip and punched his fist into his hand. "No, I call that business. A deal. I offer, you take. You go away happy, you feel you made out. All of a sudden, here you are back, crying you didn't mean it, you sold too much for the price. Too bad! I got ethics: I don't screw my client for a crybaby."

"I'm not a crybaby. I'm just a poor shnook trying to scratch out a living. But who are you? You're a big-time operator from another world with all kinds of gimmicks going for you, buttons you can press, angles I can't even begin to figure."

"You had these angles, these gimmicks, you wouldn't use them?"

"Certain things I wouldn't use, certain things I wouldn't do. Don't laugh, Eksar, I mean it. I wouldn't hustle a guy in an iron lung no matter how much of a buck was in it. And I wouldn't hustle a poor shnook with a hole-in-the-wall office and leave him looking like he's sold out his entire planet."

"Sold out isn't the word for it," he said. "That receipt you signed will stand up anywhere. We got the legal machinery to make it stand up, and we got other machinery, too, planet-size machinery. Once my client takes possession, the human race is finished, it's *kaput*, gone with the wind, forget about it. And you're Mr. Patsy."

It was hot in that hotel room doorway, and I was sweating like crazy. But I was feeling better. First that ethics pitch, now this routine of trying to scare the hell out of me. Maybe his deal with his client wasn't so good, maybe something else, but one thing I knew—Eksar wanted to do business with me. I grinned at him.

He got it. He changed color a little under all that dirt. "What's your offer, anyway?" he asked, coughing. "Name a figure."

"Well, I'll admit you're entitled to a profit. That's only fair. Let's say thirty-one hundred and five. The twenty-seven you paid, plus a full fifteen percent. Do we have a deal?"

"Hell no!" he screamed. "On all three deals, you got a total of thirty-two hundred and thirty dollars out of me—and you're offering thirty-one hundred five to buy it back? You're going down, buddy, you're going down instead of up! Get out of my way—I'm wasting time."

He turned a little and pushed me out of the way. I banged across the corridor. He was *strong!* I ran after him to the elevator—that receipt was still in his pocket.

"How much *do* you want, Eksar?" I asked him as we were going down. Get him to name a price, then I can bargain from it, I figured.

A shrug. "I got a planet, and I got a buyer for it. You, you're in a jam. The one in a pickle is the one who's got to tickle."

The louse! For every one of my moves, he knew the countermove.

He checked out and I followed him into the street. Down Broadway we went, people staring at a respectable guy like me walking with such a Bowery-type character.

I threw up my hands and offered him the thirty-two hundred and thirty he'd paid me. He said he couldn't make a living out of shoving the same amount of money back and forth all day.

"Thirty-four, then? I mean, you know, thirty-four fifty?"

He didn't say anything. He just kept walking.

"You want it all?" I said. "Okay, take it all, thirty-seven hundred—every last cent. You win."

Still no answer. I was getting worried. I had to get him to name a figure, any figure at all, or I'd be dead.

I ran in front of him. "Eksar, let's stop hustling each other. If you didn't want to sell, you wouldn't be talking to me in the first place. You name a figure. Whatever it is, I'll pay it."

That got a reaction. "You mean it? You won't try to chisel?"

"How can I chisel? I'm over a barrel."

"Okay. It's a long, long trip back to where my client is. Why should I knock myself out when I can help somebody who's in trouble? Let's see—we need a figure that's fair for you and fair for me and fair all around. That would be—oh, say, sixteen thousand."

So there it was. I was booked for a thorough bath. Eksar saw my face and began laughing. He laughed himself into a coughing fit.

Choke, you bastard, I thought, *choke! I hope the air of this planet poisons you. I hope you get gangrene of the lungs.*

That sixteen thousand figure—it was exactly twice what I had in the bank. He knew my bank account cold, up to the last statement.

He knew my thoughts cold, too. "You're going to do business with a guy," he said, between coughs, "you check into him a little."

"Tell me more," I said sarcastically.

"All right. You got seven thousand, eight hundred and change. Two hundred more in accounts receivable. The rest you'll borrow."

"That's all I need to do—go into hock on this deal!"

"You can borrow a little," he coaxed. "A guy like you, in your position, with your contacts, you can borrow a little. I'll settle for twelve thousand. I'll be a good guy. Twelve thousand?"

"Baloney, Eksar. You know me so well, you know I can't borrow."

He looked away at the pigeon-green statue of Father Duffy in front of the Palace Theater. "The trouble is," he said in a mournful voice, "that I wouldn't feel right going back to my client and leaving you in such a jam. I'm just not built that way." He threw back his twitching shoulders—you knew, he was about to take a beating for a friend, and he was proud of himself. "Okay, then. I'll take only the eight thousand you have and we'll call it square."

"Are you through, you mother's little helper you, you Florence Goddamn Nightingale? Then let me set you straight. You're not getting any eight thousand out of me. A profit, yes, a little skin I know I have to give up. But not every cent I own, not in a million years, not for you, not for Earth, not for anybody!"

I'd been yelling, and a cop walking by came in close for a look. I thought of calling out "Help! Police! Aliens invading us!" but I knew it was all up to me. I calmed down and waited until he went away, puzzled. But the Broadway we were all standing on—what would it look like in ten years if I didn't talk Eksar out of that receipt?

"Eksar, your client takes over Earth waving my receipt—I'll be hung high. But I've got only one life, and my life is buying and selling. I can't buy and sell without capital. Take my capital away, and it makes no difference to me who owns Earth and who doesn't."

"Who the hell do you think you're kidding?" he said.

"I'm not kidding anybody. Honest, it's the truth. Take my capital away, and it makes no difference if I'm alive or if I'm dead."

That last bit of hustle seemed to have reached him. Listen, there were practically tears in my eyes the way I was singing it. How much capital did I need, he wanted to know—five hundred? I told him I couldn't operate one single day with less than seven times that. He asked me if I was really seriously trying to buy my lousy little planet back—or was today my birthday and I was expecting a present from him? "Don't give your presents to me," I told him. "Give them to fat people. They're better than going on a diet."

And so we went. Both of us talking ourselves blue in the face, swearing by everything, arguing and bargaining, wheeling and dealing. It was touch and go who was going to give up first.

But neither of us did. We both held out until we reached what I'd figured pretty early we were going to wind up with, maybe a little bit more.

Six thousand, one hundred and fifty dollars.

That was the price over and above what Eksar had given me. The final deal. Listen, it could have been worse.

Even so, we almost broke up when we began talking payment.

"Your bank's not far. We could get there before closing."

"Why walk myself into a heart attack? My check's good as gold."

"Who wants a piece of paper? I want cash. Cash is definite."

Finally, I managed to talk him into a check. I wrote it out, he took it and gave me the receipts, all of them The twenty for a five, the Golden Gate Bridge, the Sea of Azov—every last receipt I'd signed. Then he picked up his little satchel and marched away.

Straight down Broadway, without even a good-by. All business, Eksar was, nothing but business. He didn't look back once.

All business. I found out next morning he'd gone right to the bank and had my check certified before closing time. What do you think of that? I couldn't do a damn thing: I was out six thousand, one hundred and fifty dollars. Just for talking to someone.

Ricardo said I was a Faust. I walked out of the bank, beating my head with my fist, and I called up him and Morris Burlap and asked them to have lunch with me. I went over the whole story with them in an expensive place that Ricardo picked out. "You're a Faust," he said.

"What Faust?" I asked him. "Who Faust? How Faust?"

So naturally he had to tell us all about Faust. Only I was a new kind of Faust, a twentieth-century American one. The other Fausts, they wanted to know everything. I wanted to own everything.

"But I didn't wind up owning," I pointed out. "I got taken. Six thousand one hundred and fifty dollars worth I got taken."

Ricardo chuckled and leaned back in his chair. "O my sweet gold," he said under his breath. "O my sweet gold."

"What?"

"A quotation, Bernie. From Marlowe's *Doctor Faustus*. I forget the context, but it seems apt. '*O my sweet gold.*' "

I looked from him to Morris Burlap, but nobody can ever tell when Morris Burlap is puzzled. As a matter of fact, he looks more like a professor than Ricardo, him with those thick Harris tweeds and that heavy, thinking look. Ricardo is, you know, a bit too natty.

The two of them added up to all the brains and sharpness a guy could ask for. That's why I was paying out an arm and a leg for this lunch, on top of all my losses with Eksar.

"Morris, tell the truth. You understand him?"

"What's there to understand, Bernie? A quote about the sweet gold? It might be the answer, right there."

Now I looked at Ricardo. He was eating away at a creamy Italian pudding. Two bucks even, those puddings cost in that place.

"Let's say he was an alien," Morris Burlap said. "Let's say he came from somewhere in outer space. Okay. Now what would an alien want with U.S. dollars? What's the rate of exchange out there? How much is a dollar worth forty, fifty light years away?"

"You mean he needed it to buy some merchandise here on Earth?"

"That's exactly what I mean. But what *kind* of merchandise, that's the question. What could Earth have that he'd want?"

Ricardo finished the pudding and wiped his lips with a napkin. "I think you're on the right track, Morris," he said, and I swung my attention back to him. "We can postulate a civilization far in advance of our own. One that would feel we're not quite ready to know about them. One that has placed primitive little Earth strictly off limits—a restriction only desperate criminals dare ignore."

"From where come criminals, Ricardo, if they're so advanced?"

"Laws produce lawbreakers, Bernie, like hens produce eggs. Civilization has nothing to do with it. I'm beginning to see Eksar now. An unprincipled adventurer, a star-man version of those cutthroats who sailed the South Pacific a hundred years or more ago. Once in a while, a ship would smash up against the coral reefs, and a bloody opportunist out of Boston would be stranded for life among primitive, backward tribesmen. I'm sure you can fill in the rest."

"No, I can't. And if you don't mind, Ricardo—"

Morris Burlap said he'd like another brandy. I ordered it. He came as close to smiling as Morris Burlap ever does and leaned toward me confidentially. "Ricardo's got it, Bernie. Put yourself in this guy Eksar's position. He wraps up his spaceship on a dirty little planet which it's against the law to be near in the first place. He can make some half-assed repairs with merchandise that's available here—but he has to buy the stuff. Any noise, any uproar, and he'll be grabbed for a Federal rap in outer space. Say you're Eksar, what do you do?"

I could see it now. "I'd peddle and I'd parlay. Copper bracelets, strings of beads, dollars—whatever I had to lay my hands on to buy the native merchandise, I'd peddle and I'd parlay in deal after deal. Until I'd run it up to the amount I needed. Maybe I'd get my start with a piece of equipment from the ship, then I'd find some novelty item that the natives would go for. But all this is *Earth* business know-how, *human* business know-how."

"Bernie," Ricardo told me, "Indians once traded pretty little shells for beaver pelts at the exact spot where the Stock Exchange now stands. Some kind of business goes on in Eksar's world, I assure you, but its simplest form would make one of our corporate mergers look like a game of potsy on the sidewalk."

Well, I'd wanted to figure it out. "So I was marked as his fish all the way. I was screwed and blued and tattooed," I mumbled, "by a hustler superman."

Ricardo nodded. "By a businessman's Mephistopheles fleeing the thunderbolts of heaven. He needed to double his money one more time and he'd have enough to repair his ship. He had at his disposal a fantastic sophistication in all the ways of commerce."

"What Ricardo's saying," came an almost-soft voice from Morris Burlap, "is the guy who beat you up was a whole lot bigger than you."

My shoulders felt loose, like they were sliding down off my arms. "What the hell," I said. "You get stepped on by a horse or you get stepped on by an elephant. You're still stepped on."

I paid the check, got myself together and went away.

Then I began to wonder if maybe this was really the story after all. They both enjoyed seeing me up there as an interplanetary jerk. Ricardo's a brilliant guy, Morris Burlap's sharp as hell, but so what? Ideas, yes. Facts, no.

So here's a fact.

My bank statement came at the end of the month with that canceled check I'd given Eksar. It had been endorsed by a big store in the Cortlandt Street area. I know that store. I've dealt with them. I went down and asked them about it.

They handle mostly marked-down, surplus electronic equipment. That's what they said Eksar had bought. A walloping big order of transistors and transformers, resistors and printed circuits, electronic tubes, wiring, tools, gimmicks like that. All mixed up, they said, a lot of components that just didn't go together. He'd given the clerk the impression that he had an emergency job to do—and he'd take as close as he could get to the things he actually needed. He'd paid a lot of money for freight charges: delivery was to some backwoods town in northern Canada.

That's a fact, now, I have to admit it. But here's another one.

I've dealt with that store, like I said. Their prices are the lowest in the neighborhood. And why is it, do you think, they can sell so cheap? There's only one answer: because they buy so cheap. They buy at the lowest prices; they don't give a damn about quality: all they want to know is, how much mark-up? I've personally sold them job-lots of electronic junk that I couldn't unload anywhere else, condemned stuff, badly wired stuff, stuff that was almost dangerous—it's a place to sell when you've given up on making a profit because you yourself have been stuck with inferior merchandise in the first place.

You get the picture? It makes me feel rosy all over.

There is Eksar out in space, the way I see it. He's fixed up his ship, good enough to travel, and he's on his way to his next big deal. The motors are humming, the ship is running, and he's sitting there with a big smile on his dirty face: he's thinking how he took me, how easy it was.

He's laughing his head off.

All of a sudden, there's a screech and a smell of burning. That circuit that's running the front motor, a wire just got touched through the thin insulation, the circuit's tearing the hell out of itself. He gets scared. He turns on the auxiliaries. The auxiliaries don't go on—you know why? The vacuum tubes he's using have come to the end of their rope, they didn't have much juice to start with. *Blooie!* That's the rear motor developing a short-circuit. *Ka-pow!* That's a defective transformer melting away in the middle of the ship.

And there he is, millions of miles from nowhere, empty space all around him, no more spare parts, tools that practically break in his hands—and not a single, living soul he can hustle.

And here am I, walking up and down in my nine-by-six office, thinking about it, and *I'm* laughing my head off. Because it's just possible, it just could happen, that what goes wrong with his ship is one of the half-dozen or so job-lots of really bad electronic equipment that I personally, me, Bernie the Faust, that I sold to that surplus store at one time or another.

That's all I'd ask. Just to have it happen that way.

Faust. He'd have Faust from me then. Right in the face, Faust. On the head, splitting it open, Faust.

Faust he wants? *Faust* I'd give him!

AFTERWORD

I have written stories like "Child's Play" and "The Flat-Eyed Monster" by, in effect, reading them for the first time as I wrote them—finding out with some fascination what happens on a given page only when I have completed the page. But for "Bernie the Faust," I used the technique of what I call *mining* for a story.

Lester del Rey had told me of the newspaper reporter back in the Depression who had offered people a twenty-dollar bill for a dollar—and found no takers. We both felt there was a story there somewhere, and he told me that if I could do it, I was welcome to it.

I made a number of tries at it, off and on, over several years, and, finally, in 1960, it began to take off. I wrote and wrote, page after page after page, trying to find out what the story wanted to say to me. I called the piece "The Giveaway Show," and when I finished the first draft, it was thirty-three thousand words long and it plunged in several different directions, like a maddened horse.

But I had found the direction I liked, and I began again with the title, "Bernie the Faust."

This version worked out to be twenty-five thousand words in length, which was too short for a novel and too long for a novelette, in other words, unsaleable according to the publishing conventions of science-fiction magazines of the day. After two months of rewriting, I had it down twelve thousand, five hundred words—a novelette. I sent it to my then agent, one of the most important general fiction agents of that time; she had told me she was going to sell me to *Harper's* and *The New Yorker* and points north; she sent it back to me by return post. "Don't just tear this up, Phil," she said, "but keep it near you and look at it from time to time, and ask yourself, 'How could I, a gifted professional writer, come to write such a piece of shit?'"

Well. I had to recover something for all that work, so I sent it around to the magazines with which I regularly dealt, from *Galaxy* on down, four-cents-a-word markets down to a half cent. They all bounced it, with comments ranging from the regretful to the pitying.

I acquired a new agent, Henry Morrison. I showed him—and apologized for showing it to him—"Bernie the Faust." To my astonishment—he liked it. He liked it so much, he sent it to *Playboy.* To my further astonishment, A.C. Spectorsky, the editorial director of *Playboy,* also liked it.

"The only problem," Henry Morrison told me over the phone, "is that Spec feels, as it stands, it's still too long for *Playboy*. If you can cut it down to, say, eighty-five hundred or nine thousand words, he'll definitely buy it."

"I can't do it, Henry," I said. "There's no fat at all left in the piece. All there is is the humor basic to the story itself. No fat—just bone."

"Good enough. I wouldn't ask you to damage the story. But, as your agent, I have to tell you that they're thinking of using it as what they call a front-of-the-book piece. That would mean five thousand dollars. I do have to tell you that."

Then I must tell you who are reading this that the most money I had ever received up to then for a story was seven hundred dollars—and that was for something twenty-three thousand words long. Five thousand dollars! And remember, please, we are talking about the year 1962… I mean, five *thousand* dollars?

"I don't care," my wife, Fruma, said to me. "With all the rejections, it's still a *good* story. You cut it up and tear it to pieces, and I swear I'll leave you."

And she went to bed, I into my study to begin trying to cut. A word here, a sentence there, once in a while a short paragraph. But no block cuts that I could see—none of the necessary big deletions. I came to the end of the story with a hundred and ten words gone, and began again. A couple of words here, maybe a sentence or two there, a longish speech by a not-too-important character. Maybe the character himself? The talkative notarizing druggist shrank to three short appearances.

When Fruma looked in on me next morning, the story was no longer twelve thousand, five hundred words long. Nor was it nine thousand words or eight thousand words long. It was a shade over five thousand, five hundred words.

"Where did it all go to?" Fruma asked after reading. "All the good stuff is still there. It's even better now."

I agreed. I pretty much still agree.

Playboy bought it for five thousand dollars. It was reprinted in several best-of-the-year anthologies in the U.S. and in Britain. I'm still proud of my double-*luftmensch* story.

The version printed here has had a couple of small cuts added—about five or six hundred words worth.

WRITTEN 1960——PUBLISHED 1963

ه

BETELGEUSE BRIDGE

You tell them, Alvarez, old boy; you know how to talk to them. This isn't my kind of Public Relations. All I care about is that they get the pitch exactly right with all the implications and complications and everything just the way they really are.

If it hurts, well, let them yell. Just use your words and get it right. Get it all.

You can start with the day the alien spaceship landed outside Baltimore. Makes you sick to think how we never tumbled, doesn't it, Alvarez? No more than a hop, skip and a jet from the Capitol dome, and we thought it was just a lucky accident.

Explain why we thought it was so lucky. Explain about the secrecy it made possible, how the farmer who telephoned the news was placed in special and luxurious custody, how a hand-picked cordon of M.P.s paced five square miles off into an emergency military reservation a few hours later, how Congress was called into secret session and the way it was all kept out of the newspapers.

How and why Trowson, my old sociology prof, was consulted once the problem became clear. How he blinked at the brass hats and striped pants and came up with the answer.

Me. I was the answer.

How my entire staff and I were plucked out of our New York offices, where we were quietly earning a million bucks, by a flying squad of the F.B.I. and air-mailed to Baltimore. Honestly, Alvarez, even after Trowson explained the situation to me, I was still irritated. Government hush-hush always makes me uncomfortable. Though I don't have to tell you how grateful I was for it later.

The spaceship itself was such a big surprise that I didn't even wet my lips when the first of the aliens *slooshed* out. After all those years of streamlined cigar-shapes the Sunday Supplement artists had dreamed up, that colorful and rococo spheroid rearing out of a barley field in Maryland looked less like an interplanetary vessel than an oversized ornament for a what-not table. Nothing that seemed like a rocket jet anywhere.

"And there's your job," the prof pointed. "Those two visitors."

They were standing on a flat metal plate surrounded by the highest the republic had elected or appointed. Nine feet of slimy green trunk tapering up from a rather wide base to a pointed top, and crested with a tiny pink and white shell, Two stalks with eyes on them that swung this way and that, and seemed muscular enough to throttle a man. And a huge wet slash of a mouth that showed whenever an edge of the squirming base lifted from the metal plate.

25

"Snails," I said. *"Snails!"*

"Or slugs," Trowson amended. "Gastropodal mollusks in any case." He gestured at the roiling white bush of hair that sprouted from his head. "But, Dick, that vestigial bit of coiled shell is even less an evolutionary memento than this. They're an older—and smarter—race."

"Smarter?"

He nodded. "When our engineers got curious, they were very courteously invited inside to inspect the ship. They came out with their mouths hanging."

I began to get uncomfortable. I ripped a small piece off my hangnail. "Well, naturally, prof, if they're so alien, so different—"

"Not only that. Superior. Get that, Dick, because it'll be very important in what you have to do. The best engineering minds that this country can assemble in a hurry are like a crowd of Caribbean Indians trying to analyze the rifle and compass from what they know of spears and windstorms. These creatures belong to a galaxy-wide civilization composed of races *at least* as advanced as they; we're a bunch of backward hicks in an unfrequented hinterland of space that's about to be opened to exploration. Exploitation, perhaps, if we can't measure up. We have to give a very good impression and we have to learn fast."

A dignified official with a briefcase detached himself from the nodding, smiling group around the aliens and started for us.

"Whew!" I commented brilliantly. "Fourteen ninety-two, repeat performance." I thought for a moment, not too clearly. "But why send the army and navy after *me*? I'm not going to be able to read blueprints from—from—"

"Betelgeuse. Ninth planet of the star Betelgeuse. No, Dick, we've already had Dr. Warbury out here. They learned English from him in two hours, although he hasn't identified a word of theirs in three days! And people like Lopez, like Mainzer, are going quietly psychotic trying to locate their power source. We have the best minds we can get to do the learning. Your job is different. We want you as a top-notch advertising man, a public relations executive. You're the good impression part of the program."

The official plucked at my sleeve and I shrugged him away. "Isn't that the function of government glad-handers?" I asked Trowson.

"No. Don't you remember what you said when you first saw them? *Snails!* How do you think this country is going to take to the idea of snails—giant snails—who sneer condescendingly at our skyscraper cities, our atomic bombs, our most advanced mathematics? We're a conceited kind of monkey. Also, we're afraid of the dark."

There was a gentle official tap on my shoulder. I said *"Please!"* impatiently. I watched the warm little breeze ruffle Professor Trowson's slept-in clothes and noticed the tiny red streaks in his weary eyes.

"Mighty Monsters from Outer Space. Headlines like that, prof?"

"Slugs with Superiority Complexes. *Dirty* Slugs, more likely. We're lucky they landed in this country, and so close to the Capitol, too. In a few days, we'll have to call in the heads of other nations. Then, sometime soon after, the news will be out. We don't want our visitors attacked by mobs drunk on superstition, planetary isolation or any other form of tabloid hysteria. We don't want them carrying stories back to their civilization of being shot at by a suspendered fanatic who screamed, 'Go back where you came from, you furrin seafood!' We want to give them the impression that we are a fairly amiable, fairly intelligent race, that we can be dealt with reasonably well."

I nodded. "Yeah. So they'll set up trading posts on this planet instead of garrisons. But what do I do in all this?"

He punched my chest gently. "You, Dick—you do a job of public relations. You sell these aliens to the American people!"

The official had maneuvered around in front of me. I recognized him. He was the Undersecretary of State.

"Would you step this way, please?" he said. "I'd like to introduce you to our distinguished guests."

So I stepped this way please, and we went all across the field and clanked across the steel plate and stood next to our gastropodal guests.

"Ahem," said the Undersecretary politely.

The nearer snail bent an eye toward us. The other eye drew a bead on the companion snail, and then the great slimy head arched and came down to our level. The creature raised, as it were, one cheek of its foot and said, with all the mellowness of air being pumped through a torn inner tube, "Can it be that you wish to communicate with my unworthy self, respected sir?"

I was introduced. The thing brought two eyes to bear on me. The place where its chin should have been dropped to my feet and snaked around there for a second. Then it said, "You, honored sir, are our touchstone, the link with all that is great in your noble race. Your condescension is truly a tribute."

All this tumbled out while I was muttering "How," and extending a diffident hand. The snail put one eyeball in my palm and the other on the back of my wrist. It didn't shake; it just put the things there and took them away again. I had the wit not to wipe my hands on my pants, which was my immediate impulse. The eyeball wasn't exactly dry, either.

I said, "I'll do my best. Tell me, are you—uh—ambassadors, sort of? Or maybe just explorers?"

"Our small worth justifies no titles," said the creature, "yet we are both; for all communication is ambassadorship of a kind, and any seeker after knowledge is an explorer."

I was suddenly reminded of an old story with the punchline, "Ask a foolish question and you get a foolish answer." I also wondered suddenly what snails eat.

The second alien glided over and eyed me. "You may depend upon our utmost obedience," it said humbly. "We understand your awesome function and we wish to be liked to whatever extent it is possible for your admirable race to like such miserable creatures as ourselves."

"Stick to that attitude and we'll get along," I said.

By and large they were a pleasure to work with. I mean there was no temperament, no upstaging, no insistence on this camera angle or that mention of a previously published book or the other wistful biographical apocrypha about being raised in a convent, like most of my other clients.

On the other hand they weren't easy to talk to. They'd take orders, sure. But ask them a question. Any question:

"How long did the trip take you?"

" 'How long' in your eloquent tongue indicates a frame of reference dealing with duration. I hesitate to discuss so complex a problem with one as learned as yourself. The velocities involved make it necessary to answer in relative terms. Our lowly and undesirable planet recedes from this beauteous system during part of its orbital period, advances toward it during part. Also we must take into consideration the direction and velocity of our star in reference to the cosmic expansion of this portion of the continuum. Had we come from Cygnus, say, or Bootes, the question could be answered somewhat more directly; for those bodies travel in a contiguous arc skewed from the ecliptic plane in such a way that—"

Or a question like, "Is your government a democracy?"

"A democracy is a rule of the people, according to your rich etymology. We could not, in our lowly tongue, have expressed it so succinctly and movingly. One must govern oneself, of course. The degree of governmental control on the individual must vary from individual to individual and in the individual from time to time. This is so evident to as comprehensive a mind as yours that I trust you forgive me my inanities. The same control applies, naturally, to individuals considered in the mass. When faced with a universal necessity, the tendency exists among civilized species to unite to fill the need. Therefore, when no such necessity exists, there is less reason for concerted effort. Since this applies to all species, it applies even to such as us. On the other hand—"

See what I mean? A little of that got old quickly with me. I was happy to keep my nose to my own grindstone.

The government gave me a month for the preparatory propaganda. Originally, the story was to break in two weeks, but I got down on my hands and knees and bawled that a publicity deadline required at least five times that. So they gave me a month.

Explain that carefully, Alvarez. I want them to understand exactly what a job I faced. All those years of lurid magazine covers showing extremely nubile females being menaced in four distinct colors by assorted monstrosities; those horror movies, those invasion-from-outer-space novels, those Sunday Supplement fright-splashes—all those sturdy psychological ruts I had to retrack. Not to mention the shudders elicited by mention of "worms," the regulation distrust of even human foreigners, the superstitious dread of creatures who had no visible place to park a soul.

Trowson helped me round up the men to write the scientific articles, and I dug up the boys who could pseudo them satisfactorily. Magazine mats were ripped apart to make way for yarns speculating gently on how far extraterrestrial races might have evolved beyond us, how much more ethical they might have become, how imaginary seven-headed creatures could still apply the Sermon on the Mount. Syndicated features popped up describing "Humble Creatures Who Create Our Gardens," "Snail-Racing, the Spectacular New Spectator Sport," and so much stuff on "The Basic Unity of All Living Things" that I began to get uncomfortable at even a vegetarian dinner. I remember hearing there was a perceptible boom in mineral waters and vitamin pills....

And all this, mind you, without a word of the real story breaking. A columnist did run a cute and cryptic item about someone having finally found meat on the flying saucers, but half an hour of earnest discussion in an abandoned fingerprint-file room prejudiced him against further comment along this line.

The video show was the biggest problem. I don't think I could have done it on time with anything less than the resources and influence of the United States government behind me. But a week before the official announcement I had both the video show and the comic strip in production.

I think fourteen—though maybe it was more—of the country's best comedy writers collaborated on the project, not to mention the horde of illustrators and university psychologists who combined to sweat out the delightful little drawings. We used the drawings as the basis for the puppets on the TV show and I don't think anything was ever so gimmicked up with Popular Appeal—and I do mean *Popular*—as "Andy and Dandy."

Those two fictional snails crept into the heart of America like a virus infection; overnight, everybody was talking about their anthropomorphic antics, repeating their quotable running gags and adjuring each other not to miss the next show. ("You *can't* miss it, Steve; it's on every channel anyway. Right after supper.") I had the tie-ins, too: Andy and Dandy dolls for the girls, snail scooters for the boys, everything from pictures on cocktail glasses to kitchen decalcomanias. Of course, a lot of the tie-ins didn't come off the production line till after the Big Announcement.

When we gave the handouts to the newspapers, we "suggested" what headlines to use. They had a choice of ten. Even *The New York Times* was forced to shriek "REAL ANDY AND DANDY BLOW IN FROM BETELGEUSE," and under that a four-column cut of blonde Baby Ann Joyce with the snails.

Baby Ann had been flown out from Hollywood for the photograph. The cut showed her standing between the two aliens and clutching an eyestalk of each in her trusting, chubby hands.

The nicknames stuck. Those two slimy intellectuals from another star became even more important than the youthful evangelist who was currently being sued for bigamy.

Andy and Dandy had a ticker-tape reception in New York. They obligingly laid a cornerstone for the University of Chicago's new library. They posed for the newsreels everywhere, surrounded by Florida oranges, Idaho potatoes, Milwaukee beer. They were magnificently cooperative.

From time to time, I wondered what they thought of us. They had no facial expressions, which was scarcely odd since they had no faces. Their long eyestalks swung this way and that as they rode down shrieking Broadway in the back seat of the Mayor's car; their gelatinous body-foot would heave periodically and the mouth under it make a smacking noise, but when the photographers suggested that they curl around the barely clad beauties, the time video rigged up a Malibu Beach show, Andy and Dandy wriggled over and complied without a word. Which is more than I can say for the barely clad beauties.

And when the winning pitcher presented them with an autographed baseball at that year's World Series, they bowed gravely, their pink shell-tops glistening in the sunlight, and said throatily into the battery of microphones: "We're the happiest fans in the universe!"

The country went wild over them.

"But we can't keep them here," Trowson predicted. "Did you read about the debate in the U.N. General Assembly yesterday? We were accused of making secret alliances with nonhuman aggressors against the best interests of our own species."

I shrugged. "Well, let them go overseas. I don't think anyone else will be more successful extracting information from them than we were."

Professor Trowson wriggled his short body up on a corner of his desk. He lifted a folder of typewritten notes and grimaced as if his tongue were wrapped in wool.

"Four months of careful questioning," he grumbled. "Four months of painstaking interrogation by trained sociologists using every free moment the aliens had, which admittedly wasn't much. Four months of organized investigation, of careful data-sifting." He dropped the folder disgustedly to the desk and some of the pages splashed out. "And we know more about the social structure of Atlantis than Betelgeuse IX."

We were in the wing of the Pentagon assigned to what the brass hats, in their own cute way, had christened Mission Encyclopedia. I strolled across the large, sunny office and glanced at the very latest organizational wall-chart. I pointed to a small rectangle labeled "Power Source Subsection" depending via a straight line from a larger rectangle marked "Alien Physical Science Inquiry Section." In the small rectangle, very finely printed, were the names of an army major, a WAC corporal, and Drs. Lopez, Vinthe and Mainzer.

"How're they doing?" I asked.

"Not much better, I'm afraid." Trowson turned away with a sigh from peering over my shoulder. "At least, I deduce that from the unhappy way Mainzer bubbles into his soup spoon at lunch. Conversation between subsections originating in different offices on the departmental level is officially discouraged, you know. But I remember Mainzer from the university cafeteria. He bubbled into his soup the very same way when he was stuck on his solar refraction engine."

"Think Andy and Dandy are afraid we're too young to play with matches? Or maybe apelike creatures are too unpleasant-looking to be allowed to circulate in their refined and esthetic civilization?"

"I don't *know*, Dick." The prof ambled back to his desk and leafed irritably through his sociological notes. "If anything like that is true, why would they give us free run of their ship? Why would they reply so gravely and courteously to every question? If only their answers weren't so vague in our terms! But they are such complex and artistically minded creatures, so chockful of poetic sentiment and good manners that it's impossible to make mathematical or even verbal sense out of their vast and circumlocutory explanations. Sometimes, when I think of their highly polished manners and their seeming lack of interest in the structure of their society, when I put that together with their spaceship which looks like one of those tiny jade carvings that took a lifetime to accomplish…"

He trailed off and began riffling the pages like a Mississippi steamboat gambler going over somebody else's deck of cards.

"Isn't it possible we just don't have enough stuff as yet to understand them?"

"Yes. In fact, that's what we always come back to. Warbury points to the tremendous development in our language since the advent of technical vocabularies. He says that this process, just beginning with us, already affects our conceptual approach as well as our words. And, naturally, in a race so much further along— But if we could only find a science of theirs which bears a faint resemblance to one of ours!"

I felt sorry for him, standing there blinking futilely out of gentle, academic eyes.

"Cheer up, prof. Maybe by the time old Suckfoot and his pal come back from the Grand Tour, you'll have unsnarled a sophistry and we'll be off this 'Me, friend; you come from across sea in great bird with many wings' basis that we seemed to have wandered into."

And there you are, Alvarez; a cheap, advertising small brain like me, and I was that close. I should have said something then. Bet you wouldn't have nodded at me heavily and said, "I hope so, Dick. I desperately hope so." But, come to think of it, not only Trowson was trotting up that path. So was Warbury. So were Lopez, Vinthe and Mainzer. So was I, among others.

I had a chance to relax when Andy and Dandy went abroad. My job wasn't exactly over, but the Public Relations end was meshing right along, with me needed only once in a while to give a supervisory spin. Chiefly, I maintained close contact with my opposite number in various other sovereign states, giving out with experienced advice on how to sell the Boys from Betelgeuse. They had to adjust it to their own mass phobias and popular myths; but they were a little happier about it than I had been, without any clear idea of what public behavior to expect of our visitors.

Remember, when *I'd* started, I hadn't even been sure those snails were housebroken.

I followed them in the newspapers. I pasted the pictures of the Mikado receiving them next to their nice comments on the Taj Mahal. They weren't nearly so nice to the Akhund of Swat; but, then, when you think of what the Akhund said about them—

They tended to do that everywhere, giving just a little better than they got. For example, when they were presented with those newly created decorations in Red Square (Dandy got The Order of Extraterrestrial Friends of Soviet Labor, while, for some abstruse reason, The Order of Heroic Interstellar Champion of the Soviet People was conferred upon Andy) they came out with a long, ringing speech about the scientific validity of communist government. It made for cheering, flower-tossing crowds in the Ukraine and Poland, but a certain amount of restiveness in these United States.

But before I had to run my staff into overtime hours, whipping up press releases which recapitulated the aliens' statement before the joint houses of Congress and their lovely, sentimental comments at Valley Forge, the aliens were in Berne, telling the Swiss that only free enterprise could have produced the yodel, the Incabloc escapement in watches, and such a superb example of liberty; hadn't they had democracy long enough to have had it first, and wasn't it wonderful?

By the time they reached Paris, I had the national affection pretty much under control again, although here and there a tabloid still muttered peevishly in its late city final. But, as always, Andy and Dandy put the clincher on. Even then I wondered whether they really liked DeRoges' latest abstraction for itself alone.

But they bought the twisted sculpture, paying for it, since they had no cash of their own, with a thumb-sized gadget which actually melted marble to any degree of pattern-delicacy the artist desired, merely by being touched to the appropriate surface. DeRoges threw away his chisels blissfully, but six of the finest minds in France retired to intensive nervous breakdowns after a week of trying to solve the tool's working principles.

It went over big here:

ANDY AND DANDY PAY
AS THEY GO
Betelgeuse Business Men
Show Appreciation for
Value Received

This newspaper notes with pleasure the sound shopper's ethics behind the latest transaction of our distinguished guests from the elemental void. Understanding the inexorable law of supply and demand, these representatives of an advanced economic system refuse to succumb to the "gimmies." If certain other members of the human race were to examine carefully the true implications of...

So when they returned to the United States after being presented at the British Court, they got juicy spreads in all the newspapers, a tug-whistle reception in New York harbor and the mayor's very chiefest deputy there on City Hall steps to receive them.

And even though people were more or less accustomed to them now, they were somehow never shoved off page one. There was the time a certain furniture polish got a testimonial out of them in which the aliens announced that they'd had particularly happy and glossy results on their tiny shell toppers with the goo; and they used the large financial rewards of the testimonial to buy ten extremely rare orchids and have them sunk in plastic. And there was the time—

I missed the television show on which it broke. I had gone to a sidestreet movie theater that night to see a revival of one of my favorite Chaplin pictures; and I'd never enjoyed the ostentatious greet-the-great hysterics of *Celebrity Salon* anyway. I hadn't any idea of how long the M.C., Bill Bancroft, had waited to get Andy and Dandy on his program, and how much he was determined to make it count when the big night arrived.

Reconstructed and stripped of meaningless effusion, it went something like this:

Bancroft asked them if they weren't anxious to get home to the wife and kiddies. Andy explained patiently, for perhaps the thirty-fourth time, that, since they were hermaphrodites, they had no family in any humanly acceptable sense. Bancroft cut into the explanation to ask them what ties they *did* have. Chiefly the revitalizer, says Andy politely.

Revitalizer? What's a revitalizer? Oh, a machine they have to expose themselves to every decade or so, says Dandy. There's at least one revitalizer in every large city on their home planet.

Bancroft makes a bad pun, waits for the uproarious audience to regain control, then asks: And this revitalizer—just what does it do? Andy goes into a long-winded explanation, the gist of which is that the revitalizers stir up cytoplasm in all animal cells and refresh them.

I see, cracks Bancroft; the pause every decade that refreshes. And then, after being refreshed, you have what as a result? "Oh," muses Dandy, "you might say we have no fear of cancer or any degenerative disease. Besides that, by exposing ourselves to revitalizers at regular intervals throughout our lifetime and refreshing our body cells, we quintuple our life expectancy. We live five times longer than we should. That's about what the revitalizer does, you might say," says Dandy. Andy, after thinking a bit, agrees. "That's about it."

Pandemonium, and not mild. Newspaper extras in all languages, including the Scandinavian. Lights burning late at night in the U.N. Headquarters with guards twenty deep around the site.

When President of the Assembly Ranvi asked them why they'd never mentioned revitalizers before, they did the snail equivalent of shrugging and said the Betelgeuse IX equivalent of nobody ever asked them.

President Ranvi cleared his throat, waved all complications aside with his long brown fingers and announced, "That is not important. Not now. We must have revitalizers."

It seemed to take the aliens a while to understand that. When they finally became convinced that we, as a species, were utterly entranced with the prospect of two to four centuries of life instead of threescore and ten years, they went into a huddle.

But their race didn't make these machines for export, they explained regretfully. Just enough to service their population. And, while they *could* see as how we might like and must obviously deserve to have these gadgets, there were none to ferry back from Betelgeuse.

Ranvi didn't even look around for advice. "What would your people want?" he asked. "What would they like in exchange for manufacturing these machines for us?

We will pay almost any price within the power of this entire planet." A rumbling, eager "yes" in several languages rolled across the floor of the Assembly.

Andy and Dandy couldn't think of a thing. Sadhu begged them to try. He personally escorted them to their spaceship, which was now parked in a restricted area in Central Park. "Good night, gentlemen," said President of the Assembly Ranvi. "Try—please try hard to think of an exchange."

They stayed inside their ship for almost six days while the world almost went insane with impatience. When I think of all the fingernails bitten that week by two billion people....

"Imagine!" Trowson whispered to me. He was pacing the floor as if he fully intended to walk all the way to Betelgeuse. "We'd just be children on a quintupled life-scale, Dick. All my achievement and education, all yours, would be just the beginning! A man could learn five professions in such a life—and think what he could accomplish in that life!"

I nodded, a little numb. I was thinking of the books I could read, the books I might write, if the bulk of my life stretched ahead of me and the advertising profession were just a passing phase in the beginning of it. Then, again, somehow I'd never married, never had had a family. Not enough free time, I had felt. And now, at forty, I was so set in my ways. But a man can undo a lot in a century....

In six days the aliens came out. With a statement of price.

They believed they could persuade their people to manufacture a supply of revitalizers for us if... An *if* writ very large indeed.

Their planet was woefully short of radioactive minerals, they explained apologetically. Barren worlds containing radium, uranium, and thorium had been discovered and claimed by other races, but the folk of Betelgeuse IX were forbidden by their ethics to wage aggressive war for territorial purposes. We had plenty of radioactive ore, which we used chiefly for war and biological research. The former was patently undesirable and the latter would be rendered largely unnecessary by the revitalizers.

So, in exchange, they wanted our radioactive elements. All of them, they stated humbly.

All right, we were a little surprised, even stunned. But the protests never *started* to materialize. There was an overwhelming chorus of "Sold!" from every quadrant of the globe. A couple of generals here, a few militaristic statesmen there, managed to raise direly pointing forefingers before they were whisked out of position. A nuclear physicist or two howled about the future of subatomic research, but the peoples of the earth howled louder.

"Research? How much research can you do in a lifetime of three hundred years?"

Overnight, the United Nations became the central office of a planet-wide mining concession. National boundaries were superseded by pitchblende deposits and swords were beaten into pickaxes. Practically anyone with a good, usable arm enlisted in the mining brigades for two or more months out of the year. Camaraderie flew on the winds of the world.

Andy and Dandy politely offered to help. They marked out on detail-contour maps the spots to be excavated; that included areas never suspected of radioactivity. They supplied us with fantastic but clear line drawings of devices for extracting the stuff from the ores in which it assayed poorly, and taught us the exact use of these devices, if not their basic principle.

They hadn't been joking. They wanted it all.

Then, when everything was running smoothly, they buzzed off for Betelgeuse to handle their part of the bargain.

Those two years were the most exhilarating of my life. And I'd say everyone feels the same, don't they, Alvarez? The knowledge that the world was working together, cheerfully, happily, for life itself. I put *my* year in at The Great Slave Lake up in Canada, and I don't think anyone of my age and weight lifted more pitchblende.

Andy and Dandy came back in two huge ships, manned by weird snail-like robots. The robots did everything, while Andy and Dandy went on being lionized. From the two ships, almost covering the sky, the robots ferried back and forth in strange, spiral aircraft, bringing revitalizers down, carrying refined radioactive elements aloft. No one paid the slightest attention to their methods of instantaneous extraction from large quantities of ore: we were interested in just one throbbing thought—the revitalizers.

They worked. And that, so far as most of us were concerned, was that.

The revitalizers *worked*. Cancer disappeared; heart and kidney disease were instantaneously arrested. Insects which were introduced into the square one-story lab structures lived for a year instead of a few months. And humans—doctors shook their heads in wonder over people who had gone through.

All over the planet, near every major city, the long, patient, slowly moving lines stood outside the revitalizers, which were rapidly becoming something else.

"Temples!" shouted Mainzer. "They look on them as temples. A scientist investigating their operation is treated like a dangerous lunatic trying to break into a nursery. Not that a man can find a clue in those ridiculously small motors. I no longer ask what their power source can be—instead, I ask if they have a power source *at all!*"

"The revitalizers are very precious now, in the beginning," Trowson soothed him. "After a while, the novelty will wear off and you'll be able to investigate at your leisure. Could it be solar power?"

"No!" Mainzer shook his huge head positively. "Not solar power—solar power I am sure I could recognize. As I am sure that the power supply of their ships and whatever runs these—these revitalizers are two entirely separate things. On the ships I have given up. But the revitalizers I believe I could solve. If only they would let me examine them. Fools! So terribly afraid I might damage one, and they would have to travel to another city for their elixir!"

We patted his shoulder, but we weren't really interested. Andy and Dandy left that week, after wishing us well in their own courteous and complex fashion. Whole population groups blew kisses at their mineral-laden ships.

Six months after they left, the revitalizers stopped.

"Am I certain?" Trowson nodded at my dismayed face. "One set of statistics proves it: look at your death rate. It's back to pre-Betelgeuse normal. Or ask any doctor. Any doctor who can forget his U.N. security oath, that is. There'll be really wild riots when the news breaks, Dick."

"But *why?*" I asked him. "Did we do something wrong?"

He started a laugh that ended with his teeth clicking frightenedly together. He rose and walked to the window, staring out into the star-diseased sky. "We did something wrong, all right. We trusted. We made the same mistake all natives have made when they met a superior civilization. Mainzer and Lopez have taken one of the revitalizer engine units apart. There was just a trace of it left, but this time they found the power source. Dick, my boy, the revitalizers were run on the fuel of completely pure radioactive elements!"

I needed a few moments to file that properly. Then I sat down in the easy chair very, very carefully. I made some hoarse, improbable sounds before croaking: "Prof, do you mean they wanted that stuff for themselves, for their *own* revitalizers? That everything they did on this planet was carefully planned so that they could con us with a maximum of friendliness all around? It doesn't seem—it just can't—why, with their superior science, they could have conquered us if they'd cared to. They could have—"

"No, they couldn't have," Trowson whipped out. He turned to face me and crossed his arms upon his chest. "They're a decadent, dying race; they wouldn't have attempted to conquer us. Not because of their ethics—this huge, horrible swindle serves to illustrate *that* aspect of them—but because they haven't the energy, the concentration, the interest. Andy and Dandy are probably representative of the few remaining who have barely enough git-up-and-go to *trick* backward peoples out of the all-important, life-sustaining revitalizer fuel."

The implications were just beginning to soak in my brain. Me, the guy who did the most complete and colossal public relations job of all time—I could just see what my relations with the public would be like if I was ever connected with this shambles.

"And without atomic power, prof, we won't have space travel!"

He gestured bitterly. "Oh, we've been taken, Dick; the whole human race has been had. I know what you're going through, but think of me! I'm the failure, the man responsible. I'm supposed to be a sociologist! How could I have missed? *How?* It was all there: the lack of interest in their own culture, the overintellectualization of esthetics, the involved methods of thought and expression, the exaggerated etiquette, even the very first thing of theirs we saw—their ship—was too heavily stylized and intricately designed for a young, thrusting civilization.

"They *had* to be decadent; every sign pointed to that conclusion. And, of course, the fact that they resort to the methods of fueling their revitalizers that we've experienced—when if we had their science, what might we not do, what substitutes might we not develop! No wonder they couldn't explain their science to us; I doubt if they understand it fully themselves. They are the profligate, inadequate and sneak-thief heirs of what was once a soaring race!"

I was following my own unhappy images. "And we're still hicks. Hicks who've been sold the equivalent of the Brooklyn Bridge by some dressed-up sharpies from Betelgeuse."

Trowson nodded. "Or a bunch of poor natives who have sold their island home to a group of European explorers for a handful of brightly colored glass beads."

But of course we were both wrong, Alvarez. Neither Trowson nor I had figured on Mainzer or Lopez or the others. Like Mainzer said, a few years earlier and we would have been licked. But Man had entered the atomic age sometime before 1945 and people like Mainzer and Vinthe had done nuclear research back in the days when radioactive elements abounded on Earth. We had data and we had such tools as the cyclotron, the betatron. And, if our present company will pardon the expression, Alvarez, we are a young and vigorous race.

All we had to do was the necessary research.

The research was done. With a truly effective world government, with a population not only interested in the problem, but recently experienced in working together—and with the grim incentive we had, Alvarez—the problem, as you know, was solved.

We developed artificial radioactives and refueled the revitalizers. We developed atomic fuels out of the artificial radioactives and we got space travel. We did it comparatively fast, and we weren't interested in a ship that just went to the Moon or Mars. We wanted a starship. And we wanted it so bad, so fast, that we have it now, too.

Here we are. Explain the situation to them, Alvarez, just the way I told it to you, but with all the knee-bending and doubletalk that a transplanted Brazilian with twelve years' Oriental trading experience can put into it. You're the man to do it—I can't talk like that. It's the only language those decadent slugs understand, so it's the only way we can talk to them. So talk to them, these slimy snails, these oysters on the quarter shell, these smart-alecky slugs. Don't forget to mention to them that the supply of radioactives they got from us won't last forever. Get that down in fine detail.

Then stress the fact that we've got artificial radioactives, and that they've got some things we know we want and lots of other things we mean to find out about.

Tell them, Alvarez, that we've come to collect tolls on that Brooklyn Bridge they sold us.

AFTERWORD

This was the first—at least the first I was conscious of writing—of my "Here Comes Civilization!" stories. About the time I wrote "The Liberation of Earth," I had been thinking of a cycle that would celebrate, in future, galactic terms, what happened in our history when technologically advanced cultures moved in on technologically backward cultures, from the Aztecs to the Tahitians, from Lake Chad to Lake Titicaca.

We of Earth were to be the Indians of Manhattan Island and the creatures from Betelgeuse were to be the Dutch of Mynheers Peter Minuit and Peter Stuyvesant. And how, my fellow humans, I intended to ask, does *that* feel?

I had mentioned the idea to John Campbell at *Astounding*, but he was in the midst of his dianetics period and asked me if I couldn't work at least one good-guy *clear* into the story. Horace Gold had been begging me for stories for his new magazine, *Galaxy*, so I called him up and told him what I'd like to do. He was very enthusiastic about it; he said he particularly wanted to publish as many satires as he could get.

In fact, he wanted the story so badly that he managed to control himself and didn't do what maddened me in my later relationship with him—try to rewrite my story before I had even written it. He just said, "Please get it to me as soon as possible. I'll definitely buy it."

I wrote it, and he bought it. But he was Horace, after all. He couldn't keep his fingers out of his writers' stories. With all their quarrels and intense rivalry, he and John Campbell had something very basic in common. They both saw the writers for their magazines as so many pencils, scribbling the stories they, as editors, felt themselves no longer able to write. And although they were great editors, they were lousy, unasked-for and insistent collaborators.

Since he wanted me to continue writing for him, Horace at this early time in our relationship made very few changes in the published "Betelgeuse Bridge." He just threw an extra adverb or adjective into three or four sentences. I was furious.

But, alas...

Of course, I had a carbon copy (carbon print on yellow backup sheets in the typewriter—for all you young, computer-using readers) in my files. But, as with several other stories, I never took very close care of that carbon. It was on brittle yellow paper that began falling apart as the years went by anyway—and anyway, in those days, who really believed that I'd ever see my oh-so-commercial fiction in my own collections, and in *hard covers* yet?

The carbon copy did completely dissolve with time. And as for me, well, my memory is not so good these days. I can no longer remember exactly which three or four sentences Horace altered.

So.

So here is W. Tenn with a soupçon of Horace L. Gold thrown in.

WRITTEN 1950——PUBLISHED 1951

"Will You Walk a Little Faster"

All right. So maybe I should be ashamed of myself.

But I'm a writer and this is too good a story to let go. My imagination is tired, and I'm completely out of usable plots; I'm down to the gristle of truth. I'll use it.

Besides, someone's bound to blab sooner or later—as Forkbeard pointed out, we're that kind of animal—and I might as well get some private good out of the deal.

Why, for all I know, there is a cow on the White House lawn this very moment....

Last August, to be exact, I was perspiring over an ice-cold yarn that I never should have started in the first place, when the doorbell rang.

I looked up and yelled, "Come in! Door's open!"

The hinges squeaked a little the way they do in my place. I heard feet slap-slapping up the long corridor which makes the rent on my apartment a little lower than most of the others in the building. I couldn't recognize the walk as belonging to anyone I knew, so I waited with my fingers on the typewriter keys and my face turned to the study entrance.

After a while, the steps came around the corner. A little man, not much more than two feet high, dressed in a green knee-length tunic, walked in. He had a very large head, a short pointed red beard, a long pointed green cap, and he was talking to himself. In his right hand, he carried a golden pencil-like object; in his left, a curling strip of what seemed to be parchment.

"Now, you," he said with a guttural accent, pointing both the beard and the pencil-like object at me, "now you must be a writer."

I closed my mouth carefully around a lump of air. Somehow, I noted with interest, I seemed to be nodding.

"Good." He flourished the pencil and made a mark at the end of a line halfway down the scroll. "That completes the enrollment for this session. Come with me, please."

He seized the arm with which I had begun an elaborate gesture. Holding me in a grip that had all the resiliency of a steel manacle, he smiled benevolently and walked back down my entrance hall. Every few steps he walked straight up in the air, and then—as if he'd noticed his error—calmly strode down to the floor again.

"What—who—" I said, stumbling and tripping and occasionally getting walloped by the wall, "you wait, you—who—*who*—"

"Please do not make such repetitive noises," he admonished me. "You are sup-

39

posed to be a creature of civilization. Ask intelligent questions if you wish, but only when you have them properly organized."

I brooded on that while he closed the door of my apartment behind him and began dragging me up the stairs. His heart may or may not have been pure, but I estimated his strength as being roughly equivalent to that of ten. I felt like a flag being flapped from the end of my own arm.

"We're going up?" I commented tentatively as I swung around a landing.

"Naturally. To the roof. Where we're parked."

"Parked, you said?" I thought of a helicopter, then of a broomstick. Who was it that rode around on the back of an eagle?

Mrs. Flugelman, who lived on the floor above, had come out of her apartment with a bagful of garbage. She opened the door of the dumbwaiter and started to nod good-morning at me. She stopped when she saw my friend.

"Yes, parked. What you call our flying saucer." He noticed Mrs. Flugelman staring at him and jutted his beard at her as we went by. "Yes, I said flying saucer!" he spat.

Mrs. Flugelman walked back into her apartment with the bagful of garbage and closed the door behind her very quietly.

Maybe the stuff I write for a living prepared me for such experiences, but—somehow—as soon as he told me that, I felt better. Little men and flying saucers, they seemed to go together. Just so halos and pitchforks didn't wander into the continuity.

When we reached the roof, I wished I'd had time to grab a jacket. It was evidently going to be a breezy ride.

The saucer was about thirty feet in diameter and, colorful magazine articles to the contrary, had been used for more than mere sightseeing. In the center, where it was deepest, there was a huge pile of boxes and packages lashed down with criss-crossing masses of gleaming thread. Here and there, in the pile, was the unpackaged metal of completely unfamiliar machinery.

Still using my arm as a kind of convenient handle to the rest of me, the little man whirled me about experimentally once or twice, then scaled me accurately end over end some twenty feet through the air to the top of the pile. A moment before I hit, golden threads boiled about me, cushioning like an elastic net, and tying me up more thoroughly than any three shipping clerks. My shot-putting pal grunted enthusiastically and prepared to climb aboard.

Suddenly he stopped and looked back along the roof. "Irngl!" he yelled in a voice like two ocean liners arguing. "Irngl! Bordge modgunk!"

There was a tattoo of feet on the roof so rapid as to be almost one sound, and a ten-inch replica of my strong-arm guide—minus the beard, however—leaped over the railing and into the craft. Young Irngl, I decided, bordge modgunking.

His father (?) stared at him very suspiciously, then walked back slowly in the direction from which he had run. He halted and shook a ferocious finger at the youngster. Beside me, Irngl cowered.

Just behind the chimney was a cluster of television antennae. But the dipoles of these antennae were no longer parallel. Some had been carefully braided together;

others had been tied into delicate and perfect bows. Growling ferociously, shaking his head so that the pointed red beard made like a metronome, the old man untied the knots and smoothed the dipoles out to careful straightness with his fingers. Then he bent his legs slightly at their knobby knees and performed one of the more spectacular standing broad jumps of all time.

And, as he hit the floor of the giant saucer, we took off. Straight up.

When I'd recovered sufficiently to regurgitate my larynx, I noticed that old redbeard was controlling the movement of the disc beneath us by means of an egg-shaped piece of metal in his right hand. After we'd gone up a goodly distance, he pointed the egg south and we headed that way.

Radiant power, I wondered? No information—not much that was useful—had been volunteered. *Of course,* I realized suddenly: I hadn't asked any questions! Grabbed from my typewriter in the middle of the morning by a midget of great brain and greater muscle—I couldn't be blamed, though: few men in my position would have been able to put their finger on the nub of the problem and make appropriate inquiries. *Now,* however—

"While there's a lull in the action," I began breezily enough, "and as long as you speak English, I'd like to clear up a few troublesome matters. For example—"

"Your questions will be answered later. Meanwhile, you will shut up." Golden threads filled my mouth with the taste of antiseptics, and I found myself unable to part my jaws. Redbeard stared at me as I grunted impotently. "How hateful are humans!" he said, beaming. "And how fortunate that they are hateful!"

The rest of the trip was uneventful, except for a few moments when the Miami-bound plane came abreast of us. People inside pointed excitedly, seemed to yell, and one extremely fat man held up an expensive camera and took six pictures very rapidly. Unfortunately, I noticed, he had neglected to remove the lens cap.

The saucer skipper shook his metal egg, there was a momentary feeling of acceleration—and the airplane was a disappearing dot behind us. Irngl climbed to the top of what looked like a giant malted milk machine and stuck his tongue out at me. I glared back.

It struck me then that the little one's mischievous quality was mighty reminiscent of an elf. And his pop—the parentage seemed unmistakable by then—was like nothing else than a gnome of Germanic folklore. Therefore, didn't these facts mean that—that—that—I let my brain have ten full minutes, before giving up. Oh, well, sometimes that method works. Reasoning by self-hypnotic momentum, I call it.

I was cold, but otherwise quite content with my situation and looking forward to the next development with interest and even pride. I had been selected, alone of my species, by this race of aliens for some significant purpose. I couldn't help hoping, of course, that the purpose was not vivisection.

It wasn't.

We arrived, after a while, at something so huge that it could only be called a flying dinner plate. I suspected that a good distance down, under all those belly-soft clouds, was the State of South Carolina. I also suspected that the clouds were artificial. Our entire outfit entered through a hole in the bottom. The flying dinner plate was covered with another immense plate, upside-down, the whole making a hollow disc close to a quarter of a mile in diameter. Flying saucers stacked with goods and people— both long and short folk—were scattered up and down its expanse between great masses of glittering machinery.

Evidently I was wrong about having been selected as a representative sample. There were lots of us, men and women, all over the place—one to a flying saucer. It was to be a formal meeting between the representatives of two great races, I decided. Only why didn't our friends do it right—down at the U.N.? Possibly not so formal after all. Then I remembered Redbeard's comment on humanity and I began worrying.

On my right, an army colonel, with a face like a keg of butter, was chewing on the pencil with which he had been taking notes. On my left, a tall man in a gray sharkskin suit flipped back his sleeve, looked at his watch and expelled his breath noisily, impatiently. Up ahead, two women were leaning toward each other at the touching edges of their respective saucers, both talking at the same time and both nodding vehemently as they talked.

Each of the flying saucers also had at least one equivalent of my redbearded pilot. I observed that while the females of this people had beards too, they were exactly one-half as motherly as our women. But they balanced, they balanced…

Abruptly, the image of a little man appeared on the ceiling. His beard was pink and it forked. He pulled on each fork and smiled down at us.

"To correct the impression in the minds of many of you," he said, chuckling benignly, "I will paraphrase your great poet, Shakespeare. I am here to bury humanity, not to praise it."

A startled murmur broke out all around me. "*Mars,*" I heard the colonel say, "bet they're from Mars. H.G. Wells predicted it. Dirty little, red little Martians. Well, just let them try!"

"Red," the man in the gray sharkskin suit repeated, "*red?*"

"Did you ever—" one of the women started to ask. "Is that a way to begin? No manners! A real foreigner."

"However," Forkbeard continued imperturbably from the ceiling, "in order to bury humanity properly, I need your help. Not only yours, but the help of others like you, who, at this moment, are listening to this talk in ships similar to this one and in dozens of languages all over the world. We need your help—and, knowing your peculiar talents so well, we are fairly certain of getting it!"

He waited until the next flurry of fist-waving and assorted imprecations had died down; he waited until the anti-Negroes and the anti-Jews, the anti-Catholics and the anti-Protestants, the Anglophobes and the Russophobes, the vegetarians and the fundamentalists in the audience had all identified him colorfully with their peculiar concepts of the Opposition and had excoriated him soundly.

Then, once relative quiet had been achieved, we got the following blunt tale, rather contemptuously told, with mighty few explanatory flourishes:

There was an enormous and complex galactic civilization surrounding our meager nine-planet system. This civilization, composed of the various intelligent species throughout the galaxy, was organized into a peaceful federation for trade and mutual advancement.

A special bureau in the federation discharged the biological duty of more advanced races to new arrivals on the cerebral scene. Thus, quite a few millennia ago, the bureau had visited Earth to investigate tourist accounts of a remarkably ingenious animal that had lately been noticed wandering about. The animal having been certified as intelligent with a high cultural potential, Earth was closed to tourist traffic and sociological specialists began the customary close examination.

"And, as a result of this examination," the forked pink beard smiled gently down from above, "the specialists discovered that what you call the human race was nonviable. That is, while the individuals composing it had strongly developed instincts of self-preservation, the species as a whole was suicidal."

"*Suicidal!*" I found myself breathing up with the rest.

"Quite. This is a matter on which there can be little argument from the more honest among you. High civilization is a product of communal living and Man, in groups, has always tended to wipe himself out. In fact, a large factor in the development of what little civilization you do experience has been the rewards contingent upon the development of mass-destruction weapons."

"We have had peaceful, brotherly periods," a hoarse voice said on the opposite side of the ship.

The large head shook slowly from side to side. The eyes, I saw suddenly and irrelevantly, were all black iris. "You have not. You *have* occasionally developed an island of culture here, an oasis of cooperation there; but these have inevitably disintegrated upon contact with the true standard-bearers of your species—the warrior-races. And when, as happened occasionally, the warrior-races were defeated, the conquerors in their turn became warriors, so that the suicidal strain was ever rewarded and became more dominant. Your past is your complete indictment, and your present—your present is about to become your executed sentence. But enough of this peculiar bloody nonsense—let me return to *living* history."

He went on to explain that the Federation felt a suicidal species should be allowed to fulfill its destiny unhampered. In fact, so long as overt acts were avoided, it was quite permissible to help such a creature along to the doom it desired—"Nature abhors self-destruction even more than a vacuum. The logic is simple: both cease almost as soon as they come into existence."

The sociologists having extrapolated the probable date on which humanity might be expected to extinguish itself, the planet was assigned—as soon as it should be vacated—to the inhabitants of an Earth-like world for the use of such surplus population as they might then have. These were the redbeards.

"We sent representatives here to serve as caretakers, so to speak, of our future property. But about nine hundred years ago, when your world still had six thousand years to run, we decided to hurry the process a bit as we experienced a rising index of population on our own planet. We therefore received full permission from the Galactic Federation to stimulate your technological development into an earlier suicide. The

Federation stipulated, however, that each advance be made the moral responsibility of an adequate representative of your race, that he be told the complete truth of the situation. This we did: we would select an individual to be the discoverer of a revolutionary technique or scientific principle; then we would explain both the value of the technique and the consequences to his species in terms of accelerated mass destruction."

I found it hard to continue looking into his enormous eyes. "In every case"—the booming rattle of the voice had softened perceptibly—"in every case, sooner or later, the individual announced the discovery as his own, giving it to his fellows and profiting substantially. In a few cases, he later endowed great foundations which awarded prizes to those who advanced the cause of peace or the brotherhood of man. This resulted in little beyond an increase in the amount of currency being circulated. Individuals, we found, always chose to profit at the expense of their race's life-expectancy."

Gnomes, elves, kobolds! Not mischievous sprites—I glanced at Irngl sitting quietly under his father's heavy hand—nor the hoarders of gold, but helping man for their own reasons: teaching him to smelt metals and build machinery, showing him how to derive the binomial theorem in one part of the world and how to plow a field more efficiently in another.

To the end that people might perish from the Earth...sooner.

"Unfortunately—ah, something has developed."

We looked up at that, all of us—housewives and handymen, preachers and professional entertainers—looked up from the tangle of our reflections and prejudices, and *hoped*.

As D-day drew nigh, those among the kobolds who intended to emigrate filled their flying saucers with possessions and families. They scooted across space in larger craft such as the one we were now in and took up positions in the stratosphere, waiting to assume title to the planet as soon as its present occupants used their latest discovery—nuclear fission—as they had previously used ballistics and aeronautics.

The more impatient wandered down to survey home-sites. They found to their annoyance that an unpleasant maggot of error had crawled into the pure mathematics of extrapolated sociology. Humanity should have wiped itself out shortly after acquiring atomic power. But—possibly as a result of the scientific stimulation we had been receiving recently—our technological momentum had carried us past uranium-plutonium fission up to the so-called hydrogen bomb.

Whereas a uranium-bomb Armageddon would have disposed of us in a most satisfactory and sanitary fashion, the explosion of several hydrogen bombs, it would seem, will result in the complete sterilization of our planet as the result of a subsidiary reaction at present unknown to us. If we go to war with this atomic refinement, Earth will not only be cleansed of all present life-forms, but it will also become uninhabitable for several millions of years in the future.

Naturally, the kobolds view this situation with a certain amount of understandable unhappiness. According to Galactic Law, they may not actively intervene to safeguard their legacy. Therefore, they would like to offer a proposition—

Any nation which guarantees to stop making hydrogen bombs and to dispose of those it has already made—and the little redbeards have, they claim, satisfactory methods of enforcing these guarantees—such a nation will be furnished by them with a magnificently murderous weapon. This weapon is extremely simple to operate and is so calibrated that it can be set to kill instantaneously and painlessly any number of people at one time, up to a full million.

"The advantage to any terrestrial military establishment of such a weapon over the unstable hydrogen bomb, which is not only hard to handle but must be transported physically to its target," the genial face on the ceiling commented, "should be obvious to all of you! And, as far as we are concerned, anything which will dispose of human beings on a wholesale basis while not injuring—"

At this point, there was so much noise that I couldn't hear a word he was saying. For that matter, I was yelling quite loudly myself.

"—while not injuring useful and compatible life-forms—"

"Ah-h," screamed a deeply tanned stout man in a flowerful red sports shirt and trunks, "whyn't you go back where you came from?"

"Yeah!" someone else added wrathfully. "Can't yuh see yuh not wanted? Shut up, huh? Shut *up!*"

"Murderers," one of the women in front of me quavered. "That's all you are— murderers trying to kill inoffensive people who've never done you any harm. Killing would be just too good for you."

The colonel was standing on his toes and oscillating a portentous forefinger at the roof. "We were doing all right," he began apoplectically, then stopped to allow himself to unpurple. "We were doing *well* enough, I can tell you, without—without—"

Forkbeard waited until we began to run down.

"Look at it this way," he urged in a wheedling voice, "you're going to wipe yourselves out—you know it, we know it and so does everybody else in the galaxy. What difference can it possibly make to you whether you do it one way or another? At least by our method you confine the injury to yourselves. You don't damage the highly valuable real estate—to wit, Earth—which will be ours after you've ceased to use it. And you go out with a weapon which is much more worthy of your destructive propensities than any you have used hitherto, including atomic bombs."

He paused and spread knobbed hands down at our impotent hatred. "Think of it—*just think of it:* a million deaths at one plunge of a lever! What other weapon can make that claim?"

Skimming back northwards with Redbeard and Irngl, I pointed to the flying saucers radiating away from us through the delicate summer sky. "These people are all fairly responsible citizens. Isn't it silly to expect them to advertise a more effective way of having their throats cut?"

There was a shrug of the green-wrapped shoulders. "With any other species, yes. But not you. The Galactic Federation insists that the actual revelation of the weapon, either to your public or your government, must be made by a fairly intelligent representative of your own species, in full possession of the facts, and after he or she has had an adequate period to reflect on the consequences of disclosure."

"And you think we will? In spite of everything?"

"Oh, yes," the little man told me with tranquil assurance. "*Because* of everything. For example, you have each been selected with a view to the personal advantage you would derive from the revelation. Sooner or later, one of you will find the advantage so necessary and tempting that the inhibiting scruple will disappear; eventually, all of you would come to it. As Shulmr pointed out, each member of a suicidal race contributes to the destruction of the whole even while attentively safeguarding his own existence. Disagreeable creatures, but fortunately short-lived!"

"One million," I mused. "So arbitrary. I bet we make—"

"Quite correct. You are an ingenious race. Now if you wouldn't mind stepping back onto your roof? We're in a bit of a hurry, Irngl and I, and we have to disinfect after— Thank you."

I watched them disappear upwards into a cloud bank. Then, noticing a television dipole tied in a hangman's noose which Irngl's father had overlooked, I trudged downstairs.

For a while, I was very angry. Then I was glum. Then I was angry again. I've thought about it a lot since August.

I've read some recent stuff on flying saucers, but not a word about the super-weapon we'll get if we dismantle our hydrogen bombs. But, if someone had blabbed, how would I know about it?

That's just the point. Here I am a writer, a science-fiction writer no less, with a highly salable story that I'm not supposed to use. Well, it happens that I need money badly right now; and it further happens that I am plumb out of plots. How long am I supposed to go on being a sucker?

Somebody's probably told by now. If not in this country, in one of the others. And I *am* a writer, and I have a living to make. And this is fiction, and who asked you to believe it anyhow?

Only— Only I did intend to leave out the signal. The signal, that is, by which a government can get in touch with the kobolds, can let them know it's interested in making the trade, in getting that weapon. I did intend to leave out the signal.

But I don't have a satisfactory ending to this story. It needs some sort of tag-line. And the signal makes a perfect one. Well—it seems to me that if I've told *this* much— and probably anyhow—

The signal's the immemorial one between man and kobold: Leave a bowl of milk outside the White House door.

Afterword

I was living next door to Lester del Rey, when I wrote this, in a fifteen-dollar-a-month unheated apartment on West End Avenue in New York City. It had a bathtub in the kitchen and the absolutely boozingest lady superintendent this side of Alcoholics Anonymous. The building was later torn down to become part of the site of today's Lincoln Center. And the apartment was a tiny three-room affair at the end of one of the very longest entrance halls I have ever seen. There was perhaps twice or three times as much square footage in the entrance hall as in the apartment proper.

I used both the apartment and the entrance hallway as the opening scene of "Will You Walk a Little Faster." The title, of course, comes from Lewis Carroll, per the whiting's impatient question to the snail. And the theme...

The theme was *the* theme of science fiction, five years after Hiroshima and Nagasaki at a time when every newly built house in the suburbs proudly featured a concrete-lined bomb cellar:

Atomic doom.

I had just come back to my apartment after a visit to Lester next door. We had begun a discussion of atomic doom as a mild, rather urbane disagreement and had ended in a screaming, yelling, almost-throwing-things argument.

Lester was a maddening person to argue with. If driven into a corner he would start to Jurgenize; that is, he would start quoting authorities, most of whom he had made up on the spot (I created this verb in honor of Lester, naming it after the most colorful character of the late James Branch Cabell). Randy Garrett, during a similar battle with Lester, made a point of writing down the title of the book Lester was quoting, the name of the author and the publishing house, and even the year, goddammit, of publication—all of which Lester supplied with a *noblesse oblige* wave of his hand. These Randy then checked, not only with the New York Public Library, but also eventually with the Library of Congress itself.

He confronted Lester with the result in the presence of four other science-fiction writers. "No such book," he said triumphantly. "No record of its ever being published. No record at all, at all, at all."

Lester looked amused. He shrugged. "It's a shame about the Library of Congress," he said. "Such a shabby excuse for what it's supposed to be. So ridiculously incomplete in every important way. No, you really have to learn to use the Bodleian in Oxford for any important research. The last time I checked, they had two copies, one of them in pretty good condition."

Randy positively danced with fury and frustration. He put his left fist in his mouth and bit hard on it.

He swore he would make it a goal of his life to go to Oxford before he died, and to visit the Bodleian. Unfortunately, he later had a stroke and never did.

My argument with Lester on the subject of atomic doom had begun with Lester asking me if I was one of those people who ran around shivering and shaking about the mere existence of nuclear weapons. When I told him I was—that I *both* shivered *and* shook—he smiled and, in his best Campbellian manner, pointed out to me how unlikely it would be for anyone with the merest *soupçon* of a sense of self-preservation to use such a weapon no matter what the provocation. Who would take the chance of doing something that might well end up destroying the planet? After all, people who governed countries had gotten to where they were because of outstanding intelligence.

"Really?" I said. "Then how about Hitler in that last bunker in Berlin, with the Russians smashing their way to where he lay hidden? If a subordinate had come to him and told him of the development of a weapon that could vaporize the oncoming Russian armies but might also just possibly destroy the entire world, what do you think he would have said?"

Lester rebutted immediately with a previously unheard-of biography of Hitler that practically said in so many words *Der Führer* would have done no such thing. He added concurring opinions by two French lieutenant generals my extensive reading had failed to mention, and wound up by quoting a former associate head of the atomic energy program whose name and title I knew he had just made up out of the thinnest of air.

At this point I'm afraid I began yelling. Lester yelled back. We continued at a very high pitch until the frequently drunken woman who was the building's resident landlady was attracted by the uproar and walked in through the open doorway to ask us if we possibly had any part of a quart of Scotch that she could borrow.

I left, still yelling over my shoulder. And the moment I opened the door of my apartment and began walking up that long entrance hall, what the French call *l'esprit d'escalier* *(l'esprit du vestibule?)* came upon me and I thought of what I might have said. And, as I did, I looked about me and realized just how I might dramatize all that I could have and should have said.

Then I went into the apartment proper and sat down at my Remington typewriter and wrote out the dramatization. Because after all, an argument is an argument, but I needed the money to pay the landlady my overdue rent.

WRITTEN 1950———PUBLISHED 1951

The House Dutiful

To—to be…an unformable, lonely thought groped blindly for a potential fact…need, a need…it was—something…it was—needed…it was needed? Consciousness!

A living creature came with the pride of ownership, the triggering wistfulness for it. Unlike its first darling, this creature had notions that were bizarre and primitive, conceptually agonizing. Painful, painful, painful they were to organize into. But it had purpose again—and, more, it had desire—

Thoughtlessly, lovingly, the immense thing began to flow to the fixed-upon place, twitching awkward experimental shapes upward as it went.

The back-country Canadian road was obscure even for the biting concentration of the deluxe Caterpillar runabout. Metal treads apologized shrilly as they hit a rock that was too large and too snugly embedded in the mud. The bright yellow car canted steeply to the right and came down level again with a murky splash.

"And I was so *happy* in the dairy," Esther Sakarian moaned in histrionic recollection as she dug her unpainted, thoroughly trimmed fingernails into the lavender upholstery of the front seat. "I had my own quiet little lab, my neatly labeled samples of milk and cheese from the day's production; at night I could walk home on cement sidewalks or drop into a dry, air-conditioned restaurant or movie. But Philadelphia wasn't good enough for me! No, I had to—"

"Bad storms last night, smooth riding, usually," Paul Marquis muttered on her left. He grimaced his glasses back into correct nose position and concentrated on the difficult visual task of separating possible road from possible marsh.

"I had to come up to the Great Bear Lake where every prospector sneezes and all the men are vile. Adventure I wanted—hah! Well, here I am, using up the last of my girlhood. I spend my days purifying water for a bunch of whisky-soaked nuclear physicists. Every night I ask God: Is this by you adventure?"

Marquis sloughed the runabout around a dwarfed red spruce that grew belligerently in the middle of the damp highway. "Should be there in a minute or two, Es. Forty of the sweetest acres that anybody ever talked the Canadian government into selling. And a little bumpy hill just off the road that's a natural foundation for the Cape Cod cottage Caroline's always talking about."

The bacteriologist prodded his shoulder tenderly. "Talking about it in Boston and building it in northern Canada—a little different, don't you think? You haven't married the gal yet."

"You don't know Caroline," Marquis told her confidently. "Besides, we'll be only forty miles from Little Fermi—and the town will grow. The lode we're working on seems to be about ten times as rich as the Eldorado mine over at Port Radium. If it holds up, we'll build a uranium pile that will be a power plant for the entire western hemisphere. Business will get interested, real estate values will boom—"

"So it's a good investment, too? Sheer mysticism, like your opinion that a lifetime spent behind Beacon Street walls makes the housemaid-and-mistress combo you want in a wife."

"Now you sound like that mad medico Connor Kuntz when I beat his classic Capablancan chess with an inspirational heresy. *There's* a nineteenth-century mechanist you could be happy with; all he wants is a mate of good disposition and fair heredity who will be absorbed in her work and let him do his bone-setting in peace. I don't want a mate—I want a marriage. No servant any employment agency ever—"

"Dr. Kuntz is a mass of greasy rationalization. And I wasn't proposing to you by indirection."

"—ever sent out," he went on doggedly, "could handle the menial essentials of domestic living with the affection and grace of a wife. Machines are no substitute; you don't get omnipresent, understanding love from a machine. Not that I'm marrying Caroline just to get someone who'll kiss me while she's preparing dinners I like—"

"Of course not! It's comfortable, though, to know you'll get it just the same. Which you wouldn't if you married, say…oh, say a female bacteriologist who had work of her own to do and would be as tired as you at the end of the day. Up with the double standard; but keep it intellectual!"

The excessively thin young man slapped the car to a stop and turned with his mouth open for a blast. Esther Sakarian was one of those tidy, docile-appearing women whose remarks generated a surprising amount of frictional heat in men.

"Look here, Es," he began loudly, "social development and the relatively new integrity of the individual to one side, people still consist of men and women. Women—with the exception of maladjusted—"

"Hey, there!" Esther was staring over his shoulder with her nostrils flaring respectfully. "You've done quite a job! It doesn't look a bit prefabricated, Paul. But it must have been expensive getting priorities for those sections on the Diesel snow trains. And you banged it together in one week by yourself? Quite a job!"

"I would appreciate it if you stopped raving and told me—"

"Your house…your Cape Cod cottage! It's perfect."

"My *what?*" Paul Marquis spun around.

Esther slid the right-hand door back into its slot and stepped delicately onto the mud. "I'll bet you have it half furnished, too. And full of the crazy domestic gimmicks you're always working out. Downy old duck, aren't you? 'Come on, Es, I want to ask your advice on where to stick a house on that land I bought!' So go on and smirk: don't worry, I won't have the gall to say I knew it all the time."

Marquis watched the progress of her feminized blue jeans up the bush-infested hill toward the green and white cottage with anything but a smirk.

Finally, he swung madly over the side, slipped headlong into the mud, picked himself up and clambered on, dripping great brown chunks of Canadian soil as he thudded up the slope.

Esther nodded at him as he approached, her hand truculent on the long, old-fashioned doorknob. "What's the sense of locking doors in this wilderness? If anyone were going to burglarize, they could smash a window quite easily and help themselves while you were away. Well, don't stand there looking philosophical—make with the key, make with the key!"

"The...the key." Dazed, he took a small key chain out of his pocket, looked at it for a moment, then shoved it back violently. He ran a hand through a tangle of blond hair and leaned against the door. It opened.

The bacteriologist trotted past him as he clawed at the post to retain his balance. "Never could get the hang of those prehistoric gadgets. Photoelectric cells will be good enough for my children, and they're good enough for me. Oh, Paul! Don't tell me your sense for the fitness of things extends no further than atomic nuclei. Look at that furniture!"

"Furniture?" he asked very weakly. Slowly, he opened eyes which had been tightly closed while he leaned against the door. He took in the roomful of chairs and tables done in the sprouting-from-one-center-leg style which was currently popular. "Furniture!" he sighed and carefully closed his eyes again.

Esther Sakarian shook her sober head with assurance. "New Single-Support just doesn't go in a Cape Cod cottage. Believe me, Paul, your poetic soul may want to placate your scientific mind by giving it superfunctional surroundings, but you can't do it in this kind of a house. Furthermore, just by looking at that retouched picture of Caroline you have pasted to your Geiger counter, I know she wouldn't approve. You'll have to get rid of at least—"

He had come up to her side and stood plucking the sleeve of her bright plaid shirt. "Esther," he muttered, "my dear, sweet, talkative, analytical, self-confident Esther— please sit down and shut up!"

She dropped into a roundly curved seat, staring at him from angled eyebrows. "You have a point to make?"

"I have a point to make!" Paul told her emphatically. He waved wildly at the modern furniture which seemed to be talking slang in the pleasant, leisurely room. "All this, the house, the furniture, the accessories, was not only not built nor sent here by me, but...but wasn't here a week ago when I came out with the man from the land office and bought the property. It shouldn't be here!"

"Nonsense! It couldn't just—" She broke off.

He nodded. "It did just. But that only makes me *feel* crazy. What makes me positively impatient for a jacket laced securely up the back is the furniture. It's the kind of furniture I thought of whenever Caroline talked about building this cottage. But the point is this: I knew she wanted to stuff it full of New England antique, and—since I feel a woman's place is in the home—I never argued the point. I never mentioned buying Single-Support to her; I've never mentioned the idea to anyone. And every chair and table in this room is exactly what I thought it should be—*privately!*"

Esther had been listening to him with an expanding frown. Now she started an uneasy giggle, and cut it off before it began to throb. "Paul, I know you're too neurotic to be insane, and I'm willing to admit my leg isn't pretty enough for you to pull. But this…this— Look, the house may have been dropped by a passing plane; or possibly Charles Fort had the right idea. What you're trying to tell me about the furniture, though— It makes for belly butterflies!"

"Mine have electric fans on their wings," he assured her. "Now let's try to stay calm. Let's hold hands and go into the kitchen. If there's a certain refrigerator-sink-stove combination—"

There was. Paul Marquis gripped the sleek enamel and whistled "The Pilgrim's Chorus" through his teeth.

"I will a-ask you to c-consider this f-fact," he said at last, shakenly. "This particular rig is one which I worked out on the back of an envelope from Caroline at three-fifteen yesterday when the big dredge got kinked up and I had nothing else to do. Prior to that time, all I knew was that I wanted something slightly different in the way of an all-in-one kitchen unit. This is what I drew."

Esther patted the sides of her face as if she were trying to slap herself back into sanity ever so gently. "Yes, I know."

"You do?"

"You may not remember, Mr. Marquis, but you showed me the drawing in the mess hall at supper. Since it was too fantastically expensive to be considered seriously, I suggested shaping the refrigerator like a sphere so that it would fit into the curve of the stove. You chucked out your lower lip and agreed. The refrigerator is shaped like a sphere and fits into the curve of the stove."

Paul opened a cupboard and pulled out a rainbow-splashed tumbler. "I'm going to get a drink, even if it's water!"

He held the tumbler under the projecting faucet and reached for a button marked "cold." Before his questing finger pressed it, however, a stream of ice-cold fluid spurted out of the faucet, filled the glass and stopped without a trickle.

The physicist exhaled at the completely dry bottom surface of the sink. He tightened his fingers convulsively on the tumbler and poured its contents down his throat. A moment passed, while his head was thrown back; then Esther, who had been leaning against the smooth wall, saw him begin to gag. She reached his side just as the coughs died away and the tears started to leak out of his eyes.

"Whoo-*oof!*" he explained. "That was whisky—the finest Scotch ever to pass these tired old lips. Just as it started to pour, I thought to myself: 'What you need, friend, is a good swift slug of Scotch.' And Esther—that's what that water was! Talk about miracles!"

"I don't like this," the brown-haired woman decided positively. She pulled a small glass vial from a breast pocket. "Whisky, water or whatever it is—I'm going to get a sample and analyze it. You've no idea how many varieties of algae I've seen in the water up here. I think the presence of radioactive ore— Hullo. It doesn't work."

With thumb and forefinger, she pressed the hot and cold water buttons until the flesh under her fingernails turned white. The faucet remained impassively dry.

Paul came over and bent his head under the metal arm. He straightened and smiled impishly. "Pour, water!" he commanded. Again water spat from the faucet, this time describing a curve to where Esther Sakarian had moved the vial to permit her companion to examine the plumbing. When the vial was full, the water stopped.

"Yup!" Paul grinned at the gasping bacteriologist. "Those buttons, the drain— they're only for display. This house does exactly what's required of it—but only when *I* require it! I have a robot house here, Es, and it's mine, *all* mine!"

She closed the vial and replaced it in her pocket. "I think it's a little more than that. Let's get out of here, Paul. Outside of the obvious impossibility of this whole business, there are a couple of things that don't check. I'd like to have Connor Kuntz up here to go over the place. Besides, we'd better get started if we're to make Little Fermi before the sun goes down."

"You don't tell Kuntz about this," Paul warned her as they moved toward the already opening door. "I don't want him fussing up my robot house."

Esther shrugged. "I won't, if you insist. But Doc Kuntz might give you a line on exactly what you have here. Hit him with the extraordinary and he'll bring five thousand years of scientific banalities to bear on it. Tell me, do you notice any other change in your land since you were here last?"

The physicist stood just outside the door and swept his eyes over the tangle of bush that seasoned the glinting patches of swamp and out-cropped rock. Sick orange from the beginning sunset colored the land weirdly, making the desolate subarctic plains look like the backdrop to a dying age. A young, cold wind sprang up and hurried at them, delighting in its own vigor.

"Well, over there for example. A patch of green grass extending for about a quarter mile. I remember thinking how much like a newly mowed lawn it looked, and how out of place it was in the middle of all this marsh. Over there, where you now see that stretch of absolutely blank brown soil. Of course, it could have withered and died in a week. Winter's coming on."

"Hm-m-m." She stepped back and looked up at the green roof of the cottage which harmonized so unostentatiously with the green shutters and door and the sturdy white of the walls. "Do you think—"

Paul leaped away from the door and stood rubbing his shoulder. He giggled awkwardly. "Seemed as if the post reached over and began rubbing against me. Didn't frighten me exactly—just sort of startling."

He smiled. "I'd say this robot whatever-it-is likes me. Almost a mechanical caress."

Esther nodded, her lips set, but said nothing until they were in the car again. "You know, Paul," she whispered as they got under way, "I have the intriguing thought that this house of yours isn't a robot at all. I think it's thoroughly alive."

He widened his eyes at her. Then he pushed his glasses hard against his forehead and chuckled. "Well, that's what they say, Es: It takes a livin' heap to make a house a home!"

They rode on silently in the seeping darkness, trying to develop reasons and causes, but finding none. It was only when they clattered onto the concrete outskirts of Little Fermi that Paul started abruptly: "I'm going to get some beans and coffee and spend the night in my living house. Breckinbridge won't need me until that shipment of cadmium rods comes in from Edmonton; that means I can spend tonight and all day tomorrow finding out just what I've got."

His companion started to object, then tossed her head. "I can't stop you. But be careful, or poor Caroline may have to marry a young buck from the Harvard Law School."

"Don't worry," he boasted. "I'm pretty sure I can make that house jump through hoops if I ask it. And maybe, if I get bored, I'll ask it!"

He looked up Breckinbridge in the clapboard barracks and got a day's leave of absence from him. Then there was a discussion with the cooks, who were rapidly persuaded to part with miscellaneous packaged foodstuffs. A hurriedly composed telegram to Caroline Hart of Boston, Massachusetts, and he was thumping his way back to the house behind headlights that were willing to split the darkness but were carefully noncommittal about the road.

It wasn't till Paul saw the house clutching the top of the hill that he realized how easily he would have accepted the fact of its disappearance.

Parking the runabout on the slope so that its lights illumined the way to the top, he pushed the side back and prepared to get out.

The door of the house opened. A dark carpet spilled out and humped down the hill to his feet. Regular, sharp protuberances along its length made it a perfect staircase. A definite rosy glow exuded from the protuberances, lighting his way.

"That's *really* rolling out the welcome mat," Paul commented as he locked the ignition in the car and started up.

He couldn't help jumping a bit when, passing through the vestibule, the walls bulged out slightly and touched him gently on either side. But there was such an impression of friendliness in the gesture and they moved back in place so swiftly that there was no logical reason for nervousness.

The dining-room table seemed to reach up slightly to receive the gear he dropped upon it. He patted it and headed for the kitchen.

Water still changed into whisky at his unspoken whim; as he desired, it also changed into onion soup, tomato juice and Napoleon brandy. The refrigerator, he found, was full of everything he might want, from five or six raw tenderloins to three bottles of dark beer complete with the brand name he usually asked for when shopping for himself.

The sight of the food made him hungry; he had missed supper. A steak suffocating under heaps of onions, surrounded by beans and washed down with plenty of hot coffee was an interesting thought. He started for the dining room to collect his gear.

His haversack still rested on the near side of the table. On the far side— On the far side, there reposed a platter containing a thick steak which supported a huge mound of onions and held an encircling brown mass of beans at one corner. Gleaming silverware lay between the platter and a veritable vase of coffee.

Paul found himself giggling hysterically and shook fear-wisps out of his head. Everything was obviously channeled for his comfort. Might as well pull up a chair and start eating. He looked around for one, in time to see a chair come gliding across the floor; it poked him delicately behind the knees and he sat down. The chair continued to the appointed position at the table.

It was while he was spooning away the last of the melon he had imagined into existence for dessert—it had been exuded, complete with dish, from the table top— that he noticed the lighting fixtures were also mere decorative devices. Light came from the walls—or the ceiling—or the floor; it was omnipresent in the house at just the right intensity—and that was all.

The dirty dishes and used silverware vanished into the table like sugar dissolving into hot solution.

Before he went up to bed, he decided to look in at the library. Surely, he had originally imagined a library? He decided he couldn't be certain, and thought one up next to the living room.

All the books he had ever enjoyed were in the warm little space. He spent a contented hour browsing from Aiken to Einstein, until he hit the beautifully bound Britannica. The first volume of the Encyclopedia he opened made him understand the limitations of his establishment.

The articles he had read completely were complete, those he had read in part showed only the sections he had touched. For the rest, there was a curious blur of not-quite print which puzzled him until he realized that this was just the picture the eyes retained while the pages of a book were flipped before it.

He climbed the narrow stairs to bed.

Yawningly tired, he noted vaguely that the bed was just the width he had always wanted. As fast as he dropped his clothes to the bedside chair, they were shaken off and pushed along a writhing strip of floor to the corner closet where he imagined they were hung neatly.

He lay down finally, repressing a shudder as the sheets curled up and over him of their own accord. Just before he fell asleep, he remembered he'd spent the largest parts of the past three nights playing chess and was likely to oversleep. He'd intended to rise early and examine his delightfully subservient property in detail, but since he hadn't thought to bring an alarm clock—

Did that matter?

He raised himself on one elbow, the sheet still hugging his chest. "Listen, you," he told the opposite wall sternly. "Wake me exactly eight hours from now. And do it pleasantly, understand?"

Wakefulness came with a sense of horror that nibbled at his mind. He lay still, wondering what had shocked him so.

"Paul, darling, please wake up. Paul, darling, please wake up. Paul, darling, please—"

Caroline's voice! He leaped out of bed and looked around crazily. What was Caroline doing here? The telegram he'd sent asking her to come up and look at their new house had probably not arrived until breakfast. Even a plane—

Then he remembered. Of course! He patted the bed. "Nice job. Couldn't have done better myself." The headboard curled against his hand and the walls vibrated with a humming noise that was astonishingly like a baritone purr.

The shower, he decided, must have been one of those brilliant yearning concepts he had once entertained for a second or two and then forgotten. It was merely a matter of stepping into a roomy cubicle dotted with multitudes of tiny holes and being sprayed with warm lather which stopped the moment he was soaped up and was succeeded by plain water at the same temperature. As the lather washed away, needle jets of air dried him completely.

He stepped out of the shower to find his clothes hung outside, excellently pressed and smelling faintly of laundry. He was surprised at the laundry odor, although he liked it; but then again that's why there was an odor—*because* he liked it!

It was going to be an unusually fine day, he noted, after suggesting to the bathroom window that it open—unfortunate that he hadn't brought any light clothes with him. Then, as his eyes glanced regretfully downward, he observed he was now wearing a sports shirt and summer slacks.

Evidently his own soiled clothes had been absorbed into the economy of the house and duplicates provided which had the pleasantly adaptive facilities of their source.

The hearts-of-palm breakfast he had worked out while strolling downstairs was ready for him in the dining room. The copy of Jane Austen's *Emma* he'd been rereading recently at mealtime lay beside it open to the correct place.

He sighed happily. "All I need now is a little Mozart played softly."

So, a little Mozart—

Connor Kuntz's helicopter lazed down out of the mild sky at four o'clock that afternoon. Paul thought the house into a Bunk Johnson trumpet solo and sauntered out to greet his guests.

Esther Sakarian was out of the plane first. She wore a severe black dress that made her look unusually feminine and much less of a laboratory type. "Sorry about bringing Doc Kuntz, Paul. But for all I knew you might need a medic after a night in this place. And I don't have a copter of my own. He offered to give me a lift."

"Perfectly all right," he told her magnanimously. "I'm ready to discuss the house with Kuntz or any other biologist."

She held up a yellow sheet. "For you. Just came."

He read the telegram and winced.

"Anything important?" Esther inquired, temporarily looking away from a pink cloud which seemed to have been fascinating her.

"Oh." He crumpled the sheet and bounced it gloomily on his open palm. "Caroline. Says she's surprised to discover I intended to make my permanent home up here. Says if I'm serious about it, I'd better reconsider our engagement."

Esther pursed her lips. "Well, it is a nice long haul from Boston. And allowing that your house isn't quite a dead issue…"

Paul laughed and snapped the paper ball into the air. "Not quite. But the way I feel at the moment: love me, love my house. And, speaking of houses— Down, sir! Down, I say!"

The house had crept down the slope behind him as he spoke, extruded a bay window and nuzzled his back with it. Now, at his sharp reproach, the window was sucked abruptly into the wall. The house sidled backward to its place at the top of the hill and stood quivering slightly. The trumpet solo developed extremely mournful overtones.

"Does…does it do that often?"

"Every time I move a little distance away," he assured her. "I could stop it permanently with a direct overall command, but I find it sort of flattering. I also don't want to step on a pretty warm personality. No harm in it. Hey, Connor, what do you think?"

The doctor perspired his plump body past them and considered the noisy structure warily. "Just now—I confess I don't know."

"Better give it up, Connor," Esther advised, "or you'll rupture an analysis."

Paul slapped his back. "Come inside and I'll explain it over a couple of glasses of beer I just got thirsty enough to think about."

Five beers later, Dr. Connor Kuntz used the black beads he had in place of eyes to watch his host shimmer from the uniform of the Coldstream Guards to a sharply cut tuxedo.

"Of course I believe it. Since it is so, it is so. You have a living house here. Now we must decide what we are to do with it."

Paul Marquis looked up, halfway into a white gabardine suit. The lapels, still tuxedo, hesitated; then gathered their energies and blended into a loose summer outfit.

"What *we* are to do with it?"

Kuntz rose and wrapped his hands behind his back. slapping the knuckles of one into the palm of the other. "You're quite right about keeping the information secret from the men in the development; a careless word and you would be undergoing swarms of dangerously inquisitive tourists. I must get in touch with Dr. Dufayel in Quebec; this is very much his province. Although there's a young man at Johns Hopkins— How much have you learned of its basic, let us say its *personal* composition?"

The young physicist's face lost its grip on resentment. "Well, the wood feels like wood, the metal like metal, the plastic like plastic. And when the house produces a glass-like object, it's real glass so far as I can determine without a chemical analysis. Es, here, took—"

"That's one of the reasons I decided to bring Connor along. Biologically and chemically, the water is safe—too safe. It's absolutely pure H_2O. What do you think of my chlorophyll roof theory, doctor?"

He ducked his head at her. "Possibly. Some form of solar energy transformation in any case. But chlorophyll would argue a botanical nature, while it has distinct and varied means of locomotion—internal and external. Furthermore, the manipulation of metals which do not exist in any quantities in this region suggest subatomic reorganization of materials. Esther, we must prepare some slides from this creature. Suppose you run out to the plane like a good girl and get my kit. For that matter, you can prepare slides yourself, can't you? I want to explore a bit."

"Slides?" Paul Marquis asked uncertainly as the bacteriologist started for the open door. "It's a living thing. you know."

"Ah, we'll just take a small area from an...a nonvital spot. Much like scraping a bit of skin off the human hand. Tell me," the doctor requested, thumping on the table experimentally, "you no doubt have some vague theories as to origin?"

Marquis settled himself back in a gleaming chair. "As a matter of fact, they're a little more than that. I remembered the ore in Pit Fourteen gave out suddenly after showing a lot of promise. Pit Fourteen's the closest to here from Little Fermi. Adler, the geologist in charge, commented at the time that it seemed as if Pit Fourteen had been worked before—about six thousand years ago. Either that or glacial scraping. But since there was little evidence of glacial scraping in the neighborhood, and *no* evidence of a previous, prehistoric pitchblende mine, he dropped the matter. I think this house is the rest of the proof of that prehistoric mine. I also think we'll find radioactive ore all the way from this site to the edge of Pit Fourteen."

"Comfortable situation for you if they do," Kuntz observed, moving into the kitchen. Paul Marquis rose and followed him. "How would this peculiar domicile enter into the situation?"

"Well, unless our archaeology still has to grow out of its diapers, nobody on Earth was interested in pitchblende six thousand years ago. That would leave the whole wide field of extraterrestrials—from a planet of our sun or one of the other stars. This could have been a fueling station for their ships, a regularly worked mine, or an unforeseen landing to make repairs and take on fuel."

"And the house?"

"The house was their dwelling—probably a makeshift, temporary job—while they worked the mine. When they went, they left it here as humans will leave deserted wood and metal shacks when they move out of Little Fermi one day. It lay here waiting for something—say the thought of ownership or the desire for a servitor-dwelling—to release a telepathic trigger that would enable it to assume its function of—"

A despairing shout from Esther tugged them outside.

"I've just broken my second scalpel on this chunk of iridium masquerading as fragile flesh. I have a definite suspicion, Paul, that I won't so much as scratch it unless you give me permission. Please tell your house it's all right for me to take a tiny chunk."

"It's...it's all right," Paul said uncomfortably, then added, "only, try not to hurt it too much."

Leaving the girl slicing a long, thin strip from the western corner, they walked down the cellar steps into the basement. Connor Kuntz stumbled around peering down at the floor for some example of an obviously biological organ. He found only white-washed cement.

"Assume its function of—" he said at last. "Its function of serving! My dear fellow, do you realize this house has a sex?"

"Sex?" Paul moved aback, taken there by the thought. "You mean it can have lots of little bungalows?"

"Oh, not in the reproductive sense, not in the reproductive sense!" The plump doctor would have prodded him in the ribs if he hadn't started hurriedly up the stairs. "It has sex in the emotional, the psychological sense. As a woman wants to be a wife to a man, as a man searches for a woman to whom he can be an adequate husband—just so this house desires to be a *home* to a living creature who both needs it and owns it. As such it fulfills itself and becomes capable of its one voluntary act—the demonstration of affection, again in terms of the creature it serves. By the by, it also seems to be that theoretically happy medium in those disagreements on twentieth-century domestic arrangements with which you and Esther liven up the mess hall on occasion. Unostentatious love and imaginative service."

"Does at that. If only Es didn't make a habit of plucking my nerve-ends— Hum. Have you noticed how pleasant she's been today?"

"Of course. The house has made adjustments in her personality for your greater happiness."

"*What?* Es has been changed? You're crazy, Connor!"

"On the contrary, my boy. I assure you she was just as argumentative back in Little Fermi and on the way out here as she ever was. The moment she saw you, she became most traditionally feminine—without losing one jot of her acuity or subtlety, remember that. When someone like Esther Sakarian who has avoided the 'You are so right, my lord' attitude all her life acquires it overnight, she has had help. In this case, the house."

Paul Marquis dug his knuckles at the solid, reassuring substance of the basement wall. "Es has been changed by the house for my possible personal convenience? I don't know if I like that. Es should be Es, good or bad. Besides, it might take a notion to change me."

The older man looked at him with a deadly twinkle. "I don't know how it affects personalities—high-order therapeutic radiation on an intellectual level?—but let me ask you this, Paul, wouldn't you like to be happy at the agreeable alteration in Miss Sakarian? And, furthermore, wouldn't you like to think that the house couldn't affect your own attitudes?"

"Of course." Paul shrugged his shoulders. "For that matter, I *am* happy about Es getting some womanly sense in her head. And, come to think of it, I doubt if you or anyone else could ever convince me that the house could push mental fixations around like so much furniture. Whole thing's too ridiculous for further discussion."

Connor Kuntz chortled and slapped his thighs for emphasis. "Perfect! And now you can't even imagine that the wish for such a state of mind made the house produce it in you. It learns to serve you better all the time! Dr. Dufayel is going to appreciate this!"

"A point there. I don't go for advertising my peculiar residence and its properties—whatever they are—up and down the field of research medicine. Is there any way I can persuade you to lay off?"

Kuntz stopped his dignified little dance and looked up seriously. "Why, certainly! I can think of at least two good reasons why I should never again discuss your house with anyone but you or Esther." He seemed to consider a moment. "Rather, I should say there are six or seven reasons for not mentioning your house's existence to Dufayel or any other biologist. In fact, there are literally dozens and dozens of reasons."

Paul followed Connor Kuntz and Esther back to the copter, promising them he'd be in for duty the next morning. "But I'm going to spend my nights here from now on."

"Take it slow and easy," Esther warned. "And don't brood over Caroline."

"Don't worry." He nodded at the affectionately trembling structure. "Have to teach it a couple of things. Like not bouncing around after me when there's company. Es, think you'd like to share it with me? You'd get as much care and affection as I would."

She giggled. "The three of us—going down the beautiful years together in a perfect marriage. We won't need any servants, just you and I and the house. Maybe a cleaning woman once or twice a week for the sake of appearances if a real estate boom materializes and we have neighbors."

"Oh, we'll have neighbors all right," Paul boasted to include Connor Kuntz's suddenly whiter-than-usual face. "We'll become very rich once the new lode is traced to part of our property, and when Little Fermi is operating as the power city of the American continents we'll make another fortune selling the land for suburban development. And think of the research we'll be able to do in physics and bacteriology, Es, with the house supplying us with any equipment we can visualize!"

"You'll be very happy," Kuntz told them shortly. "The house will see to it that you're happy if it has to kill you—or, rather, your egos." He turned to the bacteriologist. "Esther, I thought you said yesterday that Paul would have to change a good deal before you could marry him. Has he changed, or has the house changed you?"

"Did I say that? Well, Paul hasn't exactly— But the house—"

"And how about that odd feeling you said the house gave you?" the doctor went on. "As if something were disconnecting wires in your brain and resplicing them according to a new blueprint? Don't you see that wiring blueprint belongs to Paul and the house is installing it?"

Paul had taken the girl in his arms and stood frowning at Kuntz. "I just don't like that idea, even if it is vaguely possible." His face cleared. "But it's vague enough to be impossible. Don't you think so, Es?"

She seemed to be struggling with an inner confusion that darted and shed sparks. "I...I don't know. Yes, I do. Impossible isn't the word for it! Why, I never heard of anything so completely— All your house wants to do is serve you. It's lovable and harmless."

"It isn't!" The physician was dancing up and down like a partridge in a net. "Admitted, it will only make psychological adjustments as required to resolve your serious inner conflicts, but remember, this house is a distinctly alien form of life. If it was ever completely controlled, the power was vested in creatures far superior to ourselves. There's danger enough, now, when it makes you think exactly as you want to think from moment to moment; but when it begins to feel the looseness of your mental reins—"

"Stow it, Connor!" Paul cut him off. "I told you I couldn't accept that line of thought. I don't want you to mention it again. It's plain ugly. Isn't it, darling?"

"And illogical." She smiled.

And Dr. Connor Kuntz was able merely to stand and think terrifying thoughts to himself.

Behind them, the house joyfully hummed a connubial snatch of *Lohengrin*.

Oh, glorious master, who will never want to leave—

While the copter wound upward into the sallow sky, and Esther waved at the dwindling figure below with the house skipping gayly to his side, Kuntz asked cautiously: "If you two intend to go on any sort of honeymoon inside that place, you'll have to get a release from the company. That won't be easy."

She turned to him. "Why?"

"Because you signed a contract, and the government is backing the company on the contract. No out for either of you. Fact is, Paul may get into some trouble with his extended vacation."

Esther pondered it for a moment. "Yes, I see. And you know, Connor, with the house and all, I was sort of planning to leave the company permanently and take up residence right away. I'm pretty sure Paul feels the same way. I hope there won't be any trouble."

Then she laughed easily, and the angular frown lines disappeared from her face. "But I don't think there will be any trouble. I think everything will go smoothly. I just *feel* it."

Shocked, Connor Kuntz realized that this unusual display of "feminine intuition" from Esther Sakarian was correct. He thought:

The house will see to it that the government voids their contracts without any trouble, because the house wants to keep them happy. It will keep them happy, giving them anything they want—except the means to get away from it. This product of some gigantic imagination has two desires actually—the desire to serve, and the desire to have a master. Having reacquired one after all these years, it will keep him, her, them, at any cost. But making adjustments in the world to keep them happy will be like knocking over the first in a row of dominoes; it will have to do more and more to keep the world from interfering.

Eventually this domestic utensil could control all humanity and make it jump at the vagrant whims of Paul Marquis and Esther Sakarian. All in the name of service! It has the power to do it, probably is nothing more itself than a collection of basic forces in temporary formful stasis. And if it does ever control the planet—why, there will be no more objection to it than Esther and Paul exhibit! This servile hunk of real estate is so far above us in capability, that it can run our world and make us think we like it. And to think I'm sitting next to one of the people whose most passing fancy could become my unalterable command! Horrible, horrible—

But by the time he had landed the copter at Little Fermi, Connor Kuntz no longer found the idea objectionable. He thought it quite in order that he could only do those things to which Paul and Esther did not object. Extremely natural, in fact.

AFTERWORD

My original reason for writing this story had little to do with science fiction as such or with making a living out of writing. I was trying to do a portrait of my two closest friends at the time, Judy Merril and Ted Sturgeon. When they saw the completed piece, they both said I had done a fine job on the other one, but I had missed completely on themselves.

I, though, felt it was a complete failure then, and I feel it is a complete failure now; I produce it here for whatever historical or personal-literary significance it might have.

To quote our great phrase-making President, Richard Milhous Nixon, let me make one thing perfectly clear: Judy and Ted never so much as contemplated marriage with each other. We were all three happily involved with different partners at the time—but I felt that bundling the two of them together helped increase dramatic tension which might in turn strengthen the portrait I was attempting.

A few last and completely minor notes. I am in the story in a sort of shadowy way: the reading matter and musical tastes I ascribe to the male protagonist were mine, rather than Sturgeon's; Connor Kuntz's character was based on that of L. Jerome Stanton, then the associate editor of *Astounding Science Fiction* (where the story eventually appeared), and the man who took Sturgeon practically out of the gutter and into his apartment when Ted came back to New York from the tropics after a bad writing slump and a painful divorce. And the house? The house was my attempt to write into existence the kind of living arrangement that Ted at the time seemed to be searching for, as he grappled with the problems of domesticity. He told me he felt it was the best part of the story. It is.

WRITTEN 1947——PUBLISHED 1948

ॐ

There Were People on Bikini,
There Were People on Attu

One day the Earth found itself surrounded by spaceships.

These spaceships were enormous and completely alien in design; they were operated by power so tremendous that their approach had not even been suspected by a single astronomer in the northern or southern hemisphere. The ships had simply materialized in uncanny multitudes all about the planet; and there they remained, with no outward signs of activity, for about twenty hours.

On Earth, naturally, there was a good deal of activity—some of it frenzied. The nations buzzed back and forth to each other, ally reaching out with moist diplomatic hand to ally, foe asking tentative, wide-eyed question of foe.

Newspapers put out extras as fast as the presses could blink, and television networks presented stammering scientists—all kinds of scientists: nuclear physicists, botanists, field archaeologists, anatomy professors—in a tousled, bewildering succession. Aimless, ugly riots broke out; churches and revival tents overflowed with worried worshipers; the suicide rate went up sharply.

A boating party on Loch Ness swore in a group affidavit that they had been approached by a sea serpent forty-eight feet long. It informed them in impeccable English that it was a citizen of the star Arcturus and had arrived exactly two hours ago. It was pro-Labor and anti-vivisection.

Everywhere, men, women, and children shaded their eyes and stared hard at those areas of the sky most distant from the sun. Peepingly, they could discern the outlines of the strange craft, hanging like so many clusters of impossibly shaped grapes. In the dark sections of Earth, the spaceships glowed all night around their edges, throwing a thin network of yellow phosphorescence against the purple heavens.

People shuffled uneasily and asked their neighbors, their leaders, even strangers: "What does it mean? What do they want?"

Nobody had the slightest idea.

A radio-controlled space vehicle, built to explore the moons of Mars, was sent up for a close look at the spaceships. Shortly after it passed the outer limits of the atmosphere, it disappeared completely, and no trace of it was ever found again. A minute or so later, every single artificial satellite orbiting the Earth also disappeared. No explosions, no blast from a new kind of ray—just, there they all were one moment, and there they were *not* the next.

It became obvious that if the creatures in the spaceships wanted to conquer Earth, to enslave or exterminate its population, there was nothing to stop them. Mankind's most powerful countermeasures would function like a fly swatter putting down a dynamite explosion.

Nonetheless, nation after nation mobilized, airmen sat tensely in jet planes that were incapable of reaching one-hundredth the height of the spaceships, gun crews of antiaircraft units piled shells near their weapons and waited for their radar operators to give them usable target instructions. IBM sites, ABM sites, *all* ballistic missile sites, were put on red alert. Martial law was proclaimed in Greenland, at Cape Horn, in the Andaman Islands.

At the same time, men of good will all over Earth pointed out that the inhabitants of the spaceships were probably creatures of good will. Their technology was much, much more advanced than the best that humanity had—why shouldn't their sociology be equally advanced? If their machines were better, why shouldn't their ethics be better, too? Be intelligent, the men of good will suggested earnestly: if these alien creatures had the means to come upon Earth so suddenly, they could probably have overwhelmed it in the same flashing instant had they so desired. No, the men of good will decided at last, humanity had nothing to fear.

Humanity, stubbornly, continued to fear.

"All those spaceships. What do they *want?*"

There was a lot of activity in war colleges and government offices that day and night. Specialists in every field that in any way related to communications were collected by military press gangs and set to work at devices that might transmit or receive messages relative to the spaceships. Radio, blinker lights, even telepathy, were tried. Nothing worked. Panic grew.

At the end of twenty hours, each spaceship simultaneously disgorged five smaller craft. These floated down to the surface of the planet and, upon landing, began to blare out from loudspeakers mounted on their bows the identical message:

"Everybody off Earth!"

In Tibet, this message was blared in Tibetan; in Norway, in Norwegian; around Lake Chad, in all the numerous Chad dialects; in certain parts of the United States of America, *"Everbody offen the Yurth! And naow!"* The message was the same wherever the smaller craft landed, only it was spoken in the tongue and idiom peculiar to the region.

"Everybody off Earth!"

For about half an hour these words were screamed at the dumbfounded humans who had gathered around the odd vessels. Then, abruptly, and all over Earth at exactly the same moment, openings appeared in various parts of these ships, and metallic creatures with dozens of metallic tentacles came out. These creatures, it was apparent to men still able to use their imaginations, could be nothing but robots, mechanical servants of thinking individuals in the spaceships that still hovered miles upon empty hundreds of miles above the atmosphere.

The robots began to collect people.

They moved to a group of people—they moved extremely fast—and reached out with their tentacles, grasping a human gently but firmly around the waist with each one. When every tentacle held a kicking, scratching, screaming human, each robot turned and marched back to its ship, repeating forcefully, though a trifle monotonously, "Everybody off Earth—*everybody!*"

The people were set down carefully in a kind of hold inside the ship, and the robot left, after snapping the aperture shut behind it. Then it gathered more people, one to each tentacle, and brought them, hysterical or fainting or rigid with terror, to the hold of its ship. As soon as the captives began to get crowded and uncomfortable, the vessel would dart upwards and be received into the larger ship from which it had come. There, the robots, still carefully, almost daintily, transferred the people in exactly the same fashion—one by one—to another, but much more immense hold in the mother ship. This hold had been fitted with tiers of cots like those of a troop transport, and every cot held a blanket and pillow made of some unrecognizable soft white material. When the transfer was complete, the small ship and its crew of robots went down for another load.

All day, all night, the loading went on. In the holds of the large mother ships, those humans already stowed huddled in groups and stared upwards distractedly. Every few minutes, the solid metal ceiling high above them developed an opening in the center, through which a bunch of wriggling, screeching people floated down. Then the ceiling melted together again and the new arrivals landed very gently on the rubbery floor, immediately asking frenzied questions of the older inhabitants.

What was going to be done with them? Why? Who was behind all this? Where were they going to be taken? Perhaps they were going to be eaten, and the vaulting hold that stretched enormously about them was a kind of extraterrestrial pantry?

No one knew. Most of them shivered, expecting the worst; a few speculated sanely; but no one knew.

All night, all day, the loading went on. It was indiscriminate. No human boundaries were recognized. A load of Portuguese fishermen was deposited in the midst of a previous load of Chinese farmers from a collective in Kwantung. The Roman Catholic fishermen sank to their knees and followed an apoplectic Methodist minister from Albuquerque, New Mexico, in prayer; the ingratiating young chairman of the collective farm bustled about organizing a Marxist study group for a squeaking crowd of stylish matrons from Johannesburg, South Africa, whose Ladies' Aid Society meeting had been picked up en masse.

When a hold contained enough people to occupy all the cots in it, the ceiling opened no more, and activity moved to another hold or another ship. Thus, half the Congress of the United States of America was dropped wholesale into the student body and faculty of the largest elementary school in Bucharest, while the other half vainly tried gaining information and establishing authority among the surrounding Madras dirt farmers and the rather puzzled inmates of a Damascus prison.

The loading went on for five days and five nights. Nothing stopped the loading; nothing delayed it. Guided missiles with nuclear warheads not only disappeared just as they arrived at target, but their sources became the very next object of attention. Every last launching site in the Arizona desert and the Siberian tundra was visited and cleared a few minutes after it fired its rockets. Here and there, military detachments fought on valiantly to the end, their commanding officers watching in stupefaction as bullets and shells bounced harmlessly off the alien robots who plodded patiently through murderous enfilading fire on their way to pick up the occupants of regimental or divisional headquarters.

A thorough job was done. Submarines were brought to the surface and emptied of their crews; men at the bottom of the world's deepest mine shafts, with their arms locked desperately about the supporting timbers, were gently but insistently pried loose by the robot tentacles and carried to a last open hold.

Every living human on Earth was taken up to the alien spaceships. But no animals. The animals all remained behind, they and the empty fields and the tall forests and the seas that swirled unendingly along the white beaches of the world.

When the loading was complete, the space fleet moved away as a unit. The acceleration was so smooth that few of the humans even suspected that they were under way. The space fleet moved away from Earth, away from our Sun, and plunged into the black gulfs of the universe.

Except for the shock of being torn from familiar environments so abruptly, the humans aboard the ships had to admit they were not too badly off. There were several water fountains in each hold; there were adequate plumbing facilities; the cots were quite comfortable and so were the temperatures maintained.

Twice each day, exactly twelve hours apart, chimes were sounded and a dozen large soup tureens materialized in the middle of the floor. These tureens were filled with thick white dumpling-like objects bobbing in a greenish liquid. The dumplings and the soup were apparently nourishing, and acceptable to the palates of a thousand different cuisines—though dismally boring as a steady diet. After everyone had eaten, the chimes sounded again and the tureens vanished; they vanished like great, moistureless bubbles. And then there was nothing to do but wander about, try to learn your neighbor's language, sleep a little, worry about the future a little—and wait for the next feeding.

If trouble started, as for example between a factory of Australian steel workers and a tribe of Zulu warriors over the favors of some nurses from a Leningrad hospital—if large trouble, incipient riot, mass fighting, ever got started—it was stopped immediately. A series of robots would materialize through the floor, one after another, each one exactly like the other. Each robot would grab as many individual belligerents as its tentacles could hold and keep them apart until the passage of time and the ridiculous position in which they found themselves brought the angry people back to a state of relative calm. Then, without making a comment or even a single illuminating gesture, the robots disappeared, exactly like the soup tureens.

They were certainly well taken care of. On that point, eventually, all agreed. But why? For what purpose?

Certainly, there seemed to be a sinister overtone to the hospitality they were enjoying. The care and concern lavished upon them, not a few noted darkly, were all too reminiscent of a farmer in a barnyard or a shepherd with a flock of fat, highly marketable sheep.

Or was it possible, the optimists argued, that these highly advanced aliens were mixing humanity in the melting pots of the holds deliberately? Having impatiently observed our squabbling and wars and homicidal prejudices, had they decided with a kind of godlike irritation to make of us one cohesive race once and for all?

It was hard to tell. No alien ever manifested himself. No robot ever said another word, once the holds were closed. Despite the best efforts of all the inhabitants of a given hold, despite the untiring ingenuity of the human race in all of the ships, there was no communication between the people of Earth and their alien hosts for the entire lengthy voyage.

All they could do was wonder—eat, sleep, talk, and wonder—as the fleet of enormous spaceships traveled on and on. They went past star system after star system, they went past worlds in gaseous birth and worlds cracked and dead.

And as the days passed—marked only by sleep periods and carefully rewound wristwatches—most people decided that the complete lack of communication, as well as the casual way they had been handled, suggested a contempt that was very disquieting.

Many great and minor changes took place among the inhabitants of the holds. The young Danish housewife who had been separated from her husband and children grew tired of fighting off the advances of the Trobriand Islanders about her and made her choice simply, in terms of the huskiest and most importunate of her suitors; the member-delegates of the United Nations Security Council gave up trying to effect a rapprochement with the gabardined followers of Chaim ben Judah-David, the wonder-working rabbi from the Williamsburg section of Brooklyn, and sat in bitter isolation in their corner of the hold, announcing from time to time that they constituted the only world government legally capable of dealing with the aliens in the name of humanity as a whole. As soon, of course, as the aliens asked for such representatives...

That was the rub, and all felt it to some degree, and felt it more and more as the days were marked off into weeks and the weeks into months. In the bowels of every one of them—diplomat and devout Hasidic Jew, pale woman from the shores of the North Sea and brown man from the wide Pacific Ocean—nervousness about the future rattled and clattered. What was going to happen to them? What could the aliens want with the whole human race?

Most of them did not know exactly when the ships came to their destination and stopped. The realization that the voyage was over came only when the holds opened above their heads and welcome sunlight roared in. Except that—once the first wildly happy cheers had died away—they noticed this was red sunlight, not yellow.

And then there was the debarkation.

Done with much less struggling, of course, much less screaming and fear-wet excitement. The robots were almost welcomed as they reversed the process of a few months ago. Men and women, with a few neurotic or superstitious exceptions, fought to be the first picked up by the hard, shining, segmented tentacles and transferred to the smaller ships that were attached to the sides of the large transports like so many baby spiders.

When the small ships landed, the human cargo enthusiastically continued to help the robots as much as it could in its own unloading. Ship after ship, now empty, sped back to the great fleet above for more humans, while those who once again found themselves standing on soil and vegetation looked about them.

It was not Earth. That alone was certain.

They were on a hard grey planet whose surface was broken by few of the hills and none of the mountains that most of them associated with topography. A rather dry-smelling grey planet, poor in oceans and barely stippled here and there with tiny, lake-like seas. A gusty grey planet without trees to shush the steady complaint of its winds. There were only broad-leaved, gritty-stemmed plants that grew ankle-high.

All the colors were wrong. The plants looked like sick blue spinach. The sun above them was a liverish bronze, old and stained. The sky was made of bile—cloudless, featureless essence of thick green bile.

And on the night side, no moon floated through the absolutely unfamiliar constellations. It was deeply dark on the night side, and with the darkness a sharp stink belched from the ground-huddled plants. The stink was spread efficiently by the ever-wandering, ever-wailing winds.

No, it was not Earth. It was not at all like Earth…Earth, so exceptionally far away.

A Finnish farmer watched a small boy from Dakar tear off a limp blue leaf and munch on it experimentally. The boy spat out the leaf with an explosion of saliva and wiped his tongue furiously upon his arm. The farmer prodded a shoe into the ground and worried: *Grey dust, that's all it is. What could I grow in it that I could eat? I don't have any seeds, but even if I did, could they grow in this damn dust?* A New Zealand sheep rancher bit deep into a fingernail as he wondered: *We didn't bring any herds with us, but say we had—what in hell would they be grazing on? No sheep in his right mind would go near those blue weeds.* A Bolivian mining engineer arose from an examination of the soil and said to his still-nightgowned wife: "My first impression, and a pretty strong one, is that this planet is rich in copper—and not much else. Not that there's anything wrong with copper, you understand, only there's just so much you can do with it. You can't make typewriters out of copper.…You can't make automobiles or airplanes out of copper."

Men looked around in vain for wood that could be used to build houses, for stone with which to raise temples and altars and idols; they saw nothing but the green sky, the blue plants, and the grey, grey soil. Fishermen peered anxiously into the tiny seas and saw nothing swimming, nothing crawling, nothing wriggling; they saw only seaweed, purplish-blue seaweed floating in thin, ragged patches.

A little boy from Chattanooga, Tennessee, toddled up to his mother where she stood talking in a low voice to a group of worried neighbors. He tugged at her skirt until he attracted her attention. "It's an ugly world, Mommy," he told her decisively. "It's an ugly, no-good world, and I don't like it. I want to go home."

She picked him up and hugged him to her, but before she could say anything—while she was still searching for words and thoughts—the robots started to build.

They came down, the robots, from the great ships hanging motionless above, each carrying a section of a prefabricated dwelling. These they fitted together rapidly into immensely long barracks, filled with the familiar cots. Each long barracks held one shipload of people; each was furnished with toilets and water-fountains which bubbled good potable water; each had multitudes of tiny loudspeakers mounted along the walls and ceilings.

When they had assembled the barracks, the robots herded the people into them. They spread their tentacles wide, and they insistently, patiently pushed people ahead of them through the entrances. So many to a barracks, irrespective of age, sex, nationality, or family connection. When a barracks had been filled, the robots shunted the very next individual—husband, commanding officer, twin sister—into another and empty barracks. They were as efficient as ever, and, by this time, most human beings had learned it was useless to oppose them. The robots did their job well, gently and courteously for non-sentient creatures, but as ever, with the single-minded purposefulness of drones.

The humans sat on the cots and waited until all of them were housed. Then the robots disappeared. In their place came the familiar soup tureens and the familiar dumplings. People everywhere ate. They ate their fill, glancing at each other sideways and shrugging their shoulders. They finished, and the tureens disappeared.

Now, for the first time, the people of Earth heard the voice of the aliens, the owners and masters of the robots, the navigators of the grape-cluster ships.

It was an explanation (at last, at *last,* an explanation!) and it came from the many little loudspeakers in the barracks. It was given simultaneously in every language of mankind—you moved about the barracks until you found a speaker emitting words you understood—and it was listened to with great, almost frantic attention.

To begin with, the aliens explained, it was necessary for us to understand how highly civilized they were. That was very important. It was the foundation, it was the basic reason for everything they had done. They were a civilized race, enormously civilized, anciently civilized, civilized beyond our most poetic dreams of civilization.

We, as a race, were on the first stumbling steps of that civilization. We were primitive, insignificant, and—if we might pardon them for saying so—slightly ridiculous. Our technology was elementary, our ethical and spiritual awareness almost non-existent.

But we were a race of living creatures and we did have a speck, a promise, of civilization. Therefore, they had no alternative: they had to save us. They had to go to all the trouble and expense we had witnessed and would witness in the future. As civilized creatures there was absolutely nothing else they could do.

We should know that not all creatures in the universe were as civilized as they. Wars were fought, weapons were used. They themselves had recently developed, purely for purposes of self-protection, a new weapon....

It was a frightful weapon, a shattering weapon, a weapon that smashed the constituents of time and space in a given area. They sincerely hoped never to have to use that weapon in actual warfare. Still, one never knew to what lengths an uncivilized enemy might go.

The weapon had to be tested.

It was impossible, given the terrible nature of the weapon, given its totally unpredictable aftereffects, to test it in any densely populated section of the galaxy. Furthermore, in order to get a clear and scientific picture of the weapon's potential military value, it was necessary to destroy an entire planet in the course of the test.

The aliens had selected the site very carefully. They had selected a sparsely populated solar system, a very unimportant planet inhabited by an extremely backward race—a race so backward, in fact, that it was just now beginning to develop space travel. They had selected, in other words, a world of no conceivable value to anybody consulted, a world that no other race in the galaxy deemed at all desirable, an absolutely useless, second-rate nonentity of a world—our Earth.

Here they would test their weapon. They would test it on a world whose total obliteration would not be noticed anywhere.

But Earth was inhabited by a race which had intelligence within, at least, the widest definition of the term. And the aliens were civilized, highly civilized, ultimately civilized. They could not just destroy another race out of hand, no matter how primitive it might be. They had a responsibility to life itself, to the future, to history.

So they had done this enormous, this expensive, this altruistic and unheard-of thing. At a cost so overwhelming that it could not be expressed at all in the limited figures of human economics, they had evacuated our entire planet.

They had carried us all the way across the galaxy (hang the expense! never mind the expense! when they did a thing, they believed in doing it right!) to another planet which, while uninhabited, was as much like Earth as anything they could find in the universe.

Its size and mass were almost exactly the same as Earth's—so we didn't have to worry about any difference in gravity. Its distance from the sun, its periods of revolution and rotation were quite similar—our day-night systems and calendars would be little altered.

All in all, a wonderful new home.

Of course, there were some changes: no two planets were exactly alike. The atmospheric elements existed here in slightly different proportions; the water, while not poisonous, was effectively undrinkable; it would not be possible for a good long time to grow any edible plants in this soil. And, no doubt we had noticed, there weren't any animals on this world, nor were the mineral resources susceptible to exploitation by any techniques we had developed to date. However, taking the good with the bad, the bitter with the sweet, one way or another, sooner or later, they knew we would manage. We had a brand new planet, a completely untouched planet, a virgin planet, all for our very own.

All we had to do was to learn how to use it properly.

Meanwhile, they would not desert us. Hadn't they told us how civilized they were?

No, however long it took us to get on our feet and become self-supporting, their robots would be there to take care of us. We could use the barracks (they were made of almost indestructible material) until we figured out a way to make some other kind of home on this world. And the soup kitchens would be running, day in and day out, serving the good white dumplings designed especially for us until we developed some other, more indigenous source of nourishment.

But all this was for the future. We had had a long, tiring trip and probably did not want to worry about practical matters right now. How about a little entertainment? Something special, something none of us had ever imagined we would see.

Television screens appeared on the ceilings of the barracks, and humans turned baffled, confused faces upwards. Outside the walls, everywhere, the wind howled stubbornly, unendingly.

This was a rare treat, the aliens explained through the loudspeakers, a once-in-a-thousand-years sort of thing. We would be able to tell our children and our children's children that we had seen it, at exactly the same time as other, much more advanced races throughout the galaxy. "Now, for the first time, and at the exact moment it occurs, you will witness the total destruction of a world—the planet Earth—in the course of an essential and epic scientific experiment."

AFTERWORD

For those readers who don't know about it:

In 1946, the United States needed a place to test the atomic bomb that had been developed and used only one year before. The Bikini Atoll in the Pacific Ocean was chosen. It consisted of thirty-six islets on a reef twenty-five miles long.

The entire population was evacuated and removed, first to Rongerik, then to Ujelang, then to Kili. Between 1948 and 1958, twenty-three atomic and hydrogen bomb tests were conducted on the atoll. In 1969, Bikini was declared safe for humans once again, and in 1974, about a hundred or so of the original inhabitants were allowed back. They were all, however, reevacuated in 1978.

But for someone, somewhere, this testing was not enough. So they went to the island of Attu in the Aleutian chain of the North Pacific, and did it all over again.

WRITTEN 1994——PUBLISHED 1994

ॐ

The Somewhat Heavy Fantastic

She Only Goes Out at Night...

In this part of the country, folks think that Doc Judd carries magic in his black leather satchel. He's *that* good.

Ever since I lost my leg in the sawmill, I've been all-around handyman at the Judd place. Lots of times when Doc gets a night call after a real hard day, he's too tired to drive, so he hunts me up and I become a chauffeur, too. With the shiny plastic leg that Doc got me at a discount, I can stamp the gas pedal with the best of them.

We roar up to the farmhouse and, while Doc goes inside to deliver a baby or swab grandma's throat, I sit in the car and listen to them talk about what a ball of fire the old Doc is. In Groppa County, they'll tell you Doc Judd can handle *anything*. And I nod and listen, nod and listen.

But all the time I'm wondering what they'd think of the way he handled his only son falling in love with a vampire...

It was a terrifically hot summer when Steve came home on vacation—real blister weather. He wanted to drive his father around and kind of help with the chores, but Doc said that after the first tough year of medical school anyone deserved a vacation.

"Summer's a pretty quiet time in our line," he told the boy. "Nothing but poison ivy and such until we hit the polio season in August. Besides, you wouldn't want to shove old Tom out of his job, would you? No, Stevie, you just bounce around the countryside in your jalopy and enjoy yourself."

Steve nodded and took off. And I mean took off. About a week later, he started coming home five or six o'clock in the morning. He'd sleep till about three in the afternoon, laze around for a couple of hours and, come eight-thirty, off he'd rattle in his little hot-rod. Roadhouses, we figured, or maybe some girl...

Doc didn't like it, but he'd brought up the boy with a nice easy hand and he didn't feel like saying anything just yet. Old buttinsky Tom, though—I was different. I'd helped raise the kid since his mother died, and I'd walloped him when I caught him raiding the icebox.

So I dropped a hint now and then, kind of asking him, like, not to go too far off the deep end. I could have been talking to a stone fence for all the good it did. Not that Steve was rude. He was just too far gone in whatever it was to pay attention to me.

And then the other stuff started and Doc and I forgot about Steve.

Some kind of weird epidemic hit the kids of Groppa County and knocked twenty, thirty, of them flat on their backs.

"It's almost got me beat, Tom," Doc would confide in me as we bump-bump-bumped over dirty back-country roads. "It acts like a bad fever, yet the rise in temperature is hardly noticeable. But the kids get very weak and their blood count goes way down. And it stays that way, no matter what I do. Only good thing, it doesn't seem to be fatal—so far."

Every time he talked about it, I felt a funny twinge in my stump where it was attached to the plastic leg. I got so uncomfortable that I tried to change the subject, but that didn't go with Doc. He'd gotten used to thinking out his problems by talking to me, and this epidemic thing was pretty heavy on his mind.

He'd written to a couple of universities for advice, but they didn't seem to be of much help. And all the time, the parents of the kids stood around waiting for him to pull a cellophane-wrapped miracle out of his little black bag, because, as they said in Groppa County, there was nothing could go wrong with a human body that Doc Judd couldn't take care of some way or other. And all the time, the kids got weaker and weaker.

Doc got big, bleary bags under his eyes from sitting up nights going over the latest books and medical magazines he'd ordered from the city. Near as I could tell he'd find nothing, even though lots of times he'd get to bed almost as late as Steve.

And then he brought home the handkerchief. Soon as I saw it, my stump gave a good, hard, extra twinge and I wanted to walk out of the kitchen. Tiny, fancy handkerchief, it was, all embroidered linen and lace edges.

"What do you think, Tom? Found this on the floor of the bedroom of the Stopes' kids. Neither Betty nor Willy have any idea where it came from. For a bit, I thought I might have a way of tracing the source of infection, but those kids wouldn't lie. If they say they never saw it before, then that's the way it is." He dropped the handkerchief on the kitchen table that I was clearing up, stood there sighing. "Betty's anemia is beginning to look serious. I wish I knew… I wish… Oh, well." He walked out to the study, his shoulders bent like they were under a sack of cement.

I was still staring at the handkerchief, chewing on a fingernail, when Steve bounced in. He poured himself a cup of coffee, plumped it down on the table and saw the handkerchief.

"Hey," he said. "That's Tatiana's. How did it get here?"

I swallowed what was left of the fingernail and sat down very carefully opposite him. "Steve," I asked, and then stopped because I had to massage my aching stump. "Stevie, you know a girl who owns that handkerchief? A girl named Tatiana?"

"Sure. Tatiana Latianu. See, there are her initials embroidered in the corner—T.L. She's descended from the Rumanian nobility; family goes back about five hundred years. I'm going to marry her."

"She the girl you've been seeing every night for the past month?"

He nodded. "She only goes out at night. Hates the glare of the sun. You know, poetic kind of girl. And Tom, she's so *beautiful…*"

For the next hour, I just sat there and listened to him. And I felt sicker and sicker. Because I'm Rumanian myself, on my mother's side. And I knew why I'd been getting those twinges in my stump.

She lived in Brasket Township, about twelve miles away. Tom had run into her late one night on the road when her convertible had broken down. He'd given her a lift to her house—she'd just rented the old Mead Mansion—and he'd fallen for her, hook, line and whole darn fishing rod.

Lots of times, when he arrived for a date, she'd be out, driving around the country-side in the cool night air, and he'd have to play cribbage with her maid, an old beak-faced Rumanian biddy, until she got back. Once or twice, he'd tried to go after her in his hot-rod, but that had led to trouble. When she wanted to be alone, she had told him, she wanted to be *alone*. So that was that. He waited for her night after night. But when she got back, according to Steve, she really made up for everything. They lis-tened to music and talked and danced and ate strange Rumanian dishes that the maid whipped up. Until dawn. Then he came home.

Steve put his hand on my arm. "Tom, you know that poem—*The Owl and the Pussy-cat?* I've always thought the last line was beautiful. 'They danced by the light of the moon, the moon, they danced by the light of the moon.' That's what my life will be like with Tatiana. If only she'll have me. I'm still having trouble talking her into it."

I let out a long breath. "The first good thing I've heard," I said without thinking. "Marriage to *that* girl—"

When I saw Steve's eyes, I broke off. But it was too late.

"What the hell do you mean, Tom: *that* girl? You've never even met her."

I tried to twist out of it, but Steve wouldn't let me. He was real sore. So I figured the best thing was to tell him the truth.

"Stevie. Listen. Don't laugh. Your girl friend is a vampire."

He opened his mouth slowly. "Tom, you're off your—"

"No, I'm not." And I told him about vampires. What I'd heard from my mother who'd come over from the old country, from Transylvania, when she was twenty. How they can live and have all sorts of strange powers—just so long as they have a feast of human blood once in a while. How the vampire taint is inherited, usually just one child in the family getting it. And how they go out only at night, because sunlight is one of the things that can destroy them.

Steve turned pale at this point. But I went on. I told him about the mysterious epidemic that had hit the kids of Groppa County—and made them anemic. I told him about his father finding the handkerchief in the Stopes' house, near two of the sickest kids. And I told him—but all of a sudden I was talking to myself. Steve tore out of the kitchen. A second or two later, he was off in the hot-rod.

He came back about eleven-thirty, looking as old as his father. I was right, all right. When he'd wakened Tatiana and asked her straight, she'd broken down and wept a couple of buckets-full. Yes, she was a vampire, but she'd only got the urge a couple of months ago. She'd fought it until her mind began to break when the craving hit her. She'd only touched kids, because she was afraid of grown-ups—they might wake up and be able to catch her. But she'd kind of worked on a lot of kids at one time, so that no one kid would lose too much blood. Only the craving had been getting stronger…

And still Steve had asked her to marry him! "There must be a way of curing it," he said. "It's a sickness like any other sickness." But she, and—believe me—I thanked God, had said no. She'd pushed him out and made him leave. "Where's Dad?" he asked. "He might know."

I told him that his father must have left at the same time he did, and hadn't come back yet. So the two of us sat and thought. *And thought.*

When the telephone rang, we both almost fell out of our seats. Steve answered it, and I heard him yelling into the mouthpiece.

He ran into the kitchen, grabbed me by the arm and hauled me out into his hot-rod. "That was Tatiana's maid, Magda," he told me as we went blasting down the highway. "She says Tatiana got hysterical after I left, and a few minutes ago she drove away in her convertible. She wouldn't say where she was going. Magda says she thinks Tatiana is going to do away with herself."

"*Suicide?* But if she's a vampire, how—" And all of a sudden I knew just how. I looked at my watch. "Stevie," I said, "drive to Crispin Junction. And drive like holy hell!"

He opened that hot-rod all the way. It looked as if the motor was going to tear itself right off the car. I remember we went around curves just barely touching the road with the rim of one tire.

We saw the convertible as soon as we entered Crispin Junction. It was parked by the side of one of the three roads that cross the town. There was a tiny figure in a flimsy nightdress standing in the middle of the deserted street. My leg stump felt like it was being hit with a hammer.

The church clock started to toll midnight just as we reached her. Steve leaped out and knocked the pointed piece of wood out of her hands. He pulled her into his arms and let her cry.

I was feeling pretty bad at this point. Because all I'd been thinking of was how Steve was in love with a vampire. I hadn't looked at it from her side. She'd been enough in love with him to try to kill herself the *only* way a vampire could be killed—by driving a stake through her heart on a crossroads at midnight.

And she was a pretty little creature. I'd pictured one of these siren dames: you know, tall, slinky, with a tight dress. A witch. But this was a very frightened, very upset young lady who got in the car and cuddled up in Steve's free arm like she'd taken a lease on it. And I could tell she was even younger than Steve.

So, all the time we were driving back, I was thinking to myself, *these kids have got plenty trouble.* Bad enough to be in love with a vampire, but to be a vampire in love with a normal human being...

"But how *can* I marry you?" Tatiana wailed. "What kind of home life would we have? And Steve, one night I might even get hungry enough to attack *you!*"

The only thing none of us counted on was Doc. Not enough, that is.

Once he'd been introduced to Tatiana and heard her story, his shoulders straightened and the lights came back on in his eyes. The sick children would be all right now. That was most important. And as for Tatiana—

"Nonsense," he told her. "Vampirism might have been an incurable disease in the fifteenth century, but I'm sure it can be handled in the twentieth. First, this nocturnal living points to a possible allergy involving sunlight and perhaps a touch of photophobia. You'll wear tinted glasses for a bit, my girl, and we'll see what we can do with hormone injections. The need for consuming blood, however, presents a somewhat greater problem."

But he solved it.

They make blood in a dehydrated, crystalline form these days. So every night before Mrs. Steven Judd goes to sleep, she shakes some powder into a tall glass of water, drops in an ice cube or two and has her daily blood toddy. Far as I know, she and her husband are living happily ever after.

Afterword

There's not much to say about this. Leo Margulies, the publisher, and Frank Belknap Long, the editor, of *Fantastic Universe* took me out to lunch and asked me to write a gothic horror piece for them. I tried to, but it wasn't in me: I had already written my one gothic horror for *Weird Tales* and had thenceforth sworn off the stuff.

Instead, I wrote a kind of purely science-fiction gothic. How successful it is, I let the readers decide. I must remind them, however, that the gimmick of the surprise ending has been only too successful. Several stories and at least two films have stolen it.

WRITTEN 1955——PUBLISHED 1956

ॐ

Mistress Sary

This evening, as I was about to enter my home, I saw two little girls bouncing a ball solemnly on the pavement to the rhythm of a very old little girls' chant. My lips must have gone gray as the sudden pressure of my set jaws numbed all feeling, blood pounded in my right temple; and I knew, that whatever might happen, I couldn't take another step until they had finished.

> *One, two, three alary—*
> *I spy Mistress Sary*
> *Sitting on a bumble-ary,*
> *Just like a little fairy!*

As the girl finished the last smug note, I came to life. I unlocked the door of my house and locked it behind me hurriedly. I switched on the lights in the foyer, the kitchen, the library. And then, for long forgotten minutes, I paced the floor until my breathing slowed and the horrible memory cowered back into the crevice of the years.

That verse! I don't hate children—no matter what my friends say, I don't hate children—but why do they have to sing that stupid little song? Whenever I'm around.... As if the unspeakably vicious creatures know what it does to me....

Sarietta Hawn came to live with Mrs. Clayton when her father died in the West Indies. Her mother had been Mrs. Clayton's only sister, and her father, a British colonial administrator, had no known relatives. It was only natural that the child should be sent across the Caribbean to join my landlady's establishment in Nanville. It was natural, too, that she should be enrolled in the Nanville Grade School where I taught arithmetic and science to the accompaniment of Miss Drury's English, history and geography.

"That Hawn child is impossible, unbelievable!" Miss Drury stormed into my classroom at the morning recess. "She's a freak, an impudent, ugly little freak!"

I waited for the echoes to die down in the empty classroom and considered Drury's intentional Victorian figure with amusement. Her heavily corseted bosom heaved and the thick skirts and petticoats slapped against her ankles as she walked feverishly in front of my desk. I leaned back and braced my arms against my head.

"Now you better be careful. I've been very busy for the past two weeks with a new term and all, and I haven't had a chance to take a good look at Sarietta. Mrs. Clayton doesn't have any children of her own, though, and since the girl arrived on Thursday the woman has been falling all over her with affection. She won't stand for punishing Sarietta like—well, like you did Joey Richards last week. Neither will the school board for that matter."

Miss Drury tossed her head angrily. "When you've been teaching as long as I have, young man, you'll learn that sparing the rod just does not work with stubborn brats like Joey Richards. He'll grow up to be the same kind of no-account drunk as his father if I don't give him a taste of birch now and then."

"All right. Just remember that several members of the school board are beginning to watch you very closely. Now what's this about Sarietta Hawn being a freak? She's an albino, as I recall; lack of pigmentation is due to a chance factor of heredity, not at all freakish, and is experienced by thousands of people who lead normal happy lives."

"Heredity!" A contemptuous sniff. "More of that new nonsense. She's a freak, I tell you, as nasty a little devil as Satan ever made. When I asked her to tell the class about her home in the West Indies, she stood up and squeaked, 'That is a book closed to fools and simpletons.' Well! If the recess bell hadn't rung at that moment, I tell you I'd have laced into her right then and there."

She glanced down at her watch pendant. "Recess almost over. You'd better have the bell system checked, Mr. Flynn: I think it rang a minute too early this morning. And don't allow that Hawn child to give you any sass."

"None of the children ever do." I grinned as the door slammed behind her.

A moment later there was laughter and chatter as the room filled with eight-year-olds.

I began my lesson on long division with a covert glance at the last row. Sarietta Hawn sat stiffly there, her hands neatly clasped on the desk. Against the mahogany veneer of the classroom furniture, her long, ashen pigtails and absolutely white skin seemed to acquire a yellowish tinge. Her eyes were slightly yellow, too, great colorless irises under semi-transparent lids that never blinked while I looked at her.

She *was* an ugly child. Her mouth was far too generous for beauty; her ears stood out almost at right angles to her head; and the long tip of her nose had an odd curve down and in to her upper lip. She wore a snow-white frock of severe cut that added illogical years to her thin body.

When I finished the arithmetic lesson, I walked up to the lonely little figure in the rear. "Wouldn't you like to sit a little closer to my desk?" I asked in as gentle a voice as I could. "You'd find it easier to see the blackboard."

She rose and dropped a swift curtsy. "I thank you very much, sir, but the sunlight at the front of the classroom hurts my eyes. There is always more comfort for me in darkness and in shade." The barest, awkward flash of a grateful smile.

I nodded, feeling uncomfortable at her formal, correct sentences.

During the science lesson, I felt her eyes upon me wherever I moved. I found myself fumbling at the equipment under that unwinking scrutiny, and the children, sensing the cause, began to whisper and crane their necks to the back of the room.

A case of mounted butterflies slid out of my hands. I stopped to pick it up. Suddenly a great gasp rippled over the room, coming simultaneously from thirty little throats.

"Look! She's doing it again!" I straightened.

Sarietta Hawn hadn't moved from her strange, stiff position. But her hair was a rich chestnut now; her eyes were blue; her cheeks and lips bore a delicate rose tint.

My fingers dug into the unyielding surface of my desk. Impossible! Yet could light and shade play such fantastic tricks? But—impossible!

Even as I gaped, unconscious of my pedagogical dignity, the child seemed to blush and a shadow over her straighten. I went back to cocoons and *Lepidoptera* with a quavering voice.

A moment later, I noticed that her face and hair were of purest white once more. I wasn't interested in explanation, however; neither was the class. The lesson was ruined.

"She did exactly the same thing in my class," Miss Drury exclaimed at lunch. "Exactly the same thing! Only it seemed to me that she was a dark brunette, with velvet black hair and snapping black eyes. It was just after she'd called me a fool—the nerve of that snip!—and I was reaching for the birch rod, when she seemed to go all dark and swarthy. I'd have made her change to red though, I can tell you, if that bell hadn't rung a minute too early."

"Maybe," I said. "But with that sort of delicate coloring any change in lighting would play wild tricks with your vision. I'm not so sure now that I saw it after all. Sarietta Hawn is no chameleon."

The old teacher tightened her lips until they were a pale, pink line cutting across her wrinkled face. She shook her head and leaned across the crumb-bespattered table. "No chameleon. A witch. I know! And the Bible commands us to destroy witches, to burn them out of life."

My laugh echoed uncomfortably around the dirty school basement which was our lunchroom. "You can't believe that! An eight-year-old girl—"

"All the more reason to catch her before she grows up and does real harm. I tell you, Mr. Flynn, I know! One of my ancestors burned thirty witches in New England during the trials. My family has a special sense for the creatures. There can be no peace between us!"

The other children shared an awed agreement with Miss Drury. They began calling the albino child "Mistress Sary." Sarietta, on the other hand, seemed to relish the nickname. When Joey Richards tore into a group of children who were following her down the street and shouting the song, she stopped him.

"Leave them alone, Joseph," she warned him in her curious adult phraseology. "They are quite correct: I *am* just like a little fairy."

And Joey turned his freckled. puzzled face and unclenched his fists and walked slowly back to her side. He worshipped her. Possibly because the two of them were outcasts in that juvenile community, possibly because they were both orphans—his eternally soused father was slightly worse than no parent at all—they were always together. I'd find him squatting at her feet in the humid twilight when I came out on the boarding-house porch for my nightcap of fresh air. She would pause in mid-sentence, one tiny forefinger still poised sharply. Both of them would sit in absolute silence until I left the porch.

Joey liked me a little. Thus I was one of the few privileged to hear of Mistress Sary's earlier life. I turned one evening when I was out for a stroll to see Joey trotting behind me. He had just left the porch.

"Gee," he sighed. "Stogolo sure taught Mistress Sary a lot. I wish that guy was around to take care of Old Dreary. He'd teach her all right, all right."

"Stogolo?"

"Sure. He was the witch-doctor who put the devil-birth curse on Sary's mother before Sary was born 'cause she had him put in jail. Then when Sary's mother died giving birth, Sary's father started drinking, she says, worse'n my pop. Only she found Stogolo and made friends with him. They mixed blood and swore peace on the grave of Sary's mother. And he taught her voodoo an' the devil-birth curse an' how to make love charms from hog liver an'—"

"I'm surprised at you, Joey," I interrupted. "Taking in that silly superstition! A boy who does as well as you in science! Mistress Sary—Sarietta grew up in a primitive community where people didn't know any better. But you do!"

He scuffed the weeds at the edge of the sidewalk with a swinging foot. "Yeah," he said in a low voice. "Yeah. I'm sorry I mentioned it, Mr. Flynn."

Then he was off, a lithe streak in white blouse and corduroy knickers, tearing along the sidewalk to his home. I regretted my interruption, then, since Joey was rarely confidential and Sarietta spoke only when spoken to, even with her aunt.

The weather grew surprisingly warmer. "I declare," Miss Drury told me one morning, "I've never seen a winter like this in my life. Indian summers and heat waves are one thing, but to go on this way day after day without any sign of a break, land sakes!"

"Scientists say the entire earth is developing a warmer climate. Of course, it's almost imperceptible right now, but the Gulf Stream—"

"The Gulf Stream," she ridiculed. She wore the same starched and heavy clothes as always and the heat was reducing her short temper to a blazing point. "The Gulf Stream! Ever since that Hawn brat came to live in Nanville, the world's been turning turtle. My chalk is always breaking, my desk drawers get stuck, the erasers fall apart— the little witch is trying to put a spell on me!"

"Now look here." I stopped and faced her with my back to the school building. "This has gone far enough. If you do have to believe in witchcraft, keep it out of your relations with the children. They're here to absorb knowledge, not the hysterical imaginings of a—of a—"

"Of a sour old maid. Yes, go ahead, say it," she snarled. "I know you think it, Mr. Flynn. You fawn all over her so she leaves you be. But I know what I know and so does that evil little thing you call Sarietta Hawn. It's war between us, and the all-embracing battle between good and evil will never be over until one or the other of us is dead!" She turned in a spiral of skirts and swept up the path into the schoolhouse.

I began to fear for her sanity then. I remembered her boast: "I've never read a novel published after eighteen ninety-three!"

That was the day my arithmetic class entered slowly, quietly as if a bubble of silence enveloped them. The moment the door shut behind the last pupil, the bubble broke and whispers splattered all over the room.

"Where's Sarietta Hawn?" I asked. "And Joey Richards," I amended, unable to find him either.

Louise Bell rose, her starched pink dress curving in front of her scrawny body. "They've been naughty. Miss Drury caught Joey cutting a lock of hair off her head and she started to whip him. Then Mistress Sary stood up and said she wasn't to touch him because he was under her pro-tec-tion. So Miss Drury sent us all out and now I bet she's going to whip them both. She's real mad!"

I started for the back door rapidly. Abruptly a scream began. Sarietta's voice! I tore down the corridor. The scream rose to a high treble, wavered for a second. Then stopped.

As I jolted open the door of Miss Drury's classroom, I was prepared for anything, including murder. I was not prepared for what I saw. I stood, my hand grasping the door knob, absorbing the tense tableau.

Joey Richards was backed against the blackboard, squeezing a long tendril of brownish hair in his sweaty right palm. Mistress Sary stood in front of Miss Drury, her head bent to expose a brutal red welt on the back of her chalky neck. And Miss Drury was looking stupidly at a fragment of birch in her hand; the rest of the rod lay in scattered pieces at her feet.

The children saw me and came to life. Mistress Sary straightened and with set lips moved toward the door. Joey Richards leaned forward. He rubbed the lock of hair against the back of the teacher's dress, she completely oblivious to him. When he joined the girl at the door, I saw that the hair glistened with the perspiration picked up from Miss Drury's blouse.

At a slight nod from Mistress Sary, the boy passed the lock of hair over to her. She placed it very carefully in the pocket of her frock.

Then, without a single word, they both skipped around me on their way to join the rest of the class.

Evidently they were unharmed, at least seriously.

I walked over to Miss Drury. She was trembling violently and talking to herself. She never removed her eyes from the fragment of birch.

"It just flew to pieces. Flew to pieces! I was—when it flew to pieces!"

Placing an arm about her waist, I guided the spinster to a chair. She sat down and continued mumbling.

"Once—I just struck her once. I was raising my arm for another blow—the birch was over my head—when it flew to pieces. Joey was off in a corner—he couldn't have done it—the birch just flew to pieces." She stared at the piece of wood in her hand and rocked her body back and forth slowly, like one mourning a great loss.

I had a class. I got her a glass of water, notified the janitor to take care of her and hurried back.

Somebody, in a childish spirit of ridicule or meanness, had scrawled a large verse across the blackboard in my room:

> *One, two, three alary—*
> *I spy Mistress Sary*
> *Sitting on a bumble-ary,*
> *Just like a little fairy!*

I turned angrily to the class. I noticed a change in seating arrangements. Joey Richards' desk was empty.

He had taken his place with Mistress Sary in the long, deep shadows at the back.

To my breathless relief, Mistress Sary didn't mention the incident. As always she was silent at the supper table, her eyes fixed rigidly on her plate. She excused herself the moment the meal was over and slipped away. Mrs. Clayton was evidently too bustling and talkative to have heard of it. There would be no repercussions from that quarter.

After supper I walked over to the old-fashioned gabled house where Miss Drury lived with her relatives. Lakes of perspiration formed on my body and I found it all but impossible to concentrate. Every leaf on every tree hung motionless in the humid, breezeless night.

The old teacher was feeling much better. But she refused to drop the matter; to do, as I suggested, her best to reestablish amity. She rocked herself back and forth in great scoops of the colonial rocking-chair and shook her head violently.

"No, no, *no!* I won't make friends with that imp of darkness: sooner shake hands with Beelzebub himself. She hates me now worse than ever because—don't you see— I forced her to declare herself. I've made her expose her witchery. Now—now I must grapple with her and overthrow her and Him who is her mentor. I must think, I must—only it's so devilishly hot. So very hot! My mind—my mind doesn't seem to work right." She wiped her forehead with the heavy cashmere shawl.

As I strolled back, I fumbled unhappily for a solution. Something would break soon at this rate; then the school board would be down upon us with an investigation and the school would go to pot. I tried to go over the possibilities calmly but my clothes stuck to my body and breathing was almost drudgery.

Our porch was deserted. I saw movement in the garden and hurried over. Two shadows resolved into Mistress Sary and Joey Richards. They stared up as if waiting for me to declare myself.

She was squatting on the ground and holding a doll in her hands. A small wax doll with brownish hair planted in her head that was caught in a stern bun just like the bun Miss Drury affected. A stiff little doll with a dirty piece of muslin for a dress cut in the same long, severe pattern as all of Miss Drury's clothes. A carefully executed caricature in wax.

"Don't you think that's a bit silly," I managed to ask at last. "Miss Drury is sufficiently upset and sorry for what she did for you to play upon her superstitions in this horrible way. I'm sure if you try hard enough, we can all be friends."

They rose, Sarietta clutching the doll to her breast. "It is not silly, Mr. Flynn. That bad woman must be taught a lesson. A terrible lesson she will never forget. Excuse my abruptness, sir, but I have much work to do this night."

And then she was gone, a rustling patch of whiteness that slipped up the stairs and disappeared into the sleeping house.

I turned to the boy.

"Joey, you're a pretty smart fellow. Man to man, now—"

"Excuse me, Mr. Flynn." He started for the gate. "I—I got to go home." I heard the rhythmic pad of his sneakers on the sidewalk grow faint and dissolve in the distance. I had evidently lost his allegiance.

Sleep came hard that night. I tossed on entangling sheets, dozed, came awake and dozed again.

About midnight, I woke shuddering. I punched the pillow and was about to attempt unconsciousness once more when my ears caught a faint note of sound. I recognized it. That was what had reached into my dreams and tugged my eyes open to fear. I sat upright.

Sarietta's voice!

She was singing a song, a rapid song with unrecognizable words. Higher and higher up the scale it went, and faster and faster as if there were some eerie deadline she had to meet. At last, when it seemed that she would shrill beyond the limits of human audibility, she paused. Then, on a note so high that my ear drums ached, came a drawn-out, flowing "Kurunoo O Stogoloooo!"

Silence.

Two hours later, I managed to fall asleep again.

The sun burning redly through my eyelids wakened me. I dressed, feeling oddly listless and apathetic. I wasn't hungry and, for the Wrst morning of my life, went without breakfast.

The heat came up from the sidewalk and drenched my face and hands. My feet felt the burning concrete through the soles of my shoes. Even the shade of the school building was an unnoticeable relief.

Miss Drury's appetite was gone too. She left her carefully wrapped lettuce sandwiches untouched on the basement table. She supported her head on her thin hands and stared at me out of red-rimmed eyes.

"It's so hot!" she whispered. "I can hardly stand it. Why everyone feels so sorry for that Hawn brat, I can't understand. Just because I made her sit in the sunlight. I've been suffering from this heat a thousand times more than she."

"You made—Sarietta—sit—in—"

"Of course I did! She's no privileged character. Always in the back of the room where it's cool and comfortable. I made her change her desk so that she's right near the large window, where the sunlight streams in. And she feels it too, let me tell you.

Only—ever since, I've been feeling worse. As if I'm falling apart. I didn't have a wink of sleep last night—those terrible, terrible dreams: great hands pulling and mauling me, knives pricking my face and my hands—"

"But the child can't stand sunlight! She's an albino."

"Albino, fiddlesticks! She's a witch. She'll be making wax dolls next. Joey Richards didn't try to cut my hair for a joke. He had orders to—Ooh!" She doubled in her chair. "Those cramps!"

I waited until the attack subsided and watched her sweaty, haggard face. "Funny that you should mention wax dolls. You have the girl so convinced that she's a witch that she's actually making them. Believe it or not, last night, after I left you—"

She had jumped to her feet and was rigid attention. One arm supporting her body against a steam pipe, she stood staring at me.

"She made a wax doll. Of me?"

"Well, you know how a child is. It was her idea of what you looked like. A little crude in design, but a good piece of workmanship. Personally, I think her talent merits encouragement."

Miss Drury hadn't heard me. "Cramps!" she mused. "And I thought they were cramps! She's been sticking pins into me! The little— I've got to— But I must be careful. Yet fast. Fast."

I got to my feet and tried to put my hand on her shoulder across the luncheon table. "Now pull yourself together. Surely this is going altogether too far."

She leaped away and stood near the stairs talking rapidly to herself. "I can't use a stick or a club—she controls them. But my hands—if I can get my hands on her and choke fast enough, she can't stop me. But I mustn't give her a chance," she almost sobbed. "*I mustn't give her a chance!*"

Then she had leaped up the stairs in a sudden, determined rush.

I swept the table out of my way and bolted after her.

Most of the children were eating their lunches along the long board fence at the end of the school yard. But they had stopped now and were watching something with frightened fascination. Sandwiches hung suspended in front of open mouths. I followed the direction of their stares.

Miss Drury was slipping along the side of the building like an upright, skirted panther. She staggered now and then and held on to a wall. Some two feet in front of her, Sarietta Hawn and Joey Richards sat in the shade. They were looking intently at a wax doll in a muslin dress that had been set on the cement just outside the fringe of coolness. It lay on its back in the direct sunlight and, even at that distance, I could see it was melting.

"Hi," I shouted. "Miss Drury! Be sensible!" I ran for them.

At my cry, both children looked up, startled. Miss Drury launched herself forward and fell, rather than leaped, on the little girl. Joey Richards grabbed the doll and rolled out of the way toward me. I tripped over him and hit the ground with a bone-breaking wallop. As I turned in mid-air, I caught a fast glimpse of Miss Drury's right hand flailing over the girl. Sarietta had huddled into a pathetic little bundle under the teacher's body.

I sat up facing Joey. Behind me the children were screaming as I had never heard them scream before. And I had to force myself not to scream, too.

Joey was squeezing the doll with both hands. As I watched, not daring to remove my eyes, the wax—already softened by the sunlight—lost its shape and came through the cracks in his tight freckled fingers. It dripped through the muslin dress and fell in blobs on the school yard cement.

Over and above the yells of the children, Miss Drury's voice rose to an agony-filled scream and went on and on and on.

Joey looked over my shoulder with rolling eyes. But he kept on squeezing the doll and I kept my eyes on it desperately, prayerfully, while the screaming went on all about me and the immense sun pushed the perspiration steadily down my face. As the wax oozed through his fingers, he began singing suddenly in a breathless, hysterical cackle.

> One, two, three alary—
> I spy Mistress Sary
> Sitting on a bumble-ary,
> Just like a little fairy!

And Miss Drury screamed and the children yelled and Joey sang, but I kept my eyes on the little wax doll. *I kept my eyes on the little wax doll drooling through the cracks of Joey Richards' strained, little fingers. I kept my eyes on the doll.*

AFTERWORD

This is my first attempt at the gothic, a form I have never been fond of—with the possible exception of some pieces by the Brontë sisters and something else, something quite else, by Mary Wollstonecraft Shelley.

But I had been an avid reader of *Weird Tales* through most of my early adolescence (let's hear it for H.P. Lovecraft!—Seabury Quinn!—C.L. Moore!—Clark Ashton Smith!), and now—in my twenties—though the avidity had been seriously modified, I was deeply flattered to learn from Ted Sturgeon that the magazine would look with favor upon a submission by me.

I gave them "Mistress Sary," and they bought it. All right, it's no *Frankenstein*, and it's certainly not even a "The Shadow Over Innsmouth," but I enjoyed seeing it appear where that fine editor, Farnsworth Wright, once gloried and drank deep.

WRITTEN 1947——PUBLISHED 1947

THE MALTED MILK MONSTER

From the moment he opened his eyes and saw the color of the sky, the shape of the clouds, the incredible topography, Carter Broun knew exactly where he was. He didn't really have to identify the blandly sweet smell which filled his nostrils, nor did he particularly have to investigate further the river of dark mahogany coursing, with the gentlest of roars, between two small, cone-shaped hills, two hills of exactly the same dimensions and sporting exactly the same vegetation.

There was just no doubt about it. Not after Carter had contemplated, for ten or fifteen awe-struck seconds, the sky of absolutely uniform and brilliant blue—bluey-blue, *that* was the color, he decided morosely—and those oval, pink-white clouds spaced so evenly across it. Not to mention those birds flapping into the narrowing distance; from here, each looked like a letter V, the arms of which had been carefully curved outward and down.

Only one place in the universe boasted such a landscape, such an atmosphere, such birds. This was The World of The Malted Milk Monster.

God help me, Carter thought, *now it's my world, too.*

That peculiar, ripping flash inside him, like some sort of lightning of the soul! He'd said goodbye to Lee at the door of her lawn-enclosed home and started down the neat suburban street to where his MG was parked. He'd been rolling the car keys around in his hand and planning the itinerary of his Friday night date with Lee—you either got a girl to your apartment by the second date, he had found, or you flunked out forever—when he'd noticed the Malted Milk Monster watching him unwinkingly from behind a hedge. Probably had followed them all the way from Goldie's Goodie Palace.

Then the flash, the mad sensation of being ripped out of his context and being shoved into another, entirely different place. And opening his eyes here.

It all came, and the knowledge was bitter, of taking your date to an ice cream parlor instead of an honest bar. But a bar didn't seem like the right follow-up to a Sunday afternoon movie in Grenville Acres. Besides, you don't take a schoolteacher to a bar on her home grounds. You pour an inoffensive soda into her, walk her home through the autumn streets, being as gentlemanly charming as possible, you decline the invitation to come in and meet the folks by mentioning the big report you have to prepare for tomorrow's Account Executive conference—a man has his work to do, and that must come first—and back you drive to Manhattan with the pleasant knowledge of a seduction intelligently initiated.

Unfortunately, you don't plan on other factors—unseen powers, for example.

There was not much point in checking but he might as well check. Once he was really certain, he could begin worrying. And working out an escape.

Carter wandered down to the mahogany river across well-cropped grass and past large tinsel-type flowers. He knelt, dipped a finger in the thick liquid and tasted it. Chocolate. Of course.

Just on the off-chance, he pinched himself long and hard, squeezingly and painfully. It hurt enough. No, he'd known he hadn't been dreaming to begin with. For one thing, in a dream you rarely realize you're dreaming.

This was real.

Chocolate syrup to drink. And for food—

The two little hills were covered with dwarf trees bearing lollipops, the cellophane-wrapped fruit varying slightly in color from tree to tree. Here and there on the level ground were bonbon bushes and sharply triangular Christmas-tree affairs from whose twigs dangled small pies, cakes and assorted cookies—most of them chocolate.

The sun beat down rosily, rosily, and none of the chocolate melted. The chocolate river, on the other hand, ran interminably and gurglingly. Whatever its sources, wherever it rose, the river evidently had plenty of reserves.

Carter was struck by an especially ugly thought. Suppose, viewing the river's effluence, suppose it *rained* chocolate! Really, one could not put anything past the Malted Milk Monster.

Lee had objected to the name.

"She's just a fat little girl. Rather brilliant, rather neurotic, too. And very curious about the strange, distinguished young man who's buying her teacher a soda."

"All right, but I've been counting," Carter had insisted. "Five chocolate malteds since we came in. *Five!* And the way she sits there at the end of the counter, never taking her eyes off us, not even when she unwraps a fresh straw!"

"Most of the children in Grenville have more spending money than is good for them. Dorothy's parents are divorced—mother's a big-time buyer, father's a vice-president of a bank—and they use their money to fight for her affections. She spends practically all of her time in Goldie's. You know, Carter, that psychological equation: when I was small and my parents loved me, they gave me food; therefore, food equals love?"

Carter nodded. He knew all about such psychological equations. As a determined and well-sexed young bachelor, he had studied Freud as intently as a second lieutenant in the First World War might have studied von Clausewitz.

"You're so damned feminine," he announced warmly, underlining the points that, with any luck at all, would shortly be at issue. "Only a gal who was woman all the way through would be able to see in that ball of lard, that pimply Malted Milk Monster—"

"She's no such thing, Carter! What a terrible nickname for such a mixed-up little girl! Although," Lee mused, swirling the long spoon about in the residual muddy bubbles of her soda glass, "although it *is* funny you should think of it. That's what—or something like it—the other kids in the class call her. They tell stories about her—

that she can make stones and flowerpots disappear just by staring hard at them. Kids are just like adults, a little more obvious, that's all. They make a witch out of the unpopular one."

He kept trying. "They never made one out of you, that's for sure. Anybody who's the slightest bit sensitive just has to look at you to know that love and loving—"

"It's so pathetic, really," she interrupted without knowing it. "I asked them to write a composition about the happiest day they could remember. Do you know what Dorothy wrote about? A day in her dream world, a day that never ever happened. And yet it was beautifully done, for a child her age. Full of affection-symbols like cake and candy. The world was supposed to smell like an ice cream parlor. Imagine! There was a finely written passage—you appreciate good writing, Carter, I know—about two cute little hills all covered with lollipop trees, each tree bearing a different flavor. And between the hills there wound a stream of purest chocolate!"

Carter gave up. He lit a cigarette and stared over Lee's earnest but nonetheless lovely head. At the grossly heavy little girl whose fat overflowed the last stool in the ice cream parlor, her mouth sucking steadily at the chocolate malted milk, her eyes as steadily sucking at his. He found himself forced to drop his glance first.

"—even when we have a drawing lesson," Lee was still on it. "She never does anything else. It's absolutely real to the poor child—so lonely, so starved for companionship! I've learned to expect that flat blue sky full of oval pink clouds, those curved-line birds, that chocolate river and all those bushes filled with goodies. Every single time! For a child of her intelligence, she's somewhat retarded graphically. She draws like a child a year or two younger. But that's to be expected: it's almost purely a verbal, a conceptual intelligence, you might say—"

You might also say the topic had created a highly annoying and useless diversion. Carter bit on the cigarette through his lips, looked up again cautiously. The Malted Milk Monster's eyes were as unwavering as ever. Such *pulling* power—what was so fascinating about him? Well, her father was a Madison Avenue type: the clothes, probably. Carter was justly proud of his wardrobe. His clothes, he knew, were in almost ostentatious good taste—they screamed restraint and expensive lowness of key.

Yes, that was it. He reminded her of her father. Her rich father.

Carter caught himself preening and stubbed out the cigarette in abrupt harsh disgust. Damn it! That was the trouble with this Madison Avenue music—you laughed at it, you kidded others about it, you even read books satirizing it—and then you found yourself singing to it. He reminded her of her father who was the vice-president of a bank and probably quite well off. Well, so what? Did that say anything good about Carter Broun? Not necessarily at all, at all. Carter Broun was just a well-educated, clever and rather lucky young man who had found his way into a well-paying, clever and extremely luck-flavored business.

A young man who had gotten so deeply involved in the superficialities of the business that when a child as obviously and horrifyingly tormented as this little girl came to his attention, all he could see was a neat gag nickname—the kind of shallow, brilliant thing you'd toss off to a client at a sales conference.

Lee, now. Lee's roots were still wrapped around the compact, squirming mass of the human race. She loved her work but she *cared* too; she certainly cared. The way she goes on! The way her eyes shine as she talks!

"—the other children were positively stupefied. Or that time I asked them to make up riddles. Do you know what Dorothy asked when her turn came? Just listen to this, Carter. She asked the class: 'Which would you rather be eaten by—a giant caterpillar, or a million tiny little lions?' Now I maintain that a girl with that much imagination—"

"That much maladjustment," he corrected. "She sounds like a very sick kid. But I'd give a lot," he mused, "to see how she'd do on a Rorschach. A giant caterpillar, or a million tiny little lions…and without even ink-blots to go on! Do you know if she's ever had any psychotherapy?"

His companion had smiled grimly. "Her parents are very well off, I told you. I suspect she's had *all* the advantages. Up to and including protracted legal battles as to whether she's to go to poppa's doctor or momma's doctor. What that girl really needs, no one can give her: a different set of parents, or, at the least, one parent who really cares for her."

Carter had disagreed. "Not so much now, not at her age. I'd say it would be much more helpful at this point to have a couple of kids who like and accept her. If there's one thing that Motivational Research brings home to you, it's what thoroughgoing social animals we humans are. Without a matrix of companionship, without the interest and approval of at least a handful of our contemporaries, we're worse than mixed-up—we aren't even people. Hermits aren't people; I don't know what they are, exactly, but they're not people. And so long as that kid is a psychological hermit, she's not really a human person. She's something else."

Somewhere in the next fifteen minutes, he knew that he had clicked with Lee. But by then he was deep in the problem of how one could help a kid like Dorothy to make friends. It had become an MR problem, dealing with the individual, however, rather than the group; and, like all MR problems, of such obsessing interest to him that nothing else mattered.

In the end, it had been Lee who had changed the subject very forcefully; it had been Lee who had to drop hints about their next date. He'd managed to get a grip on himself and began talking about what they'd do when she came into town to meet him next Friday night. All in all, it had worked out quite well.

But as they left the soda shop, Carter had thrown just one last glance behind him through the plate-glass window. The Malted Milk Monster had turned on her stool, straw still in her mouth, eyes following him like a pair of starving sharks.

And then, of course, shadowing them all the way to Lee's home. What had she done to him? How had she done it? *Why?*

He kicked angrily at a loose stone, watched it bounce into the river with a thick brown splash. Was this one of the stones Dorothy had abstracted from the real world? Again, how? Not why, though; it could well have been part of a series of controlled experiments to test the range of her powers.

Powers? Was that the word? Talent, perhaps, or catalytic capacity—that might be more descriptive.

Given a very remarkable mind, given a very strong personality embedded in a child's brain, given unhappiness, unpopularity, and general neurosis to sharpen that mind, to add even more punch to the personality—and what? *What* would develop?

He suddenly recalled his last thoughts before arriving in this lollipop world. Just after he'd left Lee, his head full of happy thoughts about Friday night, just at the very moment he'd seen the kid staring at him, he'd begun thinking about her problems again. The realization that she had followed them all the way from the soda shop out of sheer murderous loneliness had stimulated him into wondering about her mind.

There had been a sequence. First: *Gee, she's hungry for people.* Then: *Not for people in general, for kids her own age. How would you go about making kids like her? Now there's a motivation problem for you!* Then: *Well, the first question is what are her motives; what's it like in her mind?* Good professional MR unraveling technique.

And then that terrible flash, that mental rip, and he'd opened his eyes here.

In other words, he'd had something to do with it. It hadn't been all her. He'd been wide open psychologically, trying to visualize the inside of her mind, just as she had—as she had *done* something.

No, it still required something from her, for all this to have happened. And no matter what you called it—talent, powers, catalysis—she had it. And she'd used it on him.

Carter shivered suddenly, remembering the riddle she'd made up.

He was adrift in the fantasy life of that kind of kid. He wished he had paid attention to Lee's earlier discussion in the ice cream parlor instead of forcing the conversation back into more profitable channels. To get out safely, to survive, he could use every scrap of information on Dorothy that had ever existed.

After all, her most meager wishes were now the fixed and immutable natural laws under which he had to operate.

He was no longer alone, he observed. He was surrounded by children. They had seemingly materialized all around him, yelling, playing, scrambling, jumping. And where the yelling was loudest, where the games were thickest, there was Dorothy. The Malted Milk Monster. The children gamboled about her like so many fountains against a central statue.

She stood there, still staring at him. And her stare was as uncomfortable as ever. A little more so, for that matter, than he remembered it. She wore the same blue jeans and yellow cashmere sweater with smudges on it. She was taller than life-size, a bit taller than the other children. She was slenderer, too. Now, in all fairness, you could not call her more than plump.

And she had no pimples.

Carter was irritated at how fast he'd had to drop his eyes. But to keep them open and aimed at her was like looking directly into the beam of an anti-aircraft searchlight.

"Looka me, Dorothy!" the kids yelled. "I'm jumping! Looka how high I can jump!"

"How about playing tag, Dorothy?" they yelled. "Let's play tag! You choose who should be It!"

"Make up a new game, Dorothy! Make up one of the good games you always make up!"

"Let's have a picnic, huh, Dorothy?"

"Dorothy, let's have a relay race!"

"Dorothy, let's play house!"

"Dorothy, let's jump rope!"

"Dorothy—"

"Dorothy—"

"Dorothy—"

When she started to speak, every one of the kids shut up. They stopped running, they stopped yelling, they stopped whatever they were doing and turned to look at her.

"This nice man," she said. "He'll play with us. Won't you, mister?"

"No," Carter said. "I'd like to, but I'm afraid I—"

"He'll play a game of ball with us," she went on imperturbably. "Here, mister. Here's the ball. You're a nice man to play with us."

When she moved toward him, holding out a large striped ball which had suddenly appeared in her hands, the bulk of the children moved with her.

Carter was still searching for words wherewith to explain that, while he had no interest at the moment in playing a game of ball, he was much interested in a private conversation with Dorothy herself, an audience, so to speak—when the ball was thrust into his fingers and he found himself playing.

"You see, I don't usually—" he began as he threw the ball and caught it, threw the ball and caught it.

"Very busy right now, but some other ti—" he continued as he caught the ball and threw it, caught the ball and threw it.

No matter in which direction he threw the ball, no matter how many eager pairs of child hands made a grab for it, it was always Dorothy who received it and threw it back to him.

"Yay, Dorothy!" the children yelled. "This is *fun!*"

"Be glad to play with you kids as soon as I finish my—" Carter panted, finding it fantastically tough exercise.

"Yay, Dorothy! This is a real good game!"

"Such a nice man!"

"So much fun!"

Dorothy threw the ball straight up in the air and it disappeared. "Let's play leapfrog," she said. "Would you like to play leapfrog with us, mister?"

"Sorry," Carter gasped as he bent, his hands on his knees, so that she could leap over his back from behind. "I haven't played leapfrog in years and I don't intend to st—" He ran forward, placed his hands in the small of Dorothy's back, sailed across, bent forward again in expectation of her jump. "Leapfrog is one game that I never—"

They played leapfrog until he was wobbling with dizziness, until every breath felt as if it had been clawed out of his chest.

Dorothy seated herself gracefully on the ground and gathered the children in an adoring cluster. "Now we'd like to hear a story. Please, mister, tell us a story?"

Carter started an agonized protest. It was somehow transformed into the story of Goldilocks and the Three Bears, told wheezingly and punctuated with heaving gulps for air. Then he told the story of Little Red Riding Hood. Then he told the story of Bluebeard.

Somewhere near the end of that particular work, Dorothy disappeared. But the children remained, and Carter continued the story, willy-nilly. The kids began to look frightened. Some shivered, others moaned and cried.

It had been getting darker for the past few minutes, and just as Carter finished the last lines of Bluebeard and, without stopping, launched into "Once upon a time there was a poor but honest woodcutter who had two children named Hansel and Gretel," a huge black cloud slid across the sky and swooped down at them.

A terrifying scarlet face with an enormous nose and flashing white teeth came out of the cloud and roared till the ground shook. Then it stopped and began to gnash its teeth. This sounded like an explosion in a crockery warehouse.

The children screamed in pure eye-popping terror and ran. "Dorothy!" they shrieked. "Dorothy, save us! The Bad Old Man! Save us, Dorothy, save us! Dorothy, where are you?"

Carter sank to the grass, released and utterly exhausted. He was far too tired to run or even look up, far too upset to care what happened to him any more. It seemed like the first time in hours that his body was his again to command; but his body wasn't worth very much at the moment.

"Hey, Mac," a voice queried sympathetically over his head. "They givin' you a hard time?"

It was the scarlet face from the cloud. It no longer looked terrifying, merely concerned in a friendly fashion. And it was shrinking rapidly in size until it was in correct proportion to the normal human body under it. When it was a rather ordinary red and grizzled face, dirty with a few days' growth of beard around the red and busily veined nose, its owner knelt on the edge of the cloud and leaped to the ground, a distance, by this time, of half a dozen feet.

He was an oldish man of middle height, wearing a pair of solid gray pants, a torn brown shirt which hung outside it down to his hips and, on his bare feet, two frayed and filthy canvas shoes, one of which was split at the sole. He looked familiar, as every bum somehow looks like every other bum. He was archetypically the shambling, sodden derelict, a pure example of absolute human junk, but—

He was an adult.

Carter sprang up and offered his hand joyfully. It was shaken in a flabby, uncertain, half-cringing way, like a newly paroled prisoner taking his farewell of the warden.

"Could you use a drink, Mac?"

"I sure as hell could," Carter told him heartily. "Am I glad to see you!"

The derelict nodded vaguely, reached up and pulled the black cloud even closer. He fumbled inside and pulled a bottle out. It was about half full, but though the fluid it contained was the proper shade of amber, it was clear glass all the way around. No label.

He held out this beggar's choice. "Name's Eddie. What they call me Shirttail. You need a glass to drink from? Ain't no glasses."

Carter shrugged. He sterilized the open top of the bottle with the palm of his hand, put it to his mouth and took a broad gulp.

"*Whouch!*" he said.

He found himself coughing so hard that he almost dropped the bottle. Shirttail took it away from him solicitously. "Awful, ain't it?" he asked, then proceeded to belt down a third of the stuff.

Awful, Carter decided, was not quite the word for it. It tasted like whiskey, all right, somewhere way down at the bottom, but with an overlay consisting of iodine, ammonia, camphor and dilute hydrochloric acid. His tongue squirmed in his mouth like a trapped snake.

Shirttail removed the bottle from his mouth, shuddered, grimaced, and licked his lips. "That's what *she* thinks whiskey tastes like."

"Who? Dorothy?"

"Atsit. The kid—whatever she thinks something tastes like, that's what it tastes like. But it's better'n nothing, better'n no booze at all. Wanna come up to the place? We can sit a while."

He was pointing to the cloud which hung low over them, a dark and misshapen dirigible. Doubtfully, Carter grabbed some of its tenuous material and pulled himself up. It was like swimming through fog that felt solid only at the places your hands touched it.

A soaring black cavern of a room. Off in a corner—a niche, rather, since there were no corners—stood an army cot covered with ragged plaid blankets, a tableful of cracked cups and saucers and three sagging, garbagey-looking easy chairs. An unshaded light bulb hung from a thin wire over the cot and burned tinily, resentfully, in the piles of gloom. Whether or not the area behind the cot could properly be called a wall, it was covered from top to bottom with glossy pictures of naked women.

"Not my idea—hers," Shirttail explained as he clambered up through the floor. "Everything's hers, every idea, everything. What she once saw the inside of a night-watchman's shack, I figure. What to her I'm the same kinda guy as the night-watchman, so that's the layout I get. But thank God for the bottle. The pictures, far as I'm concerned, you can have, but the bottle—thank God for the bottle."

He offered it to Carter, who shook his head and hand in a *no*. They sat in two facing easy chairs, each of which immediately settled off to one side in opposite directions. Damn it, Carter thought, I *have* seen him before. But where?

"Take a slug, Mac, go ahead, take a slug. One good thing she's got here, that kid—the bottle gets full as fast as you kill it. You ain't takin' nothin' from me when you help yourself. And if you don't drink regular, you'll be talkin' to yourself. What you won't talk sense."

Carter considered the point and saw it might well be valid. He took another drink. It was fully as bad as the first, but the effects of the alcohol came through more strongly now and tended to insulate against the flavor. He sighed and swallowed some more. No doubt about it, the world—even Dorothy's world—looked better.

He handed the bottle back and studied his companion. Hardly the right type for this place, when you came right down to it. A bum. A very average old bum. Why him as The Bad Old Man?

"How long have you been here?" Carter asked him.

Shirttail shrugged and stared loose-lipped over the top of the bottle. "A year, maybe. Two years, maybe. What there's no way to figure. Sometimes winter one day, sometimes summer tomorrow. What even my beard don't grow no more after I came. I feel like years and years *and* years and years. Worsen stir, worsen anything. The things I been through here, Mac, the things I been through!"

"Bad?" Carter asked sympathetically.

"*Bad?*" Shirttail indicated just how bad by rolling his red eyes in an emphatic upward arc. "Bad don't come near. I got to go out and scare those kids whenever she wants me to. What I'm in the sack, what I got other things on my mind, don't make no difference. Dorothy gives out with a think: 'Come a-runnin' and start a-scarin'.' I got to drop whatever I'm doin'. I'm in the sack, what the hell, I got other things on my mind, I got to drop it and start a-scarin'. I blow up big like you just saw me, I got to scream and bang my choppers, I got to zoom on down. Then the kids yell: 'Dorothy, save us!' and she starts takin' me apart. What I mean apart. The things she's done to me, *biff! bam! pow! pam!*, slapped me silly, up, down, around, every which way, for a-scarin' those kids! What it wasn't my idea in the first place. I just do it 'cause she gives out with a think and makes me do it."

"Ever try resisting, refusing?" Carter inquired. "I mean what happens if you say no?"

"Mac, you don't say no. You just don't. Everything here goes her way. When she itches, you scratch. When she sneezes, you wipe your nose. What I used to call her all kindsa names to myself, just to pass the time—Mac, I don't remember a single one now. I try to remember one dirty name and I can't, to save my skin. She's just Dorothy. That's all I can call her. You know what I mean? Everything goes her way, even inside your head. The only leeway you get is to stay the kinda guy she sees you as in the first place. But otherwise it's her way, and the longer you stick around, the more her way it is."

Carter remembered with dismay how little he had wanted to play ball or leapfrog and how thoroughly he had played. Worse, how he had told stories when he had intended to protest. And worse yet, he hadn't—even in his own mind—used the phrase The Malted Milk Monster for some time now! He had thought of her, had referred to her, only as Dorothy.

"And the longer you stick around—"

He had to get out of here, had to find some way to smash out of this world—fast.

Shirttail was offering the bottle again. Carter refused it impatiently. Escape, breaking out, that came first. And for that he'd need his mind at its clearest. The alternative was being slowly absorbed, psychologically as well as physically, into Dorothy's dream world, until even his thoughts would be only slightly eccentric versions of her image of him, and he would be caught, like a fly immortalized by amber, in whatever habitation and whatever role she visualized for The Nice Man.

The Nice Man! He shivered. What a way to spend the rest of his life! No, now, while he was still more or less himself, Carter Broun, while his brain still glittered with the edge of a bright young motivational research executive in the real world, *now* was the time to break through.

The real world. As good a name for it as any other. Carter was a mystic never and a Freudian only when the occasion suited him. His credo was simple: anything that *is* is real. So…

Postulate a cosmos sufficiently long in extension and sufficiently broad in possibility, and there has to be room somewhere in all its infinities for every kind of world that Man could imagine.

Or a child dream up.

And suppose a child, out of overpowering longing and loneliness, out of some incredible innate talent, perhaps, is able to break through the folds of cosmic enormities into the one cranny where its dream world exists as a tangible, everyday truth. Not much of a step from there to switching other individuals, adults even, stones and flowerpots certainly, from one universe to the other. The original supposition, Carter decided, was the difficult one. Once that was accepted, the others were easy.

In an unlimited number of parallel worlds, to find the true home of one's mind…

Was that what Dorothy had done? And, in that case, which would be the dream world, which the real? You could probably die in either with equal ease—so *that* was no criterion.

Well, what difference did it make? The real world, for Carter, was the world from which he had been pulled, the world in which he had standing, individuality and personal purpose. The world he liked and intended to return to. And this, this other world, no matter how substantial unto itself in its peculiar space-time matrix, was the dream world—the world he must flee. The world that he had to prove, against the logic of his very senses, did not exist—by leaving it, or by destroying it somehow.

Destroying…

He stared hard at Shirttail. No wonder the derelict had looked so familiar!

It had been the briefest glimpse, weeks ago, possibly months, but the word brought back the sententious caption under that unforgettable photograph.

A tabloid newspaper on a print-wet, newly arrived pile he'd noticed over his shoulder as he'd been passing the newsstand at 53rd Street, just off Madison. And he'd had to stop and take another look at the photograph spreading its shock value over a sector of the front page. A MAN WHO DESTROYED HIMSELF was the caption's headline.

The caption went on to explain, in the most appalled journalese, that this was what you might expect to look like if you spent the rest of your life not working, sleeping in doorways, and drinking, instead of eating, your meals. "Even hardened interns and nurses at the hospital averted their faces from this terrible thing that had once been a man."

But the photograph *did* show a terrible thing that had once been a man. He was shown in the alley as he'd been found, shown just as the stretcher was being lifted, and you weren't likely to forget him for a long, long time.

The worst part of it was that he was alive. The eyes stared into the lens of the camera without any pretense of seeing. There was no mark on the face or body, no blood, nothing but dirt, and yet you had the feeling that this was a man who had fallen out of a window ten stories up or been hit by a car speeding at ninety miles an hour—and not been killed. Not completely killed, anyway, just partially killed.

The body lay and the eyes stared and the man was alive, but nothing more than that could be said. Looking at the picture, you suddenly thought of complex organic compounds that were almost living creatures but had not yet made the grade. The flabby, sheer nonconsciousness of this yet-sentient creature made catatonia seem in comparison a rather jolly, extremely active state.

According to the caption, he had been found looking like this in an alley; he had been removed to a large city hospital, and, after ten hours, the doctors had not been able to do a single thing with him. No response at all.

Carter remembered the picture well. It had been a picture of Shirttail.

Somewhere, at this very moment, possibly in a hospital in Grenville Acres, before the eyes of a terrified, a nauseated Lee, there was another body that bore a physical resemblance to one Carter Broun, but that in every important respect looked exactly like that horrible photograph. A body that was barely alive, that would not respond to any stimuli, that could do no more than exist—since its consciousness was elsewhere.

Here, in Dorothy's private chocolate-candy world.

He had to get out of this place. No matter what, he was *going* to get out of this place. Only he'd need something close to dynamite. Psychological dynamite.

"—even cut my throat," Shirttail was going on heavily. "Oh, I maybe coulda cut my throat at the beginning, if I'da thoughta it. Too late now: I'm stopped cold any time I try. What I tried starving myself, but no go. Only candy to eat inna first place. Anybody can kick candy—it don't do no good, though. You don't hafta eat here, don't even hafta breathe. You stop breathin', you don't croak. Fact, Mac, fact. I done it. Hours and hours you can hold your breath: nothin' happens. Nothin' happens but what she wants to happen. And that's all. That's it."

Carter suggested, desperately trying to drag an elementary idea out of the concept of parallel universes, "How about the two of us getting together here and talking things over, just as we're doing? If we mapped out some workable sort of plan right now, it would be something she wouldn't like to have happen—but if we did, it would be real—it would have happened."

"Mac, you still don't get it. If you and me are together talkin', then some way or other that's the way *she* wants it. What she figures we go together, like, and we oughta be talkin' or bein' together. Meanwhile, she's workin' it out. What she's gonna do next. What we ain't gonna like it one damn bit, but so what?—far's she's concerned."

Carter frowned, not at Shirttail's last remarks, but at an unexpected and highly uncomfortable corroboration. He had suddenly felt an enormous tugging sensation in both his mind and body. Something was pulling at him to leave the cloud and descend to the candied surface.

Dorothy was coming back. She wanted him on the spot once more. She had a new sequence. Carter fought the tug grimly. He began to perspire.

The tug grew stronger. And stronger.

He squeezed his hands into tight, painful fists. "The Malted Milk Monster," he forced himself to say between clenched teeth. "Remember—*The Malted Milk Monster.*"

Shirttail looked up, intrigued. "Hey," he said. "Do me a favor, Mac—cuss her out. It'll do me good, honest, to hear a coupla good, first-class cuss words. Even if I won't remember them worth a damn, I'd still like to hear them again, just for old time's sake. Hey, Mac?"

Carter, threshing about in the chair, elbows digging into his sides, immersed in his own private struggle, shook his head. "No," he gasped. "Can't. Not now."

"I know. It's tough. What I mean, tough. Like when I first come, I used to battle it out the same way, every time I feel her give out with a think. I battle and I battle, and it's no go. I been moochin' all day, see, up and down the East Fifties, Sutton Place, all like that. I been moochin' for the price of a flop, for the price of a shot, but not a chance. What it's so cold, my back's draggin' the sidewalk, but the whole goddam world's got its pocket buttoned. Comes night, no flop. The whole night, I carry the banner. I stay awake, I keep walkin', what I don't wanna freeze. Five, six o'clock in the mornin', there's this can, there's half a fifth right on top in a bagfulla garbage. I hit it, oh, I hit it good."

Against his most determined mental opposition, Carter found himself getting to his feet. He knew his face was turning purple with the effort. He had to stop her now. He had to. It was the only way to invalidate her world.

But the Malt—*Dorothy* was calling him.

Shirttail rubbed a trembling filthy forefinger up and down the neck of the bottle. "And then I see this little alleyway between the buildings, what there's supposed to be a gate locking it off but it's been left open. I go in, it's dark, but there's a grating, hot air coming up from a basement, and I'm outa the wind. Sack time. What I think I'm one lucky old bum, but it's the last time I think about luck. I wake up, it's light, there's this kid, this Dorothy lookin' at me. Lookin', lookin'. She's got a big ball in her hands and she's standin' there lookin' at me. She points to the bottle.

"'That's my daddy's bottle,' she says. 'He threw it out last night, after the party. But it's his bottle.' I don't want no trouble with kids in this neighborhood, and I don't like the way it feels the way she looks. 'Scat, kid,' I say, and I sack out again. What I wake up next, here I am. I got the bottle and that's all I got. Mac, from that time on, it's rough. What I mean, *rough.* She had things here then, big things, things with legs and all kindsa—"

As if he were willing and even desirous of doing it, Carter turned his back on The Bad Old Man and began walking down through black fog. Behind him, the words continued to splash out like liquid from a steadily shaken glass. Carter's legs walked in direct contradiction to the nerve impulses they were receiving.

He couldn't refuse, couldn't resist. That much was obvious. As well try to refuse, to resist, the flood of forty days and forty nights, or the sun that Joshua made to stand still. Another way. He must find another way to fight. Meanwhile, he had to come as she demanded.

Dorothy was waiting for him on a patch of well-mown grass near a pink and green bonbon bush. As he came down beside her, she glanced away from him for a moment and at the dark cloud.

It disappeared.

What happened to Shirttail, Carter wondered—had he been wiped out for good? Or temporarily relegated to some sort of Limbo of reverie?

And then he really saw Dorothy—and the changes she had made.

She was still wearing the blue jeans, but the cashmere sweater was clean, perfectly clean. A bright, brand-new yellow. And she was taller. And she was even more slender than she had been before.

But that yellow cashmere sweater!

It was filled with two impossibly protruding breasts that belonged on a poster in front of a cheap movie house announcing the triumphant attributes of a Hollywood love goddess.

The rest of her body was still childlike, seemingly even more so than when he had first seen her, but this was due to the caricature effect of that incredible bosom.

Except—

Yes, except for the smear of red across her lip, the lumps of mascara at the tips of the eyelashes and the clashing, smashing colors on her fingernails. Did this mean—

He shook his head uncertainly, irritably. He hadn't counted on anything like this. Whatever it was.

"So," Dorothy simpered at last. "We meet again."

"It was meant to be," Carter found himself breathing. "We two have a common destiny. We live under the same strange star."

Talk about your precocious kids! But where did she get the dialogue, he wondered frantically—movies? Television drama? Books? Or out of her own neurosis-crammed head? And what did he represent in it? *Her* role was obvious: she was blatantly competing with Lee.

There was a struggling wisp of uncombed thought: Lee and who else? But over and around it was the horrified knowledge that he was saying things he would never say of his own volition. How soon before he'd he *thinking* such clichés?

And there was a memory at the back of his mind—he had a name for her that was very much his own creation, very hard to remember, but he had to remember it, something like, rather like, let's see now—*Dorothy.* The only name for her there was.

But that hadn't been it. No.

He thought in pitiful, despairing wing-flaps, like an ostrich trying to fly. *Awful, awful.* He had to touch his own real personality somehow. He had to break through. *Shatter—*

"Is your love then so strong, so truly true?" she demanded. "You have not forgotten me after all this time? Look into my eyes and tell me so. Tell me that your heart still belongs to me alone."

No, I won't, he groaned. He looked into her eyes. *I can't! Not such absolute baloney. And she's a kid—a little girl!*

"Do you doubt me, my darling?" he said softly, the sentences coming out of him in so many punched-out breaths. "Don't ever, *ever* doubt me. You are the only one for me, forever and always, as long as there is a sky overhead and an earth beneath. You and I, forever and always."

He had to *stop.* She was getting complete control over him. He said whatever she wanted him to say. And he was going to think it, too. But he couldn't prevent the words from flowing out of his mouth, once it was his turn, once she had finished and was waiting—

Dorothy looked off into the distance toward the two hills of equal height. Her eyes were misty, and, in spite of himself, Carter felt a catch in his throat. *Ridiculous! And yet how sad…*

"I almost feared your love," she mused. "I grew lonely and came to believe—"

Now. While she was doing the talking. While the full force of her mind was not turned compellingly upon him. Make it real. That's the way to bust this dream world. Make it real.

He reached for her.

"—that you had forgotten and found another. How was I to know—"

He grabbed at her.

He made it real.

There was an instant when the ground shook under his feet, when there was ripping sound from one end to another of the solid blue sky. There was just one instant when he exulted.

Then Dorothy turned wide, terror-stricken eyes at him. And screamed!

Her scream was the loudest thing in the universe. It went on and on and on, deafeningly. Yet he wasn't deafened, because he heard it all, every bit of it from the beginning, in each and every note of its immense range, all of its skull-powdering volume, all of its volcanic fear.

Not only Dorothy screamed. The candy trees screamed. The cookie bushes screamed. The two hills screamed. The chocolate river stood up between its screaming banks and screamed. The stones, the very air screamed.

And the ground fell apart and Carter Broun dropped into it. He dropped for centuries, he dropped for eons, he dropped for galactic eternities. Then he stopped dropping, stopped screaming himself, took his hands from his ears and looked around.

He was inside a dull gray, perfectly spherical, perfectly featureless vault. There were no doors and no windows, no seams and no cracks anywhere in the curving surface all about him. It was absolutely impenetrable and absolutely soundproof.

It had to be, he began to realize, as he scuttled dizzily around and around inside it. It had to be impenetrable and soundproof. It had to be at the bottommost bottom of the dream world, so that no sight and no sound from it should ever reach Dorothy's consciousness.

It was a total repression, this chamber of her mind, built to hide the deadly dangerous memory that was himself—built to last as long as Dorothy lasted.

AFTERWORD

One way to explain this story is to point out that, as Picasso had his blue period, I had my Bronx-school-teacher period. For about two years of my life, I seemed to be involved only with females who were elementary-school teachers and who lived in the farthest yay Bronx. The late-evening trips I took with them from my apartment in lower Manhattan's Greenwich Village! The long, well-nigh interminable, rattling subway rides to their cliff-like apartment-houses and back! I dreamed of meeting at least one young woman who lived in a suburb—but, unlike my protagonist here, I never did.

And then, of course, there was the fat little girl who came up to my chair one evening, at a dinner party, and asked me the question about a giant caterpillar and a million tiny little lions. Her parents were so proud.

I put it together in a pure fantasy tale aimed at *Beyond,* the sister magazine to Horace Gold's *Galaxy.* But Horace told me he needed it as science fiction for *Galaxy;* he was over-stocked on fantasy for *Beyond.* I poked at it and pried at it, discontentedly, finally putting it aside to work on something else.

On a summer evening in 1958, on one of his rare trips to New York, I showed the piece to Fredric Brown, who immediately suggested that I use the science-fiction rationale of his own delightful *What Mad Universe.* I did, and Horace bought the story.

All right—isn't that an explanation? Now here's another, absolutely equally true:

I read Florence Becker Lennon's *Victoria Through the Looking Glass,* and was deeply impressed by that Freudian investigation into Lewis Carroll.

Then I sat down immediately and reread all of *Alice.* I reread it all three separate times in a single session. I decided that I hated Freud.

Then I started writing "The Malted Milk Monster."

WRITTEN 1957——PUBLISHED 1959

THE HUMAN ANGLE

What a road! What filthy, dismal, blinding rain! And, by the ghost of old Horace Greeley, what an idiotic, impossible assignment!

John Shellinger cursed the steamy windshield from which a monotonous wiper flipped raindrops. He stared through the dripping, half-clear triangle of glass and tried to guess which was broken country road and which was the overgrown brown vegetation of autumn. He might have passed the slowly moving line of murderous men stretching to right and left across country and road; he might have angled off into a side road and be heading off into completely forsaken land. But he didn't think he had.

What an assignment!

"Get the human angle on this vampire hunt," Randall had ordered. "All the other news services will be giving it the hillbilly twist, medieval superstition messing up the atomic world. What dumb jerks these dumb jerks are! You stay off that line. Find yourself a weepy individual slant on bloodsucking and sob me about three thousand words. And keep your expense account down—you just can't work a big swindle sheet out of that kind of agricultural slum."

So I saddles my convertible, Shellinger thought morosely, and I tools off to the pappy-mammy country where nobody speaks to strangers no-how, "specially now, 'cause the vampire done got to three young 'uns already." And nobody will tell me the names of those three kids or whether any of them are still alive; and Randall's wires keep asking when I'll start sending usable copy; and I still can't find one loquacious Louise in the whole county. Wouldn't even have known of this cross-country hunt if I hadn't begun to wonder where all the men in town had disappeared to on such an unappetizing, rainy evening.

The road was bad in second, but it was impossible in almost any other gear. The ruts weren't doing the springs any good, either. Shellinger rubbed moisture off the glass with his handkerchief and wished he had another pair of headlights. He could hardly see.

That dark patch ahead, for instance. Might be one of the vampire posse. Might be some beast driven out of cover by the brush-beating. Might even be a little girl.

He ground into his brake. It was a girl. A little girl with dark hair and blue jeans. He twirled the crank and stuck his head out into the falling rain.

"Hey, kid. Want a lift?"

The child stooped slightly against the somber background of night and decaying, damp countryside. Her eyes scanned the car, came back to his face and considered it. The kid had probably not known that this chromium-plated kind of postwar auto existed. She'd certainly never dreamed of riding in one. It would give her a chance to crow over the other kids in the 'tater patch.

Evidently deciding that he wasn't the kind of stranger her mother had warned her about and that it would be less uncomfortable in the car than walking in the rain and mud, she nodded. Very slowly, she came around the front and climbed in at his right.

"Thanks, mister," she said.

Shellinger started again and took a quick, sidewise glance at the girl. Her blue jeans were raggedy and wet. She must be terribly cold and uncomfortable, but she wasn't going to let him know. She would bear up under it with the stoicism of the hill people.

But she was frightened. She sat hunched up, her hands folded neatly in her lap, at the far side of the seat right up against the door. What was the kid afraid of? Of course, the vampire!

"How far up do you go?" he asked her gently.

" 'Bout a mile and a half. But that way." She pointed over her shoulder with a pudgy thumb. She was plump, much more flesh on her than most of these scrawny, share-cropper kids. She'd be beautiful, too, some day, if some illiterate lummox didn't cart her off to matrimony and hard work in a drafty cabin.

Regretfully, he maneuvered around on the road, got the car turned and started back. He'd miss the hunters, but you couldn't drag an impressionable child into that sort of grim nonsense. He might as well take her home first. Besides, he wouldn't get anything out of those uncommunicative farmers with their sharpened stakes and silver bullets in their squirrel rifles.

"What kind of crops do your folks raise—tobacco or cotton?"

"They don't raise nothing yet. We just came here."

"Oh." That was all right: she didn't have a mountain accent. Come to think of it, she was a little more dignified than most of the children he'd met in this neighborhood. "Isn't it a little late to go for a stroll? Aren't your folks afraid to let you out this late with a vampire around?"

She shivered. "I—I'm careful," she said at last.

Hey! Shellinger thought. Here was the human angle. Here was what Randall was bleating about. A frightened little girl with enough curiosity to swallow her big lump of fear and go out exploring on this night of all others. He didn't know how it fitted, just yet—but his journalistic nose was twitching. There was copy here; the basic, colorful human angle was sitting fearfully on his red plastic seat.

"Do you know what a vampire is?"

She looked at him, startled, dropped her eyes and studied her folded hands for words. "It's—it's like someone who needs people instead of meals." A hesitant pause. "Isn't it?"

"Ye-es." That was good. Trust a child to give you a fresh viewpoint, unspoiled by textbook superstition. He'd use that—"People instead of meals." "A vampire is supposed to be a person who will be immortal—not die, that is—so long as he or she gets blood and life from living people. The only way you can kill a vampire—"

"You turn right here, mister."

He pointed the car into the little branchlet of side road. It was annoyingly narrow; surprised wet boughs tapped the windshield, ran their leaves lazily across the car's fabric top. Once in a while, a tree top sneezed collected rain water down.

Shellinger pressed his face close to the windshield and tried to decipher the picture of brown mud amid weeds that his headlights gave him. "What a road! Your folks are really starting from scratch. Well, the only way to kill a vampire is with a silver bullet. Or you can drive a stake through the heart and bury it in a crossroads at midnight. That's what those men are going to do tonight if they catch it." He turned his head as he heard her gasp. "What's the matter—don't you like the idea?"

"I think it's horrid," she told him emphatically.

"Why? How do you feel—live and let live?"

She thought it over, nodded, smiled. "Yes, live and let live. Live and let live. After all—" She was having difficulty finding the right words again. "After all, some people can't help what they are. I mean," very slowly, very thoughtfully, "like if a person's a vampire, what can they do about it?"

"You've got a good point there, kid." He went back to studying what there was of the road. "The only trouble's this: if you believe in things like vampires, well, you don't believe in them good—you believe in them nasty. Those people back in the village who claim three children have been killed or whatever it was by the vampire, they hate it and want to destroy it. If there are such things as vampires—mind you, I said 'if'—then, by nature, they do such horrible things that any way of getting rid of them is right. See?"

"No. You shouldn't drive stakes through people."

Shellinger laughed. "I'll say you shouldn't. Never could like that deal myself. However, if it were a matter of a vampire to me or mine, I think I could overcome my squeamishness long enough to do a little roustabout work on the stroke of twelve."

He paused and considered that this child was a little too intelligent for her environment. She didn't seem to be bollixed with superstitions as yet, and he was feeding her *Shellinger on Black Magic*. That was vicious. He continued, soberly, "The difficulty with those beliefs is that a bunch of grown men who hold them are spread across the countryside tonight because they think a vampire is on the loose. And they're likely to flush some poor hobo and finish him off gruesomely for no other reason than that he can't give a satisfactory explanation for his presence in the fields on a night like this."

Silence. She was considering his statement. Shellinger liked her dignified thoughtful attitude. She was a bit more at ease, he noticed, and was sitting closer to him. Funny how a kid could sense that you wouldn't do her any harm. Even a country kid. Especially a country kid, come to think of it, because they lived closer to nature or something.

He had won her confidence, though, and consequently rewon his. A week of living among thin-lipped ignoramuses who had been not at all diffident in showing *their* disdain had made him a little uncertain. This was better. And he'd finally got a line on the basis of a story.

Only, he'd have to dress it up. In the story, she'd be an ordinary hillbilly kid, much thinner, much more unapproachable; and the quotes would all be in "mountain" dialect.

Yes, he had the human interest stuff now.

She had moved closer to him again, right against his side. Poor kid! His body warmth made the wet coldness of her jeans a little less uncomfortable. He wished he had a working heater in the car.

The road disappeared entirely into tangled bushes and gnarly trees. He stopped the car, flipped the emergency brake.

"You don't live here? This place looks as if nothing human's been around for years." He was astonished at the uncultivated desolation.

"Sure I live here, mister," her warm voice said at his ear. "I live in that little house over there."

"Where?" He rubbed at the windshield and strained his vision over the sweep of headlight. "I don't see any house. Where is it?"

"There." A plump hand came up and waved at the night ahead. "Over there."

"I still can't see—" The corner of his right eye had casually noticed that the palm of her hand was covered with fine brown hair.

Strange, that.

Was covered with fine brown hair. Her palm!

"What *was* that you remembered about the shape of her teeth?" his mind shrieked. He started to whip his head around, to get another look at her teeth. But he couldn't.

Because her teeth were in his throat.

Afterword

There was once a wonderful magazine called *Famous Fantastic Mysteries*. It published a short novel and three or four short stories every month, most of them reprints of delightful pieces that had been overlooked by the readership or unjustly forgotten. It was a much-loved magazine.

Its editor was an elderish lady by the name of Mary Gnaedinger. Her taste and editorship were impeccable. She was, if that were possible, loved even more than the magazine. You knocked your knees a bit, if you were in the fantasy or science-fiction field, when you spoke of Mary Gnaedinger.

Ted Sturgeon, who was my first agent and perhaps the very best agent I ever had, invited me to supper one night. "You've heard," he said, "of an editor's lunch? Well, this is an agent's supper. It's for six o'clock, and please, please, don't be late. Important!"

He was living in the Village then with Ree, a talented poet and one of his high-school sweethearts, whom he called his "dark lady of the sonnets." For what it's worth, I once wrote a strange little murder mystery short about the two of them; I called it "Murdering Myra."

Ree didn't cook, but then she didn't have to. Women had to fight Ted Sturgeon for the kitchen stove: he was a gourmet cook.

Ted had prepared a meal calculated to outrage me (I am very conservative when it comes to food; I add a new dish to my cuisine promptly every eleventh year). Over the strange tropical fruits he had found and the peculiar-looking sauce on the beef, he explained the reason for that night's invitation.

Mary Gnaedinger had called him earlier in the day. She was desperate. An entire issue of *Famous Fantastic Mysteries* had been lost on the way to the printer in Ohio. The novel was no problem—she had two bound copies of that in her own bookcase—but she had no other copies of the three short-story reprints, and she was unable to find them anywhere in the short deadline she had been given by the publisher. She needed three short stories, the exact length of the missing three, and she needed them in twenty-four hours.

"That's why it was so important you come on time," Ted said. He had phoned Ray Bradbury in California (*expensive* in those days), and Bradbury had agreed to write one of the 2,100-word pieces immediately and ship it to Mary air-mail special-delivery.

"You and I," Ted told me, "will write the other two, and I'll take them to Mary in the morning."

I remember I grimaced unhappily. "But, damn it all, Ted, I don't have a single idea in my head!"

"Nonsense," he said. "Are you a writer, or aren't you a writer? You will use Ree's typewriter, and I will use my typewriter, and we'll sit back to back, and each of us will write a short and delightful fantasy for Mary."

"About *what?*" I wailed. "For the love of God, Montresor, about *what?*"

Ted thought. "You'll write about vampires," he said finally. "Mary loves stories about vampires. You'll find a new angle about vampires and write about that. Now, let's get started. Remember, we've only got tonight."

Then he put two chairs back to back. In front of one chair was his typewriter table, and on it was his Royal portable. In front of the other chair was Ree's typewriter table and Ree's Royal portable. He sat down before his typewriter and began typing immediately. Ree made coffee, which was all Ree ever did around a kitchen.

What the hell could I do? I sat down with my back to him and began typing as if I really knew what I was doing.

I wrote a story I called "The Human Angle."

Ted wrote a story he called "So Big."

Mary had all three pieces late the next day. I don't remember what Bradbury called his story. I do remember it as a very good story, though.

WRITTEN 1948——PUBLISHED 1948

ॐ

Everybody Loves Irving Bommer

Irving Bommer had been wistfully following a girl in a green frock when the absolutely fantastic thing happened to him.

A compliment.

The gypsy woman, who sat on and overflowed the stone step in front of her soiled little shop, leaned forward and called: " 'Ey, Mistair!" Then, as he broke his plodding stride to consider her and the window full of dream-books and numerology texts, she cleared her throat with the sound of lumpy oatmeal being stirred.

" 'Ey, Mistair! You, the 'ansome wan!"

Irving rocked on one foot, came to a dead stop and watched the girl maneuver the green frock around the corner and out of his life.

For the moment, he was paralyzed. He could not leave the neighborhood of that delectable compliment even—even if Humphries himself, the housewares buyer of Gregworth's, had materialized from behind an invisible counter and snapped his fingers.

But then, of course. Some people thought it was funny. Some people, especially women... His pale cheeks slowly ripened as he cudgeled his slow brain to find a retort both clever and devastating. "A-a-ah!" he began extemporaneously.

"Come 'ere, 'ansome mistair," she commanded, with no trace of mockery. "Inside, you gat what you wan' so badly. I 'ave it."

What he wanted badly? How did she know? Even he, Irving Bommer, had only the vaguest conception. Yet, he found himself following her wide, swinging body through the doorway into a store drearily furnished with three folding chairs and a bridge table on which rested a cracked crystal ball. Five children of astonishingly overlapping ages played in front of a torn bedsheet which curtained off the back room. At a peremptory bawl from the woman, they tumbled out of sight through the sheet.

As he settled into a folding chair that immediately leaned into a forty-five-degree angle with the floor, Irving Bommer wondered hazily what he was doing there. He remembered that Mrs. Nagenbeck had told him when he first rented a room from her: "Never keep *no* supper for *no* boarder at *no* time" and, since today had been monthly inventory in the housewares department, he was both late and hungry. Still...

You never knew what these gypsies might come up with. They were certainly a discerning bunch. They had standards of beauty that weren't poured out of the Hollywood mold; they came of a race that had been cosmopolitan since Pilate; they could recognize things like nobility of soul and—well, perhaps even handsomeness—worldly, mature handsomeness, you could call it.

"Well, uh," he essayed a chuckle. "What do you have that I—that I—uh—want so badly? A dream book to clean up on the races? Never play the races. And I never have my fortune told, either."

She stood before him in multifidious flesh and multitudinous colorful clothing, examining him gravely out of tiny, tired black eyes. "No," she said at last. "For you no fortune I tal. I geeve this."

There was a medicine bottle in her outstretched hand, a bottle filled with a bubbly purple liquid which changed to a rich red and then a somber blue under the shadow-thick twilight pressing in from the shop window.

"What—what is it?" he asked, though he knew suddenly there was but one thing he could be offered.

"Belong my 'osban. Many years he take to make eet. He 'ave this, he die. Bot you, ees deeferen. You entitle. Eet geeve you woman."

Irving Bommer started at the insult. He tried to laugh, but gasped his belief, his desire, instead. Woman!

"You mean it's a potion—a love philter?" His voice cracked between the conflict of ridicule and acceptance.

"Pheeltair. Wan I see you, I know you need. You 'ave moch onhoppiness. Vairy leetle hoppy. Bot remembair, use only to take bock what 'as been taken. Your blood on drop from pheeltair makes drop from pheeltair yours. Wan drop at time. Ten dollars, please."

That did it. Ten dollars! For some colored water she'd mixed up in the back room. Just because he'd been gullible enough to walk inside. Not for Irving Bommer. He was nobody's fool.

"I'm nobody's fool," he told her, finding the thought good enough to articulate. He stood up and shook himself.

"Leesen!" The gypsy woman's voice was hoarse and commanding. "You being fool now. You need. I could osk feefty, I could osk a tousand. I osk ten because thot is price, because you 'ave ten, because you need. And I—I don' need now. Don' be fool. Take eet. You be—you be really 'ansome."

Irving found the sneer wouldn't stay put, that the door was too far away. Very slowly, he counted out ten dollars, leaving himself only two until payday. Even the recollection of the fantastically expensive bottle of aftershave lotion he had been persuaded to purchase last week didn't inhibit him. He—just had to...

"Wan drop of blood wan you use," the woman called after him as he hurried out of the shop. "Good luck, mistair."

By the time he had walked the two long blocks to his boarding house, the wildly hopeful elation had subsided into the usual abiding humiliation.

"What a sucker, what a sucker!" he raged as he slipped into the back entrance of Mrs. Nagenbeck's boarding house and climbed the stairs. Irving Bommer, the all-time champ of suckers! Show him anything and he bought it. Love philters!

But when he had slammed the door of his thin little room behind him, when he had tossed the small bottle viciously to the bed, he bit his lips and drooled two huge tears out of his near-sighted eyes.

"If only I had a face instead of a comic drawing," he bawled. "If only—oh, dammit!"

Then his mind, being relatively sane, refused to deal any longer in these terms. *Let us daydream,* said his mind to his reeling subconscious; *let us daydream and imagine how pleasant it could be.*

So he sat on the bed, his chin nursing blissfully on one drawn-up knee, and dreamed of a correctly created world where women schemed for his attention and fought for his person; where, unable to win him privately, they shared him willy-nilly with equally determined sisters. Through this glorious place, he wandered familiarly, pleased as always by the way the rules kept changing in his favor.

Sometimes he was the only male left alive after an atomic catastrophe; and sometimes he reclined on purple cushions, puffing on his hookah while a harem full of breath-taking houri waited adoringly; and yet other times, dozens of men—all their faces curiously reminiscent of Humphries, the housewares buyer—watched in stolid despair as Bommer the rich, Bommer the successful, Bommer the incredibly couth, escorted their wives, fiancées, and special girlfriends out of rather roomy limousines into a bachelor's apartment so multiplex as to occupy the whole of a Park Avenue building.

Now and then, there might be a sequence—a painless one!—with a plastic surgeon, which talented gentleman, having committed his masterpiece, would die of satisfaction before he could mar his work by duplicating it. Frequently, Irving Bommer would postpone the difficult choice between a statuesque, glowing blonde and a pert little redhead long enough to ponder upon such events as his having grown past six feet two inches with no noticeable tremors, as his shoulders having broadened, his feet unflattened, his nose diminished, and straightened. While he enjoyed the new resonance of his voice and the catchy heartiness of his laughter, while he was proud of his perfect, ever-poised wit and his exact, all-purpose education, it was to his splendid physical attributes that he found himself continually returning. That head of hair which spilled carelessly over his bald spot, that third set of teeth miraculously growing past the ruins of yellowed enamel and cheap bridgework, that stomach, no longer catching the eye through a bubbly paunch, but decently hidden behind a wall of muscle. That stomach! In it were now to be found only the finest vintage wines, the tastiest dishes prepared by the most expert chefs, the most succulent, the most delicious...

With an abrupt gulp, Irving Bommer swallowed the saliva which had collected in his mouth and realized he was violently hungry.

According to his watch, the kitchen would be dark and empty; it was accessible by way of the back staircase which passed his room in its creaking descent.

Mrs. Nagenbeck, however, when aroused by an unauthorized raid on her larder, tended to combine the most significant characteristics of each of the Three Furies in one harmonious whole. Why, Irving Bommer quivered, if she caught him—

Well, friend, that's a chance we'll just have to take, his stomach interposed harshly. Sighing with trepidation, he went noisily downstairs on the top-most tips of his toes.

Feeling around in the darkness, he touched the refrigerator padlock. He frowned hungrily. A careful search of the kitchen and some emphatic shin-barking, however, netted him three-fourths of a salami, half a loaf of rye bread, and a heavy triangular-bladed knife of the type which is indispensable when boarding a Spanish galleon from a British privateer.

Oke, said his stomach, licking its duodenum. *Let's start!*

A light clicked on in the room behind the kitchen. Irving stopped in mid-slice, his body absolutely still, but his heart and still-talkative stomach somersaulting against each other like a pair of acrobats in a rousing vaudeville finale. As whenever he was frightened, he began to perspire so profusely that his feet slid around in their tight shoes.

"Who's there?" Mrs. Nagenbeck called. "Anyone in the kitchen?"

Declining to answer her, even in the negative, Irving Bommer fled upstairs damply, with his food, knife, and now thoroughly confused internal anatomy.

Back in his room, fingers on the light switch, he gasped for a moment, listened for a moment, then smiled. He had left no traces.

He sauntered leisurely to the bed, eating a slice of salami off the knife with wonderfully unselfconscious courage. The purple medicine lay where he had thrown it. It looked red; it also looked slightly blue; then again, sometimes…

He sat down and started to unscrew the bottle cap with the thumb and forefinger of his right hand and slowly raised two sloppy eyebrows at the difficulty. *So,* he thought, *we shift the knife to the right hand, sort of holding the blade under our armpit, get a good grip on the bottle with our left hand, and strenuously twist the cap. Meanwhile, we continue to munch.* Under our armpit, the knife blade squirms anxiously, trying to get a good sight on a valuable organ.

The cap was stuck fast. Maybe you weren't supposed to open it. Maybe you smashed the bottle and used it all at once. He could worry about it later, in any case. At the moment, he had salami, he had rye bread. And two dollars instead of twelve.

He started to put the bottle down, giving it an irritated half-twist back and forth to show that he wasn't through with it. The cap loosened. Bommer unscrewed it all the way, more than a little startled. He'd never known they made medicine bottles with left-hand threads.

Odd smell. Like—like a soaped, scrubbed, and freshly diapered infant who had abruptly decided that a full bladder was not half so pleasant as an empty one; and the liquid in the bottle was blue. He smelled again. No, more like a very hairy man who'd spent a busy afternoon with pick and shovel and couldn't see any sense in taking a bath today and smashing one of his most cherished personal traditions. Yet as Irving Bommer meditated at the glass vial now, it shone with a flashing scarlet. As he brought it under his nose for one last sniff, he marveled at how he had misjudged the odor: unpleasant it was, very much so, but you could identify it easily. It was…not exactly stale tobacco smoke…no, nor a recently manured field—

He spilled a little on his left palm. Purple.

A fist clump-clump-clumped on his door. "Hey, there!" Mrs. Nagenbeck yelled. "You, Mr. Bommer! Open this door! I know what you got in there. You got my food in there. Open that door!"

At Irving Bommer's convulsion, the knife under his armpit made a wild leap for freedom and glory. It aimed at a wrist where, with any luck, the whole left hand might be severed (and wouldn't that accomplishment put a certain haughty meat-cleaver in its place!). Unfortunately, the hand had jerked down instinctively to shove the salami and rye bread under the pillow. The knife clattered to the floor, content—but not happy—with a tip of the fourth finger and a sliver of pinky.

"If you don't open this door right now, this instant, this second," Mrs. Nagenbeck announced through the keyhole which she had pressed into service as a megaphone, "I will kick it down, I will break it down." Having achieved Ossa, she cast about for Pelion. "I will smash it and charge you for a door, two hinges and whatever woodwork is damaged. Not to mention the food you got in there and you're making unhygienic by touching. Open the door, you Mr. Bommer!"

He shoved the knife under the pillow after the food and jerked a blanket over them all. Then, recapping the medicine bottle, he walked toward the door sucking his bleeding fingers and perspiring insanely.

"Juzza second," he begged, the words clotting in his mouth.

"Then there's the lock," Mrs. Nagenbeck brooded. "A good lock today costs four, five, six dollars. And where's the labor costs I pay to the carpenter for his work in putting it on? If I have to break this door, if I have to crash my own…"

Her voice died into a curious mumble. Irving Bommer heard two sounds like the anticipatory wheezes of a locomotive before he managed to unlock the door.

Mrs. Nagenbeck stood there in her lavender dressing gown, her brows knit and her papery nostrils flared.

The salami! With her boarding-house experience, she could probably track it to the correct corner of the pillow by aroma alone.

"What a funny…" Mrs. Nagenbeck began uncertainly, hostile lines leaving her face with much regret. "What a strange smell! Such an unusual odor—so peculiar, so— Oh, you poor boy, Mr. Bommer—you hurt?"

He shook his head, bewildered by the completely alien expression on her face. It wasn't anger, yet it certainly looked dangerous. He retreated into the room. Mrs. Nagenbeck followed him, her voice experimenting with various sounds and winding up with something mighty like a coo.

"Let me see the hurt fingers, the ripped part, the scratch, the bruise," she said shyly, pulling his left hand from his mouth with sufficient force to loosen five teeth. "Oo-ooh, does it hurt? You got iodine antiseptic or mercurochrome peroxide antiseptic? And a styptic pencil antiseptic? And gauze bandages for wrapping and dressing?"

Overcome by her startling shift of mood, Irving Bommer indicated the medicine chest with his nose.

She continued to make the strange, embarrassing noises as she dressed the wound, for all the world like a saber-tooth purring. Every once in a while, when her lifted eyes met Irving Bommer's, she smiled with a quick exhalation. But when, holding his hand up for a last inspection, she suddenly planted a lingering, groaning kiss in the palm, he became frightened.

He strode to the door, pulling Mrs. Nagenbeck by the precious hand. "Thanks a lot," he told her. "But it's late. I have to be getting to bed."

Mrs. Nagenbeck let go. "You want me to leave," she stated reproachfully.

At his nod, she swallowed, smiled bravely and walked out sideways, practically scraping the buttons off his vest.

"Don't work too hard," her sad face was saying as he closed the door upon it. "Someone like you shouldn't have to kill themselves to death working at a job. Good night, Mr. Bommer."

The lush purple of the little vial winked at him from the bed. The love potion! He had spilled a drop in his palm and, after his fingers were cut, had involuntarily clenched his hand. The gypsy woman had said that a drop of his blood mixed with a drop of the potion would make that drop his very own. Evidently that had happened: Mrs. Nagenbeck was aflame. He shuddered. Mrs. Nagenbeck. What kind of a love philter—

But what was sauce for Mrs. Nagenbeck undoubtedly would be sauce for other, younger, more desirable females. Like that lazy-eyed girl behind the cutlery counter, or the sparkling minx in salad bowls and baking dishes.

A knock on the door.

"It's only me, Hilda Nagenbeck. Look, Mr. Bommer, I got to thinking, salami and rye bread are pretty dry. Besides, they make you thirsty for something to drink. So I brought up two cans of beer."

He smiled as he opened the door and took the two cans. Time had not stood still with Mrs. Nagenbeck. What had been a-budding in her eyes before was now in glorious bloom. Her soul stood on her lashes and waved at him.

"Thank you, Mrs. Nagenbeck. Now, go right to bed. Go ahead."

She nodded quickly, obediently, and plumped down the passage, casting a yearning glance backward with every step.

It was with straighter, prouder shoulders that Irving Bommer applied the requisite opening pressure to a can of beer. Mrs. Nagenbeck was not much, certainly; but she pointed the way to a more interesting future.

He was handsome now—to any woman with a mildly sensitive nose.

Only trouble, there was so little of the stuff; the bottle was terribly small. Who knew how long the effect lasted? And he had so much to catch up with.

As he finished the second can of beer, much, much pleased with himself, he suddenly hit on the solution. Beautiful! And so simple.

First, he poured the contents of the medicine bottle into the empty can. Then, stripping off the bandages, he inserted his two injured fingers into the triangular bottle and scraped the newly formed scar tissue off against the raw metal. In a moment, there was a satisfactory flow of blood into the can, a flow which he stimulated by repeated scrapings.

When he felt he had the mixture as before, he shook the can a few times, dressed his now messy fingers and poured the whole noisome collation into the large, economy-size bottle of aftershave lotion he had purchased a week before. The bottle was fitted with an atomizer.

"Now," he said, as he tossed the knife and rye bread to the bureau, turned out the lights, crawled into bed and began munching on the salami, "now, let them watch out for Irving Bommer!"

He forgot to set the alarm and was awakened only by the ablutionary matins of the man in the room next door. "Twenty minutes to dress and get to work," he muttered as he threw the sheets apart and leaped to the wash basin. "No breakfast!"

But Mrs. Nagenbeck met him downstairs with an arch smile and a tray. Disregarding his protestations, she insisted he have "at least a bite to chew on in his mouth."

As he frantically forked the scrambled eggs from the soup bowl to his face, jerking his head to avoid Mrs. Nagenbeck's furtive kisses like the human target in a baseball-throwing sideshow, he wondered what had happened to his prim, forbidding landlady since the last time he'd seen her.

The last time he'd seen her...

Seizing the opportunity of Mrs. Nagenbeck's departure for a jar of caviar ("so you can have a spread on your bread with your coffee"), he pounded back upstairs to his room.

He ripped off his shirt and tie and, after thinking a bit, his undershirt. He pointed the nozzle of the atomizer at himself and squeezed the rubber bulb. He sprayed his face, his hair, his ears, his neck, his chest, his back, his arms, his navel. He even pushed the nozzle under his belt and sprayed around in a complete circle. When his hand began to knot with the unaccustomed exercise, he desisted at last and began to dress. The odor almost sickened him, yet he felt amazingly light-hearted.

Before he left the room, he shook the huge bottle. Still at least nine-tenths full. So there was another bargain he was making pay off. Before he was through, a lot of things and a lot of people were going to pay off!

The gypsy woman was standing in front of her bedraggled shop when he passed. She started to smile, stopped abruptly, and shouted a slippery phrase at her children, who ran inside. Backing into the store, she held her nose and wailed at him lugubriously: "You use too moch! You not suppose use all at wance!"

He tipped her a careless salute as he hurried on. "I didn't. There's lots more where this came from!"

His train was crowded, but he saw a vacant seat from the subway platform. He hit the knot of people clustered about the opening doors and literally untied them. Dodging recklessly into the train, almost singing with self-confidence and happiness, he squeezed past two fairly determined women, expertly kicked a brisk, old fellow in the shins to distract him, and was sliding into the seat when the train started.

The lurch threw him off balance and enabled a porcelain-faced young lady of twenty or twenty-five—a rank outsider—to slip in under his probing posterior. By the time he had straightened and turned around, she was grinning at him smugly with a tiny but extremely red mouth.

If there is one thing an habitual subway rider learns, it is that Kismet underground is forever inscrutable, seating some and placing others always among the standees. Irving Bommer reached for the overhead bar, adjusting himself to the hard subway law of supply and demand.

The girl's face was twisted as if she were about to cry. She shook her head in spasms, staring up at him and biting her lips. She was breathing very loudly.

She stood up suddenly and indicated the seat with a courtly gesture. "Won't you take it, please?" she asked with a voice positively awash in milk and honey. "You look tired."

Irving Bommer sat down, acutely conscious of the heads turning in their direction. His neighbor, a somewhat plump nineteen, began sniffing and slowly, incredulously, moved her shining eyes from her historical novel to his face.

The girl who had given him her seat swung in close, though all the other standing passengers were leaning the other way just then. "I'm positive I met you somewhere before," she began with some uncertainty, then more and more rapidly as if she were remembering the words: "My name is Iphigenia Smith and, if you tell me yours, I just know I'll be able to recall exactly where we were introduced."

Irving Bommer sighed deep in his inmost psyche and leaned back. Biology and he had at last developed a rendezvous.

He led a small parade to the employees' entrance of Gregworth's Department Store. Rendered inconsolable by the refusal of the elevator operator to admit customers into the rickety elevator intended solely for personnel, they clustered about the shaft and watched him ascend as if he were Adonis and the winter solstice were approaching.

Humphries caught him scribbling his name on the sign-in pad. "Seven minutes late. Not too good, Bommer, not too good. We want to make an effort to get in on time, don't we? We want to make a real effort."

"Forgot to set the alarm," Irving Bommer mumbled.

"We aren't going to use that one, are we? Let's be adults in Gregworth's; let's face up to our mistakes and try to do better." The buyer pulled his perfectly knotted tie just a fraction tighter and frowned. "What in the world is that smell? Bommer, don't you bathe?"

"A woman spilled something on me in the subway. It'll wear off."

Having made good his escape, he wended his way past pots, pans, and pressure cookers to dicers, graters, and peelers, where he took up his regular station. He had just begun to set the counter up for the day's business when the gong announced that the outside world was now able to enter and secure Gregworth's Greater Bargains.

A hand sliding tremulously across his lapels distracted him. Doris, the blonde, beautiful salad bowls and baking dishes, was leaning across his counter and caressing him. Doris! She who usually made loud, unpleasant sounds whenever he aimed a bright cliché at her!

He grabbed her chin. "Doris," he said sternly, "do you love me?"

"Yes," she breathed. "Yes, darling, *yes*. More than *any*—"

He kissed her twice, first quickly, then with more savor as he observed she didn't leap away, but moaned deliriously instead and writhed a whole row of projecting nickel-plated graters out of position.

Fingers snapping loudly made him jerk back and push her away.

"Now, now, now, now," said Humphries, glaring at Irving Bommer with a slight uncertainty. "We have a time and a place for everything, don't we? Let's be business-like; we have customers to wait on. Let's attend to private matters after closing time."

The girl shot the buyer a look of purest hatred, but at Irving's dismissing wave and Humphries's further finger-snaps, she turned away slowly, saying in a low, insistent tone: "I'll wait for you after work, Irving darling. I'll go home with you. Everywhere, forever…"

"Don't know what happened to that clerk," Humphries mused. "Used to be the steadiest salad bowls and baking dishes." He turned back to Irving Bommer, seemed to struggle with himself, then began mildly: "In any case, Bommer, let us not go off the deep end. Customers are coming up; let's start pushing graters, let's move our slicers." He picked up a bone handle attached to a long, twisted blade and flourished it at an early group of women shoppers congregated around Irving's counter. "The latest way to cut grapefruit, oranges, and melons, ladies. The only way. Why have old-fashioned straight and severe lines around your servings?" His voice, which had been contemptuous, soared away to contemplate the lotus: "With the new Hollywood Dream Slicer you cut your grapefruit, oranges, and melons easily and efficiently. No more losing valuable, vitamin-filled juices; no more melon stains on delicate lace tablecloths. And above all, you have attractive scalloped edges. Children love to eat interestingly cut grapefruit, oranges—"

"Is that what he's selling?" asked a huge woman with a musclebound jaw. Humphries nodded.

"Then I'll take one. If he gives it to me."

"I'll take two. Will he give me two?"

"Five! I want five. I asked first and you didn't hear me."

"Now, ladies," Humphries beamed. "Let's not push, let's not squabble. There are more than enough Hollywood Dream Slicers to go around. See, Bommer, see," he hissed, "what a little sales talk can do for us? Let's not miss one of these sales; let's hustle."

He walked away happily, snapping his fingers at surrounding counters whose female custodians were all leaning disturbingly in the same Bommertropism. "Let's straighten up, girls; let's be brisk and meet the Business Day. And, at that," he mused, as he toddled back to his office to insult the first batch of manufacturers' representatives, "at that, it looks like a banner day in dicers, graters, and peelers."

How right he was, he did not begin to suspect until shortly before lunch hour, when the chief stock clerk burst in on him and screamed, "You gotta put more men on, Humphries. The stock department can't carry the load!"

"Load? Which load?"

"The load to and from Bommer's counter, that's which load!" The chief stock clerk threw away a handful of hair and danced around the desk. "I have all my men assigned to that one counter, not a man on inventory, not a man receiving, and as fast as we get the stuff to him, he sells it. Why didn't you tell me you were going to have a giveaway sale on dicers, graters, and peelers? I'd've ordered more stuff from the warehouse instead of having to yip at them every half-hour. I'd've asked Cohen in modernistic furniture or Blake in children's sport clothes to lend me a coupla men!"

Humphries shook his head, "There's no sale in dicers, graters, and peelers, not a giveaway sale, nor a seasonal sale nor even a plain bargain sale. Get a grip on yourself, man; let's not fall apart under unexpected pressure. Let's take a look and find out what is what."

He opened the door of his office and immediately exhibited the formal technique of standing aghast. Housewares was jammed with a gasping, surging mass of females, aimed at the dicers, graters, and peelers counter. Irving Bommer was completely hidden behind a flood of permanent waves and crazily perched hats but, from time to time, an empty carton would sail out of what Humphries approximated as his geographic position and a thin, cracked voice could be heard calling: "Get me more dicers, Stock, get me more! I'm running out. They're getting restless!" Every other counter on the floor was deserted—by clerks as well as customers.

Bellowing, "Hold them, Bommer; hold them, boy!" the buyer shot his cuffs and charged in. As he worked his way past women clasping whole cartons of potato peelers to their laboring breasts, he observed that the peculiar odor emanating from Bommer was now noticeable even at a distance. And it had grown stronger, more pungent...

Irving Bommer looked like a man who had gone down into the Valley of the Shadow and had seen much more there to fear than such picayune things as Evil. His collar was open, his tie flapped over one shoulder, his glasses hung from the opposite ear, his eyes were streaked madly with red, and sweat bubbled from him so furiously that his clothes appeared to have been recently withdrawn from an enthusiastic washing machine.

He was very badly frightened. While he had wares with which to distract them, the adoration was relatively passive. But as soon as his stock ran low, the women began to concentrate on his person again. There was no obvious rivalry among them; they merely pushed against each other to get a better view. In the beginning, he had told a few to go home and they had obeyed; now, though they seemed willing to do as he told them in every other respect, they absolutely refused to leave his presence. The affection they displayed had become more insistent, more determined—and more united. Dimly, he realized that this was due to his prodigious rate of perspiration—the sweat mixed with the love potion and diluted it still more, spread his odor still further abroad.

And the caresses! He had never known how painful a feminine touch could be. Every time he reeled down the counter to fill an order, hands—dozens of them—

would reach out and stroke his arms, his chest, any part of his body that was accessible. Multiplied by the three hours it had been going on, the gentle touches had begun to feel like so many roundhouse punches.

He almost wept when Humphries slid into the counter by his side. "You got to get me more stock, Mr. Humphries," he babbled. "All I got left are eggplant graters and a few cabbage dicers. When they go, I go."

"Steady, boy, steady there," the buyer told him. "This is our test; let's meet it like a man. Are we going to be an effective, dependable clerk, or a reed that no large retailer dares lean upon? Where are those salesgirls? They should be behind the counter, helping you. Well, it'll be a while before we get another shipment. Let's take a break; let's try to interest them in towel racks and toiletware."

"Hey," an arm encased in mouton reached across the counter and tapped Humphries on the shoulder. "Move, I can't see him."

"One moment, madam, let's not get impatient," Humphries began brightly, then stopped before the murderous look in the woman's eyes. She—and the others around her, he noticed—looked quite capable of shoving a Hollywood Dream Slicer into his heart without tremor. He gulped and tried to shoot his cuffs.

"Look, Mr. Humphries, can I go home?" Irving asked him tearfully. "I don't feel at all well. And now that the stock is gone, there's not much point in my sticking around."

"Well," the buyer considered, "we can't say that we haven't had a busy day, can we now? And if we don't feel well, we don't feel well. Of course, we can't expect pay for the afternoon, but we can go home."

Irving said, "Gee, thanks." He started for the counter exit, but Humphries caught him by the elbow.

He coughed. "Just thought I'd tell you, Bommer, that that odor isn't offensive at all. Quite pleasant, in fact. Hope I didn't offend you by my thoughtless remark anent your bathing."

"No, that's all right. You didn't offend me."

"I'm glad. I shouldn't like to offend you. I want you to like me, Bommer, I want you to feel that I'm your friend. Really, I—"

Irving Bommer fled. He dodged through the female multitude, and everywhere they moved back to make way for him, everywhere they reached out and touched—just touched!—some part of his pain-flooded anatomy.

He broke free long enough to get into the service elevator and shivered at the hungry, despairing moan that went up when the elevator doors closed in the earnest faces of the advance guard. As he descended, he heard a girlish voice sing out: "I know where he lives, everybody! I'll take you to his home!"

They were so damned cooperative, he groaned. He'd always dreamed of being a male god, but he'd never anticipated that one of a god's characteristics is that he is worshipped unselfishly.

He ran out of the elevator on the ground floor and hailed a taxi, observing that the girl operator had followed him out unswervingly and was also getting one. As he gave frenzied directions to the driver, he saw that all over the street women were climbing into cabs and commandeering buses.

"Hurry, hurry," he chattered at the driver. "Fast, fast, fast."

"I'm doing the best I can, fella," the man told him over his shoulder. "I observe traffic regulations. Which is more than I can say for those dumb dames back there."

Peeping despairingly through the rear window, Irving Bommer saw a complete disregard of red lights, arm-flailing policemen, and intersecting traffic as the cars behind him charged on. Every time his driver stopped, they picked up more motorized femininity.

And yet the sweat poured out of him more luxuriantly than ever as his fear increased, and yet the effluvium of Irving Bommer spread more widely through the streets.

He'd take a bath when he got home—that's what he'd do—he'd take a shower with some strong soap and wash the awful stuff off. But he'd have to hurry.

The taxi's brakes shrieked with the effort of gripping the wheels. "There you are, mister. This is as far as I can go. Some sort of riot going on."

As he paid the driver, Irving Bommer looked ahead and winced. The street was black with women.

The bottle of aftershave lotion—that's what it was. There was an open nozzle on it, and some of the odor had seeped out. The bottle was nearly full, so it must have been quite powerful. Still, if just leakage could do this…

The women stood about in the street, in the yard, in the alleyway, their faces turned up to his room like dogs who had treed a possum. They were very patient, very quiet, but every once in a while a sigh would start up and swell to the volume of shell-fire.

"Listen," he told the driver. "Wait for me. I may be back."

"That I can't promise. Don't like the looks of the mob."

Irving Bommer pulled his jacket over his head and ran for the entrance of his boarding-house. Faces—startled, happy faces—began turning in his direction.

"That's him!" he heard Mrs. Nagenbeck's hoarse voice. "That's our wonderful Irving Bommer!"

"Heem! Heem!" That was the gypsy woman. "The 'ansome wan!"

"Make way there," he yelled roughly. "Get out of my way." Reluctantly, adoringly, the mob moved back and made a path for him. He pushed the front door open just as the first of the pursuing vehicles roared around the corner.

There were women in the hall, there were women in the parlor and the dining room, there were women all the way up the stairs to his room. He pushed past them, past their swimming eyes and agonizing caresses, and unlocked the door of his room. He slammed it shut.

"Got to think, think," he patted his wobbling head with a feverish hand. A bath wouldn't be enough, not while the huge bottle of aftershave lotion remained to disseminate its fearful contents. Pour it down the drain? It would mix with water, dilute still further. Besides, he might get female sewer rats charging at him next. No, the potion had to be destroyed. How? *How?*

The furnace in the cellar. There was alcohol in the aftershave lotion, and alcohol burned. Burn the stuff, then take a shower fast, not using puerile soap but something truly effective like lye—or sulphuric acid. The furnace in the cellar!

He plumped the bottle under his arm like a football. Outside, he could hear a hundred automobile horns honking, a thousand female voices sighing and muttering of their love. In the distance, very faintly, was the sound of police sirens and the disgusted, amazed voice of the law, trying to move that which was thoroughly determined to be immovable.

The moment he unlocked the door, he felt he had made a mistake. Women poured in as if the combination of the potion, his perspiration and the seeping bottle were absolutely irresistible.

"Back," he roared. "Get back! I'm coming through!"

More slowly than before, more reluctantly, they let him out. He fought his way to the head of the stairs, his body twisting and writhing every time a soft hand wavered in his direction. "Clear the stairs, dammit, clear the stairs!"

Some retreated, others didn't. But he could go down. Holding the bottle tightly, he started forward. A young, barely nubile girl extended her arms lovingly. He threw his body to one side. Unfortunately, his right foot had started down on the first step. He teetered on his left. His body moved forward; he squirmed for balance. A gray-haired matron started to caress his back and he arched it out.

Too far. He fell, the bottle shooting out of his sweaty grasp before him.

He hit a couple of steps on the way and finally piled painfully on the ruins of the bottle. He realized his chest was very wet.

He looked up and managed to scream just once as the torrent of yearning, of adoring, of beseeching faces closed over him.

That's why they have a hunk of blood-stained linoleum buried in White Willow Cemetery. And that immense monument above it was raised by enthusiastic public subscription in a single hour.

AFTERWORD

Why do writers go through dry periods—"slumps"? Obviously there may be as many answers to this as there are writers, but creative depletion and the need for recharging must relate to most. Several years after I became a professional, I had an agent who persuaded me to write money-making but utterly unchallenging fiction. (You'll find the whole story elsewhere in these Afterwords.) It was the only time in my life when I really tried to become a hack writer. I didn't realize then that I utterly lacked the necessary talent. Well, I made a good income for a while, then stopped writing completely.

I mean completely. I found that when I sat at the typewriter, nothing at all would come out—not even a business letter, not a list of Things To Be Done. My psyche was simply opposed to anything that had to do with literary expression. This went on for two years, and I found myself working at miscellaneous nonwriting jobs in order to pay the rent.

(All right, as slumps go, this would hardly compete with Lester del Rey's. Lester claimed here, as elsewhere, to have outdone every other writer: a slump seven-and-a-half years long made my two-year one look puny. But, as I told Lester, you could still starve to death on puny.)

I had almost given up thinking of myself as a writer, and was working as a waiter—in a place called Meyer's Goodie Shoppe!—when one night, as we were sweeping up, a title occurred to me. "Everybody Loves Irving Bommer"? I couldn't wait to get home to start writing it, to find out what such a story would be about.

I wrote it in a seven-hour stretch, before I went to bed. And it ended the slump—that slump, anyway.

But that's only a very small part of the story about the story. I eventually wrote many other stories, many other articles; I completed a novel and became a professor at Penn State; and I retired from Penn State. Ten years after I retired, I turned on the television one night.

And there was Irving Bommer. As a movie. On screen.

The title was different, yes, and the protagonist was not the ugliest man in town, yes, and yes, yes, there were other differences—but the Gypsy woman was still there offering a potion that was irresistible to a womanless man, and the protagonist used the potion as a spray, and yes, yes, there were other remarkable similarities to my story. The basic plot gimmicks of the fantasy seemed to be all mine.

I was angry. Through my nephew, David Klass, who is a well-established screenwriter, I got the name of a Hollywood lawyer. I called the lawyer.

He told me I didn't have a chance; there was no satisfaction to be had. Assuming I was right in all the similarities I had noted, there was still the matter of California law as it related to the statute of limitations.

In California, the Hollywood moguls had wisely seen to it that you had three years to raise any issue that might have to do with plagiarism. Three years and absolutely no more.

I now was well beyond that three-year limitation. The movie I was seeing on television was a rerun, a possibly nineteenth or twentieth or thirty-fifth rerun. I should have seen more movies, the lawyer suggested: I should have seen this movie the week it was released. There was absolutely nothing, the lawyer told me, I could do.

But I could burn. And burn. *And* burn.

I tell you, it was enough to put a writer in a slump.

WRITTEN 1950——PUBLISHED 1951

For The Rent

A Matter of Frequency

Dr. Amadeus Ballyhock pointed with pride across the enormous campus of Meg, Beth, & Hal Thurman University.

"*There,*" he breathed to the eager group about him. "That completely streamlined building decorated with diagonal stripes. The glory of M.B. & H.T.U. and the very latest addition to our magnificent educational facilities. The Dimenocommunaplex!"

"A whole building," the young woman at his right said in man-pleasing awe. "And one machine!"

The university president smiled affably from her to the rest of his visitors. His broad chest expanded visibly under the expensively tailored clear-glass shirt he wore. "Yes. *One* machine."

"The only thing, sir," an extremely handsome fellow who was the star of *Tuesday's TV Tabloid* said uncertainly, "the only thing, doctor, is that the Dimenocommunaplex can hardly be considered educational. I mean—since it won't be used for teaching. I mean—it's a research tool, isn't it? For a Nut?"

All the other journalists looked thoughtful at this and began to scratch well-shampooed heads with extremely well-manicured fingernails.

"You know, Steve," the pretty girl commented slowly, "I think you have something there. If it's for a Nut, it can't be very educational. It's *Opening New Frontiers* stuff, not the kind of material any sponsor is paying for. When a Nut is involved in a story, you have to take notes; it gets so technical. And once you take notes, what happens to the spontaneity of good TV journalism?"

"There isn't any, Laura," the young man nodded. "Not with notes that you have to read from in order to explain things. I mean—no human interest. Then you might as well get back to dry-as-dust *paper* reporting, like they used to have in the old days."

"The days of the Nuts," someone else said. "The twentieth century." Everybody shuddered.

Dr. Ballyhock shook himself abruptly. "Not at all," he said loudly. Then, as they all looked at him, he repeated reassuringly: "Not at all! *Not at all!*"

"How do you mean, sir?" Steve asked. "Anything with a name like Dimenocommunaplex must be a Nut project."

"Quite. But, first of all, my dear fellow, the Nut involved is under careful guard and the supervision of some of our poorest minds. And may I comment here, parenthetically and with pride, on our faculty and student body, which this year possesses the very lowest average intelligence quotient of any college in the entire country?"

"You don't say!" Laura looked around enthusiastically. "That *is* worth a plug on *my* show. I like to talk about *progress*. It makes my audience feel we're advancing, kind of. Know what I mean?"

"I certainly do," Dr. Ballyhock told her, smiling warmly at the pleasing curves of her body, completely visible through the green-tinged transparent frock she wore. "Now, you journalists will need to take no notes on the Dimenocommunaplex, for the simple but entirely sufficient reason that none of you will even begin to understand its operation. It has been made so thoroughly a Nut project that only the most degraded Nuts can figure out how it works. Humans, like you, me, and your TV audience, can do no more than describe its operation and effects—if any."

There was a general sigh of relief. Steve came forward and offered his hand. "My apologies, doctor. I really didn't mean to imply that—that—that—well, *you* know."

Dr. Ballyhock nodded. "Quite. A journalist reaching millions of sets cannot be too careful. We have had more than enough of Nut thinking in this country! Now that we understand each other again, may I suggest that the explanation of the educational significance of the Dimenocommunaplex wait until we are all on our scooters and on our way to it? The experiment is due to begin at four-thirty sharp. And an unstable individual is being kept waiting."

They mounted the gaily colored little conveyances again, pulled the beribboned handlebar switches, and floated off to the agreeable accompaniment of tiny silver bells clustered on the miniature rear bumpers.

"What is the significance of the Dimenocommunaplex educationally?" the university president began once more from his position in the lead scooter. "Well, first there is the merely visual interest of the student body in such a very complex piece of machinery. We will give one credit for every hour spent in the building looking at the apparatus. Surely this is not an unpleasant or, should I say, *nutty* way of spending one's compulsory college time? Surely that group entering the Arithmetic Building will prefer it to the hour they must now willy-nilly spend on Long Division and Decimals? These youngsters may go on to acquire a doctorate in Administration like mine; they will then have to harness and be responsible for the dangerous mental energies of from ten to a hundred Nuts. What better place for them to meet the creatures than in their early college years?"

"And the rest of the educational aspect is communication," Laura said. "At least, that's what I read in the university throwaway my studio received. Dimensional communication. What's that?"

"That's a Nut's phrase," Dr. Ballyhock shrugged; "a Nut will therefore have to explain it. My intelligence quotient is well below the hundred-and-twenty danger point, I am happy to say. Dimensional communication? It would seem to imply communication between the dimensions. What good that would do, I cannot imagine. But, as with all Nut developments, you never can tell. It might lead to this, or it might lead to that. For example, the scooters we are on at the moment are powered by a kind of radiant energy discovered by an astronomical Nut who was fooling around with cosmic rays. Another less degraded Nut—one who was almost human, in fact—applied it to vehicles in an engineering design that enabled normal human technicians to manufacture scooters for the rest of us. That's why all the expense we go to in feeding and taking care of Nuts is so very necessary. You never know when one of their attacks of applied science—or even an absolute fit of pure science, for that matter—is going to lead to something useful."

"Or dangerous!" This came from a young matron floating at the edge of the group. "Remember atomic bombs, philosophy, dynamite—all those terrible things Nuts used to make in the old days?" She pulled the pink glassite jacket about her shoulders and shuddered fastidiously.

"The old days. That's just the point. Remember your history, please," Dr. Ballyhock admonished. "First man domesticated life in the form of the lower animal to provide him with food. Then he domesticated matter in the form of machines to do his work for him. Then came his greatest and most recent achievement! He domesticated mind in the form of Nuts to do his *thinking* for him."

They arrived at the striped building with backswept buttresses and alighted. Steve pointed to a barbed-wire-enclosed compound of low and old-fashioned brick buildings directly behind it. "Is that the Nut school, doctor? I mean, I know you have one on your campus. I did a human-interest exposé on it three years ago."

"Yes. Please don't look so upset, ladies. The creatures are not in a dangerously large quantity, and they are very well guarded. Our national educational laws still require universities to maintain at least one college—with separate but equal facilities—for those pathetically high IQs, but the day is not too far distant, I hope, when they will all be segregated—as most of them already are—in safe and sound institutions under the unblinking supervision of Nut specialists."

The guard swung the barred doors open at Dr. Ballyhock's nod.

Inside, the building—which was one room and one electronic machine—looked as if a wire-spinning spider had danced out an all-time arachnidan masterpiece within its walls. Banks of transformers awaited action about their compact cores; tubes, spattered like raindrops upon a huge metal plate in the center of the room, sat energyless and unwinking.

Near the metal plate was a heavily laden switchboard at which stood a man, unkempt, somewhat hairy, and scowling. Delicate metallic threads encircled both his ankles and disappeared into a hole in the floor: it was evident that, as he walked away from the hole, they unwound from a subterranean spool; and, as he came closer to it, the slack was pulled in. Two guards walked with him; the one on his right carrying an efficient little blaster, the one on his left a tiny radio switch which controlled the action of the restraining thread.

"Ladies and gentlemen of the TV tabloids," the president intoned. "This is Physics Nut 6B306, or, as he was entered on his birth certificate, Raymond J. Tinsdale. He was born of entirely normal parents who had no suspicion of his mental flaws until a series of clever childish inventions forced them to a child-test administrator, who revealed the truth."

"How awful!" Laura moaned. "It almost makes you not want to have children; it could happen to anybody!"

Dr. Ballyhock nodded gravely. "It could. The consolation is that the freak would be well taken care of for the rest of its life: the parents would never have to see it again. And, of course, we use them in a kind of occupational therapy upon each other."

"The zoo," said Physics Nut 6B306 bitterly. "The traveling zoo come to look at people. And now they'll want to be entertained. Does it matter to them that my rig isn't even ready?"

"Now, now, now," the president warned. "Don't get obstreperous, or we'll have to deprive you of equipment and books for a week. Please start explaining what it is you have here. And, guard! Make him put on his shirt. There are ladies present!"

As he squirmed back into the shirt proffered by the guard, Physics Nut 6B306 shook his head. "The atmosphere itself is air-conditioned; the seasons are controlled; every blasted tinted garment is completely transparent—yet you can't take a single scrap off, no time, no place! What a world!" He beat a fist into an open palm and sighed. "All right. We call this rig a Dimenocommunaplex. Not because we want to, but we had to call it something, and JoJo here thought we should christen it the Ballyhocker. So it's a Dimenocommunaplex. It's intended for interdimensional communication."

"Like the fourth?" Steve suggested brightly.

"No, not like the fourth. There are an infinite number of dimensional universes, coexisting with us but neither in our time nor in our space. They adjoin us on the entropy gradient."

A rustle of inattention and discomfort. "Nut words like entropy," someone muttered. "Entropy *gradient!* Make him start."

"Entropy might be defined as the increasing randomness of energy," Physics Nut 6B306 went on more rapidly as he tried to ignore Dr. Ballyhock's signals. "The rate at which our universe is proceeding to its own space-time death. A universe whose entropy gradient is steeper would be imperceptible to our senses and instruments. In that case, furthermore, all radiation in it would operate at much higher frequencies than in our universe. How *much* higher, we can only estimate. And since this is a communicative—"

"Please begin," the president ordered. "We are normal humans and interested in results, not explanations. Theory can come later."

"The problem in communicating with such an adjoining universe," the guarded man went on defiantly, "is chiefly one of finding the correct frequency at which their equivalent of, say, electromagnetic or radio wave patterns occur. Going up past our highest conceivable frequencies with the interdimensional translating device I have developed, we might still create only heat waves in their plenum. Approximation is all we can do each time; continued careful experimentation must go on. In turn, assuming intelligent creatures in such an adjoining universe, their problem would be to find a sufficiently low frequency (in their terms) with which they could reach us. Again, they would—"

"I'm getting confused," Laura said plaintively. "Make him begin."

Dr. Ballyhock gestured, and the guard holding the radio switch poised a hand over it suggestively. Physics Nut 6B306 bit his lip and walked over to the switchboard. He pulled one switch forward a single notch and released a little automatic device which beeped twice, then four times, then eight. A pause and it beeped three times, nine times, and twenty-seven.

"Control, that's the answer," the president of M.B. & H.T.U. remarked complacently. "Back in the old days, creatures like that lived in and around normal humanity and wreaked fearful harm, what with constant uncomfortable changes and strange ideas all the time. Progress began with the appointment of lay commissions to supervise science, but we still had a long way to go before we reached our present perfect control. Today, just as we use machines to check on other machines and dogs to herd sheep, we use one kind of Nut as a control on other kinds. A Psychological Nut, for example, devised the tests with which we check this specimen periodically to make certain he is not contemplating anything dangerous. A Mechanical Engineering Nut designed the self-winding spool that—"

"Is it over?" Laura asked. "I mean, the experiment?"

"Yes, it's over!" Physics Nut 6B306 told her. "We have transmitted a signal that can be evaluated as the product of mathematically advanced creatures by any intelligent organisms in an adjoining universe that happen to receive it. Now we must wait for a possible reply. The reply may come on any radio frequency; in fact, since the creatures transmitting to us will be approximating our much lower entropy gradient, it may come as sound. We must be careful—"

"I don't think that was very interesting," Laura told him. "No human interest in that beeping thing. And why did you only pull one switch a teensy-weensy bit?"

"That beeping thing," the Nut explained with the massive patience his kind were so likely to assume in conversation with normal humanity, "gives the square and the cube of two and three respectively, a fact likely to be constant and known in any spacetime. I pulled only one switch just the one notch because, since we don't know which is a communicable frequency in the universe we are trying to reach, we want to run as little risk as possible of doing any harm. In a week, if there is no answer, we will try another frequency, then another, until we receive a reply."

"Why, if you'd have told me that before, I'd have been able to help you! You have a problem in communication here. That's *my* field," Laura beamed. "Now step aside, please, so that I can—"

As she strolled toward him, the Nut waved his arms wildly, his face contorting. "No!" he yelled. "You—"

Dr. Ballyhock snapped his fingers, and the unarmed guard moved rapidly. There was a snap and a flash of metallic thread. The Nut lay groaning on the floor near the thread-hole. His feet twitched.

"You must understand," the good doctor told him gently, "that science serves humanity, not vice versa. Laura Bisselrode is one of the most communicative faces and newsiest voices on the *TV Sunday Supplement*. She will not only bring that necessary ingredient of human interest into your experiment for her audience, but will probably solve your problem."

Physics Nut 6B306 turned his face the floor and howled.

"Now, first," Laura explained happily, "I'll open all these other switches. There's no point in not having network coverage when it's available. We might as well use *all* of these—uh, frequencies."

The man on the floor began beating his head against it.

"Then, instead of that nasty old beeping thing, I'd use my lovely, well trained voice, which is adored up and down the nation. Human interest, they used to tell us back in telecasting school, Steve, remember?"

"Right!" Steve affirmed. "Human interest before news interest!"

"Hello, *you,*" the girl crooned roguishly into the mike. "This is Laura Bisselrode from the other end of the entropy gradient. We have a little universe just like your little universe, and we wonder if you'd mind dropping what you're doing for a moment and just tell us in a few simple words just how it feels to—"

She opened her mouth to scream, staggered, and dissolved into the writhing floor with the other humans in the building, with the equipment, with the building itself. All up and down the campus of Meg, Beth, & Hal Thurman University, buildings and students and faculty sank into the bubbling soil; all over the planet, mountains toppled, seas solidified and boiled away. The very air roiled and rattled in unmanageable chunks. And then, in that brief instant of communication, all was over, and the strangely altered earth was still; the completely lifeless world had assumed a stable form.

Girdling the planet now, like a realistic equator, was a peculiar wavy line which ran across the beds of what had been seas, which undulated past the base of what had been mountains. The wavy line was a message in a language and an orthography which had never before been seen in the universe—a message writ large indeed in the very molecules of matter. Its authors, you see, had been in a great hurry and had had to approximate a frequency.

Rough translation:

"Would you kindly stop doing your equivalent of *quoongling*? It is giving us our equivalent of severe headaches."

The Ionian Cycle

The tiny lifeboat seemed to hang suspended from its one working rear jet. Then it side-slipped and began to spin violently downwards to the sickly orange ground of the planet.

Inside the narrow cabin, Dr. Helena Naxos was hurled away from the patient she was tending and slammed into a solid bulkhead. The shock jolted the breath out of her. She shook her head and grabbed frantically at an overhead support as the cabin tilted again. Jake Donelli glared up from the viewscreen where the alien earth expanded at him and yelled across the control table:

"Great galaxies, Blaine, soft-jet! Soft-jet before we're pulped!"

The tall, balding archaeologist of what had once been the First Deneb Expedition waved tremulous hands at the switches before him.

"Which—which button do you press?" he quavered. "I f-forget how y-you soften those forward things."

"You don't press any—oh, wait a minute."

The spaceman tore the restraining straps away and bounded out of his seat. He seized the projecting edges of the table and made his way strainingly around it as the lifeboat spun faster in great swoops.

Dr. Archibald Blaine was squeezed against the back of his chair when Donelli reached him.

"I forgot the button," he mumbled.

"No button, Doc. I told you. You jerk this toggle—like so. You haul this switch over—like so. Then you turn the little red wheel around twice. Does it. Whew! Now things are smoother!"

Donelli let go of the table as the forward softening jets caught on and straightened the vessel into a flat glide. He walked back to the main control bank, followed by Blaine and the woman biologist.

"The sea?" Helena Naxos asked at last, lifting her eyes from the viewscreen. "That *is* the sea?"

"Nothing else but," Donelli told her. "We used up all but about a cupful of fuel trying to avoid falling into this system's sun—if you can call two planets a system! We're operating the cupful on the one main jet left unfused when the *Ionian Pinafore* blew up. Now we've overshot the continent and we're riding above the sea without a paddle. Good, huh? What'd he say the sea was made of?"

Dr. Douglas Ibn Yussuf propped himself on his uninjured elbow and called from his bunk:

"According to the spectroscopic tabulations you brought me an hour ago, the seas of this planet are almost pure hydrofluoric acid. There is a good deal of free fluorine in the atmosphere, although most of it is in the form of hydrofluoric acid vapor and similar combinations."

"Suppose you save some of that good news," Donelli suggested. "I know all about hydrofluoric acid being able to eat through almost anything and its grandmother. Tell me this: how long will the Grojen shielding on the hull stand up under it? An estimate, Doc."

With puckered brow, the Egyptian scientist considered. "If not replaced, say anywhere—oh, anywhere from five terrestrial days to a week. Not more."

"Fine!" the pale spaceman said happily. "We'll all be dead long before that." His eyes watched the viewscreen.

"Not if we find fuel for the converter and tanks," Blaine reminded him sternly. "And we know there's contra-uranium on this world—a little, at any rate. The spectroscope showed it. That's why we headed here after the disaster."

"So we know there's fuel here—good old compact Q. Okay, if we landed on one of the continents maybe we'd have scratched a miracle on the chest and found some Q before the converter conked out. Then we could have repaired the other jets and tried to get back to a traffic lane, powered up the transmitter and radioed for help, done all sorts of nice things. But now that we're going to do our fall on the first island I see, what chance do you think we have?"

Blaine looked angrily at his two colleagues and then back at the small, squat spaceman with whom destiny and a defective storage tank aboard the *Ionian Pinafore* had thrown them.

"But that's ridiculous!" he said. "Landing on an island will reduce our chances of finding contra-uranium from an improbability to an impossibility! It's rare enough in the universe, and after we've been fortunate enough to find a planet containing it, Jake, I demand—"

"You demand nothing, Doc," Donelli told him, shoving belligerently up against his lean academic frame. "You demand nothing. Back on the expedition ship maybe the three of you were big-time operators with your degrees and all, and I was just Jake—broken from A.B. to Ordinary Spaceman for drunkenness when we lifted from Io. But here, I'm the only man-jack with a lifeboat certificate and the laws of space put me in supreme command. Watch your language, Doc: I don't like to be called Jake by the likes of you. You call me Donelli from here on in, and every once in a while, you call me *Mr.* Donelli."

There was a pause in the cabin while the archaeologist's cheeks puffed out and his frustrated eyes tried to pluck a reply from the overhead.

"*Mr.* Donelli," Helena Naxos called suddenly. "Would that be your island?" She gestured to the viewscreen where an infinitesimal blot upon the sea was growing. She smoothed her black hair nervously.

Donelli stared hard. "Yeah. It'll do. Suppose you handle the forward jets—uh, Dr. Naxos. You saw me explaining them to Blaine. I wouldn't trust that guy with a falling baseball on Jupiter. 'I forgot which button,' " he mimicked.

She took her place on the opposite side of the control table as Blaine, with tightened facial muscles, went over to Ibn Yussuf's bunk and whispered angrily to the injured man.

"You see," Donelli explained as he moved a lever a microscopic distance, "I don't want to hit an island any more than you folks do, Dr. Naxos. But we can't afford to use up any more fuel crossing an ocean as big as this. We may be able to make another continent, yes, but we'll have about fifteen minutes of breathing time left. This way, the converter should run for another two, three days, giving us a chance to look around and maybe get some help from the natives."

"If there are any." She watched a dial needle throb hesitantly to a red mark. "We saw no cities on the telescanner. Although, as a biologist, I confess I'd like to investigate a creature with a fluorine respiration. By the way, Mr. Donelli, if you will allow me to call you Jake, you may call me Helena."

"Fair enough—hey, you watching that dial? Start softening jets. That's right. Now over to half. Hold it. Hold it! Here we go! Grab something, everybody! Dr. Yussuf— lie flat—flat!"

He flipped the lever over all the way, slammed a switch shut and reached frantically for the two hand grips on the control table.

An emery wheel seemed to reach up and scrape the bottom of the hull. The emery wheel scraped harder and the whole ship groaned. The scrape spread along the entire bottom half of the lifeboat, rose to an unbearably high scream in sympathy to which every molecule in their bodies trembled. Then it stopped and a vicious force snapped their bodies sideways.

Donelli unstrapped himself. "I've seen chief mates who did worse on the soft jets— Helena," was the comment. "So here we are on good old— What's the name of this planet, anyway?"

"Nothing, so far as I know." She hurried over to Dr. Ibn Yussuf, who lay groaning in the cast which protected the ribs and arm broken in the first explosion of the *Ionian Pinafore*. "When we passed the system on our way to Deneb a week ago, Captain Hauberk named the sun Maximilian—after the assistant secretary-general of the Terran Council? That would make this planet nothing more than Maximilian II, a small satellite of a very small star."

"What a deal," Donelli grumbled. "The last time I had to haul air out of a wreck, I found myself in the middle of the Antares-Solarian War. Now I get crazy in the head and ship out on an expedition to a part of space where humanity's just thinking of moving in. I pick a captain who's so busy buttering up to scientists and government officials that he doesn't bother to check storage tanks, let alone lifeboats. I haul air with three people—no offense, Helena—who can't tell a blast from the Hole in Cygnus and they get so cluttered up trying to seal the airlocks that, when the secondary explosion pops off from the ship, it catches us within range and blooies most of our jets and most of our Q. Then, to top it off, I have to set down on a planet that isn't even on the maps and start looking for the quart or two of Q that may be on the surface."

Helena Naxos eased the scientist's cast to a more comfortable position and chuckled. "Sad, isn't it? But ours was the only boat that got away at that. We were lucky."

Donelli began climbing into a spacesuit. "We weren't lucky," he disagreed. "We just happened to have a good spaceman aboard. Me. I'll scout around our island and see if I can find any characters to talk to. Our only hope is to get help from the folks here, if any. Sit tight till I get back and don't touch any equipment you don't understand."

"Want me to come with you—er, Donelli?" Dr. Blaine moved to the spacesuit rack. "If you meet anything dangerous—"

"I'll make out better alone. I've got a supersonic in this suit. And Doc—you might forget which button. Great galaxies!"

Shaking his helmeted head, Donelli started the airlock machinery.

The orange ground was brittle underfoot, he found, and flaked off as he walked. Despite the yellow atmosphere, he could see the complete outline of the island from the hill near the ship. It was a small enough patch of ground pointing reluctantly out of an irritated sea of hydrofluoric acid.

Most of it was bare, little dots of black moss breaking the heaving monotony of orange. Between the ship and the sea was a grove of larger vegetation: great purple flowers on vivid scarlet stems that held them a trembling thirty feet in the stagnant air.

Interesting, but not as interesting as fuel.

He had noticed a small cave yawning in the side of the hill when he climbed it. Sliding down, now, he observed its lower lip was a good bit from the ground. He started to enter, checked himself abruptly.

There was something moving inside.

With his metal-sheathed finger, he clicked on the searchlight embedded in his helmet, and with the other hand, he tugged the supersonic pistol from its clamps in the side of his suit and waited for its automatic adjustment to the atmosphere of the planet. At last it throbbed slightly, and he knew it was in working condition.

They needed favors from the inhabitants, but he didn't intend to do any careless dying, either.

Just inside the cave entrance, the beam of his light showed a score of tiny maggot-like creatures crawling and feeding upon two thin blankets of flesh. Whatever the animals they were eating had been, they were no longer recognizable.

Donelli stared at the small white worms. "If you're intelligent, I might as well give up. I have an idea we can't be friends. Or am I prejudiced?"

Since they ignored both him and his question, he moved on into the cave. A clacking sound in his headphones brought him to a halt again, squeezing a bubbling elation back into his heart.

Could it be? So early and so easy? He drew the screen away from the built-in Geiger on his chest. The clacking grew louder. He turned slowly until the flashlight on his head revealed a half-dozen microscopic crystals floating a few inches from one wall.

Contra-uranium! The most compact superfuel discovered by a galaxy-exploring humanity, a fuel that required no refining since, by its very nature, it could occur only in the pure state. It was a fuel for whose powerful uses every engine and atomic converter on every spaceship built in the past sixty years had been designed.

But six crystals weren't very much. The lifeboat might barely manage a take-off on that much Q, later to fall into the hydrofluoric sea.

"Still," Donelli soliloquized, "it's right heartening to find some so near the surface. I'll get an inerted lead container from the ship and scoop it up. But maybe those crystals have a family further back."

The crystals didn't, but someone or something else did.

Four large, chest-high balls of green, veined thickly with black and pink lines, throbbed upon the ground at the rear of the cave. Eggs? If not eggs, what were they?

II

Donelli skirted them warily, even though he saw no opening in any of them. They were anchored to the ground, but they were unlike any plants he had seen in nine years of planet-jumping. They looked harmless, but—

The back of the cave divided into two tunnels which were higher and wider than their parent hollow. Smooth all around, Donelli might have taken them for the burrows of an immense worm, had he not noticed the regularly spaced wood-like beams crossed upon each other at intervals in both shafts. The tunnels extended a good distance ahead, then curved sharply down and away from each other.

This was mining, this was engineering! Primitive, but effective!

Donelli hated to use up power in his helmet-transmitter, but he might run into trouble and it was essential that the three scientists learn of even the small amount of Q in the cave. After all, the creatures who built these tunnels might not know enough chemistry to appreciate his inedibility before they sampled him.

He turned on his headset. "Donelli to ship! Good news: I've found enough Q to keep us breathing until *after* this atmosphere burns through our Grojen shielding. We'll be able to sit around in our spacesuits for at least three days after the ship is eaten out from under us. Nice? You'll see the crystals about halfway into the cave. And don't forget to use an inerted lead container when you pick them up."

"Where are you going, Jake?" He recognized Helena's voice.

"Couple of tunnels at the rear of the cave here have regulation cross-supports. That's why we didn't see any cities when we came down. The smart babies on this world live underground. I'm going to try to talk them into a reciprocal trade treaty—if we have anything they want to reciprocate with."

"Wait a minute, Donelli," Blaine shouted breathlessly. "If you meet any intelligent aliens, it's more than possible they won't understand Universal Gesture-Diagram. This is an unexplored fluorine-breathing world. I'm an experienced archaeologist and I'll be able to communicate with them. Let me join you."

Donelli hesitated. Blaine was smart, but he sometimes fumbled.

Helena came back on. "I'd suggest you take him up on it," her steady voice said. "Archibald Blaine may get switches confused with buttons, but he's one of the few men in the galaxy who knows all nine of Ogilvie's Basic Language-Patterns. If these miners of yours don't respond to an Ogilvie Pattern—well, they just don't belong in our universe!"

As Donelli still hesitated, she developed her point. "Look, Jake, you're our commander and we accept your orders because you know how to cuddle a control board and we don't. But a good commander should use his personnel correctly and, when it comes to dealing with unknown extraterrestrials, Blaine and I have training that you've been too busy to acquire. You're a spaceman; we're scientists. We'll help you get your Q, then we'll take orders from you on how to use it."

A pause. "All right, Blaine. I'll be moving up the right-hand tunnel. And Helena— see that his spacesuit is all buttoned up before he leaves the ship? He can catch an awful cold in that yellow air."

The squat, pale spacehand took a firm grip on his sound pistol and walked delicately into the shaft. The ground here was of a firmer consistency than that on the surface: it supported his weight without either chipping or sagging. That was good. Nothing could come at him through the walls without his detecting it first.

He ducked under a cross-beam, his light momentarily pointing down. When he straightened again, he saw he had company.

At the far end of the tunnel, where it slanted down, several long, segmented beings were moving slowly toward him. There was only the faintest rustle in his headphones as they approached.

Donelli noticed with relief that only one of them had a weapon, a crude hand-ax without a handle. Come to think of it, though, an ax-head thrust forcefully might penetrate not his suit but—what was more dangerous—the Grojen shielding, leaving the metal exposed to the corrosive atmosphere. Not so good. But they didn't seem hostile.

As they arrived within a few feet of him, their speed decreased almost to immobility, but their three pairs of three-clawed limbs pushed them to his side. Then they stopped, and the long, thin, hairy appendages on their heads brushed against his suit inquiringly and without fear. Their toothless mouths opened and made low gobbling sounds to each other.

They evidently had a language. Donelli saw the flat membrane on their backs that was obviously an ear, but he looked in vain for eyes. Of course, living underground in darkness, they were blind. A fat lot of help Universal Gesture-Diagram would be, even if they could understand it.

Something about the sectioned length of the bodies stretching behind them, something about their rich ivory color, was familiar. Donelli's mind tugged at his memory.

A terrific crash sounded in his ear phones. The three burrowers stiffened around him. Donelli turned and swore.

Blaine had entered the tunnel and smashed into one of the cross-beams. He was stepping over the fallen log now. His spacesuit seemed undented, but his self-confidence had not fared so well. Also a little bubble of earth formed over the area which had rested on the beam end.

The natives had rubbed their head filaments upon the ground as if examining its intentions. Now, before Donelli could get started, they scampered down the tunnel toward the fallen support. Working in perfect coordination, without any apparent orders, they quickly lifted and inserted it in its former position. Then they began brushing against Blaine.

"Deep space, Doc," Donelli moaned as he came up.

"Sh-h-h—quiet!" The archaeologist had bent over the nearest burrower and was clicking his metal-enclosed fingers in an odd rhythm over its ear patch. The animal curved away for a moment, then began a low, hesitant gobbling to the same rhythm as the finger-clicks.

"Can—can you talk to it?" Donelli found it difficult to see the old man as any-thing but a doddering ineffectual.

"Ogilvie Pattern Five. Knew it. *Knew* it! Those three-clawed feet and the sharp curve of the ax. Like to investigate the material of the ax—noticed the pointed tip right off. Had to be an Ogilvie Five language. Can I talk to it? Of course! Just need a minute or two to establish the facets of the pattern."

The spaceman's respect for the academic life grew rapidly as he saw the other two aliens edge under the metallic hand and commence gobbling in turn.

They were joining the conversation, or the attempt at one. Blaine began to stroke the side of one of the creatures with his other hand. The gobbling acquired a note of surprise, became staccato.

"Amazing!" Blaine said after a while. 'They mine everything, and completely refuse to discuss the existence of surface phenomena. Most unusual, even for an Ogilvie Five. Do you know where they get their supporting beams? From the roots of plants. At least, that's what they seem to be from their description. But—and this is what the Galactic Archaeological Society will consider significant—they cannot seem to grasp the concept of plant blossoms. They know only of the roots and the base of the stem. Their social life, now, is strangely obscure for so elementary a culture. But perhaps it might better be termed simple? Consider the facts—"

"You consider them," Donelli invited. "I'm thinking of the Q we need. All this spacesuit power drain is cutting so many hours off our total breathing time. Find out what they'd consider a good trade and ask them to move up into the cave ahead so that I can show them what contra-uranium looks like. We'll supply them with inerted lead containers for picking up the stuff. How far do their tunnels run?"

"All around the planet, I gather. Under the sea and under the continents in a cross-ing, branching network. I don't anticipate any difficulty. Being the dominant intelli-gent life-form of the planet, and not particularly carnivorous, they're really quite friendly."

Blaine's fingers clicked questioningly at the nearest alien and he stroked its side with short and long rolls of his hand. The creature seemed confused and gobbled to its companions. Then it moved back. Blaine clicked and stroked once more.

"What's the matter, Doc? They look angry now."

"My suggestion of the cave. It's evidently under the strongest of taboos. These are barbarians, you understand, just emerging into a religious culture-matrix, and a powerful taboo takes precedence over instinct. Then, too, living in the tunnels, they are probably agoraphobic—"

"Look out! They're trying to pull some fancy stuff!"

One of the aliens had scuttled under Blaine's feet. The archaeologist tottered, crashed to the ground. The other two burrowers grasped his long arms between their claws. Blaine struggled and rolled desperately, looking like a confused elephant attacked by jackals.

"Donelli," he gasped, "I can't talk to them while they're holding my arms. They're—they're carrying me!"

The pair of burrowers were dragging the old man's body down the tunnel with gentle but insistent tugs. "Don't worry, Doc. They won't get by me. That must have been one powerful taboo you broke when you mentioned the cave."

As Donelli advanced to meet the group, the alien who had upset the archaeologist scurried ahead to confront him. A forward claw held the small ax-head well back for a thrust.

"Look, fella," Donelli said placatingly. "We don't want any trouble with you, but we aren't carrying too much power right now, and the Doc's suit would run down in no time if you took him any deeper. Now why don't you act business-like and let us show you what we need?"

He knew his words carried no meaning in themselves, but he had had enough experience of unusual organisms to know that a gentle attitude frequently carried the conviction of its gentleness.

Not here, though. The claw snapped forward suddenly and the ax-head spun toward his visored face with unexpected velocity. Donelli jerked his head to one side and felt the pointed tip of the weapon scratch the side of his helmet. The slight buzzing in his right ear was replaced by an empty roaring: that meant the ear phone had gone dead, which in turn meant the Grojen shielding had been chipped off, leaving the hydrofluoric vapors free to eat through the metal.

"This is no good. I guess I'll have to—" The burrower had retrieved the ax in a lightning scamper and had it poised for another throw. As Donelli brought his supersonic up, he marveled at the creature's excellent aim despite its lack of vision. That long, hairy filament waving from the top of its head evidently served to locate his movements better than the finest radarplex on the latest spaceships.

Just before he blasted, he managed to slip the intensity rod on the top of the tube down to nonlethal pitch. The directional beam of high-frequency sound tore down at the burrower and caught it with the claw coming around again. It stopped in mid-throw, stumbled backwards, and finally collapsed into unconsciousness upon the orange ground. The ax-head rolled out of its opened claw.

Blaine protested with a grunt as he was dropped by the other two. They ran up to the fallen burrower and edged around his body insistently. Donelli held his supersonic ready for further developments.

What happened took him completely by surprise.

In a series of movements so rapid that he could hardly follow it visually, one of the aliens snatched up the ax-head while the other lifted the creature Donelli had blasted to its back. They rolled up the slope of the tunnel and scurried past him on either side, the fluorine atmosphere almost crackling with their passage. By the time the spaceman had whirled, they were gone down the far end of the shaft where it dipped into the interior of the planet.

"They sure can hurry when they feel they have to," Donelli commented as he helped the older man to his feet. "Which is what I have to do if I want to get back to the ship before I start sneezing hydrofluoric acid."

While they sped as rapidly as the heavy suits would permit up the tunnel and through the cave, Blaine wheezed an explanation: "They were quite friendly until I mentioned the cave. There seems to be so much sacredness connected with it in their minds that my mere invitation to go there reduced me from an object of great interest to one of the most abysmal disgust. They were indifferent to any wants of ours in reference to the place. Any suggestion of taking them along is enough to precipitate a violent attack."

Donelli wondered if he were imagining the smarting sensation in his eyes. Had fluorine started to seep in already? Fortunately, they were at the mouth of the cave.

"Not so nice," he said. "The Q around here isn't enough to make our ship give out with a healthy cough, and we'll need their help to get any more. But we can't tell them what we want unless they go to the cave with us. Besides, after this fracas, they may be a trifle hard to meet. Why were they carrying you away?"

"To sacrifice me to some primitive deity as a placative measure, possibly. Remember they are in the early stages of barbarism. The only reason we weren't attacked immediately is because they are easily the dominant life-form of this world and are confident of their ability to cope with strange creatures. Then again, they might have wanted to investigate me—to dissect me—to examine my potentialities as food."

They rang the airlock signal and clambered in.

III

Hastily Donelli stripped off his spacesuit. There was a thin scar on the metal of the helmet where the Grojen shielding had been scratched away and HF vapor eaten in. A little longer out there and he would have been most definitely dead.

"Hullo!" For the first time, he noticed that almost one-third of the cabin was taken up by a great transparent cage, one corner of which was occupied by a relaxed red creature with folded black wings. "When did the vampire kid arrive?"

"Ten minutes ago," Helen Naxos replied. She was adjusting a temperature-pressure gauge at the side of the cage. "And he—she—it—didn't arrive: I carried it inside.

After Dr. Blaine left, I went over the island with the telescanner and noticed this thing flying in from the sea. It went right to those purple flowers and began cutting off sections of the petals and putting them in a sort of glider made out of vines and branches that it was towing. The things obviously cultivate vegetation. That patch out there is one of their gardens."

"Imagine!" the archaeologist breathed. "Another civilization in embryo—avian, this time. An avian culture would hardly build cities. But this is a culture where the glider comes before the wheel."

"So you put on a spacesuit and went out to get it." Donelli shook his head. "You shouldn't have done that, Helena. That creature might have packed a wallop."

"Yes, I considered the possibility. But I didn't know if you two were going to hit anything important, and this winged thing looked like it might prove to be the link between us and this world. Its ability to fly, in particular, while we are grounded could prove valuable. It was fairly quiet when I approached, neither scared nor angry, so I tried the little Ogilvie I know—Pattern One. Didn't work."

"Of course not," Dr. Blaine told her positively. "This is obviously Ogilvie Language-Pattern Three. Consider the hinged wings, the primitive glider you mentioned, the husbandry of flowers. It has to be an Ogilvie Three."

"Well, I didn't know that, Dr. Blaine. And it wouldn't have helped me much if I had. Ogilvie is a little too rich for a poor female biologist's blood. At any rate, after communication broke down—or never got started—this thing ignored me and prepared to fly away with its loaded glider. I squeezed some supersonic at it—low-power, of course—brought it down and came in to ask Dr. Ibn Yussuf's advice on how to build a compartment that would permit us to keep it in the ship without killing it by oxygen poisoning."

"Must have used up an awful lot of Q, Helena! I notice you have pretty elaborate temperature and pressure controls as well as HF humidifiers and in-grav studs. And that loudspeaker system is wasteful."

Dr. Ibn Yussuf groaned up in his bunk and called across the cabin. "It does reduce our supply of contra-uranium to the danger point, Donelli, but, under the circumstances, we thought we were justified. Our only hope is to get aid from the inhabitants of this planet, and we can't get aid unless we can hold them long enough to explain our position and wants to them."

"You have something there," Donelli admitted. "I should have made a stab at bringing back one of those specimens we ran into, not that it would have done much good from the way they acted. Hope you have more luck with this avian character. Treat him—her—it—lovingly, for he—she—it's—our last chance."

Then he and Blaine told her about the burrowers.

"I wish I had been with you," she exclaimed. "Think of it: two barbaric civilizations—one on the surface and the other in the tunnels—developing in complete unconsciousness of each other on the same planet! The burrowers know nothing of the avians, do they, Dr. Blaine?"

"Absolutely nothing. They even refuse to discuss the matter. Surface life is a completely alien concept to them. Their agoraphobia—fear of open places—probably has much to do with their reluctance to accompany us to the cave or even the tunnel entrance. Agoraphobia— *Hm-m-m.* Then these winged creatures might well be claustrophobic! That would be a catastrophe! We'll find out in a moment. It's opening its eyes. Where is that loudspeaker arrangement?"

Helena moved competently to the microphone and tucked a lever past several calibrations. "You may know its Ogilvie Pattern, Doctor, but it takes a biologist to give the sound frequency at which it can hear best!"

As Blaine began experimental dronings and buzzings into the instrument, the creature inside the transparent cage opened its wings in a series of hinged movements and revealed the whole rich redness of its small body. It crawled under the loudspeaker and spread open a mouth that was slit up and down instead of sideways. The black wings beat slowly as it gained interest, reflecting cheerful yellow streaks in their furrows. The two tentacles under its jaw lost their stiffness and undulated in mounting excitement.

This would take some time. Donelli walked to the telescanner and faced Dr. Douglas Ibn Yussuf.

"Suppose we get this fellow to cooperate. Where's a good place to tell it to look for Q?"

The chemist lay back and considered. "You are familiar with Quentin's theory of our galaxy's origin? That once there were two immense stars which collided—one terrene, the other contra-terrene? That the force of their explosion ripped the essence of space itself and filled it with ricocheting terrene and contra-terrene particles whose recurring violence warped matter out of space to form a galaxy? According to Quentin, the resulting galaxy was composed of terrene stars who are touched every once in a while by contra-terrene particles and go nova. The only exception is contra-uranium, the opposite number of the last element in the *normal* periodic table, which will not explode as long as it is isolated from the heavy elements near its opposite number on the table. Thus, in a fluorine atmosphere, with a bromide soil and—"

"Look, Doc," Donelli said wearily, "I learned all that in school years ago. Next you'll be telling me that it's thousands of times more powerful than ordinary atomic fuels because of its explosive contra-terrene nature. Why is it that you scientists have to discuss the history of the universe before you give a guy an answer to a simple question even in a crisis like this?"

"Sorry, son. It's difficult to break the habits of an academic lifetime, even in times of a deadly emergency. That's your advantage; you're accustomed to operating against time, while we like to explore a problem thoroughly before attempting a mere hypothesis. Science is a caution-engendering discipline, you see, and—

"All right. I won't digress into a discussion of the scientific attitude. Where would you find contra-uranium on a planet that's been shown to possess it? Near the surface, I'd say, where the lighter elements abound. You've already found some in a cave on this island? That would indicate that it was forced explosively to the surface, the only place it could exist, when the planet was in a formative state. If there is other contra-uranium on this world, there must be other caves like the one here."

Donelli waved him to silence and bent over the telescanner. "Good enough. Deep space, Doc, that was *all* I wanted to know! Now I'll see how much I can find out before I use up the dregs of our power."

He swept the beam across the sickly sea and up the coastline of the continent until he saw a dark spot in the orange ground. Then, nudging the telebeam into the cave, he saw at last the few shimmering crystals that meant precious Q. He tried other apertures here and there, convincing himself that, while there was little enough in any one cave, the planet as a whole possessed more than they required. The sight of all the unobtainable Q on the telescanner screen made Donelli sweat with exasperation.

He made another discovery. Leading down, in the rear of every cave, was at least one tunnel that denoted the presence of the burrowers.

"If only we could have made them understand," Donelli murmured. "All of our problems now would have been orbital ones."

He rose and turned to see how his shipmates were doing with the winged alien. "Great galaxies, what did you *do* to it?"

The avian was back in a cornet of the fluorine-filled compartment, its hinged black wings completely screening its body from sight. The wings pressed down harshly as if the creature were attempting to shroud itself out of its environment.

Dr. Archibald Blaine, his hands cupped over the microphone, was *chuk-chuking* urgently, droning repetitiously, humming desperately. No apparent effect. The black wings squeezed tighter into the corner. A fearful, muffled gulping came over the loudspeaker in the wall.

"It was the mention of the cave, again," Helena Naxos explained, her pleasant face betraying worry. "We were doing fine, going from howdy-do's to how've-ye-been's— the girlie was beginning to tell us all about her complicated love life—when Dr. Blaine asked if she had ever been inside the cave. Period. She crawled away and started to make like the cover of a hole."

"They can't do this to us!" Donelli yelled. "This planet is practically crawling with Q which we can't get because we don't have the Q to cross a hydrofluoric acid sea. The only way we can get it is for these babies to haul it over, either underground through tunnels or across the sea. And every time Blaine starts talking about the caves where the Q is lying around, they go neurotic on him. What's the *matter* with the caves? Why don't they like them? *I* like the caves!"

"Take it easy, Jake," Helena soothed. "We're up against a basic taboo in two separated cultures. There must be a reason for it. Find the reason and the problem is solved."

"I know. But if we don't find it soon, we'll be nothing but fancy fluorine compounds."

The woman returned to Dr. Blaine. "Is it possible you could reawaken her interest by offering some gift? A superior glider for example, or power-driven flight."

"I'm working on it," he replied testily, withdrawing his mouth from the microphone. "To creatures on the threshold of civilization, however, superstition takes precedence over mechanical innovations. If it's *only* superstition—that's another thing we don't know. Could it be the contra-uranium crystals they're afraid of?"

Dr. Ibn Yussuf raised himself on his sound arm. "That is doubtful. Their chemical composition contains no elements heavier than barium, according to the spectroscope. Thus no contra-atomic chain reaction would be set off by their bodies coming in contact with the crystals. Perhaps the mere existence of the crystals upsets them."

Blaine frowned. "No. Unlikely. There would have to be a factor intimately related to them in some way. If I could only attract her attention! No matter what I say, she just lies there and gurgles." He went back to his urgent buzzing, frantically using a lifetime of archaeological knowledge.

Donelli looked at the fuel indicators. His lips flattened into a grimace.

"I'll have to go out there and pick up those Q particles in the cave. That cage you built may make that avian comfortable, but it sure drained us dry."

"Wait, I'll go with you," Helena suggested. "Maybe I can discover what makes these fearsome caves so fearsome."

She donned a spacesuit. Donelli, after a rueful glance at his corroded helmet, dragged another metallic garment out of the locker and used its headpiece instead. They both inspected their supersonics carefully. He approved her casual efficiency.

"You know," her voice said into his headphones as they trudged toward the hill, "if Dr. Blaine is able to talk some sense into that creature and we manage to jet to a regular traffic lane and get rescued, he'll make quite a smash before the Galactic Archaeological Society with his two coexisting but unrelated civilizations. I'll get some fair notice myself with the little I've been able to deduce about these creatures biologically without resorting to dissection. Even Ibn Yussuf, bedridden as he is, has been doing some heavy thinking on the chemistry of a bromide soil. And you—well, I imagine you want to get back to a place where you can hurry up and get drunk."

"No."

Her helmet turned toward him in surprise and question.

"No," he continued. "If we get out of this, I'm going to take advantage of the lifeboat law. Heard of it?"

She hadn't. Her eyes glowed intently and curiously behind her visor.

"The lifeboat law's one of the oldest in space. Any spaceman—Able or Ordinary—who, under a given set of circumstances, is entitled to assume command of a vessel and successfully brings that vessel to safety may, at his written request, be issued the license of a third officer. It's called the lifeboat law because that's what it usually pertains to. I have the experience. All I need is the ticket."

"Oh. And what would you do as a third officer? Get drunk whenever you left Io?"

"No, I wouldn't. It's hard to explain—maybe you can't understand—but as a third mate, I wouldn't get drunk. An A.B. or an ordinary spaceman, now, there's so much tiresome, unimportant work facing you whenever you leave a port that you just have to get drunk. And the longer you've been in space, the drunker you get. As a third mate, I wouldn't drink at all—except maybe on vacations. As a third mate, I'd be the driest, stiffest guy who ever was poisoned by a second cook. I'd be a terror of a third mate, because that's the way things are."

"Look at that!" Helena had paused with her back to the mouth of the cave.

IV

Jake Donelli turned and looked back at the ship. Across it, in the grove of fleshy purple flowers, were at least a dozen winged creatures like the one Blaine was attempting to interest in conversation. Far over the sea were many dots that grew larger and re-solved into even more of the avians. Some of them towed gliders lightly behind them. Others carried light tubes. Blow-guns?

"Wonder how they knew about Susie," the spaceman mused. "Was it because she didn't come back at the usual time that the posse was organized? Or are they telepathic?"

"A combination, possibly. They certainly seem to know when one of them is in trouble. You wouldn't say they're acting belligerent?"

"Nope. Just flexing what passes for their muscles. They don't know whether we intend to serve Susie fricasseed or boiled. Better duck inside."

The biologist became her crisp self the moment she saw the white worms. "Wish I could tell exactly what it is they're eating. Now suppose I make a loose guess. Yes, it could well be. Jake, where are those other eggs?"

"Other eggs? Back there. Funny kind of eggs."

She slipped ahead of him, her searchlight picking out the chest-high globules. With a muttered exclamation, she bent down and examined one closely. It was slowly splitting along a pink vein. Donelli waited hopefully.

"No." She straightened. "It doesn't add up. Even assuming, as would seem pos-sible, that those small creatures in the front are the live young of the burrowers and these are the eggs of the avians, it still doesn't explain their relative distance from the usual habitat of their parents. If they *were* the young of each species, the positions should be reversed. With their strong taboos and respective phobias, the avians would not fly so far into the cave, and the burrowers would not crawl so close to the surface. Furthermore, they would inevitably have passed each other at some time and know of each other's existence. Then too, while birth taboos are common among all primi-tive races, they hardly have the force of the psychoses which seem to affect both spe-cies relative to this and other caves. I'd need a good deal of study and many, many careful notes to work this problem out."

"Continu-um!" he swore. "This isn't a research paper for some scientific society or other. We're in a hurry. This is a matter of life and death, woman! Can't you put some pressure into your thinking?"

She threw up her arms in their ungainly wrappings helplessly. "I'm sorry, Jake. I'm trying hard, but I just don't have enough facts on which to base an analysis of two separate, unfamiliar societies. I'm not a sociologist; I'm a biologist. So far as these creatures are concerned, I've just reached the threshold."

"That's all we do—stand around on the threshold," Donelli muttered. "Here are these caves, the threshold to our survival if we can get these babies to pick up the Q and bring it to us. The avians fly around the threshold of the underground but won't go in, while the borrowers crawl around the threshold of the surface but won't go further if you give them the place."

"And both races are on the threshold of civilization. I wonder how long they have been there?"

The spaceman slung the inerted lead container to the ground, preparatory to catching up the crystals of contra-uranium.

"What's the matter with them anyway, that they're so afraid of the caves? What do they think will happen to them after they cross the threshold?"

"What—do—they—think—will—happen," Helena repeated slowly. "What are we all afraid of, the fear intrinsic to any living animal? But how—the eggs—why, of course! *Of course!*"

She bent toward him briefly and Donelli felt his helmet *clang*.

"Sorry," she said. "I forgot. I tried to kiss you. What beautiful reasoning, Jake!"

"Huh?" He felt absurdly clumsy in his ignorance—and guilty.

"I'll have to work the details out as I go. Dr. Blaine—once I give him your premise—he'll be able to help. Isn't it wonderful how removal of one stone from the pyramid of obscurity sends the whole structure tumbling down? Now, Jake, do you think you could go into those tunnels and fetch me a live but slightly stunned burrower? We'll need one, you know."

"I—I guess I can. Where do you want him?"

"It, Jake, *it!* Bring it right here to the middle of the cave. I'll be waiting for you. Hurry!"

She ran out of the cave toward the ship. Donelli watched her go, decided he couldn't recall any particularly clever remarks he had made, set his supersonic for its lowest frequency, and moved to the tunnels.

He paused before the intersection. He and Blaine had had their little scrap with the borrowers in the right-hand one, and an elaborate trap might have been set there against their return: accordingly, he chose to walk down the shaft on his left.

It was much like the other shaft. Carefully carved cross-beams were set up at intervals, while the sides were smooth and round. He came to the sharp slope and moved more cautiously. If he slipped into a hole, there was no telling how far he might fall.

The slope became steeper. Donelli's helmet light suddenly exposed another, more complicated intersection ahead in the form of six tunnel entrances. In front of one, two burrowers were chipping the end of a large root out of the tunnel ceiling.

As his search beam hit them, they whirled simultaneously and waved the hairy appendage at him for the barest fraction a second. Then, both sprang for the tunnel entrance in a flick of ivory bodies.

Donelli thought he had missed. He had brought up his weapon just as they leaped. But one fell to the floor, the ax-head dropping. The creature was not completely unconscious, gobbling weakly at him as he approached. Donelli slung it over his shoulder and started back. The creature squirmed limply in his grasp.

There was an odd, insistent patter behind him, a sound of many legs. Pursuit. Well, they wouldn't dare follow him into the cave. He wished the suit weren't so heavy, though. He kept turning his head to look at the empty shaft to the rear. Nasty to be overcome from behind, under the suffocating earth of an alien planet.

Even though the burrower stiffened with fear when he reached the cave, he felt better. The pattering grew louder, stopped, came on slowly.

Helena Naxos and Blaine were squatting near the four large veined balls, the avian, weakly fluttering, between them. They held a supersonic over it. The winged creature had evidently had a dose of sound like that of Donelli's captive. Blaine was speaking persuasively, in that hum-drone language, with little apparent effect.

"Put it right down here, next to the other one," Helena ordered. "With a little time and a little imagination, we may get out of this fix. Too early to tell just yet. Jake, you'll have to act as sort of armed guard at this conference. We mustn't be disturbed. Susie's playmates are too frightened to come in, but they've been making all kinds of fuss since we carried her out of the ship and into the cave."

"I'll take care of it," the spaceman promised.

He gasped with sheer astonishment when he reached the entrance of the cave. The saffron sky was obscured by multitudes of black-winged avians dipping in short angry circles. A swarm of the avians had surrounded the lifeboat and, as he watched, they lifted it slightly off the ground in the direction of the sea. This was no attempt to placate a deity, he decided, but sheer vindictiveness—revenge for the unspeakable tortures they imagined the humans were venting on the prisoner.

The supersonic low-power beam rolled them off the ship in a huge stunned mass. Their places were immediately taken by others. Donelli sprayed them off too.

They left the ship alone after that, and came in flying low at him with their blow tubes in their mouths. Jagged darts shrilled nastily all around him. He felt one bounce off his chest and hoped vaguely that they were less effective than the weapons of the burrowers on Grojen shielding. He moved back into the shadow of the cave.

Helena, Dr. Blaine, and the two aliens came up behind him and gathered round the white worms near the entrance.

"Pretty dangerous here," he told them. "These avians of yours are an accurate bunch of snipers."

"No help for it," she replied. "We're getting close. I don't think they'll keep blowing darts after they get a glimpse of Sister Susie. We'll be safe so long as we're near her. Suppose you do something about the other side. Those burrowers are throwing an awful lot of stuff awfully far."

He moved past them toward the rear, noting that both the winged and clawed creatures were no longer under the influence of the supersonics but were listening intently to Dr. Blaine as he alternately hummed at one and clicked at the other. They almost watched Helena gesture to the white worms and their grisly meal and back to them.

At least we've got their interest, Donelli thought grimly.

He began to cough. No mistake this time, there was HF vapor seeping into his suit through some scratch. Fluorine was eating at his lungs. Well, he didn't have time to feel sick.

The ivory-colored animals had rigged up a primitive ballista just a few feet from the end of the tunnel and were pegging ax-heads into the cave at fairly respectable velocities. The missiles were easy to side-step, but Donelli's head was getting heavy and he lost his footing once or twice. As fast as his supersonic would sweep them away from the ballista, they would crowd back again with stubborn determination. A slow, evil fire built itself in Donelli's chest and spread nibbling fingers along his throat.

He looked over his shoulder. No more darts were coming in at the rapt group near the cave mouth. Evidently the avians were possessed of more love for one of their number than the burrowers. He had just started to turn his head when a heavy object struck the back of his helmet. He dimly perceived he was falling. It seemed to him that the burrower which he had captured leaped over him and rejoined its fellows, and that Susie flew out to a clustered bunch of avians and that they all buzzed and hummed like idiots.

What a waste of time, he thought as the fire began to consume his brain. Helena let them go.

It seemed to him that Helena and Dr. Blaine were hurrying to his side through a shimmering mist of yellow agony. It also seemed to him that one of the chest-high balls split up along a pink vein and something came out.

But he was sure of nothing but the painful, choking darkness into which his body twisted, nothing but the agony in his chest....

He woke with a spaceman's certain knowledge of riding a smooth jet. His body felt deliciously light. He tried to sit up, but he was too weak to do more than turn his head. Two men had their backs to him. After a while he identified them as Dr. Archibald Blaine and Dr. Douglas Ibn Yussuf. Dr. Yussuf was out of his cast and was arguing in an animated fashion with Blaine over a white ax-head imprisoned in a plastic block.

"Why, I'm in Dr. Yussuf's bunk," Donelli muttered stupidly.

"Welcome back," Helena told him, moving into range of his watery eyes. "You've been pretty far away for a long, long time."

"Away?"

"You ate enough hydrofluoric acid to etch a glass factory out of existence. I made my biological education turn handsprings to save that belligerent life of yours. We used up almost every drug on the ship, and Dr. Yussuf's organic deconverter-and-respirator, which he built and used on you, is going to make him the first physical chemist to win a Solarian Prize in medicine."

"When—when did we take off?"

"Days ago. We should be near a traffic lane now, not to mention the galactic patrol. Our tanks are stuffed with contra-uranium, our second jet is operating in a clumsy sort of way, and our converter is functioning as cheerily as any atomic converter ever did. After the help we gave them with their own lives, the population of

Maximilian II was so busy bringing us Q that we ran out of inerted lead containers. From considering us the personifications of death, they've come to the point where they believe humans go around destroying death, or at least its fear. And it's Jake Donelli who did that."

"I did, did I?" Donelli was being very cautious.

"Didn't you? That business about the threshold of life and death being the caves was what I heard you develop with my own ears. It was the only clue I needed. The caves related not only to the sacredness of birth, but—more important to the primitive mind—to the awful terror of death. A threshold, you called it. And so it was, not only between life and death, but between the burrowers and the avians. Once I had that, and with a little scientific guessing, it was simple to figure out why the eggs were laid in apparent reverse order—those of the burrowers near the front, and those of the avians at the rear—and why they had never met each other."

The spaceman thought that over and then nodded slowly.

"Simple," Donelli murmured. "Yes, that might be the word. This little shred of scientific guessing you did, just what did it amount to?"

"Why, that the avians and the burrowers were different forms of the same creature in different stages of the life-process. The winged creatures mate just as their powers start to decline. Before the young hatch, the parents seek out a cave and die there. The young, those white worms, use the parental bodies as food until they have grown claws and can travel down to the tunnels where they become adolescent burrowers.

"The burrowers, after all, are nothing but larvae—despite the timbering of their shafts and their mining techniques, which Drs. Blaine and Yussuf consider spectacular. They can be considered sexless. After several years, the burrower will return to the cave. In the belief of its fellows it dies there, since it returns no more. It spins a cocoon—that's what those large green balls were— and remains a chrysalis until the winged form is fully developed. It then flies out of the cave and into the open air, where it is accepted by the so-called avians as their junior. It evidently retains no memory of its pre-chrysalis existence.

"Thus you have two civilizations unaware of each other, each different and each proceeding from the same organism. So far as the organism was concerned in either stage, it went to the cave only to die, and, from the cave, in some mysterious fashion, its own kind came forth. Therefore, a taboo is built up on both sides of the threshold, a taboo of the most thoroughgoing and binding nature, the mere thought of whose violation results in psychosis. The taboo, of course, has held their development in check for centuries, perhaps for millennia. Interesting?"

"Yeah!'

"The clue was what was important, Jake. Once I had it, I could relate their life-cycle to the *Goma* of Venus, the *Lepidoptera* of Earth, the *Sislinsinsi* of Altair VI. And the clincher was that one of the winged forms hatched out of a cocoon just after I'd finished explaining what was, up to that moment, only my hypothesis."

"How did they take it?"

"Startled at first. But it explained something they were very curious about and swept away an immense weight of ugly fear. Of course, they still die in the caves, to all intents and purposes. But they can see their lives as a perfect reproductive circle with the caves as a locus. And what a reciprocity they can work out—they are working out!"

"Reciprocity?" Donelli had almost moved to a sitting position.

Helena wiped his face with a soft cloth. "Don't you see? The burrowers were injuring the avian gardens by nibbling at the roots. They will now use only the roots of old, strong plants which the surface creatures will designate and set aside for them. They will also aid avian horticulture by making certain the roots have plenty of nourishing space in which to grow. In return, the avians will bring them surface plants which are not available to tunnel creatures, while the burrowers provide the surface with the products of their mines and labors underground. To say nothing of the intelligent rearing they can now give their young, though at a distance. And when the fluorescent light system that Dr. Ibn Yussuf worked out for them becomes universal, the avians may travel freely in the tunnels and guide the burrowers to the surface. The instinctual and haphazard may shortly be supplanted by a rich science."

"No wonder they broke their backs getting Q. And after working that out for them, all you did was repair the ship, fix me up, take off and set a course for the nearest traffic lane?"

She shrugged her shoulders. "Dr. Blaine helped quite a bit with the take-off. This time, he remembered the buttons! By the way, as far as the record is concerned, he and I maneuvered the ship off the ground under your direct supervision."

"Oh, so?"

"Just so. Right, Dr. Blaine?"

The archaeologist looked up impatiently. "Of course. Of course! There has not been one moment, since the disaster aboard the *Ionian Pinafore,* when I have not been under Mr. Donelli's orders."

There was a pause in which Dr. Blaine muttered to Dr. Yussuf over the ax-head.

"How old are you, Helena?" Donelli asked.

"Oh—old enough."

"But too clever, eh? Too educated for me?"

She cocked her head and smiled at him out of a secret corner of her face. "Maybe. We'll see what happens after we get back to the regular traffic lanes. After we're rescued. After you get your third mate's ticket. Here—what are you laughing at?"

He rumbled the amusement out of his throat. "Oh, I was just thinking how we earned our Q. By teaching a bunch of caterpillars that butterflies bring babies!"

HALLOCK'S MADNESS

"A most singular case," mumbled Dr. Pertinnet, walking a dignified hop-scotch among the checkered tiles of the sanitarium waiting room. "Can't be unique, of course—nothing's ever unique: must have been someone like Hallock in medical history. Just never recorded."

Ransom Morrow sighed good-naturedly and heaved himself over to the little doctor. He reached down and plucked at a white sleeve.

"Hey, Doc, remember me? I've been recorded. Not in the *Psychiatrist's Weekly Monitor*, but in your appointment book. Nila said you wanted some help. And now that I managed to get on the subject of Nila, how is she and where is she? My expedition's trotting off to Uganda in a week, and I want to do my Christmas shopping early."

Dr. Pertinnet blinked at him until recognition widened his weak scholarly eyes. "Ransom, my boy! Glad to see you. Miss Budd is taking care of the patient. Hallock—you know, Hallock the explorer. She said you once worshipped him; her idea to call you."

"Hallock? *Wells W. Hallock?*" Morrow whistled a slow bar of recollection. "The greatest of them all. Before Peary, before Johnson, before Livingston. And for sheer dogged searching, before even old Ponce de Leon. Mom used to tear his books out of my hands; I had to read them at night under a blanket with a flashlight. He got me interested in broken cities and forgotten temples. Why, if it weren't for Hallock—"

He broke off and stared down at the old man. "What's the matter with him? And what can I do?"

"Trauma! Nothing definite, nothing we can name, but it is quite obviously driving him psychotic. And unlike most cases of this sort, he realizes it and wants help desperately. But he seems to feel that our help is worse than nothing at all; he keeps saying that psychiatry will complete the tragedy that curiosity began. He's resisted all our efforts so violently that we've been forced to resort to—well, to the straitjacket."

Ransom Morrow shook his head. Wells W. Hallock in a straitjacket! Huge, fearless Hallock, who had shot his way out of the underground temple in northern India where the original, primitive *Thuggee* was practiced, who penetrated to the vampire cult of Lengluana and took flashbulb photographs! Hallock, who had laughed at superstition and dream-fancies and roared his way into the inaccessible, twilit corners of the world!

An attendant was handing a white envelope and a sheet of beworded paper to Dr. Pertinnet. "That's the complete report, Doctor," he said. "We checked the original analysis as you requested, but the results were the same. No injurious substances— definitely *Phoenix dactylifera,* however. And we still haven't found the cat."

"Then find her. Find her!" The attendant backed out in a flurry of *sirs* and *buts.* "Valuable experimental animal like that—allowing it to escape and run around as if—"

"You still haven't told me how I can help."

The doctor stuffed the envelope and paper into a pocket of his gown. "Of course. Fact is, I don't know myself. Miss Budd mentioned your name to Hallock, told him it was his influence that started you exploring. Now, he insists on seeing you. Says only you can help him, understand him. Pretty usual fixation under the circumstances, except that he never heard of you before. Miss Budd suggested that we call you in any case. He might make a useful slip, if you can win his confidence. I don't see any harm in it, just so you don't get him overexcited."

They walked down a long, silent, antiseptic corridor. Dr. Pertinnet paused before a smooth door.

"Understand," he placed a friendly hand on Ransom's shoulder, "understand, we can't have any affectionate hijinks between you and Miss Budd in that room. This case is difficult enough, what with Dr. Risbummer—my predecessor in the case— suddenly taking it in his head to disappear without leaving a trace of his notes. And now the cat. We just can't have any more tomfoolery. Straight scientific investigation."

"Gotcha, Doc," the young man grinned. "I'll save my research on Nila for this evening. Meanwhile, lead on. I'm agape and agog but not aglow."

They entered a large, airy room that shrieked of hospital austerity. A screen, a night table, a small chair, and a large bed were its only furniture. Nila Budd, trim, blonde, and hygienically beautiful in her starched white uniform, sat on the chair doling spoonfuls out of a china bowl to a weatherbeaten face.

She paused as they came in, and smiled briefly at Ransom. Then she dropped the spoon into the bowl and set it on the table near a tiny chest made of incredibly yellowed ivory. She walked up to them while the man lying on the bed watched her curiously out of great, deep-sunk eyes. He seemed strangely free, as if the buttoned sheets which restrained his immense body were somehow not significant, somehow didn't matter…

"I did as you suggested with the sedative, Doctor," she whispered. "He's been fairly docile all day, no trouble at all. Hello, Ran."

"Hi." He attempted a brief embrace, but she evaded him and walked over to where the doctor stood looking down at Hallock.

"I've brought you an old admirer," the doctor was saying. "This is Ransom Morrow. Your books inspired him to become an explorer. He's leaving for Uganda next week in search of—of—"

"Of a paleolithic Hamitic civilization around Lake Albert," Ransom finished, walking over to the bed. "I'm honored to meet you, sir."

Wells W. Hallock raised his head and stared at the younger man. His hair, cut long and free in the style affected by men of the old West, was no longer the shiny black of a thousand pictures; it was white, thin, and straggled. But his eyes were proud.

"And it's an honor to meet you, Mr. Morrow," he said at last, in a voice so hoarse that Ransom had to bend over the bed to catch the carefully shaped syllables. "I've heard of your work in North Africa and Ethiopia. But Dr. Pertinnet is very wrong when he says my books made you an explorer. It was curiosity that did it—divine, satanic curiosity—like the curiosity which brought me to this. Your curiosity, Mr. Morrow—it can save me, do you hear, it can save me! Only we must have weapons— an elephant rifle, machine guns, machetes, hand grenades—"

"Hallock!" The psychiatrist cut in on the sharply rising voice. "If you go on this way, I'll have to ask Mr. Morrow to leave. Now lie back and relax. That's right, rela-a-ax."

The explorer dropped his head to the pillow. "You had the *Fruit* analyzed, didn't you?" he asked suddenly.

Dr. Pertinnet was flustered. "Y-yes. We did. Surprisingly enough, it contains nothing that might be termed a drug." He set the envelope down on the ivory chest and unfolded the sheet of paper given him by the orderly. "Of course, it's difficult to be certain in its present dried condition, but it appears to be nothing more than a variety of *Phoenix dactylifera*. In other words, a date. Common, ordinary fruit of the date palm."

"Common, ordinary—"

The man on the bed tilted his chin at the ceiling and laughed soundlessly. "You call the *Fruit* a common, ordinary date! What would you call the Gates of Hell, Doctor—doors or railings? Would you look at them and say, 'Why, here's a fence that needs whitewashing?'" He coughed for a moment and continued his feverish whispering. "And what happened when you gave a bit to the cat? Have you found the cat yet?"

"Why, no. How did you know we gave a piece to a cat?" the doctor asked him suddenly. "Has she been in here? We've searched the hospital— Nurse, have you seen the cat?"

"No, Doctor," Hallock broke in before Nila could answer, "the nurse hasn't seen the cat. But I have. She's a badly frightened little pussy by now—if she isn't dead. You gave her a pretty large piece, you know. She won't be able to get back. And she hasn't seen any of the larger things yet, just the two-headed snake and the portions of the giant centipede and—"

The doctor leaned over and gripped the explorer's shoulder through the thick sheets. "Where is the cat, Hallock?" he asked in a soothing voice. "Where did you see her last?"

"Here," the man on the bed whispered. "Here. In my head. In my horrible brain. Where I go when you make me fall asleep. Where I meet Dr. Risbummer, cowering and gibbering to himself. Only he isn't Dr. Risbummer any more, but a poor, mad, crippled thing who clings to me for protection, who begs me not to have nightmares because he's tired of running, because he's afraid he'll fall and get caught sometime."

"Hopeless!" Dr. Pertinnet straightened. "Most unfortunate about Dr. Risbummer's disappearance. Not only don't we have his diagnosis available, but the whole affair has strengthened Hallock's hallucinations. Given them substance, as it were." He moved toward the door. "If we could only find Risbummer!"

"You can, damn it, you can!" Hallock strained against the sheets. "Give him a chance. Just don't stick any more of those needles into me, don't put me to sleep any more."

"I told you there would be no further hypodermics, unless you made them necessary. The sedative for tonight has already been administered; Miss Budd mixed it with the broth she fed you."

Ransom, licking his dry lips, decided he would never forget the look of furious horror that distended Hallock's eyes.

"You fool! You crazy, crazy, *crazy* fools!" He writhed on the solid bed as if he wanted to dissolve through it. "I begged—"

"Now, then, Mr. Hallock," Nila told him, "you do need sleep."

"Sleep!" The massive head dropped back to the pillow. "Oh, go away. Go away."

"Miss Budd," the doctor called as he pushed the door open. "I'd like to see you for a moment."

"Right with you, Doctor." She touched Morrow's arm before slipping after him. "I go off duty in an hour, Ran; hang around and say nice stuff to my patient."

Hallock watched the nurse leave. "Like her a lot?" he whispered.

"Yeah."

"She's a nice girl. And a good nurse. But she doesn't take to the idea of your wandering off to Uganda and similar points unknown?"

"That's right, sir. Calls it adolescence in longer pants." Morrow dropped to the chair. He was still finding difficulty in associating this heroic wreck with the Wells W. Hallock he had read about—crisp, cynical, fearless…

"She may be wrong. And she may be right. There are those among us who walk wide arcs around horror, who obey the simpler, more important precepts of their religion. And then, Morrow, there are the whistling fools who rush in where even fallen angels fear to tread. People like you and people like me, may the gentle God have mercy on us."

His voice was so hoarse that hardly one recognizable sound broke the rhythmic, rustling sentences. Ransom found himself leaning close to the tough, wrinkled face framed on three sides by long white hair.

"I'm sorry," the old explorer chuckled somewhere in his throat. "My voice *is* hard to hear. You see, I—well, I scream too much."

There was a brief silence while he breathed heavily and fidgeted his head about on the pillow. Down the hall, a clock ticked in regular hammer-strokes.

"You're an explorer because you have a curiosity that eats at your insides night and day. But how much curiosity do you really have, Ransom Morrow? Enough to wander willingly through a land that has never been mapped, through a land never meant to be mapped? A land filled with creatures that are unfortunately not inconceivable, whose greatest horror is that they *have* been conceived and exist in the mind of an imaginative, foolhardy idiot! Have you the curiosity to do that and come to the rescue of a pitiful hulk whom only you can save before the ministrations of kindly doctors and sympathetic nurses send him stumbling forever into the abyss of the unutterable?" He paused, coughed soundlessly, smiled. "I'm sorry. To leave out the drama, have you the curiosity to eat a slightly mildewed dried date?"

"From there?" Morrow jerked his fascinated eyes to where the white envelope reposed on the ivory chest.

"Yes. From there. It's the Fruit, Morrow, the Fruit of the Tree. Only you must be careful—you mustn't, like Risbummer—a little—a taste—" His eyes closed as his voice trailed away. Suddenly they opened again, and he whispered rapidly, as if each word were measured in years of life. "Must help me, Morrow—knives—guns. Gets worse each time. Fools gave—me sedative. Can't fight— tied down—but dangerously close—dangerous—must get help—some way—some—way—" This time his lids slid shut, and his breathing slowed to a sleeping regularity.

Ransom watched the determined muscles of his face relax and grow gentle. Then he rose and tiptoed to the small table.

The chest was well known to any reader of Hallock's books. Given to him by a Buddhist lama for services rendered and friendship tendered, the hard yellow box had once contained the crowning, though fragmentary, jewels of every expedition. It had once held that bit of stone from Java—the earliest artifact definitely known to have been made by human hands; the tiny, primitive steam engine assembled by the priests of ancient Egypt had once rattled against its hard corners. Now?

Morrow picked up the envelope and flipped back the cover of the chest.

A handful of dry, olive-shaped objects lay on the creamy surface of the bottom. Dr. Pertinnet's dates! Ransom smiled. Outside the room, the little doctor's voice was detailing dreary instructions to Nila's occasional bubble of assent.

Slowly he reached for the envelope, pried it open with thumb and forefinger, and peered inside.

More dates. No, only one this time. Rather, what was left of the one used in the analysis.

A black powder residue of the brittle fruit streaked the lower edge of the envelope. Ransom dug his finger into it idly. Some powder wedged into the nail. He brought his hand up and sniffed the stuff.

Strange! He felt—dizzy. What a—a *warm* odor!

He steadied himself against the table and reached for a pinch of the powder. He brought it near his nostrils. He paused for a moment, then shrugged his shoulders and inhaled deeply.

The lights went out and the floor dissolved.

He was falling, falling through endless space and eternal twilight. Fear swathed itself about him like an oversized blanket. He beat his arms frantically against the dark as he somersaulted slowly.

Round and round he went; round and round and down. Always down into the hungry gloom. He was startled to find that he was screaming; he closed his mouth with difficulty.

There he was sitting on the bottom. Bottom of what? And when had he hit? There hadn't even been a thud; at the rate he was falling—what was it: thirty-two feet per second?—he should have broken at least every other bone. He felt his body carefully; nary a bone.

But when had he hit?

He rose on the hard, gray surface and stared into the shifting darkness. Something—something was moving.

A camel with a long, scaly tail that ended in a human head broke from the shadows and raced past him. Ransom whirled in time to see it disappear into the dark again, the smiling head bumping evenly against its shanks.

"Sqgg," breathed Ransom Morrow.

As if in answer, he heard a musical whine on his right. He turned. A cat! Nothing else? No saber-teeth, no pink worms instead of hair? Nope, just an everyblessedday ordinary cat! A snow-white cat with the tiniest black saddle.

It lay on its belly, all four feet braced, regarding him intently. "Miauu?" it questioned.

Ransom knelt and snapped his fingers at it. "Here, puss," he called. "Here, puss, puss, puss."

Red gums rolled back to display a lion's maw in miniature. It lunged forward and snapped. Ransom jerked his hand away and leaped to his feet. "You are certainly one suspicious feline," he said, examining his fingers ruefully. "Not that I blame you—here!"

He jumped as two sets of voices—one human—began screaming.

The camel had wandered into what appeared at first to be a bramble patch. Only, as Ransom squinted ahead desperately, he saw it wasn't brambles that curled round it with hairy strength and dragged it to a many-eyed darker blot of head in the center. It was a huge spider—or a collection of fantastically large spiders with only one head but with the slavering evil and obscene legs of them all.

Long neck distended, the camel was bellowing its terror deafeningly, while, at the other end, the human head screamed almost recognizable words as it bit and tore at the extremities of the incredible arthropod.

Ransom backed away slowly, his hands slipping the leather belt off his waist. Not much of a weapon in this place, but he had to have something in his hands!

As the great dripping mouth in the center took its first bite of the camel, a bluish light began to break. Ransom looked around for the cat.

It was rubbing against the scrawny legs of an old man dressed in the flapping rags of a once-white laboratory smock.

The old man placed a hand foolishly against the side of his face. "Y-you aren't Hallock," he mumbled.

"No," Ransom told him. "But I'm not one of the citizens of this place, either." He stepped toward him.

With a look of complete fear, the old man moved back a few steps. Then he turned and ran. The cat loped after him easily, its smooth stride contrasting with his determined staggering.

Ransom cursed and began to follow. The old man and the cat grew fainter, though the light was much stronger now. After a moment, they had disappeared. The multilegged spider had also vanished. He was alone in a well lit emptiness.

"Now what?" he asked himself.

"Now what *what?*" Nila's voice questioned. He spun around. She was bending over Hallock's sleeping head on the hospital pillow. The severe room was back, white and reassuringly normal. Down the corridor, the noisy clock still ticked.

"Where have you been? You know my patients can't be left alone. We just stepped outside the door for a moment, and you took it into your head to go sightseeing. Can't you forget that explorer's itch long enough to do an old man a simple human kindness? And while I'm on the subject, how did you get out of here? The doctor and I were standing right against the door all the time."

He braced himself against her words. The ivory chest still sat heavily on the small night table; the envelope hung precariously over one edge, a tiny trace of powder oozing out of it. Ransom adjusted the envelope and noticed that his belt was in his hands.

Slowly he threaded it back around his waist. "You say I wasn't in the room when you got back?" he asked at last. "Then where was I?"

"That's the point; the door's the only exit, the windows are all barred, and I looked under the bed and behind the screen. Where *did* you go?"

He smiled bleakly. "Oh, somewhere east of the sun and west of the moon. Pretty goshawful place. Has the doctor left?"

"Yes. He looked in to make certain that Hallock was asleep, couldn't find you, and toddled off to his lab. Ran," she moved close to him, "you look upset. I've never seen such strain on your face. Maybe you better wait for me downstairs."

"Check." He stopped at the door. His right hand was scratched. "That cat," he asked, "the one Pertinnet fed some of Hallock's fruit. The one that disappeared. Was it mostly white with a tiny black saddle near the tail?"

"Yes." He was upset at the sudden whiteness of her face. "Did you see it?"

"Um-m-m. Sorta. Kinda." He went downstairs.

When she joined him a half-hour later, trim in her blue nurse's coat, he had transferred the bulk of a pack of cigarettes from his pocket case to several ashtrays, charring them only slightly in transit. She glanced deductively at his face, then linked her warm arm to his. "Come on, Ran. Let's get out of this place. I want to play."

So they played. At a good restaurant, in the balcony of the best musical comedy of the season, around the dance floor of a dimly lit night club. "Some playing," she commented while a white-coated band stuttered suave music. "When we came in, I almost told the head waiter, 'Pardon my corpse.'"

"I'm sorry. Just not up to snuff tonight, Nila. Would you like to go home?"

She turned to him at the door of her apartment hotel. "All right, Ran, so you saw the cat. Did you see Risbummer, too?"

He spread his feet apart and took a deep breath. "What—what did Risbummer look like?"

"About the same size and weight as Dr. Pertinnet. Old, a little helpless, as if he had reached enough of a second childhood to need a mother again. He had a small acid burn on the tip of his nose."

Ransom blinked his eyes and tried to remember. Did the old man have a small burn on his nose? Maybe. Maybe not.

"I don't know; I really couldn't say. Look here, you and the doctor, you really believe Hallock's story! You don't think he's insane!"

Nila looked down at her shoes, considered. "This is top-secret, Ran; but I'll tell you. We *have* to believe Hallock to a certain extent. His mind is definitely affected—that we know—but how much is traumatic, induced by his strange experiences, and how much is the strange experience itself…? Dr. Pertinnet has his scientific reputation to consider: he can't go off quarter-cocked until he is absolutely certain of his facts. Meanwhile, we've been treating Hallock as a regular patient and keeping our suspicions from everybody, even you. We feel there may be some other explanation for Hallock vanishing so frequently—"

"Vanishing? You mean he disappears from the bed?"

She nodded. "And reappears on it again ten or fifteen minutes later, right inside his straitjacket. The first time it happened, Jenny, the night nurse, threw a fit up and down the corridor. Dr. Pertinnet smoothed her down and told me to take over till morning. It happened twice while I was on duty. We've managed to keep it quiet; Jenny takes it in her stride now. You see, Hallock only disappears when he's had a sedative. At all other times, he lies fairly still and chatters about his dates."

"I know," Ransom brooded. "They aren't. Dates, I mean. I tasted a bit of one, or rather, I smelled at it. That's what sent me to—wherever I went."

"You didn't! Why, Ran, that's crazy; it's dangerous! We don't know exactly—but Dr. Risbummer is supposed to have eaten one, and he—we only wanted you to get some information from Hallock, to—"

"Sort of a scientific stool pigeon," he snarled. "That gallant old codger is battling something infernally alien and ugly with every ounce of his used-up strength, and all you can do is shoot sedatives in him so he'll perform some more intriguing tricks. No. From here on out, I play Hallock's ball. If he wants guns and knives, he gets 'em; though I can't quite see—"

"But, Ran! You'll ruin everything. At first, we thought the Fruit had something—but since Dr. Pertinnet had it analyzed, we've been forced to drop that line. But if you show Hallock you believe him, we'll never find out what causes his disappearances, what brought on his neurosis. Don't you see what I mean?"

"No, I don't. First, you can get negative analyses a hundred times from Sunday, but it still is the Fruit which somehow activates the whole situation. If either you or Dr. Pertinnet had submitted it to the most elementary analysis of all, you'd have found it to be so, if only you'd have done what Risbummer did—tasted it! Now—well, now you've called me in, and I'm going to do my gosh-damned best to help the old guy. I don't know how exactly, not yet, but I'm going to hit it realistically, honestly."

She laughed at him. "Realistically! The greatest romantic of them all talking about realism! Ransom Morrow, who goes trotting off into the African equivalent of a haunted house because the ordinary, adult world doesn't give him enough thrills. Don Quixote tilted at windmills, but you—you make them up!"

"Now, look, Nila. There's no call—"

"Yes, there is," she told him fiercely. "You insist on slandering the only realism I'll accept, the realism of science, which must be skeptical if it's to be of any use. Perhaps you've discovered something of value by your reckless experiment; perhaps we've overlooked an important item in limiting ourselves to a chemical investigation of the Fruit. Perhaps, I say. But you are still a layman, whom we called in as a layman, and not as a research director. You're worse than the average at that because of your tendency to fly off the handle. In the future, you'll be barred from the hospital—and from Hallock. I'll convey your *experiences* to the doctor and let him make what he can of them." She paused with her hand on the door. "And perhaps I'll see what I can make of them."

Ransom grabbed her shoulders. "What do you mean? What will you do?"

She shook his arm away. "I don't know yet. But as a nurse, it's my case. I'll do as I think best for the patient."

Then she stepped resolutely away from him and into the lobby. He watched her cross into an elevator and move to the rear without once looking back at him.

White glare from the street light made him conspicuous and awkward. He walked for half a block talking to himself, and finally called a cab.

This was the nastiest quarrel he'd had with Nila. Of course, it hadn't been the one incident; it was the whole pattern of his coming jaunt to Uganda and her unquenchable opposition.

But Hallock! Poor, poor Hallock. Trapped by a misstep in the suddenly-become-reality of his own nightmares and held there by a series of stumbling, peering psychiatrists. And what nightmares! None of the humdrum kind that brought you awake in a fog of fear and the desperate desire to flick on the light switch, but nightmares filled with incredibly nasty monstrosities whose abilities to inflict injury and even death were disturbingly possible.

And Risbummer? And the cat? What invitation had they answered to find themselves in this world of half-tone horror? And the others—all the others there must have been who nibbled at the Fruit…

Dawn chilled outside his bedroom window before Ransom Morrow finally, reluctantly fell asleep. He had no dreams, but he slept late. He would have slept later, had not the telephone awakened him.

"Morrow? This is Dr. Pertinnet. I'm at the hospital. Uh—did Miss Budd discuss our patient with you last night? Did she mention any specific plans relative to him?"

"Discuss patient?" Ransom yawned a thick gob of sleep out of his mouth. "What you talking about?"

"She can't be found anywhere. First time it's happened. She's a very conscientious nurse. The night nurse said she took over in the morning, while Hallock was still sleeping off his sedative. I came in an hour ago and found Hallock awake, Miss Budd gone. There's no sign of her at all, just a half-eaten date on the floor which Hallock says—"

It was as if there was a definite *click* in the back of his brain. His mind churned away the clouds, tore into full wakefulness. "Hallock! Does he say she's eaten the Fruit?"

"Ye-e-es." The doctor's voice had uncertain edges. "He says she was curious about it when he woke this morning, and he persuaded her to eat a date. He claims she's eaten so much that she's now a permanent part of his nightmares, and only you can get her out. Of course, it's all preposterous, but since I can't find her anywhere, and since you and she—"

"Yeah! Well, hold on to your stethoscope: I'll be right over!" He slammed down the phone and dressed with flying fingers.

All the tightly packed equipment for his expedition into the African wilderness was in the next room. Ransom thanked a dozen minor deities that he was the youngest member of the group and as such was burdened with most of the armament, which covered every imaginable emergency. He telephoned for a taxi, selected three awkwardly shaped, oilskin-wrapped bundles, and staggered downstairs with them.

The cabbie helped him tug them into the car. His eyes grew round when he felt the muzzle of a submachine gun and the pointed ends of cartridges through one set of wrappings. They grew rounder when Ransom slammed the door and yelled out the hospital address. "First time," he muttered as he settled behind the wheel, "first time I ever seen an accident go to the *right* place to happen."

Dr. Pertinnet met him in the corridor as he dragged the heavy bundles behind him. "Why, wh-what's that?"

"Pills and poultices," Ransom told him. "Tincture of nitroglycerine. Nice strong medicine that's good for what ails Hallock. I think it may cure him. Here, Doc, take this one. It's bulky and keeps getting in my way."

He pushed into the old explorer's room with the doctor laboring and protesting behind him. A plump nurse blocked his way to the bed.

"Shoo, girl. Go away. Scat. This is man's work. Take yourself a toddle." He pushed past her determined opposition. At a signal from the doctor, she left the room, her nose high and her shoulders shrugging.

Ransom knelt and began to tear the wrappings off the weapons. He stared up at Hallock, smiling from the bed. "I'm ready. Map it out."

"Good," came the whispered reply. "I'm sorry I had to talk Miss Budd into danger, my boy, but I'm getting desperate. I spend more and more time in my dreams now, with greater risk of never returning. I counted on you to act immediately so that the nurse wouldn't spend too much time alone, but I swear I never intended for her to eat that much of the Fruit. I swear I intended for her to come back."

"It's done now. Doctor, give him a sedative. Don't look at me like that—*give him a sedative!*"

As the doctor unfastened the blanket and swabbed Hallock's arm, Morrow asked, "What do I have to do to get Nila back? And Dr. Risbummer?"

"I'll tell you; I'll be with you…there. We must kill the mother—the Brood Mother of Fancies and Horrors. You have the weapons?"

"Everything short of a portable hydrogen bomb. Rifle—high-powered Winchester—Tommy gun, two machetes, and a batch of hand grenades. Manage?"

The old explorer lay back and stared at the ceiling. "Wonderful! If only I'd had the sense years ago, myself… None of this would have happened. I'd never have reached this helpless, horror-ridden state." His whispers became almost inaudible as his mind wandered under the influence of the sedative.

"In Mesopotamia, far south of Dinra, where the desert turns to broken rock that looks like rubble left over from the making of the world… None of the native guides will go there, although there is a legend that the Garden of Eden and that treasure unheard of… *Treasure!* There is nothing but the tree—you pick through the sharpest rocks…and there is the tree—"

"The tree?" It was the doctor, breaking his staring silence.

"The Tree of Knowledge of Good and Evil," Hallock said softly, without lowering his gaze. "Not the way it is in the Bible…although some ancestor of man must have eaten of its fruit…it grows in a deep, rocky cleft where the sun cannot reach it and where no water flows…and yet it thrives…the summit is a magnificent crown of large feather-shaped leaves—purple, red and gold—and the Fruit…dozens of species of fruit, over a half of them unrecognizable, all on the same tree…not of this earth, that tree—yet who knows what creatures have eaten of it in the past, and what the Fruit eaten by a hairy Adam and his Eve. I could not know, God help me…"

His voice stopped. Dr. Pertinnet tiptoed over to see if he was asleep. Suddenly, the whispers began again. The old explorer's eyes bulged, and he licked his dry lips.

"I could not know…and I didn't care…I picked the dates from the top because I recognized them, and I thought I would be safe…I thought I would be safe!…How was I to know which fruit had already been eaten by man…and then it began!… I lived in my own dreams, the dreams of my past…but only for a moment…it was pleasant…then …but when I gave some to the camel driver, and he disappeared into the dream…then when I saw the Brood Mother and what she sent forth in my mind…I could not know which fruit was already eaten by man…I could not know…what kind of men we would be…what kind if a different fruit had been eaten then…if the one I picked had been eaten…a race living in its dreams… strange powers…what some races have eaten…a dinosaur nibbling at the top…monstrosities of all geologic time eating of it…how was I to know which…which fruit…"

He was asleep.

Morrow said "Whew!" He glanced at the doctor, who was licking his lips and staring at the man on the bed.

"Coming with me?"

The doctor was startled. "Where? How?"

"Into Hallock's madness, or his mind. Comes to the same thing. Want to come along? I need a gun bearer."

"Now look here, Morrow! I've stood around and let this foolishness go on—"

"It's not foolishness," Morrow interrupted. "You should know that by now. You can't find Nila, and I can. You can't give an adequate reason for Hallock's disappearances, and I can. You don't dare taste any of that fruit which your lab says is chemically pure, while I—"

"Oh, all right. All right. I'll admit this situation has its unusual side…"

"The understatement of the millennium. Now wrap this grenade belt around your waist and pick up those cartridge boxes. See if you can slip a machete under your right arm—tha-a-at's right. I'll carry the guns and the other machete." Morrow pulled two dates out of the ivory chest on the night table.

He grinned at the doctor, who was bent almost double under the weight of the armament. "How do you know," the old man grumbled, "that, assuming we go anywhere, we will arrive with this—this confounded arsenal?"

"Don't know. I just assume it from Hallock's instructions and the fact that I carried all my clothes with me on my last visit. Here, have a date. Go on, take it!"

The psychiatrist took the fruit, turned it around doubtfully, and finally, following Ransom Morrow's example, popped it in his mouth.

"Mmmm, good," he said. "Tastes just like—"

They were falling. Down and down, around and around. All about them, the curiously shifting darkness. Morrow felt the pressing fear, the screaming desire to run away and panic.

"—just like a fruitcake the hospital dietician makes when she's in a good mood," the doctor was saying. His voice was quite calm, with the slightest edge of wonder to it. "Interesting that this should begin by a falling sensation. I think that the most reasonable explanation may be—"

They had landed. Again there was no memory of the actual moment of contact. The doctor rose and brushed nonexistent dust from his white hospital gown. He looked around nearsightedly and continued.

"The most reasonable explanation may be found in Freud. Not the Freud of declining mental powers, but the earlier, more acute scientist."

Ransom Morrow shook his head and began to divest the doctor of his weapons. "Doc," he said, "you are one nerveless wonder."

"Eh? Quite. Now on the subject of a falling sensation, Freud would have it that— *Risbummer!*"

He had turned and noticed the old man in tattered gown, who stood watching him fearfully. "Risbummer! So this is where you've been keeping yourself! Where are your notes, man?"

"My—notes?"

"Yes, your notes on the Hallock case. Come, come, we need them badly. Inexcusable to go away without leaving your notes available to the staff. I've been through the hospital files three times and your office twice. Where did you put them?"

The other passed his hand through his sparse hair. "My notes. Did—did you look in my cigar box? I seem somehow—I—I think I left them in the cigar box. I'm—I'm sorry for the trouble you've had."

"That's quite all right," Pertinnet told him magnanimously. "Just so we get them into the files eventually." The two men moved off to one side, conversing in low tones, for all the world like two physicians at a sickbed. Risbummer *did* have a nose-burn.

"Old home week in Hallock's subconscious," Ransom said to himself. He finished loading the rifle and stood up. "Nila," he called. "Hey, Nila!"

He was surprised at the speed with which his call was answered. A hysterical figure in white dashed out of the darkness and flung herself against his chest. He held her, soothed her, kissed her. "You aren't hurt?" he asked anxiously.

"No, I'm not hurt. But this place—this awful, *awful* place!" She stopped sobbing and straightened her hair. "I must look—*oh!* As bad as Risbummer. He ran away when he first saw me, but the cat was friendly and after a while so was he. He was in a broken state when I arrived: it's wonderful what a little human conversation will do."

"Well, you aren't merely human," Morrow assured her. He glanced over her head and stiffened. That pith helmet, those tropical shorts, that flowing black hair—it was Wells W. Hallock, but the Hallock of fifteen, of twenty years ago. The cat rubbed affectionately against his khaki wool socks.

"Some tableau!" Hallock said in the booming voice of youth. "Pertinnet and Risbummer are holding a consultation; Budd and Morrow are holding each other. All the stuff come through?" He walked forward briskly.

While the two doctors came up to watch, he selected a machete and loaded the submachine gun; he hung two grenades from his belt.

"Don't mind if I take the Tommy?" he asked. "I know the vulnerable spots better than you. Let the docs carry the ammo."

He moved off into the lifting gloom, and Morrow hurried up beside him. "Where are we going? I don't want to take Nila where there's any danger."

"Well, the location keeps changing, but we'll get there soon. And don't worry about Nila: she's safest with you. You two, along with Pertinnet and Risbummer, are stuck here, by the way: you've all eaten too much of the Fruit. Your only hope is to wipe out the Brood Mother. From what I've seen, all this stuff will dissolve with her. I don't know whether we have enough equipment to sock it to her, but if we haven't—" He shrugged.

Nila walked directly behind them, looking about fearfully at the uglinesses slipping by in the darkness. The doctors brought up the rear, struggling under the heavy boxes of ammunition. The cat roamed on the outskirts of their little group, never moving off too far.

"How is it that you keep your youth?" Morrow asked.

"I don't know. It's one of the things I don't understand about this whole affair: I'm always as young as when I first tasted the Fruit. But that's just one puzzler. Another is why everyone who eats the Fruit winds up in my dream rather than in their own.

Possibly because I was the first to eat it, and when it was fresh from the plucking at that. It's convenient to stay young, though, and I've often thought that if it weren't for these horrors barging about— Hello!"

A tiny, red head supported on a flexible stalk of a neck waved down out of the gray shadow. There were three eyes in the head and a kind of sucking proboscis for a mouth. The other end of the stalk protruded from a bulging red mass some ten yards away.

As the head descended lazily, Ransom pumped a shot into the center eye. He heard Hallock let go with a burst from the machine gun, and the head, severed from the neck, fell and dissolved into red liquid as it fell. Almost immediately, a new head began to take form on the thin, twisting neck.

"Get the body—there!" Hallock was yelling.

Ransom pulled a grenade from his belt, ripped the pin out with his teeth, and lobbed it at the main body of the creature. Then—"Drop!" he yelled.

They all fell flat as the terrific concussion sent bits of steel and red, writhing flesh over their heads. When they rose, the monstrosity was gone.

"You fool!" Hallock was raging. "You wild-eyed, trigger-happy fool! Wasting good grenades on a creature like that when we could have finished it with cartridges. We'll need all of our grenades for the Brood Mother." He took stock morosely. "Only five left. They'll have to do."

"Wasn't that the Brood Mother?" Morrow asked. He was still unsteady, but he put a reassuring arm around Nila.

"That? The Brood Mother? Why, that was just one of her minor offspring—part of a nightmare I had ten years ago in Tunis. When you see the Brood Mother—*you'll recognize her!*"

"How?"

"She just couldn't be anything else! Let's go."

Nila walked up and slipped her arm on Ransom's shoulder. "If we meet one of mama's bigger boys, I want to be as close to you as I can get, Ran," she whispered.

"Steady," Ransom warned. "I'm about ready to go off the deep end myself. But we've got to hold steady." He followed Hallock.

Behind him, he heard the doctors wheezing under the weight of the cartridges. "Did you notice the peculiar manifestation of the color red in that monster, Risbummer?" Dr. Pertinnet was saying. "Remember what Piscoodberry says about the occurrence of red in dreams of the mentally unstable?"

"Do you mean Piscoodberry *On Simulated Hypnotism* or the Piscoodberry monograph on *The Primary Colors and the Subconscious?*"

"The monograph, of course! Where are your thoughts, Risbummer? What else could I mean but the monograph? Now, according to Piscoodberry…"

Their voices became low and professionally confidential. Ransom and Nila grinned at each other. They felt better as they moved along behind Hallock.

The number of distorted creatures around them seemed to increase, but nothing moved out to disturb them. They were watched by hundreds of crazy eyes in all kinds of fantastic faces.

An odor, perceptible for the last few minutes, became suddenly stronger. It was something which could only be described as a stink. "Although," said Ransom, "it smells like the great grand-daddy of all stinks. Like everything filthy and foul concentrated in one place." The light had grown until there was almost perfect visibility.

The cat had been moving stiffly in front of their group. It stopped, stared ahead, and began to hump its back. A violent, hating hiss shot from its teeth. Then it slowly retreated until it backed into Hallock's legs. It crawled behind him.

Hallock stopped and peered ahead. "This is it," he said in a low, frightened voice. "The Brood Mother. Load up and get ready."

The two men saw to their weapons, made certain their grenades were easily detachable and would not catch on any part of their clothing. They stuck the machetes through their belts. Nila helped with the clips of cartridges.

"You stay here," Ransom whispered. He turned to the doctors, who were standing near him in wistful helplessness. He gave Pertinnet one of his grenades. "Take care of her." Then as Hallock squared his shoulders and sighed, he moved up beside him.

"*Götterdämmerung*," Hallock said. "The last big battle."

They walked forward gingerly, in step, a foot moving slowly ahead after the other one had found firm purchase. The cat padded at their side, its belly hugging the ground.

The stench tore at their nostrils. Solid waves of odor came at them in stronger and stronger layers. Ransom scratched at the stock of his Winchester, trying desperately to see what lay ahead.

Then they saw it.

An immense carpet of living flesh, cradled in its own slime, lay before them. Miles long—and miles wide. A great expanse of flat, undulating tissue, green and yellow and sickly orange. Every now and then, some monstrosity would float up to the side of the organic carpet and move away from it. It was breeding before their unbelieving eyes.

Back and forth it soughed in the thick goo, and the odor arising from it was indescribable. And then, Ransom saw it was not entirely flat: at regular intervals, there were gaping mouths set flush with the surface, opening and closing spasmodically.

Hallock rushed forward, and Ransom, licking lips that tasted like dehydrated cardboard, moved with him. He knew they should go slowly, stalk it and not fire until they knew just where to strike. But he was hypnotized by the horror of the thing, by Hallock, and he ran at it like a madman.

Hallock stopped at the edge of the slime and tore the grenades off his belt. He pulled the pins and threw them in long looping arcs far into the monster. There were explosions and bits of awful flesh splattered about them.

Then Hallock was on his knees, screaming curses and laughter and spraying bullets into the expanse of living matter.

There was an answering scream from ten thousand throats. A vast ripple ran across the blanket of flesh, from mouth to mouth. Then—the far side lifted. Higher and higher—the monster was rearing from the slime!

Ransom got off a grenade as he saw it come up. One mouth winked out into a dripping hole. Then he was beside Hallock, firing into it as it rose.

Those mouths—they weren't only mouths, they were part of individual faces with discernible eyes and noses—they were gaping red mouths and horrible faces, but they reminded Ransom of something he couldn't quite remember.

"Get that center bulge," Hallock was gasping. "Looks like a vital spot!"

Ransom squeezed off a shot right into the palpitating scarlet blob at the exact middle of the creature. It ricocheted! Armor!

He pulled the pin out of his last grenade. Slime dripped down on them. He threw the grenade. It exploded far above the red spot.

They cursed in unison and began to stumble backward, firing as they went. The monster undulated forward, the gaping mouths at the top swinging down closer.

Ransom remembered the grenade he had given Pertinnet. He turned and ran back to where he had left Nila and the two doctors. He dropped his Winchester as he ran, not bothering to retrieve it.

Nila stared over his head at the awful thing coming down and forward. "Ran, oh, Ran," she moaned.

Pertinnet was examining the grenade, turning it over and over in his hands. "Strange device," he observed. "No discernible trigger mechanism. Simplicity should be one of the chief factors—"

Ransom plucked the grenade from his hands and whirled. Hallock was firing straight up now, burst after burst of bullets that had as little effect as wads of paper. He ran out of ammunition or the gun jammed, and he dropped it. He swept the machete from his belt.

"Back, Hallock," Ransom called. "Get back!" The older explorer didn't seem to hear him, but moved ankle-deep into the slime.

Ransom pulled the pin, took dead aim at the red spot and threw. The entire red bulge seemed to open outward as the grenade hit it. The monster screamed again, a perfect chord of screams. It folded back, and in upon itself.

As it rolled back, Hallock stepped onto the surface, swinging his machete like a lunatic. He sliced great hunks out of it before the edge behind him curled inward, carrying him with it—shrieking in horrible pain—wrapped in huge agonizing mouths.

The world cracked. Millions of unmatched cymbals clashed against each other in a discordant rattle of sound. Great splinters of grayness came smashing down all around them.

Ransom grabbed at Nila as he felt himself fall. They turned and twisted down through a dissolving murk. On both sides, he could see fragments of bloated green bodies floating off into spiraling vapor, red and violet areas writhing off into nothingness. Pertinnet and Risbummer, also clutching each other, were floating down slowly some distance away.

Nila huddled her warm and frightened body closer to his. "Those faces," she whimpered. "Those faces! Do you know whose they were? Hallock! Awful! How unbelievably awful!"

They *were* Hallock, Ransom remembered now. Ten thousand infernally grotesque caricatures—all the faces of the Brood Mother—were Wells W. Hallock's own face. And in that last moment, as he stepped into the creature, Hallock must have known it!

They came to rest in the midst of dazzling whiteness. They shut their eyes against the glare, opened them cautiously again. The glare subsided. Objects appeared indistinctly, became clearer, resolved into the sharp outlines of reality.

Then—no more obscene shapings, no more distorted vision. They were back in the hospital room, all of them, Ransom and Nila still shuddering with excitement. Dr. Pertinnet was unbuttoning the restraining blanket. He placed it carefully around the gory, broken mess on the bed.

"I—I'll get some sedatives for all of us," he said at last. Risbummer followed him through the door.

"Dr. Pertinnet and his sedatives!" Nila cried hysterically.

Ransom crossed to the table and lifted the small ivory chest. "This may not be in the best interests of scientific investigation, Nila, but I think we should destroy what's left of this stuff."

She grabbed the chest from him. "We certainly should," she agreed. "I'll dump it into the hospital incinerator. I'm through with dates for the rest of my life. But—of course—I'll settle for rice."

"A deal." He grinned at her. "If anyone should ask, a character by the name of Ransom Morrow has now had enough adventure to last clear through his grandchildren!"

She walked unsteadily through the door. A moment later Ransom heard the incinerator door open. He lit a cigarette and smiled at the cat. It was lucky not to have a human memory.

Then he stopped smiling. Because the cat had something round and black in its teeth. *And it wasn't a mouse.*

RICARDO'S VIRUS

Graff Dingle stolidly watched yellow mold form around the stiletto hole in his arm. He smelled the first faint jasmine odor of the disease and glanced up to where the sun glowed unhappily behind a mass of dirty clouds and wind-driven rain.

Dingle kicked morosely at the Heatwave thug left behind to ambush him, and the charred body turned soughingly in the mud. "Be seeing you, bully-boy, in about five and a half hours. Your electroblast may have missed me, but it cooked my antiseptic pouch into soup. It made that last knife-thrust really rate."

There was a dumb dryhorn blunder, Graff reflected, sneering at himself out of a face that was dark from life-long exposure to a huge sun. Bending over an enemy before making certain he was burned to a crisp.

But he'd had to search the man's clothing for a clue to the disappearance of Greta and Dr. Bergenson and—even above Greta—the unspeakably precious cargo of lobodin they'd been flying in from Earth.

So I'll pay for my hurry, he thought. *Like you always do in the Venusian jungle.*

Ricardo's Virus was viciously prompt: six hours after its light, saffron globules had formed in an open wound, you were dead. And no frantic surgery, no pathetic attempts at drainage, could save you. Graff should know. His parents, his brothers and sisters had been a small fraction of the New Kalamazoo death totals due to cuts and scratches observed too late for antisepsis. The virus had accounted for most of three generations of Venusian colonists, including Vilfredo Ricardo himself, the first man to set hesitant foot on the swampy planet. Ricardo had merely skinned his hand on his new flagpole.

Nasty to die of the filthy mold before he knew what had happened to the Bergensons. Not that he had a personal interest in the matter any more, for Greta wouldn't be marrying a corpse when she could pick any one of a hundred extremely live and woman-hungry pioneers. But her father was the only doctor in the tiny settlement. And the loss of the lobodin meant Ricardo's Virus would tuck many more New Kalamazoo colonists into seepy graves before the year was out.

A speck grew large in the sky. Graff involuntarily moved into the shade of a giant rosebush as his oversharp instincts asserted themselves.

Yes, it was a terry all right. Friendly?

The pterodactyl landed lightly on a frond of the opposite fern. Its absurd, leathery forehead wrinkled at him. Graff noted that it was barely out of range of his electroblast. Intelligent, sure enough, and an unusually fearless specimen to perch this close to man.

At any other time, he would have been intrigued by the opportunity of making friends with one of the intelligent winged reptiles who had learned to speak man's languages and, with good reason, shun his works. Now, he had other things on his mind.

Like dying painfully in a few hours.

Graff looked up sharply as enormous bat-like wings ceased their rustle.

The lizard-bird's long, sloping forehead wrinkled even further. Its beak opened and closed several times. It cleared its throat.

"City?"

Then it was civilized, too. What had induced it to leave its communal eyrie in the San Mountains? The terries had avoided men for over fifty years. Many was the time that Graff, intent on stalking meat for the colonists, had been startled by a flock of pterodactyls winging overhead and shouting curses down at him in the three languages of the early settlers.

"City?" the question was repeated more insistently. "Heatwave or New Kalamazoo?"

"New Kalamazoo."

A relieved nod of the triangular head. "This I thought. You wish knowledge which Heatwave man has man and girl from shif?"

Graff's whole body tensed. "Yes! Do you know?"

Another nod. "This I know. Name is Fuvina."

"Fuvina?" The hunter repeated it with a frown. He knew the names of most of Heatwave's big shots; some were political criminals, escaped from Earth. Others were former residents of his own town who had left in search of an easier living than the continual struggle with marshy soil and carnivorous jungle.

But he couldn't recall any Fuvina. Possibly a new arrival; possibly one of the smaller fry who had recently killed and looted his way to the top of bloody Heatwave society. Fuvina? Fuv—

Of course! The not-quite-flexible pterodactyl beak was incapable of labial sounds like *p* and *b*, and transformed them into the labiodentals *f* and *v*. Pubina! Max Pubina had left New Kalamazoo in a hurry three years ago after cutting some farmer's throat in a boundary dispute and, by combining organized raids on isolated families with the smuggling of the illicit Venusian dunging drug to Earth, had become a power of sorts.

"You mean Pubina?"

"This I said. Fuvina. He and other Heatwave men took man and girl from shif and placed them in own shif. Also took vig green vottle. Left one Heatwave man hidden here. Then flew that way in own shif." A fantastically large and fleshy wing gestured south. "Them I follow. Where Heatwave men stof, I see. Then I come vack."

The terry drew an immense swallow of air to compensate for his long speech and shook himself. The great fern trembled in sympathy.

Graff stepped forward from the rosebush and inspected his informant closely. "Thanks. But I don't see why you're interested."

The toothed beak, which was half as long as a man, opened uncertainly. "Vecause," the lizard-bird explained in a low voice, "Heatwave men have caftured my mate vefore attacking New Kalamazoo sky-shif. In cage they fut her for shivment to Earth. This I can do nothing about fy myself. Vut them I follow, hofing to find way to rescue her."

"And you figure that if you help me find my friends, I'll help you save your mate from the sideshows on Earth? Well, I will, *if*—"

A big, complex *if*, with as many tendrils as sucking ivy. If he lived long enough, and, if he did, if he would be sane enough—considering the agonizing last hour of Ricardo's Virus infection—to do anything constructive once he arrived at Pubina s jungle hideout. If a man, guided by a pterodactyl flying overhead, could pick his way on foot through a completely unexplored section of swamp and have enough juice left in him when he emerged to take the prize of the century away from the toughest collection of cutthroats on an extremely tough planet.

He clenched his fist as the cramps began in his left hand—the cramps that would spread slowly throughout his body until they ended in fatal convulsions some five hours from now. If a one-armed man could do all this, and do it with just one portable electroblast...

He cursed sharply, suddenly, as he realized he'd been holding the electroblast in his hand ever since he'd given the Heatwave thug that finishing jolt. That was after he'd been stabbed, after the man's first wild blast had burned Graff's antiseptic pouch into a mess of fused glass vials and blackened fabric. Without immediate application of the ten different antiseptic solutions.

But now! He inspected the bright metal of the coils anxiously. Might still do. Just might. He holstered the blaster with infinite tenderness and stooped over the blackened body that had almost disappeared into the mud. The man's electric gun was far too wet to be of any use, but Graff fumbled around in the soggy soil until he located the stiletto.

He straightened and grinned at the long blade, its steel already reddening from the pervasive rust of Venus.

"Where is the ship?" he asked. "The ship my friends were in?"

The terry nodded at a flat and soggy expanse. "Under there. Heatwave sky-shif wait here high uf. When New Kalamazoo shif come, Heatwave shif fly down fast ufon it. New Kalamazoo shif hit mud hard. This I see. Then Heatwave men take your friends away and New Kalamazoo shif sink in mud. Altogether are four Heatwave men, vesides Fuvina. You kill one, so now are only three, vesides Fuvina." The flying reptile breathed heavily again. Its scaly claws moved restlessly about on the branch.

Call that a break, Graff decided. Four men to handle. Might have been twenty. Either Pubina had a smaller gang than had been believed, or he was playing the whole thing really smart. Toughs, especially Venusian ones, would really chop each other to merry hell over the first laboratory sample of a vaccine that promised immunity from Ricardo's Virus. A break to balance the loss of the ship.

Or was it? All he had was the terry's word. Could be that the entire yarn about his mate being captured for export to the terran amusement parks was nothing more than a story made up by Pubina to play on a colonist's sympathy. The terry might be working for Pubina some way or other. Who knew anything about pterodactyls? Who knew if they experienced anything like love or loyalty?

Graff stared at the unwinking reptilian eyes, at the tapering ugly beak, both completely devoid of expression. Add another *if*.

"All right, MacDuff," he said at last, "lead on."

"We go in vig curve," the terry told him, flapping its wings monstrously in preparation for flight. "Eight, nine hours for you. Other way take half time, vut—"

"Vut nothing!" Graff broke in. He massaged his left forearm, which had begun aching in sympathy with the hand. "Let's use the shortcut."

"It too hard for you, too dangerous! River cuts across—"

"So I'll get my feet wet. I'm not in a position to be worried by pneumonia. Let's head for the straight and narrow, MacDuff. I'm in a hurry."

The creature cocked its head to one side, dropped its wings in a gesture like a shrug, and moved off the fern in a soaring glide southward. When it was about three hundred feet up, it circled back to make certain that Graff was following.

Now if you ever go to Venus, the Polar Continent is probably where you'll live for the duration of your stay. Not only is its temperature and annual rainfall the lowest on the planet (which makes it just a shade more uncomfortable than the Amazonian jungle), but also it is the most heavily populated stretch of land—averaging close to one person every thirty square miles.

But if you find yourself on the Polar Continent, you will be advised, and well-advised, to stay away from the Southern Peninsula. This is not merely because it is a dank and deadly swamp, but chiefly because of the Black River, which winds through the peninsula, doubling back on itself, crossing through itself and becoming a tributary of itself a dozen times over, like a living surrealist corkscrew.

The Black River rises somewhere in the unscalable peaks of the San Mountains and comes roaring into the flatlands with a tremendous velocity. Just before reaching the peninsula, however, it is joined by the Zetzot River, and the two of them make a combination that is really in a hurry. Even if there were no rain at all (which is definitely not the case!), there would be a perpetual mist over the Southern Peninsula. And by the time the Black gets through doubling back on itself, giving itself a shove, so to speak—well, the reason no one knows exactly where the river empties into the Jefferson Sea is because the entire area is completely obscured by an opaque steaming fog which boils about for miles on either side.

Nor is that all. Certain animals like to wallow in the swamp created by the Black. And most of them are very large. Creatures which can survive in the swamp of the Southern Peninsula are quite tough, quite dangerous, and most uniquely suited to their environment. There are snakes and insects and carnivorous plants galore, not to mention the huge creatures who live in quicksand and have yet to be classified. One of the smallest animals of the peninsula is a dark little fish which swims back and forth in the Black itself. Venusian colonists have christened it the sardine, possibly because it is the size of a terrestrial sardine. Its habits, however, resemble those of the South American piranha. It travels in large schools and eats its way through anything.

All in all, the Southern Peninsular Swamp is an ideal home for a baron of crime who wants to get away from it all. The *all* doesn't include law, of course. On Venus, each man writes his own code of laws with the weapon he finds handiest.

The trouble was, Graff Dingle reflected as he found a ford and leaped across the screaming waters to the opposite bank, the trouble was that his folks and people like them had come to Venus to get away from lawlessness of the international kind, only to hit the inevitable individual lawlessness of a frontier.

Ordinarily, a frontier is slowly and surely transformed from rowdy wide-openness into suburban quietude by the increase in population—but population doesn't increase in really dangerous spots; that's why the people of New Kalamazoo worked so hard and so long to make their settlement large enough to merit the establishment of a university. A university would mean laboratories and research facilities to investigate Ricardo's Virus and all the lesser plagues peculiar to Venus, the plagues which took more lives yearly than jungle monsters and murderous Heatwavers combined; and a university would mean an increase in population, and law and order.

But Earth hadn't been interested. The study of Venusian diseases was an exotic subject hardly touched upon in Terran medical schools. Earth had been far too busy manufacturing artificial diseases to supplement atom bombs and hydrogen bombs.

Earth had, however, investigated the Venusian plagues with a view to their use in biological warfare. And out of the investigation, as an accident, as a byproduct, had come lobodin. A vaccine, not a serum. No good for Graff right now, for he was almost two full hours into the yellow death.

He worked his left arm around slowly, wincing with each turn, his eyes on the terry above him circling southward in the damp murky sky. At the same time, he tried to plant the broad soles of his boots on mud that wasn't quicksand, on rotten twigs that wouldn't crack too loudly. He knew his blood was now completely infiltrated with the obscene little yellow specks.

Pubina was probably trying to force Dr. Bergenson to inject the vaccine into him, ridiculing the old man's protests that all the bottle held was a starter culture, just enough so that with weeks of careful tending they might have sufficient vaccine to immunize the children.

It had been so expensive and difficult for the little colony to send Dr. Bergenson and Greta to Earth, where his reputation and connections had enabled him to wheedle a spoonful of the precious stuff out of a government laboratory! Pubina hadn't been able to get it, for all of his bribes and underworld contacts. But the bribes and underworld contacts had served another purpose: Pubina had discovered when the Bergensons were due to return—and that was all he really needed.

Graff noticed abruptly that the terry was falling rapidly back at him. Could he be trying to warn—

A shriek gave him the answer. Less than a quarter-mile away, a brontosaurus squatted its tremendous bulk in a shallow pool and regarded him from the end of an undulating snake-like neck. The animal screamed again, and Graff froze.

He watched the incredibly heavy reptile scramble to its feet and desperately tried to think. It wasn't a brontosaurus charge you had to be afraid of, but what usually traveled in its wake. A brontosaurus was herbivorous and, for all its size, extremely timid. It was ridiculous, possibly, but the mountain of living flesh was probably screaming in terror at the sight of him. You only had to control yourself and think while the great beast charged.

Because a brontosaurus meets danger by running into it. It is so massive that it is virtually unstoppable once in motion. You can blast its stupid little head off and it will keep running for another twenty minutes, powered by the bundle of nerve cells just under the spine. You just have to stand still and remember that it is much more frightened than you and is trying to trample you to death before you can bite it.

Graff stood his ground, bending his knees slowly, until the behemoth was only twenty-five feet away. Then he straightened suddenly and leaped off to the right, then again, further, and again, still further to the right.

Screaming insanely, the tons upon tons of flesh roared past, absolutely unable to halt itself. Its momentum carried it up a small hill, and Graff could hear it bellowing down the other side. It wouldn't return.

But something else was on its way. There's always a meat-eater in the wake of a brontosaurus. Sometimes there are several. The *kind* of carnivore was very important to Graff right now. He had an electroblast which he wasn't certain would work in an emergency and whose diminished power he'd certainly need later. And he had a stiletto.

He heard the beast thumping its way through the luxuriant weeds of the swamp. A moment later it had broken into the clear, had seen him, and was loping toward him easily with all the confidence of a powerful creature which sees an easy meal in sight.

A shata. No larger than a terran wolf. But if a brontosaurus can be said to be all body-bulk and very little head, the shata is just the reverse. Twelve rows of teeth, and jaws which open wide enough to admit a sheep. Regretfully and a little uncertainly, Graff holstered the electroblast and balanced the stiletto on his palm. He'd hunted lots of shata in his time, but never with a knife.

He began weaving about, conscious of his awkwardness. The knots in his left side constantly made him misjudge his body and slip off balance. And here he was hoping to take four men at a time—

As he expected, the shata was confused by his peculiar motion. It slowed to a dead stop, then slunk before him, growling. It moved in half-circles, coming in closer each time. Graff waited until it was directly in front of him. He stood still, and immediately the shata sprang, jaws gaping.

The palate. Just behind the palate is the brain. It means sticking half your arm into a fearful set of jaws, but do it right.

Graff let the rigid, distended head slide off the knife and into the mud. He wiped his blade on the green fur, standing out like so many spikes, and grimaced. A nice specimen. Shatas were good eating, too.

Well, he wasn't a hunter any more. He was a dead man looking for a coffin. He was swamp-bait if he collapsed in this weedy muck.

The terry skimmed by with his head turned questioningly.

"I'm fine," Graff reassured him. "How much farther?"

"Vetween one and two of your hours." The lizard-bird curved up and ahead, leathery wings beating slowly.

Graff plodded on. He should arrive with about an hour and a half of life left. That would give him a half-hour to an hour at most in which to operate consciously and more or less effectively. After that, there would be half an hour of writhing agony, leading into unconsciousness. After that, he would be dead.

He'd hate to leave life. It meant leaving the thrill of tracking your quarry on the bracing slope of Mount Catiline where the dodle breeds in the Season of Wind-Driven Rains; it meant leaving a wild new world that was just a-borning as far as humanity was concerned; it meant leaving Greta Bergenson.

It also meant leaving wealth. Now that lobodin had been developed, the colonization of Venus would begin in earnest. He was the last alive of a numerous family who had homesteaded half the Galertan Archipelago into their possession. He was heir to all the rich, fertile, and deserted islands his father and brothers had claimed. With Ricardo's Virus taken care of, future Venusian farmers would pay well for those scattered spots of soil in the Jefferson Sea.

Following the terry, he hit the river again. He started downstream, looking for a ford as he had before. The Black was rather wide at this point, and he wasted fifteen precious minutes before he found a bank that curved near enough to the opposite one to permit a leap. He went into the weeds to get a running start.

A shadow plummeted past him.

"Vack," the terry screamed. "Get vack! Don't jumf here. Gridnik!"

Graff paused and peered across the river. Sure enough, there was the brown and white nest on the opposite bank where he would have landed. As he watched, a single gridnik droned out, looking like a winged red ant but with the size and disposition of a large, cornered rat.

"Thanks, MacDuff," he muttered, moving away. Well, there was no help for it. He didn't have time to look for another ford. He'd have to swim.

He waited on the crumbling bank until a dozen blue flashes swept past under him. "Sardine" schools were usually far enough apart to permit a fast swimmer to get through between them. When the tiny blue fish were fifty feet away, he dived.

The force of the river knocked the breath out of him. He fought his way through the torrent. His flailing hands touched a projecting piece of rock, and he hauled himself painfully up the bank.

Graff noted gratefully that his head was clearer. The gnawing headache had diminished somewhat under the impact of the water.

The pterodactyl alighted near him. "There," it said, pointing ahead with a yellow claw. "Fuvina."

But the hunter was interested in something else. He removed his electroblast and examined its coils ruefully. The tight holster was supposed to be fairly waterproof, but it had not been intended for protecting a weapon in the Black River.

He started to throw it aside, but held it as he remembered how few cards he held in his hand.

Max Pubina's hideout was a large prefabricated job that must have cost a medium-sized fortune to import from Earth across some thirty million miles of empty space. The outlaw's house covered the top of a rise, and the soil around it was sufficiently high over the swamp proper to resemble the fine farmland of New Kalamazoo. Rich jungle growths were held at bay by a patch of sandy ground completely surrounding the house. It made it impossible for anyone or anything to creep up to the walls unobserved. Graff Dingle knew how expensive it must have been to sterilize so large an area of ground.

Crime does not pay, he mused. *Except on Venus.*

He reconnoitered the place cautiously, keeping well under cover. The man-made yard was empty. There was no one outside the house or the rocketship hangar attached to it. He could see the blunt nose of Pubina's sleek craft in the otherwise-deserted hangar. But they probably had guards posted at the windows.

A long white line traced a curve in his path. Graff stepped over it gingerly, glancing to the left. Sure enough, hidden in thick bushes was the mass of white filaments that was the bulk of the sucking ivy. Touch the trigger-vine, however gently, with your foot…

He came back to the terry. "Listen, MacDuff," he said, "I want you to stay out of trouble as long as possible. When I need you, I'll need you bad. Meanwhile, on the wing or on the ground, you're a sucker for an electroblast with that wingspread. But you could be useful as a lookout. I wouldn't like to be outflanked."

A grave nod of the narrow beak. "This I do." The reptile soared up in a high spiral over the house.

Now. He had to get into the house across thirty-five feet of open ground, under the electroblasts of four highly proficient murderers. How?

The headache returned, stronger than ever, and Graff swayed dizzily. Red roaring fires tore up and down his left side. He'd never make it. Swamp-bait, that's all he was, bait for the mud of the Black.

He straightened then and laughed. Bait? Well, that was one way to hunt.

The hunter strode toward the house, across the creeper of sucking ivy, counting each step. He stopped under cover of a sweeping fern just outside the sandy expanse.

"Pubina!" he yelled. "I've come for the Bergensons."

There was a flicker at one of the windows. "Who are you?"

"Graff Dingle of New Kalamazoo. Listen, Pubina, I'll trade the rest of our lobodin for Greta Bergenson and her father."

A pause while they digested this. Then: "Send one of your men in, and we'll talk it over, Dingle."

"Can't. I'm alone. Send one of your men out with the Bergensons, and I'll give you the lobodin."

No reason for Pubina to be certain that the Bergenson lobodin represented the first and only shipment. And what he claimed to have would raise the quantity to the point where all of the outlaws could be vaccinated.

The terry came down behind him and whispered gently, "Three men leave house from rear. Two coming around on left, one on right. Man on right has clearer fath, so will ve here first."

Graff gestured assent with the electroblast. He heard the terry take off again.

Pubina was being safe and cozy. Sending his henchmen while he held the fort himself!

He heard a soggy clump to the right and grinned. Why, the man was making more noise than a dryhorn freshly arrived from Terra! When he saw the black waterproof jumper through the high weeds, he stepped out from under the fern and moved backwards. He held the electroblast out, as if it worked.

The outlaw's face, lined with years of dunging inhalation, broke into a lunatic smile. Since Graff wasn't looking at him, he deduced Graff hadn't seen him. Pubina's henchman took larger steps. Graff backed.

He counted as he retreated. He counted slowly, taking steps that were uniform and even, looking off to the side of the outlaw, trying to keep his tortured body from making a deadly misstep.

There! He breathed gustily as he saw he'd passed the white line. The outlaw crept forward, crouching, trying to get close enough for a certain blast. He too noticed the trigger-vine and stepped daintily across it.

Graff whirled to face him then, electroblast at the ready. The man jumped—and one boot dug into the creeper!

He barely had time to scream. A haze of white tendrils whipped around him, each armed with thousands of microscopic suckers. A moment later, the bloodless husk that had been a human was being dropped from the sucking ivy's clutches, rattling like so much paper.

The scream had been heard. Graff's jungle-trained ears caught the whispers of the other two men on his left as they conferred worriedly. If only he had a decent weapon. Anything besides the stiletto! He could take such dryhorns with an old-fashioned pistol!

But he didn't have a pistol. All he had was twenty-seven years of experience on Venus as a native-born citizen. So he began to run.

He stopped after a moment and listened. The crashes behind him indicated he was being pursued. If he was afraid, the outlaws had evidently decided, he was weak enough to chase. Graff ran toward the Tuscany.

By the time he reached the river, he was weaving from side to side and sobbing. The exertion magnified his pain a thousand fold. His pursuers were getting closer. Desperately, he trotted downstream.

They were quite close now. He heard them chuckling and calling to each other triumphantly—but there was the gridnik nest!

He waited just a moment, poised on the bank of the river, until they broke into the clear, almost within electroblast range. Then, as they caught sight of him and increased their speed, he hurled his useless weapon into the striped little dome—and jumped.

When he came threshing out of the water, twenty feet further down the bank, the hideous swarm of insects were still gorging themselves. Graff crept away, nauseated. He rubbed his eyes against the darkness welling within them.

"MacDuff!" he called, his voice crackling with agony. "MacDuff!"

The terry swept down to his side.

"Listen, pal, I haven't got much time left, so we'll have to hurry. No more fancy stuff. Think you can fly in the rear windows or something, by way of diversion? It'll give me time to cross the sandy stretch."

Without a word, the lizard-bird went away. Graff came to the edge of the arid soil surrounding the pre-fab and waited.

He saw the enormous shadow tilt down behind the house and heard the crash of breaking glass. He threw himself forward. Sand boiled away from his boots. His head wobbled as if his neck had ceased to exist. Must be getting close to deadline time, Graff decided. A few minutes more at most before he caved in completely. He drew the stiletto out, holding it with difficulty in a twitching hand.

There was a yell inside the house and the sizzle of an electroblast bolt. As he smashed into the door, he heard the electroblast go off again.

He saw a huge cage holding a fluttering pterodactyl as he tottered into the living room. Dr. Bergenson and Greta were tied to chairs with long coils of fongool vine. Greta's pink overall-jumper was ripped, and there was the mark of a man's hand on her face. Pubina stood under a charred hole in the ceiling where his first blast had gone wild. At his feet, a hole neatly burned in one wing, writhed MacDuff, awaiting the finisher.

Pubina whirled to face Graff, his electroblast coming up swiftly. The hunter staggered toward him, fully conscious of his lack of speed, his almost infantile weakness. Knots of pain pulled at his knees.

The Heatwaver's forefinger flicked down on the firing button. MacDuff lifted himself on his one good wing and lunged at the boot before him. His long beak closed on Pubina's ankle. There was a horrible bony crunch, and the outlaw cursed, turning to beat down at the reptile.

Graff reached them, almost falling against Pubina. For a moment, he couldn't coordinate his arm muscles enough to use the stiletto; then, sinking his teeth deep into his own lip, he drove the thin blade ahead. Pubina shrieked and fell, the stiletto throbbing in his side.

Deciding to let MacDuff finish him, even if the terry was making a mess of it, Graff bent over clumsily and retrieved the electroblast Pubina had dropped. He almost went over backwards as he straightened.

Placing one foot in front of the other intently, he walked to the Bergensons. He slid like a man walking on banana skins. Darkness roiled all about him now, and every cell in his body seemed to writhe.

The bottle containing the vaccine was on a table, he noticed. It was still full; the shining hypodermic beside it was empty. Good.

Very carefully, he burned off the fongool vine with the electroblast at low power. Greta rushed toward him, but he slipped and fell at her feet.

"Darling," he heard her sob; it sounded as if her voice were on the other side of the Jefferson Sea. "You're infected! Oh, Graff, Graff! The lobodin won't work on an infected case!"

"I know," he muttered thickly, and let his head loll round to where the terry was inching along the floor to the cage in the corner. The last thing he saw was the neat little hole in the wing.

"Be seeing you, MacDuff," Graff whispered as the darkness came down, pin-pointed with multitudes of exploding yellow dots…

That was why he was so surprised when he opened his eyes to see the terry perched by his bed with a neat patch of gauze taped to one wing.

"How in hell did you pull through, MacDuff?" he asked.

"The same as you," the lizard-bird told him. 'We are voth natives of Venus."

"Huh?" He raised himself waveringly on one elbow. He was lying in the Bergenson home in New Kalamazoo. They must have used Pubina's rocketship to fly back. "What do you mean—*native*?"

"Just what he says, Graff." Greta pushed open the screen-door and bustled in with a pile of linen. "You were both born on Venus. Father says that you must have had all kinds of skin abrasions as an infant: your body developed a natural immunity to Ricardo's Virus. We'll still use the vaccine on everybody else, including the children, just to be on the safe side. But Father has felt for a long time that the blood of the pioneers would adjust to its environment. When you got sick but didn't die, you proved it."

"Well, I'd like to point out," Graff said, as he sat up to permit Greta to change his sheets, "that I am very, very happy to have given your father a chance to prove that theory."

MacDuff closed a lidless eye in an assenting reptilian wink.

THE PUZZLE OF PRIIPIIRII

The bravely questing light of Hartwick's helmet beam disclosed the tunnel abruptly becoming five more as it dipped sharply down. He halted, perplexedly scratching his transparent visor with a metal-gloved hand.

Unable to stop short, Boule, the expedition's photographer, tripped into him, cursed, and cursed again as the three scientists piled up against his back with weirdly echoing crashes of spacesuit against spacesuit.

"Careful, Hartwick, careful!" Lutzman's bass voice warned into their headsets from the rear. "Another tangle like that, and we'll rip the line to Bhishani."

The guide nodded abstractedly at the bioareologist. He spent a long, careful glance at the faintly fluorescing cable connecting the loops in their suits and stretching lengthily behind them through corridor after intersecting corridor to the assistant archaeologist on the surface. The cable was their link with life.

"Five more branchings," he stated at last, pointing ahead.

"An honest-to-Minotaur labyrinth," Punnello, the senior archaeologist, muttered as he extricated himself from between Boule and Lutzman and peered over Hartwick's shoulder. "We differ from Theseus only in that we use an insulated wire instead of a spool of thread."

"And that we won't find a Martian version of the bull-man monster in the heart of this neurotic temple," the bioareologist pointed out. "Not that I look forward to it; he'd be rather hungry after—how long?"

Punnello shrugged his shoulders resoundingly. "At least a quarter of a million years since Priipiirii had a worshipper. No, from those wall friezes we've been passing, I'd say he was as crustacean as the race which conceived him."

"Which isn't very crustacean according to Earth standards," Lutzman observed. "Why does he continually change his sex? When we dug away the sand and stepped through that first trapdoor on the roof, there was a large statue of him as a male in front of the cross-passage. After the first level, there were only female representations; they became hermaphrodite and later neuter. Down here, he shifts back and forth through all four in each frieze. And yet the Priipiirii ideogram on each of his pictures is unmistakable.

"Why, for that matter, isn't there an occasional hint of the daily life of the average mortal, such as we found in the other temples? They showed their gods being worshipped and occasionally disregarded; here, there is a steady reiteration of Priipiirii only—Priipiirii at work and at play, as it were. Odd, that business of play, considering how evil other Martians thought him."

"Don't *you*?" Boule asked suddenly. "I've been snapping flash shots of this jovial character in all his phases, and I like him less all the time. I don't know why ancient Mars tabooed him, but he sure radiates the impression of happy executioner. Frankly, I'm sorry I came on this jaunt. I don't relish wandering around in the place where the Martian devil was worshipped, and I still haven't accepted those trapdoors on the roof of the temple—as if the inhabitants knew it would be buried by the desert one day."

Hartwick paused in the middle of an impatient gesture at the five tunnels ahead of them and swept his helmet light through the gloom until it came to rest on Boule's visored face. Back in Bubbleburg, when he'd been commissioned to lead an expedition to the fabled temple of Priipiirii, the Martian Archaeological Foundation had assured him that the scientists of the party would all be picked, psycho-certified men.

But they'd said nothing about guaranteeing the photographer's stability, the desert guide remembered uncomfortably. Boule was one of the few lens-hounds in the archaeological paradise that the dead planet had become: he'd taken pictures of the early excavations at Gulthum and Yeyarneh when the first mumbling hints of the Priipiirii cult had been noticed; he was a logical choice.

"Very possibly, they suspected the end of their canal civilization would invite the desert to creep forward again," Punnello suggested. "I'll admit it is rare to the point of nonexistence for a race to build with a view to its own extinction, but remember what a highly intellectualized—rather than mechanicalized—culture the Martians enjoyed. They were definitely telepathic, probably prescient, too. And the reason why Priipiirii frightens you so, seems so alive—"

"If you don't also feel he's alive, why use the present tense?"

"Hah?" The archaeologist's jaw sagged against his facepiece.

"All right!" Hartwick's voice interrupted brusquely. "The big question right now has nothing to do with whether this purple crayfish has horns or a forked tail. Down which of these five holes do you professors want to be led? The slope is getting sharper all the time, so we have to be twice as careful as a trip to Mercury. And if we meet any reincarnations, Boule, don't forget that you, Lutzman, and Punnello each have deadly little kazoos in your mitts, and I'm carrying a bazooka."

I only wish you weren't holding any *sort of rocket weapon, Boule,* he added to himself. *Talk like that in a place like this!*

The archaeologist turned to Lutzman. "Considering the one-sided sensory orientation of the architects, I think we might as well continue bearing hard to the left. Seems correct, up to now."

"Left?" Lutzman turned from a frowning examination of a mural depicting Priipiirii swimming twistedly in a canal—the back of his thorax and the front of his abdomen submerged. "Not necessarily if—"

They all spun round as the hideous clatter began in their rear. The bioareologist stepped forward and squinted up the incline that slanted past multitudinous passageways to the desert surface.

"It's Bhishani!" he shouted. "Must have fallen through the trapdoor and couldn't get to his feet in time!"

Hartwick wasted a quick glance for the sake of certainty at the limb-threshing figure rolling toward them like a compact avalanche. "Get over to the wall!" he yelled. "If he hits us—"

He ran to his right, dragging Boule with him, while Lutzman and Punnello scrambled to the opposite side. Before either pair could correct their error, the Hindu archaeologist bounded into the taut cable connecting them across the tunnel and snapped them around him in a churning conglomeration of bodies.

They bounced hurtfully through the center corridor, ricocheted against a slanting wall, and crashed agonizingly to rest upon four red idols on the floor of a spherical room.

Hartwick was on his feet first, testing his suit for leaks and using muscle-flexes to determine if any of his bones were broken. Finding nothing, he reached down and angrily turned Bhishani on his back. "Do you realize what you've done?"

The assistant archaeologist's face sickened to blue under its smashed visor. "Felt a tug on the line," he gasped thinly into his headset. "Lifted trapdoor—leaned over—slipped—not my fault—why did you tug on—" His throat rattled in the almost airless cold.

"Hey, Lutzman!" the guide snapped at the Martian biologist, who was groaning himself into an upright position. "Fast! Help me work his headscreen over the crack in the visor."

Together, they tugged at the round piece of metal at the top of the helmet. The headscreen, too, had been bent by the fall. It was stuck tight. Hartwick abruptly stopped working on its broken hinges and tore it out of place. He fitted it rapidly around the visor and snapped the emergency clips into position. But by the time he saw the rip in Bhishani's oxygen tank, the man's body had relaxed out of life.

"Poor guy," Boule muttered. "Gone just like that."

Punnello was also on his feet. "Perhaps—some of our oxygen—"

"Not a chance," the guide told him. "Mars is too fast for you."

"I can't understand how he felt a tug on the line. If any of us pulled at it, the others would have noticed."

"Work it out tomorrow," Hartwick invited. "Meanwhile, the only way we can be sure of getting out of this lunatic maze is by following the cable while it still reaches to the surface. Let's go!"

He started for the tunnel opening where the wire lay slack, his companions following. The line was piled inside the tunnel mouth, coil upon scrambled coil!

"Bhishani must have torn it loose when he fell in," Lutzman almost squeaked. He regained control of his voice. "And the desert wind blew it down."

Hartwick nodded and kept going. "It's still roaring. You can feel the rattle of sand on your visor. We can find the trapdoor that way."

He stopped a moment later as the wind disappeared. "Trapdoor must have been blown shut. But the sand makes a track."

The winding path of sand drifted down casually, lazily—but completely. It went past them into the room of four idols and collected in little piles upon the harsh stone floor. Ahead of them, they could see that the tunnels were perfectly clean under the glare of their helmet beams.

"You can't call this an accident," Boule began in a high voice.

"Shut up! I think I can remember the turns we took. We simply reverse them going back. Let's keep moving before it gets hazy."

With Hartwick leading, they raced up the weirdly offshooting corridors in their ungainly spacesuits. Their helmet lights made the rapidly successive friezes of the temple's god seem like a jerky motion picture. Suddenly, the guide slowed to a walk.

"What's the matter?" Punnello gasped from the rear.

"No slope. It's gone level, and we should still be climbing."

They came round a curve in the tunnel—and into the spherical room. Bhishani's body lay near one of the idols. Piles of sand....

One by one, they filed in. Boule said huskily, "A circle."

Hartwick rang a fist against his open metal palm. "Look," he said at last. "Maybe I'm hearing the flutter of bat wings in my bell tower, but I have the odd idea that the maze was rearranged."

"Obviously," Punnello nodded. "The gradient which was present everywhere when we came down has disappeared. But I suggest—and for other reasons than because that way madness lies—that we temporarily gloss over that explanation of our failure to escape—er, to reach the trapdoor. I suggest we concentrate on things like routes."

"It does seem—" the bioareologist cleared his throat. "No."

Boule walked over to the four idols and examined the table at which they sat. "Saea! They're playing a game of saea. *Saea!*"

Hartwick, having observed him remove his kazoo from its holster, unslung his bazooka cautiously. "Know anything about saea, docs?" he asked, his eyes on the photographer. "Does it help?"

"Not very much," Punnello said slowly as he too looked down at the odd altar. "Directions for play have been deciphered in every Martian ruin, but it's a little too rich for our cerebral blood. The rules are a cross between chess and the Japanese game of *Go,* with the addition of crevices where pieces can be held out of play for a varying number of moves. Why a sculptured problem in saea, now?"

Lutzman moved up. "And do you notice who the players are? Our old friend Priipiirii—all four of him!" He swept an arm around at each enormous scarlet idol. "Masculine, feminine, hermaphrodite, neuter."

"Red's the Martian color of death, isn't it?" the guide inquired.

Punnello nodded abstractedly. "And life. In fact, the combination of the two expresses it better. Here, perhaps— Suppose we work on less metaphysical subjects. Much safer, at the moment."

They agreed rather hastily. Hartwick drew a stylus and a sheet of recordio film from his flank canister; the four of them squatted on the floor near the body of the assistant archaeologist and discussed the matter of routes. They argued about each turn they had taken until they were all convinced of each one. The guide copied the list backwards, in the order which they would come across the intersections while returning. Then, they left the room again, carefully reversing each change of direction.

Fifteen minutes later they were back. They discussed the list, made a few alterations and once more left through the tunnel in which the cable was piled.

The sixth time they came back, Hartwick scaled the sheet of recordio out into one of the tunnels. It spun away, drifted easily back, and floated to the floor.

"One last idea," he said. "This *has* to work."

"What's the use?" Boule demanded. "Let's admit what we're all thinking and really get someplace."

Hartwick tightened his grip on the bazooka. "I don't know," he said with a grim attempt at humor. "Are we all thinking?"

The archaeologist shrugged. "We start with the premise that we are the first humans in this temple, and that no humans on Mars have any desire to do us harm."

"Check," the guide told him softly. "Just carry that ball, doc."

"We accept, though on less evidence, that there are no extrasolar creatures operating here, since there was no indication of this site being disturbed and no one has previously observed such creatures in the system. Furthermore, there is no race in the system, other than humanity, which possesses intelligence. Finally, for almost a hundred thousand years, the only animal life which has existed on Mars is the extremely primitive polar beetle. Therefore, the tugging at the line, the death of Bhishani, the loss of the wire path to the surface, all of our difficulties—including the apparent rearrangement of the labyrinth—may be laid to mechanical contrivances which the temple's builders left behind them out of viciousness or religion.

"Such contrivances are not rare in Terrestrial temples, especially of this type. However, we have the fact that Martians tended more to things intellectual—the esthetic and philosophical, say—than to material enterprise. All that we have seen on Mars supports this view: it would seem to be accentuated among this particular people, where, with the exception of the trapdoors, not one remotely mechanical device has been observed. And if you add the almost sentient malevolence with which we have been frustrated, *logic* leaves only—"

"Only what?"

"Priipiirii," Lutzman finished very gently for the archaeologist. "Priipiirii, an evil deity."

"Well, I'll be— I've been sitting on that notion like crazy, but I never thought a bunch of scientists could swallow it!"

"Reject the implausible," Punnello intoned as if the words were a hymn, "and what is left is the plausible."

"It's true, isn't it?" the photographer demanded. "You feel he's alive, he's near us, don't you?"

Hartwick looked from one helmeted face to the other, his beam stabbing three separate times around their heads to the curved walls. Then he sat down.

"All right. I'll admit I believe it. But why should I?"

"Well," the archaeologist sank his head on his chest and minced a tiny, meditative circle. "It has been suggested that the powers ascribed to some of the Terrestrial deities really existed, at one time or another, in some form or another; that the very act of widespread belief in a particular god called forth *something* like that god with *some* of his powers on a *temporary* basis. Now, generally, this theory may well be grit for the herds; but here, where you have a race intellectualized out of all human conception, that had achieved a philosophical level higher than the scientific one we may reach in a thousand years, a race that had telepathy, possibly prescience of a sort, and various mental facets outside the scope of our imagination—such a race might well create a living god from its collective mind. A sort of racial super-*id*."

"But why would they need a god? With all that mental equipment, I just can't see them praying exactly."

"Prayer and sacrifice, and the granting of favors thereby, is only one of the uses of a divinity. He can fill certain psychological needs which the race may even recognize as such. For example, the warlike inhabitants of Asgard rarely gave boons to suffering Norsemen; they carried on a constant heaven-shattering warfare, however, in the last great battle of which humanity was merely an inconsequential ally. They typified the precarious, bloody existence of the race which had conceived them: they were satisfactory."

"I see that. But how did we get Priipiirii into the psychic flesh again?"

"By thinking about him, by believing in him. Those wall friezes were probably not designed for that purpose, but seeing them helped solidify our mental pictures of the god. I think Boule was the first affected, since it was his job to take photos of the most significant sculptures. All of us were slightly, as these people knew how to pack an esthetic wallop—but Boule most of all. When he came to believe that Priipiirii was alive—well, Bhishani felt a tug on the line."

Hartwick exhaled against his visor. "Okay, I'll ride along. But we have a little problem of diminishing oxygen. We do what?"

"Find out what he wants," Boule replied loudly. "And give it to him. Sacrifices, propitiation—"

The archaeologist shook his head. "Not sacrifices, necessarily. Propitiation, if we can deduce enough of his innate qualities to make it possible. But that will be very difficult, considering the alien quality of his former worshippers, the very little data and time we have available for deductions— Hello! Speak of the devil, and you do get data!"

Above their heads, in the exact center of the room, a violet cloud had appeared. Luxuriously, it formed itself into the familiar figure of Priipiirii—masculine version.

Invisible fear dripped through their airtight suits and drenched their skins.

Lutzman rose, his eyes narrowed. "Why do you suppose he shows himself? Because we all admit belief in him now? Because he wants to gloat over our helplessness? Because he's vain? He doesn't seem interested in making any overt move—all he can do, hanging up there like that, is confuse the issue. He's a very damn puzzling god."

"He wants worshippers, he wants sacrifices," Boule insisted. "All of the dying-god cults on Earth follow that pattern. It *must* be the same on Mars. Changing from sex to sex—I read somewhere that was a manifestation of what they call a dying-god. Right, Punnello?"

"No. Occasionally there is a hint of hermaphroditism or feminization in some of the dying gods Earth has known in the past. But not all four forms at once. Not even on Mars—"

"What's to prevent us from no longer believing in him?" Hartwick wanted to know. "Then he and his powers no longer exist."

"With all these statues and pictures around you? Hah! That's like that game— 'don't think of a white horse!' No, we have to work out the component parts of his nature. This race engaged in both sex and agriculture in a very offhand—or offclaw—way, so he couldn't be a regenerative deity. Now, can anyone say what's *really* intellectual?"

No answer. They stared up at the carelessly undulating horror.

"I want to examine his solidity," Lutzman observed suddenly and slipped his kazoo from its holster. Boule and Hartwick both leaped at him—a moment tardily.

The tiny rocket shell whizzed through the hovering monster and exploded against the domed ceiling. A crack appeared in the highly polished stone, was wiped abruptly clean again as Priipiirii shot over toward it. He raced around the inner room as if inspecting it for further damage. Finding none, he resumed his position.

Hartwick had reached Lutzman first and plucked his weapon away with a muscled grab. Out of the corner of his eye, he saw Boule jerk to a stop and level his kazoo at the specialist in Martian biology.

He swung back again fast, desperately. Boule pressed the firing stud and threw himself aside. The rocket hissed past Hartwick; an immense gong seemed to ring in their headphones as Lutzman exploded before he could scream.

The guide tottered past Boule, sickeningly off balance. He knew the gun was centered on his back, that momentum was carrying him too fast in the heavy suit to permit him to turn and fire first. And there were three more rockets in the kazoo's chamber....

He cursed all unstable photographers and the dim-witted archaeological foundations that permitted them to go on such highly charged expeditions without adequate psychological probing. He heard the sibilant exhalation of a shell, and his body tried to hold itself together against the moment when it would be ripped apart.

Then there was the explosion—and he was still alive.

Hartwick turned slowly. There were clean bits of metal and ugly shreds of flesh all over the room. Outside of the twisting, somehow exultant Priipiirii, he and Punnello were alone.

The archaeologist sheathed the kazoo with which he had killed Boule before he could fire at Hartwick. "Sacrifice," he mumbled distractedly. "He was trying to sacrifice you as well as Lutzman for having blasphemed. The fool! I tried to tell him Terrestrial standards of divinity didn't apply. He was so desperate of his own life, so anxious to placate— Imagine trying to propitiate a god with the subtle origins of Priipiirii by a hideously blunt sacrifice!"

"Blunt or no, that little rumpus sure cut down our strength. By any other name, they're still sacrifices—and from the look of that crayfish, I'd say he was enjoying them. Thanks for the shot, doc."

Punnello nodded and grimaced at the crustacean god, who was now writhing in unmistakable ecstasy. "Evil, evil. Yet it's obvious there's no direct malice involved. With his powers—consider the ease with which he patched the hole in the ceiling— he could undoubtedly dispose of us in unnumbered horrific ways. Somehow or other, we *are* giving him the kind of worship he wants—how? The god of the most advanced and most decadent of the mind-stretching Martians—from what we've deciphered in the other tombs, we know that his people were both detested and immensely re- spected. But what is he?"

Hartwick frowned. "Look, I've been wondering. All those pictures of him we saw as we came down, the ones you said made us believe in him. Couldn't they have been put there just for that purpose?"

"No. Much more likely, they were meant to help the creatures who worshipped him, by giving them clues as what to expect. It just occurred to me: this god or super- Martian, who was created out of the united aspirations and interests of a race, prob- ably destroyed it. There is every indication that he is highly egocentric; the other temples hinted at his destructiveness. They didn't discuss *him*, however; almost as if they were too close to worship themselves."

The guide nodded and pulled a long stick of chalk from his flank canister. "Save it. I don't think you could work out his nature if you stood on your head and walked around on your ears. Who knows what in space those brainy crayfish considered holy? And if we did figure it out, how much chance would we have of giving him what he wants? No, let it ride. I said I had one last idea as to how to crack this joint—let's try it."

Gently, Punnello smiled at the chalk. "Oh, that. No, I'm afraid it won't work. If he can rearrange the maze, if he can repair holes we make in the stone with our rocket shells—"

He walked slowly to the four idols sitting about their involved game. "Somehow, I'm positive that this is the answer. Why all four manifestations of Priipiirii playing saea against each other? Why an altar which is nothing more than a problem in saea? If we can solve the problem, now, it might loosen something essential in the god's powers. There had to be a reason for this stone game."

"Listen, doc," Hartwick urged. "I've seen too many archaeologists talking through the top of their heads because they tried to learn saea. And this problem they set up here is bound to be ultimate stuff. Give it the go-by, and come with me."

Punnello hadn't heard. He was standing before the board, studying the carved pieces carefully. From time to time, he made motions with a metal-covered hand.

Hartwick shrugged and strode into the cable-littered tunnel. He bent over and made a cross on the floor every ten steps. "If my oxygen holds out, I should make it," he pondered. "No more circle-walking."

After he had gone a hundred feet, he gave up and wandered aimlessly: Chalk cross-marks had appeared on the floor ahead, in every tunnel....

When he arrived in the spheroid room again, he walked directly to Punnello's gesticulating figure. He froze when he saw the archaeologist's contorted face, now screaming at the four red idols, now raised in anguish to the god floating in his carnate purple. He understood the muted gibberings he had been hearing in the headset for the past fifteen minutes—and had dismissed as Punnello's necessary self-communion over the saea problem.

Punnello stood before the immutable saea problem—and was mad.

The guide clenched his fist fiercely, then sighed and opened his fingers wearily. There was nothing to strike, nothing to grip, nothing....

He dropped to the floor and spread himself on his back. The moment he lay down, Priipiirii left the insane archaeologist to undulate over him.

"What *are* you?" he wondered, noticing the first faint foulness in his oxygen supply. "What do you want? Why do you tear us down this way, when we've done nothing to you? You aren't the kind of god who would punish for desecration of his temple?"

As if in reply, the deity went through all of his sexual forms, ending up as masculine once more. Hartwick watched, cursing.

His sanity began to slip into the narrow chasm of the problem. He got a grip on it by reverting to practical approaches. Lutzman had taken a shot at it. Perhaps—

His oxygen already was dangerously low.

He shot at it several times. Useless. Weapons were useless here. Lutzman shouldn't have tried. If Lutzman hadn't been killed, he might have been able to work out the god's desires from crustacean psychology.

An angle! His mind, fogged by the poisons his respiratory system was inhaling in lieu of air, groped desperately. What—what would be a highly intellectualized crustacean viewpoint? Not really crustacean, though—Martian biology was so different that bioareology was the name of the science here—Lutzman, now, Lutzman might have....

Desperate struggling through the night that was coming down over his brain. It was such torment to breathe—to think—crustacean—that was it—all he had to do was work out something peculiarly crustacean—

Priipiirii replied again. This time, he became a fish, a mammoth, a Martian polar beetle, in turn. Then himself again.

Hartwick's mind, Hartwick's life, slipped out too fast for him to hold on. Faster—

Above him, the god watched the approaching extinction of his last worshipper—which meant his own extinction, too—with courteous delight. Faster and more ecstatic grew his squirmings over the two dying lunatics in the temple of a dead and decadent race. So sweet to receive again obeisance from insanity!

For was not Priipiirii most gloriously and intricately the God of Puzzles?

Dud

So there I was. Set. The war was over, and the moment the *Sunstroke* landed on Earth, I would hand my prisoners over to some official of the War Crimes Tribunal and be a full-fledged civilian again. I would be free to drink the wine, sing the song, and—well, you know what I mean—all set.

The communicator on the beautiful pastel ceiling showed the mileage remaining—two million. Why, that was a hop, a skip, and a burp! It had been a fairly pleasant trip—the *Sunstroke* was a private luxury yacht requisitioned for the needs of the Terran Navy in bringing my peculiar charges to justice. I hoped I'd be able to afford a vessel like her someday. When I had been a civilian for a long, long—

My eyes drooped shut. Jimmie Trokee would be waking me in four hours to take over the watch on the prisoners. And I'd have to be super sharp. I dozed.

"Mr. Butler!" I twitched up to a squat. Captain Scott's huge head was glaring from the communicator. "Report to the bridge on the double. On the double, Mr. Butler!" He faded rosily.

I tilted the bed, got out, and dressed. Five years in the service and you develop certain reflexes toward orders. It was only after I'd walked through the doorap that I remembered to stop and curse.

"What does that spacehound mean by talking to me like that? I'm Army, not Navy. Not even that, I was discharged before we took off. And my only responsibility is to and for the prisoners. I've got to make a couple of fine distinctions for the old boy."

All the same, I started for the bridge. But not before I walked to the end of the corridor to see how our Martians were getting along.

Jimmie Trokee, my junior, was lounging against the doorap of the combination prison-stateroom. He dropped the cigarette quickly and ground it out.

"Sorry, Hank. But honestly, everything's under control. Rafferty and Goldfarb stopped their chess game so I could get a smoke. They won't miss a trick."

"Sure," I said. "I do the same thing, myself. Your lungs get awful dry in that joint. How are our friends feeling? Still taking baths?"

He grinned. "Didangul took five during my watch. His two pals spelled him in the pool. Only a Martian could loll in the water like that with a probable death sentence hanging over his scaly head!" His face tightened. "But when they aren't bathing, they fool around with that converter and whistle at each other."

"I know, I don't like it either. But the white-haired boys at headquarters cleared their request for the gadget. Said they couldn't possibly make anything dangerous with one that size. It's all part of this coddle-them-before-you-kill-them idea. The condemned Martians surrounded a hearty supper."

"Yeah. I don't get it. When I think of what Didangul did to the boys of the Fifteenth Army. Of course, they can't spit a weapon out of the converter. All they've been getting is tiny hunks of neutronium that not even the three of them can lift. Yet—"

"Mr. Butler," a communicator shrilled down the hall, "Captain Scott says if you aren't on the bridge in two minutes, he'll send a detail to drag you up by the short hairs."

Jimmie got angry. "Who does he think he is? You don't take orders from that guy. He's Navy!"

"He's the captain of the ship," I reminded him. "You know, power of life and death in empty space. I better get going."

"Well, don't take any guff from him," Jimmie called after me. He waved his hand at the doorap and walked through.

I adjusted my tunic before walking through the heavy panel leading to the bridge, and straightened the Eagle over Saturn on my chest. The first PX our occupation forces had established on Mars was stale out of civvies; I was wearing my uniform home. And Scott was death on sloppy uniforms.

Then I caressed the panel and started through. Whop! I massaged my nose and blasted the Terran Navy from heck to brunch. Why they had to remove a perfectly good doorap and substitute an old-fashioned hingie, just because of naval tradition—

I felt around for the doorknob and walked in, still aching in the olfactory. Nobody so much as batted a wink of sympathy at me. Everyone but Cummings the quartermaster was clustered around one of the five great visiscreens in the bridge. I sighed.

"Mr. Butler," Captain Scott called over his shoulder, "if your manifold social obligations will permit you to comply with my suggestions, would you care to stroll up to the screen for a moment?"

I glared at the back of his shaggy head and light blue fatigues. Then, very obviously, I strolled up to the screen beside Lieutenant Wisnowski, the astrogator. I heard Scott rub his teeth against each other, and Wisnowski twisted a quick grin at me.

There wasn't much on screen that meant anything to me. A fairly large disc of Earth, the moon approximately the same size, lots and lots of little lights that were stars or meteors or fireflies.

"What do you expect me to—" I began.

"This part," Wisnowski said, whirling a little doohickey with a handle. A section of the screen in front of me seemed to spread out, and the little white lights got thicker.

There was an odd something moving there, a something with an irregular shape and all kinds of protruding edges. Dark brown in color, it seemed to jerk itself along. I'd never seen anything quite like it before.

"Small asteroid? Meteor?"

"Neither," Scott told me. "It's not on any chart, and this area is mapped to twelve decimal places. The speed and movement—jerky movement, you notice—disqualify it as a solar body. Besides, it's been following us."

My mind danced to the Martians below. "Rescue party?"

"Hardly think so." The captain walked to the middle of the room, where Cummings sat alertly before his hundred switches. "Forty, five-nine, forty. The object has no discernible jets."

"Forty, five-nine, forty," Cummings mumbled through his wad of tobaccogum. He flipped three switches toward him, moved two others back. He peered at the slowly revolving "grampus" on the ceiling. "Forty, five-nine, forty. On arc."

"Well, if it has no jets, how can it be following us?" I asked reasonably. "I don't know how far off it is, but—"

"Over three hundred thousand miles." Captain Scott had returned to the visiscreen and was studying it intently. I was amazed at the look of worry on his old, space-pale face. "Much too far away for gravitation to be asserted, if that's what you can't understand, Mr. Butler.

"The *Sunstroke* may have been a large yacht, but it makes a very small naval vessel, and that thing is too tiny for any real attraction to exist. Yet it moves at approximately our number of gyros, and—see there, now!—it changes course with us."

Sure enough, it did. As the *Sunstroke* curved into its new arc, the celestial bodies on the screen seemed to slant away. All but our new little friend. One of its great uneven edges came round slowly, and the whole mass moved into relatively the same position on the screen it had held before.

"Lock the magnification, Mr. Wisnowski."

The astrogator pushed on the doohickey, and it clicked into permanent place. He and the captain hurried back to the chart table. The second officer, after an anxious look at the grampus, moved to the door and left the bridge. Not before another sidelong glance at the thing in the visiscreen. "I'll check battle stations, sir."

"Good. And you might sound a secondary alert. I called you to the bridge, Mr. Butler, because I believe this—whatever it is—is definitely related to your distinguished prisoners. Perhaps—"

"In that case, I insist you radio Earth immediately. Or a military base on the moon. They'll send whatever help—"

"Mr. Butler! You insist? You? Until such time as you can carry five red jets on your shoulders, I give all the orders on this ship!" He had whirled to face me angrily, his lips curved into each other. The old boy was mad down to his bottom gyro.

But I still had statements to make for publication. "You're master in all spatial matters," I told him, trying to imitate his bluster, "but I'm directly responsible to the War Crimes Tribunal and, through them, to the Solar Council for the safe delivery of these prisoners. Didungal is the only one of the four peritic tetrarchs we caught—"

"I don't care if he is the chief embezzling field-marshal in the whole blasted Terran Army, I still give all orders on this ship. I can prove that to you, if necessary, by throw-

ing you into the brig, the real brig—not the fancy home away from home those lizards are enjoying.

"You have chosen to become a civilian, Mr. Butler—though you still prefer the
uniform—and, as far as I'm concerned, you are merely a civilian employee of the
government charged with seeing that three sensitive Martians don't catch colds or
commit suicide. You take orders from me and my officers—is that clear?"

Deeply inhaling, I thought of pointing out that all of us "civilian employees" were
the most frequently wounded and decorated men in the entire Third Corps, who had
elected to take their discharges on Mars, and who had volunteered to guard the most
vicious criminals of the Peritic War on their way home because no occupation troops
could be spared. But—I grimaced, but didn't unzip.

"Good." Some of the sudden red lines in Scott's face faded to pink, and he picked
a book off the chart table. "I won't use the radio—as you call it, in army slang—because of the *Jetsam* incident. You've heard of it? The *Jetsam*, a small scout operating
off Deimos about a week before the armistice, reported via radarito that it was being
followed by a strangely shaped object that matched its speed but seemed to maintain
its distance.

"It broke in on its own message to announce that the object had accelerated since
transmission started and was now approaching very rapidly. A moment later, the entire
Deimos beachhead was shaken by a tremendous spacerip blast. Nothing of the *Jetsam* or its crew was ever found."

"M-m-m-m. Spacerip yet. Atomic channels aren't bad enough. So you won't use
the radio—oops, radarito—because you're afraid it'll help set off this mine, or anyway excite it to increase its speed. But a mine doesn't make sense. If it's anything that
new, the Martians haven't had time to plant it. They've cleared from this area since
long before the Battle of the Southern Hemisphere."

"Not on this side of the moon," the captain pointed out. "There are still guerilla
bands of Martians holding out in forgotten mountain forts on the moon. It may be
a loose mine—or a new-fangled sort of proximity shell. It may be practically anything. It's probably a dud, in any case, but that doesn't make it less dangerous. It might
be one of our own weapons. The Martians are essentially imitators. They haven't
discovered a single scientific principle for themselves."

I smiled at him and shook my head. "Don't go falling for our propaganda, Captain. The Martians are, each and every one of them, better scientists than any five
thousand humans. Just because they weren't interested in mechanics until we caressed their scales with all sorts of nasty weapons. Why, the gyrospeed drive your ship
is using was copied from a Martian derelict in the war's first stages."

'I wasn't aware that was publicly accepted, Mr. Butler," he said, his thin body very
erect in the blue uniform. "Mr. Wisnowski, how many gyros are we turning?"

"Five, I think."

"You think?"

"Five, I know," Wisnowski amended after a hasty glance from the grampus to
his charts.

"Raise it to nine. I know it's over our limit, but tell the engine room we'll hold that acceleration only until we've shaken this dud, if it is a dud."

Captain Scott walked swiftly past me to the visiscreen and opened the book in his arms. He turned the metallic pages slowly, staring with desperate intentness first at the illustrations and then at the weird brown object in the magnified portion.

Wisnowski raised the engine room on the communicator and ordered the nine gyros. He closed the switch on their surprised yelps.

"Don't mind the old cometcatcher," he whispered. "'He won't take any backtalk from even an ex-Army guy. It's a shame we have to have two separate services in the first place. Crazy jurisdictional squabbles in the middle of a war, whether a battle is deep-space or planet-based. It's silly and positively twentieth-century."

I agreed with him. "But the captain was way off base when he said I had to prevent my Martians from committing suicide. Catching colds yes; committing suicide, no. If a Martian could ever bring himself to voluntarily slither off into the great moist beyond, we'd have lost the war a month after Antarctica was gouged out.

"They've been civilized too long and enjoy life too much for that. They'd have stayed civilized, too, if we hadn't objected to their dreaming in their baths and insisted on showing them the delights of pugnaciousness. How their placidity used to annoy us!"

Wisnowski nodded. "Most soldiers I've talked to feel the same way. I remember how everyone was intrigued when the first two Martians were persuaded to attend an old-fashioned heavyweight fight at Madison Square Garden."

"Sure. We're responsible for changing an attitude a million years old. And then, the people we used to colonize Mars! The supermen philosophers of Germany and Japan we didn't have the nerve to kill after the second atomic war."

"Drop to six gyros," Captain Scott called. "This thing has increased its acceleration to match ours. I hope you're keeping an accurate account of all this in the rough log, Mr. Wisnowski."

"Yes sir, I am. Very accurate." Wisnowski blushed, passed the order down to the engine room and began to write very rapidly. I was glad I'd never served under such a commander. "Almost forgot about it completely," he whispered, after a while, his eyes glued to the log.

"My dad told me how the government sold the idea 'Let those brilliant but mis-guided men build a new life for themselves on a new world. They will help them-selves become better in the struggle with this hostile planet—they will help human-ity stretch its empire farther into space.' Empire—phtaaa!"

"Well, the only ones they helped with their muscle-man methods and garish ideas were the peritic Martians, who simply modified super with Martian instead of man. In thirty years, the Perites grew from an obnoxious little cult to a major political party. When Martian scientists began toying with weapons instead of new ways of making water spray off their scales, humanity just—"

"Nine gyros!" Scott yelled. "Get back to nine gyros!"

"Raise it to nine again," Wisnowski flashed into the communicator. "And no ar-gument! What's up, sir?"

He ran to the captain's side; I scuttled after him. Scott pointed a shaking finger at the screen. The brown mass had grown larger. More details of its odd, broken shape could be seen. "Look at that! It increased its acceleration to match our limit, but when we cut to six, it stayed at nine. Now I'm sure it's a dud—some sort of naval proximity shell.

"There's nothing in the naval bulletin about it; just some vague notes like, 'It's believed the Martians have been attempting to develop an improved proximity fuse using a spacerip-type warhead, which will adjust its speed to that of the pursued object, making landing and deceleration impossible.' Of course, we can't think of deceleration if that ungodly pebble will stay at our maximum. But the desk-bound idiot writing the bulletin doesn't mention a countermeasure!"

"Probably had no idea what it was like." Wisnowski made faces at the screen. "Just wanted to let commanders know it might be around sometime. Then they're on their own."

Even Cummings had lifted his eyes from the hundred switches and was chewing his tobaccogum at the deadly missile uneasily. I couldn't understand all this crazy concern and decided to say so.

"The *Sunstroke* is fitted with atomic channels, isn't it? Why don't you just reach out and bop it one?"

"Mr. Butler," the captain enunciated in slow irritation, "you evidently haven't been out in deep space since the Battle of Deimos, if you think you can blast a late-model proximity shell. They are all adjusted to absorb sufficient power from the blast to reach the ship of origin in a fantastic spurt before they explode. No, we can't blast it; but we can't hold nine gyros for long, either! This has us where the hairs are long, short and middle-sized."

I remembered hearing about that new principle—temporary immunity and total absorption—they'd been building into the latest proximity shells, but I was so deep in underground operations around Grinda City at the time that I'd hardly bothered to file the information.

"But just a moment, Captain; this is a dud, isn't it? And a dud is a shell that hasn't exploded. So how can it—"

"A dud is a shell that hasn't exploded—yet. And in the case of a naval proximity shell, it's one that has failed to be attracted to a target, very possibly because it hasn't encountered one—yet. Mr. Wisnowski, what is your opinion?"

Wisnowski rolled his lower lip under his teeth and jabbed at his chin. I waited, more than a little anxious myself. This total absorption deal—that explained partially why radio couldn't be used, why we couldn't get away in lifeboats.

Any additional expenditure of energy would be used by the missile to increase its speed, already equal to the ship's maximum. It also meant that, since every man-made object in space radiated a certain amount of energy as it streaked through the vacuum, these nasty playthings must eventually catch their targets. But what did they use for jets?

"With your permission, sir," Wisnowski was saying, "I'd like to take a red herring out."

"Was hoping you'd say that, Mr. Wisnowski. We are well into the period for considering desperate measures. But I would never order a man into a red herring. If you hadn't volunteered, I myself—"

"Hold your lanyards," I told both of them. "We had red-herring maneuvering way back in Army basic. I'm supercargo on this wagon, just a valet to the Martians, so why shouldn't I carry the ball? I don't want to do anything that sounds like volunteering, but Wisnowski here has three wives, while I—"

"Haven't even got one. But you will have when you get back to civilian Terran jurisdiction—new law. With all the guys that got knocked off in the war, how do you think there will be a next human generation if people like you hang on to their individuality so hard? Anyway, Butler, you're on your way out of the service, and the captain would want this to be a strictly Navy job." He started out before I could get my formal protest exhaled.

"Send the second officer in to relieve you," Captain Scott called after him. "And have a detail bring up that Martian fellow—Dangdang something."

I whirled on him. "My instructions were to keep Didangul under close guard in the cabin!"

"Under the emergency powers vested in me," the captain barked, "I hereby invalidate your instructions. I'm positive this is a snake trick, and, if anything happens to Mr. Wisnowski, I intend to burn the secret out of them—Terran Justice Code or no Terran Justice Code!"

"Not a chance. Those babies, and especially a character like Didangul, can take more punishment than you can deliver before they'll crack. And they're smart enough to know that if they're hurt too badly, it won't do you any good to get away from that dud, because you'll be blasted by Edict twenty-two, thirty-four of the War Crimes Tribunal as soon as we hit Earth."

The second officer came in and took his position at the screen, his coal-black face twisted with worry. I knew how he felt. Under normal circumstances, a red herring was just a refined way of committing suicide while making certain your dependents received a posthumous medal. You took an open single-seater out and circled the proximity shell until you attracted it.

Then, when it changed its course and barged after the lifeboat, you jetted yourself out of the seat and just floated around in your spacesuit until the ship picked you up. If you were still around, that is. A spacerip covers a prodigious area, atomic channels almost as much.

With this gadget on our trail, it would be a little different. For one thing, the missile was already moving at almost as many gyros as the single-seater could turn; that meant that there wouldn't be much of a time gap between the attraction and the impact. Add to that fact that this new shell was almost certainly using spacerip, and Wisnowski stood a slightly better chance of being picked up by the ship afterwards than I did of getting a royal flush in spades the next time I played a hand of stud poker.

I slapped the second officer's back awkwardly. Wisnowski was evidently one of the more popular characters on the *Sunstroke*.

Somebody slammed against the door and began cursing in most colorful Afghan. I chuckled—Jimmie Trokee was also being reminded of the naval prejudice against dooraps on ships' bridges.

Then the door opened and Jimmie backed in, his Stifflitz at the ready, followed by nineteen feet of wet, angry, and superbly insolent lizard. Rafferty sauntered in behind the twitching tail with another Stifflitz.

"Goldfarb's keeping an eye on his two pals," Jimmie told me over his shoulder. "Want me to tie him up?"

"Yeah. You'd better."

Jimmie made an adjustment in his weapon and sprayed the Martian with a web of fine, low-power Stifflitz threads. When the former tetrarch was reduced to a mere waggling of the head and jaws, my junior handed the weapon to me and started out with Rafferty. "He's in your hands now, chief," he cracked, with a nod to me. Didangul said something which wouldn't have been printable even if it had been translatable.

"What's he saying?" the captain asked. Didangul had been whistling at the ceiling. I waited until he repeated it, then I was almost afraid to translate. "He says he has been pulled out of his bath most unceremoniously and is feeling chilled all over. He says he is highly susceptible to colds and will probably catch one now. He wants to know if this is the vaunted democratic justice of Earth."

"And this is the monster who slowly dehydrated fifteen thousand men in his own palace a week before he bothered to make a formal declaration of war! The slimy— When I think of all the water headquarters diverted from their own supplies just so these blisters could be comfortable on their way to trial— Ask him if he knows anything about that lump of whatnot out there."

I whistled Scott's question at the Martian and listened intently to the answer. All I knew was the pidgin, and Didangul was perversely using literary Martian with all of its triple images and expanded noun phrases.

"He says he does. Probably one of his friends on the moon. Says we can't possibly escape it, no matter what we do. Says he will trade information on the only countermeasure for an ironbound opportunity to get away. By ironbound, he says he means give his fellow-prisoners a lifeboat and two hostages. After he's told us the countermeasure, he'll enter the lifeboat, and the hostages will be released. He won't have to worry about pursuit since the ship will be limping after traveling for so long at nine gyros."

"He doesn't, eh? Tell him to go straight to—to the Sahara! I wonder how this snake would stand up under a steady bath of medium power Stifflitz? Or some neurone tickling—Martians are as cowardly as Ionian Skelnicks."

"Even more so," I shrugged. "But only when it involves somehow the voluntary choice of self-destruction. They're fairly hardy—Perites especially—under torture. This individual knows enough about Terran government to understand we run as much risk by killing him as we do by kissing that proximity shell. On the basis of that knowledge, I don't think he'd ever crack, even if I could sanction such persuasion."

"What about psychological prodding? I understand the water needs of so-called civilized Martians are fantastically high. Perhaps some sort of a thirst treatment—"

I considered that. "First, there's the difficulty that Didangul here has just come from a combination bath and drinking party. We don't have nearly enough time for him to generate sufficient thirst—"

There were two flat noises from the nose of the ship. "Mr. Wisnowski has just jetted," the second officer reported.

Captain Scott and I hurried to the blue screen, where a tiny orange dot moved in a straightening arc towards the jagged shell. It curved away after a while and shot off in the direction opposite the *Sunstroke*'s flight.

"The shell isn't following," Scott breathed. "The lifeboat has failed to attract it! Impossible!"

But it hadn't. Wisnowski, evidently noticing the failure of the maneuver, turned back to the shell in a diminishing spiral. The jagged brown mass completely ignored his tiny vessel. It continued following us in obstinate quest of self-destruction.

"The crazy fool! He intends to—he's trying to— Where in blazes is that communicator?"

Scott seized the curving panel with both hands and brought his great head almost inside it.

"Mr. Wisnowski! Are you trying to crash-explode that shell? Answer me, Mr. Wisnowski. This is your commanding officer speaking!" The astrogator's face appeared in the curve of the panel. "It's all that's left, sir. I can't get it to follow the lifeboat. I'll set it off and—"

"I'll break you, Wisnowski, I'll reduce you to third-class messman! I will not have my officers taking it upon themselves to throw their lives away, do you hear? Return to ship immediately. Immediately, Wisnowski! Don't you know that such an advanced weapon as this can't be detonated by a mere crash of an extraneous body? And your lifeboat is obviously irrelevant to the ship's course."

The lifeboat's spiral continued. Two or three more complete curves, and—

"I know there isn't much chance of detonating it, sir, but just the barest possibilities now—"

"Are matters that only I determine," the captain yelled. "We need you as astrogator, Wisnowski. Our only chance of evading impact depends on your presence on the bridge with me. I vitally need your help in formulating decisions. Return to ship, Wisnowski, or I promise by all that's holy to strip your uniform down to underwear!"

There was a moment of silence after this somewhat complicated threat. Then the speck of orange angled sharply away from the oncoming shell. It moved back towards the ship. We all breathed loudly again.

A few moments later, there was another high note and slight thud as the lifeboat entered the *Sunstroke*.

Captain Scott walked over to the chart table and poured himself a tumbler of water from the carafe.

Hearing a rattle behind me, I turned, bringing the Stifflitz up. Didangul, tightly wrapped in the golden threads, was stretching a yearning claw at the water bottle.

Greedy! He'd practically just emerged from a bath, but get a Martian anywhere near water, in sight of wet stuff—

He saw my sneer and straightened. "After this fiasco, are the humans prepared to bargain?" he whistled.

I didn't bother to answer. How he knew what we had been doing puzzled me for a moment. No Martian, peritic or of any other cult, had ever deigned to learn so primitive a language as Universal Terran. Then I remembered he'd seen the whole operation in the screen; these babies were much more than normally intelligent.

"We're worse off than before," Scott was worrying. "The radiation from the lifeboat has increased the shell's acceleration to approximately nine and one-tenth gyros. It won't be long now. Hear that rumbling? The *Sunstroke* wasn't built to stand up under such strain."

I listened; the strange creaking noise underfoot had been growing in intensity. Sweating, I started for the water myself. Then I stopped.

"What is it?" the captain whispered. "Idea?"

"Sorta kinda. I was just thinking what water means to a Martian, a highly civilized one like Didangul. It represents survival in essence. Water is one of the triple images in the Martian noun for life. It has the connotation of the ultimate in luxury, the reward of the rich, the reason for striving for worldly success. An aristocratic Martian scientist will consider any investigation but the question of the irrigation of their desert lands as demeaning beyond all conception. I was wondering—"

"But you said they weren't thirsty enough!"

"Oh, Didangul isn't thirsty, all right. But water is something more than a physical need. It's an emotional, intellectual requirement. Especially water in their neighborhood that they aren't using. I wonder how much of a need it is! It was enough to make them dehydrate fifteen thousand living humans merely to get at the water imprisoned in their bodies. I'm going to try something."

Carelessly, I walked to the chart table and poured myself a drink. I smacked my lips after I had finished and sighed happily. Then I strolled back to the enormous Martian, sloshing the water in the carafe. I held it up to him silently.

He shuddered and tried to straighten. Then painfully, almost pitifully, he strained both claws against the tight threads in the direction of the water bottle. The well-tended, pointed nails scraped horribly against the glass.

"Very fine water," I whistled. "Very wet. Moist. Very, very wet. Nice water to feel fine against your skin, Didangul. Cool and wet water to slide happily down your throat. You can have it, Didangul, to splash around in, to drink, to give you moist and lovely pleasure. What must we do to avert the explosion?"

His great green tail attempted to curl back upon his head. He opened his long jaws, closed them again. His eyes were fixed fiercely, unwinkingly upon the container I held just out of his reach.

He whistled a few bars, and I leaned forward intently. Just a meaningless babble of yearning—no recognizable words.

Wisnowski came in and stopped near the door as he grasped the scene. He was still wearing part of a spacesuit.

I shook the carafe again, letting the water splash about inside. "Nice wet water for you, all moist and damp for you. How do we stop the shell?"

Another uncommunicative whistle, another convulsive wriggle. Didangul seemed to want that water more than I've ever seen any living thing want anything. "Only trouble," I said aloud, "is that his psychological block against divulging information which will prevent his escape seems as strong and maybe a little stronger than his desire."

"Lots of humans can be forced to give secondary info when the most brutal torture won't extort a particular secret," Wisnowski said suddenly. "Even a Martian has an unconscious. Try asking him something that doesn't seem so obviously important—ask him what kind of shell it is."

I brought the water bottle up to Didangul's reptilian snout. "Plentiful moisture," I trilled. "Delightful wetness. Just tell us how the shell works, and you will bathe and drink deep. We don't want to know how to evade it—just its nature. Tell us its nature, Didangul, for this swirling water you see and may have. Why does it follow us? Why didn't it follow the lifeboat? All this wetness for you alone."

An awkward whistle. Then a few more, his whole being concentrated on the water bottle. "The shell—gravity—artificial gravitation—no power source, no jets—just artificial, magnified attraction to—to neighboring body of greatest mass." He halted, wheezed, writhed and went on, "—greatest mass moving at variable acceleration as all non-celestial bodies—lifeboat's mass smaller than ship's—let have water—let me—need it—need—"

I translated. "Does it help?"

"Yes!" Captain Scott said emphatically. "Artificially magnified gravitation! Must have been one of their last, desperate spurts of scientific development before the end. All we have to do is get a greater mass out of the ship than remains in it—leave, say, only the personnel, the hull and the radarito—attach our gyros in automatic operation to this greater mass and send it off in a different arc than the ship's. Then, after the spacerip, we radarito a lunar base for help—"

"Excuse me, sir," Wisnowski broke in. "We couldn't possibly weld it all together in time. And if we don't weld, the individual pieces we accumulate will spread out in space as fast as they are pushed through the ports. The drive won't affect the entire mass. It'll only send the individual fragment it's attached to in a different arc."

I remembered the gadget that headquarters had cleared at the Martians' request. The converter—neutronium! "They've been fiddling with it ever since the voyage started, Captain! That's the price—the gadget they were going to give us for their freedom. But it's only one small converter. You'd need a skilled industrial mechanic to convert a sufficient quantity of ship's mass into neutronium—"

The second officer had come up. "With your permission, Captain Scott, I believe I could handle it. I specialized in industrial naval techniques at the academy. Converters are my own potatoes."

"Take over, then. Requisition any of the crew to help as you see fit."

The second officer barged out. I leaned a bit too close to Didangul. He seized the carafe. Captain Scott tore over and ripped it out of his claws.

"We'll need all the mass we can spare, Mr. Butler. That water these lizards have been wallowing in will be going into the converter." He chuckled. "Let them drink soup."

Wisnowski made a wry face as the Martian drooped in a corner. "I feel sort of sorry for the guy. After all the grilling he's been through, the least we could do is let him wet his whistle."

"Ship emergency," the captain was declaring into the communicator panel. "Heads of departments will extend every cooperation to the second officer and see that he has all the men and materials he requires to adequately complete his task.

"All personnel whose work is no longer essential will report to the bridge immediately. The prisoners will be bound carefully and also brought up here. We are facing a spacerip, men. We don't know exactly what its effects will be or whether our hull can withstand it. Our only hope for survival is to get everyone into the bridge, which is in the exact center of the ship; this will provide a maximum of bulkhead armor."

Three hours later, Cummings called abruptly. "Captain Scott, these beetles are trying to walk away with the grampus and the hundred switches!"

Three weary electricians stood near the quartermaster. "Orders," said one of them laconically, brandishing an electronics wrench.

"Just a moment," the captain hurried over. "We've got to set the best possible course first. Uh—thirty-nine, five-eight, thirty."

"Thirty-nine, five-eight, thirty," Cummings repeated. "On arc, you danged blacksmiths!" He skipped off the control dais as the electricians began tearing the equipment out of the floor and ceiling.

The bridge was getting crowded with everybody from the mess detail, their hands still greasy, to the sleepy dog watch. Jimmie Trokee came in and got the other two tightly bound Martians up against a wall with Didangul.

Rafferty and Goldfarb were howling about the loss of their chess-board. The creaking of the ship was now a definite whine as the bulkheads seemed to vibrate in place. I prayed that the second officer would get the necessary mass into the converters before the ship shook itself apart.

"Mr. Wisnowski," the captain was yelling above the din of irritated mumbling as men shoved against each other. "Mr. Wisnowski, I hope you're keeping a record of this in the rough log."

"Sorry, sir," Wisnowski called. "The rough log just went into the converter. And that's the chart table going out now."

Captain Scott stared after the two men pushing their way out through the crowd and shook his head. "Well, give orders then that the visiscreens are to be left in place. If we live through it, this may be man's only chance to describe a spacerip at short range."

Hmmm, I thought. That was so. I jostled through cursing spacemen and got my face up against the quivering screen. Captain Scott was already there. Together, we watched the huge, uneven mass which filled half the screen grow even larger.

"If that second officer doesn't hurry—" the captain began. "I haven't thanked you, as yet, for your assistance, Mr. Butler. I'll forward a complete report to Terran Army Command if and when we land. A complete report." Then he smiled at me. I didn't like that smile.

A terrific thudding boom from somewhere. A thick, palpitating blob of orange which was the ship's gyrospeed drive appeared on the screen behind the tiny coruscating dot that signified neutronium. It arced away and past the proximity shell. Everyone stopped breathing.

Slowly, very slowly, one oddly outlined edge of the shell turned around. The entire evil contraption seemed to revolve on its axis. Then—I noticed it was growing smaller. It was pursuing the neutronium!

Feet pounded in the corridor outside as the second officer came in with the last of the engine room crew.

"Wish we had enough spacesuits to go around," the captain said restlessly. "Of course, the Navy reinforced the *Sunstroke* to withstand anything short of direct hit on a vital spot with atomic channels. I'd take this ship into practically anything, even—"

Sound abruptly disappeared in the room. A tremendous orange glow spilled across the screen. It was followed by an expanding cone of the ugliest, deepest, most hopelessly depressing black the mind of man ever shudderingly refused to imagine.

I found my muscles were locked in place. I seemed to have jelled into a creature of no time, no movement, and slow, impossibly tortured thought. Then my body slammed against the screen, whipped away from it.

Sound—horrible screaming sound as if the very universe was shrieking—battered my head with the insane force of a mallet in the hands of a lunatic, as every electron in the ship fought to maintain its identity. I crawled abjectly into unconsciousness with a last, frantic impression of men's bodies rolling off the wrinkled screen. The screen held that fantastically blinding spot of white light where space, ripped apart, was pathetically trying to roll back upon itself. Empty space, never meant to be opened....

"Butler's all right," Wisnowski was yelling. My head was on the hard bump of his knee. The screens were hanging in dripping shards of plastic around the bridge. Men crawled to their feet, groaning. The floor had bellied up into an immense, irregular mound.

"Everyone's okay," Wisnowski said as he helped me to my feet. "Couple of broken bones and maybe some internal injuries, but nothing to cry about. Nobody killed. But the ship—the old man's keening over it. Second officer just came back and reported that not one square inch of the hull is left. The bridge and half the center level are intact—rest of the vessel is breathing vacuum."

"The radarito?"

"Oh, we got the auxiliaries functioning. They're raising a lunar base now. The spacerip would have attracted attention in any case. We're all set. Just a matter of time now, before the rescue party gets here."

I saw to my prisoners. They were dry, unhappy, and a little bruised in their golden bonds. But they were in sound enough condition to be executed as soon as the formalities of trial were over. I was all set. I'd even won the approbation of a jet-happy naval character like Captain Scott.

Only I didn't figure just how much of his approbation I'd won. On his recommendation, Terran Army Command revoked my discharge when we reached Earth. Yeah—revoked my discharge! They said I'd proved my value in handling the Martians too much for them to let me go until the trial was over. They said Captain Scott's recommendation showed I was far too useful, a man of far too high caliber. Spacewash!

That was five years ago. Didangul and his scaly friends were convicted all right, but they still have fifty-four of their sixty-one points of appeal to be considered. They're fighting for their lives with the best legal talent available—they're not so dumb themselves. I've been trying to figure—if seven points of appeal are turned down in five years, how long before fifty-four—

I had to go and be clever, I tell myself as I cry over the discharge they gave me on Mars hanging on the barracks wall. A discharge? A dud, brother, a dud.

CONFUSION CARGO

Captain Andreas Steggo had commanded a light negship in the late war before peace and retirement had given him the master's position aboard the Sagittarian Line's *Reward.* He was big, slightly brutal and accustomed to absolute obedience from his crews.

On the other hand, the crew hastily signed on by the Aldebaranian office were all ex-cargo jockeys of the twenty-five-planet system thrown out of work by the sudden cessation of hostilities. They were rough, fast-thinking and terrifically independent.

Excepting myself, there were no passengers. The voyage was to be especially long—two months; the cargo was particularly nasty—ten tons of stinking viscodium.

Anyone with half an ounce of brain would have known there would be trouble. Unfortunately the requirements for an official of the Sagittarian Line include a university degree and galactic license; nothing about half an ounce of brain.

First we discovered the viscodium, instead of being sealed in dellite drums, was stored in a large tank with an overflow lid. That made for economy in shipping space, but also for certain discomfort in such useful functions as breathing. I'd lie awake at sleep period thinking of what would happen if the lid fell off and the green slime came churning through the loose hatches.

Then one of the loading pipes developed a leak under the strain of acceleration. The *Reward* was an old ship and she had been hastily serviced for this, her first trip in five years. Breen, the ship's welder, burst the pipe while repairing it and we tossed him, stiff within the congealed mass of viscodium, through an airlock. No second welder either; so when the plumbing...

After the burial service, a delegation from the crew visited Captain Steggo and accused him of negligence in not having the loading pipes inspected for residual viscodium immediately after the take-off. They demanded their protest be logged. Steggo had all five of them clapped in restrainons. He then announced that full-dress discipline would be observed until we arrived; all ship's officers were to go armed at all times. I heard angry men in cheap *hwat* suits muttering after that about punishment half-meals and longer watches for a smaller active crew.

Mr. Skandelli, the chief engineer, visited me and offered a sawed-off shmobber. I looked at the foot-long weapon and declined. "Never touch the stuff."

"More than this may be touched before we warp in," he said grimly. "When Aldebaranian riff-raff gets snappish, I start using the armory. And passengers are classed with officers."

"That's no compliment on the *Reward*."

He looked at me, holstered the shmobber and left.

An hour later, I was presented with the captain's compliments and asked to attend him on the bridge. The whole business was beginning to annoy me more than slightly, but under the peculiar circumstances of my status I didn't feel like arousing any unnecessary antagonism. I went, determined not to be enlisted on either side—if it had come to choosing sides.

Steggo overflowed a huge armchair. A faint stubble covered his chin which, considering the cheapness of a depilosac, was unnecessarily filthy.

"Mr. Skandelli tells me you have no desire to be classed with the officers. However," he waved a huge paw to forestall my objections, "that's beside the point. You are Dr. R. Sims, late of Naval Research?"

"Yes. Robert Sims, physical chemist grade 2, Aldebaranian Project CBX-19329." I tried to keep my voice from quavering. This man wanted to bollix my papers.

He smiled and studied my questionnaire. "I am interested, Dr. Sims, in why a person of your standing chooses to travel on an uncomfortable cargo ship when the fastest negships and government cruisers are at his disposal."

"I am going home to visit my family, whom I haven't seen in more than three years." I hoped my voice sounded confident. "Naval employees are not allowed aboard negships for matters of personal convenience. It would be six months before obtainable priorities would get me a cabin on a reconverted liner. Since my leave starts immediately, the *Reward* looked damn good."

Papers rustled as he held them up to the light. "The seal is genuine enough. Ordinarily, the matter would not have come to my attention. But remember, we are still traveling under the mercantile sections of the articles of war. After your amazing outburst to Mr. Skandelli—who approached you at my instigation, by the way—I thought you merited looking into."

"I told Mr. Skandelli what any passenger in his right mind would have. Having paid for my passage, my protection is in your hands and not in mine." I touched the door button. "May I go?"

"One moment." He turned his massive head slowly. "Mr. Ballew, bring in the prisoners."

Ballew was the astrogator. He was a thin, fair-haired fellow who had been hunched over his charts during the interview. He grimaced and left, returning in a few seconds with five men.

The first of them was the tallest man I'd ever seen, not excluding the captain. The yoke of the restrainon about his neck barely seemed able to cover his body with its lines of force. His head was free to permit breathing, and the machine had been adjusted above his knees, enabling him to shuffle along in an odd, broken-legged fashion. The other four were likewise yoked.

Steggo introduced them to me.

"Ragin, whom I have logged as the leader of an abortive mutiny. The other woebegone gentlemen have names I either can't pronounce or don't choose to remember."

I waited, wondering how I came into this situation.

Suddenly the tall man spoke. The words seemed to come with difficulty because of the restrainon pressing upon his diaphragm. "You'll remember us, Steggo, if I have to hunt you straight across the galaxy."

The captain smiled. "A shmobber squad on Earth will quiet you. And it *will* be shmobbers for you after my report is in."

Ragin glared and shuffled rapidly across, the small room. His intention was obviously to hurl himself against the captain. Steggo lurched out of his chair and placed it in front of the moving man. Ragin hit the chair, bounced off it and was hurled against a bulkhead. I heard the thud as his head smashed into metal. The astrogator helped him to his feet.

"That, too, will go into the log," Steggo puffed. "Now, Dr. Sims, if you will please come this way."

I followed him, disagreeably conscious of the murderous thoughts swirling about in the bridge.

He walked to the ship's visor, fiddled with the dial and snapped it on. I gasped.

"That, as you see, is the hold. I was looking through at the hold where our Mr. Ragin and his little playmates were being kept. I thought I saw somebody bending over Ragin, feeding him. Mr. Skandelli was sent to investigate with the second officer and my suspicions were proven correct. The ship was then searched and six others found. Five of these are the wives of these men here; two belong to other members of the crew who are now being placed in restrainons themselves."

"Women!" I muttered. "Aboard a ship. Stowaways!"

"Ah, you are familiar with the mercantile sections of the articles of war. 'Any person of the feminine gender found aboard a ship engaged in interstellar flight without naval or military guard shall be subject to death or such other punishment as a court martial may direct.' That is the law, is it not?"

"But, Captain," I protested. "That law was directed against members of the Fino Feminist League who cooperated with the enemy during the war. It has never been used against civilians."

"Which is not to say it does not apply to civilians. I am fully aware that women have participated in our government during the entire conflict and even served with distinction during the Battle of the Dead Star. But the law is specific. It considers the costly sabotage at the time we were attacked and forbids women aboard ships on a blanket basis."

His heavy face seemed unusually thoughtful. He snapped off the visor.

"What do you want me to do?"

He pointed to the open log. "I've entered the entire incident; the fact that these men and two others, prior to the attempt at mutiny, did willfully smuggle their wives on board, in knowing violation by all parties concerned of space law." Ragin snorted heavily in the background. "I want you to sign the entry, testifying to the physical presence on ship of these women."

"But I'm not an officer. I'm not even an employee of the line!"

"That is precisely why I want your signature. It provides disinterested evidence. If you refuse, in the light of the emergency conditions now revealed as well as your semi-official naval status, I shall be forced to conclude you favor the mutinous elements. You will then be placed—"

He didn't have to finish. I signed.

Steggo followed me courteously to the door. "Thank you. Dr. Sims. Mr. Ballew, please assemble the court martial."

Ballew had turned a fiery red. "But, sir, you aren't going to court-martial them before we reach Earth!"

"I am, Mr. Ballew. And you will sit on the court. Remember the mercantile sections: 'Any merchant ship in priority categories 1AA, 1AB or 1AC, whether proceeding with or without military or naval escort, shall be considered to be on military or naval status for the purpose of discipline at the discretion of the master.' A viscodium cargo is sufficiently delicate to place us in category 1AC. And our Dendro drive prohibits radio communication even if a ship this size carried an interstellar transmitter, which it doesn't. Please assemble the court."

As Ballew, breathing hard, hurried from the bridge, I thought of what a space lawyer we had for a captain. He'd probably been an administration officer until near the end when the bottom of the barrel was carefully scraped. Early retirement usually pointed to such a background. Mr. Discipline, himself!

"You appreciate the fact, Captain, that the priority categories as well as the mercantile sections which you quote so glibly were all wartime measures?"

"I do. Wartime measures which have not yet been repealed. Now, Dr. Sims, if you would return to your cabin?"

I left, trying to throw some passing comfort at Ragin while the door closed behind me. He was staring at my parplex jumper oddly, his brows knitted as if he were trying to decide something very important. I was wearing the naval *pi* with three palms.

My cabin had been searched. Officers or crew? I didn't know. It was no fun being a neutral, as many small and sorrowful planets have discovered.

The suitcase and toilet articles had been hastily rifled, clumsily put back into place. I felt the head of the bed. The invisible blusterbun still reposed on the top of the ledge. Obviously no search scanners or even colored powder had been employed.

Amateurs. A stellective would have used powder, at least.

I pocketed the tiny, completely transparent weapon and stretched out on the bed. My toilet articles caught my eye. The half-empty container of depilosac had been probed for hidden articles. White drippings of the stuff stained the red shelf. Well, they hadn't found anything there.

Nothing incriminating had been found in the suitcase either; I had selected its contents with great care. Rather a nice touch that, choosing something old-fashioned like a suitcase instead of a modern space-saving collapsicon.

But if this mess got down to really sharp brass tacks, all my precautions wouldn't be worth a gram of plutonium in an atomic furnace. Damn Steggo anyway. Damn him and his mercantile sections. Damn Ragin. Damn the war.

I fell asleep in a wave of homesickness for Earth.

Weapons coughed brokenly at the stern of the ship. I came awake with my hand on the blusterbun. Somebody ran past my cabin screaming. The lights went off, came back on, then went off again.

I hit the floor of the bed as my pneumastic mattress was turned off too. Something rattled against the outside bulkhead and passed down the spaceship. Meteor dust? Not this far out. Probably Steggo turning on the gas sprinkler system. Or the mutineers.

So this was a mutiny. I had been in an atomic explosion and a devastating space negation in my time. I had been in the photonite plant on Rigel VIII when molecular joint lubricant was spilled against the dome, allowing our air to leak out into space. Now I was in a mutiny.

Fingers tapped on my door in a frantic message. I threw it open.

The man lying outside was evidently a crew member. He had a gaping, smoking hole instead of his chest.

"Jobal!" he almost whispered. "Please, please, Jobal—" He seemed to belch; when he didn't move I realized it was a death rattle. I moved his hand gently and closed the door. I went back to the side-board of the bed and sat down.

Who was Jobal? A friend? His wife, sweetheart? One of his gods? I must have sat in the darkness for an hour. After a while I noticed the ship was silent again. There was only the rolling hum of the Dendros.

Footsteps became louder and stopped outside my door. There was the sound of a man stepping over the body. Then the door was flung open and two huge Aldebaranians strode in. They leveled still-throbbing shmobbers at my waist.

"Captain Ragin wants to see you."

There. So the score was in. And now, I imagined, all bets were being paid. And which side was I supposed to be on? I walked carelessly to the door, keeping the pocket in which I had the blusterbun away from them.

Ragin sat in Steggo's chair. He didn't fill it as completely, but he looked just as dominant as the captain. Ballew pored over his charts in a corner. Except for the splash of blood on the floor, the room was as I had left it.

"Hello, Dr. Sims," Ragin grinned through puffed lips. Ballew didn't look up. "Some changes been made."

"For the better, I hope." I waited.

"Yeah. We think so." He looked behind me at my guards. "He's been searched?"

"Well—" one of them began.

"We didn't think—" the other fumbled.

"Great exploding novas! What do you blastheads think this is—a meeting of the Aldebaranian Benevolent Association?" He was on his feet snarling at them, his head almost two feet above mine.

"I can save you the trouble—er, Captain." I flipped the blusterbun from my pocket and held it out, butt foremost.

He stared uncomprehendingly at my outstretched hand for a few moments. Then he reached forward gingerly and took the invisible weapon.

A smile twisted his mouth as he ran his fingers over its intricacies. "Well, I'll be washed by a comet's tail! A blusterbun! Dainty and deadly. I've heard about these things but I never hoped to have one. How does a civilian rate it?"

"Naval research," I reminded him.

Coolly, he appraised me. "Maybe. Maybe not. I'll still have to have you searched." The guards came up.

I moved away. "Now, wait a moment. I gave you my weapon. Had I wanted to, I could have shot you with the same motion before your zombie friends decided to swallow or wipe their mouths. I carry documents on my person that I most definitely don't want seen until I reach Earth. Unless I'm mistaken, you want some favor of me. If you read those documents, all deals are automatically off; and you'll be in a mess about five times as disagreeable as a mutiny."

He took time to chew on that. Finally: "OK. Not that you can kill more than one man even if you have another weapon. If you start shooting, you'll be thoroughly butchered. And we do want a good deed out of you."

A tall, blonde woman came in with a tray. She prodded me with it. Catching on, I took a cup of hot liquid. Aldebaranian *hialiau* juice. Things were looking up.

"Elsa and I were just married. I wasn't going to leave her to what that fat sadist calls justice. The boys were all for mutiny thirty-six hours after we cleared Booma City, but I held them down until our wives were discovered. We've been miners and independent freightmen; we're not used to this sort of disciplinary guff."

My chin pointed at the red mess on the floor. "Steggo?"

"No. One of our boys. We've been careful to keep this a completely bloodless mutiny as far as the officers were concerned. As a result, there've been more casualties on our side than there should have been. We lost four men."

"Five," one of my guards broke in. "There was another stiff outside this guy's cabin. Couldn't see in the dark, but it felt like Rildek."

Ragin nodded. "Five, then. We'll have a roll call after we get the power turned back on. Running the ship on auxiliaries now. Now what I want you to do, doctor, is sign a document testifying to the background of the mutiny as you know it, as well as an affidavit stating that when last seen by you Steggo and his officers were all alive and in as good condition as could be expected."

"If I see them in that state, I will."

"You will. We're letting them go in a small lifeboat, with enough to last until they reach a base. If you want to, you may join them. This *is* a mutinous ship."

"No, thank you." I tried to sound casual. "I'll stay here."

He studied me. "I thought you'd say that. There's something terrifically phony about you, doctor, but I don't have time to figure it out."

I smiled. "I'm grateful for your lack of time." Then I put my cup on the floor. "But your word on this. I can take your word, because the fact you didn't kill Steggo and his officers indicates that you don't intend to turn pirate. Whatever your plans may be, will you tell me on your honor that you will see to it that I eventually reach Earth or Earth's authority?"

He pumped my hand in a pulverizing grip. "Word of honor. On my honor as a— a mutineer." We both grinned.

On the way to the airlock, the man behind me suddenly pushed his shmobber into my back. Startled, I stopped.

"My idea," Ragin said. "When Steggo reaches civilization, he'll tell the story his way. I want him to think you were detained aboard by force. It'll give your testimony more legality and protect you as well. I don't think you want to be investigated."

I thanked him. Quite a guy, this Ragin.

Ex-Captain Steggo, Chief Engineer Skandelli, and five other officers lay on the floor of the little lifeboat, restrainon yokes about their necks. The fat man glared up madly.

"Cast me adrift in a small boat, will you, Ragin? Well, I'll pull through somehow. I'll see you dissolving under the biggest thermons in the galactic navy!"

My guard bent over and spat in his face.

"You'll pull through, all right," Ragin said soberly. "You have twelve collapsicons containing every conceivable need." He smiled. "And after you we get rid of that unholy viscodium."

He made rapid adjustments on the restrainons, setting them to automatically turn off the binding lines of force within a half-hour. As he stooped over Skandelli, I noticed the chief was wearing a bandage over his chest.

"Do you want to make a little bet, fellow?" the engineer said softly. "I'll bet you my arms against your guts that before we're picked up you'll be warming a cot in a Terran prison."

Ragin smiled down at him. "Now that's no way to talk, Skandelli. After you locked yourself in the Dendros and gave my men all that trouble in blasting you out! Some of them had such nice plans for you; they'd just adore keeping you on the *Reward* to play with."

Skandelli turned a creamy white and shut up.

"All set. Get ready to cast off. This guy," he indicated me, "stays with us. So does Ballew. They're hostages."

As the airlock closed, I heard Steggo's wild shriek, "Dr. Sims, we'll be back, we'll be back, we'll be—"

There was a *whoosh* as the lifeboat arced away.

Ballew typed the papers on the basis of Ragin's written notes. We were alone on the bridge. Obviously, we were trusted.

I looked at Ballew's sullen, pale face. He was young for an officer, even aboard a cargo ship. What was in this for him? I asked him.

"Oh, I don't know," he said, rolling the last sheet out of the machine. "I ran away to sea first because I'd read a lot of books. The great ancients: Conrad, London, Nordhoff and Hall. Then I read books about space—*Mallard's Travels,* Soose, Jon Iim. So I thought I was in too limited a medium and went to astrogation school. But space is as dull as the sea."

I clucked sympathetically and ran my fingers over the smooth finish of the chair. "Things generally are, to a romantic. And you expected to find something really interesting in a mutiny?"

He flushed and I remembered how he had looked when the captain had been roaring at him. "Nothing like that. I knew Ragin on Aldebaran VI—Nascor, that is—and I'd gone on a couple of hunting trips to Aldebaran XVIII with some of the other members of the crew. When I signed on as astrogator I told them of the crew shortage and they came a-running. I even helped them stow their wives aboard." He stared at me defiantly.

Of course, I nodded to show I thought this was no crime under the circumstances. The boy went on.

"I'd never traveled with Steggo before, but I'd heard of him. When he started to pull this mercantile section stuff, I told Rildek and Gonda—Gonda was the guy watching over you all the time—and they passed the word. Tore in here in the middle of the court martial and took over the ship. Steggo was planning to toss those guys and their women through an airlock!"

"Not a particularly nice thing to do, but the Fino Feminists did manage to wreck three squadrons at the beginning of the war. These men knew that women are strictly forbidden to be present on a ship without official escorts; why in the name of the Curvature did they bring them?"

He shrugged. "Well, they wanted to build a home in a system where every foot of ground wasn't worth its weight in galactic credits. Aldebaran is almost all ore and almost all staked out. The Solarian asteroids have become pretty cheap during the war; they thought they'd pool their capital and buy one. But the women had to come or they'd be spending half their capital on fares. Aldebaran-Sol is an expensive trip."

"Don't I know!" I read the stuff he had typed and signed it. "Now I imagine they plan to hole up on Otho or one of the obscure little suns near it."

The papers were tucked in the astrogator's desk. "Don't know where exactly, except that it must be an uninhabited system and preferably unexplored. You'll be set on a course for Sol. If the ship is found in good condition and no murders are committed, the affair doesn't come under the jurisdiction of the galactic navy, especially since it's being demobilized. And you know how much time the Aldebaranian Patrol will spend on a mutiny."

"About as much time as it takes to move the papers from the 'missing in space' to the 'wanted for mutiny' file. But you'll have trouble over women. Only seven of them."

"Maybe." He stretched, and the blue parplex tightened over a meager chest. "The galaxy is big and business will be hell-bent for expansion after the war. We'll always be able to slip off and get a job somewhere when things cool off."

Ragin came in heavily and thumbed through the charts. He selected one of them and studied it, swearing softly to himself.

Ballew looked at him inquiringly and continued. "Me, I have the satisfaction of helping my friends against a son of a bilge pump. I also get to know whether life on a desert planetoid is all it's cracked up to be."

"You'll get to know what a thermon tastes like," the tall man snarled suddenly. "Sol was this ship's original course, eh?"

The fair-haired kid had jumped to his feet. "Y-yes," he stuttered. "B-but I th-thought you could operate steering Dendros. I laid out a new course and all you had to do was steer to it."

"We can operate steering Dendros, all right." Ragin grimaced. "When they're steerable." His hand flashed up, holding emptiness. My blusterbun.

"After you, doctor. I hope for your sake you *are* a physical chemist."

I walked ahead of him to the engine room. He gestured me inside. I was not feeling exactly immortal just then.

There was a little bubble of men around the double mass of convoluted machinery in the center. The bubble disintegrated as we came up and I stared at the green transparency for two minutes before I understood.

"Skandelli!" I shouted. "That's what he meant by that threat in the lifeboat. And that's what I heard rushing by the outside bulkhead during the mutiny."

"Yeah. The rotten bushaleon holed up in here for an hour. One of the loading pipes runs under the floor plates to the storage tank. He blasted a piece out of it and as soon as the holding pressure went down far enough, the stuff came crawling out over the Dendros. Of course, it congealed faster than it could come out of the small opening, so at least the ship wasn't flooded. Not that it makes much difference to us."

I squatted and touched the cold stuff experimentally. Hard as dendraloid itself. "I'm afraid you're out of luck, Ragin. You can't steer with clogged Dendros, and if I know viscodium, you'll never get them unclogged. This ship goes to Sol."

"Maybe the ship does," he said easily. "But you don't."

Their set faces frightened me. "I have your word of honor! And I thought you were one man who wouldn't break it."

"I'm sorry, doctor, but this is one time when my word will have to be plumb disintegrated. We gave most of our high-neutron fuel to that bunch in the lifeboat and we couldn't hope to make an uninhabited system unless we brought the ship close to it first. If we get to Sol I might be able to cook up something like an atomic explosion to account for Steggo and his officers as well as the five crew members who were shmobbered off.

"Ballew will back me up. As an officer, his testimony will be useful. *If* we all tell our stories straight, and *if* Steggo hasn't been picked up yet, we *might* be able to get away with it. But you're an outsider; we could never take a chance on your suddenly remembering what your civics teacher said. No, you either unstick those Dendros or become our first planned corpse."

Sharp muzzles jabbed into my back. "But, Ragin—I'm a physical, not a mucilaginous chemist. Do you know what viscodium is? There's a joke in the student labs: what viscodium hath joined together, no man can put asunder. It takes on the physical properties of whatever it congeals around and dendraloid is the hardest substance in the galaxy. If you try to split the block, you split the Dendros, too. The manufacturers are still working on a softener. They warn people not to use the stuff unless they intend it to be permanent."

"Well, Dr. Sims, you better start inventing," the leader said over his shoulder. He paused at the exit hatch. "You have exactly three weeks, figuring on Terran time."

"No! Why don't you tell me the unit of liquid measure is the Sirian drom? Something I don't know, I mean." I wasn't being sarcastic; I was scared.

Three weeks to solve a problem that had the best men defeated. No lab and no equipment. And me, a neutronium specialist!

"Run down to the medicine chest and see if there's any scaralx aboard," I told one of my guards. It had proven effective in treatment of people suffering from viscodium cancer, the result of a liquid drop touching the skin.

The man tore out of the engine room. I found a morose satisfaction in the discovery that I would get cooperation.

He came back with a container of scaralx which said in large letters: DANGER! THIS COMPOUND IS TO BE TAKEN ONLY AS THE PHYSICIAN PRESCRIBES! DO NOT USE INTERNALLY.

I opened the container feverishly. There were five aspirin tablets and an eyedropper inside.

Four days later, Ragin looked in on me on his daily tour of inspection. I had gotten around to using banked thermons. My eyes were red with fatigue. They let me go to my cabin whenever I wanted, but I hadn't been able to sleep. I was going to solve this problem and get to Earth in one piece, or I was going to burst my frontal lobe.

"How's it going, doc?" the big man asked.

"Not so good," I grunted. "I don't dare use too much juice for fear of melting the machinery. I've been trying to run it on an alternating current generator so that the heat is applied only to the surface in short bursts. But this stuff conducts too damn fast. I'll solve it somehow, though."

"Attaboy," he encouraged. "That's the old scientific spirit."

He wilted under my glare. "Sorry. I've no call to be funny. I wish those slobs— Steggo and Skandelli—were here. They'd have their mouths washed with viscodium, they would. Although," he considered, "they probably despise us just as much as we do them. You're the only innocent bystander."

The women, dressed in gay Aldebaranian frocks, were peering anxiously through the hatch. I thought of how much workable Dendros meant to them. After all, their claim was as just as mine.

"Forget it."

"You see," he explained anxiously, "this is a democracy we have here, a democracy of the purest kind because it's still close to the conditions which produced it. I'm only the leader; and even if I wanted to set you free because I trust you, the rest of the men can't feel that sure."

"I understand. You have a sound mind, Ragin. A pity only Solarians and Sagittarians are allowed in galactic government."

"Yeah. That's what I kept telling them."

Everybody laughed and tension dissolved. Gonda leaned over his shmobber and said to a neighbor: "See, what did I tell you—the doc *is* a good guy!"

The tall mutineer came over and stood at my side. Together we stared at the stubborn viscodium, green and immovable.

We all perspired quietly in useless, repetitious thought.

"It beats the living shavings out of me," Ragin said finally, "how that goo won't let us make any adjustments in the Dendros that will turn us away from the Solarian Patrol, but keeps them working the way they were set."

"Property of the substance," I yawned wearily. "In order to steer you must use the Dendros as moving parts; viscodium between the parts precludes that. However, Dendros merely vibrate through the space warp on straight drive; the viscodium, having assumed the characteristics of the substance to which it adheres, vibrates along with it, actually adding to its efficiency. If the Dendros stop, so does the viscodium. Any activity of the bound object automatically becomes an activity of that filthy, hardened slime."

"Suppose you change the makeup of the Dendros, then. You could negate them and take the whole business apart with hyper-tongs. After we got rid of the viscodium, the boys would reassemble the machines and make 'em solid. No?"

I shook my head. "No. Space negation is dangerous enough with the proper equipment and under the proper conditions. Here, you'd just save the Solarian Patrol a lot of grief by tearing a hole right through the ether. Besides, you can't negate dendraloid. Of course, if you could change the physical properties of dendraloid enough to pick the viscodium off, you'd be set. But any way I figure it, you wind up without any motors at all."

"And with the ship carrying no transmitter, that would not be nice. No matter what these damned bushaleons are doing to us, we have to keep them in good condition. I have the boys oiling them internally every six hours. That's the minimum period according to the manual."

When I could get my tongue disentangled from my teeth, I grabbed his arm. "Oil them? What kind of oil?"

He looked down, puzzled. "Machine oil. Not the Terran kind—"

"You poor, broken blasthead!" I yelled. "Is there any molecular joint lubricant on this filthy, meteor-broken scow?"

A light of purest joy broke over his face. He snapped out an order.

One of the men scurried to a cabinet and peered inside. At his triumphant shout everybody exhaled gustily.

"Use the mittens," I called to him. "There should be a pair of insulated mittens next to the case."

The Aldebaranian came staggering back with a container whose walls were made of thinnest neutronium. Inside it splashed the most beautiful purple liquid I'd ever seen. Molecular oil!

It meant a reprieve from the negative space foundries for the men. It meant a reprieve from imprisonment with Fino Feminists for the women. As for me—it meant reprieve...

"Dig up a couple of loading pipes," I ordered. "Clean ones. They're the only things that have linings to take the stuff. You can make one of them into a funnel and cup it under the whole block of Dendros and solid viscodium. Then run a pipe from the funnel to an airlock and if it works we can pump the goo right out into space."

"If it works!" Ragin caroled. "It's got to work! We're down to our last electron in this pot. It's got to work!"

It worked.

We poured the purple liquid into a vat of Sirian machine oil. Then we squirted the mixture, at the highest pressure we could generate, along the Dendro input pipes under the floor plates. It took a while for the super lubricant to work its way through the heavy colloid. Then the outside of the machinery shone with a sudden purple sheen as oil oozed through the molecules of dendraloid.

Ragin yelled and pounded my back.

Slowly the viscodium changed from green to purple, the color of the machine oil. It became softer and softer, as the physical characteristics of the object it gripped changed from solid to liquid. Finally, it flowed evenly into the funnel. We heard it gurgling through the loading pipe on the way to the airlock, moving slower and becoming more viscous as it went.

One of the mutineers volunteered to crawl under the Dendros. While we watched breathlessly, he held the neutronium container under the tapering, bottom point of the drive motors. He caught every drop of the molecular joint lubricant in the container. Naturally—he had to.

Ballew turned from his charts and said, "I hope you won't get angry, but the men are—well, insistent that you stay in your cabin while the lifeboats are leaving. It isn't that they don't trust you, but—"

"They feel my conscience will help my mouth in depriving the Solarian Patrol of information if I don't know where they're heading. I understand."

He smiled at me out of poor teeth. "That's it. While you were prying the viscodium loose, I was a prisoner on the bridge. And I've known these men for years. They felt that as an officer, I didn't have the same size stake as say Ragin has, with his wife involved the way she is. They were right. That's why I'm staying aboard with you. I'm going on to Sol."

"Are you that confident I won't inform on you?"

A rustle of charts as he turned one around. There was a youthful grin on his face. "Yes. You see, we had your cabin searched before the mutiny. Nothing important was found. Except for half a container of *unused* depilosac dissolving in the waste chamber."

I stopped breathing and sat up straight. What a stupid slip!

"Ragin claimed it meant nothing. I didn't think so. I thought about it and thought about it until I came to the one possible solution. Now I know you have just as much interest in my not talking about this trip as I have in your keeping quiet. So I'm going on to Sol and after the patrol finishes its routine check—it won't be more than that with Ragin taking all responsibility in the log—I'll go my way and you'll go yours, *Doctor* Sims."

"Have you told anyone else?"

"Only Ragin, just after you finished with that mess in the engine room. He didn't believe it at first."

I bounded out of the room. Ragin was in his cabin with his wife. They were packing.

When I entered, he was almost halfway through the ninety-five volumes of the *Encyclopaedia Galactica*. As each volume passed into the force field of the collapsicon, it diminished to one-twentieth of its original size and mass. I stared at the miniature books lying at the bottom of the mechanical valise.

The Aldebaranian woman left quietly in response to her husband's signal. I cleared my throat. "Don't open that thing suddenly when you start unpacking, or you'll think an avalanche hit you."

He shifted uncomfortably. "I know. I've used collapsicons before." There was a silence.

"And how do you expect to live on a bare planetoid? You can't grow food where there isn't oxygen."

"Oh, we sunk our money in extractors. We'll be able to suck enough raw elements out of whatever we hit to get started. After that it's a matter of our own ingenuity."

"And the books are for your children?"

"Yeah. Elsa wants a lot of them. And I'm going to see they grow up with all the knowledge the galaxy has available."

Ragin coughed. "By the Hole in Cygnus, doctor, why couldn't you wait? A naval employee, too! Six months and the liners would be running again, and everything would be open and above-board."

"I have a son in a naval hospital on Earth," I told him. "We haven't seen each other in three years and I still couldn't get a priority. He may be dead in six months."

"Yes, that would be it. But your papers—"

"My papers refer to Dr. R. Sims, physical chemist, of naval research, Aldebaranian Project CBX-19329. Horkey, my superior, made them out for me just that way, gave me an indefinite leave of absence, and wished me luck."

He squeezed my hand in a last, friendly mangle and accompanied me to the door. "Don't worry about Ballew. He's a good kid. The only reason he mentioned his discovery at all was because he decided to go to Sol and he wanted you to know how secure he felt. He's read too many books, maybe."

Before they left, the mutineers showed Ballew and me how to set the Dendros. In the end, he worked out the charts and I tended the machinery. Just as well—I felt safer that way.

"You know," Ballew said lazily as he waited for the Solarian warpers to pull us into the system. "All I can think of is a little old bar in New York. A little old bar where I'm going to get stinking drunk."

He was cute. Personally, I was dreaming of Max's Salon in Chicago. Max's where I, Roberta Sims, Sc.D., Ph.D., Ga.D., would be getting a glorious terrestrial permanent wave.

After my hair had grown back, of course.

Afterword: For the Rent

"A Matter of Frequency"
"The Ionian Cycle"
"Hallock's Madness"
"Ricardo's Virus"
"The Puzzle of Priipiirii"
"Dud"
"Confusion Cargo"

These stories were all written in the late 1940s and published either then or in the early 1950s. Ted Sturgeon had been my agent almost from the beginning, and he was at the time quite bitter over his relationship with John W. Campbell, Jr., the editor of *Astounding Science Fiction* (then far and away the premier magazine in the field). He felt that John had forced him to become too much of a sprocket-and-gear writer, instead of the style-accenting fantasist he started out to be. He particularly envied Ray Bradbury, who had had so much trouble selling Campbell that he had developed a good relationship with the other editors in the field and had produced such a great volume of highly personalized science fiction.

Ted also felt that being part of Campbell's stable was what was responsible for his constant financial difficulties. "John can only take so much from any one writer," he'd say, "especially these days when *Unknown* is dead and he has only a single magazine. The newsstands are full of other science-fiction magazines; there's enough market there to make a decent living. I don't want you to make the mistake I did, Phil. Now, when you're beginning, is the time to spread out and sell as many different things to as many different editors as there are."

The trouble was that for the most part I didn't enjoy reading these science-fiction magazines that were south of Campbell nearly as much as I enjoyed reading *Astounding Science Fiction.* I also couldn't be nearly as proud of being published in them as I was of appearing in Campbell's magazine. But Sturgeon was both my agent and my mentor: he had written an awful lot—an awful lot of very good stuff—and all I could point to was two or three passable stories in *Astounding.*

Obviously, Ted Sturgeon *knew.*

So I bought and read all these other markets, the so-called "BEM" magazines (after the Bug-Eyed Monsters and scantily clad females on their covers—covers hilariously described by S.J. Perelman in his classic essay, "Captain Future, Block that Kick!"). They not only had lurid covers but what you had to call lurid titles as well: *Marvel* and *Startling* and *Thrilling Wonder.* Science fiction in those days was a pulp field, and pulp magazines had to have titles that yelled at you from the newsstand.

The work that appeared in them was paid for at very low rates—frequently on publication, rather than acceptance—and appeared beside letter columns, as I've noted elsewhere, filled with material written by raucous fans. These letters by fans, mostly juvenile, like Chad Oliver, Bob Tucker, Rickey Slavin, and Marion "Astra" Zimmer (which was what she then called herself, before becoming Marion Zimmer Bradley), ranged from strident judgments of a given "ish" of the "mag" to scholarly chidings of a writer for referring to Jason's centaur tutor as Charon rather than Chiron.

Close to the bottom, in terms of payment and cover art and general fan hysteria, was *Planet Stories*, which featured titles like "Beneath the Red World's Crust" and "Valkyrie from the Void" and "The Thing of Venus." (My all-time favorite was one particular cover story, "When Kohonnes Screamed.")

Pretty poor stuff, you might think. And you would be somewhat wrong. Because though the magazine paid poorly—and only on publication—it also featured many splendid and to-be-anthologized stories by Leigh Brackett and Poul Anderson and the young Ray Bradbury—Bradbury when he was at his powerful, most colorful best.

Now, instead of using these magazines as I had up to then, as no more than rescue markets, I tried very hard to write for them. And I did well. I actually made a fair living out of writing, which was more than Ted had ever done, and I was doing it within a couple of years after my first publication.

I felt I was earning while I was learning, and so I tried to write just about every kind of science-fiction story.

(There were some science-fiction types I never attempted, however. One of them, fortunately, was the telepathy story. I say "fortunately," because the definitive stories of that type were still to be written, the stories that were so good, that only a blind, deaf, and dumb writer would try do a science-fiction telepathy story after them. I refer, of course, to the two masterpieces of the genre —Alfie Bester's *The Demolished Man* and Bob Silverberg's *Dying Inside.*)

Ted Sturgeon never did make a real livelihood out of writing, not until there were magazines in the field with the quality and paying level of *Galaxy* and *The Magazine of Fantasy & Science Fiction,* and not until he began to write novels. He was perhaps one of the best agents I ever had, but he became completely discouraged at some point and took himself and his entire client list—Jim Blish, Damon Knight, A. Bertram Chandler, Judy Merril, Chandler Davis, Ree Dragonette, me—to Scott Meredith.

Scott had started his own agency only a short time before, and was still at the period where he couldn't even afford to hire a messenger (so that he and his brother, Sidney, used to change secretly to sloppy clothes in the afternoons and deliver manuscripts to editors themselves). He was, however, already writing advertising for the agency in *The Writer's Digest*, advertising that was so effective that it almost immediately pulled in scores of reader's-fee clients and even professional writers like P.G. Wodehouse.

The *Writer's Digest* advertising also pulled in Ted, and one interview with Scott convinced Ted that he'd at last found the agent he himself should have been. He shipped all of us over to the great man, assuring us that at last we would be represented by someone capable of transforming us into *real* commercial writers, people who made a living out of what they did, instead of dabbling and starving as he, Theodore Sturgeon, had done.

Well, as I said, Ted *knew*—we all absolutely agreed on that. We all turned to and tried to satisfy this new agent by writing for as wide a range of markets as possible, everything from *Ranch Romances* to *Spicy Hockey Stories.* Jim Blish even got a job doing reader's-fee criticisms for Scott, helping would-be writers become professionals by introducing them to the Scott Meredith Plot Skeleton, a sure-fire way, it was claimed, to achieve a sale to the pulp-story magazines. Jim analyzed story after story by wannabes this way for several years until he finally cracked up and spent one long afternoon writing a very lengthy criticism on James Joyce's *Finnegans Wake,* pointing out to the verbose Dubliner all the ways the book missed out again and again on the crucial twists and turns of the Plot Skeleton.

And I? Under Scott's direction, I not only wrote for the lower-level science-fiction magazines, but I branched out for publications all over the newsstands of the day. Scott had a number of what might be called captive editors—editors of western, sport, detective, and love-story magazines, paying a cent a word or a half-cent a word, who bought their entire table of contents from Scott with the understanding that he would never, never fail to fill up one of their issues. You had to write a lot to do well. I wrote a lot.

You might say I had become a hack. You would be wrong.

You would be wrong because I failed. It turned out that I just didn't have the utterly necessary talent of a hack. I don't think anyone ever tried harder to become a hack writer, or failed more miserably. You had to be born with the genes of hackhood. So I made a very good living for a couple of years, then I suddenly stopped. I mean *stopped*—end of action, *fini,* no more and nothing. I found I couldn't even sit at the typewriter and write a love letter or a note to my grocer. I hated the act of writing. I hated trying to think of a story. I hated the very idea of stories so much that for several months I even stopped reading anything but the daily newspaper.

I felt that I had spent the last two years drinking my own vomit.

I left Scott, who was becoming a major literary agent: he represented the likes of Norman Mailer and Arthur C. Clarke and, to the best of my knowledge, they swore by him. To support myself, I worked at a number of odd jobs (and I do mean "odd"—everything from department-store cookware demonstrator to disease specialist in a tropical fish hatchery to stickman in a nickel-and-dime gambling joint on Times Square).

When at long, long last I began writing again, I swore I would never put typewriter key to paper again unless I *meant* it, meant it in some important way that had to do with either learning or stating something that counted. I really took an oath before God; I was that grateful for the interesting words that were coming out of me once more.

Most of these stories, however, were written when Ted Sturgeon, rather than Scott, was my agent (I wrote little science fiction in my Scott Meredith days). I did not make a lot of money with Sturgeon, I just got by. But I *was* getting by—paying the rent regularly, for instance. And above all, as I said, I felt I was earning while I was learning. I suspect that Ray Bradbury and Poul Anderson also felt at the time that they were earning while they were learning. I read them today and feel they learned one hell of an esthetic lot.

Not that I would say that any of the pieces by me in this section were of a quality comparable with their best work—not at all. But my editors and publishers here wanted a *complete* collection and, after much argument, I've let them have it. What the hell, these pieces are still mine, and once I was even quite proud of them.

I started "A Matter of Frequency" immediately after Fred Pohl told me that the phrase "entropy gradient" was Cyril Kornbluth's all-time favorite and that Cyril was determined one day to find out what if anything it meant. The phrase struck me as a science-fiction version of *"Twas brillig...,"* and I felt it fitted the story I was writing just then. I just went ahead and lifted it from Cyril. And then Cyril, when we met, was nice enough to tell me that he had enjoyed the story and that he felt it complemented his brilliant novelette, "The Marching Morons," published just about the same time. It made me feel a shade less guilty.

Now, "The Ionian Cycle" (I've no idea where the title came from: it's the magazine editor's, not mine; I've long ago forgotten what my title was) was a piece that, except for the "great galaxies" language and the somewhat enforced love interest, I know I thought was pretty good when I wrote it: it's really a Campbell solve-the-problem story, though Campbell never had the opportunity to accept or reject it.

I was never exactly proud of "Hallock's Madness." As I read it now, I see it as heavily influenced by writers like H. Rider Haggard, and somehow not quite making it. I picked up the idea later, however, in a story that I think was much better and that I sold to Horace Gold's *Galaxy*—"The Malted Milk Monster."

"Ricardo's Virus" is a pure *Planet* story. For it, I borrowed the Venusian landscape and fauna I used in the much more original "Venus and the Seven Sexes." And it and "The Puzzle of Priipiirii" were written as I was coming out of a totally unrewarding (and unrewarded) love affair: nothing was making much sense to me at the time—I was love-lorn, and every popular song seemed to have been written with the intention of making me wince as much as possible. I still had to pay the rent, though.

Another Campbell kind of story, *Dud*, gets the ship out of a jam in the manner, if not the quality, of a Malcolm Jameson piece. I liked Jameson then and read every one of his stories in *Astounding* at least two or three times as soon as I got the magazine. Today, however, I can't remember the details of a single one of them.

And finally, "Confusion Cargo." The story I wrote, my first attempt at an action piece, was originally titled "Glutinous Mutiny" (the editor told me over the phone that he loved the title and would therefore buy the story without reading it. Then he changed the title to "Confusion Cargo"!) and was planned as the first of a series parallelling Nordhoff and Hall's Bounty trilogy. "Glutinous Mutiny" was to be followed by "Men Against Space" and, finally, "Pitcairn's Asteroid."

I lost interest and never did the two sequels, something for which I am today rather grateful.

Two last notes on this one. As I now reread the piece, I am impressed by how much glittering sci-fi (as opposed to science fiction) I managed to pack into it: "negship," "visco-dium," "dellite," "restrainons," "*hwat* suits," "sawed-off shmobber"—and that's just in the first eight paragraphs!

But second, and as to science fiction: The editors of what was, after all, a true-blue, down-to-Mars pulp magazine, told me they were rather uncomfortable with a *female* protagonist in an action story, not to mention some crazy kind of feminist organization that was sufficiently bellicose actually to cooperate with the enemy in a war.

Fortunately for my first attempt to sell outside of Campbell, however, they felt there was just enough shoot-em-up in the narrative to cover such loopy and subversive ideas.

That's the lot: seven stories written primarily to pay the rent and buy some food. They're not really all that bad, and they're fairly good examples of a lot of science fiction of the period, but I only hope the reader will agree with my editors and publishers about the wisdom of including them here —and not agree with me.

の

Beating Time

The Discovery of Morniel Mathaway

Everyone is astonished at the change in Morniel Mathaway since he was discovered, everyone but me. They remember him as an unbathed and untalented Greenwich Village painter who began almost every second sentence with "I" and ended every third one with "me." He had all the pushing, half-frightened conceit of the man who secretly suspects himself to be a second-rater or worse, and any half-hour conversation with him made your ears droop with the boastful yells he threw at them.

I understand the change in him, the soft-spoken self-deprecation as well as the sudden overwhelming success. But then, I was there the day he was "discovered"—except that isn't the right way to put it. To tell you the truth, I don't know how to put it really, considering the absolute impossibility—yes, I said *impossibility*, not improbability—of the whole business. All I know for sure is that trying to make sense out of it gives me belly-yammers and the biggest headache this side of calculus.

We were talking about his discovery that day. I was sitting, carefully balanced, on the one wooden chair in his cold little Bleecker Street studio, because I was too sophisticated to sit in the easy chair.

Morniel practically paid the rent on his studio with that easy chair. It was a broken-down tangle of filthy upholstery that was high in the front of the seat and very low in the back. When you sat in it, things began sliding out of your pockets—loose change, keys, wallets, anything—and into the jungle of rusty springs and rotting woodwork below.

Whenever newcomers came to the place, Morniel would make a big fuss about showing them to "the *comfortable* chair." And as they twisted about painfully trying to find a spot between the springs, his eyes would gleam and he'd get all lit up with good cheer. Because the more they moved about, the more would fall out of their pockets.

After a party, he'd take the chair apart and start counting the receipts, like a store owner hitting the cash register the evening after a fire sale.

The only trouble was, to sit in the wooden chair, you had to concentrate, since it teetered.

Morniel couldn't lose—he always sat on the bed.

"I can't wait for the day," he was saying, "when some dealer, some critic, with an ounce of brain in his head sees my work. I can't miss, Dave, I know I can't miss; I'm just too good. Sometimes I get frightened at how good I am—it's almost too much talent for one man."

"Well," I said, "there's always the—"

"Not that it's too much talent for me," he went on, fearful that I might have misunderstood him. "I'm big enough to carry it, fortunately; I'm large enough of soul. But another, lesser guy would be destroyed by this much totality of perception, this comprehension of the spiritual *gestalt,* as I like to put it. His mind would just crack wide open under the load. Not me, though, Dave, not me."

"Good," I said. "Glad to hear it. Now if you don't *mi*—"

"Do you know what I was thinking about this morning?"

"No," I said. "But, to tell you the truth, I don't really—"

"I was thinking about Picasso, Dave. Picasso and Rouault. I'd just gone for a walk through the pushcart area to have my breakfast—you know, the old the-hand-is-quicker-than-the-eye Morniel—and I started to think about the state of modern painting. I think about that a lot, Dave. It troubles me."

"You do?" I said. "Well, *I* tend to—"

"I walked down Bleecker Street, then I swung into Washington Square Park, and while I walked, I was thinking: Who is doing really important work in painting today, who is really and unquestionably great? I could think of only three names: Picasso, Rouault—and me. There's nobody else doing anything worthwhile and original nowadays. Just three names out of the whole host of people painting all over the world at this moment: just three names, no more. It made me feel very lonely, Dave."

"I can see that," I said. "But then, you—"

"And then I asked myself, why is this so? Has absolute genius always been so rare, is there an essential statistical limitation on it in every period, or is there another reason, peculiar to our own time? And why has my impending discovery been delayed so long? I thought about it for a long time, Dave. I thought about it humbly, carefully, because it's an important question. And this is the answer I came up with."

I gave up. I just sat back in my chair—not too far back, of course—and listened to him expound a theory of esthetics I'd heard at least a dozen times before, from a dozen other painters in the Village. The only point of difference between them was on the question of exactly who was the culmination and the most perfect living example of this esthetic. Morniel, you will probably not be amazed to learn, felt it was himself.

He'd come to New York from Pittsburgh, Pennsylvania, a tall, awkward boy who didn't like to shave and believed he could paint. In those days, he admired Gauguin and tried to imitate him on canvas; he'd talk for hours, in the accents that sound like movie Brooklynese, but are actually pure Pittsburgh, about the *mystique* of folk simplicity.

He got off the Gauguin kick fast, once he'd taken a few courses at the Art Students League and grown his first straggly blond beard. Recently, he had developed his own technique, which he called smudge-on-smudge.

He was bad, and there were no two ways about it. I say that not only from my opinion—and I've roomed with two modern painters and been married for a year to another—but from the opinions of pretty knowing people who, having no personal axe to grind, looked his work over carefully.

One of them, a fine critic of modern art, said after staring slack-jawed at a painting which Morniel had insisted on giving me and which, in spice of my protests, he had personally hung over my fireplace: "It's not just that he doesn't say anything of any significance, graphically, but he doesn't even set himself what you might call *painterly* problems. White-on-white, smudge-on-smudge, non-objectivism, neo-abstractionism, call it what you like, there's nothing there, nothing! He's just another of these loudmouth, frowzy, frustrated dilettantes that infest the Village."

So why did I spend time with Morniel? Well, he lived right around the corner. He was slightly colorful, in his own sick way. And when I'd sat up all night, trying to work on a poem that simply wouldn't be worked, I often felt it would be relaxing to drift around to his studio for a spot of conversation that wouldn't have anything to do with literature.

The only trouble—and the thing I always forgot—was that it almost never was a conversation. It was a monologue that I barely managed to break in on from time to time.

You see, the difference between us was that I'd been published, even if it was only in badly printed experimental magazines that paid off in subscriptions. He'd never been exhibited—not once.

There was another reason for my maintaining a friendly relationship with the man. And that had to do with the one talent he really had.

I barely get by, so far as living expenses are concerned. Things like good paper to write on, fine books for my library, are stuff I yearn for all the time, but are way out of my reach financially. When the yearning gets too great—for a newly published collection by Wallace Stevens, for example—I meander over to Morniel's and tell him about it.

Then we go out to the bookstore—entering it separately. I start a conversation with the proprietor about some very expensive, out-of-print item that I'm thinking of ordering and, once I've got all of his attention, Morniel snaffles the Stevens—which I intend to pay for, of course, as soon as I'm a little ahead.

He's absolutely wonderful at it. I've never seen him so much as suspected, let alone caught. Of course, I have to pay for the favor by going through the same routine in an art-supply store, so that Morniel can replenish his stock of canvas, paint and brushes, but it's worth it to me in the long run. The only thing it's not worth is the thumping boredom I have to suffer through in listening to the guy, or my conscience bothering me because I know he never intends to pay for those things. Okay, so I will, when I can.

"I can't be as unique as I feel I am," he was saying now. "Other people must be born with the potential of such great talent, but it's destroyed in them before they can reach artistic maturity. Why? How? Well, let's examine the role that society—"

And that's exactly when I first saw it. Just as he got to the word "society," I saw this purplish ripple in the wall opposite me, the strange, shimmering outline of a box with a strange, shimmering outline of a man inside the box. It was about five feet off the floor and it looked like colored heat waves. Then there was nothing on the wall.

But it was too late in the year for heat waves. And I've never had optical illusions. It could be, I decided, that I had seen the beginnings of a new crack in Morniel's wall. The place wasn't really a studio, just a drafty cold-water flat that some old occupant had cleared so as to make one long room. It was on the top floor and the roof leaked occasionally; the walls were covered with thick, wavy lines in memory of the paths followed by the trickling water.

But why purple? And why the outline of a man inside a box? That was pretty tricky, for a simple crack in the wall. And where had it gone?

"—the eternal conflict with the individual who insists on his individuality," Morniel pointed out. "Not to mention—"

A series of high musical notes sounded, one after the other, rapidly. And then, in the center of the room, about two feet above the floor this time, the purple lines reappeared—still hazy, still transparent and still with the outline of a man inside.

Morniel swung his feet off the bed and stared up at it. "What the—" he began.

Once more, the outfit disappeared.

"W-what—" Morniel stuttered. "What's going *on?*"

"I don't know," I told him. "But whatever it is, I'd say they're slowly zeroing in."

Again those high musical notes. And the purple box came into view with its bottom resting on the floor. It got darker, darker and more substantial. The notes kept climbing up the scale and getting fainter and fainter until, when the box was no longer transparent, they faded away altogether.

A door slid back in the box. A man stepped out, wearing clothing that seemed to end everywhere in curlicues.

He looked first at me, then at Morniel.

"Morniel Mathaway?" he inquired.

"Ye-es," Morniel said, backing away toward his refrigerator.

"Morniel Mathaway," the man from the box said, "my name is Glescu. I bring you greetings from 2487 AD."

Neither of us could think of a topper for that one, so we let it lie there. I got up and stood beside Morniel, feeling obscurely that I wanted to get as close as possible to something I was familiar with.

And we all held that position for a while. Tableau.

I thought to myself, 2487 AD. I'd never seen anyone dressed like that. Even more, I'd never *imagined* anyone dressed like that and my imagination can run pretty wild. The clothing was not exactly transparent and yet not quite opaque. Prismatic is the word for it, different colors that constantly chased themselves in and out and around the curlicues. There seemed to be a pattern to it, but nothing that my eyes could hold down and identify.

And the man himself, this Mr. Glescu, was about the same height as Morniel and me and he seemed to be not very much older. But there was a something about him— I don't know, call it *quality,* true and tremendous *quality*—that would have cowed the Duke of Wellington. Civilized, maybe that's the word: he was the most civilized-looking man I'd ever seen.

He stepped forward. "We will now," he said in a rich, wonderfully resonant voice, "indulge in the twentieth-century custom of shaking hands."

So we indulged in the twentieth-century custom of shaking hands with him. First Morniel, then me—and both very gingerly. Mr. Glescu shook hands with a peculiar awkwardness that made me think of the way an Iowan farmer might eat with chopsticks for the first time.

The ceremony over, he stood there and beamed at us. Or, rather, at Morniel.

"What a moment, eh?" he said. "What a supreme moment!"

Morniel took a deep breath and I knew that all those years of meeting process servers unexpectedly on the stairs had begun to pay off. He was recovering; his mind was beginning to work again.

"How do you mean 'what a moment'?" he asked. "What's so special about it? Are you the—the inventor of time travel?"

Mr. Glescu twinkled with laughter. "*Me?* An *inventor?* Oh, no. No, no! Time travel was invented by Antoinette Ingeborg in—but that was after your time. Hardly worth going into at the moment, especially since I only have half an hour."

"Why half an hour?" I asked, not so much because I was curious as because it seemed like a good question.

"The skindrom can only be maintained that long," he elucidated. "The skindrom is—well, call it a transmitting device that enables me to appear in your period. There is such an enormous expenditure of power required that a trip into the past is made only once every fifty years. The privilege is awarded as a sort of Gobel. I hope I have the word right. It *is* Gobel, isn't it? The award made in your time?"

I had a flash. "You wouldn't mean *Nobel,* by any chance? The Nobel Prize?"

He nodded his head enthusiastically. "That's it! The Nobel Prize. The trip is awarded to outstanding scholars as a kind of Nobel Prize. Once every fifty years—the man selected by the gardunax as the most pre-eminent—that sort of thing. Up to now, of course, it's always gone to historians and they've frittered it away on the Siege of Troy, the first atom-bomb explosion at Los Alamos, the discovery of America—things like that. But *this* year—"

"Yes?" Morniel broke in, his voice quavering. We were both suddenly remembering that Mr. Glescu had known his name. "What kind of scholar are you?"

Mr. Glescu made us a slight bow with his head. "I am an art scholar. My specialty is art history. And my special field in art history is…"

"*What?*" Morniel demanded, his voice no longer quavering, but positively screechy. "What is your special field?"

Again a slight bow from Mr. Glescu's head. "You, Mr. Mathaway. In my own period, I may say without much fear of contradiction, I am the greatest living authority on the life and works of Morniel Mathaway. My special field is you."

Morniel went white. He groped his way to the bed and sat down as if his hips were made of glass. He opened his mouth several times and couldn't seem to get a sound out. Finally, he gulped, clenched his fists and got a grip on himself.

"Do—do you mean," he managed to croak at last, "that I'm famous? *That* famous?"

"Famous? You, my dear sir, are beyond fame. You are one of the immortals the human race has produced. As I put it—rather well if I may say so—in my last book, *Mathaway, the Man Who Shaped the Future:* 'How rarely has it fallen to the lot of individual human endeavor to—' "

"That famous." The blond beard worked the way a child's face does when it's about to cry. "*That* famous!"

"That famous!" Mr. Glescu assured him. "Who is the man with whom modern painting, in its full glory, is said to have definitely begun? Who is the man whose designs and special manipulations of color have dominated architecture for the past five centuries, who is responsible for the arrangement of our cities, the shape of our every artifact, the very texture of our clothing."

"Me?" Morniel inquired weakly.

"You! No other man in the history of art has exerted such a massive influence over design or over so wide an area of art for so long a period of time, To whom can I compare you, sir? To what other artist in history can I compare you?"

"Rembrandt?" Morniel suggested. He seemed to be tying to be helpful. "Da Vinci?"

Mr. Glescu sneered. "Rembrandt and Da Vinci in the same breath as you? Ridiculous! They lacked your universality, your taste for the cosmic, your sense of the all-encompassing. No, to relate you properly to an equal, one must go outside painting, to literature, possibly. Shakespeare, with his vast breadth of understanding, with the resounding organ notes of his poetry and with his tremendous influence on the later English language—but even Shakespeare, I'm afraid, even Shakespeare—" He shook his head sadly.

"Wow!" breathed Morniel Mathaway.

"Speaking of Shakespeare," I broke in, "do you happen to know of a poet named David Dantziger? Did much of his work survive?"

"Is that you?"

"Yes," I told the man from 2487 AD eagerly. "That's me, Dave Dantziger."

He wrinkled his forehead. "I don't seem to remember any— What school of poetry do you belong to?"

"Well, they call it by various names. Anti-imagist is the most usual one. Anti-imagist or post-imagist."

"No," said Mr. Glescu after thinking for a while. "The only poet I can remember for this time and this part of the world is Peter Tedd."

"Who is Peter Tedd? Never heard of him."

"Then this must be before he was discovered. But please remember, I am an art scholar, not a literary one. It is entirely possible," he went on soothingly, "that were you to mention your name to a specialist in the field of minor twentieth-century versifiers, he could place you with a minimum of difficulty. Entirely possible."

I glanced at Morniel, and he was grinning at me from the bed. He had entirely recovered by now and was beginning to soak the situation in through his pores. The whole situation. His standing. Mine.

I decided I hated every single one of his guts.

Why did it have to be someone like Morniel Mathaway that got that kind of nod from fate? There were so many painters who were decent human beings, and yet this bragging slug...

And all the time, a big part of my mind was wandering around in circles. It just proved, I kept saying to myself, that you need the perspective of history to properly evaluate anything in art. You think of all the men who were big guns in their time and today are forgotten—that contemporary of Beethoven's, for example, who, while he was alive, was considered much the greater man, and whose name is known today only to musicologists. But still—

Mr. Glescu glanced at the forefinger of his right hand where a little black dot constantly expanded and contracted. "My time is getting short," he said. "And while it is an ineffable, overwhelming delight for me to be standing in your studio, Mr. Mathaway, and looking at you at last in the flesh, I wonder if you would mind obliging me with a small favor?"

"Sure," Morniel nodded, getting up. "You name it. Nothing's too good for you. What do you want?"

Mr. Glescu swallowed as if he were about to bring himself to knock on the gates of Paradise. "I wonder—I'm sure you don't mind—could you possibly let me look at the painting you're working on at the moment? The idea of seeing a Mathaway in an unfinished state, with the paint still wet upon it—" He shut his eyes, as if he couldn't believe that all this was really happening to him.

Morniel gestured urbanely and strode to his easel. He pulled the tarp off. "I intend to call this—" and his voice had grown as oily as the subsoil of Texas—"*Figured Figurines Number 29.*"

Slowly, tastingly, Mr. Glescu opened his eyes and leaned forward. "But—" he said, after a long silence. "Surely this isn't *your* work, Mr. Mathaway?"

Morniel turned around in surprise and considered the painting. "It's my work, all right. *Figured Figurines Number 29.* Recognize it?"

"No," said Mr. Glescu. "I do not recognize it. And that is a fact for which I am extremely grateful. Could I see something else, please? Something a little later?"

"That's the latest," Morniel told him a little uncertainly. "Everything else is earlier. Here, you might like this." He pulled a painting out of the rack. "I call this *Figured Figurines Number 22.* I think it's the best of my early period."

Mr. Glescu shuddered. "It looks like smears of paint on top of other smears of paint."

"Right! Only I call it smudge-on-smudge. But you probably know all that, being such an authority on me. And here's *Figured Figurines Number—*"

"Do you mind leaving these—these figurines, Mr. Mathaway?" Glescu begged. "I'd like to see something of yours with color. With color and with form!"

Morniel scratched his head. "I haven't done any real color work for a long time. Oh, wait!" he brightened and began to search in the back of the rack. He came out with an old canvas. "This is one of the few examples of my mauve-and-mottled period that I've kept."

"I can't imagine why," Mr. Glescu murmured, mostly to himself. "It's positively—" He brought his shoulders up to his ears in the kind of shrug that anyone who's ever seen an art critic in action can immediately recognize. You don't need words after that shrug; if you're a painter whose work he's looking at, you don't *want* words.

About this time, Morniel began pulling paintings out frantically. He'd show them to Glescu, who would gurgle as if he were forcing down a retch, and pull out some more paintings.

"I don't understand it," Mr. Glescu said, staring at the floor, which was strewn with canvases tacked to their wooden stretchers. "This was obviously before you discovered yourself and your true technique. But I'm looking for a sign, a *hint,* of the genius that is to come. And I find—" He shook his head dazedly.

"How about this one?" Morniel asked, breathing hard.

Mr. Glescu shoved at it with both hands. "Please take it *away!*" He looked at his forefinger again. I noticed the black dot was expanding and contracting much more slowly. "I'll have to leave soon," he said. "And I don't understand at all. Let me show you something, gentlemen."

He walked into the purple box and came out with a book. He beckoned to us. Morniel and I moved around behind him and stared over his shoulder. The pages tinkled peculiarly as they were turned; one thing I knew for sure—they weren't made out of paper. And the title-page...

The Complete Paintings of Morniel Mathaway, 1928-1996.

"Were you born in 1928?" I demanded.

Morniel nodded. "May 23, 1928." And he was silent. I knew what he was thinking about and did a little quick figuring. Sixty-eight years. It's not given to many men to know exactly how much time they have. Sixty-eight years—that wasn't so bad.

Mr. Glescu turned to the first of the paintings.

Even now, when I remember my initial sight of it, my knees get weak and bend inward. It was an abstraction in full color, but such an abstraction as I'd never imagined before. As if all the work of all the abstractionists up to this point had been an apprenticeship on the kindergarten level.

You had to like it—so long as you had eyes—whether or not your appreciation had been limited to representational painting until now; even if, in fact, you'd never particularly cared about painting of *any* school.

I don't want to sound maudlin, but I actually felt tears in my eyes. Anyone who was at all sensitive to beauty would have reacted the same way.

Not Morniel, though. "Oh, *that* kind of stuff," he said as if a great light had broken on him. "Why didn't you tell me you wanted *that* kind of stuff?"

Mr. Glescu clutched at Morniel's dirty tee-shirt. "Do you mean you have paintings like this, too?"

"Not paintings—*painting.* Just one. I did it last week as a sort of experiment, but I wasn't satisfied with the way it turned out, so I gave it to the girl downstairs. Care to take a look at it?"

"Oh, yes! Very, very much!"

Morniel reached for the book and tossed it casually on the bed. "Okay," he said. "Come on. It won't take more than a minute or two."

As we trooped downstairs, I found myself boiling with perplexity. One thing I was sure of—as sure as of the fact that Geoffrey Chaucer had lived before Algernon Swinburne—nothing that Morniel had ever done or had the capacity of ever doing could come within a million esthetic miles of the reproduction in that book. And for all of his boasting, for all of his seemingly inexhaustible conceit, I was certain that he also knew it.

He stopped before a door two floors below and rapped on it. There was no answer. He waited a few seconds and knocked again. Still no answer.

"Damn," he said. "She isn't home. And I did want you to see that one."

"I *want* to see it," Mr. Glescu told him earnestly. "I want to see anything that looks like your mature work. But time is growing so short—"

Morniel snapped his fingers. "Tell you what. Anita has a couple of cats she asks me to feed whenever she's away for a while, so she's given me a key to her apartment. Suppose I whip upstairs and get it?"

"Fine!" Mr. Glescu said happily, taking a quick look at his forefinger. "But please hurry."

"Will do." And then, as Morniel turned to go up the stairs, he caught my eye. And he gave me the signal, the one we use whenever we go "shopping." It meant: "Talk to the man. Keep him interested."

I got it. The book. I'd seen Morniel in action far too many times not to remember that casual gesture of tossing it on the bed as anything but a casual gesture. He'd just put it where he could find it when he wanted it—fast. He was going upstairs to hide it in some unlikely spot and when Mr. Glescu had to take off for his own time—well, the book would just not be available.

Smooth? Very pretty damned smooth, I'd say. And Morniel Mathaway would paint the paintings of Morniel Mathaway. Only he wouldn't paint them.

He'd *copy* them.

Meanwhile, the signal snapped my mouth open and automatically started me talking.

"Do you paint yourself, Mr. Glescu?" I asked. I knew that would be a good gambit.

"Oh, no! Of course, I wanted to be an artist when I was a boy—I imagine every critic starts out that way—and I even committed a few daubs of my own. But they were very bad, very bad indeed! I found it far easier to write about paintings than to do them. Once I began reading the life of Morniel Mathaway, I knew I'd found my field. Not only did I empathize closely with his paintings, but he seemed so much like a person I could have known and liked. That's one of the things that puzzles me. He's quite different from what I imagined."

I nodded. "I bet he is."

"Of course history has a way of adding stature and romance to any important figure. And I can see several things about his personality that the glamorizing process of the centuries could—but I shouldn't go on in this fashion, Mr. Dantziger. You're his friend."

"About as much of a friend as he's got in the world," I told him, "which isn't saying much."

And all the time I was trying to figure it out. But the more I figured, the more confused I got. The paradoxes in the thing. How could Morniel Mathaway become famous five hundred years from now by painting pictures that he first saw in a book published five hundred years from now? Who painted the pictures? Morniel Mathaway? The book said so, and with the book in his possession, he would certainly do them. But he'd be copying them out of the book. So who painted the original pictures?

Mr. Glescu looked worriedly at his forefinger. "I'm running out of time—practically none left!"

He sped up the stairs, with me behind him. When we burst into the studio, I braced myself for the argument over the book. I wasn't too happy about it, because I liked Mr. Glescu.

The book wasn't there; the bed was empty. And two other things weren't there—the time machine and Morniel Mathaway.

"He left in it!" Mr. Glescu gasped. "He *stranded* me here! He must have figured out that getting inside and closing the door made it return!"

"Yeah, he's a great figurer," I said bitterly. This I hadn't bargained for. This I wouldn't have helped to bring about. "And he'll probably figure out a very plausible story to tell the people in your time to explain how the whole thing happened. Why should he work his head off in the twentieth century when he can be an outstanding, hero-worshipped celebrity in the twenty-fifth?"

"But what will happen if they ask him to paint merely *one* picture—"

"He'll probably tell them he's already done his work and feels he can no longer add anything of importance to it. He'll no doubt end up giving lectures on himself. Don't worry, he'll make out. It's you I'm worried about. You're stuck here. Are they likely to send a rescue party after you?"

Mr. Glescu shook his head miserably. "Every scholar who wins the award has to sign a waiver of responsibility, in case he doesn't return. The machine may be used only once in fifty years—and by that time, some other scholar will claim and be given the right to witness the storming of the Bastille, the birth of Gautama Buddha or something of the sort. No, I'm *stuck* here, as you phrased it. Is it very bad, living in this period?"

I slapped him on the shoulder. I was feeling very guilty. "Not so bad. Of course, you'll need a social security card, and I don't know how you go about getting one at your age. And possibly—I don't know for sure—the FBI or immigration authorities may want to question you, since you're an illegal alien, kind of."

He looked appalled. "Oh, dear! That's quite bad enough!"

And then I got the idea. "No, it needn't be. Tell you what. Morniel has a social security card—he had a job a couple of years ago. And he keeps his birth certificate in that bureau drawer along with other personal papers. Why don't you just assume his identity? *He'll* never show you up as an imposter!"

"Do you think I could? Won't I be—won't his friends—his relatives—"

"Parents both dead, no relatives I ever heard about. And I told you I'm the closest thing to a friend he's got." I examined Mr. Glescu thoughtfully. "You could get away with it. Maybe grow a beard and dye it blond. Things like that. Naturally, the big problem would be earning a living. Being a specialist on Mathaway and the art movements that derived from him wouldn't get you fed an awful lot right now."

He grabbed at me. "I could paint! I've always dreamed of being a painter! I don't have much talent, but there are all sorts of artistic novelties I know about, all kinds of graphic innovations that don't exist in your time. Surely that would be enough—even without talent—to make a living for me on some third- or fourth-rate level!"

It was. It certainly was. But not on the third- or fourth-rate level. On the first. Mr. Glescu-Morniel Mathaway is the finest painter alive today. And the unhappiest.

"What's the matter with these people?" he asked me wildly after his last exhibition. "Praising me like that! I don't have an ounce of real talent in me; all my work, *all,* is completely derivative. I've tried to do something, *anything,* that was completely my own, but I'm so steeped in Mathaway that I just can't seem to make my own personality come through. And those idiotic critics go on raving about me—and the work isn't even my own!"

"Then whose is it?" I wanted to know.

"Mathaway's, of course," he said bitterly. "We thought there couldn't be a time paradox—I wish you could read all the scientific papers on the subject; they fill whole libraries—because it isn't possible, the time specialists argue, for a painting, say, to be copied from a future reproduction and so have no original artist. But that's what I'm doing! I'm copying from that book by memory!"

I wish I could tell him the truth—he's such a nice guy, especially compared to the real fake of a Mathaway, and he suffers so much.

But I can't.

You see, he's deliberately trying not to copy those paintings. He's working so hard at it that he refuses to think about that book or even discuss it. I finally got him to recently, for a few sentences, and you know what? He doesn't actually remember it, except pretty hazily!

Of course he wouldn't—he's the real Morniel Mathaway and there is no paradox. But if I ever told him that he was actually painting the pictures instead of merely copying them from memory, he'd lose whatever little self-confidence he has. So I have to let him think he's a phony when he's nothing of the sort.

"Forget it," I go on telling him. "A buck's a buck."

AFTERWORD

Body or soul, often both, I was an inhabitant of New York's Greenwich Village from the late '40s to the middle '60s, the period in which I wrote most of these stories. I knew twenty or thirty versions of Morniel Mathaway, all of them as convinced (they claimed) of their own greatness; a lot of them far more predatory than my fictional character here.

Two of the most decent and most promising had been friends of mine since high school, Harold Paris and Irving Amen. I have always believed that one of the pair would be celebrated as a master for at least a couple of centuries.

And he—I won't identify him any further—was the talented original of Morniel, up to and including the remark about Picasso and Rouault. He was also, when much older, one of the originals of Mr. Glescu.

Let me add here that when I first knew these two guys back at Abraham Lincoln High School, although I already planned on being a writer, I lived with a far greater affinity for painting. If you had asked me then to choose between being Shakespeare and Rembrandt or Jonathan Swift and Paul Cézanne, I would have ground my teeth and pulled at my hair and finally come down in each case on the side of the painter.

But over the years I had to learn that whatever talent I was granted lies with literature and not at all with art. So much for the other model for Mr. Glescu.

Alas.

WRITTEN 1954——PUBLISHED 1955

&

SANCTUARY

The cry was in a deep voice, a breathless, badly frightened voice. Hoarse and urgent, it rose above the roar of the distant mob, above the rattle of traffic; it flung itself into the spacious office on the third floor of the Embassy and demanded immediate attention.

His Excellency, the Ambassador from 2219 AD—the sole occupant of that office—was a man of relaxed bearing and a wonderfully calm face. His eyes transmitted the unvarying message that all things were essentially simple—and could be further simplified. It was, therefore, quite remarkable how that cry from the grounds below made him look suddenly uncertain.

He rose and moved to the window with unaccustomed haste. A tall, bearded man, whose clothes were torn and whose body was badly bruised, had just leaped onto the Embassy lawn from the surrounding high fence. The bearded man pointed the forefingers of both hands at the third-floor office of the Ambassador from 2219 AD and shrieked again:

"*Sanctuary!*"

There was an answering shriek from the mob cascading down the street toward him. The bearded man looked over his shoulder once, then dashed forward across the lawn. His feet could be heard pounding up the steps of the Embassy. Downstairs, a heavy door slammed behind him.

The Ambassador from 2219 AD bit his lip. Well, the fellow had made it. Now *his* problems began.

He turned a dial on his wrist communicator. "All Embassy personnel," he said. "Attention! This is the Ambassador speaking. Bolt and barricade all street doors immediately! Barricade all windows on the street level that are not protected by bars. All female personnel and the fugitive who has just entered will be sent up to the second floor. Havemeyer, take charge of the first floor. Bruce, take charge of the second floor—and keep the fugitive under careful guard. Dodson, report to me."

He turned the dial another notch. "Police Department? This is the Ambassador from 2219 AD. A fugitive has just entered the building, requesting sanctuary. From the looks of the mob behind him, I'd say that your normal detail down here will be inadequate to protect us. You will have to send reinforcements."

The policeman's snort was as much anger as surprise. "*You're* giving sanctuary to Henry Groppus and you want us to protect you? Listen, I *live* in this time! It's as much as my life is worth to—"

243

"It's as much as your job is worth if a riot detail isn't down here in two minutes. Two minutes, I said. It is now precisely twenty-seven minutes past six o'clock."

"But listen!" The voice from the dial seemed almost hysterical. "That's Henry *Groppus* you have in there. Do you know what he *did?*"

"At the moment, that's not relevant. If his request for asylum isn't honored, he will be returned to the proper authorities. I am asking protection for the Embassy from 2219 AD, for its property and personnel, which, like all Embassies and their staffs, enjoy extraterritorial status and immunity. It's your responsibility to see that we get it."

The Ambassador clicked off and drew a deep breath. His calm was returning and once more his eyes announced that all complex matters could be refined down to simple ones—and handled.

As he turned to the window again, Dodson, his First Secretary, came in and stood respectfully at his shoulder.

Together, they stared down at the mob, the relaxed, observant older man and the slender, alert young one who split his gaze between the scene below and his chief.

As far as the eye could see, in all directions, the street was the color of the yelling mob. It had pushed right up against the fence, so hard and so tight that those in front were unable to climb it as they had intended, but were jammed, screaming their agony, into the iron bars.

"The police detail on duty, sir," Dodson said in a low voice. "They weren't able to hold them back for more than a few seconds. But they gave us time we needed. Everything downstairs should be secure, sir."

The Ambassador grunted.

Now the fence was giving way. It bent slowly, steadily inward, like a black flower closing. And then it was down here and the mob spilled over it, down there and a thick wave of mob washed across the lawn, down everywhere, mob over it everywhere, mob rushing toward the building in which they stood, mob maddened and swirling all about them and breaking thunderously against the walls.

For just a moment, Dodson was looking contemptuously down through the window. "2119 AD!"

The Ambassador grunted again. The grunt could be taken any one of several ways.

The frenzied, directionless noise from below abruptly changed in quality. It became steady, rhythmical. At the peak of each pulsation, there was an enormous thump. After a while, the thumps were followed by a ripping sound.

"Sir!" Havemeyer's voice came in suddenly on the wrist communicator. "The front door's beginning to give way. All right if we move up to the second floor?"

"By all means. And as soon as you're up there, you and Bruce see to it that the doors, front and rear, are barricaded. Then I want you to stand by the destructive fuses on the Embassy files. If the mob breaks into the second floor, see to it that the files go."

"Right, sir."

"Do you think, sir, that there's any chance—" Dodson had begun, when the sound of a dozen sirens made them look up.

The riot squad was coming down from the sky on flying platforms, two men to a platform. Soupy yellow stuff flowed out of the nozzles of the canisters each policeman carried, flowed out and bubbled into the mob.

The Ambassador looked at his watch. "One minute and fifty seconds," he said comfortably. Then he went back to his desk.

Dodson stood at the window, watching the mob stumble back across the Embassy lawn in chokes and gasps. Above all, he was fascinated by the number of individuals who, in the midst of their choking, stopped and turned and shook their fists at the building behind them.

When he could tear himself away, he described them to his chief.

"They evidently feel pretty strongly, sir," he suggested. "This is no ordinary mob."

"No, it's no ordinary mob. And Groppus is no ordinary criminal. Send him in. Tell Havemeyer and Bruce to start straightening up the place. I want an itemized statement on all damage to be forwarded to the Secretary of State before five o'clock."

"Yes, sir." Dodson paused near the door. "You know, sir, the staff received him inside as something of a hero."

The Ambassador looked up, his calm eyes slightly intent. "Of course they did. How did you feel about him, Dodson—criminal or hero?"

The secretary's face went immediately blank as his burgeoning diplomat's mind tried to blunt the question. "Well, of course, sir, he's both—both criminal and hero."

"Yes, but which is he chiefly? Take a stand, Dodson. How did *you* feel about him? Off the record, naturally."

"Well, sir," the young man began, then hesitated. "I think the dictum that applies here is *When in Rome...* We are, in effect, in Rome. Therefore, Henry Groppus should undoubtedly be considered a criminal."

"Yes," the Ambassador said thoughtfully. "In Rome. All right, send him in, send him in."

Dodson left. The Ambassador sat back and stared at the ceiling—calmly. Then he got up and paced back and forth across the office—calmly. Then he went back to his desk, opened a heavy, gray-bound book, skimmed through a few pages in it and finally leaned forward, drumming his fingers on the polished desktop—calmly, very calmly.

His wrist communicator buzzed. He flipped it on.

"Your Excellency, this is the Secretary of State," said a formal, moistureless voice.

"Good afternoon, Mr. Secretary," said the Ambassador, with equal formality. "What can I do for you?"

"Your Excellency, according to information just received by my office, a certain Henry Hancock Groppus has escaped from the jail cell in which he was awaiting execution and taken shelter in your Embassy. I must ask you if this is true."

"That is true, Mr. Secretary, except for one small detail. At the time he entered the Embassy, he was not being pursued by lawfully constituted authority, but by an unlawful and ungoverned mob."

The voice in the communicator coughed an extremely dry cough. "I cannot regard this detail as being relevant, Your Excellency. In the name of the government of the United States of America of 2119 AD—to which government you are accredited and whose laws you are bound to respect—I must ask you to surrender the person of Henry Hancock Groppus, convicted felon, to the justice of his country and his time."

"And I, Mr. Secretary," the Ambassador replied with equal dry urbanity, "as a representative and servant of United Earth of 2219 AD, must respectfully decline until I have had time to study the situation."

"In that case, Your Excellency, I regret to have to inform you of the extreme displeasure of my government and our determination to take whatever steps are necessary to secure the person of Henry Hancock Groppus."

"Noted, Mr. Secretary," said the Ambassador.

There was a silence. "May I speak to you on the private channel, Your Excellency?"

"You may, Mr. Secretary. One moment, please."

The Ambassador from 2219 AD pressed a button on his desk which locked his door and lit a *Do Not Disturb* indicator. Then he swung around and switched on the big screen behind his desk.

A heavy-set balding man appeared on it. "Hi, Don," he said. "This is one big stink we're in."

"I know, Cleve," the Ambassador sighed. "A bigamy case. Capital offense."

"Bigamy, hell! Polygamy, Don boy! That's what this joker's been convicted of, *polygamy*. Advocating, abetting and encompassing polygamy. You just don't *go* any lower."

"In your time, you mean. In 2119."

"In our time, yes. That's the time we're living in right now. The time that has to face the problem of one woman to every ten men because of the genetic imbalance created by the last world war. All right, so we haven't licked the Uterine Plague yet. We won't lick it for another fifty years, according to you, though you won't tell our medics how we finally will solve it."

The Ambassador gestured wearily at the screen. "You know as well as I, Cleve, there are things that Temporal Embassies can do and there are things they can't do."

"Okay. Good. No argument. You boys take your orders and have your problems. But we've got problems, too. Gigantic ones. We've got a social code that was designed in the days when there were equal numbers of men and women, and it's splitting at the seams everywhere. We've got to persuade hundreds of millions of normal men that it's right and proper for them to lead lives of the most maddening frustration if we want to keep civilization from dissolving into hand-to-hand battles. We've got them persuaded—about as well persuaded as a herd of rutting elephants. And along comes this Henry Groppus and his handful of crackpot Mendelists, making strange, sudden noises in the rear of the herd and—"

"Slow down, Cleve. Take a deep breath. I know the kind of problems your time is facing, perhaps better than you. I know it from the history I studied in school, and, since I've arrived here in 2119 as Ambassador from the Next Century, I've seen it sharp and bloodily clear, at first hand. I know what an explosive danger the Mendelist philosophy is. I couldn't be more sympathetic, I assure you.

"Nonetheless, Cleve, you're an important government official; you're not the man in the street. 2119 is grappling with the social effects of the Uterine Plague, and to 2119 it looks like the biggest thing that ever was. But 2119 is just a drop in the historical bucket. And so, for that matter," he added in all fairness, "is 2219, my own period. Be just to your position and your intellect; look at the thing in perspective."

The Secretary of State made a sluicing motion at the top of his bald head. "What perspective? How perspective?"

"Simply this, as an example. Take an Englishman of the upper middle class, a rich merchant, let us say. In the time of the Tudors, he'd be all for increasing the powers of the king, all for an absolute monarchy, all for a very strong central government— the things that would damage his superiors, the feudal nobility, the most. A century later, when the nobility had been pretty much reduced to so much court decoration, his great-great-grandson would be fighting the absolutism of the Stuarts tooth and nail, insisting that the people had a right to call their king to account and that any government which was dictatorial deserved to be overthrown.

"And a hundred years or so after that, under the Hanoverian George III, *his* great-great-grandson, looking across the channel to France, observing that the *very* common people there in the course of taking the same drastic action with *their* king had completely bollixed up industry, banking and commerce—he would be exclaiming his pious horror over regicides and calling for laws that would strengthen the government and keep revolutionaries in their place."

"The point being," said the Secretary of State, "that most social values are conditioned by the time, place and prevailing political climate. Is that what you mean by perspective?"

"Exactly," the Ambassador said.

The bald-headed man stared angrily out of the screen. "I wish I weren't so upset. It's my misfortune to forget every dirty word I know when I get really mad. And this calls for— Look, Don, I don't know very much about 2219, what's important, what's sacred, what's not to be touched. The rules of your outfit forbid you to give us a very clear picture of your time—and you're a close-mouthed character to begin with. But I'd give the goddam front lobe of my brain to see how you'd behave if some Henry Groppus of the twenty-third century did the future equivalent of polygamy in *your* neck of the woods.

"You'd perspective *him*, you would. Now I'm not going to beat about the bush any more. Enough history, enough philosophy. Our government wouldn't last a week if we let Mendelists get away with preaching their vicious nonsense, let alone committing overt acts. I hate to have to put it this way, Don, but the man is the vilest of criminals. You're going to hand him over to us."

Smiling calmly, the Ambassador from 2219 AD said, "I repeat: he's a criminal in *your* terms. Beyond that, I repeat: I have to study the situation. He had escaped from prison; he was being pursued by a lynch mob; he took asylum in our Embassy, which is legally an enclave of 2219 in the present-day United States, an extension of our time and government into yours. Don't talk to me as if I were your office boy's assistant, Cleve."

"A criminal is a criminal," the bald-headed man went on doggedly. "*This* criminal has got to be brought to justice. I've asked you for him on the record and off the record. Next step is formal extradition papers. And the step after that—well, I won't like to do it, but I will."

"I wouldn't like you to do it, either," said the Ambassador calmly and softly.

Their eyes locked. The Secretary of State spread his hands. "Well, there it is," he muttered, and he clicked off.

Dodson and Groppus had been waiting patiently outside. When the Ambassador unlocked the door and nodded them in, he looked the bearded man over carefully.

A thoroughly bewhiskered, messily eyebrowed and well-muscled person, perhaps a jot past middle age, he stood clumsily tall and stiffly erect in a manner slightly reminiscent of a military cadet who had arrived at the academy just the evening before.

His eyes were mild and apologetic, not at all fanatic and intense. They had a tendency to blink if you stared at them too hard. His hands were the most vibrant part of him. Even in comparative repose, when he was listening or thinking, they kept going through the repertoire of the fluid, underlining gestures of the practiced sidewalk exhorter.

"I suppose you know, Mr. Groppus, that you are already the subject of a rather acrimonious controversy between your government and my Embassy?" said the Ambassador.

"Not *my* government. I don't recognize it as mine. I don't admit its jurisdiction over me."

"Unfortunately, it feels differently. And it is larger, more powerful and more numerous than you. Please sit down."

Henry Groppus lowered his head and shook it from side to side slowly, a negative gesture that could make its point the entire length of a meeting hall. "I prefer to stand, thank you. I always stand. Size, power, numbers—since the beginning of time, those three have been trying to correlate with right and wrong. So far, they haven't succeeded."

Nodding, the Ambassador murmured, "Very true. But, on the other hand, they do exceedingly well with life and death. Which, of course, brings us back to the present moment and you. As a convicted criminal under sentence of—"

"I am *not* a criminal."

"You aren't? In that case, Mr. Groppus, we have all been misled. I really must beg your pardon. Suppose you tell me then: how, precisely, do *you* visualize your role?"

"As a political refugee! I come here, persecuted and cast out, to my true home and nation. I claim spiritual citizenship in 2219."

"Spiritual citizenship? That's hardly the best kind. But putting that complex question aside for the moment, let me ask you, Mr. Groppus: what has given you the impression that my era shares your beliefs? The first rule of all Temporal Embassies is to transmit no information about the technological status and social attitudes of their own time to the period in which they are accredited. I fail to see what basis you have for—"

"I always suspected that the future would be Mendelist, but I couldn't be really sure. When the mob broke into the jail to lynch me and I got away from them, this was the only place I could think of hiding in. Now that I've been here for a while and seen you people—I *know!* The next century belongs to us!"

The Ambassador looked completely startled and unbelieving, as if he'd stubbed an emotion on a projecting rock. He shot a quick, questioning glance at his First Secretary.

"I'm sorry, sir," Dodson said in a low, rapid voice. "Bruce. It was his fault. He was so busy barricading the second floor against the mob that he neglected to take proper precautions. Some of the clerks came up to the prisoner during the excitement and got into conversation with him. By the time I reached him, the damage had been done."

"Some of the clerks—" His Excellency fought with himself for a moment, then squirted out an immense, protective cloud of calm. He said, after a deep breath, "I was under the impression that my staff was composed of trained employees, regularly briefed as to their responsibilities. Well trained. Down to the very lowest echelons."

"Yes, sir, but these were three youngsters on their first extratemporal assignment. I'm not trying to make excuses for them, but it's been very dull at the Embassy these last few months, especially for romantic kids who came out all hot and bothered at the idea of seeing history come alive and happen. And then, all of a sudden, there's a lynch mob and a siege of the Embassy. They find themselves standing next to an actual twenty-second-century Mendelist Martyr in the flesh. Well, you know how it is, sir. They started out by asking excited, admiring questions—and ended up answering them."

The Ambassador nodded gravely. "Groppus is the man to do just that. But after this affair has been cleared up, Vice-Consul Bruce and those three clerks will be the subject of an investigation and a report through Temporal Embassy channels clear to the end of the line."

Groppus, meanwhile, had wound himself up and was now running strong.

"It had to be! It had to be!" he chanted, pacing up and down the office, his torn clothes whipping in the breeze created by his gesticulating hands. "We carried the word to the people and told them it had to be. If the Uterine Plague means that nine-tenths of all female children are still-born, does it follow that the remaining precious tenth should marry at random? No, we said. Such a thought stinks in the nostrils of evolution!

"It's not enough to require every prospective husband to show a certificate of fecundity. We must go further! We must march under the slogan of a maximum genetic potential in every marriage. After all, we are not living in the darkness of the twentieth and twenty-first centuries! With modern eugenic methods, we can know exactly what we are getting in every fetus conceived. But even *that* is not enough. We must—"

"All right," said the Ambassador from 2219 AD wearily, dropping into his chair and frowning at the desktop. "I am quite familiar with the sentiments. I had them drummed into me all through childhood, and I had to memorize and repeat them all through my adolescence."

"*Even that is not enough!*" repeated the bearded man, his voice rising majestically. "We must go further yet, we told them. We must turn a curse into a blessing, the Uterine Plague into a true genetic revival! If only the best should be allowed to reproduce, why not the *best* of the best? And if only the best of the best—if only the smallest, most refined nugget of mankind is to be allowed the privileges of further heredity—" here his voice sank to a dramatic whisper, before suddenly soaring up again—"surely we will not presume to impose the ancient, outworn limitation of one woman, one wife, one mate at a time?

"Surely the race—stumbling and floundering in a deadly biological morass—deserves more than this mote, this snippet of aid? Doesn't the next, the smaller generation, deserve the best of the previous, the larger generation, whatever custom may whine and morality may squeak to the contrary? We don't preach sexual monopoly: we preach sexual salvation! And I say to you—"

"Oh, Dodson, please take him out!" the Ambassador begged. "I have to think, and these grammar school recitations are giving me a headache!"

At the door, Groppus abruptly slid from his dizzy forensic heights and landed springily on his feet. "So you won't allow them to extradite me, Your Excellency? You won't relinquish me to the justice of these primitives?"

"I haven't decided one way or the other. There's more at stake than your person. I have to consider the matter carefully."

"*Consider?* Are you for light or for darkness? Are you for the future or the past? What is there to consider? I am a spiritual citizen, a philosophical forefather of 2219 AD. I have the *right* to sanctuary here—I *demand* that you give me asylum!"

The Ambassador stared at him calmly. "Neither spiritual citizenship nor philosophical forebears are included in the category of duties for which I am responsible. And I would like to point out to you, Mr. Groppus, that under international law—from which the body of extratemporal law is derived—a fugitive's rights of asylum are never implicit, but are dependent entirely upon the determination of the state to which he flees or the embassy of refuge *in each separate case.*"

Dodson closed the door on the bearded man's dawning expression of consternation.

When he returned, having deposited Groppus with guards who were going to be very self-consciously uncommunicative, the Ambassador told him of the threat contained in the Secretary of State's last comment.

The young man swallowed. "That seems to imply that—that shortly after we're served with extradition papers, sir, a forcible entry of the Embassy will be made in order to remove the prisoner. But that's unheard of!"

"It may be the sort of thing that isn't talked about much, but it certainly isn't unheard of. It would mean, of course, that the Temporal Embassy would be permanently withdrawn from the United States of this era."

"Would they risk *that*, sir? After all, it's their link with the future! We can't give them all the information they want, but we do give them whatever knowledge the

Temporal Embassies in our own time say is safe. And we take nothing in return. It would be idiotic for them to break relations."

The Ambassador studied a page in the gray-bound book on his desk.

"Nothing which *must* be done is idiotic," he said, largely to himself. "Precedent after precedent. A matter of finding the right kind of spurious legality in which to cloak such action. And who is to say what is spurious or not about the reasons a sovereign state gives for taking drastic measures, if it believes that the measures are essential to its survival? A case like this, so intricately involved with mass frustration and the most basic problems of individual male egos..."

Dodson was watching him closely. "So we give up the fugitive? I thought we would have to from the very beginning, if you'll pardon me for saying so, sir. He is a criminal, no doubt about it. But it *is* going to be an uncomfortable business, very much like turning in a forefather, at that. He thinks so much like us."

The young man rubbed a hand reflectively against a clean-shaven chin. "Even looks like us—I mean the way we looked back home in 2219, before we were anachronized for the Embassy in this period. It's amazing in how many petty and minor ways, as well as large and important ones, Groppus has anticipated our age."

His Excellency stood up and stretched at great length. "Nonsense, Dodson, nonsense! Don't confuse cause with effect and real history with dramatic personalities. Henry Groppus didn't grow whiskers because he envisioned the possibility that every man in our time will—that's not the way it works at all. We go about bearded because our entire civilization is based on the Genetic File. And the concept of the Genetic File had its roots among the ideas of the twenty-second-century Mendelists—a maladjusted anti-social bunch who wore whiskers in a non-whiskered time as part of their general protest.

"Put the utopian babblings of Henry Groppus up against the hard, workaday facts on the Genetic File in our age—do you see any real correspondence? Here and there, clumsily—as in Groppus advocating compulsory polygamy, or genetic aristocrats, and in our society allowing an occasional, gifted man, under special circumstances, to take more than one wife. The sad truth about political saints of any given past is that nobody but a scholar will take the trouble to read their complete works and try to see them whole. But all this to one side: the Mendelists *are* political saints in our time and we can't turn one of them in."

"I'm afraid I don't follow you, sir," Dodson objected. "You said just a moment ago that the present-day United States government felt so strongly about this matter that it was prepared to recover fugitives by force, even at the cost of breaking diplomatic relations with our time. Well, sir? And then there's paragraph 16a of the Temporal Embassy By-laws: '...and above all the duty of respecting the laws, the customs and the mores peculiar to the time in which an Embassy is accredited and of giving no offense whatsoever thereto'. "

The Ambassador from 2219 AD began emptying his desk, explaining gently over his shoulder: "By-laws are one thing, Dodson. Natural laws are another. And the first and most fundamental natural law of a public servant is this: don't bite the hand that feeds you. Don't offend the sensibilities of the government officials who employ you. And above all, don't offend the sensibilities of the public who employs *them*. If I turned Groppus in, I would receive the heartfelt appreciation of this period—and never get another diplomatic appointment from 2219 AD. That's the basis on which I finally made my decision.

"So we simplify things. We close down the Embassy before even the extradition warrant arrives, and we leave, with all our personnel, papers and our precious fugitive, through the emergency chrondromos in the basement. Back in our time, we make the necessary explanations, they make the necessary apologies to this period, and, after a necessary interval has elapsed and memories have dimmed a bit, a new Temporal Ambassador from 2219 AD is appointed—one who will swear upon his arrival that he would absolutely never dream of obstructing justice. Everyone's face is saved."

He chucklingly prodded the astonished First Secretary in the ribs with the gray-bound Casebook of Extratemporal Law. "Jump, my boy, jump! The Embassy has to be ready to move out of here in an hour. And Havemeyer has to check out the scientific problems involved in bringing Henry Groppus into the future! And you have to write out a visa for him."

Three weeks later—or, to be exact, one hundred years and three weeks later—Dodson called on the Ambassador, who was packing busily, having just been appointed to the Embassy on Ganymede. Both men scratched from time to time at newly sprouted hair on their faces.

"Have you heard, sir? About Groppus? He finally did it!"

"Did what, my boy? The last I heard, he was going from triumph to triumph. Adoring crowds everywhere. A speech at the Monument to the Mendelist Martyrs. Another speech on the steps of the North American Genetic File, tearfully hailing the concrete reality of a dream hallowed in blood—or some such moist metaphor."

The young man shook his head excitedly. "That's what I mean. After the speech on the steps of the North American Genetic File last week, he went inside with a flourish and made out an application for a fatherhood certificate—just in case, he explained, he ran into a woman he wanted to marry. Well, this morning the Genetic File completed its regulation chromosome survey on him—*and he was turned down!* Too many unstable patterns, said the voucher. But that's nothing, sir, nothing! What do you think he did fifteen minutes ago?"

"I don't know." The Ambassador shrugged. "Blew up the Genetic File?"

"That's *exactly* what he did! He made up the explosive himself, he said. He claimed he had to free mankind from the tyranny of eugenic red tape. He destroyed the File completely, sir!"

He sat down heavily.

The Ambassador's face had gone white. "But," he whispered, "but—the Genetic *File!* The only complete genetic record of every individual in North America! The basis of our civilization!"

"Isn't it— Isn't it—" Dodson gave up trying to express the calamity in words. He clenched his fists. "He's under heavy guard. But I can tell you this, sir, and I'm not the only one who feels that way—he'll never live to face sentence. Not if I know 2219 AD!"

The cry was in a deep voice, a breathless, badly frightened voice. Hoarse and urgent, it rose above the roar of the distant mob, above the rattle of traffic; it flung itself into the spacious office on the third floor of the Embassy and demanded immediate attention.

His Excellency, the Ambassador from 2319 AD—the sole occupant of that office—was a man of tense bearing and an extremely strained face. His eyes transmitted the unvarying message that all things were essentially complex—and might be further complicated. It was, therefore, not at all remarkable how that cry from the grounds below made him look suddenly uncertain.

He rose and moved to the window with his usual haste. A tall, bearded man, whose clothes were torn and whose body was badly bruised, had just leaped onto the Embassy lawn from the surrounding high fence. The bearded man pointed the forefingers of both hands at the third-floor office of the Ambassador from 2319 AD and shrieked again:

"*Sanctuary!*"

AFTERWORD

A century ago, any American could have described Thomas Jefferson quite easily. He was above all one of the great Founding Fathers, pretty much a secular saint. Today he's still a Founding Father, of course, but many see him as a libertine and a bit of a hypocrite, especially with regard to slavery.

And take the great African-American statesman and writer, W.E.B. Du Bois. In 1900, most white Americans who knew of him would have described him as a vicious trouble-maker, if not an out-and-out revolutionary. A century later, he's seen as a courageous visionary and an important leader.

Sitting Bull? Victoria Woodhull? During my adolescence, I read about them as terrifying or comical figures. Now, in my elder years, I see them as anything but.

It was such metamorphoses in viewpoint, as one era succeeds another, that have always fascinated me and that led to "Sanctuary." It also led me to coin the term "temporal provincialism" in my first anthology, *Children of Wonder*, in 1953.

But "Sanctuary" has an even more specific accent. It seems to be about the governmental organization of time travel, but it's actually quite nakedly about history. It's my belief that all good science fiction, from H.G. Wells and Aldous Huxley to Cliff Simak, Brian Aldiss, and Connie Willis, is about history—past history, future history, or alternate history—even when i *seems* to be about developments in technology, theology, or information management.

In other words, the *science* in science fiction is actually history. Nothing more and nothing other.

WRITTEN 1956——PUBLISHED 1957

෴

ME, MYSELF, AND I

"Don't you think you might look up from that comic book long enough to get interested in a last-minute briefing on the greatest adventure undertaken by man? After all, it's your noodle neck that's going to be risked." Professor Ruddle throbbed his annoyance clear up to his thin white hair.

McCarthy shifted his quid and pursed his lips. He stared dreamily at an enameled wash-basin fifteen feet from the huge, box-like coil of wire and transparencies on which the Professor had been working. Suddenly, a long brown stream leaped from his mouth and struck the brass cold-water faucet with a loud *ping*.

The professor jumped. McCarthy smiled.

"Name ain't Noodleneck," he drawled. "It's Gooseneck. Known and respected in every county jail of the U.S.A., including here in North Carolina. 'Gooseneck McCarthy, ten days for vagrancy' is the way it goes, or 'Gooseneck McCarthy, drunk and disorderly, twenty days.' *Never* Noodleneck." He paused, sighted, and the cold-water faucet *pinged* again. "Looky, Bub, all I asked was a cup of coffee and maybe a piece of breakfast. Time machine's your notion."

"Doesn't it mean anything that you will shortly be one hundred and ten million years in the past, a past in which no recognizable ancestors of man existed?"

"Nope. It don't mean anything."

The former chairman of the physics department at Brindlesham Business College grimaced disgustedly. He stared through thick lenses at the stringy, wind-hardened derelict whom he was forced to trust with his life's work. A chipped-granite head set on a remarkably long, thin neck; a narrow body whose limbs were equally extended; clothes limited to a faded khaki turtleneck sweater, patched brown corduroy pants and a worn-out pair of once-heavy brogans. He sighed.

"And the fate of human knowledge and progress depends on you! When you wandered up the mountain to my shack two days ago, you were broke and hungry. You didn't have a dime—"

"Had a dime. Only had a hole in my pocket, too. Somewhere around here in this room, that dime is."

"All right. All right. So you *had* had a dime. I took you in, gave you a good, hot meal and offered to pay you one hundred dollars to take my time machine on its maiden voyage. Don't you think—"

Ping! This time it was the hot-water faucet.

"—that the very least you could do," the little physicist's voice was rising hysterically, "the very least would be to pay enough attention to the facts I make available to insure that the experiment will be a success? Do you realize what fantastic disruption you might cause in the time stream by one careless slip?"

McCarthy rose suddenly and the brightly colored comic magazine slid to the floor in a litter of coils, gauges, and paper covered with formulae. He advanced toward the Professor, whom he topped by at least a foot. His employer gripped a wrench nervously.

"Now, Mister Professor Ruddle," he said with gentle emphasis, "if'n you don't think I know enough, why don't you go yourself, huh?"

The little man smiled at him placatingly. "Now don't get stubborn again, Noodleneck—"

"Gooseneck. Gooseneck McCarthy."

"You're the most irascible person I've ever met. More stubborn even than Professor Darwin Willington Walker, the head of the mathematics department at Brindlesham Business College. He insisted, in spite of the irrefutable evidence I brought to bear, that a time machine would not work. 'Great inventions,' he kept saying, over and over and over, 'do not from small paradoxes grow. And that's all time travel will ever be: a collection of small and very intricate paradoxes.' As a result, the college refused to grant an appropriation for my research and I had to come out here to North Carolina. On my own time and money, too." He brooded angrily on unimaginative mathematicians and parsimonious trustees.

"Still ain't answered my question."

Ruddle looked up. He blushed a little under the fine, wild tendrils of white hair. "Well, it's just that I'm rather valuable to society what with my paper on intrareversible positrons still uncompleted. Whereas everything points to the machine being a huge success, it's conceivable that Walker considered some point which I've—er, overlooked."

"Meaning there's a chance I might not come back?"

"Uh—well, something like that. No danger, you understand. I've gone over the formulae again and again, and they are foolproof. It's just barely possible that some minor error, some cube root that wasn't brought out to the furthest decimal…"

McCarthy nodded to himself. The nod had an *as-I-suspected* finality. "If'n that's so," he announced, "I want that check before I leave. Not taking any chances on something going wrong and you not paying me."

Professor Ruddle looked at him carefully and moistened his lips. "Certainly, Noodleneck," he said. "Why—why, of course!"

"Gooseneck. How many times do I have to tell you it's Gooseneck McCarthy? Only make the check out to me with my real first name."

"Which is?"

"Huh? Oh, you have to know now, I guess. Only kinda don't spread it around. It's, uh—" the tall vagrant's voice dropped to a delicate whisper, "—it's *Galahad*."

The physicist added a final scribble to the green paper rectangle, ripped it out and handed it to McCarthy. Pay to the order of Galahad McCarthy one hundred dollars and oo cents. On the Beet and Tobacco Exchange Bank of North Carolina.

Ruddle watched while the check was carefully placed in the outer breast pocket of the ancient sweater. He picked up an expensive miniature camera and hung its carrying strap around his employee's neck. He patted the camera. "Now, this is fully loaded. Are you certain you can operate the shutter? All you do—"

"I know all right. Fooled around with these doohickeys before. Been playing with this 'un for two days. You want me to step out of the machine, take a couple of snaps of the scenery, and move a rock."

"And nothing else! Remember, you're going back a hundred and ten million years and any action on your part might have an incalculable effect on the present. You might wipe out the whole human race by stepping on one furry little animal who was its ancestor. I think that moving a rock slightly will be a good first innocuous experiment, but be careful!"

They moved toward the great transparent housing at the end of the laboratory. Through its foot-thick walls, the red, black, and silver equipment in one corner shone hazily. An enormous lever protruded from the maze of wiring like a metallic forefinger.

"You should arrive in the Cretaceous Period, the middle period of the age of reptiles. Most of North America was under water, but geological investigation shows an island on this spot."

"You been over this sixteen times. Just show me what dingus to pull and let me go."

Ruddle executed a little dance. "Dingus!" he screeched. "You don't pull any dingus! You gently depress—*gently*, you hear—the chronotransit, that large black lever, thus sliding the quartzine door shut and starting the machine. When you arrive you lift it—again *gently*—and the door will open. The machine is set to go back a given number of years, so that fortunately you have no thinking to do."

McCarthy stared down at him easily. "You make a lot of cracks for a little guy. I'll bet you're scared stiff of your wife."

"I'm not married," Ruddle told him shortly. "I don't believe in the institution." He remembered. "Who was talking about marriage? At a time like this… When I think of allowing a stubborn, stupid character like yourself to run loose with a device having the immense potentialities of a time machine— Of course, I'm far too valuable to be risked in the first jerry-built model."

"Yeah," McCarthy nodded. "Ain't it the truth." He patted the check protruding from his sweater pocket and leaped up into the machine. "I'm not."

He depressed the chronotransit lever—gently.

The door slid shut on Professor Ruddle's frantic last word, "Goodbye, Noodleneck, and be *careful*, please!"

"Gooseneck," McCarthy automatically corrected. The machine seemed to jerk. He had a last, distorted glimpse of Ruddle's shaggy, white head through the quartzine walls. The Professor, alarm and doubt mixed on his face, seemed to be praying.

Incredibly bright sunlight blazed through thick, bluish clouds. The time machine rested on the waterline of a beach to whose edge the lushest jungle ever had rushed—and stopped abruptly. The semi-transparent walls enabled him to see enormous green masses of horsetails and convoluted ivy, giant ferns, and luxuriant palms, steaming slightly, rich and ominous with life.

"Lift the dingus *gently*," McCarthy murmured to himself.

He stepped through the open doors into an ankle-depth of water. The tide was evidently in and white-flecked water gurgled around the base of the squat edifice that had brought him. Well, Ruddle had said this was going to be an island.

"Reckon I'm lucky he didn't build his laboratory shack fifty or sixty feet further down the mountain! I might be real wet."

He sloshed ashore, avoiding a little school of dun-colored sponges. The professor might like a picture of them, he decided. He adjusted the speed of the lens and focused it on the sponges. Then some pictures of the sea and the jungle.

Huge leathery wings beat over a spot two miles in from the edge of the luxuriant vegetation. McCarthy recognized the awesome, bat-like creature from drawings the Professor had shown him. A pterodactyl, the reptilian version of bird life.

McCarthy snapped a hasty photograph and backed nervously toward the time machine. He didn't like the looks of that long pointed beak, so ferociously armed with jagged teeth. Some living thing moved in the jungle under the pterodactyl. It plummeted down like a fallen angel, jaws agape and slavering.

McCarthy made certain that it was being kept busy, then moved rapidly up the beach. Near the edge of the jungle, he had observed a round, reddish rock. It would do.

The rock was heavier to budge than he had thought. He strained against it, cursing and perspiring under the hot sun. His feet sank into the clinging loam.

Abruptly the rock tore loose. With a sucking sound it came out of the loam and rolled over on its side. It left a moist, round hole out of which a centipede fully as long as his arm scuttled away into the underbrush. A nauseous stink arose from the spot where the centipede had lain. McCarthy decided he didn't like this place. Not at all.

Might as well head back.

Before he depressed the lever, the tramp took one last look at the red rock, the underside somewhat darker than the rest. A hundred bucks worth of tilt.

"So this is what work is like," he soliloquized. "Maybe I been missing out on something."

After the rich sunlight of the Cretaceous, the laboratory seemed smaller than he remembered it. The Professor came up to him breathlessly as he stepped from the time machine.

"How did it go?" he demanded eagerly.

McCarthy stared down at the top of the old man's head. "Everthin' OK," he replied slowly. "Hey, Professor Ruddle, what for did you go and shave your head? There wasn't much of it, but that white hair looked sorta distinguished."

"Hair? Shave? I've been completely bald for years. Lost my hair long before it turned white. And my name is Guggles, not Ruddle—*Guggles:* try and remember that for a while. Now let me see the camera."

As he slipped the carrying strap over his head and handed the instrument over, McCarthy pursed his lips. "Coulda *sworn* that you had a little patch of white up there. Coulda sworn. Sorry about the name, Prof; we never seem to be able to get together on those things."

The Professor grunted and started for the darkroom with the camera. Halfway there, he stopped and almost cringed as a huge female form stepped through the far doorway.

"Aloysius!" came a voice that approximated a corkscrew to the ear. "Aloysius! I told you yesterday that if that tramp wasn't out of my house in twenty-four hours, experiment or not, you'd hear from me. Aloysius! You have exactly thirty-seven minutes!"

"Y-yes, dear," Professor Guggles whispered at her broad, retreating back. "We—we're almost finished."

"Who's that?" McCarthy demanded the moment she had left.

"My wife, of course. You must remember her—she made our breakfast when you arrived."

"Didn't make my breakfast. Made my own breakfast. And you said you weren't married!"

"Now you're being silly, Mr. Gallagher. I've been married for twenty-five years and I know how futile it is to deny it. I couldn't have said any such thing."

"Name's not Gallagher—it's McCarthy, Gooseneck McCarthy," the vagrant told him querulously. "What's happened here? You can't even remember my last name now, let alone my first; you change your own name; you shave your head; you get married in a hurry; and—and you try 'n tell me that I let some female woman cook my breakfast when I can rassle up a better-tastin', better-eatin'—"

"Hold it!" The little man had approached and was plucking at his sleeve eagerly. "Hold it, Mr. Gallagher or Gooseneck or whatever your name is. Suppose you tell me exactly what you consider this place to have been like before you left."

Gooseneck told him. "And that thingumajig was layin' *on* that whatchmacallit instead of under it," he finished lamely.

The Professor thought. "And all you did when you went back into the past was to move a rock?"

"That's all. One hell of a big centipede jumped out, but I didn't touch it. Just moved the rock and headed back like you said."

"Yes, of course. H'mmm. That may have been it. The centipede jumping out of the rock may have altered subsequent events sufficiently to make me a married man instead of a blissful single one, to have changed my name from Ruddle to Guggles. Or the rock itself. Such an intrinsically simple act as moving the rock must have had much larger consequences than I had imagined. Just think if that rock had not been moved, I might not be married! Gallagher—"

"McCarthy," the tall vagabond corrected resignedly.

"Whatever you call yourself—listen to me. You're going back in the time machine and shift that rock back to its original position. Once that's done—"

"If I go back again, I get another hundred."

"How can you talk of money at a time like this?"

"What's the difference between this and any other time?"

"Why, here I am married, my work interrupted, and you chatter about— Oh, all right. Here's the money." The Professor tore his checkbook out and hastily scribbled on a blank. "Here you are. Satisfied?"

McCarthy puzzled over the check. "This isn't like t'other. This is on a different bank—The Cotton Growers Exchange."

"That makes no important difference," the Professor told him hastily, bundling him into the time machine. "It's a check, isn't it? Just as good, believe me, just as good."

As the little man fiddled with dials and adjusted switches, he called over his shoulder. "Remember, get that rock as close to its original position as you can. And touch nothing else, do nothing else."

"I know. I know. Hey, Prof, how come I remember all these changes and you don't, with all your science and all?"

"Simple," the Professor told him, toddling briskly out of the machine. "By being in the past and the time machine while these temporal adjustments to your act made themselves felt, you were in a sense insulated against them, just as a pilot suffers no direct, personal damage from the bomb his plane releases over a city. Now, I've set the machine to return to approximately the same moment as before. Unfortunately, my chronotransit calibrations can never be sufficiently exact— Do you remember how to operate the apparatus? If you don't—"

McCarthy sighed and depressed the lever, shutting the door on the Professor's flowing explanations and perspiring bald head.

He was back by the pounding surf off the little island. He paused for a moment before opening the door as he caught sight of a strange transparent object just a little farther up the beach. Another time machine—and exactly like his!

"Oh, well. The Professor will explain it."

He started up the beach toward the rock. Then he stopped again—a dead-stop this time.

The rock lay ahead, as he remembered it before the shifting. But there was a man straining at it, *a tall, thin man in a turtleneck sweater and brown corduroy pants.*

McCarthy got his loosened jaw back under control. "Hey! Hey, you at the rock! Don't move it. It's not supposed to be moved!" He hurried over.

The stranger turned. He had the ugliest face McCarthy remembered having seen on a human being; his neck was ridiculously long and thin. He examined McCarthy slowly. He reached into his pocket and came out with a soiled package. He bit off a chew of tobacco.

McCarthy reached into his pocket and came up with an identically soiled mass of tobacco. He also took a bite. They chewed and stared at each other. Then they spat, simultaneously.

"What do you mean this rock ain't supposed to be moved? Professor Ruddle told me to move it."

"Well, Professor Ruddle told me *not* to move it. *And* Professor Guggles," McCarthy added as a triumphant clincher.

The other considered him for a moment, his jaw working like a peculiar cam. His eyes traveled up McCarthy's spare body. Then he spat contemptuously and turned to the rock. He grunted against it.

McCarthy sighed and put a hand on his shoulder. He spun him around. "What for you have to go and act so stubborn, fella? Now I'll have to lick you."

Without changing his vacant expression to one of the slightest hostility, the stranger aimed a prodigious kick at his groin. McCarthy dodged easily. That was an old stunt! He'd done that himself, dozens of times. He chopped out rapidly against the man's face. The stranger ducked, moved away, and came back fighting.

This was a perfect spot for the famous McCarthy one-two. McCarthy feinted with his left, seemingly concentrating all his power at the other's middle. He noticed that his opponent was also making some awkward gesture with his left. Then he came up out of nowhere with a terrific right uppercut.

WHAM!

Right on the—

—on the button. McCarthy sat up and shook his head clear of bright little lights and happy hums. He had connected, but—

So had the other guy!

He sat several feet from McCarthy, looking dazed and sad. "You are the stubbornest cuss I ever saw! Where did you learn my punch?"

"Your punch!" They rose, glowering at each other. "Listen, Bub, that there is my *own* Sunday punch, copyrighted, patented and in-corporated! But this ain't getting us nowhere."

"No, it ain't. What do we do now? I don't care if I have to fight you for the next million years, but I was paid to move that rock and I'm going to move it."

McCarthy shifted the quid of tobacco. "Looky here. You've been paid to move that rock by Professor Ruddle or Guggles or whatever he is by now. If I go back and get a note from him saying you're not to move that rock and you can keep the check anyways, will you promise to squat still until I get back?"

The stranger chewed and spat, chewed and spat. McCarthy marveled at their perfect synchronization. They both spat the same distance, too. He wasn't such a bad guy, if only he wouldn't be so stubborn! Strange—he was wearing a camera like the one old Ruddle had taken from him.

"OK. You go back and get the note. I'll wait here." The stranger dropped to the ground and stretched out.

McCarthy turned and hurried back to the time machine before he could change his mind.

He was pleased to notice, as he stepped down into the laboratory again, that the Professor had rewon his gentle patch of white hair.

"Saaay, this is gettin' real complicated. How'd you make out with the wife?"

"Wife? What wife?"

"The wife. The battle-axe. The ball and chain. The steady skirt," McCarthy clarified.

"I'm not married. I told you I consider it a barbarous custom entirely unworthy of a truly civilized man. Now stop babbling and give me that camera."

"But," McCarthy felt his way very carefully, "but, don't you remember takin' the camera from me, Professor Ruddle?"

"Not Ruddle—Roodles, *Roodles*. Oo, as in Gooseface. And how could I have taken the camera from you when you've just returned? You're dithering, McCarney, I don't like ditherers. Stop it!"

McCarthy shook his head, forbearing to correct the mispronunciation of his name. He began to feel a vague, gnawing wish that he had never climbed aboard this merry-go-round.

"Look, Prof, sit down." He spread a great hand against the little man's chest, forcing him into a chair. "We're gonna have another talk. I gotta bring you up to date."

Fifteen minutes later, he was winding up. "So this character says he'll wait until I get back with the note. If you want a wife, don't give me the note and he'll move the rock. I don't care one way or t'other, myself. I just want to get out of here!"

Professor Ruddle (Guggles? Roodles?) closed his eyes. "My," he gasped. Then he shuddered. "Married. To that—battle-axe! That st-steady skirt! No! McCarney—or McCarthy—listen! You must go back. I'll give you a note—another check—here!" He tore a page from his notebook, filled it rapidly with desperate words. Then he made out a check.

McCarthy glanced at the slips. " 'Nother bank," he remarked wonderingly. "This time The Southern Peanut Trust Company. I hope all these different checks are gonna be good."

"Certainly," the Professor assured him loudly. "They will all be good. You go ahead and take care of this matter, and we'll settle it to everybody's satisfaction when you return. You tell this other McCarney that—"

"McCarthy. *Hey!* What do you mean—'this other McCarney'? I'm the only McCarthy—only Gooseneck McCarthy, anyway. If you sent a dozen different guys out to do the same job…"

"I didn't send anyone but you. Don't you understand what happened? You went back into the Cretaceous to move a rock. You returned to the present—and, as you say, found me in somewhat unfortunate circumstances. You returned to the past to undo the damage, to *approximately* the same spot in space and time as before—it could not be exactly the same spot because of a multitude of unknown factors and because of the inescapable errors in the first time machine. Very well. You—we'll call you You I—meet You II at the very moment You II is preparing to move the rock. You stop him. If you hadn't, if he hadn't been interrupted in any way and had shifted that stone, he would have been You I. But because he—or rather you—didn't, he is slightly different from you, being a You who has merely made one trip into the past and not even moved the rock. Whereas you—You I—have made two trips, have both moved the rock yourself and prevented yourself from moving it. It's really very simple, isn't it?"

McCarthy stroked his chin and sucked in a great gasp of air. "Yeah," he mumbled wildly. "Simple ain't the word for it!"

The Professor hopped into the machine and began preparing it for another trip. "Now as to what happened to me. Once you—You I again—prevented You II from moving that rock, you immediately precipitated—not so much a change as an *unchange*—in my personal situation. The rock had not been shifted—therefore, I had not been married, was not married, and, let us hope, will never be married. I was also no longer bald. But, by the very fact of the presence of the two You's in the past, by virtue of some microscopic form of life you killed with your breath, let us say, or some sand you impressed with your feet, sufficient alterations were made right through to the present so that my name was (and always had been!) Roodles and your name—"

"Is probably MacTavish by now," McCarthy yelled. "Look, Prof, are you through with the machine?"

"Yes, it's all ready." The Professor grimaced thoughtfully. "The only thing I can't place is what happened to that camera you said I took from you. Now if You I in the personification of You II—"

McCarthy planted his right foot in the small of the little man's back and shoved. "I'm gonna get this thing settled and come back and never, never, *never* go near one of these dinguses again!"

He yanked at the chronotransit. The last he saw of the Professor was a confused picture of broken glassware, tangled electrical equipment, and indignantly waving white hair.

This time he materialized at the very edge of the beach. "Gettin' closer all the time," he mumbled as he stepped out of the housing. "Now to hand over the note, then—"

Then—

"Great sufferin', two-tailed, explodin' catfish!"

There were two men fighting near a red rock. They wore identical clothes; they had identical features and physical construction, including the same lanky forms and long, stringy necks. They fought in a weird pattern of mirror-imagery—each man swinging the same blows as his opponent, right arm crossing right, left crossing left. The man with his back to the rock had an expensive miniature camera suspended from his neck; the other one hadn't.

Suddenly, they both feinted with their lefts in perfect preparation for what hundreds of small-town law officials had come to curse as "the Gooseneck McCarthy One-Two." Both men ignored the feint, both came up with their right hands and—

They knocked each other out.

They came down heavily on their butts, about a yard apart, shaking their heads.

"You are the stubbornest cuss I ever saw," one of them began. "Where—"

"—did you learn my punch?" McCarthy finished, stepping forward.

They both sprang to their feet, stared at him. "Hey," said the man with the camera. "You two guys are twins!"

"Wait a minute." McCarthy stepped between them before their angry glances at each other could be translated into action. "We're all twins. I mean triplets. I mean— Sit down. I got somethin' to tell you."

They all squatted slowly, suspiciously.

Four chaws of tobacco later, there was a little circle of dark nicotine juice all around them. McCarthy was breathing hard, all three of him. "So it's like I'm McCarthy I because I've seen this thing through up to where I stop McCarthy II from going back to get the note that McCarthy III wants from Ruddle."

The man with the camera rose and the other followed, "The only thing I don't get," he said finally, "is that I'm McCarthy III. Seems to me it's more like I'm McCarthy I, he's McCarthy II—that part's right—and *you're* McCarthy III."

"Uh-uh," McCarthy II objected. "You got it all wrong. The way I look at it—now see if'n this doesn't sound right—is that I'm McCarthy I, you're—"

"Hold it! Hold it!" The two men who had been fighting turned to McCarthy I. "I know I'm McCarthy I!"

"How do you know?" they demanded.

"Because that's the way Professor Ruddle explained it to me. He didn't explain it to you, did he? I'm McCarthy I, all right. You two are the stubbornest hooligans I've seen and I've seen them all. Now let's get back."

"Wait a minute. How do I know I still ain't supposed to move this rock? Just because you say so?"

"Because I say so and because Professor Ruddle says so in that note I showed you. And because there are two of us who don't want to move it and we can knock you silly if'n you try."

At McCarthy II's nod of approval, McCarthy III glanced around reluctantly for a weapon. Seeing none, he started back to the time machines. McCarthys I and II hurried abreast.

"Let's go in mine. It's closest." They all turned and entered the machine of McCarthy I.

"What about the checks? Why should you have three checks and McCarthy II have two while I only got one? Do I get my cut?"

"Wait'll we get back to the Professor. He'll settle it. Can't you think of anythin' else but money?" McCarthy I asked wearily.

"No, we can't," McCarthy II told him. "I want my share of that *third* check. I got a right to it. More'n this dopey guy has, see?"

"OK, OK. Wait'll we get back to the lab." McCarthy I pushed down on the chronotransit. The island and the bright sunlight disappeared. They waited.

Darkness! "Hey!" McCarthy II shouted. "Where's the lab? Where's Professor Ruddle?"

McCarthy I tugged at the chronotransit. It wouldn't move. The other two came over and pulled at it too.

The chronotransit remained solidly in place.

"You must've pushed down too hard," McCarthy III yelled. "You busted it!"

"Yeah," from McCarthy II. "Who ever told you that you could run a time machine? You busted it and now we're stranded!"

"Wait a minute. Wait a minute." McCarthy I pushed them back. "I got an idea. You know what happened? The three of us tried to come back to—to the present, like Professor Ruddle says. But only one of us *belongs* in the present—see what I mean? So with the three of us inside, the machine just can't go anywhere."

"Well, that's easy," said McCarthy III. "I'm the only real—"

"Don't be crazy. I know I'*m* the *real* McCarthy; I *feel* it—"

"Wait," McCarthy I told them. "This isn't gettin' us any place. The air's gettin' bad in here. Let's go back and argue it out." He pushed the lever down again.

So they went back a hundred and ten million years to discuss the matter reasonably. And, when they arrived, what do you think they found? Yep—exactly. That's exactly what they found.

AFTERWORD

"Me, Myself, and I" is in a sense actually my first professional story, although the first one to be published was, of course, "Alexander the Bait."

I wrote "Me, Myself, and I" in 1941 as one of my earliest attempts to break into magazine science fiction, shortly before I went into the army. The day I completed a satisfactory version of the piece on my typewriter, I picked up a copy of Street & Smith's *Astounding* and, to my chagrin and some degree of horror, read "By His Bootstraps" by Anson MacDonald.

The chagrin had to do with the time-travel paradox of "By His Bootstraps"—very much the same as the one I had used in "Me, Myself, and I." I would look as if I were copying another writer. The horror? Well, for a couple of years now I had been trying to write publishable science fiction, only to find that every time I got a good idea, it immediately appeared in print (obviously written six months or more earlier), and in a better form, under the name of Robert Heinlein. I felt I had been trapped in the lag end of a telepathic hookup with one man, and now it seemed I was connected in much the same way with yet someone else, one Anson MacDonald.

It would not have made me feel much better, I don't think, to have learned that they were actually the same person.

Well, I flipped the story into a desk drawer and went off to World War II. Years later, when I told my first agent, Ted Sturgeon, about it, he told me I had been an idiot and asked to see the manuscript. He made a suggestion or two about buffing it, and sold it for me the very first time out. He did, however, continue to call me an idiot.

WRITTEN 1941——PUBLISHED 1947

It Ends with a Flicker

It was a good job and Max Alben knew whom he had to thank for it—his great-grand-father.

"Good old Giovanni Albeni," he muttered as he hurried into the laboratory slightly ahead of the escorting technicians, all of them, despite the excitement of the moment, remembering to bob their heads deferentially at the half-dozen full-fleshed and hard-faced men lolling on the couches that had been set up around the time machine.

He shrugged rapidly out of his rags, as he had been instructed in the anteroom, and stepped into the housing of the enormous mechanism. This was the first time he had seen it, since he had been taught how to operate it on a dummy model, and now he stared at the great transparent coils and the susurrating energy bubble with much respect.

This machine, the pride and the hope of 2089, was something almost outside his powers of comprehension. But Max Alben knew how to run it, and he knew, roughly, what it was supposed to accomplish. He knew also that this was the first backward journey of any great duration and, being scientifically unpredictable, might well be the death of him.

"Good old Giovanni Albeni," he muttered again affectionately.

If his great-grandfather had not volunteered for the earliest time-travel experiments way back in the nineteen-seventies, back even before the Blight, it would never have been discovered that he and his seed possessed a great deal of immunity to extra-temporal blackout.

And if that had not been discovered, the ruling powers of Earth, more than a century later, would never have plucked Max Alben out of an obscure civil-service job as a relief guard at the North American Chicken Reservation to his present heroic and remunerative eminence. He would still be patrolling the barbed wire that surrounded the three white leghorn hens and two roosters—about one-sixth of the known livestock wealth of the Western Hemisphere—thoroughly content with the half-pail of dried apricots he received each and every payday.

No, if his great-grandfather had not demonstrated long ago his unique capacity for remaining conscious during time travel, Max Alben would not now be shifting from foot to foot in a physics laboratory, facing the black market kings of the world and awaiting their final instructions with an uncertain and submissive grin.

Men like O'Hara, who controlled mushrooms; Levney, the blackberry tycoon; Sorgasso, the packaged-worm monopolist—would black marketeers of their tremendous stature so much as waste a glance on someone like Alben ordinarily, let alone confer a lifetime pension on his wife and five children of a full spoonful each of nonsynthetic sugar a day?

Even if he didn't come back, his family was provided for like almost no other family on Earth. This was a damn good job and he was lucky.

Alben noticed that Abd Sadha had risen from the straight chair at the far side of the room and was approaching him with a sealed metal cylinder in one hand.

"We've decided to add a further precaution at the last moment," the old man said. "That is, the scientists have suggested it, and I have—er—I have given my approval."

The last remark was added with a slight questioning note as the Secretary General of the United Nations looked about rapidly at the black market princes on the couches behind him. Since they stared back stonily, but offered no objection, he coughed in relief and returned to Alben.

"I am sure, young man, that I don't have to go into the details of your instructions once more. You enter the time machine and go back the duration for which it has been preset, a hundred and thirteen years, to the moment after the Guided Missile of 1976 was launched. It *is* 1976, isn't it?" he asked, suddenly uncertain.

"Yes, sir," one of the technicians standing by the time machine said respectfully. "The experiment with an atomic warhead guided missile that resulted in the Blight was conducted on this site on April 18, 1976." He glanced proudly at the unemotional men on the couches, very much like a small boy after completing a recitation before visiting dignitaries from the Board of Education.

"Just so." Abd Sadha nodded. "April 18, 1976. And on this site. You see, young man, you will materialize at the very moment and on the very spot where the remote-control station handling the missile was—er—handling the missile. You will be in a superb position, a superb position, to deflect the missile in its downward course and alter human history for the better. Yes."

He paused, having evidently stumbled out of his thought sequence.

"And he pulls the red switch toward him," Gomez, the dandelion-root magnate, reminded him sharply, impatiently.

"Ah, yes, the red switch. He pulls the little red switch toward him. Thank you, Mr. Gomez, thank you very much, sir. He pulls the little red switch on the green instrument panel toward him, thus preventing the error that caused the missile to explode in the Brazilian jungle and causing it, instead, to explode somewhere in the mid-Pacific, as originally planned."

The Secretary General of the United Nations beamed. "Thus preventing the Blight, making it nonexistent, as it were, producing a present-day world in which the Blight never occurred. That is correct, is it not, gentlemen?" he asked, turning anxiously again.

None of the half-dozen men on couches deigned to answer him. And Alben kept his eyes deferentially in their direction, too, as he had throughout this period of last-minute instruction.

He knew who ruled his world—these stolid, well-fed men in clean garments with a minimum of patches, and where patches occurred, at least they were the color of the surrounding cloth.

Sadha might be Secretary General of the United Nations, but that was still a civil-service job, only a few social notches higher than a chicken guard. His clothes were fully as ragged, fully as multicolored, as those that Alben had stepped out of. And the gnawing in his stomach was no doubt almost as great.

"You understand, do you not, young man, that if anything goes wrong," Abd Sadha asked, his head nodding tremulously and anticipating the answer, "if anything unexpected, unprepared-for occurs, you are not to continue with the experiment but return immediately?"

"He understands everything he has to understand," Gomez told him. "Let's get this thing moving."

The old man smiled again. "Yes. Of course, Mr. Gomez." He came up to where Alben stood in the entrance of the time machine and handed the sealed metal cylinder to him. "This is the precaution the scientists have just added. When you arrive at your destination, just before materializing, you will release it into the surrounding temporal medium. Our purpose here, as you no doubt—"

Levney sat up on his couch and snapped his fingers peremptorily. "I just heard Gomez tell you to get this thing moving, Sadha. And it isn't moving. We're busy men. We've wasted enough time."

"I was just trying to explain a crucial final fact," the Secretary General apologized. "A fact which may be highly—"

"You've explained enough facts." Levney turned to the man inside the time machine. "Hey, fella. You. *Move!*"

Max Alben gulped and nodded violently. He darted to the rear of the machine and turned the dial which activated it.

flick!

It was a good job and Mac Albin knew whom he had to thank for it—his great-grandfather.

"Good old Giovanni Albeni," he laughed as he looked at the morose faces of his two colleagues. Bob Skeat and Hugo Honek had done as much as he to build the tiny time machine in the secret lab under the helicopter garage, and they were fully as eager to go, but—unfortunately for them—they were not descended from the right ancestor.

Leisurely, he unzipped the richly embroidered garment that, as the father of two children, he was privileged to wear, and wriggled into the housing of the complex little mechanism. This was hardly the first time he had seen it, since he'd been helping to build the device from the moment Honek had nodded and risen from the drafting board, and now he barely wasted a glance on the thumb-size translucent coils growing out of the almost microscopic energy bubbles which powered them.

This machine was the last hope of 2089, even if the world of 2089, as a whole, did not know of its existence and would try to prevent its being put into operation. But it meant a lot more to Mac Albin than merely saving a world. It meant an adventurous mission with the risk of death.

"Good old Giovanni Albeni," he laughed again happily.

If his great-grandfather had not volunteered for the earliest time-travel experiments way back in the nineteen-seventies, back even before the Epidemic, it would never have been discovered that he and his seed possessed a great deal of immunity to extra-temporal blackout.

And if that had not been discovered, the Albins would not have become physicists upon the passage of the United Nations law that everyone on Earth—absolutely without exception—had to choose a branch of research science in which to specialize. In the flabby, careful, life-guarding world the Earth had become, Mac Albin would never have been reluctantly selected by his two co-workers as the one to carry the forbidden banner of dangerous experiment.

No, if his great-grandfather had not demonstrated long ago his unique capacity for remaining conscious during time travel, Mac Albin would probably be a biologist today like almost everyone else on Earth, laboriously working out dreary gene problems instead of embarking on the greatest adventure Man had known to date.

Even if he didn't come back, he had at last found a socially useful escape from genetic responsibility to humanity in general and his own family in particular. This was a damn good job and he was lucky.

"Wait a minute, Mac," Skeat said and crossed to the other side of the narrow laboratory.

Albin and Honek watched him stuff several sheets of paper into a small metal box which he closed without locking.

"You will take care of yourself, won't you, Mac?" Hugo Honek pleaded. "Any time you feel like taking an unnecessary risk, remember that Bob and I will have to stand trial if you don't come back. We might be sentenced to complete loss of professional status and spend the rest of our lives supervising robot factories."

"Oh, it won't be that bad," Albin reassured him absentmindedly from where he lay contorted inside the time machine. He watched Skeat coming toward him with the box.

Honek shrugged his shoulders. "It might be a lot worse than even that and you know it. The disappearance of a two-time father is going to leave an awful big vacancy in the world. One-timers, like Bob and me, are all over the place; if either of us dropped out of sight, it wouldn't cause nearly as much uproar."

"But Bob and you both tried to operate the machine," Albin reminded him. "And you blacked out after a fifteen-second temporal displacement. So I'm the only chance, the only way to stop the human race from dwindling and dwindling till it hits absolute zero, like the tired old Security Council seems willing for it to do."

"Take it easy, Mac," Bob Skeat said as he handed the metal box to Albin. "The Security Council is just trying to solve the problem in their way, the conservative way: a worldwide concentration on genetics research coupled with the maximum preservation of existing human lives, especially those that have a high reproductive potential.

We three disagree with them; we've been skulking down here nights to solve it *our* way, and ours is a radical approach and plenty risky. That's the reason for the metal box—trying to cover one more explosive possibility."

Albin turned it around curiously. "How?"

"I sat up all last night writing the manuscript that's inside it. Look, Mac, when you go back to the Guided Missile Experiment of 1976 and push that red switch away from you, a lot of other things are going to happen than just deflecting the missile so that it will explode in the Brazilian jungle instead of the Pacific Ocean."

"Sure. I know. If it explodes in the jungle, the Epidemic doesn't occur. No Shapiro's Mumps."

Skeat jiggled his pudgy little face impatiently. "That's not what I mean. The Epidemic doesn't occur, but something else does. A new world, a different 2089, an alternate time sequence. It'll be a world in which humanity has a better chance to survive, but it'll be one with problems of its own. Maybe tough problems. Maybe the problems will be tough enough so that they'll get the same idea we did and try to go back to the same point in time to change them."

Albin laughed. "That's just looking for trouble."

"Maybe it is, but that's my job. Hugo's the designer of the time machine and you're the operator, but I'm the theoretical man in this research team. It's my job to look for trouble. So, just in case, I wrote a brief history of the world from the time the missile exploded in the Pacific. It tells why ours is the worst possible of futures. It's in that box."

"What do I do with it—hand it to the guy from the alternate 2089?"

The small fat man exasperatedly hit the side of the time machine with a well-cushioned palm. "You know better. There won't be any alternate 2089 until you push that red switch on the green instrument panel. The moment you do, our world, with all its slow slide to extinction, goes out and its alternate goes on—just like two electric light bulbs on a push-pull circuit. We and every single one of our artifacts, including the time machine, disappear. The problem is how to keep that manuscript from disappearing."

"Well, all you do, if I have this figured right, is shove the metal box containing the manuscript out into the surrounding temporal medium a moment before you materialize to do your job. That temporal medium in which you'll be traveling is something that exists independent of and autonomous to all possible futures. It's my hunch that something that's immersed in it will not be altered by a new time sequence."

"Remind him to be careful, Bob," Honek rumbled. "He thinks he's Captain Blood and this is his big chance to run away to sea and become a swashbuckling pirate."

Albin grimaced in annoyance. "I *am* excited by doing something for the first time in my life besides sitting in a safe little corner working out safe little abstractions. But I know that this is a first experiment. Honestly, Hugo, I really have enough intelligence to recognize that simple fact. I know that if anything unexpected pops up, anything we didn't foresee, I'm supposed to come scuttling back and ask for advice."

"I hope you do," Bob Skeat sighed. "I hope you do know that. A twentieth-century poet once wrote something to the effect that the world will end not with a bang, but a whimper. Well, our world is ending with a whimper. Try to see that it doesn't end with a bang, either."

"That I'll promise you," Albin said a trifle disgustedly. "It'll end with neither a bang *nor* a whimper. So long, Hugo. So long, Bob."

He twisted around, reaching overhead for the lever which activated the forces that drove the time machine.

flick!

It was strange, Max Alben reflected, that this time travel business, which knocked unconscious everyone who tried it, only made him feel slightly dizzy. That was because he was descended from Giovanni Albeni, he had been told. There must be some complicated scientific explanation for it, be decided—and that would make it none of his business. Better forget about it.

All around the time machine, there was a heavy gray murk in which objects were hinted at rather than stated definitely. It reminded him of patrolling his beat at the North American Chicken Reservation in a thick fog.

According to his gauges, he was now in 1976. He cut speed until he hit the last day of April, then cut speed again, drifting slowly backward to the eighteenth, the day of the infamous Guided Missile Experiment. Carefully, carefully, like a man handling a strange bomb made on a strange planet, he watched the center gauge until the needle came to rest against the thin etched line that indicated the exactly crucial moment. Then he pulled the brake and stopped the machine dead.

All he had to do now was materialize in the right spot, flash out and pull the red switch toward him. Then his well-paid assignment would be done.

But...

He stopped and scratched his dirt-matted hair. Wasn't there something he was supposed to do a second before materialization? Yes, that useless old windbag, Sadha, had given him a last instruction.

He picked up the sealed metal cylinder, walked to the entrance of the time machine and tossed it into the gray murk. A solid object floating near the entrance caught his eye. He put his arm out—whew, it was cold!—and pulled it inside.

A small metal box. Funny. What was it doing out there? Curiously, he opened it, hoping to find something valuable. Nothing but a few sheets of paper, Alben noted disappointedly. He began to read them slowly, very slowly, for the manuscript was full of a lot of long and complicated words, like a letter from one bookworm scientist to another.

The problems all began with the Guided Missile Experiment of 1976, he read. There had been a number of such experiments, but it was the one of 1976 that finally did the damage the biologists had been warning about. The missile with its deadly warhead exploded in the Pacific Ocean as planned, the physicists and the military men went home to study their notes, and the world shivered once more over the approaching war and tried to forget about it.

But there was fallout, a radioactive rain several hundred miles to the north, and a small fishing fleet got thoroughly soaked by it. Fortunately, the radioactivity in the rain was sufficiently low to do little obvious physical damage: All it did was cause a mutation in the mumps virus that several of the men in the fleet were incubating at the time, having caught it from the children of the fishing town, among whom a minor epidemic was raging.

The fleet returned to its home town, which promptly came down with the new kind of mumps. Dr. Llewellyn Shapiro, the only physician in town, was the first man to note that, while the symptoms of this disease were substantially milder than those of its unmutated parent, practically no one was immune to it and its effects on human reproductivity were truly terrible. Most people were completely sterilized by it. The rest were rendered much less capable of fathering or bearing offspring.

Shapiro's Mumps spread over the entire planet in the next few decades. It leaped across every quarantine erected; for a long time, it successfully defied all the vaccines and serums attempted against it. Then, when a vaccine was finally perfected, humanity discovered to its dismay that its generative powers had been permanently and fundamentally impaired.

Something had happened to the germ plasm. A large percentage of individuals were born sterile, and, of those who were not, one child was usually the most that could be expected, a two-child parent being quite rare and a three-child parent almost unknown.

Strict eugenic control was instituted by the Security Council of the United Nations so that fertile men and women would not be wasted upon non-fertile mates. Fertility was the most important avenue to social status, and right after it came successful genetic research.

Genetic research had the very best minds prodded into it; the lesser ones went into the other sciences. Everyone on Earth was engaged in some form of scientific research to some extent. Since the population was now so limited in proportion to the great resources available, all physical labor had long been done by robots. The government saw to it that everybody had an ample supply of goods and, in return, asked only that they experiment without any risk to their own lives—every human being was now a much-prized, highly guarded rarity.

There were less than a hundred thousand of them, well below the danger point, it had been estimated, where a species might be wiped out by a new calamity. Not that another calamity would be needed. Since the end of the Epidemic, the birth rate had been moving further and further behind the death rate. In another century...

That was why a desperate and secret attempt to alter the past was being made. This kind of world was evidently impossible.

Max Alben finished the manuscript and sighed. What a wonderful world! What a comfortable place to live!

He walked to the rear dials and began the process of materializing at the crucial moment on April 18, 1976.

flick!

It was odd, Mac Albin reflected, that these temporal journeys, which induced coma in everyone who tried it, only made him feel slightly dizzy. That was because he was descended from Giovanni Albeni, he knew. Maybe there was some genetic relationship with his above-average fertility—might be a good idea to mention the idea to a biologist or two when he returned. *If* he returned.

All around the time machine, there was a soapy gray murk in which objects were hinted at rather than stated definitely. It reminded him of the problems of landing a helicopter in a thick fog when the robot butler had not been told to turn on the ground lights.

According to the insulated register, he was now in 1976. He lowered speed until he registered April, then maneuvered slowly backward through time to the eighteenth, the day of the infamous Guided Missile Experiment. Carefully, carefully, like an obstetrician supervising surgical robots at an unusually difficult birth, he watched the register until it rolled to rest against the notch that indicated the exactly crucial moment. Then he pushed a button and froze the machine where it was.

All he had to do now was materialize in the right spot, flash out and push the red switch from him. Then his exciting adventure would be over.

But...

He paused and tapped at his sleek chin. He was supposed to do something a second before materialization. Yes, that nervous theoretician, Bob Skeat, had given him a last suggestion.

He picked up the small metal box, twisted around to face the opening of the time machine and dropped it into the gray murk. A solid object floating near the opening attracted his attention. He shot his arm out—it was *cold,* as cold as they had figured— and pulled the object inside.

A sealed metal cylinder. Strange. What was it doing out there? Anxiously, he opened it, not daring to believe he'd find a document inside. Yes, that was exactly what it was, he saw excitedly. He began to read it rapidly, very rapidly, as if it were a newly published paper on neutrinos. Besides, the manuscript was written with almost painful simplicity, like a textbook composed by a stuffy pedagogue for the use of morons.

The problems all began with the Guided Missile Experiment of 1976, he read. There had been a number of such experiments, but it was the one of 1976 that finally did the damage the biologists had been warning about. The missile with its deadly warhead exploded in the Brazilian jungle through some absolutely unforgivable error in the remote-control station: the officer in charge of the station was reprimanded and the men under him courtmartialed, and the Brazilian government was paid a handsome compensation for the damage.

But there had been more damage than anyone knew at the time. A plant virus, similar to the tobacco mosaic, had mutated under the impact of radioactivity. Five years later, it burst out of the jungle and completely wiped out every last rice plant on Earth. Japan and a large part of Asia became semi-deserts inhabited by a few struggling nomads.

Then the virus adjusted to wheat and corn—and famine howled in every street of the planet. All attempts by botanists to control the Blight failed because of the swiftness of its onslaught. And after it had fed, it hit again at a new plant and another and another.

Most of the world's non-human mammals had been slaughtered for food long before they could starve to death. Many insects, too, before they became extinct at the loss of their edible plants, served to assuage hunger to some small extent.

But the nutritive potential of Earth was steadily diminishing in a horrifying geometric progression. Recently, it had been observed, plankton—the tiny organism on which most of the sea's ecology was based—had started to disappear, and with its diminution, dead fish had begun to pile up on the beaches.

Mankind had lunged out desperately in all directions in an effort to survive, but nothing had worked for any length of time. Even the other planets of the Solar System, which had been reached and explored at a tremendous cost in remaining resources, had yielded no edible vegetation. Synthetics had failed to fill the prodigious gap.

In the midst of the sharply increasing hunger, social controls had pretty much dissolved. Pathetic attempts at rationing still continued, but black markets became the only markets, and black marketeers the barons of life. Starvation took the hindmost, and only the most agile economically lived in comparative comfort. Law and order were had only by those who could afford to pay for them and children of impoverished families were sold on the open market for a bit of food.

But the Blight was still adjusting to new plants and the food supply kept shrinking. In another century…

That was why the planet's powerful individuals had been persuaded to pool their wealth in a desperate attempt to alter the past. This kind of world was manifestly impossible.

Mac Albin finished the document and sighed. What a magnificent world! What an exciting place to live!

He dropped his hand on the side levers and began the process of materializing at the crucial moment on April 18, 1976.

flick!

As the equipment of the remote-control station began to take on a blurred reality all around him, Max Alben felt a bit of fear at what he was doing. The technicians, he remembered, the Secretary General, even the black market kings, had all warned him not to go ahead with his instructions if anything unusual turned up. That was an awful lot of power to disobey; he knew he should return with this new information and let better minds work on it.

They with their easy lives, what did they know what existence had been like for such as he? Hunger, always hunger, scrabbling, servility, and more hunger. Every time things got really tight, you and your wife looking sideways at your kids and wondering which of them would bring the best price. Buying security for them, as he was now, at the risk of his life.

But in this other world, this other 2089, there was a state that took care of you and that treasured your children. A man like himself, with *five* children—why, he'd be a big man, maybe the biggest man on Earth! And he'd have robots to work for him and lots of food. Above all, lots and lots of food.

He'd even be a scientist—*everyone* was a scientist there, weren't they?—and he'd have a big laboratory all to himself. This other world had its troubles, but it was a lot nicer place than where he'd come from. He wouldn't return. He'd go through with it.

The fear left him and, for the first time in his life, Max Alben felt the sensation of power.

He materialized the time machine around the green instrument panel, sweating a bit at the sight of the roomful of military figures, despite the technicians' reassurances that all this would be happening too fast to be visible. He saw the single red switch pointing upward on the instrument panel. The switch that controlled the course of the missile. Now! Now to make a halfway decent world!

Max Alben pulled the little red switch toward him.

flick!

As the equipment of the remote-control station began to oscillate into reality all around him, Mac Albin felt a bit of shame at what he was doing. He'd promised Bob and Hugo to drop the experiment at any stage if a new factor showed up. He knew he should go back with this new information and have all three of them kick it around.

But what would they be able to tell him, they with their blissful adjustment to their thoroughly blueprinted lives? They, at least, had been ordered to marry women they could live with; he'd drawn a female with whom he was completely incompatible in any but a genetic sense. Genetics! He was tired of genetics and the sanctity of human life, tired to the tips of his uncalloused fingers, tired to the recesses of his unused muscles. He was tired of having to undertake a simple adventure like a thief in the night.

But in this other world, this other 2089, someone like himself would be a monarch of the black market, a suzerain of chaos, making his own rules, taking his own women. So what if the weaklings, those unfit to carry on the race, went to the wall? His kind wouldn't.

He'd formed a pretty good idea of the kind of men who ruled that other world, from the document in the sealed metal cylinder. The black marketeers had not even read it. Why, the fools had obviously been duped by the technicians into permitting the experiment; they had not grasped the idea that an alternate time track would mean their own nonexistence.

This other world had its troubles, but it was certainly a livelier place than where he'd come from. It deserved a chance. Yes, that was how he felt: his world was drowsily moribund; this alternate was starving but managing to flail away at destiny. It *deserved* a chance.

Albin decided that he was experiencing renunciation and felt proud.

He materialized the time machine around the green instrument panel, disregarding the roomful of military figures since he knew they could not see him. The single red switch pointed downward on the instrument panel. That was the device that controlled the course of the missile. Now! Now to make a halfway interesting world!

Mac Albin pushed the little red switch from him.

flick!

Now! Now to make a halfway decent world!

Max Alben pulled the little red switch toward him.

flick!

Now! Now to make a halfway interesting world!

Mac Albin pushed the little red switch from him.

flick!

…pulled the little red switch toward him.

flick!

…pushed the little red switch from him.

flick!

…toward him.

flick!

…from him.

flick!

Afterword

I had two ignoble reasons for writing this story, and a third which might be considered moderately acceptable.

First, I had long wanted to use a title that rang a change on T.S. Eliot's lines in *The Hollow Men:*

> *This is the way the world ends*
> *Not with a bang but a whimper.*

Second, I had long wanted to try something special in the way of a time-travel paradox—a *reductio ad absurdum,* say.

And third, I have always believed that no matter how history were modified, no matter how it forked, the Thoreauvian insight would still hold true. The mass of men would still lead lives of quiet desperation.

WRITTEN 1956———PUBLISHED 1956

ॐ

The Girl with Some Kind of Past.
And George.

You know George.

He says one minute there was nothing in his living room but him and his TV and his VCR and the picture window overlooking half of the city, and the next minute there was this beautiful red-headed girl in a kind of shining red playsuit hovering in the air over his head. Not really hovering, not floating, but kind of all sprawled out every which way and staring down between her legs at him. Well, you know George.

George says she was making this musical sound, or something was making this musical sound, like a small synthesizer with hiccups; then she disappeared.

George says there was about three seconds of silence, just him and his VCR and his TV, then hiccup, hiccup, and she's sitting on the couch beside him, all red playsuit and beautiful long legs.

You know, he's right? It's hard to think of something to say when a girl pops into your room like that?

But you know George.

"Gin, maybe, with just the teensiest bit of vermouth?"

The girl opened first her eyes, then her mouth at him, both very wide. She nodded.

"I don't have any olives," George told her, getting up. "But I have the funniest little green onions. You'll like them."

The girl nodded again and rubbed something on her chest. Nice chest, George says. "You are good," she said. "I didn't quite expect that. You are very, very good."

"Why shouldn't I be?" George asked. He took a good look at her while he was mixing the drinks at his bar. She was still staring at him, all big hazel eyes and nice chest. The red playsuit was not really a playsuit, he noticed. It was not the actual color red, either, he says, but somehow like red, if you know what he means. I don't. George says it was kind of a rosy fog that was vibrating all over the best parts of her very nice body, and it had tiny, transparent rosy knobs every couple of inches that kept popping up and then disappearing. He couldn't see anything that looked like a zipper anywhere.

"George Rice?" the girl said slowly, tentatively. She had a nice voice, too; it came from deep in her diaphragm with plenty of breathing. "You are George Rice?"

"That's it. You're on the button," George told her. "You wanted George Rice, kid, you got George Rice." He came back with the drinks, found some coasters, and put the drinks on the whatchamacallit table next to the couch. The VCR had been running *Casablanca* all this time through the TV, so he turned it off.

The girl picked up her drink, sipped it, made a face, then nodded. She sipped some more and nodded some more. "I'm Antoinette Donnelly. This is—what? 1994? 1995?"

"Still 1994," George said. Now he took a good long look at her: she was unarguably juicy as hell. "You're a time traveler, right?"

"The first. The very first."

"Are you the inventor of time travel?"

"One of," the girl said. She put down her drink and studied it hard for a bit. Then she gave a quick little shudder and a long exhale and turned back to George. She was sitting with both feet solidly planted on the floor, not the way a girl usually sits on a couch, you know, all curled up.

"There are five of us," she explained. "I'm the youngest, the healthiest, the smoothest reflexes. And I had the best reason for going to our first logical target area, this time and place."

"The best reason?" George swirled his drink around—you know, the thoughtful, snotty way he does. But whatever he looked like, he says, he was feeling as if he had a hole in his chest and he was breathing through the hole. "Me?"

The girl walked over to the picture window and stared down the twenty or so floors. She tapped on the window and scratched at it. "Glass?"

"That's it," George said. "Glass." He tried to drink some gin and found he couldn't swallow. He set the drink on the table. "I was the reason? I mean, was I the reason?"

She came back and sat down on the couch. She wrapped her hands around her right knee and pulled it back up against her belly and rocked back and forth, just like a real girl. "Yes, I've always been terribly curious about what you were like when you were a young man. What was the name of that television special you were watching? Hasn't color television been developed yet?"

"Sure. This is a color set. I wasn't watching a TV special; it was a movie— *Casablanca*. It was made in black and white: it's a thirties or forties film. I don't like the colorized version. Why me? What did I—I mean, what will I—oh, hell, where do I stand in your time? What does history say about me? Why me? Hey? Huh? Why me?"

She shook her head at him reproachfully. "Don't do that. Be nice. I only have so very few hours before the spirillix goes down. And the skindrom's very weak on this trip. I want to see a lot and ask a lot, and I have to keep careful measurements of the chroniates in this room. So be nice. Please try not to be selfish and personally inquisitive."

George stared at this Antoinette, this Antoinette Donnelly. Who the hell did she think she was?

Still, he figured, still— There was that unarguably juicy body. And the interesting information she evidently had about him. Better go easy. Later on, maybe—

"I will try," George told her, spreading his arms out in a great, truth-embracing gesture, "not to be selfish and personally inquisitive. It'll be hard, but I'll try. Any questions that I'm *allowed* to ask? Like, maybe, *when* are you from? How far in the future?"

She nodded. "A century. Just about. We thought that a century was long enough to avoid any—you know—complications, and long enough to look like a real voyage to the past."

"Look like to whom?"

"Oh, the Institute. People like that. But, of course, you were the other reason. For me, anyway."

"Of course." So they were back to him again. But he was not supposed to be personally inquisitive, now wasn't he? Bull*shit!* He felt like telling her to go measure her chroniates.

And then it hit him that the problem was also bullshit. The problem just couldn't be that difficult to solve. I mean, she knew what his achievement was: it was bound to be on her mind all the time. George represented something very, very special to her. She'd be thinking about him and his achievement every single second.

To be that famous and not know what you were famous for! To be so famous that the first time traveler went straight for you as soon as she got a chance! If that were so, it had to be incredibly big big-time, Moses-level, Shakespeare-level, Einstein-level. Maybe even bigger than that.

His autograph—what might that not be worth! The postcard he'd just scribbled to Lonnie Santangelo vacationing in Sweden—they could be bidding lunatic sums for it at an auction in some future version of Sotheby's. Where he planned to have dinner this evening could be an item of information that a biographer a century from now would give almost anything to know.

For that matter, he himself would give almost anything to know. Why waste time farting with this or doodling with that when you could be practicing the thing that was going to continue crashing like cymbals across the world long after you were dead? He had to find out.

And to all this, Antoinette Donnelly was the key. Very damn fortunately.

She was pure girl, after all, George says. You know—touch the right part at the right time in just the right way, and she's bound to react. By which, George says he means *in this case,* let her see a little bit of what he's become famous for. The first beginnings of that later big stuff.

So where to begin?

He wandered casually over to the bookcase and took his alto recorder off the top shelf, making casual conversation as he walked. "So you're from the end of the twenty-first century. Must be a pretty wonderful time to be living in."

"Not at all," she laughed. "It feels to us just as your time does to you. Except for— Well, maybe I'd better not go into that. Anyway, most of what's important to us had already begun in your period. You know, computer networking, leveraged buyouts, gene splicing, all that sort of thing."

"Oh, sure, sure." He blew the dust off the recorder and put it to his lips. First he tootled a couple of bars of "Greensleeves," then he said, "Hey, what do you think of this?" and went into the rock number. You remember, the one he and Lester Pittstein wrote and tried to peddle about four years ago?

He kept his eyes on her face as he played it. Not much. As a matter of fact, she got off the couch and went over to the bookcase beside him. She seemed a hell of a lot more interested in his paperbounds than in what he was playing.

"This just came out, didn't it?" she said, pulling a suspense novel off the shelf and opening it to the copyright page. "He's still doing nothing but hard-boiled mysteries?"

George put the recorder away and freshened her drink. It was obvious that she wasn't much used to liquor. Despite the little she had had, there was already a faint glow to her. Believe me, if George says so, he knows.

"I started to write a suspense novel once," he said, thinking, maybe she's giving me a lead? "Want to look at the first chapter?"

"Uh-uh. Where's your—your *bathroom?*"

When she'd closed the door behind her, George sat down and began thinking hard. Obviously, it was not music and it was not literature. He was famous for something else. But what? Well, there were lots of other possibilities.

Money? Was he to become one of the great multi-billionaires of all time? How do you work into that, George wondered? Perhaps start talking about stocks and bonds?

Sure. Try to be smooth! "Hey, isn't it odd how well the utilities are doing today?" Or— "Anything you especially like about four-year debentures, Antoinette, old kiddo?"

Crap.

No, better stick to the logical, the things he'd actually experimented with, the things he was a little bit good at.

Meanwhile. He freshened her drink a little bit harder. He set out the green onions near her glass and got some thirsty-making stuff from the refrigerator, you know, a plateful of real spicy salami, some hot peppers, stuff like that, to put around and near her glass.

And he turned on *Casablanca* again—maybe? just possibly?—and turned it off fast: it was at the airport scene with Conrad Veidt and Claude Rains, not to mention Bergman and Bogey. Too damn much renunciation in that scene, George says. A renunciation mood is just plain blind alley, he claims.

When she came back, she pursed her lips at the salami. "I thought you people were afraid of foods like this. Isn't it full of what you call phlogiston?" She took a bite. "But it *is* good."

George was pleased that she washed it down with another mouthful of vermouth-flavored gin. "Phlogiston? What are you talking about?"

"Caloricol, phlogisterol—something like that. You have this superstition that having it in your food is going to kill you early."

"Oh, cholesterol. No, I don't bother with that. At least not at my age. Try the peppers. They're good too."

And while she tried the peppers, he tried her with other fame possibilities among his interests. Lots else. The only thing she seemed interested in was the pair of limericks he'd written way back when for his college humor magazine. But it turned out not to be the limericks.

There was a pen-and-ink caricature of him on the page facing the limericks. Now *that* grabbed her. Antoinette kept staring at it, turning it this way and that way. She seemed fascinated by it.

"I didn't do it," George told her. "Somebody—I don't remember his name—he was only a freshman who'd wandered into the office... Do you think it's that fine?"

"Not particularly. It's just that the resemblance is so strong."

"Resemblance? You mean between me now and me then?"

"No. Between you then and him then. Him at your age."

"Him? Who?"

"Your father. You both looked exactly alike at twenty."

"You've seen pictures of my father?"

"Of course. Do you have one of your mother here? I'd love to see which is the picture you've kept of your mother."

Her eyes were sparkling away, and only part of it was the gin. She'd been doing all right with the gin, George noticed, but he had the distinct feeling it was not her usual drink. She seemed unfamiliar with it, and she was pouring it down a bit too fast. Still, all to the good.

He hauled out a picture of his mother. Antoinette Donnelly practically jumped at it. "I've never seen this one," she squealed. "Oh, how lovely, how unexpected."

George says he was just beginning to come out of his bafflement. Why his parents? Well, if a man is maximum famous, there are all sorts of biographies written about him; there are chapters on his parents, there'd be pictures of his parents in the illustration section, you know, all the interesting stuff about his origins.

She was still crooning over his mother's photograph. And you know, he says, it was just a very ordinary studio shot. He listened to her go *oh!* and *ah!* and make the kind of breath-kissy sounds girls do when they're all overcome, and then, suddenly, she said something. She definitely *said* something.

"My ancestor," she said. "My very own ancestor."

"Your wha-at?"

"My ancestor. My great-great-great-grandmother."

George says it hit him harder than the gin was hitting her. He says he went all kinds of rubbery. "Your ancestor," he got out after a while. "That makes me…"

"My great-great-grandfather. Exactly. How do you do, great-great-granddad?"

She shook hands with him, you know, solemn-comical. George says he didn't feel he had much muscle in the arm she was shaking.

"Is that the reason you came back to see me?" he asked.

The question seemed to upset her a little bit. "Most of," she said. Then she thought for a second or two and grimaced. "Some of," she added.

Naturally, George took a good hard look at her now. There seemed to be a real family resemblance, but he wasn't sure how much he was reading into it. On the other hand, there'd been no red hair in the family, none at all that he remembered. And Antoinette Donnelly's hair was bright red, flame red, almost orange. Well, maybe he was going to marry a red-headed woman. Or maybe his son would. Or his grandson.

But here he'd been half-planning to put it to her—his own great-great-granddaughter. Wow.

And then he thought, why wow? First, who would know? Second, was it really incest? She was a lot farther away, relationwise, than a second cousin, say. And nobody objected to anyone making it with a second cousin. What an opportunity! It was his chance to make it with the next century—something no cocksman before him had ever done.

He freshened her drink again and took a sip from his—just to keep things looking right.

And the point was also to get the information out of her. George says it hit him that what he had to do was both. And he knew he could. If he got her loose enough to get her into bed, she'd nine chances out of ten be loose enough to tell him what he wanted to know. There's nothing like the aftermath of the sack to make a person feel like talking.

You know George. He knows.

"Would you like to see a picture of the two of them together?"

"Oh, yes."

"It's in the bedroom. Bring your drink with you."

And that's all it took, George says.

He says he got the framed wedding picture out of a bureau drawer and, while she crooned over it, he got his arm around her waist, and then she fast slurped the rest of her drink down, and he fast slurped at the base of her throat and the side of her throat and then on down. He says he didn't even have to push her into bed. She flowed.

The big problem was that jumpsuit or playsuit she was wearing. George says that trying to remove it reminded him of way back in his teens and the first time he'd tried to get a brassiere off a girl while kissing her passionately and all the time acting suave and man-of-the-world. That red stuff just wouldn't come off her, no matter how he pulled or pushed or got his fingers inside. There was no catch, no hook anywhere, that he could find.

She had to do it for him—just like with that first girl and that first brassiere. She just put her finger on one of the little knobs or buttons, and the whole garment let out a wheeze and shriveled up into a little red bump on her right shoulder.

And off they went.

How good was she? Not great, George says. Not at all bad; just not great. And, he says, sex in the twenty-first century is still pretty much sex as we know it. If you've been in one century, he figures, you've been in them all. Maybe the two biggest differences are how many clothes you have to take off and what you do about birth control. She looked like a level-headed female so he decided he could trust her on birth control.

That left the incest angle, and I asked him about that. He says that making it with your great-great-granddaughter from the twenty-first century is not much different from making it with your clothes-designer neighbor from across the hall.

If that's what he says, that's what it is. You have to figure he knows.

They had two, three rolls, and she seemed to get a little drunker with each roll. When it was all over and they lay apart, George looked her over carefully. A real fine body—and you know what? He says she was still clutching the wedding picture of his parents in one hand. As a matter of fact, up to a few seconds ago, she'd been banging away at the sheets with it.

He got up, took it away from her and put it back in the bureau drawer.

This Antoinette Donnelly. She was still breathing hard. "You are fantastic," she said. "You are absolutely fantastic, Mr. George Rice."

"Thanks," he said with as much of a modest smirk as George can manage. "My father thanks you. My mother thanks you. And I thank you." He took her drink off the night table and handed it to her. Keep her loose.

She drank some—you know, sex always makes me thirsty too—and held up a hand. There was a wiggly black dot inside her wrist. "Ooch," she said. "It's late."

George figured it was now or never to move. "You're not going without at least giving me a hint?" he whimpered—you know how George does. "Just a hint? Not even that?"

She seemed to say something to the red bump on her right shoulder. There was a fast wheeze or something and the red playsuit kind of boiled up and out and over her body. She was obviously thinking hard.

"You are so very, very good," she grinned. "You even know exactly how to ask for something you have no right to ask."

"No right? Aw, come on." He bent down and kissed her. "I've got a perfect right. A great-great-grandfather's right."

She giggled. "Some great-great-grandfather!"

He walked back to the living room with her. Feeling great. It was obvious she couldn't refuse him, couldn't hold back. He was probably strutting a bit as he walked. You know George.

"Come on. Why did you have to see me? What's so great about me?"

"Well, to begin with there are—I mean, were—your parents. Their accomplishments."

"My parents? What are you talking about? They were all right, they led okay lives, but, hey, they didn't *do* very much. What accomplishments?"

"Well, for just one thing, your mother's critical study of the academic novel. That by itself is a pretty big item."

"Mom's book? Oh, no. She had to have it published by a vanity press. It cost her four thousand dollars. And it came out a year after she died."

Antoinette shrugged. "So? It's still definitive. The seminal study of the academic novel of the twentieth century. Everything else takes off from that."

"My God. And Dad? Poor old nutty Dad? Don't tell me his matchbook collection, or his beer can collection.... Hey, don't tell me that."

At this point, the girl touched a couple of raised knobs on her playsuit. A kind of tinkling started up. "Well," she said, "if you're talking about his famous seven collections—the ones he left to his local branch of the public library—if you're talking about those, that's exactly what I do have to tell you."

"Famous. You said famous. Those crappy collections? I mean you couldn't walk around in our basement because of that junk."

"Yes, I said famous. Of course, I meant his accompanying monograph as much as the collections themselves. There's a two-year course at most universities based on that monograph: *Popular Culture and Its Industrial Base*. Well, actually only half of it is based on your father's monograph; the other half has to do with the extension into musical theory that one of your children did late in life."

"Which one of my children? How many kids will I have? Will they—"

"No. I can't go into that kind of detail about future events. Surely you can see why?" She rubbed hard on a reddish button and the tinkling developed into a definite and noticeable rhythm. A kind of hiccuppy rhythm. "I wish I could. I'd particularly like to tell you about my grandmother, one of your granddaughters. So much of her research on the speed of light as a sometime constant has been the background of all my work on time travel. Although, her cousin's theories, I'd say, are also really—"

"Cousin! That's one of my descendants, too, right? I hear what you're telling me. From my parents down, quite a goddam family!"

"Oh, yes, quite a family. A genetic delight, a eugenic fantasia. A family that's been scrutinized exactly as the Bachs of Germany have been scrutinized."

And now she was playing around with a whole bunch of those rosy buttons. Back and forth. Up and down. It almost sounded like a tune. And it was getting loud.

But George was paying no attention to that. He was hot on the trail now.

"And of that whole famous family, you picked me to come back to. Me you wanted to see. Just me!"

She was concentrating on those buttons, but she looked up, a little annoyed. "Of course you were the one I wanted to see. You have to be the most interesting one of the lot."

George grabbed her shoulders and began shaking her. "*Why?* You've got to tell me *why*. What did I do? What *will* I do?"

"Please!" She pushed him away hard. George says she had a lot of power for something her size. "Please! You'll defuse the spirillix. It's already falling fast."

George bounced back. "Come on. Don't do this. Tell me why. Why me particularly?" He says his voice had gotten hoarse. He was practically yelling in a whisper.

She looked up from the buttons and stared at him. "Don't you see? Surely you know!"

"Know what? What's special about me? *What?*"

"You're the only one in the family, the only one for a whole bunch of generations who achieved nothing, absolutely nothing. And, when I was given the chance, I just had to find out why."

"Nothing? Nothing at all?" George says his two lips tasted like paper.

"Nothing at all. I've been puzzled by it all my life. Nor am I the only one in my time who finds it baffling. The articles! The hypotheses! And I found out why just two minutes or so after I arrived. It's so obvious."

"Obvious?" George says he croaked out.

"Yes. You're just too good at what you do do." She gestured toward the bedroom. "The way you managed me into there. And the way— How could there be room for any other skill?"

Those musical sounds got very loud and very fast. And then she was gone. George says like a bubble bursting, a bubble bursting where no bubble had been.

And that's all. I mean, that's all, folks.

It's a pretty weird story, you have to admit. It's not a story every guy would tell about himself.

But he says Antoinette Donnelly missed the whole point. He says the record will damn well show he was first-rate at *something*. He grins like a cat when he says that.

Well, you know George.

AFTERWORD

I think this is not at all a bad story. In fact, it has some rather really good bits. But I couldn't figure out a way to end it. When my agent, Virginia Kidd, began pointing out to me that it had been a long time since I had given her a chance to show me her marketing ability, out of sheer shame I finished up the piece and sent it to her. She sold it immediately.

I still don't quite like the ending. I need help, I feel, with the last couple of paragraphs. I've never found that help.

Can you, do you think…

WRITTEN 1987———PUBLISHED 1993

෨

FLIRGLEFLIP

Banderling, you are a fathead!

Yes, yes. I know. It is rather improbable that this message will reach you in the years that remain of your smug life; but if something, some new discovery—an unexpected warp in the plenum, say—should bring these pages to the surface, I want Thomas Alva Banderling to know that I consider him the most dilated, augmented, and amplified fathead in the history of the race.

Excepting myself, of course.

When I consider how happy I was puttering around my collection of dolik and spindfar, how splendidly my paper on Gllian Origins of Late Pegis Flirg-Patterns was progressing—when I recall that bliss, only to be recalled in turn to the filthy, dripping necessities of my present vocation, I tend to become somewhat unacademic in my opinions of Banderling. What chance do I have now of ever returning to the creamy towers of the Institute rising in plastic beauty from the septic Manhattan soil?

I like to dream of the scholarly exhilaration I felt the day we of Field Party Nineteen returned from Mars with a shipload of punforg out of the Gllian excavation. I like to muse on my delighted reacquaintance with the problems I had left unsolved when the field trip was offered me. Banderling and his obscene radiation depressor? Why, that night was the first time I really noticed him!

"Terton," he asked suddenly, his face focusing sharp and studious in the screen of my benscope, "Terton, could you look in at my lab for a moment? I need an extra pair of hands."

I was startled. Beyond occasional meetings at Institute Assemblies, Banderling and I had had little reason for conversation. And it was fairly rare for an Associate Investigator to call on a full Investigator for mechanical assistance, especially when their fields were so different.

"Can't you get a labtech or a robot?" I asked.

"All the labtechs have gone. We're the only ones left in the Institute. Gandhi's Birthday, you know. I told my robot to package himself two hours ago when I thought I was leaving."

"Very well," I sighed, necklacing both my flirgleflip and the dolik I had been examining with it. As I walked into the benscope, giving my necklace the required tugs for the opposite wing of the Institute, I had already ceased to wonder at the oddity of Banderling's request.

The dolik on which I bad been working, you see, was the so-called Thumtse Dilemna—a thoroughly fascinating business. Most of my colleagues inclined toward Gurkheyser's statement of the problem when he discovered it at Thumtse over fifty years ago. Gurkheyser declared that it couldn't be dolik because of the lack of flirg-pattern; and it couldn't be spindfar because of the presence of flirg in minute quantities; therefore it was a consciously created paradox and, as such, had to be classified as punforg. But, by definition, punforg could not exist at Thumtse....

I wander. Once more I forget the reactions of my audience to this subject. If only this were not so, if only on this one point— In any case, I was still considering the Thumtse Dilemma when I stepped out of the benscope into Banderling's lab. I was not at all prepared psychologically to make the obvious deductions from his nervousness. Even if I had, who could have imagined such psychotic behavior from an Associate Investigator?

"Thanks, Terton," he nodded, his necklace jangling with the gadgetry that physicists seem to find necessary at all times. "Would you hold that long bar away from the turntable and press into the grid with your back? Right." He sucked at the knuckles of his right hand; with his left, he flipped a toggle and clicked a relay shut. He turned a small knob past several calibrations, frowned doubtfully and moved it back to an earlier mark.

The turntable before me—a wheel-like affair whose spokes were resistor coils and whose hub was an immense mesotronic tube—began to glow and whirl softly. Behind me, the grid was vibrating gently against my shoulder blades.

"There's—uh, nothing dangerous in what I'm doing?" I asked, moistening my lips at the roomful of fully operating equipment.

Banderling's little black beard shot up scornfully and the very hairs on his chest seemed to quiver. "What could be dangerous?"

Since I didn't know, I decided to feel reassured. I longed for Banderling's help in the process, but he was moving about rapidly now, sneering impatiently at meters and slapping at switches.

I had almost forgotten my uncomfortable position and the bar I was holding, and was considering the middle passage of my paper—the section where I intended to prove that the influence of Gll was fully as great as Tkes upon later Pegis—when Banderling's booming voice thrust a question into my consciousness.

"Terton, don't you often feel unhappy that you live in an intermediate civilization?"

He had stopped in front of the turntable and put his overlong hands truculently upon his hips.

"What do you mean—the Temporal Embassy?" I asked. I'd heard of Banderling's views.

"Exactly. The Temporal Embassy. How can science live and breathe with such a modifier? It's a thousand times worse than any of those ancient repressions like the

Inquisition, military control, or university trusteeship. You can't do this—it will be done first a century later; you can't do that—the sociological impact of such an invention upon your period will be too great for its present capacity; you should do this—nothing may come of it now, but somebody in an allied field a flock of years from now will be able to integrate your errors into a useful theory. And what do all these prohibitions and restrictions accomplish; whose ends do they serve?"

"The greatest good of the greatest number in the greatest period of time," I quoted firmly from the Institute prospectus. "That humanity may continually improve itself by reshaping the past on the basis of its own historical judgment and the advice of the future."

He nodded a sneer at me. "How do we know? What is the master plan of those ultimate humans in that ultimate future where there is no temporal embassy from a still later period? Would we approve of it, would we—"

"But Banderling, we wouldn't even understand it! Humans with minds compared to which ours would look like elementary neural responses—how could we grasp and appreciate their projects? Besides, there seems to be no such ultimate future, merely temporal embassy after temporal embassy sent by each age into the preceding one, the advice of each embassy based on the best historical hindsight of the period from which it came. Temporal embassies extending always into the past from the improving future, temporal embassies without end." I paused, out of breath.

"Except here. Except in an intermediate civilization like ours. They may go out to infinity as far as the future is concerned, Terton, but they stop in our time. We send nobody into the past; we receive orders, but give none of our own."

I puzzled over Banderling as he examined the greenly sparking mesotronic tube and made an adjustment among his controls which excited it still further. He had always been considered a bit of a rebel at the Institute—by no means bad enough for a Readjustment Course, however—but surely he knew that the organization of the Institute itself was the first suggestion made by the Temporal Embassy when our age durated into its time-fix? I decided that the present difficulty with his equipment had irritated him out of normal reasoning processes. My mind trotted back to important items like spindfar problems, and I began to wish that Banderling would relieve me of the long bar so that I could denecklace my flirgleflip.

Not that I believed the Thumtse Dilemna could conceivably be spindfar. But it was possible, I had suddenly realized, for flirg—

"I've been told to call off work on my radiation depressor." The physicist's morose voice sliced into my thoughts.

"This machine, you mean?" I inquired rather politely, concealing my annoyance both at his interruption and the sudden inexplicable increase of warmth in the room.

"Hum. Yes, this machine." He turned away for a moment and came back with a modified benscope projector which he placed in front of me. "The Temporal Embassy merely suggested that I stop, of course. They suggested it to the Institute administration, which put it in the form of an order. No reason given, none at all."

I clucked sympathetically and moved my perspiring hands to another position on the bar. The vibration of the grid had almost worn a checkerboard callus into my back; and the thought of being involved in an experiment with revoked equipment when I could be doing constructive investigation into dolik, spindfar, and even punforg made me almost pathologically unsocial with impatience.

"Why?" Banderling demanded dramatically, throwing opened palms up in the air. "What is there about this device which requires an ultimatum to stop its progress? I have been able to halve the speed of light, true; I may be able to reduce it even further in the tube, possibly to zero, eventually. Does such an increase of man's scientific powers seem dangerous to you, Terton?"

I pondered the question and was happy to be able to answer in all honesty that it didn't. "But," I reminded him, "there have been other direct revocations of projects. I had one. There was this dolik which was most curiously flirgled, evidently a product of Middle Rla at the peak of its culture. I had no more established the Rlaian origin when I was called to—"

"What have these infernal, incomprehensible thingumajigs to do with the speed of light?" he blasted at me. "I'll tell you why I was ordered to stop work on my radiation depressor, Terton, after eleven years of mind-breaking research. This machine is the key to time travel."

The offense I had decided to take was forgotten. I stared at him. "Time travel? You mean you've discovered it? We have reached the point where we are permitted to send a temporal embassy of our own into the past?"

"No. We have reached a point where journeying in time is possible, where a visit to the past may be made, where we are able to set up an embassy in a previous period. But we will not be allowed to do it! Instead, I drop my radiation depressor so that a century later, say, when the Embassy approves, some other physicist will build a machine using my notes and research—and be credited by history as the father of time travel."

"Are you sure that it's time travel? Possibly only a—"

"Of course I'm sure. Haven't I been measuring duration-gap since the first indication of electromagnetic dampening? Didn't I lose two mesotronic tubes before the reverse field had even approached optimum? And didn't I duplicate the experience of the tubes with over fifteen rabbits, none of which have reappeared? No, it's time travel, Terton, and I have to drop it. Officially, that is."

His tone confused me. "What do you mean, 'officially'?"

Banderling drew a universal necklace across the screen of the benscope until it began to pulsate. "Well, by officially— Terton, would you mind lifting the bar to your chest? A little higher. Fine. We'll be all set in a moment. Suppose someone from the present should be sent into the past as a result of a laboratory accident? Time travel would be an accomplished fact; the man who had built the machine that had accomplished it would be the accredited discoverer—the Temporal Embassy and all its plans notwithstanding. That would cause repercussions clear to the last dwindling curvature of time!"

I shivered, despite the extreme warmth of the lab at this point. "It would," I agreed. "If anyone were fool enough to try it. Seriously, though, do you really think your radiation depressor could send a man from our time into the past and bring him back?"

The physicist put the necklace aside as the benscope achieved optimum pulsation. "I couldn't effect the return with my equipment. But the Temporal Embassy would take care of that. Why, even they have only emissaries operating in the pre-intermediate civilizations—highly trained operatives working secretly and under great difficulties to make the necessary alterations in cultural evolution without the dislocation that would be caused by a Temporal Revelation to primitives. Anyone from our time who wandered into a previous period would be brought back in a hurry. And since the Temporal Embassy permits itself only advisory functions in an intermediate civilization like ours, he'd be brought back alive with a suggestion to Administration that he be shut up somehow. But no matter what happened after that, the secret would be out, the mission would be accomplished. Administration would probably shrug its bureaucratic shoulders and decide to accept the existence of time travel with its attendant Advanced Civilization status. Administration wouldn't object to that at all, once the thing was done. And the temporal embassies would ricochet irritation ahead for a couple of million years; but they'd have to revise their plans. Their grip on history would be broken."

I saw it. Fascinating! Imagine solving once for all the Thumtse Dilemna by watching its creation! And what fantastic new knowledge of the flirglers themselves? We knew so little. I would be particularly interested in the relationship of punforg to—

Unfortunately, the dream was only that. Banderling's radiation depressor had been revoked. He would work on it no more after tonight. Time travel was for another age. I slumped unhappily against the grid.

"That's it, Terton!" the physicist yelled delightedly. "It's passing optimum!" He picked up the universal necklace and held it over the screen of the benscope.

"I'm glad it's working again," I told him. "This grid has been punishing my back. Banderling, I have research of my own to do."

"Don't forget your training," he warned me. "Keep your eyes open and make careful mental notes of everything you see until you're picked up. Think how many investigators in your wing of the Institute would scramble to be in your place, Terton!"

"My place? Helping you? Well, I don't know—"

Then the turntable canted toward me in a flash of oozing green light; the bar seemed to melt into my chest and the grid to flow down my rigid back. Banderling's face tilted out of recognizable perspective through shimmering heat waves. A great goblet of ear-piercing sound poured over my head and numbed my mind. Something enormous, irresistible, punched at me hard and snapped the bubble of consciousness. Nothing was left but a memory of Banderling's grin.

And I was cold. I was very cold.

I stood on a ridiculously stony thoroughfare, looking at a scene from Mark Twain, Washington Irving or Ernest Hemingway—one of the authors of *that* period, in any case. Brick buildings were scattered carelessly over the landscape like a newly discovered trove of spindfar; metal vehicles crawled noisily past on both sides of me; people walked on the raised stone sections near the ugly little buildings with leather clogs laced tightly to their feet and bandages of various fabrics wrapping their bodies.

But above all, it was cold. Why, the city wasn't even air-conditioned! I found myself shivering violently. I remembered some drawing I had seen of an urchin shivering in just such a scene. Medieval New York. 1650 to 1980, I believe.

Abruptly I remembered the last moments in the lab. And understood.

I raised my fists to my face. "Banderling!" I shrieked at them. "Banderling, you are a fathead!"

This, so far as I can remember, was the first time I used a remark which was to become a cliché with me. Let me repeat it nonetheless, out of a full heart and an aching body—fathead! Fathead!

Somewhere, a woman screamed. I turned and saw her looking at me. Other people were laughing and pointing. I gestured impatiently at them, sank my head on my chest and tried to return to consideration of my predicament.

Then I remembered.

I didn't know exactly when I was, but one thing all of these pre-intermediate civilizations had in common: a clothes fetish with severe penalties for those who disregarded it.

Naturally, there were reasons. I wasn't certain which of them was most important here. For example, there was evidently no thermostatic control of the atmosphere in this area, and the season was the cooling third of the four ancient natural ones.

A gesticulating group had congregated on the raised cement surface facing me. A burly figure in blue, primitive weapons dangling from his belt, shouldered his way out of the crowd and started rapidly in my direction.

"Hey, character," he said (approximately). "Whadaya think this is? Free show? Huh? C'mere!"

As I said, I approximate. I found I was terribly afraid of this savage.

I retreated, whirled, and began to run. I heard him running behind me. I ran faster; I heard him do likewise.

"C'mere!" a voice bellowed. "I said c'mere!"

Was I in an era when burning at the stake was used on those who ran contrary to the psychotic edicts of society? I couldn't remember. I considered it essential, however, to find the privacy necessary for concentration on my next move.

I found it in a dark corner of an alleyway as I galloped past a building. A large metal receptacle with a cover.

There was no one close to me at the moment. I dodged into the alleyway, removed the cover, jumped into the receptacle and got the cover back over my head just as my pursuer puffed up.

Such an incredibly barbarous period! That receptacle—unspeakable, unspeakable....

I heard a pair of feet trotting up the alley, coming back. After a while, several more pairs of feet arrived.

"Well, where did he go?"

"S'elp me, sergeant, he musta gone over that nine-foot fence in back there. I coulda sworn he turned in here, coulda sworn!"

"An old guy like that, Harrison?"

"Pretty spry for an old guy, even if he was a gejenerate. Gave me a run."

"Gave you the slip, Harrison. Guy probably took off from some sanitarium or other. Better find him, men, before he terrorizes the neighborhood."

The feet slapped off.

I decided that my temporary escape from capture was balanced by the notice I had attracted in what seemed to be the higher echelons of the city's officialdom. I tried desperately, but futilely, to remember some of my Terran history. What were the functions of a sergeant? No use. After all, sixty years since I had studied the subject....

Despite my intense olfactory discomfort, I couldn't leave the receptacle. It would be necessary to wait quite a while, until my pursuers had given up the chase; it would also be necessary to have a plan.

Generally speaking, I knew what I must do. I must somehow discover an emissary of the Temporal Embassy and request a return to my own period. Before I could go about finding him, though, I would have to equip myself with such standard equipment as clothes.

How did one go about getting clothes in this period? Barter? Brigandage? Government work-coupons? Weaving them on one's own loom? Banderling and his idiotic idea that my specialty would be useful in such a world! That fathead!

The cover of the receptacle lifted suddenly. A very tall young man with a vague and pleasant face stared down at me. He rapped on the metal of the lid.

"May I come in?" he inquired courteously.

I glared up at him, but said nothing.

"The cops are gone, Pop," he continued. "But I wouldn't get out just yet. Not in your uniform. I'll lay chick if you tell me all about you."

"Wh-who are you? And what do you want?"

"Joseph Burns, a poor but honest newspaperman." He considered for a moment. "Well, poor, anyway. I want any such story as you may have to give. I was in that crowd on the sidewalk when the cop started to chase you. I ambled along behind. You didn't look like the kind of nut who enjoys parading his glorious nakedness. When I got to the alley, I was too tired to follow law and order any more. So I took a rest against the wall and noticed the garbage can. Ecce you."

I shuffled my feet in the soft, stinking mass, and waited.

"Now, lots of people," he went on, twirling the lid absently and looking down the street, "lots of people would say, 'Joe Burns, what if he isn't a nut? Maybe he just tried to draw to an inside straight in a strip-poker game.' Well, lots of people are sometimes right. But did I or did I not I see you materialize out of relatively empty air in the middle of the street? That's what I care about, Pop. And if so, how so?"

"What will you do with the information?"

"Depends, Pop, depends. If it has color, if it has that certain—"

"For example, if I told you I came from the future."

"And could prove it? In that case, I would spread your name and photograph across the front page of the lowest, dirtiest, most thoroughly misinforming sheet in all this wide land. I refer to the eminent journal with which I am associated. Honest, Pop, did you come from the future?"

I nodded rapidly and considered. What better way to attract the attention of a temporal emissary than by letting him know through an important public communication medium that I could expose his existence in this era? That I could destroy the secrecy of the Temporal Embassy in a pre-intermediate civilization? I would be sought out frantically and returned to my own time.

Returned to scholarship, to dolik and spindfar, to punforg and the Thumtse Dilemna, to my quiet laboratory and my fascinating paper on Gllian Origins of Late Pegis Flirg-Patterns....

"I can prove it," I said swiftly. "But I fail to see the value to you of such a situation. Spreading my name and photograph, as you put it—"

"Don't worry your pretty white thatch about that angle. Joseph Burns will do right well with a tabloid tango about a guy from the future. But you have to get out of that can first. And to get you out of it you need—"

"Clothes. How does one get clothes in this period?"

He scratched his lower lip.

"Well, money is said to help. Not crucial, you understand, but one of the more important factors in the process. You wouldn't have a couple of odd bills somewhere? No-o-o, not unless you have an unrevealed marsupiality. I could lend you the money."

"Well, then—"

"But after all, how much suiting can be purchased in these inflationary times for a dollar twenty-three? Let's face it, Pop; not much. I don't get paid until the day after tomorrow. Besides, if Ferguson doesn't see much value in the yarn, I won't even be able to squeeze it onto my swindle sheet. It wouldn't do to fetch one of my suits down, either."

"Why?" The great quantity of wordage from above and garbage from below was having a very depressing effect on me.

"First, because you might be hauled away by the sanitation department before I returned, and converted into hollyhock vitamins. Then, you're somewhat stouter than me and a good deal shorter. You don't want to attract attention when you step out into this cop-infested thoroughfare; and, in my suit, believe me, Pop, you would. Add to all this the fact that the brave boys in blue may return at any moment and search the alley again— Difficult situation, Pop, most difficult. We face an impasse."

"I don't understand," I began impatiently. "If a voyager from the future appeared in my period, I would be able to help him make the necessary social adjustments most easily. Such a minor item as clothes—"

"Not minor, not minor at all. Witness the ferment in the forces of law and order. Hey! That hammer-shaped ornament, there, the one on your necklace—it wouldn't be silver by any chance?"

Twisting my chin with difficulty, I glanced down. He was pointing at my flirgleflip. I took it off and handed it to him.

"It may well have been silver before it was renucleied for flirgling purposes. Why, does it have any special value?"

"This much silver? I hope to win the Pulitzer Prize it does. Can you spare it? We can get at least one used suit of clothes and half an overcoat out of it."

"Why, I can requisition a new flirgleflip at any time. And I use the large one at the Institute for most of the important flirgling in any case. Take it by all means."

He nodded and replaced the cover of the can over my head. I heard his feet going away. After a lengthy interval in which I developed several surprisingly colorful phrases in regard to Banderling, the garbage-can cover was lifted again and some garments of crude blue cloth dropped upon my head.

"The pirate in the second-hand store would only allow me a couple of bucks on your gimmick," Burns told me as I dressed. "So I had to settle for work clothes. Hey, button those buttons before you step out. No, these. *Button* them. Oh—let me."

Having been properly fastened into the garments, I climbed out of the receptacle and suffered the reporter to tie shoes to my startled feet. Shoes—these were the leather bandages I had observed. My fingers itched for a crude flint axe to make the shambling anachronism complete.

Well, possibly not a flint axe. But a weapon like a rifle or crossbow did seem in order. Animal pelts and vegetable fibers all over my skin. Ugh!

Glancing nervously up and down the street, Burns led me by the arm to a badly ventilated underground chamber. There he flailed a path into an extremely long and ugly sectional conveyance—a subway train.

"I see that here, as elsewhere in your society, only the fittest survive."

He got a better grip on one man's shoulders and moved his feet into a more comfortable position on another's toes. "Howzat?"

"Those who are not strong enough to force their way inside are forced to remain where they are or to resort to even more primitive means of transportation."

"Honest, Pop," he said admiringly, "you'll make terrific copy. Remember to talk like that for Ferguson."

After an appreciable interval of discomfort, we emerged from the train—somewhat like two grape pips being expectorated—and clawed our way to the street.

I followed the reporter into an ornate building and stopped with him in front of a distinguished old man who sat in a small cubicle wrapped in dignified, thoughtful silence.

"How do you do, Mr. Ferguson?" I began immediately, for I was pleasantly surprised. "I am very happy to find in Mr. Burns's superior the obvious intellectual kinship which I had almost—"

"Lay off!" Burns whispered fiercely in my ear as the old man backed away. "You're scaring the pants off the guy. Fourth floor, Carlo."

"Gee, Mr. Burns," Carlo remarked as he pulled a black lever and the cubicle containing the three of us shot upward, "you sure do come in with characters. What I mean, *characters.*"

The newspaper office was an impossible melange of darting humanity exhibiting complicated neurosis patterns among masses of paper, desks, and primitive machines that I later learned were typewriters. Joseph Burns placed me on a wooden bench and scurried inside a glass-paneled office after various ritualistic wavings of the arm and crying of such phrases as "hiya tim, hiya joe, whadaya know abe."

After a lengthy period during which I almost became ill in the atmosphere of perspiration and frenzy, he came out followed by a small man in shirt sleeves who had a tic in his left eye.

"This him?" the small man asked. "Uh-huh. Well, it sounds good, I don't say it don't sound good. Uh-huh. He knows he sticks to this future gag no matter how they try to break him down, and if he does break, nobody's to know we were in on it. He knows it, huh? He looks good for the gag, just old enough, just enough like a crazy prof. It looks good all around, Burns. Uh-huh. Uh-huh, uh-huh."

"Wait till you hear his line," the reporter broke in. "Talk about color, Ferguson!"

"I am unfamiliar with my prismatic possibilities," I told them coldly. "But I must own to a great disappointment that the first representative individuals of the pre-intermediate civilization to hear a coherent account of my origins persist in idiotic droolings—"

The small man's left eye rapped out an impatient tic. "Can that free copy. Or save it for Burns: he'll take it down. Listen, Joey boy, we got something good here. Uh-huh. Two days before the World Series start and not a stick of red-ink news in the town. We can let it run all over the front page, more if it bounces up enough argument. I'll take care of the milking—the regulation comments by the university guys and science societies all around your copy. Meanwhile, you haul whozis here—"

"Terton," I told him desperately. "My name."

"Terton. Uh-huh. You haul Terton here over to a good hotel, get a decent suite and start dragging copy out of him. Keep him isolated until tomorrow morning when there should be a nice thick smell started up. Tomorrow morning, uh-huh. Bring him over again and I'll have a bunch of psychs all ready to swear he's crazy and another bunch crying with tears in their eyes that he's normal and every word sounds like the truth. Get a couple of pics taken of him before you leave."

"Sure, Ferguson. Only trouble, the cop might recognize him as the guy who turned up stark naked in the street. He claims that nobody wears clothes in his period. The police department would have him certified and in Bellevue in no time."

"Lemme think." Ferguson walked around a swift little circle, scratching his nose and winking his eye. "Then we'll play it heavy. For keeps. Uh-huh, for keeps. Find out what he claims his job is—I mean, was—I mean, is going to be—uh-huh, and I'll have a couple of specialists in the same field lined up and insisting that he sounds just like one of them a thousand years from now."

"Just a moment," I insisted. "A thousand years is fantas—"

Tic went Ferguson's eye. "Get him out of here, Joey boy," he said. "He's your baby. I got work to do."

Not until we were in the hotel room was I able to convey to the reporter my extreme disgust at the stolid lunacy of his culture. And his attitude before Ferguson. Why, he had acted as if he shared Ferguson's opinions!

"Take it easy, Pop," the young man told me, his long legs spilling carelessly over the arm of a garishly upholstered couch. "Let us avoid bitterness and reproach. Let us live out our wealthy two days in harmony. Sure, I believe you. But there are certain proprieties to be observed. If Ferguson suspected that I ever believed anybody, let alone a guy who walks through busy office traffic on Madison Avenue with his bare skin hanging out, it would be necessary for me to seek gainful employment not only with another firm, but possibly in another occupation. Besides, all you care about is attracting the attention of one of these temporal emissary queebles. To do that, you feel you have to threaten him with exposure, you have to make a splash. Believe me, Pop, with the wire service tie-up we have, you'll make a splash that will moisten the ears of Eskimos fishing peacefully off Greenland. Australian Bushmen will pause between boomerangs to ask each other—'What's with this Terton character?' "

After much reflection, I agreed. As a result of Banderling's fatheaded use of me as a thrown gauntlet, I had to adjust myself to the customs of a ridiculous era. As they say, when in 200 AD...

By the time Burns had finished questioning me, I was exhausted and hungry. He ordered a meal sent up, and despite my repugnance for the badly cooked meal in unsanitary glazed pottery, I began eating as soon as it was set before me. To my surprise, the taste sensations were rather pleasant.

"You'd better crawl into the sack as soon as you've finished blotting up calories," Burns advised from the table where he was typing. "You look like a hundred-yard man who's just tried to cop the cross-country crown. Bushed, Pop, bushed. I'll run the copy over to the office when I get it done. I don't need you any more tonight."

"The facts are sufficient and satisfactory?" I yawned.

"Not quite sufficient, but very satisfactory. Enough to give Ferguson a bunch of happy gurgles. I only wish— Oh, well, the date business for example. It would help out a lot."

"Well," I said sleepily, "I can think a bit more about 1993."

"No. We've been through that from every angle. Let it ride. Get yourself some sleep, Pop."

The newspaper office had changed its population quality when Burns and I walked in. An entire section of the huge floor had been roped off. Signs had been posted at regular intervals reading "FOR SCIENTISTS ONLY." Between them were other signs extending a welcome to "THE VISITOR FROM 2949," announcing that "THE NEW YORK BLARE SALUTES THE FAR FUTURE" and minor obscure comments concerning such things as "HANDS ACROSS THE TIMESTREAM" and "THE PAST, PRESENT, AND THE FUTURE ARE ONE AND INDIVISIBLE WITH LIBERTY AND JUSTICE FOR ALL!"

Various elderly gentlemen milled about in the roped enclosure into which I was half jostled, half guided. What I had come to recognize as flashbulbs were expended blindingly and in quantity by troops of photographers, some of whom lay prone on the floor, while others contorted on chairs, and still others hung suspended from trapeze-like affairs attached to the ceiling.

"It's sizzling and bubbling, Joey boy," Ferguson babbled as he writhed his way up to us and put several sheets of ink-fresh newspaper into the reporter's hands. "Some say he's a nut, uh-huh, and some say he's a resurrection of the prophet Nehemiah; but everybody in town is buying the paper. Two full days before the World Series and we've got a solid newsbeat. The other rags have their tongues hanging out for a look-in—they can kiss my basket. Nice slew of copy, uh-huh, nice angles. I had some trouble finding a couple of archaeologists who'd swear Terton was a member of the guild, but Ferguson never fails—we got our men." Ferguson's left eye momentarily lost its tic and developed a positive oscillation. "Look," he growled hoarsely, as he pushed me into a seat, "don't go prima donna on us now. No fancy stuff, see! Uh-huh. That's right. You just stick to your story for today and tomorrow and you'll get yourself a nice hunk of the publisher's dough. If you're good enough, maybe you can even last through the first two games of the Series. Stick to your story—you came from the future, and that's all you know. Uh-huh, and stay away from facts!"

As he clapped his bands, calling the assembled scientists to attention, Joseph Burns slid into the chair next to mine.

"Sorry about the archaeologist complication, Pop. But remember my copy is edited thoroughly at this end. What you told me just doesn't look good on paper. Martian archaeologist is close enough for the masses. If I were you, I'd stay away from any detailed description of your occupation. It'll densify the air no end."

"But Martian archaeologist is wholly inaccurate!"

"Come now, Pop, you seem to forget that your primary objective is to attract attention, enough attention so that you'll be considered a dangerous big-mouth and sent back to your time. Well, glance to your right and occasionally to your left. Lots of attention, no? This is the way to do it: huge heads and lurid lines."

I was still considering my reply when I noticed that Ferguson had finished introducing me to the scientists, most of whom wore thin little curled smiles. "Uh-huh, and here he is! Terton, the man from the impossibly far future. He will speak to you himself, he will answer your questions. *The New York Blare* requests, however, that questions be brief and limited in number; just for the first day, gentlemen. After all, our guest is tired and upset after his long, hazardous journey through time!"

The dignified questions sputtered at me as I rose to my feet. "Exactly what year do you claim as your origin, Mr. Terton? Or is the figure 2949 correct?"

"Quite incorrect," I assured the questioner. "The actual date in terms of a translation from the Octet Calendar which we use— Now, what *was* that rule about translating from the Octet?"

"Could you explain the construction of a rocket motor of your period?" someone asked as I was deep in the complicated and unfamiliar methodology of calendar mathematics. "You speak of interplanetary flight."

"And interstellar flight," I added. "And *interstellar* flight. Except that rockets are not used. A complicated propulsion method called the space pressure spread is employed."

"And what exactly is a space pressure spread?"

I coughed embarrassedly. "Something which, I am afraid, I had never the slightest interest in investigating. I understand it is based on Kuchholtz's Theory of the Missing Vector."

"And what—"

"Kuchholtz's Theory of the Missing Vector," I told them with a good deal of firmness, "has been the one thing that attracted my mind even less than the operation of a space pressure spread."

So it went. From triviality to triviality. These primitive though well-meaning savants, living as they did at the very dawn of specialization, could not even faintly appreciate how cursory my education had been in everything but my chosen field. In their period of microscopic knowledge and rudimentary operational devices it was already difficult for one man to absorb even a generalization of total learning. How much more so in my time, I tried to tell them, with separate biologies and sociologies for each planet—to mention but one example. And then, it had been so many years since I had touched upon the elementary sciences! I had forgotten so much!

Government (as they called it) was almost impossible to illustrate. How can you demonstrate to twentieth-century savages the nine levels of social responsibility with which every child has thoroughly experimented before reaching adolescence? How can you make clear the "legal" status of such a basic device as the judicialarion? Possibly someone from my time deeply versed in this period's tribal lore and superstitions might, with the aid of rough parallels, give them a glimmering of such things as communal individuality or mating by neurone-pattern—but not I. I? Good cause had I to berate Banderling as the chuckles rippled higher.

"I am a specialist," I cried at them. "I need another specialist like myself to understand me."

"You need a specialist all right," a brown-clothed, middle-aged man said as he rose in the back row. "But not like you. Like me. A psychiatrist."

There was a roar of agreeing laughter. Ferguson rose nervously and Joseph Burns came quickly to my side.

"This the man?" the psychiatrist inquired of a blue-clad figure who had just entered the office. I recognized my chief pursuer of the day before. He nodded.

"Him, all right. Runnin' around nood. Should be ashamed. Or committed. I dunno which, honestly I don't."

"Just a moment," one of the scientists called out as Ferguson cleared his throat. "We've spent this much time; the least we can do is find out what he claims as his specialty. Some form of archaeology—Martian archaeology, no less."

At last. I drew a deep breath. "Not Martian archaeology," I began. "Not *archaeology*." That had been Banderling's misconception! Behind me, Burns groaned and slumped back into his chair.

"I am a flirgleflip. A flirgleflip is one who flips flirgs with a flirgleflip." There was a loud intake of breath.

I discussed my profession at great length. How the first dolik and spindfar discovered in the sands of Mars had been considered nothing more than geological anachronisms, how the first punforg had been used as a paperweight. Then Cordes and that almost divine accident which enabled him to stumble upon the principle of the flirgleflip; then Gurkheyser who perfected it and may rightly be considered the father of the profession. The vistas that opened as the flirg-patterns were identified and systematized. The immense beauty, created by a race that even living Martians have no conception of, which became part of man's cultural heritage.

I told of the commonly accepted theory as to the nature of the flirglers: that they were an energy form which at one time attained intelligence on the red planet and left behind them only the flirg-patterns which were vaguely equivalent to our music or non-objectivist art; that being energy forms they left permanent energy records of all kinds in their only material artifacts—dolik, spindfar, and punforg. I told proudly of my decision at an early age to dedicate myself to flirg-patterns: how I was responsible for the system of using present-day Martian placenames to identify the sites on which the artifacts were found in their loosely scattered fashion. Then, modestly, I mentioned my discovery of an actual contrapuntal flirg-pattern in some dolik—which had resulted in a full Investigatorship at the Institute. I referred to my forthcoming paper on *Gllian Origins of Late Pegis Flirg-Patterns* and became so involved in a description of all the facets of the Thumtse Dilemna, that it seemed to me I was back at the Institute giving a lecture—instead of fighting for my very identity.

"You know," I heard a voice say wonderingly near me, "it almost sounds logical. Like one of those double-talk hits or the first verse of Jabberwocky, it almost sounds as if it exists."

"Wait!" I said suddenly. "The sensation of flirg-pattern is impossible to describe in words. You must feel it for yourself." I tore open the rough cloth of my upper garment and pulled the necklace out. "Here, examine for yourselves the so-called dolik of the Thumtse Dilemna with my flirgleflip. Observe—"

I stopped. I was not wearing the flirgleflip! I'd forgotten.

Joseph Burns leaped up. "Mr. Terton's flirgleflip was exchanged for the suit of clothes he is now wearing. I'll volunteer to go out and buy it back."

My gratitude went with him as he picked his way through the amused scientists.

"Listen, guy," Ferguson told me wetly. "You'd better do something fast. Burns isn't a genius: he may not be able to work up a good out. There's an alienist here—uh-huh, I said an alienist—and they'll shove you behind soft walls if you don't come up with something new. You're looking so bad, all our men are sitting on their tongues. They're afraid for their reps."

One of the younger scientists asked for the necklace. I handed it to him, the dolik still attached. He scrutinized both objects, then scratched them with his fingernail. He returned them to me.

"That necklace—ah—was what you claimed could send you or teleport you any-where on Earth, I believe?"

"Through a benscope," I pointed out. "You need benscope receivers and transmitters."

"Quite. And the small thing is what you call a—hum—a dolik. Thumbnail's Dilemna, or some such. Gentlemen, I am an industrial chemist, as you know. That necklace, I am convinced—and chemical analysis would merely confirm my visual impressions—is nothing more than a very fine spun glass. Nothing more."

"It's been renucleied for use with a benscope, you fool! What difference does the nature of the material make, when it's been renucleied?"

"Whereas the dolik," the young man went on equably, "the Martian dolik is really a treasure. Something quite unique. Oh, yes. Old red sandstone such as the average geologist can find almost anywhere on Earth in fifteen minutes. Old red sandstone!"

It was a while before I could make myself heard again. Unfortunately, I lost my tem-per. The idea of anyone referring to the Thumtse Dilemna as old red sandstone al-most made me insane. I shouted at them for their bigotry, their narrowness, their lack of knowledge. Ferguson stopped me. "You'll get yourself put away for sure," he whispered. "You're almost frothing. Uh-huh, and don't think it'll do the sheet a bit of good for you to be dragged out of here in a straitjacket." I took a deep breath.

"Gentlemen," I suggested. "If any of you were suddenly to find yourselves in an earlier century, you would have great difficulty in using your specialized knowledge with the primitive equipment you would then find available. How much more must I—"

"You have a point there," a man with a stout face admitted. "But there is one thing, one means of identification always open to a traveler from the future."

"What's that?" Several academic necks were craned at him.

"Dates. Historical events. Things of this month or this year. The significant occur-rences. You claim to regard this period as your past. Tell us of it. What will happen?"

"Unfortunately—" I made an unhappy gesture and the laughter sped forth anew, "my Terran history is very fragmentary. One brief course in childhood. I was brought up on Mars, and even Martian history is rather vague to me. Historical dates I never could assimilate. As I told Joseph Burns last night, I remember only three around this general period."

"Yes?" Their interest was substantial now.

"First, 1993."

"What happens in 1993?"

"I don't know, I regret to say. But it seems to have some great significance. Possibly a plague, an invention, the date of a masterpiece. Or possibly a date which was men-tioned to me casually and which I've retained. Not very useful, in any case. Then August, 1945. The atom bomb. Mr. Burns says this isn't particularly useful either since it is already several years in your past. Please remember, that I have great difficulty with your calendar."

"What's the third date?" a voice called.

"1588," I told him hopelessly. "The Spanish Armada."

Chairs scraped. The scientists rose and prepared to leave. "Hold 'em," Ferguson shrilled at me. "Say something, do something." I shrugged.

"One moment." It was the young industrial chemist. "I think we can settle the hash of this hoax most definitely. I noticed in Mr. Burns's lurid little article that you said you had played on the Martian sands as a child. What were you wearing at the time?"

"Nothing." I was puzzled. "Some warm clothing. Nothing else."

"No helmet of any sort, say?"

"No, none at all."

He grinned. "Just some warm clothing. Yet we know that the temperature at the equator rarely rises above freezing. We also know that there is—practically speaking—no oxygen on Mars. The spectroscope has continually confirmed this over the years. Warm clothing, no oxygen helmet. Hah!"

I puzzled after their retreating, contemptuous backs as they left. This was one point I couldn't understand at all. What if their instruments showed only minute quantities of oxygen on Mars and a temperature below freezing? I had played in the Martian desert as a boy. I had been there and I remembered it very clearly. *No* oxygen helmet, *some* warm clothing. These savages and their instruments!

"Better scram fast," Ferguson told me, the tic in his left eye batting unhappily. "The cop and the alienist are still out in the corridor. It don't look good for you and it won't look good for the sheet if they wrap you up. Better get out with the service elevator. Uh-huh, the service elevator."

I went down to the street, pondering how the temporal emissaries would get in touch with me now. Evidently, in Joseph Burns's words, I hadn't made a sufficiently great "splash." Or had it been enough? Possibly one of the scientists was a temporal emissary, observing me and preparing to send me back to my own time before I could cause any more disruption in this period.

"Hi, Pop. I called the office. Tough go."

"Burns!" I turned in relief to the young man lounging against the wall of the building. The only friend I had made in this crazy, barbaric era. "You didn't get the flirgleflip. They'd bartered it, or sold it, or lost it."

"No, Pop, I didn't get the flirgleflip." He took my arm gently. "Let's walk."

"Where?"

"Find a job for you, an occupation into which you can fit your futuristic talents."

"And what would that be?"

"That is the problem, the nasty, difficult problem. Not many flirgles to be flipped in this period. That's all you can do well and you're too old to learn another profession. Yet a man must eat. If he doesn't, he gets odd feelings and strange, mournful quaverings in his abdomen. Ah, well."

"Evidently, you were wrong about the temporal emissary."

"No, I wasn't. You attracted their attention. You've been contacted."

"By whom?"

"Me."

I would have stopped in astonishment directly in the path of a scudding vehicle if Burns's pressure on my arm hadn't kept me moving.

"You mean you're a temporal emissary? You take me back?"

"Yes, I'm a temporal emissary. No, I don't take you back."

Completely confused, I shook my head carefully. "I don't—"

"You don't go back, Pop. First, because this way Banderling is accused of destroying the rights of a communal individual—namely you. This way the Institute decides that the radiation depressor will bear years of investigation and development before anything but completely stable individuals are allowed near it. Eventually time travel will be discovered—and in the proper period—as the result of a textual cross-reference to Banderling's radiation depressor. Second, you don't go back because it is now impossible for you to blab loudly about temporal emissaries without getting into a walled establishment where they make guests wear their sheets like overcoats."

"You mean it was all deliberate, your meeting me and worming the flirgleflip out of my possession and convincing me that I must make a splash, as you put it, so that I am maneuvered into a position where nobody in this society will believe me—"

We turned right down a narrow street of little cafes. "I mean even more than that was deliberate. It was necessary for Banderling to be the kind of person he is—"

"A fathead?" I suggested bitterly.

"—so that the radiation depressor would be put on the shelf a sufficient number of years as a result of the 'Terton Tragedy.' It was necessary for you to have the profession and background you do, completely unfit for the needs of this period, so that you will be able to make no appreciable alteration in it. It was further necessary—"

"I thought you were my friend. I liked you."

"It was further necessary for me to be the kind of person I am so that your confidence would be won by me as soon as you—er, arrived and the project began to work properly. Also, being the kind of person I am, I am going to be very uncomfortable at what I did with you. This discomfort is probably also necessary for another facet of the Temporal Embassy's plans. Everything fits, Terton, into everything else—even the temporal embassy at the end of time, I suspect. Meanwhile, I had a job to do."

"And Banderling? What happens to him when I fail to return?"

"He's barred from physical research, of course. But since he's young, he will manage to develop a new profession. And the mores of your era being what they are, he will become a flirgleflip—replacing you in the community. He will have a Readjustment Course first, however. Which reminds me—I've been concentrating so hard on getting you a job you can do, I forget important things."

I mused on the irony of Banderling's supposed revolt being part of the plans of the Temporal Embassy. And on the pathos of my spending what remained of my lifetime in this insane age. Suddenly I noticed that Burns had detached the dolik from my necklace.

"One of those oversights," he explained as he pocketed it. "You shouldn't have taken it with you, according to our original plans. Now I'll have to see that it's returned as soon as I get you settled in your job. That dolik is the Thumtse Dilemna, you know. The schedule calls for its problem to be solved by one of your colleagues at the Institute."

"Who solves it?" I asked with great interest. "Masterson, Foule, Greenblatt?"

"None of them." He grinned. "According to the schedule, the Thumtse Dilemna is solved finally by Thomas Alva Banderling."

"Banderling," I cried as we paused in front of a grimy restaurant which had a Dishwasher Wanted sign in the window. "Banderling? That fathead?"

AFTERWORD

Some stories just don't work. I rewrote this one several times, and I never could make it even slightly better. Really, when it comes to the creative act, there does not seem to be any rule that holds true all the way down the line.

I have written full-length stories in one night and done no more beyond the first draft than correct spelling mistakes—and been reasonably proud of the result. I have written and rewritten others over the years and have come to consider them among my best. And, conversely, stories that I've ripped hot from my typewriter and immediately sent off to an agent or editor have, upon later rereading, turned out to be things that I've wanted to hide under sofa cushions or behind wallpaper. And so have been pieces that I've worked and reworked and changed and buffed and polished until there's nothing left but a single subordinate clause from the original draft.

Lovely, lovely babies and dismal miscarriages—they all come up in their turn and have to be accepted as my very own.

The notion that precipitated "Flirgleflip" seemed to be a good one: temporal embassies from every century to the century before, working, on the basis of known historical results, to improve the future (and, of course, no longer being sent back to a period when knowledge that time travel was possible might have deleterious consequences). The thought of creating an occupation or future profession that would be close to meaningless in the present also intrigued me (as, for example, what would the Egyptians of 500 AD be able to make of a twenty-first-century exobiologist or computer technician or particle physicist?).

But the story *qua* story never took off. Upon reexamination more than half a century later, I wonder if I've found the reason. After all, I cut out a whole lot of subordinate clauses, but I did always keep the first line. That's because the story, whatever it is, seems to unroll precisely from the agonized exclamation, "Banderling, you are a fathead!" and repeat that in the inevitable conclusion.

No, that first line belongs as first line.

Still... If I did put "Flirgleflip" in my word processor now... If I did try one last rewrite, taking out the first line and substituting another one...

Ahh...

WRITTEN 1947——PUBLISHED 1950

Errand Boy

Yes, I'm the Malcolm Blyn who phoned you from the village. Mind if I come in and take a seat—I won't take up much of your time? Thanks. Now, here's the story, and if you're the man I've been tearing the country apart for, there's a million in it—

No, please! I'm not selling gold mine stocks or a patent for an internal combustion atomic engine: I'm not selling anything. I'm a salesman all right—been one all my life and I know I look like a salesman right down to my bottom adjective—but today I'm not selling anything.

Today I'm buying.

If you have the stuff, that is. The stuff the errand boy said you or someone with your— Listen! I'm not crazy, believe me till you hear it all! Please sit down and listen. He wasn't an ordinary errand boy; he was an errand boy like Einstein is an accountant. The errands he ran! But you must understand…here, have a cigar.

Here's my card. *Blyn's Wholesale Paints and Painters' Supplies*—that's me—*Any Quantity of Any Paint Delivered Anywhere at Any Time.* Of course, by "anywhere" we mean the continental United States only. But it looks good on the card. Salesmanship.

That's me, a salesman. Give me something to sell: an improvement, a service or a brand-new crazy novelty gimmick—I guarantee to get people tearing the lining out of their pants pockets. I've always kept Emerson's famous wisecrack framed on my office wall, you know: "If a man can write a better book, preach a better sermon, or make a better mousetrap than his neighbor, though he builds his house in the woods, the world will make a beaten path to his door." Solid stuff. And I'm the guy that gets them interested in beating a path in the first place.

I'm good. I want you to understand that. I can put it over, whatever it is you've got—if only you're the guy that's got it. But I must have something to put over, something good. No hot air. No, I'm not accusing you of putting out the hot air. I don't know yet what you put out—raise chickens, mostly? Yeah. So listen.

Five weeks ago this coming Wednesday, we had a rush job. Three hundred gallons of flat white to the Expando Construction Corporation, an outfit I'd been trying to sell ever since they started up after the war. Eleven o'clock, and they wanted it delivered to their new development over in north Jersey by noon, so their men could start slapping it on the walls right after lunch.

I was out on the floor of the warehouse lighting a fire under Hennessey, my foreman, so he'd light a fire under his crew. Cans of paint were being stacked and shipped as fast as the bank says no to an extension of your loan, men were rolling this way, guys were hustling that way—when I heard Hennessey make a crack.

"Hey, that new errand boy's been gone a long time. Kid must have given up." About a dozen men stopped working and laughed for a while. They could see it was supposed to be funny—Hennessey was their boss.

"Since when do we have a new errand boy?" I stopped Hennessey in his tracks. "I do all the hiring and firing around here. Any new personnel have to go on the books—a dozen different ones these days. Do you want to get me into trouble? Haven't you ever heard of Social Security? Child Labor Laws? How old is the kid?"

"Aw, Mr. Blyn, how should I know? They all look alike to me. Maybe nine, maybe ten, eleven. A lot thinner than most kids I've seen, but a lot healthier. Looks—sorta rich."

"Well, if he's that young, he's got no business in the warehouse district this early in a weekday. Probably on the hook. I'll have the New York Board of Education on my neck as well as the working papers people. Don't I have enough trouble, Hennessey, with two road-happy truck drivers who use a Pennsylvania map to get lost in New Jersey, without—"

"I didn't hire him, honest. He come around here asking for a job in that funny voice like kid stars have in the movies. He says he's willing to start at the bottom and prove himself, he feels he's bound to rise, he's got the will to win, all he wants is a chance. I tell him the way business has been lately, we wouldn't hire Alexander Graham Bell to run our switchboard. He says he doesn't care; he wants to get a foot on the ladder of success. He'll work for nothing."

"So?"

"So, I make out I'm thinking—at ten this morning, things were slow on the floor—and finally I say I'll give him a crack at trying out for errand boy. I hand him an empty can and say I want it filled with green paint—it should have orange polka dots. I'm testing him, see? He grabs the can and takes off. He won't bother us any more. You shoulda seen the guys after he left, Mr. Blyn: they fit to died."

"Hold me up," I said. "I'm getting weak myself. Almost as funny as the time you locked Whalen in the washroom with a stink bomb. That reminds me—you'll be taking orders from Whalen if your crew doesn't get that truck loaded and out of here in ten minutes."

He wiped his hands on his overalls and started to say something. Then he changed his mind and began yelling up and down the warehouse. He asked his men if they didn't think it was time to crawl out of their coffins, he told them to get their asses behind every dolly that wasn't being used, he got the place hissing where before it was only humming.

One thing about Hennessey: he might have been a practical joker from way back when he found all the amusing things you could do with diapers; but he was one crackerjack foreman. The way he made those monkeys hustle reminded me of the way I fit a fountain pen in a customer's hand just before he begins to purse his lips.

Then the kid walked in.

"Hey, Ernest," somebody yelled. "Look. Ernest's back."

Work stopped. The kid walked in, breathing hard, and set the can down in front of Hennessey. He was dressed in a white blouse, patched corduroy pants and high-laced brown shoes. But I'd never seen corduroy like that before, or that kind of white broadcloth in a shirt. The material seemed to be very thin—and, well, rich somehow. That's the only way to describe it. Like expensive imitation iron.

"Glad you're back, kid," Hennessey told him. "I've been needing a left-handed paintbrush. Shop around and see if you can pick one up for me. But it must be left-handed."

A couple of characters on the loading platform started to chuckle. The kid started out. He turned at the big sliding doors.

"I'll try, sir," he said in a voice like he had a flute in his throat. "I'll do my best. But this paint—I couldn't find any green paint with orange polka dots. This only has red polka dots. I hope it will do."

Then he left.

For a moment we all stared at the patch of sidewalk where he'd been standing. Then I laughed; in a second the roars were bouncing off the second-story ceiling. The men just stood there with dollies and paint stacked on them, laughing their heads off.

"Hennessey, the wise guy!" someone yelled.

"All I could find was green paint with red polka dots!"

"Please, sir, I hope it will do. Wow!"

"Did that kid let you have it!"

"Poor Hennessey!"

Hennessey stood there, his great big fists hanging at his sides and no one to use them on. Suddenly he noticed the can of paint. He drew his right leg back and came tearing at it with a kick that would have sent it into Long Island Sound. Only he missed it. He just touched a corner of the can—rocking it enough to spill a drop—missed his footing and came smashing down on his great big backside. The roars got louder as he scrambled to his feet.

In a second, the laughter had stopped cold and everyone and his brother was hustling again. Not a man in that warehouse wanted to attract Hennessey's attention after his joke had bounced back at him.

Still chuckling, I strolled over and looked at the can. I wanted to see what junk the kid had used to fill it. Looked like water. The liquid in the can was mostly transparent, with little brown flecks floating around. Not paint, certainly—no kind I knew.

I glanced at the floor where a drop had been spilled when my foreman tried to kick the can.

I began strangling on a howl.

The junk the kid had used to fill the can—the junk had been green paint with red polka dots. *Red polka dots!*

No doubt at all: a little oval puddle dripped up to the side of the can; the warehouse floor now had a spot painted green with red polka dots. And this kid—this errand boy—this Ernest—had found it somewhere.

One thing I told you I can tell. Saleability. I can tell the saleable something in somebody else's dream at night when I'm sleeping on the other side of town. I can sniff it—but, you know all that. But do you know how saleable that kind of paint would be? Sell it as a sure-fire novelty to manufacturers, sell it as a gimmick to guys who putter around their own home, sell it as a brand-new idea in design to interior decorators. It's a natural; it's a gold mine.

But I had to move fast. I picked up the can by the wire handle; I scuffed the paint spot carelessly with my foot. Luckily, it seemed to take a long time to dry: it mixed with the dust on the floor and lost its color. I walked out into the street where Hennessey was standing near the truck watching his crew load.

"What did you say that kid's name was? Ernest?"

He looked up. "Yeah," he brooded. "Ernest. Didn't give me his last name. But if he ever shows his wise puss around here—"

"OK. I have an important business appointment. Take over until I get back and get that flat white out." I turned and started in the direction the kid had gone. I knew Hennessey was staring at the can of paint I carried swinging from my left hand. He was wondering what I wanted with it, with the kid. Let him wonder, I told myself. Give Hennessey the curiosity; I'll take the profit.

I caught sight of the kid about three blocks away; he was going east, in the direction of the park. He stopped in front of a hardware store, thought a moment, walked in. By the time he came out again, I'd caught up with him. He was shaking his head unhappily.

We walked side by side for a while before he noticed me. I couldn't get over those clothes of his. Even the old-fashioned high shoes he was wearing weren't made out of anything I'd ever seen; the material hugged his foot like another layer of skin; it wasn't leather, I was sure of that.

"No luck?" I asked.

He jumped and stared a bit. Then he seemed to recognize the face as one of those that had been staring at him a while ago. "No. No…er, luck. The distributor said he was very sorry but he was just this moment fresh out of left-handed paintbrushes. Exactly what they all said when I asked them for the paint with the polka dots. I don't mean any offense, but…but this *is* an inefficient method of circulating goods."

I watched his face while he said that. Really meant every word of it. What a kid! I stopped and scratched my head. Should I come right out and ask him where he'd found the paint, or should I let him talk into the secret as most people will usually do?

He had turned pale and then begun blushing. I didn't like to see that in a boy. That musical soprano voice was bad enough, his thinness for a kid his size—he was almost as tall as me—I could take; but a boy who blushed had just never met a real school bully.

"Look, Ernest," I began. I reached out and put my hand on his shoulder, you know, fatherly-like. "Ernest, I—"

Zing! He jumped backward as if I'd gone to work on his neck with a can opener. And blush! Reminded me of a bride who'd led a full life and was doing her rosy best to convince the groom's mother at the altar that she hadn't.

"Don't *do* that," he said, shaking himself all over.

Better change the subject. "Nice outfit, you've got there. Where did you get it?" Subtle, you know. Catch him off guard.

He looked down complacently. "It was my costume in the school play. Of course, it was a little off-period, but I thought—"

His voice trailed away awkwardly like he'd just realized he was breaking a lodge secret. This thing had angles, all right.

"Where do you live?" I shot at him fast.

"Brooks," he came right back.

I thought that over. No, it couldn't be. "Brooks?"

"Yes, you know—Brooks. Or maybe it's Bronklyn?"

I stroked my chin, trying to work it out. He was shuddering again.

"Please," he said in that high voice. "Please. Do you have to skinge?"

"Do I have to what?"

"Skinge. Touch your body with your hands. In a public place, too. Spitting and belching are bad enough—though most of your people avoid it. But everyone—everyone is always skingeing!"

I took a deep breath and promised him I wouldn't skinge. But if I wanted to see his hole card, I'd have to flip mine over first. "Look, Ernest, what I wanted to say...well, I'm Malcolm Blyn. I—"

His eyes widened. "The robber baron of the warehouse!"

"The *what?*"

"You own Blyn's Paints. I saw your name on the door." He nodded to himself. "I've read all the adventure stories. Dumas...no, Dumas isn't right...Alger, Sinclair, Capon. Capon's *The Sixteen Salesmen,* there's one fully conscious book! I read it five times. But you wouldn't know Capon, would you? He wasn't published until—"

"Until when?"

"Until...until...oh, I can tell you. You're one of the ruling powers: you own a warehouse. I don't come from here."

"No? Where do you come from?" I had my own ideas on that. Some overeducated rich kid—a refugee, maybe, to account for his accent and slenderness.

"From the future. I shouldn't have done it; it may mean my being set back a whole responsibility group, but I just had to see the robber barons with my own eyes. Wolf bait! I wanted to see them forming pools, freezing out competitors, getting a corner on—"

"Hold the economics, Jackson! From the future, did you say?" This kid was getting too big for his corduroy britches. *Corduroy* britches?

"Yes. According to the calendar of this time...let me see, and this part of the world, it would be...oh, the year 6130. No, that's still another calendar. According to *your* calendar I came from 2369 AD. Or is it 2370? 2369, I think."

I was glad he'd settled the point to his satisfaction. I told him so, and he thanked me. And all the time, I was thinking: if this kid's crazy, or if he's lying, how come paint that brushes out green with red polka dots? And how come his clothes? They hadn't been made in any factories I'd ever heard of. Check.

"This paint…that come from the future…from your time?"

"Well, the shops were all out of it, and I wanted to prove myself to Hennessey…he's a real swashbuckler, isn't he? I went home and probed the spirillix, and finally I found—"

"Spirillix? What spirillix?"

"The spirillix—the rounded usicon, you know. Your American scientist Wenceslaus invented it just about this time. I *think* it was just about this time—I remember reading of the trouble he had getting it financed. Or was it this time? Yes, I think—"

He was starting another of those debates with himself. I stalled him off. "OK. What's the difference, a hundred years more or less. This paint: do you know how it's made, what's in it?"

"How it's made." He swung a high-booted foot around in a little circle and studied it. "Well, it's hydrofluoric acid, of course. Triple-blasted. Although the container didn't mention the number of times it had been blasted. I *assume* it was triple-blasted, though—"

"Sure, sure. What do you mean—blasted, triple-blasted?"

A mouthful of perfect white teeth flashed out as he laughed right up and down the scale. "I wouldn't know that! It's all part of the Schmootz Dejector Process—my conditioning is two whole responsibility groups behind the Schmootz Process. I may never even reach it if I do well enough in self-expression. And I like self-expression better than conditioning; I only have two hours now, but—"

He raved on and on about how he was persuading some committee or other to give him more self-expression; I concentrated on worrying. This wasn't so good. I couldn't expect to import much more of the paint from this kid's hunting ground; my only hope was analysis of the sample he'd given me. And with this hydrofluoric acid and triple-blasting deal that didn't look so good.

Figure it out. Man has had steel for a long time now. But take some heat-treated steel from the best factory in Gary or Pittsburgh back to the time of that chemist character Priestley. Even if he had a modern lab available and knew how to use the equipment in it he wouldn't be able to find much useful information. He'd know it was steel maybe, and he might even be able to tell how much carbon, manganese, sulphur, phosphorus and silicon it contained—in addition to iron—if someone gave him a briefing on modern elementary chemistry, that is. But how it had acquired its properties, where its elasticity and tensile strength came from—the poor guy wouldn't know from nothing. Tell him "heat-treatment," "inward combustion of the carbon," and all he'd be able to do is open and close his mouth like a fish in Fulton Market wondering what happened to all the water.

Or spun glass. They had glass way back in ancient Eygpt. Shove some of that shiny fabric we have at them, though, even say it's *spun* glass. They'd say, "Yah, sure. Have another piece of pie."

So I had the paint. One can of it hanging from my sweaty little palm. But it looked like a one-shot proposition unless I could be foxy grandpa himself—or, considering the kid, foxy great-great-great-grandpa.

Standing in front of me was the greatest errand boy a greedy businessman ever saw. And let me tell you I'm greedy; I admit it. But only for money.

How to swing it? How to turn this kid's errands into nice, bulging mounds of green paper with lots and lots of zeros on them? I didn't want him to get suspicious or upset; I didn't want him to feel I was using him as the tool I intended using him as.

I had to be a salesman; I had to sell him a bill of goods. I had to get him running the errands right, with a maximum of profit to all concerned, especially me.

Carelessly, I started walking in the direction he'd been going. He swung along beside me. "Where's your time machine, Ernest?"

"Time machine?" His delicate face wrinkled. "I don't have any time ma— Oh! You mean the chrondromos. Time machine—what a thought! No, I sunk a small chrondromos for my own personal use. My favorite father is an assistant engineer on the main chrondromos—the one they use for field trips? I wanted to go unsupervised for this once, no carnuplicators or anything. I wanted to see the ragged but determined newsboys rising steadily to riches. I wanted to see the great, arrogant robber barons like yourself—perhaps, I thought, I might even come across a real economic royalist! And I might get involved in some great intrigue, some market manipulation where millions of small investors are closed down and lose their last shred of— what is it again?—margin?"

"Yeah, they lose all their margin. Where did you sink this—this chrondromos?"

"Not where—*when*. I sank it after school. I'm supposed to be having self-expression now, so it doesn't make much difference. But I hope I can get back before a Census Keeper winds a total."

"Sure you can. I wouldn't worry about it. Uh...can I use this chrondromos of yours?"

He laughed real hard at my foolishness. "How can you? You have no conditioning, not even responsibility group two. No, you wouldn't know how to begin to unstable. I'll be glad to get back. Not that I haven't enjoyed myself. Wolf bait! To think I met a robber baron! This has been one fully conscious experience."

I dug into my tweed jacket and lit a baronial cigarette. "Guess you wouldn't have much trouble finding a left-handed paintbrush."

"Well, it might be difficult. I've never heard of one before."

"One thing I was wondering." I flicked ashes elaborately onto the sidewalk. "Do you have anything that sees ahead in time?"

"A revolving distringulatrix, you mean? There's one at the main chrondromos. I don't know how it works; they don't allow anyone from responsibility group four near it—you have to be at least six or seven."

Nasty. It had looked good. I might be able to persuade the kid to ferry back and forth with a couple of more cans of paint—but it would never amount to much. Especially if I couldn't get an analysis that would enable me to produce the stuff with present-day methods. But if I could get a gadget from the future—something I wouldn't have to sell, something I could make a million out of just by using it myself—like a dingus for seeing into the future, predicting race results, elections, sweepstake winners....

The dingus was there all right. This revolving distringulatrix. But the kid couldn't lay his hands on it. Nasty, I tell you.

"What about books? Got any books lying around the house: chemistry books, physics texts, pamphlets on industrial methods?"

"I don't live in a house. And I don't study from books. Not chemistry or physics anyway. That's all handled by conditioning. I had six hours of conditioning last night—examinations are coming, you know."

My tongue knotted with the frustration of it. Millions of bucks walking next to me and I didn't know how to turn it into cash. Ernest had evidently seen all he wanted to see of the present, at least temporarily—hadn't he met a real, live, robber baron?—and he was heading home to mama and self-expression.

There must be an angle, somewhere!

"Where'd you plant your chrondromos? I mean, where's its other end come out?"

He waved ahead. "Behind a big rock in Center Park."

"Central Park, you mean. Mind if I tag along, watch you leave?"

He didn't. We padded across Central Park West and turned up a little unpaved path. I pulled a dry bough off a tree and switched it across my ankles; I just had to think of something before he took off. I began to hate the can of paint; it was light enough, but it looked like such a puny item to get out of the whole deal. Especially if it couldn't be analyzed.

Keep the kid talking. Something would turn up.

"What kind of government do you have? Democracy, monarchy—"

There he went laughing at me again! It was all I could do not to smash him across the face with the switch. Here I was losing fortunes right and left, and he thought I was making like a comic!

"Democracy! But you would think in political terms, wouldn't you? You have to consider your sick individuals, your pressure groups, your— No, we passed that stage long before I was born. Let me see, the last president they manufactured was a reversibilist. So I imagine you could say we are living in a reversibilism. An unfulfilled one, though."

That helped a lot. Solved everything. I sort of dropped down into a moony yearning for an idea, any kind of an idea. Ernest skipped along chattering about things with unpronounceable names that did unbelievable deeds. I thought unprintable words.

"—I get in responsibility group five. Then there are the examinations, not at all easy this time. Even the trendicle may not help."

I cocked an ear at him. "What's with this trendicle? What does it give out?"

"It analyzes trends. Trends and developing situations. It's really a statistical analyzer, portable and a little primitive. I use it to determine the questions I'll be asked in the examinations. Oh, I forgot—you probably have the scholarship superstitions of your period. You don't believe that the young should anticipate questions based on the latest rearrangements in the world, on the individual curiosities of their in-structors. There it is!"

High up on a little wooded hill was a gray and careless rock formation. And, even at that distance, I could see a transparent, shimmering blue haze behind the largest rock.

Ernest beat it off the road and scurried up the hill. I choked after him. There wasn't much time; I had to think it out fast—this trendicle looked like the goods.

I caught up to him just as he reached the large rock. "Ernest," I wheezed, "how does your trendicle go?"

"Oh, it's simple. You punch all available facts into it—regular keyboard, you know—it analyzes them and states the only possible result or shows the trend the facts indicate. Built-in Skeebee power system. Well, goodbye, Mr. Blyn."

He started for the blue haze where it was thickest on the ground. I wrapped my paw around his chest and pulled him back.

"There you go again. Skingeing!" he wailed.

"Sorry, kid. The last time. How would you like to be in on a really big deal? Before you go back, you might like to see me get control of an international trust. I've been planning it for some time—one of the biggest bull markets. Wall Street has never seen my secret gilt-edged because I have a broker planted in Chicago futures. I'll hurry it along and do it today, just so you can see how we robber barons operate. The only thing is, this trendicle deal will make it sure-fire and I'll be able to do the whole thing much faster. What a spectacle! Hundreds of banks failing, I get a corner on synthetic rubber, the gold standard crashes, small investors frozen and down to their bottom margin! You'll see it all. And if you get the trendicle for me, why I'd let you handle the capitalization."

His eyes shone like brand-new dimes. "That would be fully conscious! Think of my getting involved in financial battle like that! But it's so risky! If a Census Keeper winds a total and finds I've been subtracted— If my guide catches me using a chron-dromos illegally—"

I'm a salesman, I told you. I know how to handle people. "Suit yourself," I said, turning away and stepping on my cigarette. "I just thought I'd offer you the chance because you're a nice kid, a bright boy; I think you'll go far. We robber barons have a lot of pride, you know. It isn't every errand boy I'd trust with anything as important as capitalization." I made as if to walk away.

"Oh, please, Mr. Blyn!" He sprinted around in front of me. "I appreciate your offer. If only it weren't so dangerous— But danger, that's the breath of life to you, isn't it? I'll do it. I'll get you the trendicle. We'll rip the market open together. Will you wait?"

"Only if you hurry," I said. "I have a lot of manipulating to do before the sun goes down. Take off." I set the can of paint on the grass and crossed my arms. I swished the dry bough back and forth like the widget kings go in for—scepters.

He nodded, turned and ran into the blue haze just behind the rock. His body sort of turned blue and hazy too as he hit it; then he was gone.

What an angle! I mean, *what an angle.* You get it, don't you? This trendicle—if it was anything like the kid described it—could practically be used the way I said I was going to use it, in that fast double-talk shuffle I'd handed him. Predict movements of the stock market up and down—sideways even!; anticipate business cycles and industrial trends; prophesy war, peace and new bond issues. All I'd have to do would be to sock the facts into it—all the financial news, let's say, of the daily paper—and out would come multitudes of money. Was I set!

I threw my head back and winked at a treetop.

Honestly, I felt drunk. I must have been drunk. Because I'd stopped figuring. Just shows—never stop figuring. Never!

I wandered up to the shimmering blue haze and put my hand out toward it. Just like a stone wall. The kid had been giving me the straight goods on this conditioning deal.

He was a nice kid. Ernest. Nice name.

Nice.

The haze parted and Ernest ran out. He was carrying a long, gray box with a cluster of white keys set in one end. Looked like an adding machine that had been stretched.

I plucked it away from him. "How does it work?"

He was breathing hard. "My guide...she saw me...she called me ...I hope she didn't see me go into the chrondromos...first time I've disobeyed her...illegal use of chrondromos—"

"Sure," I said. "Sure. Very sad. How does it work?"

"The keys. You punch the facts out on the keys. Like the ancient—like your typewriter. The resulting trend appears on the small scanner."

"Pretty small. And it'll take a terrifically long time to type out a couple of pages of financial news. Those stock listings, especially. Don't you people have anything that you just show the paper to and it burps out the result?"

Ernest looked puzzled. Then, "Oh, you mean an *open* trendicle. My guide has one. But it's only for adults. I won't get an open trendicle until responsibility group seven. With good leanings toward self-expression."

There he went on that self-expression gag. "Then that's what we need, Ernest. Suppose you trot back and pick up your guide's trendicle."

I've never seen so much shock on anyone's face in my life. He looked as if I'd told him to shoot the president. The one they just manufactured.

"But I told you! It isn't mine—it's my guide's!"

"You want to be in charge of capitalization, don't you? You want to see the greatest coup ever pulled in Wall Street—lambs fleeced, bears skinned, bulls broken? Go back to your guide—"

"You are discussing me?" A very sweet, very high voice.

Ernest twisted around. "Wolf bait! My guide," he fluted.

A little old lady in a nutty kind of twisted green dress was standing just outside the haze. She was smiling sadly at Ernest and shaking her head at me. I could tell the difference.

"I hope you are satisfied, Ernest, that this period of high adventure was in reality very ugly and peopled by individuals infinitely small. We've become a little impatient with the duration of your unstabling, however. It's time you returned."

"You don't mean—the Census Keepers *knew* all along that I was illegally using a chrondromos? They allowed me to do it?"

"Of course. You stand very high in self-expression; an exception had to be made in your case. Your involved and slightly retarded concepts of the romantic aspects of this era made it necessary to expose you to its harshness. We couldn't pass you into responsibility group five until you had readjusted. Come, now."

It was about time for me to break into the conversation. Between Ernest and the old lady, it sounded like a duet with fife and piccolo. Such voices!

"Just stay unstabled a second," I said. "Where do I come into all this?"

She turned hostile eyes to me. "I'm afraid you don't. We are removing it from you. The various items you have received from our time…you should never have gone so far, Ernest…will also be removed."

"I don't see it that way." I reached out and grabbed Ernest. He struggled, he had muscles in the strangest places; but I had no trouble holding on to him. I lifted the bough threateningly over his head.

"If you don't do just as I tell you, I'll hurt the boy. I'll—I'll skinge all over him!" Then I had an inspiration. "I'll demobilize him! I'll fragisticate every last bone in his body."

"Just what do you want?" she asked very quietly in that thin voice.

"That trendicle you have. The one without keys."

"I'll be back shortly." She turned with a tinkle of the green dress and faded back into the chrondromos. Just like that.

One of the neatest deals I'd ever swung. Just like that! And guys work for a living.

Ernest writhed and twisted and shuddered, but I held him. I wasn't letting him go, no sir! He represented millions of dollars.

The blue haze shimmered again and the old lady stepped out. She carried a circular black thing with a handle in the center.

"Now, that's more like—" I started to say as she pulled the handle.

And that was all. I couldn't move. I couldn't even wiggle the hairs in my nose. I felt like my own tombstone.

The kid darted away. He picked up the small trendicle where I'd dropped it on the grass and ran to the old lady. She reached up with her free hand. She was speaking to him:

"A definite pattern, Ernest. Selfishness, cruelty, little wisdom. Avarice without the faintest signs of a social—" Her hand came down and the blue haze disappeared. I bounded forward, but there was empty air behind the rock. As if they'd never been there.

Not quite.

The can of paint still sat on the ground where I'd parked it. I chuckled and reached for it. There was a sudden flicker of blue.

The can disappeared. A musical voice said, "Ooops. Sorry!"

I whirled. Nobody there. But the can was gone.

For the next half hour, I almost went crazy. All that stuff I could have had. All the questions I could have asked and didn't. All the information—money-making information—I had missed.

Information. Then I remembered. Wenceslaus. The kid had said someone named Wenceslaus had invented the spirillix about this time; had a lot of trouble financing it. I don't know what it is: maybe it stuffs ballot boxes; maybe it enables you to scratch your left elbow with your left hand. But whatever it is, I made up my mind right then, I'm going to find it and sink every penny I have into it. All I know about it is that it's some sort of gimmick; it does things—and it does them good.

I got back to my office and began hiring detectives. You see, I'd already figured that it wouldn't be enough to check phone listings—my Wenceslaus of the spirillix might not have a phone. He might not even call the gadget a spirillix; that could be the name Ernest's people fastened on it.

Well, I didn't go into detail with the detectives. I just told them to find me people named Wenceslaus or close to it, anywhere in the country. I interview them myself. I have to tell them the whole story, so they'll get the feel of the thing, so they'll be able to recognize the spirillix if they've invented it.

That's where you come in, Mr. Wantzilotz. Anyone with a name so close can't be missed. Maybe I didn't hear Ernest right; maybe the name was changed, later.

Now you've heard the story. Think, Mr. Wantzilotz. Are you working on anything besides raising chickens? Are you inventing anything, improving on anything—

No, I don't think a homemade mousetrap is quite what I want. Have you written a book, maybe? Thinking of writing one? Developing a new historical or economic theory—the spirillix might be anything! You haven't?

Well. I'll be going. You don't have any relatives of the same name who fool around with tools and stuff—no? I've got a lot of people to visit. You'd be amazed at the number of Wenceslauses and variations there are—

Wait a minute. Did you say you'd made—you'd invented a new mousetrap?

Here, have another cigar. Sit down. Now tell me, this mousetrap of yours—just how does it work? It catches mice, yes. But exactly what does it *do?*

AFTERWORD

I wrote this story immediately after "Child's Play" was accepted by John W. Campbell, and I used the time-travel vocabulary and background of "Child's Play." I was dreaming of having my own special series in *Astounding*—my own version of Asimov's Empire, Heinlein's Future History, or H. Beam Piper's Paratime Police. It was cheeky of me, I eventually decided, and gave it up.

My greatest source of pride, though, when I had completed the story, was that it came out exactly as I had visualized it, the first time I had managed such a feat. I had yet to learn—as I did many years later, upon listening to a radio broadcast interview with E.M. Forster—that the most exciting and creative experience for a writer was to look upon a finished piece of work and say, "Now, where on earth did that come from?" And to realize that, to continue quoting Mr. Forster, "It came from nowhere on earth."

"Errand Boy" did not make nearly the splash that "Child's Play" did. The only strong reaction was from a paint manufacturing company. They informed me in a letter forwarded from *Astounding* that they had found the passage in which Ernest brings back paint from the future very interesting and profitable. They had experimented and found that they could actually produce in the present day a green paint with orange polka dots. It seemed to be marketable.

Did I have any other money-making ideas for paints, they wanted to know?

I wrote back and told them that there was something I wanted to know in my turn. What would be in it for me?

They were apparently too shocked at my crass commercial attitude to reply.

WRITTEN 1947———*PUBLISHED 1947*

A Lamp
for Medusa

A LAMP FOR MEDUSA

"And thence came the Son of Danae, flaming with courage and spirit;
Wise Athena brought him thus to the fellowship of these stalwart men.
He slew the Gorgon and winged back, bringing to the islanders
The head with its writhing snake-locks, the Terror that froze to stone."
—Pindar, *Pythian Odes*

The bit of parchment on which the words were written in large, blotty letters had a bad smell. Like everything else in the apartment, Percy S. Yuss thought bitterly. He turned the parchment around in his fingers—annoyed at the strange discomfort he experienced in handling it—and grunted in disbelief.

Its back still had a few fine brown hairs clinging to the badly tanned surface. Someone had evidently gone to the trouble of killing an animal and skinning it, merely to write a translation of a long-dead poet's little-known verse.

Such eccentrics as these three rooms had known!

He dropped the handkerchief-size square of dead tissue on the floor, with the rest of the fantastic garbage, that varied from a ballet dancer's worn white slippers to four wooden chair legs which had evidently been chopped off with an exceedingly sharp axe—to judge from the unbelievable smoothness of the cut-away surface.

What an amazing and varied collection of junk! He shook his head as he shepherded the stuff into a great pile with the broom he'd discovered in the kitchen. A man's safety razor, a woman's curling iron, notebook upon notebook filled with strange and unrecognizable scripts. Not to mention the heap of locked suitcases on the top of which he'd just chucked his own battered valise.

In these days, one did not look gift apartments in the foyer, so to speak. Still, he couldn't help wondering why these previous tenants hadn't bothered to come back for their possessions. He found himself tingling uncomfortably, as when he'd first seen the parchment.

Maybe they hadn't paid their rent. No, that couldn't be. It was such a wonderfully small rent, that even people who didn't own a half interest in a mildly bankrupt hashhouse wouldn't have too much trouble raising it. It had been the lowness of the rental figure that had made Percy scramble frantically in his wallet for the thirty-five dollars' worth of cumshaw the superintendent had demanded. After years of tramping from dismal furnished room to dingy sublet to get at long last a place as cheap as this in his own name!

Percy sighed the smug, deeply happy sigh of the happy householder. It smelled, it was badly littered and would require at least two full days to get clean, but it was his, all his. Enthusiastically, he bent his back into the broom again.

The hall door opened and Mrs. Danner walked in without knocking. From the living room, where he was scraping the rubbish together, Percy saw the rather badly used-up old lady, who served as a combination janitor, building superintendent and renting agent, stagger into his kitchen. A half-empty fifth of whiskey swung restlessly from one bony hand as a kind of liquid epitaph to thirty-five dollars that had once been in Percy's possession and was no longer.

She leaned against a wall, first patting it gently so that it wouldn't get frightened and leap away. "Good old, lovely old, moneymaking apartment," she muttered. "They come and they go, they come and they go, but you're always left for me. And every time they come, little Marybelle Danner gets another ten bottles. Darling, gorgeous old apartment, you're my *splurfsk!*"

The last word, Percy realized as he walked sternly into the kitchen, was not an entirely novel term of endearment coined on the spot by Mrs. Danner, as much as it was a very ordinary word dissolved beyond recognition into the hearty gulp of whiskey with which she frequently punctuated her sentences.

"Pretty apartment!" she continued, rubbing her back against the filthy wall like a kitten which had grown to lanky old age without ever having become a cat. "The owners don't pay me enough to feed the teensiest canary, my children don't care what becomes of their sweet old ma, but you watch out for me, don't you? You won't let me *sturvleglglg*. Every single time a new tenant—"

She lowered the bottle with which she had been preparing a new and moister period. She leaned forward from the hips, blinking madly through worn, red-lined eyes. "You still here?"

"Yes, I'm still here," Percy told her angrily. "After all, I just moved in this morning! What are you doing in my apartment?"

Mrs. Danner straightened. She waved her head from side to side like a bewildered gray banner. "How can he still be here?" she asked the neck of the bottle in a confidential whisper. "It's been over four hours since he took possession. None of the others ever stayed that *lurngsht*." She wiped her lips. "Not one of them!"

"Look here. I paid one month's rent in advance. I also gave you a big hunk of cash under the table, even though it's illegal. I have to work pretty hard for my money in a hot and stinking little luncheonette that seems to go further into the red with every bit of business we do."

"Too bad," Mrs. Danner told him consolingly. "We should never have elected Hoover. I voted for Al *Smiglugglug*. He wouldn't have let the Kaiser get away. He'd have got Eisenhower after him. Here. You need a drinkie before you disappear."

"The reason," Percy went on patiently, "that I paid you all this cabbage was so I could have an apartment of my own. I don't want you walking in without knocking. This is my place. Now was there anything you wanted?"

She batted her eyes mournfully at him, took another shot, belched, and started for the door. "All I wanted was the apartment. But if it isn't ready yet, it just isn't *reyurmph*. I can wait another hour or two if I have to. I'm no *purksk*."

The new tenant closed the door behind her very carefully. He noticed again that there was an area of splintered wood around the place where the lock had been—as if it had been necessary to break the door down upon the last occupant.

What did that point to? Suicide, maybe. Or Mrs. Danner's mention of disappearances—could that be taken seriously? It would explain all that queer junk, all those full suitcases, as if people had just been moving in when—

When what? This was the scientific twentieth century, and he was in one of the most civilized cities on the face of the Earth. People didn't just walk into a cold tenement flat on the West Side and vanish. No, it wasn't logical.

Anyway, he'd better get a lock on the door before he left for work. He glanced at his watch. He had an hour and a half. Just enough time to take a quick bath, buy the lock, and screw it on. He'd finish cleaning the place tomorrow.

The bath was a tiny, four-foot affair that stood high on angle-iron legs beside the kitchen sink. It had a huge enamel cover that was hinged to the wall. There was more junk piled on the cover than there had been on the floor. With a sigh, Percy began to carry the stuff into the half-clean living room.

By the time he was through, the other room was a mess again and he was hot, tired, and disgusted. Trust Percy Sactrist Yuss to get this kind of bargain, he thought angrily as he wedged the cover up against the wall, filled the little bathtub with water, and began to undress. A dark, dirty apartment, filled with the garbage of countless previous tenants, and not only had he had to pay extra money to get the place, but now it seemed there was a curse on it, too. And a curious drunken female superintendent who would probably let him have all the privacy of a hot suspect in the Monday morning police line-up.

He took a towel and a fresh bar of soap from his valise. His mood grew blacker as he realized his feet had become coated with a kind of greasy grime as a result of standing on the kitchen floor. The place probably had vermin, too.

Bending down to brush off his feet so that he wouldn't carry the soil requirements of a potato patch into the bathtub, he noticed a scrap of white on the floor. It was the parchment with the fragment of classic poetry laboriously traced out on one side. He'd scuffed it into the kitchen while tramping back and forth.

As he glanced at it cursorily once more, another peculiar electric shiver went through him.

"...*He slew the Gorgon and winged back, bringing to the islanders*
The head with its writhing snake-locks, the Terror that froze to stone."

Who was it who had slain the Gorgon? Some character in Greek mythology—but who exactly he just couldn't remember. For some reason, the identity and the name escaped him completely. And usually he had a fine memory for such little items.

Twenty years spent working out crossword puzzles after a frenzied day dealing them off the arm in dining cars was almost the equivalent of a college education.

He shrugged and flipped the parchment away. To his annoyance, it bounced off the upright bathtub cover and into the water. Trust his luck! He hung the towel on a crossbar of the tall bathtub legs and climbed in, having to duck his head and twist his shoulders down laboriously to avoid the wooden dish-closets set on the wall some three feet above the tub.

His knees were well out of the water in the little bathtub, practically digging into his chest. Washing himself under these conditions was going to be real cozy!

It was impossible now to recapture the earlier mood of exultation at having an apartment of his own. He felt he'd been taken, as he'd felt all through his life after being persuaded to go into some scheme or other. Like buying a half-interest in a restaurant which the sheriff already regarded with fond proprietary interest.

"I'm not even taken," he said unhappily. "I give myself away!"

And on top of everything, the plug leaked! The level of water sank rapidly down to his hips. Cursing his parents for being attracted to each other in the first place, Percy reached forward to jab it more securely in place. As he did so, the parchment, floating face up on the water, caught his eye.

Long strands of hair now trailed it wetly, and the words were beginning to dissolve in the water. He wasn't interested in it; more, he felt very strongly that he shouldn't be interested in it, that here, in this bit of archaic verse, was more living danger than he had ever known in his screamingest nightmares. He felt that strange tingle begin again in the inner recesses of his body, and he knew that his instincts to toss it away had been right, that the curiosity that impelled him to read it every time he picked it up was utterly, terribly—

"And thence came the son of Danae—"

Almost against his will, his mind wondered. *Thence?* Where *thence?* Somehow, he felt he knew. But why should he feel that way? He'd never read a line by Pindar before. And why should he be wondering about it in the first place? He had other troubles, lots of them.

His hand swept the parchment up like a particularly disgusting insect. Up and over the side of the bathtub. Right into the bluish waves that billowed all around him.

Into the sea.

He hardly had time to let his jaw drop. Because the bathtub began to sink. Percy was bailing before he realized he was doing it.

This time the water was bubbling into the tub. With a convulsive gesture of his entire body that almost threw him over the side, he clamped his left foot down hard upon the defective plug and splashed the tepid mixture out with two threshing, barely cupped bands.

In spite of his inaccurate roiling and tossing, he had the tub all but emptied in a matter of seconds. A thin trickle of sea water still lounged out from between his toes.

He reached over the side, noticing uncomfortably that the rim was a bare two inches above the sea's restless surface. Yes, the towel was still in place, knotted intricately around the cross-bar. It was soaking wet, but it made a magnificent reinforcement for the plug. With fingers that had sharpened into a remarkable deftness under the grinding surprise of the moment, he jabbed corners of the towel all around the edges of the rubber plug.

Not perfect, but it would hold back the waters. Now, where was he?

He was in a bathtub which—temporarily at least—was floating in a warm and only slightly choppy sea, a sea of the deepest, most thrilling azure he had ever seen. Ahead, an island rose in a mass of incredibly stately and delicately colored hills.

Behind him there was another strip of land, but it was lost in a gentle mist and was too far away for him to determine whether it was an island or the outstretched finger of a continent.

To the right, there was more blue sea. To the left—

Again he almost fell out of the tub. Some fifty feet off to the left was quite the largest sea serpent he had ever seen in or out of the Sunday Supplements.

And it was humping along the waves directly at him!

Percy leaned forward and paddled madly at the water on both sides of his tub. What a world, he thought, what an insane world for a quiet man to find himself in! What had he ever done to deserve—

He heard a peculiar rattle of sound, like a cement mixer gargling, and looked up to see the monster staring down at him through unwinking eyes. It was, the back of his mind gibbered, all of two feet in diameter: no doubt it could swallow him without even gulping. A row of bright red feathers plumed up from the top of its head as the great mouth opened slowly to reveal countless rows of jagged, fearful teeth.

If only he had a weapon! A knife of any sort, a stone, a club... Percy clambered upright in the tub, his fists clenched desperately. As the mouth opened to its fullest width and the forked tongue that looked as sharp and deadly as a two-headed spear coiled back upon itself, he lashed out with his right arm, putting into the blow all the strength of cornered despair.

His fist caught the beast on its green lower lip.

"Ouch!" it said. "Don't do that!"

It swirled away from him so vehemently that his little enameled craft was almost swamped. Licking its lip with its flickering tongue, it paused to stare back at him indignantly over a glistening coil.

"That hurt, you know! All I wanted to do was say, 'Welcome, son of Danae,' and you have to go and bop me one! You won't make many friends acting like that, I can tell you!"

The monster swam a bit further away and curved to face the goggling Percy standing limply in his bathtub.

"You didn't even ask if I was working for the snake-mother or Poseidon or whatever! Maybe for all you know I'm an independent operator. Maybe I have a bit of information that would save your life or the life of someone pretty important to you. No, all you can do is hit me," the creature sneered. "And on the lip, which as everyone knows is my most sensitive part! All right, son of Danae, if that's the way you want it, that's the way it's going to be. I won't help you."

With a kind of rippling shrug that threaded disdainfully from the enormous head down to the thin delicacy of a tail, the sea serpent dived. And was gone.

Percy sat down carefully, feeling the hard sides of the tub as caressingly as if they were his own sanity.

Where in the world was he? Or, rather, where out of it was he? A man starts to take a bath in his new apartment and winds up in—in— Was that how the others had gone?

He stared over the side through the clear sea. The legs of painted angle-iron which had supported the bathtub were sheared off cleanly about halfway down. Fortunately, the faucets had been shut off; the pipes were also cut. Like something else. He remembered the chair legs back in the apartment.

Four chair legs minus a chair. Somewhere, then, in this world there might be a chair without legs. Containing someone who had purchased an apartment from Mrs. Danner.

Percy realized suddenly that there was a very bad taste in his mouth. An awful taste, in fact.

Of course. The soap. When he'd started bailing upon arrival in this weird place, he had a cake of soap in his hand. He'd stuck it in his mouth. And up to now he hadn't had a really peaceful moment in which to remove it.

He extracted the somewhat soggy pink bar from his teeth with a distinct lack of relish and washed his mouth out carefully with sea water. As he did so, he noticed that he had drifted much closer to the island. There was evidence of life somewhere behind the beach, a few slowly moving human beings and a cluster of huts or houses— at this distance, it was hard to tell which.

What were his resources in dealing with this new world? He considered them ruefully. A slightly used cake of soap. An extremely wet bath towel. A round rubber plug, too badly worn to do its job properly. And a bathtub, if he could move it once he got to shore.

Then, of course, there was himself. "Like if the natives go in for human steak," he grimaced.

A sea serpent that talked! Whose dignity had been injured, who had even gone so far as to— Wait a minute! What had it called him?

Son of Danae.

But he wasn't!

"Go tell the sea serpent," he told himself fiercely. He remembered the verse on the bit of parchment abruptly: *"The head with its writhing snake-locks—"*

"I've got to get out of here!" he commented restlessly and with tremendous conviction, glancing from the rocking tub to the placid rolling sea from which anything might be expected.

For a moment, when the net flapped down upon his shoulders, Percy had the frantic idea that he'd been overheard by some deity who had hurried to cooperate. He struggled, threshing wildly against the coarse, knotted fibers that tore at his skin. Then, as he felt the entire tub caught in the huge skein and being drawn rapidly toward shore, he relaxed into *now what?* hopelessness and tried to see what had happened.

He had drifted in front of a cliff-like promontory of the island. A group of men dressed in loincloths were dancing about on the edge of the cliff, cheering an enormous, richly clad fellow who, from a precarious foothold halfway down the steep face, had flung the net and, with dexterous twists of wrist and forearm, was now hauling it in.

"Attaboy, Dictys!" one of them yelled as the tub beached, turned over and, with Percy crashing around under it, was dragged up the side of the cliff. "You got it all right, all right."

"That Dictys," another commented admiringly. "He's death on sea monsters. This'll be the third he caught this week."

"The fourth," Dictys corrected as he scrambled to the top of the cliff with the bathtub and the net-enclosed man both securely on his shoulder. "You forgot the pygmy mermaid—half-woman, half-sardine. I count it even though she was kind of small. But this'll be the best of the lot. I've never seen anything like it before."

He unwound the net rapidly with long-practiced gestures. Percy climbed out of the tub and flopped on the ground. He felt like a bag of well gnawed bones.

Dictys picked him up with a huge hand, held him out for inspection. "This isn't a monster," he said in evident bitter disappointment. "It comes apart: half of it is a man and the rest is a round sort of chest. And I thought it was something really unusual! Oh, well," he mused, lifting Percy over his head with the obvious intention of throwing him back into the sea. "You can't hit it all the time."

"Maybe," suggested an oldster on the edge of the group, "maybe he is a monster. He could have changed into a man just now. He might know that if he's a monster we'd put him in your brother's zoo, but if he's a man we'd throw him back because we've got lots of people here already."

The tall man nodded thoughtfully. "You might have something there, Agesilaus. I'd hate to go back to King Polydectes empty-handed. Well, there's an easy way of finding out."

What kind of world is this? Percy was frantic "—if he's a man we'd throw him back because we've got lots of people here already!"

And what kind of test were they going to apply?

He noticed that the well dressed fisherman had unsheathed the great single-bladed sword he wore on his back. He ground the point of it into Percy's chest interrogatively.

"You better change to your particular monstrous form fast, sonny. Because you're not going to have the pleasure of being returned to the drink. Instead, I'm going to cut you up into six distinct and separate slices in just a few seconds. You'll be *much* better off in my brother's cages. Now then, what exactly are you?"

Percy beat against his forehead with an open palm. What was he supposed to do—develop a quick-change routine on the spot that included wings, flippers, and a Siamese twin? Because if he didn't, he was evidently going to become cutlets.

"All right," Dictys said, frowning. "Go ahead—be stubborn. See what it gets you."

He whirled the bronze blade experimentally around his head, then curved it back for a tremendous stroke.

Percy swallowed as he saw it glint redly at him. "I'll talk," he babbled. "I'll tell you about myself! I'm—I'm—"

What could he tell them that would make sense in their terms? What kind of lie could he compose in a hurry that they would believe? They wanted him to make like a monster.

Monster! He'd talked to a—

The words boiled rapidly out of his lips. He had no time to weigh them. "I'm the man the sea serpent welcomed as the son of Danae." He hoped it would at least give the big fellow pause.

It did.

Dictys lowered his sword and stepped back staring. "The—the son of Danae? The one who's going to kill the Gorgon?"

"The same." Percy nodded with the self-conscious grandeur of a celebrity discovered by the nightclub emcee at a ringside table. "The…the famous Gorgon killer. The—the man who brought the islanders the head with the writhing snake-locks, the Terror that—"

"Who will bring, you mean," Dictys corrected him. "It's not done yet. Well, well, well. You're kind of scrawny for that sort of job, even if you do have red hair. What's your name?"

"Percy. Percy S. Yuss."

"Right!" Agesilaus yelped from the rear. He came hurrying up, his beard floating behind him like an oversized white woolen necktie. "It figures, Dictys, it figures! Right on the dot of the prophecy. His name's Perseus, he has red hair, you caught him in a fishnet—everything happened exactly the way the oracle said—"

Dictys thrust out his lower lip and shook his head. "Oracles are one thing. Muscles are another. Nobody's going to tell me that this weakling is going to tackle the beast that frightens the bravest men and even other monsters, no matter how powerful. Look at him—he's quivering with fear already!"

This was not exactly true. Percy had become chilled standing on the windy hillside in nothing but his wet skin. There was, besides, an emotional reaction to all his recent experiences setting in. But there was also a mounting discomfort at the way they were discussing his capabilities as a Gorgon killer. He'd thrown in the sentence merely as a means of distracting Dictys temporarily; now it seemed they couldn't get off the subject. The beast that frightened men and gods!

He thought back wistfully to a few minutes ago when he'd been riding a serpent-infested sea in a leaky bathtub. Ah, those were carefree, happy times!

"His name's not even Perseus," Dictys was arguing. "It's Persaesus or something.

You're not going to tell me that this bedraggled bumpkin will become the most famous hero of all time?"

Agesilaus nodded vehemently. "He certainly will! As far as the name's concerned, I think it's close enough. Sometimes the oracle gets names mixed up. But here's the chest in which the oracle said Perseus would arrive with his mother, Danae, after King Acrisus of Argos tossed them into the sea."

"Yes, but the oracle said the infant Perseus," another loin-clothed man broke in. "Didn't she?"

"Well," Agesilaus hedged. "Sometimes the oracle gets ages mixed up, too." The old man looked a little now as if he were no longer certain about oracular dependability on any matter.

Percy found himself sympathizing with him. Agesilaus was evidently pleading his case, but he wasn't certain which way he'd be worse off, if the old man won or lost.

Dictys came in fast for the argumentative kill. "If King Acrisus of Argos, according to the oracle, threw Perseus and his mother into the chest, then where is Danae? And another thing, Agesilaus. Argos is that way," he pointed with a braceleted hand. "Northwest. This fellow came from the east. No, he's an impostor trying to cash in on the prophecy. And I don't like impostors."

He reached down for a couple of lengths of rope with which several of the men had been repairing holes in the net. Before Percy could get a word of protest out of his slowly opening mouth, he was tripped expertly and tossed to the ground. In a moment, he was tied up as tightly as an expensive Christmas present.

"What's the penalty for impersonating a hero?" Dictys asked Agesilaus. The packaging job completed, he removed his knee from the gasping young man's back and rose.

"For impersonating a hero," the old man said thoughtfully, with an unsatisfied frown still creasing his face, "the penalty's the same as for blasphemy. Cooking over a slow fire. In fact, since your brother, King Polydectes, reformed the legal system, practically every crime is punishable by cooking over a slow fire. Your brother says it makes it easier for him to pass sentence that way. He doesn't have to remember a whole calendar of complicated punishments."

"That's why we call him Wise King Polydectes," one of the younger men exclaimed, and everyone nodded enthusiastically.

"Listen—" Percy began screaming from the ground. Dictys stuck a handful of grass into his mouth. There was enough loose soil attached to make the gag a verb as well as a noun. He was so busy strangling that he had little energy for observation and less for an attempt to escape when two of the men slung him to a pole and began carrying him downhill over highly uneven ground.

"Hi, there, Menon," he heard someone call as he was borne choking and sneezing along a dusty road. "Whatcha got?"

"Don't know for sure," the forward bearer replied. "I think it's kettle bait."

"You don't say! This crime-wave gets more frightening every week!"

By the time Percy had worked the last of the foliage out of his mouth, they had passed through the huge gateway of a stone-walled citadel and into a cluster of small but surprisingly well built brick houses.

His pole was placed in two forked sticks set upright in the main thoroughfare of the town. He dangled from the tight ropes, feeling his blood grinding to a halt.

A group of curious men and women gathered around asking questions of his two guards.

"Is that the latest monster Dictys has caught?" a woman wanted to know. "He doesn't seem to be very unusual." She poked experimentally at choice spots on his naked body. "Practically normal, I'd say."

"Stew-job," the bearer said laconically. "Nice tender stew-job."

As far as was possible in his tightly laced condition, Percy writhed. No, this couldn't be happening to him—this just couldn't be! A man doesn't start taking a bath in a new apartment and wind up in a world where everything from burglary to barratry is punished by—

"I will not consider that thought," his mind announced. "I know when I'm well off."

Certain things were clear to him, though, disagreeably clear. He had somehow fallen into a past which had never really existed, the time of the Greek mythos. Never really existed? The sea serpent's indignation had been real enough, and so were the ropes with which he was bound. So, he suspected, would be the punishment, if he were found guilty of impersonating a hero.

Odd, that. The serpent addressing him as the son of Danae, who was evidently the mother of Perseus. His own name, which formed a combination of syllables remarkably like the Gorgon killer's. The bit of parchment he'd found in the apartment which evidently had helped precipitate him into this mess, and the subject of the snatch of poetry written upon it. The way he'd come close to the legend in various other ways, such as the arrival by sea—

No! When his trial came up, he wanted to plead absolute innocence, that he had no knowledge whatever of the Perseus prophecy and no interest at all in it. Otherwise, thinking all those other thoughts could only lead in one direction....

He shivered violently and vibrated the pole briefly.

"Poor fellow, he's cold!" a girl's voice said sympathetically.

"That's all right. King Polydectes will warm him up," a man told her. Everyone guffawed. Percy vibrated the pole again.

"I never said I was Perseus!" the bound young man broke out despairingly. "All I did was tell your Dictys that the sea serpent—"

"You'd better shut up," the bearer who had been called Menon advised him in a confidential, friendly manner. "For trying to influence the jury before a trial, you can have your tongue torn out by the roots—whether you're eventually found guilty or innocent."

Percy decided to keep quiet.

Every time he opened his mouth, he put the local criminal code in it. He was getting deeper and deeper into the most fantastic trouble and didn't have the slightest idea how to go about getting out of it. Or how he'd gotten into it in the first place.

Mrs. Danner. He hated Mrs. Danner, how he hated that profiteering old female souse! She, if anyone, was responsible for his present situation. She'd evidently known that the apartment was some kind of exit apparatus; when she'd walked in unannounced, she had expected to find the place empty. If only he'd given a little more attention to her gleeful maunderings!

How long had people been noticing that sign outside the tenement entrance? "Three-Room Apartment for Rent. Very Cheap. Immediate Occupancy!"

How many had run in and excitedly paid her the thirty-five dollars "renting fee" she demanded, then bolted home to gather up enough personal belongings to take formal possession? And then, a few moments after entry, while measuring the bedroom for furniture arrangements perhaps, or considering the walls relative to a daring color scheme idea, or prying loose a badly stuck window—had suddenly fallen through into this world of magic and violence?

How long had Mrs. Danner been making a good thing out of this apartment, how many "renting fees" had she acquired? Percy didn't know, but he thought dreamily of coming upon her some time in a locked room. Forgetting his painfully bound hands and feet for a moment, he mused gently on the delightful softness of her throat under a pair of insistent thumbs.

Although she couldn't be the whole answer. She didn't know enough about anything outside of the latest quotations on whiskey-by-the-case-F.O.B.-distillery to have created the peculiar chronological trap that the apartment contained. Who was it then? Or what? And, above all and most important, why?

Dictys had come up, surrounded by his bully-boys in semi-sarongs.

"A bad day," he told the townsfolk. "Didn't catch a single solitary horror. Just this fake hero."

"That's all right, Dictys," the man who had previously expressed confidence in the king's thermal reliability reassured him. "He'll still be a good excuse for a party."

"Sure," someone else chimed in. "With an execution, the evening won't be entirely lost."

"I know, I know," Dictys admitted morosely. "But I wanted a specimen for the zoo. An execution won't be the same thing at all."

While most of the surrounding individuals applauded the extremely commendable detachment of so scientific an attitude, Percy saw a man with a voluminous white mantle push out to the front of the group and look at him more closely and curiously than anyone else had. The man had a peculiarly bright saffron skin, Percy noticed, when a fold of the cloak came down from his face for a moment.

"What made you think he was a monster?" the man asked Dictys, putting the fold carefully back in place.

"The chest he was riding, from the cliff, it looked like part of him. It was round and white and had all kinds of metal pieces sticking out. I've never seen anything like it before—and I've been to the mainland twice."

"Where is the chest?"

The large man pointed over his shoulder with a thumb the size of a small banana. "Oh, we left it on the cliff with the rest of the stuff he had in it. You can never tell about strange pieces of furniture: sometimes they come alive or burst into flame or— *Say!* Are you a stranger in town?"

The white-cloaked man dropped a hand to his mid-section. He passed it once across his abdomen and, as Dictys advanced truculently upon him, he disappeared.

There were breaking bubbles of comment all through the crowd.

"What was that?"

"Where in the world did he go, Eunapius?"

"I don't know but, if you ask me, he wasn't all human."

"Mama, I wanna go home!"

"Sh-h-h, Leontis. There may be a cooking today. You wouldn't want to miss that, would you?"

"What do you think he was, Dictys?"

Their leader scratched his matted hair. "Well, he couldn't have been what I thought he was, just an ordinary stranger passing through. I wanted to grab him and put him under arrest. If he was a stranger or a wandering merchant and had forgotten to register with the commander of the palace guard, he'd have been liable to the Foreigner's Penalty Tax."

"You mean all his goods impounded and his right arm burned off before his face?"

"More or less, at the discretion of the guard commander. But I think he must have been either a wizard or a major monster. In fact, from the color of his skin, I'd say he was a human-type monster. Wasn't it gold?"

Agesilaus nodded. "It was gold, all right. What they call on the mainland the *Olympian* type of monster. Those aren't supposed to be too bad. According to the mainlanders, they help men lots of times."

"When they help men, it's for their own good reasons," Dictys growled. "Not that I have anything against major monsters," he explained hurriedly to Agesilaus. "They have their own private quarrels, and men should stay out of them if they don't want to get badly hurt."

From the anxious speed with which he had added the last remark, Percy deduced a certain real fear of what the man called "major monsters." Evidently, minor monsters were something else again, since Dictys had been fishing for them, and the king maintained a kind of zoo. But why had the golden-skinned stranger been so interested in him? Had he something to do with Percy's arrival here?

He had long lost all feeling in his wrists and ankles and was wondering dizzily if they intended to keep him hanging in the village square as a kind of permanent decoration, when there was a musical clank of metal armor and an uneven tramping of feet.

A very hoarse voice said, "King Polydectes of Seriphos will see the prisoner now."

Percy sighed with real gusto as two men shouldered his pole again and began jouncing him along the main avenue. Not only was he going to go to a place where his side of the story could be heard at last, but he now knew the name of the island kingdom on which his errant bathtub had stumbled so unceremoniously.

Seriphos. He went through his memory rapidly. No, he didn't know anything about an island called Seriphos. Except what he had learned in the past hour or so. That it was fairly close to the Greek mainland and therefore in the warm Aegean Sea. And that it was awaiting the fulfillment of an ancient legend to the effect that the Gorgon killer Perseus was to land there sometime before starting out on his heroic quest.

Also, that it had a judicial system that bore a close resemblance to a power saw.

He was carried up a single step and into a courtyard with an enormous ceiling supported by four massive pillars of stone. Menon slipped the pole out of the rope loops at his hands and feet, and the other bearer cut his bonds with a few generous slashes of a long bronze knife.

They stood him on his feet and stepped back. "Feel better now?"

Percy pitched forward on his face. He bounced hard on the painted cement floor.

"His legs," Menon explained to his buddy. "They've fallen asleep."

"Always happens," the other said professionally. "Every damn time."

The return of circulation was grim, swirling agony. Percy moaned and rolled about on the floor, rubbing his wrists and ankles with hands that felt like wooden boards. A few people came over and squatted down beside him for a moment to stare at his face or watch his struggles. No one offered to help.

After a while, he was able to bow-leg painfully upright. His guards grabbed him and shoved him between them against a pillar.

Most of the townspeople had followed him into the hall. The news was spreading, it would seem. Every few moments someone else came in—butchers with their dripping meat cleavers, peasants with their scythes, women carrying rush baskets filled with berries and vegetables.

The newcomers would have him pointed out to them. Then they would either smile and nod slowly in satisfaction, or they would turn and run out fast, in evident haste to get Cousin Hybrias or Aunt Thea before all the fun was over.

In the middle of the courtyard, beside a blackened hearth roughly the size of the entire apartment which Percy had so recently vacated, a man sat on an enormously wide stone throne.

At first glance, he seemed to be lolling in a large number of strangely shaped cushions. Closer examination, however, revealed the cushions to be a fine collection of young and pretty girls who varied as much in their coloring as they did in their interest in the affairs of state going on before them. One extremely pretty blonde who formed part of the king's foot-stool was snoringly sound asleep. Another, a gorgeous Negro girl, most of whose body was obscured by a large masculine shoulder, was expostulating vehemently into the monarch's right ear and waving her hand at a moaning figure prostrate before the throne.

"See here, Tontibbi," the king told her at last in a highly exasperated voice, "I've got my own system of punishments, and I don't want any decadent females from an over-civilized part of the world to be suggesting changes all the time, no matter how imaginative they might be. We're rough-and-ready folk here on Seriphos, and we go in for simple entertainments. And if you African snobs want to go around calling us barbarians, well, go right ahead. We're proud of the name."

The dark girl scowled and subsided back into the recesses of the great throne. The assembled crowd applauded vehemently.

"That's the way, Polydectes. You tell these stuck-up foreigners where to get off!" an elderly farmer cheered.

"Well," Polydectes said slowly and thoughtfully. "The way I see it—why shouldn't what was good enough in my father's day be good enough for me?"

"Don't you just love the way he puts things?" a beaming housewife remarked to her neighbor. "I think it's lovely to have a king who's so clever with words!"

"Besides," her friend replied, "I don't understand all this crazy desire for change all the time. What could be better than disposing of criminals by cooking them over a slow fire? The way King Polydectes's chef does it, we usually get four or five hours out of the weakest man. He starts after supper, and by the time he's through, it's quite dark, and everyone feels like having a good night's sleep after a fine, enjoyable evening. Personally, I wouldn't dream of asking for anything more."

Percy felt his stomach turn in a slow, rocking half-circle. The man who was lying before the king screamed a little bit and tried to grind his face into the cement floor.

What kind of people were they anyway? They talked of the most horrible things with the same equanimity as if they might be discussing the latest movie or wrestling match they'd seen the night before on television.

Well, of course, public executions were the closest these people came to such things as movies or television. Percy remembered stories he'd read in the newspapers of crowds turning out to attend hangings in various parts of the United States. That was the twentieth century! And an execution was still a sufficiently fine spectacle for many men to bring their dates, for some women to bring their children, and for a few enterprising businessmen to hawk tiny replicas of the gallows on which a fellow human was frantically kicking his life away.

All of which was well and good, but didn't help him very much in his present predicament. If only he could figure out some approach which these people would honor, if only he could learn a little bit about their ideas of right and wrong in time to do himself some good!

He strained to catch every detail of what was going on. He needed clues as to their courtroom procedure. Would he get a lawyer to defend him? He doubted it from what he'd seen so far. Yet there had been talk of a trial, there had been mention of a jury. There was a little frozen comfort in these civilized institutions no matter how they were applied, he decided.

And then he wasn't so sure.

"I'm getting tired of this," the king broke into the prostrate prisoner's broken-hearted babble. He lifted his head and waved vaguely at the assembled crowd. "Hey, jury! Any of you willing to insist on this man's innocence?"

"Uh-uh. Guilty!"

"Guilty as hell!"

"The low-down beast! Cooking's too good for him. Hey, Brion, what'd he do?"

"How should I know? I just came in. Must have been something bad, or he wouldn't be on trial."

"Guilty, guilty, guilty! Let's get on to the next case. That looks good!"

"Raise the prisoner for sentencing," King Polydectes commanded. Two guards leaped forward and lifted the writhing, pleading man. The king pointed a forefinger solemnly at the ceiling. "By virtue of the power vested in me by me," he intoned, "I hereby sentence you to—to…just a minute now. To—"

"To cooking over a slow fire," the Negro girl behind him said bitterly. "Is it ever anything else?"

Polydectes pounded a barrel-like fist angrily into his open palm. "You better be careful, Tontibbi! You'll go into the kettle yourself, if you don't watch out! You might have spoiled the whole legality of the trial! All right, take him away," he said in disgust. "You heard what she said. Do it."

"I'm sorry, Polydectes," the girl murmured contritely. "I get so bored! Go ahead, sentence him yourself."

The king shook his head unhappily.

"Naa-a-ah! There's no pleasure in it anymore. Just try to control yourself from now on, huh?"

"I will," she promised, snuggling down again.

As they lifted the vaguely struggling man by his arms, Percy gasped in horror. He understood why he hadn't been able to make out any of the prisoner's words—his tongue had been torn out! There were great drying crusts of blood all over his face and still more coming down his chin to his chest. The man was obviously so weak from loss of blood that he could hardly stand by himself, but so terrified by the agonizing imminence of his doom that he had been desperately trying to make himself understood in some way. His hands waved hopelessly, and a dreadful tongueless moan kept rolling out of his mouth as he was dragged, his toes plowing thin furrows in the dust of the floor, off to a small room which was probably the execution antechamber.

"See?" Menon said to Percy, who was feebly massaging his belly. "He tried to influence the jury before trial. From what I hear, they were the soldiers."

It began to make a kind of highly disagreeable sense, Percy decided. Every citizen on the island—soldiers, civilians, policemen, noblemen, whatever—was a potential member of the jury in any criminal case. The fact that these people took the responsibilities of office rather lightly by the standards of the world he had just left was not as important as their right to crowd into any trial and participate in the verdict. Therefore, if you were arrested on Seriphos for an offense, no matter how flimsy the accusation, you must, above all, not protest your innocence. The man who arrested you would be a talesman, and the punishment for violating this particular law was swift and comprehensive. He began to feel a surprising glow of gratitude for the gag that Dictys had stuffed in his mouth. Why, the man had actually been human even though, instead of pulling Percy's tongue out, he had virtually shoved it down his throat.

But how could you defend yourself when people like these brought you to trial?

"Next case!" the king roared. "And let's cut it short. We're all getting hungry, and there's a pretty good execution scheduled for after supper. I don't like to keep my people waiting."

"And that's why we call him Good King Polydectes," a woman murmured as Percy was dragged before the throne and flung down hard.

"Charged," a somewhat familiar voice said above his head, "with impersonating a hero, i.e., Perseus, who, according to the legend—"

"I heard the legend, Dictys," his brother said grumpily. "We went all through it in the previous case. Let's find this man guilty, too, and start to adjourn. I don't know why there are so many Perseuses these days and so few fake Heracleses or Theseuses. I guess it's like anything else: someone starts a fad, and before you know what's happened, everybody's doing it."

Dictys's curiosity had been aroused. "What do you mean you went all through it in the previous case?"

"Oh, a couple of my soldiers were on duty up on the hills investigating a report that those small-size monsters, the flying ones, you know which I mean…?"

"Harpies? You mean the ones with heads of girls and the bodies, wings, and claws of birds, don't you?"

Polydectes sighed. "Those. It's wonderful to have a brother who knows his monsters so well. I get all mixed up whenever I try to keep them straight in my head. I just have a simple rule: if it has no more and no less than two arms, two legs, and one head, then it's human. Otherwise, it's a monster."

"That leaves out the golden-skinned Olympians. They're not human, either. I don't know exactly what they are, but a lot of people would classify them with the major monsters."

"And a lot wouldn't," the king pointed out. "So there you are. Where exactly it is that you are, I don't know, but— Anyway, there's been a couple of reports lately that these things, these harpies, have been smuggling contraband into the island from the air and cutting into the royal revenues of Seriphos. I sent a squad up to Mount Lassus to look into the matter. They were settling down to a little meal before going into action, when this man came blundering down the hill. They arrested him as soon as he told them he was Perseus. After they arrested him, of course, and he still tried to argue, they punished him on the spot for jury-tampering under my edict of last summer. Now, I felt they might have been a bit too zealous, but— What is this fellow still doing here? Didn't we find him guilty?"

"Not yet," Dictys assured him. "You haven't asked the jury. But that's all right. I'm in no hurry."

"Well, I am." The monarch spread his hands out at his eager people. "Guilty, eh?"

"Oh, sure!"

"Guilty ten times over!"

"His crimes show in his face, every one of them!"

"Hooray for Just King Polydectes!"

Just King Polydectes beamed. "Thank you, my friends, thank you. Now, as for the sentencing—"

Percy leaped to his feet. "What kind of a trial is this anyway?" he raged. "You might give a man a chance for his life!"

King Polydectes shook his head in amazement. He leaned forward to stare at Percy closely, almost squashing a feminine footstool who had just begun to stretch. He was as large as his brother but, since his waist competed burstingly with his height, the effect was overpowering. Also, while most of the people on the island—male and female—seemed to dress in a negligent sheepskin or sagging loincloth, the two royal brothers wore richly dyed woolen garments, and the king sported what must once have been a clean tunic of the finest linen.

"I don't know what's upset you, young fellow, but you've had all the chance for your life that the laws of Seriphos allow. Now, why don't you be quiet about it and take your punishment like a man?"

"Listen, please listen!" Percy begged. "Not only am I not a citizen of Seriphos, but I'm not even a citizen of this world. All I want is the chance of finding a way back, practically anything that—"

"That's the whole point," the king explained. "Our laws are not made for citizens—at least not the ones about cooking over a slow fire. Citizens who go wrong get thrown off cliffs or strangled outside the walls at high noon, things like that. Only non-citizens get punished this way. This is how I keep my people happy to be under my rule. Now do you understand? Let's not have any more trouble, huh? Let's be grown-up about paying the penalty for our crimes."

Percy grabbed at his hair, pulled out an exasperated clump, and jumped on it. "Look, the way this whole thing started—I won't begin with Mrs. Danner—it's impossible, insane to stand here and watch what— Just a minute." He took a deep breath, conscious of the necessity to remain calm, to be very, very persuasive—to be, above all, *reasonable*. "There was a slight misunderstanding when I met your brother. A sea serpent—" he paused for a moment, took a deep breath and went on "—an honest-to-gosh real sea serpent came up to me in my—in my floating chest and welcomed me as the son of Danae. So when I was asked by Dictys who I was—"

"You needn't go on," Polydectes advised him. "The testimony of a sea serpent is not admissible evidence."

"I was not talking—"

"What I mean is, it's not admissible evidence from the sea serpent himself. So it certainly is not admissible when you repeat it to us."

"All I was trying to say—"

"Of course," the king stuck out his lower lip and nodded his head thoughtfully, "if it was a land serpent, it might be a little different matter."

Percy paused in the midst of a frantic peroration, intrigued in spite of himself. "It would?" he asked curiously.

"Certainly. Depending on the exact type of land serpent. The oracular type, now, we'd certainly listen to what a pythoness has to say with a good deal of respect. Or the very intelligent and friendly walking kind the legends tell about. But none of this applies to you. You're charged with impersonating Perseus and circulating the impression that you have the courage to kill the Gorgon. For such a crime, a sea serpent is no good as a character witness. Besides, you've already been found guilty."

"I'm not even arguing with the idea that—"

"Dictys," the king said with a gesture of infinite weariness. "Rule him out of order."

An enormous fist came down on the top of Perseus's head. He felt as if his brains had been rammed down his nostrils. When he could see clearly again through the reddish haze, he was grabbing at the floor, which seemed to be curling away from him.

"I don't see why we can't have two executions the same day," Dictys was saying angrily. "Both of these men claimed to be Perseus. As you said, we're having a regular rash of this impersonation lately. Well, a good way to discourage it would be a slam-bang double cooking. A sort of two-course execution. All you have to do is pass sentence on him now, let me attend to details like getting a slave to clean the pot between acts, and—"

"Who's king around here, me or you?" Polydectes roared.

"Oh, you are, you are. But—"

"No buts. You're just a grand duke, and don't you forget it, Dictys. Now, I say we'll have just one execution tonight, the man who was caught first. Then tomorrow, we'll have this man in for an official sentencing. It'll give me another excuse to have a throne-room reception, which I like, and will insure that we'll all have something to keep us cheerful on another night."

"All right," Dictys said morosely. "But how many times does it happen that we get two stew-jobs on the same day?"

"All the more reason for spreading them out over a period of time," the king insisted. "Guards, take this man away! You see, Dictys, the way I feel about it is—waste not, want not."

And that, Percy thought bitterly as two huskies with hands like iron claws began dragging him out of the pillared chamber, that's why they call him Philosophical King Polydectes!

At the end of the hall, a grate was abruptly lifted from the floor, and he was dropped into the hole like a handful of garbage. The hole was deep enough to knock him out again.

He managed to roll over on his back after a while, nursing his bruises with aching arms. Whatever else was the matter with it—and that came to a good deal!—this was certainly the least gentle of possible worlds.

There was a little light slanting in from the grate. He started to stagger over to it, to get a somewhat better idea of his cell. Something hit him in the stomach, and he sat down again.

"You just try that again, mister," a girl's soft voice told him in definite accents, "and I'll really wreck you."

"I beg your pardon?" Percy asked the dead gloom stupidly.

"Don't worry about my pardon. You just stay on your side of the cell, and I'll stay on mine. I've had all I want or am going to take of loose-fingered guys who want to find out how much of what a girl has where and don't think twice of finding out right away. I never saw such a place!" Her voice had been riding up the scale with every word; when she came to the last one, she began crying.

After thinking the matter over carefully, Percy started to crawl in the direction of the sobs. "See here…" he began gently.

This time she hit him in the eye.

Cursing more fluently than he had ever known he could, he moved to the opposite wall and sat down against it with sternly folded arms. After a while, however, the bitterness got to be too much for silence. He began by cursing the entire human race, limited it to women in general and, after a nod at the girl across from him, he concentrated on Mrs. Danner. He put so much feeling into the business that his maledictions became surprisingly expert, almost worthy of an ecclesiastical body discussing one of their number.

He suddenly felt the girl's wet face nuzzling against his shoulder. He leaped into the corner. "Let me tell you, lady," he almost spat out, "that I don't want to touch you any more than—"

"You just mentioned Mrs. Danner's name," she said. "I heard you. Apartment 18-K?"

"Right! But how…" Slowly the answer dawned on him. "Oh, you're an alumnus, too!"

"I'll kill that woman!" she said through clenched teeth. "The first day I was here, I said I'd beat every dollar bill and every shot of whiskey that she enjoyed on my money out of her if I ever got back. The second day, I said if I only got back, I wouldn't pay any attention to her, I'd be so busy kissing things like city sidewalks and big six-foot cops and plumbing equipment. The third day, I didn't think of her at all, I was so busy trying to remember what it was like in the city. But today, I know I'm not going back, not ever, so all I do is pray that somehow I will figure out a way of killing her, that somehow—"

She began crying again, great gusty sobs that sounded as if her shoulders were being torn out of place.

Very, very gingerly, the young man returned to her side and patted her on the back. After a while, he took her in his arms and caressed her face gently. Some terribly rough garment she was wearing irritated his own scratched skin.

"It could be worse," he assured her, although privately he wondered what miracle would be necessary to achieve that state. "It could be a lot worse, believe me. Meanwhile, we've found each other. Things won't be nearly so bad with someone to talk to. We're compatriots or comtimeriots or something. My name's Percy S. Yuss. The 'S' stands for Sactrist. I used to own half of a restaurant that our creditors owned two-thirds of. Who are you?"

"Anita Drummond," she said, straightening with a slightly self-conscious giggle and wiping her eyes with her peculiar dress. "Ann. I used to be a ballet dancer. Or, rather, I was still studying to be one, getting a little work here and there. That apartment was a godsend. It just fitted my budget. I plumped myself down in the one chair the place had and gloried in a home at last! Then I notice a piece of parchment on the floor with some poetry on it. I started to read it, stopped, and then began to doze with my eyes on the words. When I woke, I was halfway up a plowed hillside, the chair didn't have any legs, and some old peasant and his wife were saying spells over me to make me vanish before I put a charm on their crops. As soon as they saw me open my eyes, they both jumped on my head, tied me down, and carried me into their hut. And they wouldn't listen to a word I had to say! Uh—by the way, if you want to—to be a little more presentable, there's a pile of castoff clothes in that corner there."

Percy ambled over and found a half-dozen badly worn sheepskin tunics. He selected one which smelled strongly but seemed to have fewer inhabitants than the others, and came back. Somehow, wearing clothes again helped restore his confidence. He hadn't had much opportunity to think about the various aspects of nudism since his arrival *sans* wardrobe in this thoroughly mad world, but he felt for the first time that there was a possibility of outwitting his captors now that he was dressed almost as well as they.

Ann continued her story. She was describing how all the inhabitants of a village on the far side of the island had been called into a conference on methods of disposing of the witch.

"There was a real tug-of-war going on between the drive-a-stake-into-her-and-be-done-with-it school and the burn-her-and-then-only-then-can-you-be-sure faction, when a seneschal or chamberlain or whatever he was of King Polydectes's court happened to pass by. He was out hunting some small monsters. Furies, I think. Or perhaps they were Sirens. He saw me, and before any of the village could say anything, he— Percy, look!"

He jerked his head around to follow her pointing finger. Dusk had been sliding down over the grating at a steeper and steeper incline. There was little more than the most delicate of rosy glows from a sun which had done more than its share of shining and wanted only to rest.

There was a man's head on the other side of the grating. His fingers pressed hard upon his lips. Percy nodded to show that he understood. Slowly the man faded, like smoke dissipating under a gentle summer breeze. Then he was gone.

But the grate lifted slowly, silently, and closed again in a moment. Percy had the eerie sensation of something very heavy that was floating down in the lazy circles that a feather would assume. Without thinking about it, he covered Ann's mouth with his own hand. Even so, her gasp was almost audible when, abruptly, a man wearing a suit vaguely reminiscent of renaissance Italy appeared before them.

He made an adjustment on the extremely thick metal-studded belt he wore, gave them the slightest inclination of his head by way of greeting, and said: "My name is Hermes."

Ann removed Percy's hand from her mouth. "Hermes!" she whispered. "The messenger of the gods!"

"Exactly."

The smile came and went so fast on that aristocratic face that Percy was not quite sure it had ever been. He stared closely at the man's visible skin in the almost non-existent light. It looked golden. "Weren't you the fellow in the white mantle who disappeared when Dictys began asking you questions?"

Hermes nodded. "I suspected who you were, but I had to check on the so-called chest before I could be sure. I could hardly ask you questions while you were surrounded by that mob."

"What questions?" Percy asked eagerly.

"Questions which would determine whether you were the rightful Perseus, the legendary hero who is to save the world from the Gorgon race."

"Look, mister, that stuff has me in enough hot water already! My name is Percy S. Yuss. I am not the son of Danae—we never even had a Daniel in the family anywhere. I don't know this Gorgon everyone keeps raving about all the time and, if I did, I certainly wouldn't feel like killing her. I have nothing against any Gorgon, or any man—except for that fat old slob of king—"

"You're speaking too loudly," the other warned. "It's not any Gorgon we sent you against—it's Medusa herself!" His voice dropped almost to inaudibility at the name. "I spoke to Professor Gray and described the articles with which you had arrived, and he agreed that you must be a man of his own time."

"You mean there's someone else here from the twentieth century?" Ann asked eagerly.

"Where is he? In trouble, too?" Percy inquired. He was slightly bitter.

The stranger smiled. This one was long and slow, and Percy decided be didn't like it any better than the fast take. "No, he's not in trouble. He's waiting for you to give you advice on how best to conquer the Gorgon."

"Well, he'll have to run pretty far and awfully fast. I don't like the way everyone jumps when they mention that character. I don't feel like a hero, and I don't intend to be one. I've been a sucker all my life, always taking somebody else's falls, but this is one that my mother's favorite son is not going to take."

"Not even to avoid the stew-pot tomorrow?"

Percy swallowed. He'd forgotten the trial according to the laws of Seriphos since he had met Ann. Yes. There'd be another evening like this one, and then he'd be led out—

Could any risk he'd run be greater than the horrible certainty he faced in twenty-four hours? He'd seen enough of these ancient Greeks to have developed a very healthy respect for their deadly efficiency in the prosecution of what they considered to be criminal cases. It was very doubtful, for example, that these people had developed the institution of appeal, or parole...

"Not even," Hermes went on, picking each word up carefully with his teeth and holding it out for them to see, "not even for the chance to return to your own time?"

Ann squealed, and the messenger of the gods sternly told her to be quiet. He jerked at his belt, went invisible. After a while, he turned back on. When he rematerialized, he was staring anxiously up at the grating, one hand poised over his belt.

It struck Percy that this fellow was pretty nervous for a supposed deity. It also struck him that he was being offered just what he needed immediately and most desperately wanted. Did the price he had to pay sound too high? That was silly. Whatever he had to do would be worth the risk and difficulty, if somehow he could find himself back in his own era. Not to mention the desirable aspects of getting out of his present surroundings before supper-time tomorrow.

"I'll do it," he said finally. "Whatever it is you want done, I'll do it. Only listen. Any bargain I made applies to this girl as well as to me."

"Done!" The golden one held out a thin pouch. "Take this. When they lead you to execution tomorrow—"

"Hey! I thought you were going to get us out of this jam. Why can't you just take us with you?"

Hermes shook his head violently. He seemed to be extremely interested in moving on as soon as possible. "Because I can't. You don't have the—the powers. Do what I tell you, and you'll be all right."

"Listen to him, Percy!" Ann urged. "This is our only chance. Let's do it his way. Besides, he's a god. He must know his way around this mythological world."

Again Hermes smiled that quick-flitting smile. "When they take you out, make a long speech—as long as you can—about how sorry they are going to be. Whatever it is they're going to have you fight—"

"I'm not going to fight anything," Percy insisted. "I'm going to be—"

"Cooked over a slow fire. I know! But believe me, trust me, you will be led out to fight somebody or something. You make your speech and while you're talking, without anyone seeing you, you dip your hand under your garment and into this pouch. Start fondling the kernels you find there, squeeze them, rub them back and forth between the palm of your hand and the fabric of the pouch. When they start to squirm and move about of their own, get sent in, and start fighting as soon as possible! All you do then is to scatter them on the ground all around you—and stand back! Get back as far as—"

He stopped and ripped at the switch on his belt. A torch appeared on the other side of the grating and two heavily whiskered men peered in.

"Could have sworn I saw something," one of them said.

"Well, you can call the guard out and go down to look into it," the other one announced. "Me for the party."

The torchbearer straightened. "Me, too. If I saw what I thought I did, I don't want to look into it! Let the morning watch do it."

Out of the darkness came the pouch and pushed itself into Percy's hand. "Remember," they heard the whisper ascending slowly. "Don't start rubbing those kernels too early—and don't wait too long either. Once they begin moving, you've got to get into the fight fast."

The grate lifted briefly, came down again. There was a final whispered injunction: "And don't look into the pouch tonight! Don't even think of touching it until just before you have to!"

They felt a presence departing stealthily above them. Ann moved closer to Percy, and he squeezed her reassuringly.

"A big list of don'ts," he grumbled. "Time it just right, but don't try to find out what it is! It's like taking a Frenchman up to a row of medicine bottles labeled in Chinese and warning him to take some aspirin before his fever goes up any further, but not to touch the sleeping tablets because they're strong enough to kill him. What does he think I am?"

Ann leaned on him, chuckling with a slight edge of hysteria. "Do you know, Percy, this is the first, absolutely the first ray of hope I've seen since coming to this awful world? And you're grumbling because the directions aren't so clear!"

"Well, after all," his mind said logically—but privately!—"I'm the one who's going to have to fight the Gorgon!"

"I'm not really complaining," he said aloud as they sat down. "But confused directions irritate me. I always feel I'm being taken for a ride."

"Think of sitting in a restaurant," she murmured dreamily. "Or a hairdresser's. Think of going to those chic little dress shops along the Avenue and feeling all those wonderful fabrics and imagining yourself in all those lovely new styles. And all the time making believe that you're really fooling the sales girl into believing you have enough money to buy them. And any time a man you don't like makes a pass at you, you can make him stop. And if he doesn't stop, you yell, and when you yell, you get help instead of him. Oh, civilization, *civilization!*"

She was asleep in his arms. Percy patted her tenderly and prepared to go to sleep himself. He'd had a long, tiring day. Long? Just three thousand years or so!

Unfortunately, he hadn't fallen completely asleep when the execution started. Being underground somewhat and a good distance away, he couldn't see very much. But a good deal of the noise carried....

It was quite a few hours before he finally dozed off and stopped thinking about the man who had come charging down a hillside insisting he was Perseus. How many Perseuses were there in this world? It looked almost as if someone wanted the Gorgon killed very badly indeed and was sending in a good many pinch-hitters.

Who was the real Perseus? He didn't know, but it struck him then that he did know he wasn't. And he was the only one committed so far to killing the Gorgon. What, exactly, was the Gorgon? That was another good question....

Their cell had a third occupant by morning. Agesilaus.

"What did you do?" Percy asked him as he stretched painfully.

"Nothing," the old man said. He sat against the wall hunting for lice in his beard. Every time he caught one, he grinned and cracked it noisily between his teeth. "I'm here because of my brother."

"What do you mean because of your brother?"

"He committed high treason last night and had his brains knocked out according to the law the king made up a few minutes after he committed it. The king was still pretty sore, though, so he passed another law making all blood relatives co-responsible in cases of high treason. I was the only blood relative, so here I am. I'm due to get my brains knocked out today."

"Good old 'waste not, want not' Polydectes," Percy mused. "What kind of high treason did your brother commit that the king had to pass a law covering it?"

Agesilaus pored through the bottom tattered fringes of his beard. From the obvious disappointment with which he put them aside, it was clear that he considered them devoid of life. "Well, sir, my brother was the royal chef. So of course he was also the public executioner. Somewhere along the line, he must have made a mistake last night. He probably forgot to grease it properly. Because after the execution, the great cooking pot cracked."

"Cracked? You mean they can't use it any more?"

"That's just what I do mean. Broke open like a nut. Ah, you can smile, but let me tell you—that pot was the pride of Seriphos! It wasn't made of bronze or silver or gold, but—and I don't ask you to believe this—of pure *iron!* Yes, sir, this whole island wouldn't be wealthy enough to buy another pot like that. Years and years it took, in my great-grandfather's day, melting down those little meteors that our people had been collecting for generations. And at that they say it was one of the walking reptiles that finally did the casting. Do you blame King Polydectes for getting mad at my brother and all his kith and kin? I don't. Why, his predecessor, King Aurion—the one Polydectes stabbed in the back at the feast of the summer solstice—Aurion would have extended the penalties to relatives by marriage and most of the criminal's close friends."

Percy sat musing on Hermes's prediction of the night before. In all probability, it was not so much an example of accurate prophecy as a clear case of sabotage. He chuckled. Well, at least that particular fear was no longer to be lived with!

"What were these walking reptiles?" Ann asked. She'd been sitting quietly by Percy's side all through his interrogation of the old man, and had pressed his hand when he chuckled to show that she too was hoping that the rest of Hermes's promises would be realized.

"That's a hard question to answer," Agesilaus said slowly. "They must have died off completely forty, fifty years ago. In my great-grandfather's day, there were very few of them left, and they got fewer all the time. They were like the pythonesses who work with the oracles or some of the friendlier sea serpents. But they were smarter than any of them. And they had legs—some say they even had arms—and they walked about and performed wonders. Taught us how to make pottery, my grandfather told me, and how to—"

"Hey, Agesilaus!"

They all looked up to see the rope ladder come twirling down into the cell. The burly man at the top gestured impatiently to the new arrival. "Time for boom-boom. Hurry up, will you? There's going to be a bull-baiting this afternoon, and we have to clear up the arena."

"Their lives are certainly one mad round of pleasure," Ann said bitterly to Percy. "Something doing all the time!"

"Don't misunderstand us," the old man pleaded as he began to mount the ladder. "We have entirely too many people on this island, and there haven't been any wars or serious pestilences for over two generations now. What better way to cut down our numbers than by interesting executions? Polydectes calls this 'Population Control with a Smile.' "

"He would," Percy muttered. "That's why we call him Humorous King Polydectes."

Later he was ordered up the rope ladder in his turn and sentenced to combat in the theater with such monsters as would be made available by the zoo superintendent. Polydectes was evidently too morose to develop much interest even in the throne-room reception which a sentencing made inevitable. He lounged sideways on his concubine-infested seat, scowling at the wall, while a court official lackadaisically informed Percy of what he was to expect.

He was sitting thoughtfully in the execution antechamber touching the pouch under his sheepskin tunic from time to time, when Ann was hurled in.

"Monster bait, too," she nodded at him. "They're going to send us in together. Let us hope and pray that Hermes knows what he's talking about."

"How come you're under sentence, too? What did you do? Not that you can't be tossed into Condemned Row for just making the serious error of being alive."

"Well, you see, I was brought here originally from the other side of the island to become a part of Polydectes's harem."

"How did you get out of that?"

"I didn't get out of it. I'm afraid I just didn't make the grade. The king said I wasn't pneumatic enough. Although," she added with a vicious snap of her teeth, "I still think it was that jealous cat Tontibbi that poisoned his mind against me. Oh no, you don't have to look so startled, Percy," she laughed. "I didn't want to be a member of that harem at all. But it kind of hurts a girl's feelings to be told she's not good enough, when she sees all kinds of fat and sloppy creatures positively infesting the place!" She curled up beside him, still fuming.

In the late afternoon, they were given a handful of dried fruits and, while they were still munching this highly uninteresting supper, were ordered out for execution.

Percy was intrigued to see Ann for the first time in daylight. He noted with approving interest that she was one of those rare and perfect blondes whose skin is so magnificently clear as to neutralize the brightness of her hair into an overall glow of fairness which yet leaves rich hints of darker tones and deeper wells of personality beneath.

They clasped hands as they marched along a constantly curving lane that meandered around the hill on the far side of the citadel. It came eventually to a collection of stone buildings that was obviously the zoo. They were hurried past this, both of them quite happy to be moving fast after a hurried glimpse of what the cages contained. They found themselves in a small valley formed by several tiny hills.

There were seats carved out of the soil of the hills; most of these were already filled. Percy was almost certain he saw Hermes in one of the seats. At the bottom of the valley, an area had been surrounded by a high stone wall. There were ponderous gates on either side.

Ann and Percy were alternately pushed and led to one of these gates, which was tended by a pair of jumpy youths who held it slightly ajar. Percy nervously reached for the hidden pouch. Everyone was waiting for the king.

He arrived finally, accompanied by his twittering retinue. "Let the punishment proceed," he said in a flat, tired voice. It was evident that he expected little of life, now that the execution pot was gone.

Percy dipped his left hand into the pouch as a green-coated bronze sword was shoved into his right. The two boys started to pull the gates back. "I think you'd better start," Ann whispered.

He nodded. "O mighty King Polydectes of Seriphos!" he howled so suddenly that one of the youths dropped his door-ring and turned to run. The Captain of the Guard pushed him back sternly. "I beg and implore you to grant me one last favor." The *kernels* were disagreeably soft to the touch.

Polydectes waved a hand unhappily. "If it's reasonable. And if you can tell me in just a few more or less well chosen words." He leaned back irritably.

Grinding the soft little bits slowly between his fingers and against the fabric of the pouch, Percy wondered how, where to begin. Suddenly he smiled.

"You are probably wondering whether what happened to your execution pot yesterday was an accident, or whether some discontented subject was responsible for destroying the glory of Seriphos. I alone know the answer, and my request hinges on that."

"He's hooked!" Ann whispered delightedly. "Perfect, Percy, perfect!" A buzz of excitement had ripped up and down the theater's earthen rows.

"Well," the young man went on, massaging and squeezing inside the pouch as if he were a prizefighter trying to build up the powers of his fist, "let us examine what probably happened in terms of the basic function of the pot—cooking. What do we know of the effects of previous ingredients upon the structure of the pot? Do we know anything?"

The king looked confused and anxious at the same time, as if he felt that Percy had made a very important point but didn't know precisely what he had made it out of. Even the guards who surrounded them had the half-thrilled, half-frightened appearance of men who believe they stand on the brink of tremendous revelation. Percy was not quite certain whether he had felt a ripple of life on his fingertips; he decided, after a moment of waiting, that he hadn't, and continued rolling *non sequiturs:*

"Well, first of all we have sandwiches. On the menu, made to order and to go. We have various kinds of cheese sandwiches. Grilled cheese, cheese and tomato, cheese and bacon, cheese and ham. We can grill them together or separately."

He stopped as he felt a few of the tiny little lumps begin to curl around his fingers.

"If what you're trying to tell me," the king said slowly and intently, "is that my people have been illegally using the state execution pot for grilling cheese and bacon—"

"I'm not trying to tell you anything," Percy said curtly. "Let's get on with the execution."

"No, listen, son," Polydectes said warmly, "you were making sense. It was a little hard to follow, but you had a good solid point there. Somewhere, anyway. Please go on."

"Yes, do go on," one of the spectators called out. "I can understand you."

"There's nothing to understand!" He was feeling desperate. The *kernels* were leaping about in the pouch like tiny frogs frightened out of their pond. "I have nothing to tell you. I made everything up. I just wanted a delay. Now will you go on with the execution?"

"We will not!" the king said portentously. "You're trying to protect somebody. Somebody important."

The little writhing bits were now grouped at the mouth of the pouch, burrowing out to freedom. Percy looked at Ann's anxious face, saw that she understood his predicament but had no way to help him.

"Listen, Polydectes," he said hoarsely. "Why don't you give the throne to someone who's deserved it from away back? Tontibbi would make a better ruler several times over. Not only is she smarter than you, not only does she know more about civilized living, but she also—"

"Open those gates," roared Purple King Polydectes, "and throw him to the beast!"

The great portals creaked back. Ann and Percy were pushed out into the enormous sweep of stone floor. Ann managed to keep her balance, but Percy, thrown off by the arm he had been keeping under his tunic where the pouch lay against his breast, staggered forward unable to lift his head and regain his equilibrium. He tripped and came crashing down on one hand and one knee, his sword ringing on the flagstone as it spun out of his grip.

He heard Ann scream in disbelief and looked up. Racing toward them from the other gate was something that belonged on an insane artist's drawing board and nowhere else.

Waist-high it was, but over twelve feet wide, a weirdly fused conglomeration of canine, lupine, reptile, human, and something else, something, Percy immediately felt, that this planet had never bred. The thing ran on the bodies of snakes, lizards, dogs, and wolves, all of them seemingly independent living entities and all of them nonetheless joined to the main body by thick trunk-like appendages which took the place of their hind ends. Six distinct heads the thing had, each of them, including the human one, with dripping jaw thrown wide open and screaming an unrecognizable counterpoint to each other.

It was moving terribly fast. Percy leaped to his feet and, withdrawing the handful of writhing lumps from the pouch, darted toward the terrified girl.

He pulled her behind him before making his throw. A gaping crocodile mouth which had been wavering toward them was abruptly withdrawn as one of the bits fell upon it. Percy managed to throw them in a rough semi-circle, then, pushing Ann ahead, stumbling, bouncing against her and running in crazy zigzags because of the looks he kept throwing over his shoulder, he made it to the opposite wall.

They stood awed at the destruction they had let loose.

The little lumps had been kernels all right. But of such plants as only the most unholy gardener could have sown!

Wherever the seeds touched a surface, they grew—grew luxuriantly! And in a matter of seconds had put forth on their sickly white stems elephant-sized white flowers covered with irregular purple blobs. Their roots tore into and through the surface contacted like streams of flood water irresistibly seeking their way. Tremendously hungry the roots had to be to support such fantastic growth in the rest of the plant, and tremendously hungry they were. Whatever they touched died on the spot— flesh grew bloodless, normal plants turned yellow with sudden age and lack of chlorophyll, the very stone flaked and crumbled into fine dust under the probing requisitions of the sprouting root hairs.

They grew, these seeds, with the maintained momentum and direction in which Percy had thrown them. They reproduced by means of single new seeds virtually expectorated ahead by each fruitful flower.

The monster, which had turned to run, was engulfed in mid-stride and dropped in a moment—a pallid husk. The walls of the stadium, too—those on the side at which Percy had thrown the seeds—were powdered ruins in a moment.

And the entire audience, after a horrified moment of half-understanding, had risen and fled before this botanical juggernaut.

They could have stayed. It hardly reached the top rows.

Almost, it seemed, a moment after it had started to live, it became moribund. It was as if, tremendously hungry of life, it could find in this place or this world no life on which to feed, nothing whose constitution was what it needed to sustain itself. By the time that the forward blossoms were pluming open among the rapidly emptied seats, their ancestors of seconds ago on the stadium floor had turned a brittle black and begun to fall apart.

In a few minutes, except for the transparent outline of the monster lying near the dissolved gate which it had been vainly trying to regain, and the completely disintegrated length of wall over which the blossoms had passed, there was no sign of the weapon which Hermes had given Percy. A thin gray fog wandered away blindly—and that was all.

There was the abrupt sound of heels striking the ground. They turned. Hermes appeared, a slightly mocking smile on his expertly carved face.

"Well?" he asked. "Was that satisfactorily efficient, Perseus?"

"My name is Percy," the young man told him shortly. "And with that kind of power, I don't see why you don't go after the Gorgon yourself."

"Your name, for the duration of this bargain, my friend, is Perseus as far as the Olympians are concerned. With regard to power," he shrugged, "there are many different kinds. Some so old that they can be conquered only at the cost of universal destruction. Some so new," he smiled brilliantly at the two of them, "that their scope cannot as yet even be estimated. And there is the power of a legend which says a truth that must be fulfilled before the days of a world can further unwind." He nodded, in what seemed to be a prodigious self-satisfaction. "Now, if you two would kindly clasp my waist from either side, we can go on."

The thought occurred to Percy that he was remarkably cool and chipper away from the dungeons of King Polydectes. The touch of aristocratic insolence in his manner was much deeper now than it had been the previous night, when he had broken it frequently to gnaw a nervous lip at the grating above. With weapons such as he had at his disposal, why should he worry about the soldiers of a monarch as petty as Polydectes?

Could it be because the weapons were very limited in quantity and could be used only for emergencies—or to make such important bargains with people like himself as the Olympians deemed necessary? And why was it necessary to make bargains with a master hash-slinger like Percy S. Yuss? For all of Hermes's chatter about different kinds of power, it still seemed much more logical for the Olympians to knock off Medusa themselves than to provide an ordinary human with the weapons to do it.

If they could provide the weapons to do it. If they could...

He shook his head in bewilderment and grabbed Hermes's waist as Ann had already done, his arms overlapping hers. The golden one flexed his shoulders for a moment, then touched the belt lightly.

They rose, not abruptly, but with the steady insistence of a warm updraft. At two or three hundred feet, Hermes made another adjustment and began skimming south at a fair rate of speed. It wasn't difficult to maintain a grip and, since the late day was extremely mellow, this particular kind of flight was very enjoyable. Percy and Ann smiled, "Fun, isn't it?" at each other.

"This is some kind of antigravity belt, isn't it?" Percy asked.

Hermes gave him a brief, cold glance. "Don't ask such questions!" he said with the insulting emphasis of an order. He flexed his shoulders again and stared straight ahead.

Percy bit his lip. He definitely didn't like this character....

They came down on a little peninsula on the southern tip of Seriphos. There, beside a long rock-like shelf that overhung the sea, was a small and neat hut built of driftwood. After separating themselves from Hermes, the two stood uncertainly on the path for a moment.

"Professor Gray," called out the golden man. "Your fellow tourists!"

A highly energetic little old man dressed in a gray flannel suit came prancing out of the hut. "Hello, hello!" he said chirpingly. "Come inside, please do. I've been waiting quite a while for you, young fellow. Thank you very much, Hermes. You'll be back tomorrow?"

"If we can get the boots working right." The messenger shot up and away at several times the speed he had used in bringing them there.

Professor Gray took a hand of each and hauled them into his hut. "Now, sit down and make yourselves comfortable. Dinner will be ready in a moment." He indicated a full-bellied pot bubbling in the fireplace. Percy, remembering another such pot and noticing the resemblance in all but size, smiled wryly.

"What is it?" the other man asked. Despite his age, he had the quick gestures of a highly nervous sparrow. "What are you brooding about? You must tell me all your adventures, both of you."

So they did. All through dinner.

"I'm sorry. Truly sorry." Professor Gray had his hands shoved deeply into his pockets. "I had no idea—no idea at all—that my little experiment would be dragging fellow humans into such misery. My deepest apologies to both of you, especially the young lady," he asserted self-consciously. "And I certainly didn't intend to present Mrs. Danner with the equivalent of a lifetime pension."

"What little experiment?" Percy asked curiously.

"You mean to tell us that you were the first one through?" Ann asked, her eyes very wide.

"I'm afraid I mean just that." The little man walked bouncingly up and down the length of the small hut. "You see, when I retired as Head of the Classics Department at the University, I rented that apartment as a sort of laboratory. I felt it was the place where I might try some experiments with my theories of subjective time-travel, theories based more upon the ancient Greek philosophers than on our modern mathematicians. There, I thought I'd be alone, safe at least from ridicule. The only thing I didn't anticipate quite so early was my success! Simply because it is a period about which little is known by our archaeologists, I fixed my psyche during the experiment upon the time of the *older heroes,* so called. For the purpose, I used a poem by Pindar, written nine centuries after the period in which I was interested. I copied an English translation of the poem on a piece of sheepskin, to create greater subjective verisimilitude. I didn't have any warning, either, the day I sat down to try just another experiment in mental control of time."

He grinned at them, gestured with both palms. "Much to my surprise, I—well, I fell in! I was more fortunate than either of you, in that I had a plentiful supply of silver and copper coins when I arrived in the southern, less densely populated half of the island. It was inevitable that I should arrive in Seriphos, by the way, because of the poem celebrating Perseus's return here after he had acquired the Gorgon's head that I had used as a psychic time-travel tie. I was able to develop a reputation as a kind of beneficent local wizard through my knowledge of the people and the time. And I've done fairly well for a scholar, most of whose adult life has been spent in other places than the press and scramble of business: I own this hut and a substantial tract of productive land. By the standards of this community, I am quite a wealthy man.

"But there is my greatest compensation here—the close, on-the-spot study of a period which has always fascinated me. I place it, by the way, somewhere between the end of the Mycenaean and the beginning of the Achaean eras of Greek history. Roughly 1400 BC. It was a remarkable time in that, while superstition flourished, religion—important both before and after this period—was almost nonexistent. Some scholars even claim—"

"Pardon me, sir," Percy broke in, "but how did we come to follow you?"

"I think the answer is obvious. The parchment, containing the English translation of the poem which served me as a kind of target, was still in the apartment. So, therefore, was my subjective aura. And there had also been created what might be called a psycho-chronological hole in the place through which I had fallen. You young people were unfortunate enough to read the poem under these conditions and therefore followed me, arriving more or less in my neighborhood, depending on personality differences in relation to the psycho-chronological hole. I think the apartment should be fairly safe now, since Percy had the parchment in his hand when he arrived and dropped it in the Aegean Sea."

"And here we are," Percy mused, "in the world of Greek mythology."

Professor Gray shook his head emphatically. "I beg your pardon, but we most definitely are not. There never was such a place! It's entirely a world in Man's imagination. You are in a time that is to give rise to what we call Greek mythology. The actual events in this era will be the religion and mythos of the next. What form exactly they will take, I cannot say, since this is not our world nor our universe."

"What do you mean?" Percy's question was fringed with sudden panic.

"I mean that you aren't in the past at all. You are in the future, uncountable eons in the future! This is the formative period of Greek mythology on another Earth, in a space-time universe which came into being only after our own grew senile and died. Much the same things are happening to it and on it as happened to our own planet, but since it is not the same Earth, the results tend to be more and more different."

"The—the future?" Ann shook her head as if to clear it of accumulating webs. "Another space-time universe?"

"Is it really so hard to understand or believe? It isn't possible to travel backwards in time, only ahead of one's era. The past, having died, is dead forever: only the future is constantly unrolling. Since I buried myself into this particular period which, being in the past, had ceased to exist, I inevitably materialized in a parallel period in the succeeding cosmos. The ancient philosopher Anaximander of Miletus was one of the first to discuss the concept of an *Indefinite-Infinite* from which all things were drawn, including primordial atoms and planetary systems, super-galaxies and even time-streams. There is birth and death in all things, said Anaximander, and they perish into those from which they have been born. Thus there were Earths in space-time universes which existed long before our own, and barring unexpected developments in Anaximander's Indefinite-Infinite, there will be Earths in many, many succeeding space-time universes."

"And in each one," Percy muttered slowly as he began to understand, "in each one, another Perseus."

"Right!" Professor Gray beamed. "Except that he does not necessarily do the same things in the same way each time. But enough of this metaphysics! You young people are exhausted: suppose I show you to your beds. You begin a training program tomorrow, Percy—you, especially, will need your sleep."

He led Ann up a ladder into a narrow bedroom in the loft which, after her recent accommodations, she found magnificent. Percy and he bedded down near the fireplace on a soft pile of skins.

"Look, professor," Percy asked as the older man extinguished the torch, "if this isn't a world of actual mythology, then those babies aren't really gods and monsters. Yet, I saw a monster in the arena which I'd like to forget for the sake of my dreams, and I can remember other things which are even harder to explain."

"Of course. And if that thing—it was a scylla, by the way—had caught you— But while they are real, painfully so, they don't come from our universe at all."

"How's that?"

"There are universes which adjoin ours in the plenum. Every possible type of universe exists parallel with ours. Many of them have Earth-type planets and Sol-type suns positioned in their space to correspond with ours. Well, it happens that the subspatial fabric separating these universes from each other is understandably weak in their youth and grows progressively stronger as the ages pass. At one time, there was probably a constant exchange and pilgrimage of individuals taking place from one universe's 'Earth' to another. Right now, it is down in all probability to the barest of trickles as the subspatial fabric has solidified and lets little through in any place. In a little while, it will have closed or clotted completely, and all that will be left will be the memories of strange unearthly creatures to generate beautiful legends and peculiar superstitions."

Percy grunted as he chewed into the strange texture of this information. "Then the gods aren't gods at all, I guess, but what I heard one of the men who captured me call them: Olympian monsters."

"Well, yes. Monsters, in the sense that they are nonhuman intrinsically, since they evolved on a different world. But, Percy, they are very like us in so many ways! They are much more advanced scientifically at this point than is our race, and they can't be as confusingly horrible in their thought processes—no matter how bad they might get!—as—well, the Gorgon race for example. These creatures are humanoid: they therefore must come from a world and universe whose natural laws are very much like our own, and they are very much interested in helping humanity advance to their level. The people of this time call them Olympian monsters, by the way, because in our world they originate upon Mount Olympus in Northern Thessaly.

"I owe the one called Hermes a good deal: if it hadn't been for his help, I wouldn't have nearly a third of the wealth and knowledge I do. He sought me out shortly after I arrived and insisted on doing all sorts of useful little favors. I'll admit to feeling the same sort of distrust for a while which, I can see, you are experiencing. But believe me, it will be washed away by the fellow's ubiquitous friendliness! I just can't understand why later myths gave him the character of a mischievous schemer! Of course, it's entirely possible that the myths which will evolve in this world will be greatly different from the ones in our own." He nodded to himself gravely, with his head cocked at an angle, as if he were enviously imagining the kind of Greek myth with which some future Professor of Classics should have to deal.

"The Gorgon race is pretty bad in comparison, huh? If I'm going to chase over to—to—"

"Crete. Their headquarters is on the island of Crete."

"Well, can you give me some idea of what they're like?"

Professor Gray sat up, supporting his chin on his knees with his cupped hands. "I can, but please remember that what I know is a combination of archaeo-anthropological data and what I have learned about present conditions from Hermes. Almost all the more disgusting monsters, he has explained, are properly speaking members of the Gorgon race, who are themselves, however, basically reptile. The Gorgons derive from a universe or universes so different from our own even in the laws of biology and chemistry as to be virtually beyond our comprehension. Their chieftainess, for example, has a human body and a head covered with writhing snakes. Which jibes, of course, with the description of Medusa in almost all the texts.

"The only thing," he said, his delicate old face wrinkling suddenly, "that bothers me a little is the exact relationship of Medusa to the cult of the Snake-Goddess or All-Mother of ancient, matriarchal Crete. In fact, by middle Mycenaean times—just before the present era—the religion of the Triple Goddess, as she was then called, was being practiced over almost the entire Mediterranean by priestesses who not only dominated the community but had control of all agriculture and most of local industry. In the records of our world, this religion disappeared suddenly, to be replaced by the Olympic pantheon. Yet, here, in a parallel transitional period, some two centuries before the Homeric heroes, there is no sign of either religion. Very strange. Possibly neither has developed as yet; although I would give a good deal to see what conditions are like on Crete. Hermes tells me that since the Gorgons have been crowding in, the island is far too dangerous to visit on a purely social basis. Yet— Yet —

"And then there's the question of the Gorgons' reptilian form. Among the majority of ancient peoples, the serpent was the symbol of wisdom and fertility. Not until the Genesis of our Bible do we find a less flattering picture of the snake and, even then, he is still incredibly shrewd and cunning, though no longer friendly to Man. Is it possible, now—"

Percy, exhausted by his first two days in pre-Achaean Greece, fell asleep at this point, to dream that he was back in his own time and a clever, fast-talking salesman named Lucifer Beelzebub Hermes had talked him into buying a very expensive restaurant which, upon his assuming ownership, turned out to have a clientele composed exclusively of rattlesnakes who insisted on charging their meals. When he approached one of them with a suggestion that a part of the long-standing bill be paid, the creature lunged at him with an enormous and rapidly-growing set of triple poison fangs.

He was rather bitter when he woke up, even though Ann had prepared a tasty breakfast out of some local bread and cheese and five eggs from as many different types of birds. Also, Professor Gray had laid out some fairly good garments for them.

The fact remained that whatever Medusa was, however dangerous the Gorgons were, he, Percy Sactrist Yuss, was committed to ridding the world of them and would probably, in the process, rid the world of himself.

"Some people," he told Ann morosely, "have lots of different talents. I have only one—being a sucker. But I'm the best sucker, the most complete sucker, that this world—or the one before it—has ever seen. I'm actually a genius at it."

"The trouble with you," she said, surveying him judiciously over an extremely well designed water jug, "is that you think about yourself too much."

"Well, it's a good idea while there's still enough of me left around to make it worth-while."

Professor Gray trotted in and insisted on Percy's coming out to test the weapons which Hermes had been bringing for the encounter with the Gorgon. Reluctantly, Percy followed him outside into the still, strong brightness of a morning in the Eastern Mediterranean.

"This is the cap of darkness or invisibility," the little man said, handing him a collection of curved metal plates welded in a rough hemisphere and decorated with many wires and incredibly tiny transformers. "The switch is just under the brim—here!—but you'll have to be very careful about practicing with it since Hermes tells me its power supply is very low and there is little possibility of refueling for a long while. Don't gape like that, Percy, it really does work! I told you that their science was far ahead of ours."

He reached into the large wicker basket for a black object shaped like an overnight zipper bag. It had a long looping handle. Where the zipper should have been, however, there was instead a thin and hazy line that shut the bag so completely as to make it seem like one continuous piece.

Professor Gray tapped it importantly. "The *kibisis*. The satchel in which you are to place the Gorgon's head after you've cut it off. This is probably the most important single item—except for the boots—that you will be given. You see, according to legend, even after her head has been severed, Medusa still has the power to turn men into stone with a glance. Furthermore, according to Hermes, she is so unlike life as we know it that, merely with her head, she will still be capable of blasting open an ordinary container. This bag can only be opened from the *outside*. You are to place her head in the *kibisis* and keep it there until you hand it over to Hermes. And now for the major item: how are you to get her head in the first place? Well, we have a sword for you, the famous *harpe*."

He was, Percy noted with disgust, speaking with all the patronizing familiarity of a sports enthusiast or a fight manager explaining the virtues of a new defensive crouch to a young championship contender.

"This is big stuff to you, isn't it, professor? Being able to crowd yourself into a story you used to lecture about?"

"Crowd myself? But I am already in the legend! Professor Gray is as much a part of the original story as Percy S. Yuss is Perseus and Ann Drummond is Andromeda. Hesiod refers to the Graiae Sisters who have been gray since birth and who are largely responsible for the equipping of Perseus on his mission to Medusa. Well, there's only one of me and none of it is female, but it's still close enough to the real myth. As, for example, your rescue of yourself and Ann from the scylla, which is classically a monster of whirlpool and shipwreck, tallies with the original tale which has Perseus saving Andromeda from a sea-beast, though only after he's killed the Gorgon. The fact that you did arrive at Seriphos in a bathtub and as an adult contradicts Pherecydes's version in which the infant Perseus, shut inside a chest with his mother Danae, is rescued from the sea by the fisherman Dictys, brother of King Polydectes. And yet, it was Dictys's net that pulled you out of the Mediterranean....

"You see, it goes on and on agreeing with the legend here, altering it slightly there. That's the fascinating thing about myth," the old academician went on. "There's fact in it somewhere, the trick is to find that little nugget of solidity and be able to recognize it when you do. The truth might be that there was originally a Professor Gray in the actual story as it took place on our world—and his name, sex and...quantity were altered by later writers; or, possibly the truth is that there is a repeating myth in every space-time universe, a myth which has several broad generalizations which must be satisfied, but whose particulars may be filled in from almost any palette."

"You mean," Percy asked slowly, reluctantly unclasping a precious hope he had let nobody know about, "that this time Perseus might be killed by the Gorgon instead of vice versa?"

Professor Gray nodded with brain-curdling enthusiasm. "Now you're beginning to understand! Exactly. Don't you see it was always possible, just as it's possible that you aren't the right Perseus any more than I'm the right Gray—or Graiae? That's what makes this whole thing so infernally exciting!"

His pupil started to smile. Unfortunately, since he had great difficulty in lifting the corners of his mouth from under his chin, the attempt was no great success as smiles go. "Yeah," he said. "I'm beginning to see that."

"Here. Try your sword," the professor suggested, his eyes almost popping under the weight of the enormous mass of metal he was holding out to Percy with both straining arms.

Percy took it and, by tearing his back muscles slightly, was able to lay it on the ground before it fell out of his hand.

"Don't tell me I'm supposed to go fence a duel with that girder!"

"Oh, you'll get used to it, you'll get used to it! Notice that it's made of iron, not bronze? Nothing's too good for Perseus!"

"Thanks, pal, from the bottom of my—"

"Of course, on the later vases," the professor had backed into archaeology again, "especially the red-figure ones, the *harpe* of Perseus is represented in the shape of a sickle. But the earliest kind, the black-figure vases, show it as a straight sword. And a straight sword it must have been, because that's how Hermes brought it here to be held against the time when a Perseus arrived."

"Speaking of arrivals," Ann commented from the doorway of the hut, "the 8:45 is coming in on Runway One. Better move back!"

They looked up to see Hermes twirl down from the bright blue sky a little more rapidly than usual. He carried a peculiar and bulky package slung from his belt. He began walking toward them the moment his toe-tips punched the soil.

"Is he ready? I hope he's been practicing with those weapons."

"As a matter of fact," the little old man said, rubbing his forehead, "he just began to examine them. You're a little premature, Hermes: remember, these people only arrived last evening."

The golden-skinned young man nodded absent-mindedly for a moment, then bent to open his package. "I know. Unfortunately, a good deal has changed in the world since then. The Gorgons will be making their final attempt at conquest in the next twenty-four hours. Medusa must be killed before tonight."

"I won't!" Percy raved. "You just can't pull a man out of a nice, comfortable world and expect him to—to—"

"As I recall," Hermes drawled, turning around with a pair of calf-length metallic boots, "I pulled you out of a series of highly unpleasant situations. You were not too comfortable in that underground cell, and you would have been even less so the next day in a certain large cooking vessel which I destroyed. Then, there was the meeting in the arena...."

"Percy's point," said Professor Gray uncomfortably, "is that he has hardly begun to adjust to the situation, psychologically. And physically—well, he's not even able to flourish the sword as yet."

"I'll take care of those difficulties!" the messenger promised. "Here are your boots. When you rub them together like so, your mobility is multiplied by a factor of twenty. Put them on and take a drink of this."

Dubiously, Percy donned the boots that were to make him twenty times as fast. The soles vibrated underfoot in a way that was not exactly pleasant.

With even more uncertainty, he swallowed some liquid out of a long tubular flask which the golden one held out to him. He almost doubled over as the drink hit his stomach like a bursting rocket. "Whee-ew! That's potent stuff!"

A thin, smirking grin. "Wait! You've yet to find out how potent it really is. Now, I want you to pick up your sword, Percy, and remember as you do how strong you've become. Why, you're such a powerful man that I wouldn't be at all surprised to see you wave it around your head like a tiny twig fallen from a dead tree."

Percy reached for the sword, a rather silly grin on his face. It was all very well for Hermes to try to inspire him with such confidence, but he knew his capacity. A sword as heavy as that...

Only it was very light. It was the easiest thing in the world to lift and flourish. He did so, marveling at the feel of power in his arm and wrist muscles.

"Wonderful!" Professor Gray breathed. "That flask—does it contain the fabled *Nektar*, the ineffable drink of the gods?"

"After a fashion," the messenger said. "After a fashion. Now that we're all set, Perseus, suppose you gather up your armory, and we can start out."

Events got very dim after that. Percy found it hard to remember their sequence. Sometime or other, Ann had come up and said a good deal of angry nonsense to Professor Gray, who had seemed very confused. Then, just as she was about to throw her arms about his neck, Hermes took him by the hand, and they went soaring away.

His head felt a lot clearer when they were high against the clouds, racing southward across an island-dotted sea.

"Why," he said, "don't you people, with all the tremendous stuff you have at your disposal, go after the Gorgon yourself?"

"A matter of prophecy. The legend of Perseus must be fulfilled at all costs." Hermes let the words dribble out of his mouth as he peered ahead anxiously.

Vaguely dissatisfied, Percy found himself wondering if the answer made any sense after all. Like so many of the things he'd been told recently, it sounded as if a small lump of truth had been used to flavor a great steaming bowl of nonsense.

The drink must be making him feel this way, he decided. Professor Gray was an entirely sincere if slightly bumbling human being. Still...

"And why did you tell us that we'd get sent back to our own time? According to what Professor Gray says, that time is dead forever."

The golden man shook his head impatiently, and they both almost turned over. "Now, now, this is no time to look for problems and disagreements. You need another drink. Here."

He almost forced the flask to Percy's lips. Again there was an explosion in his intestines which, while not so violent as the first, had much more of an echo. He looked at Hermes with new trust and fondness. How could he ever have doubted so splendid a friend?

"Let me tell you what you will see when you force your way into Medusa's chamber," Hermes was saying with a drowse-provoking smoothness. "Medusa herself will appear to be a horrible, horrible..."

Under them, the waves raced gleefully through each other, pausing every once in a while to shake a fistful of foam at the constantly watching and disapproving sky. Percy swung lazily from the hands of the steadily talking golden man. Life was simple, he thought, when people told you what to do and what to expect. Everything had become so easy.

He looked up as he felt Hermes let go one of his hands and fumble for the switch on his cap of darkness. A moment later, the same hand made a similar gesture on its owner's wide belt.

"Making us invisible, that's what you're doing," Percy commented, nodding his head slowly. "Are we there already?"

"Yes. Sh-h-h! Please be quiet!"

Turning his head, he saw a long, greenly rich island expanding up towards them. "Why did you people have to go to so much trouble making this cap for me and all that sort of thing, when you could have given me something you already had—like the belt, for example—and I'd have been able to travel here all by myself? What I mean," he went on with large, drunken generosity, "is that you're probably a busy man, Hermes. 'Sa shame for me to drag you away from—"

"Will you shut up?" Hermes's voice was a whispered custard of fear. His eyes flickered up and down, right and left, as they dropped into an enormous, silent city built from massive blocks of gray, moss-covered stone. "We didn't give you a belt for the same reason we gave you a sword instead of a ray gun. Short supply."

"Sup—supply?" Percy asked stupidly. He scratched his head and almost knocked the cap off.

"Supply. And besides, do you think we're foolish enough to trust a human with our weapons?" Their feet touched the worn surface of a rock balcony high up on a building. Hermes pulled him behind the great finger of stone that served as one of the lintels for the doorway. Percy could feel the twitching tenseness in the body of the golden man as he hugged him to the wall and waited to make certain that no one was coming out on the balcony to investigate.

He tried to remember the last thing that Hermes had said. He found he couldn't and wished desperately that the black blobs in his mind would go away and let him think again. But he remembered that Hermes had made some sort of slip in his fright, that abruptly he had almost had the vision of—of— What?

"You need one more drink before you go inside," came the insistent whisper. Percy started to protest that he had been drinking entirely too much of this strange concoction but, as he did so, Hermes thrust the flask into his mouth. He gagged and managed to dribble the bulk of the liquid down his chest, but enough entered his stomach to provide a walloping accompaniment to the clouds which slid over his thoughts once more.

"Now, you know what you are to do. Her bedroom is the first one to the right of the corridor leading away from the balcony. Don't even try to think, Perseus: it will only lead to disaster! All of your instructions are safely buried in your mind; if you just relax and let them take over, you will do exactly the right thing every time. Remember, you can't fail! You cannot fail! Now go!"

Hermes pushed him around the lintel and down the hall. Percy stumbled the first few feet, then managed to walk upright and as stealthily as he knew he should. He wanted to turn back and argue some very important points with his guide, but somehow it was much more important to keep walking, to keep one hand on the hilt of his great sword, to have every nerve anxious and waiting....

The hall was covered with tapestry of a fabric so strange that it almost seemed logical for his eyes to be unable to focus whenever he tried to make out the design. The tapestry ended just before an archway supported by spiral stone columns. He walked in.

Almost before he saw the reclining, sleeping figure with the headful of drowsy, slightly restless serpents, he had flipped open the *kibisis* and ground his boots together to close the subsurface relays. He was speeding toward Medusa at a fantastic rate of speed across an enormous stretch of floor thoroughly as slimy as Hermes had said it would be. And along the walls, his eyes noted—yes, there were chained the groaning, writhing human captives on which the Gorgon race was constantly experimenting. All, all as Hermes had said it would be, droning the picture into his ear as they flew toward ancient Crete above the gaily splashing sea.

He hardly remembered grasping the snakes with one hand and, pulling slightly to extend the neck, lifting the heavy *harpe* behind him. The sword poured down and the chillingly ugly head came free, greasy stinking blood pouring from it. He dropped it into the *kibisis* with the snapping, sideways motion that Hermes had told him to use, flipped the lid shut and turned to run back, exactly as Hermes had told him he should.

But, in that moment before he closed the *kibisis,* a single, frantic thought had sped out of the severed head. It hit his swirling thoughts like a pebble from a sling-shot and sent them rippling in so many directions that he almost came to a full stop.

Almost. But he ran on, shaken by the awful familiarity of that mental voice. It was as if his mother had tearfully asked him to stop, to stop now, this moment, no matter what the consequences. It was as if the wisest men in the world had assembled in convention and passed a resolution addressed to him, formally requesting Percy Sactrist Yuss in the name of humanity and universal intelligence to turn somehow, before he plunged the whole world into disaster. It was as if a million tiny infants had bawled out in a terrible, unendurable agony that he alone had caused.

The voice was safely shut in the *kibisis,* but its dwindling harmonics rang on and on in his mind.

Hermes came around the lintel as he emerged on the balcony and waited for him to rub his boots back into normal speed. Then he held out a hand. "All right, give it to me."

He started to hand the *kibisis* over, but the memory of the thoughts locked inside made him pause for a moment. He swung the black bag from its long, looping handle undecidedly.

The golden-skinned man laughed. "You're not going to keep it?"

Percy didn't know what he was going to do. He certainly didn't want that head of surpassing horror for any reason that he could think of. And, certainly, wasn't he supposed to give the *kibisis* to Hermes as soon as he had filled it with the grisly contents for which it had been designed? Certainly he was. Someone had explained all that to him. But that thought he had received from the head…

"Let's not have any trouble, Percy. Give me the bag and we can start back. Your girl friend is waiting."

That was decisive. He still couldn't think as clearly as he would have wished, but he could remember. He recognized Hermes's manner now; the bitterness was still too fresh in him for forgetfulness.

It was the manner of the broker who had sold him the half-interest in a more than half-bankrupt restaurant. Just at the point when he'd started to ask the questions that had been bothering him about a series of bookkeeping entries, the man had shoved a fountain pen in his band and begun to prattle of the possibility of selling the place the very next week at a tidy profit. "Of course, I don't know if you'd be interested in getting rid of it so soon after purchase. I imagine if the profit were sufficiently high, however, you would hardly feel like holding on. Well, Mr. Yuss, as soon as we leave my office, I'll have you meet Mr. Woodward. Mr. Woodward has been interested in purchasing this restaurant for some time and, quite confidentially, I think we can get close to…" He had signed almost before he knew he had and acquired therefrom a piece of property that was more like a cash incinerator than an eating place.

And he had sworn not to be taken that way again. He recognized Hermes's manner now: it was the con man getting a little impatient at the sucker's delay and throwing out some more bait.

"No," he said. "I won't give it to you until we return. I think I want Professor Gray to look at it first."

He never knew how he realized that the tiny red tube Hermes suddenly flashed was a weapon. He leaped clumsily sideways and the stone wall section in front of which he had been standing exploded like a burst paper bag. He kicked the boot switch into operation and tore the *harpe* out of its back scabbard.

Hermes was turning the ray gun around at him with the same unpitying, contemptuous smile he had flashed so many times before, when Percy became a darting, feverish flicker of humanity. As the golden man rolled backwards to find a good shot somewhere in this incredibly fast creature who seemed to be one continuous line, his eyes grew wider and wider, his lips pulled in deeper and deeper; a fear ricocheted through him. And, when the screaming sword finally bit his head off, it rolled to the balcony floor looking just like that—thoroughly popped eyes and almost nonexistent mouth shaming the refined gold of the skin and carefully cut, artistically designed features.

Percy leaned on his sword and breathed hard. This was the second in one day! He was becoming a wholesaler!

He turned the boots off. He didn't know when he might need that extra speed again in a hurry or how much fuel they still had left in them. He stepped carefully away from the bleeding, decapitated corpse.

Abruptly the sword grew very heavy; he holstered it with difficulty. The drug was wearing off. He knew it was a drug now as the hypnosis induced by Hermes began to dissipate. The city was still the same quiet stone. But it was no longer the thing of implicit horror it had been up to a few minutes ago. Men lived here, he knew, and went about their tasks in their various human ways.

The building on whose balcony he stood was much older than the others around it. It had a distinctive style of architecture—more pillared stone and friezed decoration than even a palace should have.

He tiptoed back along the hall. There was the tapestry he remembered, except that now he could see it quite clearly. Men and women were dancing around a huge upright snake in one section; in another, a great lizard plowed a field while people walked behind it joyfully strewing flowers across the new-made furrows. In the last, a tall and beautiful woman stood before a crowd of young children and allowed a pair of small snakes to curl around her bare breasts.

He paused at the entrance to the room, reluctant to enter and confirm his suspicions. In his hands, the black *kibisis* undulated slowly as if the thing inside it were still alive. Well, there at least Hermes had told the truth.

At last he looked into the chamber. It was a large, clean room lit by three huge torches, very sparsely furnished. There were no chained humans along the walls; there were colorful murals instead which dealt with a strange nonhuman race.

There was a kind of triangular altar in the middle of the floor. On the other side of the altar, there was a high dais supporting an intricately carved wooden throne. And sagging in the throne was the headless, blood-covered body of a creature Percy had never seen before.

He brought his hand across his lips as partial understanding came to him. This was a temple. But who—or what—had he killed?

The head inside the bag moved once more. He had to find out! He snapped the *kibisis* open and—

He didn't have to take the head out. Understanding came to him then, complete and rounded, to the best of his capacity to understand—as the still-living and slowly dying thing in the bag telepathically thrummed out its history. It gave him the information he wanted without reproaches and with complete objectivity. And, as he realized what he had been tricked into doing, he almost fell to his knees.

In the almost nonexistent time it takes to feel a doubt or experience surprise, Percy came to know—

Long before Man, there had been the other mammals from which he had derived. And long before mammals, millions of years before, there had been the reptile. The reptile had eaten across the planet as herbivore and carnivore, had raced across it as thundering dinosaur and pygmy, rodent-like lizard. In a span of time beside which the reign of mammals was as a moment, the reptile had ruled the Earth with an absolute despotism in all the forms—and many more besides—that his warm-blooded successor was to achieve.

Inevitably, one of these forms laid its accent on intelligence.

A creature arose which called itself Gorgon and walked its way with pride. Great cities the Gorgons built; they captured and tamed the unintelligent dinosaurs and made cattle out of them, even to the ground-shaking brontosaurus. Those they could not tame, they destroyed for sport, much as a thoughtful simian newly arrived from the trees was to do much later. And, partly for sport, partly for burning conviction, they destroyed themselves.

War after war, superweapon after superweapon, they fought and lived through. They even destroyed the continent on which they had originated, the home of most of their science and art and all of their major industry—they saw it sink into a boiling sea, and they lived through that. Then, at last, they gathered in their shrunken numbers upon inhospitable shores and created a way of life that made war between them impossible.

There was a brief season of great cooperative achievement, an instant or two of Indian summer, before the curtain began to fall upon the Gorgons once more. Their seed had been injured by one of the latest weapons: they were no longer breeding true. In small quantities at first, the number of monsters and defectives being born increased rapidly. Almost the entire energy of the race was channeled into a frenzied biological research.

They cured every disease that had ever made them the slightest bit uncomfortable, they doubled and quadrupled their lifespan again and again, they came to such ultimately complete understanding of their bodies and minds that they were well-nigh godlike and just this side of immortality. But still, every generation, there were fewer of them....

Eventually, they made peace with their approaching racial death, and set themselves to cheat it by passing their knowledge and achievements on to another creature. This was not easy to find. First, they tended to look within the ranks of the reptiles for a successor, but they had depleted the vital energies of the best nonintelligent species as badly as they had their own. They had a brief success with the serpents and pythons but, despite increased intelligence, no amount of selective breeding or indoctrination could persuade these creatures to live communally. Second, they tried the amphibians; then, the birds—

After many trials and many errors, the Gorgons settled at last on the mammalian primate. Here, with much difficulty and heartache because of the creature's fundamentally alien orientation, they achieved success. Slowly, over the unhurried centuries, the Gorgon selected this stock, discarded that one, gently stimulated and educated, until a civilization of sorts had been achieved. A little longer and they could throw aside the mantle of godhood and teach their charges directly.

But the Olympians came.

It was true, as Hermes had told Professor Gray, that a weakness in the subspatial fabric between universes had made it possible for them to enter. He had neglected to mention that they were the first and only ones to invade this universe, they and the assorted monsters, that a completely different corpus of natural law made it possible.

Originally, they poured into Earth from almost every spot on her surface. They conquered and enslaved, killed and looted, but their chief object was land. The available space on their own highly crowded world was very limited.

And there were only a handful of Gorgons to defend mankind against them. Hurriedly, these ancient reptiles turned to their forgotten and hoary armories, brought out the weapons they had sworn never to use and plunged into combat to save, not themselves—for this they were now psychologically incapable of doing through warfare—but the infant race they guarded. And slowly over the years—while liquid fire rained upon one land and floods swept through another—the invaders were driven back and the exits sealed one by one.

The Gorgon losses had been small numerically, but devastating in proportion to their total strength. There were only three females who escaped being mortally wounded; two badly crippled males had hung on for a century before dying without viable offspring. The three remaining intelligent reptiles saw no alternative but to concentrate in the Eastern Mediterranean and provide at least a section of the human race with an accelerated course of instruction.

Then, five hundred years ago, the outsiders were heard from again. This was a remnant which, cut off on this planet by the Gorgon victory, had returned to the sealed-off Mount Olympus exit and secretly rebuilt its strength. They had attacked one awful night and wiped out Cnossus, the capital city. Wearily, the Gorgons turned back to combat. They drove the Olympians off and crushed them for the time, but were no longer strong enough themselves to wipe out completely the golden-skinned race. A degenerate fragment remained which was now, like humanity's protectors, a constantly dwindling species.

Before this had been achieved, however, every large city in Crete had been gutted and Sthenno and Euryale, Medusa's sisters, had been killed. She worked desperately now at her double task: to pass on as much of the Gorgon knowledge as humanity was capable of absorbing and to rebuild enough of the ancient weapons to prevent the one remaining danger—an Olympian attempt to break through the subspatial fabric once more and regain contact with their parent universe.

To this end, she had been preparing a multitude of weapons which men of this time, under her direction, could use against the Olympians. Unfortunately, the entire orientation of the Gorgon educational process had been opposed to war and weapons. This generation of Cretans, while superior in brains and breeding to most twentieth-century humans, were decidedly not warriors and were having great difficulty developing the martial spirit.

Medusa had been sending the priestesses through whom she governed to nearby lands in search of a people who, while possessing the requisite belligerence, were sufficiently advanced intellectually that they still could be persuaded of the necessity of joining the last campaign against the Olympians. The concept of forcing people to fight—even for themselves—was anathema to a Gorgon.

But she had been anticipated. The Olympians had evidently managed to receive some sort of message from their own world and believed that, by operating on both sides of the subspatial barrier, they could effect another breakthrough. It was probably one of the last attempts that could be made (possibly the civilization in the other universe was beginning to dissolve under the continual corrosion of war as the Gorgons' had), and they considered it essential to remove the last of the ancient reptiles to insure that they would not be interrupted.

Knowing that they were far too weak and backward now to carry off a frontal attack with any success, they must have developed the idea of using Percy as a catspaw. Probably, the head mused, one of their number—scouting among ordinary people for crumbs of information Medusa might have dropped—happened upon a superstitious myth-prophecy and decided to develop it into fact. The arrival of a young man from a previous space-time universe worked in perfectly, since no human of this period could be persuaded or frightened into attacking a Gorgon.

And, at the reason why a human assassin was needed by the Olympians, Percy's knees almost buckled.

For no Gorgon, my son, is capable of injuring a human being without committing immediate mental suicide. It would have been like a mother stabbing her crawling infant for me to have killed you, as I could have, when your harpe *sang at my throat.*

"Listen," he said desperately to the tired, dying head in the black bag, "you may not want to force people to fight for their world, but I don't have any such compunctions. I've certainly been forced to do enough things in my own life that I most definitely didn't like! Now, I know a place where there's a bunch of plenty belligerent characters—and I know a way of getting them to volunteer for the forward echelons. I want to do what I can to fix up this terrible thing I did!"

Medusa considered. He could feel her holding on to her vital energies with more and more difficulty, despite the enormous psychosomatic control practiced by the Gorgons. Her life was seeping away.

Yes, the faint thought came at last. *Yes, it might save the planet. It must be tried. Call Athena, young man. Call her with your voice.*

He hesitated for just a moment. He licked his lips. It would be kind of nasty if this was just another trap. "Athena!" he called.

Almost immediately, an old priestess hobbled down the hall to the balcony. She clapped her hands to her ears and her mouth distended in horror at what she saw, but at a rapidly telepathed order from Medusa, she controlled the scream in time.

This is no time for sorrow or anger. Weeping must come later, in its proper time and place. Meanwhile, the Olympians prepare to tear down once more the barrier between the worlds. If they succeed, there will be none of my race to stand between them and you. They must be stopped! All else must be subordinated to that necessity. So, go, call your sisters together and make ready for the things I have prepared for this day. And hurry, Athena, hurry!

An efficient nod, and the old woman had gone back down the hall calling her subordinates.

What are you going to do? the thought came.

Percy told her. There was a pause. Then, *Let it be done, then. But remember, my son, no matter what the circumstances may be, I cannot injure a human being!*

Athena returned with a dozen or so wide-eyed, frightened young priestesses whom she organized and ordered so efficiently that they had no time to do more than bite their lips occasionally at the thought of what the *kibisis* contained. Even so, they made Percy feel terrible. He had killed not merely their deity, but their wise teacher and gentle friend. And why? Because he was a sucker.

Well, he was through with that from now on, he vowed. He knew what the score was—and from here on out, he would be acting on what he knew rather than on what others told him.

Each priestess was standing on a wide metallic rug piled high with shimmering weapons that looked like spears and battle-axes, but that he knew must be disguised as such merely to be credible to the people of the period. Athena beckoned, and he stepped onto her rug. She pulled a tiny switch set in a corner box and turned a small wheel. The rug rose and soared from the huge balcony with no feeling of motion.

"The island of Seriphos," he said to Athena in reply to her questioning glance. Behind him, he could see the other priestesses, each on her flying metal carpet, strung out across the sky.

They flew over the waves at a much greater speed than he had when traveling with Hermes. This was a tremendous science he had killed, Percy thought wistfully. All these millennia of working and nurturing, and along comes a stumblebum named

Percy Sactrist Yuss who has listened to a good smart line and—

Had it happened the same way in his own previous space-time universe, he wondered? Well, there was no way of knowing. Right now, he was operating completely outside the framework of the legend—at least as Professor Gray had told it to him. Anything could happen.

They came down directly in the village square, as Percy had intended they should for maximum effect. And, while the townsfolk stood around with mouths hanging as slack as their hands, he strode toward the palace with Athena hurrying along on his right.

"I wonder," he said, out of the corner of his mouth to the black bag. "This *harpe's* getting heavier. I can't walk with as much dignity as I'd like to. Could you try some of that hypnosis stuff, perhaps...."

He strode into the pillared hall with clanking boots. He stopped against the massive column where he had been placed upon being brought to this hall as a prisoner. King Polydectes was having lunch. He rose from the long, crude wooden table at Percy's entrance and started to wipe his lips with a nearby wife's hair.

"Welcome home, Perseus, welcome home!" he said with a creaking, somewhat laborious enthusiasm. "We've been waiting for you to return!"

"Have you now?"

"Oh, certainly my boy, certainly! Ever since that tragic mistake out at the theater, we've known for certain you were really Perseus. I've punished that zookeeper horribly, I assure you! Why, he was supposed to have a hundred dancing flower-decked maidens greet you and the girl. Somehow or other, he got confused and rang in that scylla. I have absolutely no idea how he made such—"

"Can it. I'm here on business. Call everybody in who can get here fast."

Polydectes nodded vehemently and waved at Dictys with both hands. As his brother obediently sped out of the hall, the king, his eyes fastened warily on the black bag that swung at Percy's side, asked in what he evidently considered was a winning voice: "Aren't you going to say hello to your mother?"

Percy stepped back. "My—my mother?"

"Yes, she arrived this morning. When she told us her name, we realized how completely the legend had been fulfilled. We've been making her as happy as possible since, even though it has been a little—eh, a little—expensive."

He pointed to a spot halfway down the table. Percy gasped, then let it roll out into unbelieving laughter. Mrs. Danner sat in her dirty flowered housedress, her arms bent around a huge wine-skin.

"Poor little Marybelle Danner," she was mourning between slobbers. "It's all weak stuff, the best they got's like a baby's slap. And they mix it with water, yet!"

So even this much of the myth was fulfilled, too! Not a Danae but a Danner had arrived to be associated with him. And the fact that she wasn't really his mother? " 'She's somebody's mother, boys,' he said."

Obviously, if someone was needed to round out the generalities of a legend, they too "fell through," parchment or no parchment. Although he'd like very much to question Mrs. Danner on the exact mechanics of her arrival. It might be important and useful....

"Take good care of her," he ordered. "And, Dictys!"

"Yes, sir," the king's brother inquired as he reentered the hall with a substantial and highly uneasy section of the population behind him. He too kept throwing anxious glances at the *kibisis:* everyone seemed very well educated in the legend on this point. "Anything I can do for you? Anything at all? Just name it, that's all I ask, just—"

"Somewhere on the southern tip of the island," Percy told him, "you'll find an old man, together with the girl who escaped from the arena with me. I want you to find them and make them as comfortable as you can. Concentrate on nothing but making life pleasant for them until I return. If you get slack anywhere along the line, you'll hear from me. Understand?"

"I'm on my way," Dictys assured him. "Hey, Menon, Bupalus, Pataikion! This way. We've got to run. Favor for a hero, a man we all admire!"

Percy grinned as the three violently nodding men followed Dictys out of the hall. It was fun to unsucker. But he had business, important business, as the sight of the grim priestess at his back reminded him.

"Polydectes," he said, "you are about to start the first draft in the military history of Seriphos. I'm on my way to attack the Olympians, and I'd like you to furnish about fifty good fighting men to assist me in the project."

The king stilled the crowd and turned nervously back to the young man before him. "Uh...my people like to stay out of other people's fracases. That's why they call me—"

"I know," Percy told him. "I know. Only this is urgent. I want those fifty men very badly indeed. We'll give them powerful weapons such as they've never dreamed of before—and teach them their use. But this is your chance to cut down on that surplus population you're always talking about. And, as I said, it's very important to me." He patted the *kibisis* delicately as he spoke.

"Oh, in that case," said King Polydectes. "If it's urgent! Why, certainly. Captain of the Guard! Detail all twenty-eight members of the army, the ten policemen, and any twelve members of the Citizens' Reserve for duty with this famous and spectacular hero. If anyone grumbles, tell him he can choose between that and being cooked over a slow fire."

"I see you've repaired the execution pot," Percy commented.

The king shook his head unhappily. "No, it was a dead loss. And we can't get any kind of decent replacement anywhere. But we've been experimenting with barbecue recently. The results, while not perfect as yet, show a good deal of promise. I'm very hopeful."

Percy walked outside to watch the fifty men being assembled. The priestesses had broken them into very small groups and were explaining the functions of the strange new weapons to them. The men looked half-dazed and half-resentful; the fact that women were teaching them how to fight seemed especially confusing. But the presence of "the hero," and the young women's business-like approach successfully kept their attention from wandering.

The head of Medusa stirred in the open *kibisis*. *Hurry, my son. The time of my last weakness draws near.*

"One last thing," Percy assured her. He turned back to the palace entrance where Polydectes stood munching on the dripping leg of a sheep and watching the whole scene with friendly interest. I've done my part, his attitude suggested. I've given of the flower of my country. The best I have. No sacrifice can be too great....

He stared from the king to the weeping women bidding their husbands and sons goodbye, the nervous male conscripts trying to understand their instructors and obviously wondering how they had gotten into a war with Olympians, and back to the chewing monarch.

"There's one thing you haven't been told," he announced. "King Polydectes has volunteered to lead his troops into combat. King Polydectes isn't afraid of the Olympians, so long as he has our weapons to use against them. King Polydectes says, 'Damn the thunderbolts, full speed ahead!'"

"I d-do?" The chunk of mutton dropped to the ground, the sound of its fall obscured by the cheer that went up.

"You most certainly do," Percy told him. He grabbed the quivering monarch with one hand and, stroking the black bag suggestively with the other, drew him gently onto the metallic rug which Athena operated. The other priestesses followed suit with their charges. "This is why," he said in a voice that echoed back and forth across the square, "they call you Brave King Polydectes!"

They took off to the accompaniment of another wildly rattling cheer.

Once they were scudding along the curve of the Greek mainland, Athena began explaining one of the weapons to the ruler of Seriphos.

"You sight your target in the holes running lengthwise through these spears—like this. See that rock? Then, as soon as you've made your sight, you press this little button in the rear. After that, all you have to do is let go of the spear. It won't miss."

"I'm an old man," Polydectes muttered. "Toothless, worn, and feeble. In the bleak winter of my life, all I want to do is lie by the fire and watch the youths frolic and fight. Ah, youth, youth!"

Percy walloped his back heartily. "Well, we're giving you a new lease on life! You might as well pay attention, because when we come down, we'll come down fighting. And there's no turning back!"

They passed two great peaks near the coast. "Mount Pelion," Athena said, nodding at the first. "And that's Mount Ossa. Olympus is next."

My son, came the hurried thought. *I am dying fast. Grasp my head by the long hairy spines on its back and hold it in front of you when you attack. And, if you are about to be overcome, throw it at your enemies. But you must move rapidly! Already can I sense the dissolution of the impermanent interspace that keeps one world from disturbing another. Our enemies will pour through and overwhelm the pitiful striving. Remember your strength! Remember that it is greater now than when the false Olympian led you to the balcony of my temple in New Cnossus. Feel it, my son, feel it leap through you; feel your mightiness!*

And, as they neared the majestic mountain and swung into a circle of carpets for the attack, Percy felt the strength boil in his muscles. He wouldn't have any trouble wielding the *harpe* now!

The only trouble with that was that all of his weapons had been given to him by the Olympians. Wouldn't they know how to deal with them?

He seized a spear as a horde of golden-skinned men swirled off the side of the mountain and rose to meet them. Sighting somewhere in the center of the group, he pressed the button. The spear buzzed out of his hand and plunged downward, spitting three Olympians like so much *shish kebab.*

Beside him, he heard a similar noise as Polydectes let a weapon go, too. The king's success was even greater—he got four flying outsiders. Now that they were in combat, Polydectes was concentrating on nothing but the kill, the most efficient kill, as befitted a barbarian monarch.

A sheet of flame flashed down from one of the carpets as someone brought another weapon into play. An entire group of ascending Olympians vanished. They turned and sought shelter in the mountain again.

Now, they had the advantage. The long, purple cone of a ray gun raked across a carpet and exploded it. Then another shattered outward. The priestesses brought their craft up higher, out of the ray gun's obvious range.

"Won't work," Polydectes told Percy crisply, as if he'd been advising him on military strategy for the past five campaigns. "They'll come up one at a time now and burn us down. Whatever this thing is that we're flying, we've got to go in after them!"

Percy nodded. He gestured to Athena who, making an overhead motion to the other priestesses, spun the little wheel rapidly. They swooped down, the fore-part of a long parabola of carpets.

Take me now, my son, came the urgent summons. *Now!*

Percy grabbed the lizard-like head out of the bag by a lock of something on the back that was very much like green hair and held it out in front of him. He reached around and whipped out the *harpe.*

The purple rays died out. He heard screams of terror from below. "A Gorgon, a Gorgon!"

"Yes," he said grimly. "It's coming back, along with the sucker that did the job!"

They touched the ground, and he leaped down, clicking his boot switches into action. With this much extra speed, he'd match a sword against a ray gun any old time!

Except that from the mouth of the immense cave halfway up the mountain a dozen golden-skinned men poured out wearing identical boots and blasting purple cones ahead of them! And they moved so much faster than he did, their boots were either better-fueled or better-made.

Polydectes behind him accounted for one of them. And a sheet of flame flapping down from one of the nearest descending carpets burned half of the rest out of existence. He ran on toward the cave desperately trying to dodge and circle around the burst-provoking rays.

One of the Olympians angled in front of him. Percy cursed, realizing he would never be able to reach him in time to use the *harpe*. The fellow's ray gun came up.

And Medusa struck.

Percy, catching her agony in his mind, realized what the effort had cost her. But the Olympian fell forward in cracking fragments; he had been completely ossified on the spot!

So another aspect of the legend was true! Medusa could—

He was inside the cave now and had no time to think. In front of him, there was a rank of determined and armed Olympians, some sixty or seventy deep. And beyond them, over their heads, his eyes rapidly followed intricate whorls of wiring and shimmering instruments to where—at the rear of the cave—a little whirlpool of red energy was growing larger in the rocky ceiling.

At this very moment, they were acquiring reinforcements from the dread other side!

Feverishly, he poured into the attack, slashing them from before him like so many scallion heads on the restaurant cutting board. Beside him, he could hear Polydectes roaring and the men of Seriphos as they poured up.

But he couldn't make it! He'd have to climb those Olympian-filled steps. He knew it despairingly as he hacked and dodged, slew and was ripped himself. He saw that the little whirlpool had grown larger now, that a huge machine had taken shape on the other side and was coming through.

Throw me, Percy! the Gorgon abruptly screamed in his mind.

He brought his arm back and threw the head straight at the skimming scarlet circle high overhead. There was a moment of last instruction that thrummed inside his brain, then the shrill agony of dissolution as the head touched the red energy whirlpool and exploded.

The Olympians screamed their despair when the dust had blown aside sufficiently to show that the entrance was gone. It had been sealed again forever, Percy knew. Never again would they be able to pool their bits of half-knowledge and rebuild their side.

The men of Seriphos pressed in for the completion of the kill. A few Olympians managed to escape out of the cage mouth and soar away, but those who remained fought listlessly.

What were those last instructions the Gorgon had shot at his mind? *The poem! The poem!*

Which poem? The one beginning: *"And thence came the son of Danae, flaming with courage and spirit—"?*

He was standing on a sunny hilltop in the northern part of a small island. There was no one near him.

Percy looked around stupidly. What—

Then, as his mind settled slowly and he remembered the advice Medusa had frantically telepathed to him, he understood. He wasn't happy, but he understood.

Now that the Perseus sequence was over in that particular space-time universe, it was possible only to arrive at the beginning of the one in the next. And while the parchment was gone, the poem related to him, to Percy-Perseus. With that subjective aura and the psychological impetus the Gorgon had given him, he had only to remember the lines of the poem to be precipitated into the next universe.

Why? So that this time there would be no mistake. So that this time he would not be talked into slaying the last surviving Gorgon and removing from humanity the fountain of ancient peaceful wisdom which could nourish it. So that this time he would not—at long, long last—be a sucker.

He regretted it. He especially regretted the loss of Ann, whom he had hardly come to know.

But, come to think of it, wouldn't there be another Ann Drummond in this universe? Yes, and couldn't he be even more successful? He knew his way around now. He'd do that little job for the Gorgon, all right, but first Percy—or Perseus as he might as well call himself here—was going to strut a little. He was carrying a small armory, he knew his power—and he wasn't taking any con games from any man.

No, this time Seriphos was going to hear from him right at the start.

He started down the hill-side, not noticing the young man paddling furiously in a just-materialized bathtub out in the bay.

Nor did he notice the squad of King Polydectes's soldiers eating their uninteresting meal in a clump of bushes halfway down the hill. Nor, if he had seen them, would he have known that their commander was the type to have annoying strangers knocked out from behind so their fine clothes could be stolen at leisure.

Especially was their commander that type after a hot, irritating day spent fruitlessly chasing harpies in the hills by order of King Polydectes....

Afterword

So I finally did what I'd been dreaming of doing since coming out of the army in 1945: I began studying Greek. "Why in the world," my good friend Calder Willingham wanted to know, "start that, for the first time in your life at your age? At your goddam age?"

"What has age got to do with it?" I replied. "After all, there is the story about Cato. Cato began studying Greek at eighty!"

Calder spread his hands at me. "All right. But at least that guy already had a fairly good grounding in Latin."

But I went ahead with it. I intended to support my Greek habit with science-fiction stories. Unfortunately, the two just didn't mix. In several months, I was deeply in debt (something I was, anyway, in most often), and starving.

Fred Pohl learned of it, and got me an assignment that went to both problems.

The Ziff-Davis magazine *Fantastic Adventures* had bought a cover painting for a future issue. They needed a short novel to go with it.

"Perfect for you," Fred said. "They pay a very nice hunk, so long as you meet their one-week deadline. And it's all about Medusa, which is something you've been talking about for a month. Ideal, right?"

I didn't know. I stared at the cover repro Fred had brought along with him to my apartment on New York's East 95th Street (one block south of Spanish Harlem, two or three blocks north of where the *echt* rich East Side then ended), and I just didn't know. There was an undoubted Medusa head, snake locks and all, on the cover, but it was dripping blood on the boots of a fellow dressed in unquestionably seventeenth-century clothing, a fellow waving what looked like an eighteenth-century Scottish broadsword in the air in front of a fourteenth-century castle wall.

I pointed this out to Fred.

"Now don't get all technical on me," he chided. "So it's a bit off-period. All they want in the story from the cover is the cut-off Medusa head. Make believe you're seeing it not on the cover but on an authentic black-krater vase, and tell the story your way. Now, what should I say to the editor of *Fantastic Adventures?* Do you want the assignment, or don't you want the assignment?"

"I want the assignment," I said, looking at the closed door of my almost-empty refrigerator. "Thanks, Fred."

"All right," he said. "And it's due in exactly one week. That's Thursday—dead deadline."

I thanked him again, and let him out of the apartment. Then I borrowed enough money to put in a supply of bread, cheese, and Benzedrine, and went to work.

I spent two days looking for a satisfactory quote to head the piece. Where I got that particular Pindar translation, I no longer have the slightest idea—but I could find things in my salad and bachelor days that only amaze and confound me now at eighty.

Then, mumbling a prayer to my favorite god, Thoth, the Egyptian god of scribes, I began typing. I used as the locale of the opening scene, the apartment I had been living in before the one I was in now. It was the apartment I described in the story "Will You Walk a Little Faster." I left out my neighbor, Lester del Rey, but I included the drunken landlady-superintendent.

The piece began to work, and I let it have its head. It was a strange story, rather unlike anything I'd ever done before, a peculiar mixture of humor and action and alternate-world-stuff.

(Actually, it was only when George Zebrowski recently identified all the elements for me that I at last got a handle on what kind of narrative it really was: a Harold Shea story, the kind of thing that was done, and done much better, by Fletcher Pratt and L. Sprague de Camp, back about 1940, 1941.)

Doing mostly without sleep—and doing without much food, either—I got about two-thirds of the way into the novel, before it suddenly turned and bit me. The texture changed and changed radically. I felt I needed to stop writing and take a week or two off to think about how it was supposed to end.

But I couldn't. I had a deadline that would be crossed within forty-eight hours, as phone calls from the anxious editor reminded me. And I owed Fred Pohl much for the favor he had done me.

Red-eyed and muscle-cramped (and hungry!), I ploughed on. And that's what it literally felt like—ploughing a frozen field.

I finished it and took it to the Ziff-Davis office, without a rewrite or a reread. They liked it and bought it.

I was much ashamed. I felt I had, with premeditation and malice aforethought, written a piece of junk. When the issue of *Fantastic Adventures* that featured "Medusa" hit the stands, I chucked the magazine into a box under my bed and piled all kinds of miscellaneous papers on top of it. I haven't reread the novel in all these years, and I didn't want to include it in this collection. But my wife has (inexplicably) told me for a long time that she likes it; and my brother Morton—whose taste I trust almost as much as Fruma's—insists that it is nowhere nearly as bad as I think; and George Zebrowski—a critic of whom my opinion is very high indeed—George Zebrowski says…

So I finally took the magazine out of the box and reread the story.

And. Well. Hell. It's not so bad.

WRITTEN 1951——PUBLISHED 1951

✤

Essay

On the Fiction in Science Fiction

If there is one quality common above all others to both science fiction and the historical moment which has produced it, that quality is Change. Change is the recurrent motif of most science fiction: Change in human societies, human technologies, human attitudes. Change even in the very structure of human bodies and minds. And the quality of Change affects the field itself to such an extent—originating from a constantly developing and expanding audience—that today I am no longer capable of defining the medium in which I have been working for eight years, so many times have my own style and themes mutated to meet its demands.

From the point of view of any critic of conventional literature, however, science fiction can be very easily categorized: it is one of the several divisions of popular commercial fiction, of which the others are Western, detective, sports, and love stories. Such a critic would not hesitate to label such luminaries in the field as Sturgeon and Bradbury as ordinary commercial writers who happen to specialize in science fantasy and who, as such, are more interested in a steady production of material of proved saleability than in the steady derivation from their work of new, unfamiliar, and possibly unpopular creative azimuths. He would point out with a yawn, this critic, that science fiction's special literary conventions—such as Outer Space and Murdering Monsters Out to Destroy the Earth—are merely high-stepping versions of basics in Western and detective stories—the Wide Open Spaces and the Monstrous Murderer About to Destroy Our Heroine. He would go on, this critic, to nod wearily at the argument that science fiction has peculiarities shared by no other branch of letters; he would observe that every aspect of commercial writing has its eccentricities, but that eccentricities do not a literature make....

And yet, I have come to know a great many science-fiction writers of substantial talent who have, variously proportioned, the following characteristics in common: (1) They share a passionate belief in science fiction as a means of literary expression that has particular validity and significance in this age. (2) They are deeply concerned with their own development as writers in the new and untried channels of their medium. (3) They are resolutely dedicated to the proposition that while man may not live by bread alone, bread is nonetheless a good beginning and should be purchasable by arts as well as crafts.

Rather odd commercial writers, these, worrying about esthetic questions *as well as* word rates, closely questioning the integrity of each narrative performance in their field *while* exchanging market gossip and trade talk—odd, and markedly unlike their colleagues, the Shoot-Em-Down Daltons and the Love-Em-Up Desdemonas in the media immediately adjoining on the newsstands and bookstores. Admittedly this phenomenon has occurred briefly in other areas of commercial writing, the detective story, for example. But there was one Dashiell Hammett, and Raymond Chandler was hardly his prophet.

Then again, the occasional sincere and highly capable author working the well-hewn quarries of realistic crime and timeless West comes to feel an unpleasant constrictive sensation about the more imaginative places of his mind. The reverse is true of the science-fiction writer, who has infinity—literally!—at his disposal, an infinity of concept as well as of cosmos from which he must fashion dimensioned narratives that will be significant to creatures of his species, time, and place. In other words, a Dorothy L. Sayers works in a medium whose limitations are decreed by its definition, while an Olaf Stapledon or a C.S. Lewis is limited only by his skills, his sensitivity, and the thematic range of his intellect. Is it any wonder that science fiction has tended to attract those writers who are interested not only in literature but also in the proliferating problems of our time, a time which one day sees strong conventions smashed in their yellow molds and the next is witness to a revival and reunderstanding of myths centuries upon centuries old?

But then there are those, in and out of the field, who will claim that all this talk of Art and Expression-of-the-Age is so much noonday nonsense. They disagree with the dictum that science fiction has to do primarily with people—that whether the people are modern *Homo sapiens* hammering out the first rocket, twenty-fifth-century mutants hammering out the first *xxl-yyrdk,* robots trying to form labor unions, androids fighting to have the manufacturer's label removed from their backsides, or monocotyledonous Arcturians pathetically attempting to smuggle themselves past Terran Immigration disguised as lima beans, it is first and foremost with their problems and view of *themselves* as people that the SF writer has to deal successfully. It is with their characters as individuals or their collective personality as an alien community that he must grapple long before he has a story. There are still those, in other words, who feel that science fiction is essentially the field of the wonderful gimmick, the dramatized gadget, the engineer's doodle made into flesh and bone and narrative action. They crawl, these folks, out of the cave of the past and cry constantly for more science, more *science* in science fiction.

This is the group that plays Scylla to the litterateur's Charybdis. Against them, the average science-fiction writer has been able to develop only the thinnest, most pathetic defense. At least he can reply to the exotics who challenge the artistic substance of his work with the many-lunged rebuttal of *vox populi;* he can dig his fists truculently into his hips and remind sneering estheticians that that part of our heritage which today's taste would call "fine arts" was *popular* art in its own time, that the masses flocked to watch Michelangelo sculpt and crowds of standees sweated to see Euripides' latest; and that while popularity, by itself, is no guarantee of future fame, it would seem historically important enough to dim the immortality aspirations of most present-day "serious fiction," for which—according to its publishers—apathy among the buying, reading public has been growing steadily. But the critic who successfully charges the science-fiction writer with inadequate or—much, much worse—*inaccurate* science has smitten him hip, thigh, and jawbone, and left him a thing of gibbering, barely audible apologies.

There are two reasons for this: first, the fear of science fiction's being labeled an "escape" literature and, second, the heavy quantities of physics and chemistry in the early science-fiction magazines on which most of the modern writers were suckled. As a result of the latter, if it can be proved that a story contains an incorrectly computed orbital velocity or, heaven help us, a presently impossible faster-than-light speed, while the writer's ears are no longer cropped nor his nose slit, there is a general backing away from the story and a widespread tendency to regard it as "spoiled."

But consider.

Years ago, Robert Heinlein, who is an engineer and naval officer, wrote a novel entitled *Beyond This Horizon,* in which he described a future of abundance and plenty so overwhelming that the principal social problem of the day was keeping the bulk of the population amused and occupied. Then Frederik Pohl and Cyril Kornbluth, who received their training in advertising and journalism, respectively, gave us *The Space Merchants,* a portrait of a world to come wherein the economic returns have diminished so close to the vanishing point that only the wealthiest and most successful can afford a room of their own. Both books are among the best modern science fiction.

Both Ward Moore's *Bring the Jubilee* and Isaac Asimov's *Pebble in the Sky* turn to history for their inspiration, the one to depict a thoroughly believable 1953 America in which the South had won the Civil War; and the other to show the Earth, a millennium or so hence, in the same position *vis-à-vis* the galactic civilization as Judea of the first century AD to the Roman Empire. And both of these are among the best modern science fiction.

In none of these stories would a scientific error or two be of any consequence; even in the factual matter behind the specific narrative action, an inaccuracy should be considered of no more importance than the boners in Shakespearean historical plays. Of course, obvious errors can be annoying to the reader, and the writer who has any pride at all will check all doubtful items carefully. But the stories mentioned, like all good fiction, are essentially stories of human relationships, individually and communally, and no misstatements of scientific fact could rob them of this quality, nor can dozens of validating footnotes add to their stature.

And as to the charge of "escape" literature, a charge which even so respected a science-fiction personality as Fletcher Pratt found it necessary to refute in an article that appeared in a West Coast literary magazine, well, I think it's about time that we who read and write this new kind of story recognize that here is a jealous argument of very ancient lineage indeed. When, back in the eighteenth century, novels first began to appear—and flourish—in booksellers' windows, they were attacked by writers of heavy sermon-essays as instruments of the devil in that they pulled the book-buying public away from the stuff which they should have been reading for the sake of their immortal souls: heavy sermon-essays. The same thing happened when the tedious miracle play of the Middle Ages began to give way to the Elizabethan drama. In every age, entrenched intellectual privilege has attempted to preserve itself by slighting the newer and more popular forms or by attacking them outright as dangerous. But despite these efforts, the audience for miracle plays and bound volumes of sermons has contracted considerably.

The dictionary definition of *escape* that is pertinent here is "avoidance of reality." On this basis, science fiction, dealing as it does with events that have not yet occurred (or, as in the Ward Moore story, events that by a matter of historical necessity have never occurred), frequently stands accused of leading our youth astray and perverting the population in general by ladling out great quantities of verbal opiate.

But why do people read fiction in the first place—any kind of fiction? To learn more about their own irritating, unfulfilled, and insecure lives? To gather useful moral precepts by means of allegories thinly veneered with narrative? I think not.

The fiction writer is the heir of the Homeric epic poet and the Viking *skald*. His lyre has been replaced by a typewriter, true; and his voice amplified enormously by the printing press—but his role today is fundamentally the same as when the local warriors of that period, having returned from a hard day's skull-cracking and armor-denting, sat down in the great smoke-filled hall and, cutting themselves a slab of burnt boar, belched a couple of times and commanded, "Hey, fellow, you with the funny stink; take your arms off that wench and sing us a song of how brave we were in last week's battle. And it better be plenty interesting if you know what's good for you."

Today, if the writer knows what's good for him, he continues to make it plenty interesting. And realizing that few people can see the place-time segment they occupy as an intriguing phenomenon, he wanders as far afield as he can, *without jeopardizing the sense of reality.*

In that last phrase is the secret—and a paradoxical one!—of the escape element in fiction. It has to be believable. Whether the reader is a sex-starved slum kid following the slickly written, highly spiced adventures of a well-to-do, well-preserved roué; or an impotent, rich old man wallowing in the sordid details of a naturalistic novel about young juvenile delinquents; or, for that matter, an intense young girl reliving a handful of tall tales told on a fourteenth-century pilgrimage to Canterbury, all demand a feeling of reality, a feeling that it did happen, that it is happening, that—at the very least—what they are reading *could* happen.

But before that, all have demanded—and found—a literary escape hatch out of the dullness of their own lives. First, the child will climb on your knee and ask to be told a story; *then,* he will demand of you: "Is it true?" The minstrel who dared to sing of last week's battle in terms of the situation as it actually occurred would have been brained with a mead flask. No, he increased the numbers of the enemy ten- or twenty-fold; he verbally blunted the axes and broke the swords of the men to whom he was singing until it seemed to his listeners that they had practically committed suicide by getting involved in the battle in the first place; and then, by alternately extolling their stout hearts and decrying the cowardice of their opponents, he showed how, in a magnificent charge behind their invincible leader, they had carried the day and won eternal fame for themselves and the patch of hillside on which they lived. It is more than possible that when he finished, his enthusiastic audience had already forgotten that the battle had been no more than an attack on a neighboring village, the majority of whose male inhabitants had been known in advance to be away on a fishing expedition. So the minstrel was cheered to the greasy rafters for creating an interesting tale out of what was essentially a rather routine slaughter-and-rape fest—and asked to give an encore.

For an encore, he probably selected his well-known piece about the gods—strange, eternal creatures that could hurl lightning bolts from their bare hands and wrestle with serpents twice as long as the Earth, but who, in the song's opening stanzas, were sitting in *their* great, smoke-filled hall munching roast meat and listening to *their* minstrel sing of *their* wars with the mud giants to the south. And the mortal, dirty humans who heard this encore were completely fascinated and marveled delightedly at the incredible, homey parallels between their lives and the lives of their divinities.

And there, right there, is the area in which science fiction leads the literary side of its life. It is the job of the science-fiction writer to take the utterly fantastic, if need be, and make it seem as real as a copy of today's tabloid newspaper folded to the sports section. To the extent that he succeeds in this he is a good science-*fiction* writer, and to the extent that he fails to make the story believable he is a bad one, be it ever so full of faster-than-light gimmicks and fantastic individuals with triple brains and mechanical genitalia. When H.G. Wells gave us the giant children in *Food of the Gods*, he made it clear at one point that they intended to conquer humanity and take over the planet for themselves; yet he had, by then, made them so completely understandable that the reader realized them much more vividly than he did his next-door neighbors and hoped rather wistfully that they would succeed in replacing him and his comparatively minuscule fellow citizens.

Science fiction, it is true—as opposed to pure fantasy—is not supposed to deal in the impossible or utterly fantastic. In theory it originates in the best available knowledge of the day and thus should concern itself only with those events which can conceivably occur. I have always been impatient of this approach.

Does it really matter that much of Swift's *Gulliver* and most of Rabelais's *Gargantua* are based on what today's science would call fables and legends and impossibilities? Is either work rendered less valid for the child seeking pure entertainment or the adult seeking entertainment plus depth? Yet both Swift and Rabelais were among the best-educated men of their time and based their work as well as they could on such facts (and extensions of these facts) as their age could boast. The facts—the science, so to speak—have been outdated; the fiction will out-endure our civilization.

I tend to limit fantasy, in my own mind, to those stories based primarily on superstitious belief, but I find myself much troubled by this definition. The term "superstitious belief" partakes far too much of a pejorative quality. *Who* is calling *whom* superstitious, I ask, and how much careful investigation has been made of the superstition? On the one hand, you had the spectacle, a few years ago, of extremely able scientists in a science-oriented country like Germany insisting that abruptly they found themselves able to detect real differences between "races," a term which, after all, is no more than a semantic convention; on the other hand, you had Professor Rhine of Duke University looking into the hoary old superstitions of telepathy and telekinesis and coming across results which could be expressed in surprisingly positive mathematical terms. And then a madman like Fredric Brown writes a magnificent, mad yarn entitled *What Mad Universe,* based on some very acceptable modern theoretical physics, and creates a literary matrix where, as someone dazedly pointed out to me, "Anything, absolutely *anything,* could happen and yet be entirely logical!"

What then is the specific literary role of the science-fiction writer? I think it can be said to derive in equal parts from what I call the fictional quality in science and the scientific quality in literature.

Before the development of the electron microscope and sundry useful gadgets like cloud chambers and special photographic devices, it was obvious to most chemists that very definite laws governed the combinations of elements as well as more complex substances. Various laws were worked out, expressed in what were called "combining weights," to cover the observed phenomena. But the question of why the elements combined in the specific ways, weights, and quantities that they did could not be answered with the research equipment then available. So, over a century ago, an Englishman named John Dalton revived an ancient piece of Greek metaphysics, altering it to fit the observed data, and gave the world Dalton's Atomic Theory. And that's the theory which, with the necessary amendments to fit new facts as they've been discovered, is behind the modern atomic bomb. Dalton died without seeing either an atom or its path on a photographic plate, but the theory which bears his name still stands in all essentials.

A little while earlier, there was the matter of phlogiston. Unable to explain the phenomenon of combustion any other way, the alchemists and early chemists decided on an imaginary substance which had to be in all things that could catch fire. The more phlogiston, the hotter the flame. Eventually, of course, all the phlogiston would be burned away and only the original substance left. The trouble was that when Lavoisier finally burned material under laboratory conditions and weighed the residue carefully, he found that the weight increased because of the acquisition of oxygen and thus destroyed the phlogiston theory.

As a nonscientist, I have always been fascinated by both theories, one accepted even today and the other mentioned now only to be ridiculed. I have always felt that their respective originators, Dalton and Becher, were essentially poets of science. Operating from definite facts, they went beyond facts to create a scintillating explanation of how a specific part of our universe operated. With all due deference to hardheaded laboratory technicians, I call this the fictional quality in science and include in it such delightful items as Einstein's curved space and Heisenberg's uncertainty principle. The entertainment and stimulation of such theories, utterly apart from their value to science, is prodigious to a speculative mind.

But the writer, and I mean any writer here, has to be scientific in his turn. To put it very simply, if the author constructs a character who is miserly and selfish, he cannot absent-mindedly allow him to be generous at odd moments for no good reason, without destroying the inner consistency of the work. And it is this inner consistency which is the scientific quality in literature. Every good story is a kind of sealed universe, in which, as the action unfolds, the reader is made privy to the laws peculiar to it. If the author destroys a law, he must rapidly reveal a higher one, or lose the reader's confidence irrevocably.

These two seemingly contradictory qualities from both science and literature have fused in science fiction and produced a situation where the possible number of "sealed universes" the author can create has multiplied enormously in number and variety. And the author who is true to his craft and daring in it can in this way employ the facts of science to liberate himself from the facts of everyday life and go exploring all kinds of dramatic situations far beyond the dreams of literature to date.

Science fiction, thus considered, is not a mere pocket in the varicolored vest of modern writing; it is a new kind of fiction, the beginnings of a long-delayed revolution in letters consequent upon the revolutions that the last two hundred years have witnessed in science, industry, and politics. By this I do not at all mean that it is the only possible literature of the present time, just that it is the type most peculiar to it, most indicative of its larger intellectual trends. The *chansons de geste* of the eleventh and twelfth centuries faithfully reflected the rigid feudal thinking of medieval, hero-worshipping Europe. Later, when the sacred institutional framework of church and knighthood was weakened by increasing trade, broadened cultural contacts, and the beginnings of modern thought, the picaresque novel appeared as an expression of the skepticism that was then exciting the minds of men. Just so, I feel, has the present age produced out of its own grating necessities and future-mindedness a science capable of examining man in the various psychosocial arenas he can occupy—and a literature to run parallel to the science, a literature which must, like all art forms, frequently outstrip the facts which birthed it. Nor, peculiarly enough, is science per se the only proper subject of science fiction. An Oxford don, the aforementioned C.S. Lewis, constructed a magnificent and indisputably science-fictional trilogy on purely religious themes, using the extrapolative techniques of the twentieth century's most flexible medium to affirm beliefs of the thirteenth!

Here it strikes me that I have flung down gauntlets enough all around this, my very first book of short stories. I should remind the reader that I have been attempting to show the potential as well as historical placement of the field as a whole, not by any means to imply that my own thin achievements have measured up to it. In fact, I may well paraphrase Wolsey's humbling comment to the eighth Henry: this, my realm of written stories, is but in an angle of the world of science fiction. I have worked the several fields which have interested me most, to the limits of my talents, moving on whenever urged by inner restlessness or the sudden vision of a brighter green. But there are others who have ranged much further, or cultivated a single, unchanging plot much more assiduously—with truly wonderful results.

How wonderful? Has science fiction produced a Cervantes yet, or a Fielding? No, but neither did the swarming golden glory of the Elizabethan stage produce an Aeschylus. Yet, in that day, the so-called university playwrights were desperately trying to revive the classic dramatic modes. They complained that "no right comedies or right tragedies" were being written. And they must certainly have looked with contempt on thumb-ruling, money-hungry, crowd-pleasing boors like Will Shakespeare, until, of course, Shakespeare's enormous achievement became undeniable. Whether or not science fiction will eventually develop a Shakespeare, I would not dare to predict. But I do claim that it is a literature produced by our times as much as Shakespeare's was by his. And its unfortunate, frequent vulgarities can well be equated with the vulgarities and plebeian absurdities of much Elizabethan writing, both reflecting the primitive vitality of the mass audience that responded to them. It is, of course, in any age, only moribund fiction that is polished to a point of antisepsis, and that will, in losing touch with its audience, "lose the name of action." This new medium has as yet lost neither.

The human mind is lit by an elemental sense of wonder, a probing, restless curiosity that is our primate heritage and that from its beginnings has sought a knowledge, *some* knowledge, of the future. To satisfy that need there has come into being a massive and thoroughly modern creation, science fiction, the literature of extrapolative, industrial man.

Afterword

Very early in 1954, I was having a conversation with Harry Harrison, then the editor of *Science Fiction Adventures*. I said something about how nobody in the field seemed to be paying any attention to the second word in the term "science fiction": most of the arguments seemed to deal only with the "science"—how to define it and just how much of it should be in a given story.

Harry, one of the most alert human beings I've met in my life—Harry pounced. "The fiction in science fiction," he said. "A good title. Write it fast. I have an open slot for it."

I liked the title myself, and I went home and wrote it that afternoon. I put into the essay all sorts of angers and theses and rebuttals that had been percolating inside of me for years. Harry rewarded me with an adequate check and a more-than-adequate editorial lunch.

When Ian and Betty Ballantine decided to publish my first collection of short stories a year later, they insisted on using the essay as the introduction. Why not, I felt.

Well, several times since I've thought of why not. For one thing, it's much too large a topic for a single short essay. For another, the piece makes too many large and overly casual assertions abut literature, history, drama—all kinds of intellectual areas. And I've changed my mind about many of the positions it takes, so many times, so many different ways.

But.

The piece keeps getting mentioned favorably in science-fiction publications. There's apparently something in it that my colleagues rather like. One of them, Connie Willis, spoke warmly of it in her introduction to the first volume (*Immodest Proposals*) of this complete-works thingumajig.

And Jim Mann and Mary Tabasko, my editors here, both specifically want it to be included, despite the fact that it's nonfiction, unlike all the other stuff that surrounds it. And I'm not yet sufficiently senior as a writer to snap my fingers at an editor, especially, if you please, a book editors.

Finally, my thirty-four-year-old self deserves some consideration and respect. He thought it was a very good piece, and for years was quite proud of having written it.

The fact that, at eighty, I've become quite stinkingly literary and could argue a dozen points with him, shouldn't be allowed to stand in the way.

It's his piece, and, truth to tell, I always liked working with the guy.

WRITTEN 1954——PUBLISHED 1954

સ્જ

Of Men
and Monsters

"It doth not appear from all you have said, how any one virtue is required towards the procurement of any one station among you; much less that men are ennobled on account of their virtue, that priests are advanced for their piety or learning, soldiers for their conduct or valour, judges for their integrity, senators for love of their country, or counsellors for their wisdom.... I cannot but conclude the bulk of your natives to be the most pernicious race of little odious vermin that nature ever suffered to crawl upon the surface of the earth."

Jonathan Swift, *Gulliver's Travels*,
"A Voyage to Brobdingnab"

Part I: Priests for Their Learning

Chapter 1

Mankind consisted of 128 people.

The sheer population pressure of so vast a horde had long ago filled over a dozen burrows. Bands of the Male Society patrolled the outermost corridors with their full strength, twenty-three young adult males in the prime of courage and alertness. They were stationed there to take the first shock of any danger to Mankind, they and their band captains and the youthful initiates who served them.

Eric the Only was an initiate in this powerful force. Today, he was a student warrior, a fetcher and a carrier for proven, seasoned men. But tomorrow, tomorrow...

This was his birthday. Tomorrow, he would be sent forth to Steal for Mankind. When he returned—and have no fear: Eric was swift, Eric was clever, he would return—off might go the loose loincloths of boyhood to be replaced by the tight loin straps of a proud Male Society warrior.

He would be free to raise his voice and express his opinions in the Councils of Mankind. He could stare at the women whenever he liked, for as long as he liked, to approach them even, to—

He found himself wandering to the end of his band's burrow, still carrying the spear he was sharpening for his uncle. There, where a women's burrow began, several members of the Female Society were preparing food stolen from the Monster larder that very day. Each spell had to be performed properly, each incantation said just right, or it would not be fit to eat—it might even be dangerous. Mankind was indeed fortunate: plenty of food, readily available, and women who well understood the magical work of preparing it for human consumption.

And such women—such splendid creatures!

Sarah the Sickness-Healer, for example, with her incredible knowledge of what food was fit and what was unfit, her only garment a cloud of hair that alternately screened and revealed her hips and breasts, the largest in all Mankind. There was a woman for you! Over five litters she had had, two of them of maximum size.

Eric watched as she turned a yellow chunk of food around and around under a glow lamp hanging from the ceiling of the burrow, looking for only she knew what and recognizing it when she found it only she knew how. A man could really strut with such a mate.

But she was the wife of a band leader and far, far beyond him. Her daughter, though, Selma the Soft-Skinned, would probably be flattered by his attentions. She still wore her hair in a heavy bun: it would be at least a year before the Female Society would consider her an initiate and allow her to drape it about her nakedness. No, far too young and unimportant for a man on the very verge of warrior status.

Another girl caught his eye. She had been observing him for some time and smiling behind her lashes, behind her demurely set mouth. Harriet the History-Teller, the oldest daughter of Rita the Record-Keeper, who would one day succeed to her mother's office. Now there was a lovely, slender girl, her hair completely unwound in testament to full womanhood and recognized professional status.

Eric had caught these covert, barely stated smiles from her before; especially in the last few weeks as the time for his Theft approached. He knew that if he were successful—and he *had* to be successful: don't dare think of anything but success—she would look with favor on advances from him. Of course, Harriet was a redhead, and therefore, according to Mankind's traditions, unlucky: she was probably having a hard time finding a mate. But his own mother had been a redhead.

Yes, and his mother had been very unlucky indeed. Even his father had been infected with her terrible bad luck. Still, Harriet the History-Teller was an important person in the tribe for one her age. Good-looking, too. And above all, she didn't turn away from him. She smiled at him, openly now. He smiled back.

"Look at Eric!" he heard someone call out behind him. "He's already searching for a mate. Hey, Eric! You're not even wearing straps yet. First comes the stealing. *Then* comes the mating."

Eric spun around, bits of fantasy still stuck to his lips.

The group of young men lounging against the wall of his band's burrow were tossing laughter back and forth between them. They were all adults: they had all made their Theft. Socially, they were still his superiors. His only recourse was cold dignity.

"I know that," he began. "There is no mating until—"

"Until never for some people," one of the young men broke in. He rattled his spear in his hand, carelessly, proudly. "After you steal, you still have to convince a woman that you're a man. And some men have to do an awful lot of convincing, an *awful* lot, Eric-O."

The ball of laughter bounced back and forth again, heavier than before. Eric the Only felt his face turn bright red. How dare they remind him of his birth? On this day of all days? Here he was about to prepare himself to go forth and Steal for Mankind....

He dropped the sharpening stone into his pouch and slid his right hand back along his uncle's spear. "At least," he said, slowly and definitely, "at least, my woman will stay convinced, Roy the Runner. She won't be open to offers from every other man in the tribe."

"You lousy little throwback!" Roy the Runner yelled. He leaped away from the rest of the band and into a crouch facing Eric, his spear tense in one hand. "You're asking for a hole in the belly! My woman's had two litters off me, two big litters. What would you have given her, you dirty singleton?"

"She's had two litters, but not off you," Eric the Only spat, holding his spear out in the guard position. "If you're the father, then the chief's blond hair is contagious—like measles."

Roy bellowed and jabbed his spear forward. Eric parried it and lunged in his turn. He missed as his opponent leaped to one side. They circled each other, cursing and insulting, eyes only for the point of each other's spears. The other young men had scrambled a distance down the burrow to get out of their way.

A powerful arm suddenly clamped Eric's waist from behind and lifted him off his feet. He was kicked hard, so that he stumbled a half-dozen steps and fell. On his feet in a moment, the spear still in his hand, he whirled, ready to deal with this new opponent. He was mad enough to fight all Mankind.

But not Thomas the Trap-Smasher. No, not that mad.

All the tension drained out of him as he recognized the captain of his band. He couldn't fight Thomas. His uncle. And the greatest of all men. Guiltily, he walked to the niche in the wall where the band's weapons were stacked and slid his uncle's spear into its appointed place.

"What the hell's the matter with you, Roy?" Thomas was asking behind him. "Fighting a duel with an initiate? Where's your band spirit: that's all we need these days, to be cut down from six effectives to five. Save your spear for Strangers, or—if you feel very brave—for Monsters. But don't show a point in our band's burrow if you know what's good for you."

"I wasn't fighting a duel," the Runner mumbled, sheathing his own spear. "The kid got above himself. I was punishing him."

"You punish with the haft of the spear. And anyway, this is my band and I do the punishing around here. Now move on out, all of you, and get ready for the council. I'll attend to the boy myself."

They went off obediently without looking back. The Trap-Smasher's band was famous for its discipline throughout the length and breadth of Mankind. A proud thing to be a member of it. But to be called a boy in front of the others! A boy, when he was full-grown and ready to begin stealing!

Although, come to think of it, he'd rather be called a boy than a singleton. A boy eventually became a man, but a singleton stayed a singleton forever. It was almost as bad as being a bastard—the child of a woman not fully accepted by the Female Society. He put the problem to his uncle, who was at the niche inspecting the band's reserve pile of spears.

"Isn't it possible—I mean, it is possible, isn't it—that my father had some children by another woman? You told me he was one of the best thieves we ever had."

The captain of the band turned to study him, folding his arms across his chest so that his biceps swelled into greatness and power. They glinted in the light of the tiny glow lantern bound to his forehead, the tiny glow lantern that only fully accredited warriors might wear. After a while, the older man shook his head and said, very gently:

"Eric, Eric, forget about it, boy. He was all of those things and more. Your father was famous. Eric the Storeroom-Stormer, we called him, Eric the Laugher at Locks,

Eric the Roistering Robber of all Mankind. He taught me everything I know. But he only married once; and if any other woman ever played around with him, she's been careful to keep it a secret. Now dress up those spears: you've let them get all sloppy. Butts together, that's the way, points up and even with each other."

Dutifully, Eric rearranged the bundle of armament that was his responsibility. He turned to his uncle again, now examining the knapsacks and canteens that would be carried on expedition. "Suppose there had been another woman. My father could have had two, three, even four litters by different women. Extra-large litters too. If we could prove something like that, I wouldn't be a singleton any more. I wouldn't be Eric the Only."

The Trap-Smasher sighed and thought for a moment. Then he pulled the spear from his back sling and took Eric's arm. He drew the youth along the burrow until they stood in the very center of it. He looked carefully at the exits at either end, making certain that they were completely alone before giving his reply in an unusually low, guarded voice.

"We'd never be able to prove anything like that. If you don't want to be Eric the Only, if you want to be Eric the something else, well then, it's up to you. You have to make a good Theft. That's what you should be thinking about all the time now—your Theft. Eric, which category are you going to announce?"

He hadn't thought about it very much. "The usual one, I guess. The one that's picked for most initiations. First category."

The older man brought his lips together, looking dissatisfied. "First category. *Food.* Well…"

Eric felt he understood. "You mean, for someone like me—an Only, who's really got to make a name for himself—I ought to announce like a real warrior? I should say I'm going to steal in the second category—Articles Useful to Mankind. Is that what my father would have done?"

"Do you know what your father would have done?"

"No. What?" Eric demanded eagerly.

"He'd have elected the third category. That's what I'd be announcing these days, if I were going through an initiation ceremony. That's what I want you to announce."

"Third category? Monster souvenirs. But no one's elected the third category in I don't know how many auld lang synes. Why should I do it?"

"Because this is more than just an initiation ceremony: it could be the beginning of a new life for all of us."

Eric frowned. What could be more than an initiation ceremony and his attainment of full thieving manhood?

"There are things going on in Mankind, these days," Thomas the Trap-Smasher continued in a strange, urgent voice. "Big things. And you're going to be a part of them. This Theft of yours—if you handle it right, if you do what I tell you, it's likely to blow the lid off everything the chief has been sitting on."

"The *chief?*" Eric felt confused: he was walking up a strange burrow now without a glow lamp. "What's the chief got to do with my Theft?"

His uncle examined both ends of the corridor again. "Eric, what's the most important thing we, or you, or anyone, can do? What is our life all about? What are we here for?"

"That's easy," Eric chuckled. "That's the easiest question there is. A child could answer it.

"Hit back at the Monsters," he quoted. *"Drive them from the planet, if we can. Regain Earth for Mankind, if we can. But above all, hit back at the Monsters. Make them suffer as they've made us suffer. Make them know we're still here, we're still fighting. Hit back at the Monsters."*

"Hit back at the Monsters. Right. Now how have we been doing that?"

Eric the Only stared at his uncle. That wasn't the next question in the catechism. He must have heard incorrectly. His uncle couldn't have made a mistake in such a basic ritual.

"We will do that," he went on in the second reply, his voice sliding into the singsong of childhood lessons, *"by regaining the science and knowhow of our forefathers. Man was once Lord of all Creation: his science and knowhow made him supreme. Science and knowhow is what we need to hit back at the Monsters."*

"Now, Eric," his uncle asked gently. "Please tell me this. What in hell is knowhow?"

That was way off. They were a full corridor's length from the normal progression of the catechism now.

"Knowhow is—knowhow is—" he stumbled over the unfamiliar verbal terrain. "Well, it's what our ancestors knew. And what they did with it, I guess. Knowhow is what you need before you can make hydrogen bombs or economic warfare or guided missiles, any of those really big weapons like our ancestors had."

"Did those weapons do them any good? Against the Monsters, I mean. Did they stop the Monsters?"

Eric looked completely blank for a moment, then brightened. Oh! He knew the way now. He knew how to get back to the catechism:

"The suddenness of the attack—"

"Stop it!" his uncle ordered. "Don't give me any of that garbage! *The suddenness of the attack, the treachery of the Monsters*—does it sound like an explanation to you? Honestly? If our ancestors were really Lords of Creation and had such great weapons, would the Monsters have been able to conquer them? I've led my band on dozens of raids, and I know the value of a surprise attack; but believe me, boy, it's only good for a flash charge and a quick getaway if you're facing a superior force. You can knock somebody down when he doesn't expect it, but if he really has more than you, he won't *stay* down. Right?"

"I—I guess so. I wouldn't know."

"Well, I know. I know from plenty of battle experience. The thing to remember is that once our ancestors were knocked down, they stayed down. That means their science and knowhow weren't so much in the first place. And *that* means"—here he turned his head and looked directly into Eric's eyes—*"that* means the science of our ancestors wasn't worth one good damn against the Monsters and it wouldn't be worth one good damn to us."

Eric the Only turned pale. He knew heresy when he heard it.

His uncle patted him on the shoulder, drawing a deep breath as if he'd finally spat out something extremely unpleasant. He leaned closer, eyes glittering beneath the forehead glow lamp, and his voice dropped to a fierce whisper.

"Eric. When I asked you how we've been hitting back at the Monsters, you told me what we *ought* to do. We haven't been *doing* a single thing to bother them. We don't know how to reconstruct the Ancestor-Science, we don't have the tools or weapons or knowhow—whatever *that* is—but they wouldn't do us a bit of good even if we had them. Because they failed once, they failed completely and at their best. There's just no point in trying to put them together again."

And now Eric understood. He understood why his uncle had whispered, why there had been so much strain in this conversation. Bloodshed was involved here, bloodshed and death.

"Uncle Thomas," he whispered, in a voice that kept cracking despite his efforts to keep it whole and steady, "how long have you been an Alien-Science man? When did you leave Ancestor-Science?"

Thomas the Trap-Smasher caressed his spear before he answered. He felt for it with a gentle, wandering arm, almost unconsciously, but both of them registered the fact that it was loose and ready. His tremendous body, nude except for the straps about his loins and the light spear-sling on his back, looked as if it were preparing to move instantaneously in any direction.

He stared again from one end of the burrow to the other, his forehead lamp reaching out to the branching darkness of the exits. Eric stared with him: no one was leaning tightly against a wall and listening.

"How long? Since I got to know your father. He was in another band; naturally we hadn't seen much of each other before he married my sister. I'd heard about him, though: everyone in the Male Society had—he was a great thief. But once he became my brother-in-law, I learned a lot from him. I learned about locks, about the latest traps—and I learned about Alien-Science. He'd been an Alien-Science man for years. He converted your mother, and he converted me."

Eric the Only backed away. "No!" he called out wildly. "Not my father and mother! They were decent people—when they were killed a service was held in their name—they went to add to the science of our ancestors—"

His uncle jammed a powerful hand over his mouth. "Shut up, you damn fool, or you'll finish us both! Of course, your parents were decent people—how do you think they were killed? Your mother was with your father out in Monster territory. Have you ever heard of a woman going along with her husband on a Theft? And taking her baby with her? Do you think it was an ordinary robbery of the Monsters? They were Alien-Science people, serving their faith as best they could. They died for it."

Eric looked into his uncle's eyes over the hand that covered the lower half of his face. *Alien-Science people...serving their faith...do you think it was an ordinary robbery...*

He had never realized before how odd it was that his parents had gone to Monster territory together, a man taking his wife and the woman taking her baby!

As he relaxed, his uncle removed the gagging hand. "What kind of Theft was it that my parents died in?"

Thomas examined his face and seemed satisfied. "The kind you're going after," he said. "If you are your father's son. If you're man enough to continue the work he started. Are you?"

Eric started to nod, then found himself shrugging weakly, and finally just hung his head. He didn't know what to say. His uncle—well, his uncle was his model and his leader, and he was strong and wise and crafty. His father—naturally, he wanted to emulate his father and continue whatever work he had started. But this was his initiation ceremony, after all, and there would be enough danger merely in proving his manhood. For his initiation ceremony to take on a task that had destroyed his father, the greatest thief the tribe had ever known, and a heretical, blasphemous task at that…

"I'll try. I don't know if I can."

"You can," his uncle told him heartily. "It's been set up for you: it will be like walking through a dug burrow, Eric. All you have to face through is the council. You'll have to be steady there, no matter what. You tell the chief that you're undertaking the third category."

"But why the third?" Eric asked. "Why does it have to be Monster souvenirs?"

"Because that's what we need. And you stick to it, no matter what pressure they put on you. Remember, an initiate has the right to decide what he's going to steal. A man's first Theft is his own affair."

"But, listen, Uncle—"

There was a whistle from the end of the burrow. Thomas the Trap-Smasher nodded in the direction of the signal.

"The council's beginning, boy. We'll talk later, on expedition. Now remember this: stealing from the third category is your own idea, and all your own idea. Forget everything else we've talked about. If you hit any trouble with the chief, I'll be there. I'm your sponsor, after all."

He threw an arm about his confused nephew and walked to the end of the burrow where the other members of the band waited.

Chapter 2

The tribe had gathered in its central and largest burrow under the great, hanging glow lamps that might be used in this place alone. Except for the few sentinels on duty in the outlying corridors, all of Mankind was here, over a hundred people. It was an awesome sight.

On the little hillock known as the Royal Mound, lolled Franklin the Father of Many Thieves, Chieftain of all Mankind. He alone of the cluster of warriors displayed heaviness of belly and flabbiness of arm—for he alone had the privilege of a sedentary life. Beside the sternly muscled band leaders who formed his immediate background, he looked almost womanly; and yet one of his many titles was simply The Man.

Yes, unquestionably The Man of Mankind was Franklin the Father of Many Thieves. You could tell it from the hushed, respectful attitudes of the subordinate warriors who stood at a distance from the mound. You could tell it from the rippling interest of the women as they stood on the other side of the great burrow, drawn up in the ranks of the Female Society. You could tell it from the nervousness and scorn with which the women were watched by their leader, Ottilie, the Chieftain's First Wife. And finally, you could tell it from the faces of the children, standing in a distant, disorganized bunch: a clear majority of their faces bore an unmistakable resemblance to Franklin's.

Franklin clapped his hands, three evenly spaced, flesh-heavy wallops.

"In the name of our ancestors," he said, "and the science with which they ruled the Earth, I declare this council opened. May it end as one more step in the regaining of their science. Who asked for a council?"

"I did." Thomas the Trap-Smasher moved out of his band and stood before the chief.

Franklin nodded, and went on with the next, formal question:

"And your reason?"

"As a band leader, I call attention to a candidate for manhood. A member of my band, a spear-carrier for the required time, and an accepted apprentice in the Male Society. My nephew, Eric the Only."

As his name was sung out, Eric shook himself. Half on his own volition and half in response to the pushes he received from the other warriors, he stumbled up to his uncle and faced the Chief. This, the most important moment of his life, was proving almost too much for him. So many people in one place, accredited and famous warriors, knowledgeable and attractive women, the Chief himself, all this after the shattering revelations from his uncle—he was finding it hard to think clearly. And it was vital to think clearly. His responses to the next few questions had to be exactly right.

The Chief was asking the first: "Eric the Only, do you apply for full manhood?"

Eric breathed hard and nodded. "I do."

"As a full man, what will be your value to Mankind?"

"I will steal for Mankind whatever it needs. I will defend Mankind against all outsiders. I will increase the possessions and knowledge of the Female Society so that the Female Society can increase the power and well-being of Mankind."

"And all this you swear to do?"

"And all this I swear to do."

The Chief turned to Eric's uncle. "As his sponsor, do you support his oath and swear that he is to be trusted?"

With just the faintest hint of sarcasm in his voice, Thomas the Trap-Smasher replied: "Yes. I support his oath and swear that he is to be trusted."

There was a rattling moment, the barest second, when the Chief's eyes locked with those of the band leader. With all that was on Eric's mind at the moment, he noticed it. Then the Chief looked away and pointed to the women on the other side of the burrow.

"He is accepted as a candidate by the men. Now the women must ask for proof, for only a woman's proof bestows full manhood."

The first part was over. And it hadn't been too bad. Eric turned to face the advancing leaders of the Female Society, Ottilie, the Chieftain's First Wife, in the center. Now came the part that scared him. The women's part.

As was customary at such a moment, his uncle and sponsor left him when the women came forward. Thomas the Trap-Smasher led his band to the warriors grouped about the Throne Mound. There, with their colleagues, they folded their arms across their chests and turned to watch. A man can only give proof of his manhood while he is alone; his friends cannot support him once the women approach.

It was not going to be easy, Eric realized. He had hoped that at least one of his uncle's wives would be among the examiners: they were both kindly people who liked him and had talked to him much about the mysteries of women's work. But he had drawn a trio of hard-faced females who apparently intended to take him over the full course before they passed him.

Sarah the Sickness-Healer opened the proceedings. She circled him belligerently, hands on hips, her great breasts rolling to and fro like a pair of swollen pendulums, her eyes glittering with scorn.

"Eric the Only," she intoned, and then paused to grin, as if it were a name impossible to believe, "Eric the Singleton, Eric the one and only child of either his mother or his father. Your parents almost didn't have enough between them to make a solitary child: is there enough in you to make a man?"

There was a snigger of appreciation from the children in the distance, and it was echoed by a few growling laughs from the vicinity of the Throne Mound. Eric felt his face and neck go red. He would have fought any man to the death for remarks like these—any man at all—but who could lift his hand to a woman and be allowed to live? Besides, one of the main purposes of this exhibition was to investigate his powers of self-control.

"I think so," he managed to say after a long pause. "And I'm willing to prove it."

"Prove it, then!" the woman snarled. Her right hand, holding a long, sharp-pointed pin, shot to his chest like a flung spear. Eric made his muscles rigid and tried to send his mind away. That, the men had told him, was what you had to do at this moment: it was not you they were hurting, not you at all. You, your mind, your knowledge of self, were in another part of the burrow entirely, watching these painful things being done to someone else.

The pin sank into his chest for a little distance, paused, came out. It probed here, probed there; finally it found a nerve in his upper arm. There, guided by the knowledge of the Sickness-Healer, it bit and clawed at the delicate area until Eric felt he would grind his teeth to powder in the effort not to cry out. His clenched fists twisted agonizingly at the ends of his arms in a paroxysm of protest, but he kept his body still. He didn't cry out; he didn't move away; he didn't raise a hand to protect himself.

Sarah the Sickness-Healer stepped back and considered him. "There is no man here yet," she said grudgingly. "But perhaps there are the beginnings of one."

He could relax. The physical test was over. There would be another one, much later, after he had completed his Theft successfully: but that would be exclusively by men as part of his proud initiation ceremony. Under the circumstances, he knew he would be able to go through it almost gaily.

Meanwhile, the women's physical test was over. That was the important thing for now. In sheer reaction, his body gushed forth sweat which slid over the bloody cracks in his skin and stung viciously. He felt the water pouring down his back and forced himself not to go limp, prodded his mind into alertness.

"Did that hurt?" he was being asked by Rita, the old crone of a Record-Keeper. There was a solicitous smile on her forty-year-old face, but he knew it was a fake. A woman as old as that no longer felt sorry for anybody: she had too many aches and pains and things generally wrong with her to worry about other people's troubles.

"A little," he said. "Not much."

"The Monsters will hurt you much more if they catch you stealing from them, do you know that? They will hurt you much more than we ever could."

"I know. But the stealing is more important than the risk I'm taking. The stealing is the most important thing a man can do."

Rita the Record-Keeper nodded. "Because you steal things Mankind needs in order to live. You steal things that the Female Society can make into food, clothing and weapons for Mankind, so that Mankind can live and flourish."

He saw the way, saw what was expected of him. "No," he contradicted her. "That's not why we steal. We live on what we steal, but we do not steal just to go on living."

"Why?" she asked blandly, as if she didn't know the answer better than any other member of the tribe. "Why do we steal? What is more important than survival?"

Here it was now. The catechism.

"To hit back at the Monsters," he began. *"To drive them from the planet, if we can. Regain Earth for Mankind, if we can. But, above all, hit back at the Monsters...."*

He ploughed through the long verbal ritual, pausing at the end of each part, so that the Record-Keeper could ask the proper question and initiate the next sequence.

She tried to trip him once. She reversed the order of the fifth and sixth questions. Instead of *"What will we do with the Monsters when we have regained the Earth from them?"* she asked, *"Why can't we use the Monsters' own Alien-Science to fight the Monsters?"*

Carried along by mental habit, Eric was well into the passage beginning *"We will keep them as our ancestors kept all strange animals, in a place called a zoo, or we will drive them into our burrows and force them to live as we have lived,"* before he realized the switch and stopped in confusion. Then he got a grip on himself, sought the right answer in his memory with calmness, as his uncle's wives had schooled him to do, and began again.

"There are three reasons why we cannot ever use Alien-Science," he recited, holding up his hand with the thumb and little finger closed. *"Alien-Science is nonhuman, Alien-*

Science is inhuman, Alien-Science is antihuman. First, since it is nonhuman," he closed his forefinger, "*we cannot use it because we can never understand it. And because it is inhuman, we would never want to use it even if we could understand it. And because it is antihuman and can only be used to hurt and damage Mankind, we would not be able to use it so long as we remain human ourselves. Alien-Science is the opposite of Ancestor-Science in every way, ugly instead of beautiful, hurtful instead of helpful. When we die, Alien-Science would not bring us to the world of our ancestors, but to another world full of Monsters.*"

All in all, it went very well, despite the trap into which he had almost fallen. But he couldn't help remembering the conversation with his uncle in the other burrow. As his mouth reeled off the familiar words and concepts, his mind kept wondering how the two fitted together. His uncle was Alien-Science, and, according to his uncle, so had been his parents. Did that make them nonhuman, inhuman, antihuman?

And what did it make him? He knew his religious duty well: he should at this moment be telling all Mankind about his uncle's horrible secret.

The whole subject was far too complicated for someone with his limited experience.

When he had completed the lengthy catechism, Rita the Record-Keeper said: "And this is what you say about the science of our ancestors. Now we will find out what the science of our ancestors says about you."

She signaled over her shoulder, without turning her head, and two young girls—female apprentices—pulled forward the large record machine which was the very center of the tribe's religious life. They stepped back, both smiling shyly and encouragingly at Eric the Only.

He knew the smiles meant little more than simple best wishes from apprentices of the one sex to apprentices of the other, but even that was quite a bit at the moment. It meant that he was much closer to full status than they. It meant that, in the opinion of unprejudiced, disinterested observers, his examination was proceeding very well indeed.

Singleton, he thought fiercely to himself. *I'll show them what a singleton can do!*

Rita the Record-Keeper turned a knob at the top of the squat machine and it began to hum. She flung her arms up, quiveringly apart, and all—warriors, women, children, apprentices, even the chief himself—all bowed their heads.

"Harken to the words of our ancestors," she chanted. "Watch closely the spectacle of their great achievements. When their end was upon them, and they knew that only we, their descendants, might regain the Earth they had lost, they made this machine for the future generations of Mankind as a guide to the science that once had been and must be again."

The old woman lowered her arms. Simultaneously, heads went up all over the burrow and stared expectantly at the wall opposite the record machine.

"Eric the Only," Rita called, spinning the dial on the left of the machine with one hand and stabbing at it randomly with the forefinger of the other. "This is the sequence in the science of our ancestors that speaks for you alone. This is the appointed vision under which you will live and die."

Chapter 3

He stared at the wall, breathing hard. Now he would find out what his life was to be about—*now!* His uncle's vision at this moment, many years ago, had suggested the nickname he came to bear: the Trap-Smasher. At the last initiation ceremony, a youth had called forth a sequence in which two enormous airborne vehicles of the ancestors had collided.

They'd tried to cheer the boy up, but he'd known his fate was upon him. Sure enough, he had been caught by a monster in the middle of his Theft and dashed to pieces against a wall.

Even then, Eric decided, he'd rather have that kind of a sequence than the awful emptiness of a *blank* vision. When, every once in a while, the machine went on and showed nothing but a blinding white rectangle, the whole tribe knew that the youth being examined had no possibility of manhood in him at all. And the machine was never wrong. A boy who'd drawn a blank vision inevitably became more and more effeminate as he grew older without ever going out on his Theft. He tended to shun the company of warriors and to ask the women for minor tasks to perform. The machine of the ancestors looked at a boy and told exactly what he was and what he would become.

It had been great, that science which had produced this machine, no doubt about it. There was a power source in it which was self-contained, and which was supposed to be like the power behind all things. It would run almost forever, if the machine were not tampered with—although who could dream of tampering with it? In its visions were locked not only the secrets of every individual human being, but enormous mysteries which the whole of Mankind had to solve before it could work out its salvation through the rituals and powers of the ancestral science.

Now, however, there was only one small part of Mankind that concerned Eric. Himself. His future. He waited, growing more and more tense as the power hum from the machine increased in pitch. And suddenly there was a grunt of awe from the entire burrow of people as a vision was thrown upon the wall.

He hadn't drawn a blank. That was the most important thing. He had been given an authentic ancestral vision.

"Scattergood's does it again!" a voice blared, as the picture projected on the wall showed people coming from all directions, wearing the strange body wrappings of the ancestors. They rushed, men, women, children, from the four corners of the glittering screen to some strange structure in the center and disappeared into its entrance. More and more poured in, more and more kept materializing at the edges and scrambling toward the structure in the center.

"Scattergood's does it again!" the vision yelled out at them. "The sale of sales! The value of values! Only at Scattergood's three stores tomorrow. Binoculars, tape recorders, cameras, all at tremendous reductions, many below cost. Value, value, value!"

Now the vision showed only objects. Strange, unfamiliar objects such as the ancestors used. And as each object appeared, the voice recited a charm over it. Powerful and ancient magic this, the forgotten lore of Ancestor-Science.

"Krafft-Yahrmann Exposure Meters, the best there is, you've heard about them and now you can buy them, the light meter that's an eye-opener, a price to fit every pocketbook, eight dollars and ninety-five cents, tomorrow at Scattergood's, absolutely only one to a customer."

"Kyoto Automatic Eight-Millimeter Movie Cameras with an eff one point four lens and an electric eye that does all the focusing and gives you a perfect exposure every single time. As low as three dollars a week. The supply is limited, so hurry, hurry, hurry!"

Eric watched the sequence unfold, his hands squeezing each other, his eyes almost distended in reverence and concentration. This was the clue to his life, to what he might become. This was the sequence that the record machine of the ancestors, turned on at random, had vouchsafed as a prophecy of his future.

All knowledge was in that machine—and no possibility of error.

But Eric was getting worried. The vision was too strange. Sometimes there would be a vision that baffled even the wisest women. And that meant the youth who had called it forth would always be a puzzle, to himself and all of Mankind.

Let it not happen to him! O ancestors, O science, O record machine, let it not happen to him!

Let him only have a clear and definite vision so that his personality could be clear and definite for the rest of his life!

"Our special imported high-power precision binoculars," the voice roared on as a man appeared in the vision and brought one of the strange objects up to his eyes. "If we told you the manufacturer's name, you'd recognize it immediately. Seven ex fifty, only fourteen dollars and ninety-five cents, *with case*. Ten ex fifty, only fifteen dollars and ninety-five cents, *with case*. You see further, you see clearer, you pay less. You always pay less at Scattergood's. Rock-bottom prices! Skyscraper values! Tomorrow, tomorrow, tomorrow, at Scattergood's annual Week-After-Halloween Sale!"

There was a click as the vision went off abruptly to be replaced by a white rectangle on the wall of the burrow. Eric realized that this was all the clue there was to be to his life. What did it mean? Could it be interpreted?

Anxiously, now, he turned to Ottilie, the Chieftain's First Wife. He turned to her as everyone else in Mankind was now turning, Sarah the Sickness-Healer and Rita the Record-Keeper amongst them.

Only Ottilie could read a vision, only short, squat, imperious Ottilie. The Chieftain's First Wife was her title of honor and her latest title, but long before she had acquired that, long before even she had become Head of the Female Society, she had been Ottilie the Augur, Ottilie the Omen-Teller, Ottilie who could walk in her mind from the familiar, homey burrow of the present into the dark, labyrinthine corridors of the future, Ottilie who could read signs, Ottilie who could announce portents.

It was as Ottilie the Augur that she could pick out the one new-born babe in a litter of three that had to be destroyed because, in some way or other, it would one day bring death to its people. It was as Ottilie the Augur that, upon the death of the old chief, she had chosen Franklin the Father of Many Thieves to take over the leadership of Mankind since he stimulated the most propitious omens. In everything she had been right. And now, once again it was as Ottilie the Augur that she threw her arms over her head and twisted and swayed and moaned as she sought deep inside herself for the meaning of Eric's vision, it was as Ottilie the Augur and not as Ottilie the Chieftain's First Wife, for that she had been only since Franklin had ascended the Throne Mound.

The scratches and holes gouged in his body by Sarah the Sickness-Healer had begun to ache badly, but Eric shrugged off their annoyance. Could his vision be interpreted? And *how* would it be interpreted?

Whatever Ottilie saw in the vision would stick to him for the rest of his life, much closer than the dried blood upon his arms and legs and chest. How could you possibly interpret such a vision? Eric the Scattergood? That was meaningless. Eric the Value? No, that was a little better, but it was dreadfully vague, almost as bad as a blank vision.

He stared past Ottilie's writhing figure to where his uncle stood, surrounded by his band, a little to the left of the Throne Mound. Thomas the Trap-Smasher was watching Ottilie and grinning with all his teeth.

What did he find so funny, Eric wondered desperately? Was there nothing holy to him? Didn't he realize how important it was to Eric's future that his vision be readable, that he get a name to be proud of? What was funny in Ottilie's agony as she gave birth to Eric's future?

He realized that Ottilie was beginning to make coherent sounds. He strained his ears to listen. This, this was it. Who he really was. Who he would be.

"Three times," Ottilie mumbled in a voice that steadily grew clearer and louder, "three times our ancestors gave Eric his name. Three repetitions they made. Three different ways they called on him to become what their science needed him to be. And all of you heard it, and I heard it, and Eric heard it too."

Which, Eric puzzled, which among the many strange magical statements had contained his name and his life's work? He waited for the Augur to come out with it. He had almost given up breathing.

Her body relaxed now, her hands hanging at her sides, Ottilie was speaking to them in a sharp, authoritative voice as she stared at the wall of the burrow where the vision had appeared.

" 'A light meter that's an eye-opener,' the Ancestor-Science said," she reminded them. "And 'an electric eye that does all the focusing.' And 'you see further, you see clearer, you pay less,' the Record Machine told us of Eric. What the ancestors want of Eric is unmistakable, what he must be if we are to hit back at the Monsters and regain the Earth which is rightfully ours."

Thank the Record Machine, thank each and every ancestor! At least the message had been unmistakable. But what precisely had it been?

Ottilie the Augur, the Omen-Teller, turned to face him now where he stood apart from the rest of eagerly watching Mankind. He straightened up and stood stiffly to learn his fate.

"Eric," she said. "Eric the Only, Eric the Singleton, you go out now to make your Theft. If you are successful and return alive, you will become a man. And as a man you will no longer be Eric the Only, you will be Eric the Eye. Eric the Eye, Eric the Espier, Eric who seeks out the path for Mankind. Eric who hits back at the Monsters with his eye, his open eye, his electric eye, his further-seeing, clearer-seeing, less-paying eye. For this is the word of the ancestors, and all of you have heard it."

At last Eric could take a deep breath, and he did so now, noisily, in common with the whole of Mankind who had been hanging on Ottilie's words. Eric the Eye—that was what he was to be. If he was successful. And if he lived.

Eric the Eye. Eric the Espier. Now he knew about himself. It was fixed, and for all time. It was a good name to bear, a fine personality to have. He had been very fortunate.

Rita the Record-Keeper and her daughter. Harriet the History-Teller, rolled the Record Machine back into its accustomed holy place, the niche in the wall behind the Throne Mound. Despite the sacred quality of the act in which she was engaged, the younger woman could not take her eyes off Eric. He was a person of consequence now, or at least would be when he returned. Other young and mating-aged women, he noticed, were looking at him the same way.

He began to walk around in a little circle before Mankind, and, as he walked, he strutted. He waited until Ottilie, no longer the Augur now, no longer the Omen-Teller, but once more the Chieftain's First Wife—he waited until she had returned to her place at the head of the Female Society before he began to sing.

He threw back his head and spread out his arms and danced proudly, stampingly, before Mankind. He spun around in great dizzying circles and leaped in the air and came down with wrenching spasmodic twists of his legs and arms. And as he danced, he sang.

He sang out of the pride that racked his chest like a soul coughing, out of the majesty of the warrior-that-was-to-be, out of his sure knowledge of self. And he sang his promise to his fellows:

> *I am Eric the Eye,*
> *Eric the Open Eye,*
> *Eric the Electric Eye,*
> *Eric the Further-Seeing, Clearer-Seeing, Less-Paying Eye.*
> *Eric the Espier—*
> *Eric who finds and points out the way.*
> *Are you lost in a strange place?*
> *I will show you the path to your home.*
> *Does the burrow break off in too many branches?*
> *I will pick out the best one and Mankind shall walk through in safety.*
> *Are there enemies about, hidden traps, unthought of dangers?*

I will see them and give warning of them in time.
I will walk at the head of the line of warriors and see for them,
And they shall be confident and they shall conquer—
For they have Eric the Espier to lead the way and point the path!

So he sang as he danced before Mankind, under the enormous glow lamps of its great central burrow. He sang of his mission in life as just a few short auld lang synes ago he had heard Roy the Runner, at his initiation, sing of the fleetness and swiftness that he would soon be the master of; as his Uncle Thomas had sung long before that of his coming ability to detect and dismantle traps; as once his own father had sung of the robberies he was to commit, of the storerooms he would empty for the benefit of Mankind. He sang and he leaped and he whirled, and all the while the watching host of Mankind beat time with its feet and hands and played chorus in the litany of his triumph.

Then came a loud grunt from Franklin the Father of Many Thieves. The noise stopped. Eric danced to a quivering halt, his body wet all over, his limbs still trembling.

"That is what is to be," Franklin pointed out, "once the Theft has been made. But first, first comes the Theft. Always before manhood comes the Theft. Now let us speak of your Theft."

"I will go into the very home of the Monsters," Eric announced proudly, his head thrown back before the chief. "I will go into their home alone, with no companion but my own weapons, as a warrior should. I will steal from them, no matter what the danger, no matter what the threat. And what I steal, I will bring back for the use and enjoyment of Mankind."

Franklin nodded and made the formal reply. "That is good, and it is spoken like a warrior. What do you promise to steal from the Monsters? For your first Theft must be a promise made in advance and kept, kept exactly."

Now they were at it. Eric glanced at his uncle for support. Thomas the Trap-Smasher was staring off in a different direction. Eric licked his lips. Well, maybe it wouldn't be too bad. After all, a youth going off on his first Theft had complete freedom of choice.

"I promise to make my theft in the third category," he said, his voice trembling just a little.

The results were much more than he had anticipated. Franklin the Father of Many Thieves yelped sharply. He leaped off the Royal Mound and stood gaping at Eric for a while. His great belly and fat arms quivered with disbelief.

"The third category, did you say? The *third?*"

Eric, thoroughly frightened now, nodded.

Franklin turned to Chief Wife Ottilie. They both peered through the ranks of Mankind to where Thomas the Trap-Smasher stood in the midst of his band, seemingly unconcerned by the sensation that had just been created.

"What *is* this, Thomas?" the chief demanded, all ceremony and formality gone from his speech. "What are you trying to pull? What's this third category stuff you're up to?"

Thomas the Trap-Smasher turned a bland eye upon him. "What am *I* up to? I'm not up to a damn thing. The boy's got a right to pick his category. If he wants to steal in the third category, well, that's his business. What have I got to do with it?"

The chief stared at him for a few moments longer. Then he swung back to Eric and said shortly: "All right. You've chosen. The third category it is. Now let's get on with the feast."

Somehow it was all spoiled for Eric. The initiation feast that preceded a first Theft—how he had looked forward to it! But he was apparently involved in something going on in Mankind, something dangerous and unsavory.

The chief obviously considered him an important factor in whatever difficulty had arisen. Usually, an initiate about to depart on a Theft was the focus of all conversation as Mankind ate in its central burrow, the women squatting on one side, the men on the other, the children at the far ends where light was dim. But at this meal, the chief made only the most necessary ritual remarks to Eric: his eyes kept wandering from him to Thomas the Trap-Smasher.

Once in a while, Franklin's eyes met those of Ottilie, his favored and first wife, across the feast that had been spread the length of the burrow. He seemed to be saying something to her, although neither of them moved their lips. Then they would nod at each other and look back to Eric's uncle.

The rest of Mankind became aware of the strained atmosphere: there was little of the usual laughter and gaiety of an initiation feast. The Trap-Smasher's band had pulled in tightly all around him; most of them were not even bothering to eat but sat watchful and alert. Other band captains—men like Stephen the Strong-Armed and Harold the Hurler—had worried looks on their faces as if they were calculating highly complex problems.

Even the children were remarkably quiet. They served the food over which the women had said charms much earlier, then scurried to their places and ate with wide eyes aimed at their elders.

All in all, Eric was distinctly relieved when Franklin the Father of Many Thieves belched commandingly, stretched, and lay back on the floor of the burrow. In a few minutes, he was asleep, snoring loudly.

Night had officially begun.

Chapter 4

At the end of the sleep period, as soon as the chief had awakened and yawned, thus proclaiming the dawn, Thomas the Trap-Smasher's band started on its trip.

Eric, still officially surnamed the Only, carried the precious loin straps of manhood in the food knapsack the women had provided for a possible journey of several days. They should return before the next sleep period, but when one went on an expedition into Monster territory anything might happen.

They stepped out in full military formation, a long, straggling single file, each man barely in sight of the warrior immediately ahead. For the first time in his military career, Eric was wearing only one set of spears—those for himself. Extra weapons for the band—as well as extra supplies—were on the back of a new apprentice, a stripling who marched a distance behind Eric, watching him with the same mixture of fright and exhilaration Eric himself had once accorded all other warriors.

Ahead of Eric, momentarily disappearing as the dim corridor curved and branched, was Roy the Runner, his long, loose-jointed legs purposefully treading down the paces. And all the way in the lead of the column, Eric knew, was his uncle. Thomas the Trap-Smasher would be striding cautiously yet without any unnecessary waste of time, the large glow lantern on his forehead constantly shifting from wall to wall of the uninhabited burrow and then straight ahead, the heavy spear in each brawny hand ready for instant action, his mouth set to call the warning behind him if danger materialized.

To be a man—this was what it was like! To go on expeditions like this for the rest of one's life, glorious, adventure-charged expeditions so that Mankind might eat well and have weapons and live as Mankind should. And when you returned, triumphant, victorious, the welcoming dance of the women as they threaded their way through the tired ranks, giving you refreshment and taking from you the supplies that only they could turn into usable articles. Then, after you had eaten and drunk and rested, your own dance, the dance of the men, where you sang and acted out for the tribe all the events of this particular expedition, the dangers you had overcome, the splendid courage you had shown, the strange and mysterious sights you had seen.

The sights you had seen! As Eric the Eye, he would probably be entitled to a solo dance any time his band came across anything particularly curious. Oh, how high Eric the Eye would leap, how loudly, how proudly, how melodiously he would sing of the wonders the expedition had encountered!

"Eric the Eye," the women would murmur. "What a fine, fine figure of a man! What a mate for some lucky woman!"

Harriet the History-Teller this morning, for example, before they started out. She had filled his canteen for him with fresh water as if he were already an accredited man instead of an initiate going out to face his ultimate trial. Before the eyes of all Mankind she had filled it and brought it to him, her eyes downcast and light purple blushes on the rosy skin of her face and body. She had treated him the way a wife treats a husband, and many warriors—Eric thought gleefully—many full warriors with their Thefts long behind them had observed that Eric was likely to join the ranks of the Male Society and the married men almost simultaneously.

Of course, with her unlucky red hair, her bustling, domineering mother, Harriet was not exactly the most marriageable girl in Mankind. Still, there were many full warriors who had not yet been able to persuade a woman to mate with them, who watched Franklin and his three wives with unconcealed hunger and envy. How they would envy Eric, the newest warrior of all, when he mated the same night he returned from his Theft! Call him Only, then! Call him Singleton, then!

They would have litter after litter, he and Harriet, large litters, ample litters, four, five, even six at a time. People would forget he'd ever been the product of a singleton birth; other women, mates of other warriors, would wriggle to attract his attention as they now wriggled when they caught the eye of Franklin the Father of Many Thieves. He would make the litters fathered by Franklin look puny in comparison, he would prove that the best hope for Mankind's increase lay in his loins and his loins alone. And when the time came to select another chief…

"Hey, you damned daydreaming singleton!" Roy the Runner was calling from the burrow ahead. "Will you wipe that haze out of your face and pay attention to signals? This is an expedition to Monster territory, not a stroll in the women's quarters. Stay alert, will you? The band captain's sent down a call for you."

Amid the chuckles ahead and behind him—damn it, even the new apprentice was laughing!—Eric took a firmer grip on his glow torch and sprinted for the head of the column. As he passed each man, he was asked the name of the girl he'd been thinking about and pressed for interesting details. Since he kept his mouth tightly shut, some of the warriors hypothesized out loud. They were painfully close to the truth.

His uncle wasn't much gentler with him. "'Eric the *Eye!*" the Trap-Smasher growled. "Eric the Eyebrow, Eric the Closed Eyelash, you'll be known as, if you don't wake up! Now stay abreast of me and try to *act* like Eric the Eye. These are dangerous burrows and my vision isn't as sharp as yours. Besides, I have to fill you in on a couple of things." He turned. "Spread out a little farther back there," he called out to the men behind him. "Spread out! You should be a full spear-cast from the backside of the man in front of you. Let me see a real strung-out column with plenty of distance between each warrior."

To Eric, he muttered, once the maneuver had been completed: "Good. Gives us a chance to talk without everyone in the band hearing us. You can trust my bunch, but still, why take chances?"

Eric nodded, with no idea what he was talking about. His uncle had become slightly odd recently. Well, he was still the best band captain in all Mankind.

They marched along together, the light from the strange glowing substance on Eric's torch and his uncle's forehead spreading a yellowish illumination some hundred feet ahead of them. On either side, underfoot, overhead, were the curved, featureless walls of the burrow. From the center of the corridor, where they marched, the walls looked soft and spongy, but Eric knew what tremendous labor was involved in digging a niche or recess in them. It took several strong men at least two sleep periods to make a niche large enough to hold more than a handful of Mankind's store of artifacts.

Where had the burrows come from? Some said they had been dug by the ancestors when they had first begun to hit back at the Monsters. Others claimed the burrows had always been there, waiting for Mankind to find them and be comfortable in them.

In all directions the burrows stretched. On and on they went, interminably curving and branching and forking, dark and silent, until human beings stamped into them with glow lamp and glow torch. These particular corridors, Eric knew, led to Monster territory: he had been along them many times as a humble spear-carrier when his uncle's band had been dispatched to bring back the necessities of life for

Mankind. Other corridors went off to more exotic and even more dangerous places. But were there any places which had no burrows?

What a thought! Even the Monsters lived in burrows, big as they were reputed to be. But there was a legend that Mankind had once lived outside burrows, outside the branching corridors. Then what had they lived in? Just trying to work it out made you dizzy.

They came to a place where the burrow became two burrows, each curving away from the other in opposite directions.

"Which one?" his uncle demanded.

Eric unhesitatingly pointed to the right.

Thomas the Trap-Smasher nodded. "You have a good memory," he said as he bore in the direction that Eric had indicated. "That's half of being an Eye. The other half is having a feeling, a knack, for the right way to go. You have that too. I've noticed it on every expedition where you've been along. That's what I told those women—Rita, Ottilie—I told them what your name had to be. Eric the Eye, I told them: 'Find a vision for the kid that corresponds to it.'"

He was so shocked that he almost came to a halt. "You picked my name? You told them what kind of vision? That's—that's—I never heard of such a thing!"

His uncle laughed. "It's no different from Ottilie the Omen-Teller making a deal with Franklin to have a vision showing him as the new chief. He gets to be chief, she becomes the Chieftain's First Wife and automatically takes over the Female Society. Religion and politics, they're always mixed up together these days, Eric. We're not living in the old times any more when Ancestor-Science was real and holy and it worked."

"It still works, Ancestor-Science, doesn't it?" he pleaded. "Some of the time?"

"Don't be a fool. Of course it works. Without the correct ritual behind us, we wouldn't dare go out on expedition. But it doesn't work far enough, strong enough—like Alien-Science. Alien-Science is working for the Monsters. It's got to begin working for us. That's where you come in."

He had to remember that his uncle was an experienced captain, a knowledgeable warrior. Thomas the Trap-Smasher's protection and advice had brought him, a despised singleton, an orphaned child of parents that no one dared even talk about, to his present estate of almost full thieving status. It was very fortunate for him that neither of his uncle's wives had yet produced a son who survived into the initiate years. He still had a lot to learn from this man.

"Now," the Trap-Smasher was saying, his eyes still on the dimly illuminated corridors ahead. "When we get to the Monster burrows, you go in. You go in alone, of course."

Well, of course, Eric thought. What other way was there to make your Theft? The first time you stole for Mankind, you did it all alone, to prove your manhood, your courage, also the amount of personal luck you enjoyed. It was not like a regular band theft—an organized stealing of a large amount of goods that would last Mankind many sleep periods, almost a tenth of an auld lang syne. In a regular band theft, assigned to each band in rotation, a warrior had to be assured of the luck and skill of the warriors at his side. He had to know that each one of them had made his Theft—and proved himself when completely alone.

Stealing from the Monsters was dangerous enough under the best of conditions. You wanted only the cleverest, bravest, most fortunate warriors along with you.

"Once you're inside, stay close to the wall. Don't look up at first or you're likely to freeze right where you are. Keep your eyes on the wall and move close to it. Move fast."

Nothing new here. Every initiate learned over and over again, before he made his Theft, that it was terribly dangerous to look up when you first entered Monster territory. You had to keep your eyes on the wall and move in the protection of it, the wall touching your shoulder as you ran alongside it. Why this was so, Eric had no idea, but that it was so he had long ago learned to repeat as a fact.

"All right," Thomas the Trap-Smasher went on. "You turn right as you go in—*right,* do you hear me, Eric?—you turn right, without looking up, and run along the wall, letting it brush your shoulder every couple of steps. You run forty, fifty paces, and you come to a great big thing, a structure, that's almost touching the wall. You turn left along that, moving away from the wall, but still not looking up, until you pass an entrance in the structure. You don't go in that first entrance, Eric; you pass it by. About twenty, twenty-five paces farther on, there'll be a second entrance, a bigger one. You go in that one."

"I go in that one," Eric repeated carefully, memorizing his uncle's words. He was receiving directions for his Theft, the most important act of his life! Every single thing his uncle told him must be listened to carefully, must not be forgotten.

"You'll be in something that looks like a burrow again, but it'll be darker, at first. The walls will soak up light from your glow lamp. After a while, the burrow will open out into a great big space, a real big and real dark space. You go on in a straight line, looking over your shoulder at the light from the entrance and making sure it's always directly behind you. You'll hit another burrow, a low one this time. Turn right at the first fork as soon as you go in, and there you are."

"Where? Where will I be? What happens then?" Eric demanded eagerly. "How do I make my Theft? Where do I find the third category?"

Thomas the Trap-Smasher seemed to have trouble continuing. Incredible—he was actually nervous! "There'll be a Stranger there. You tell him who you are, your name. He'll do the rest."

This time Eric came to a full stop. "A Stranger?" he asked in complete amazement. "Someone who's not of Mankind?"

His uncle grabbed at his arm and pulled him along. "Well, you've seen Strangers before," he said with a loud laugh. "You know there are others in the burrows besides Mankind. You know that, don't you, boy?"

Eric certainly did.

From an early age he had accompanied his uncle and his uncle's band on warfare and trading expeditions to the burrows a bit farther back. He knew that the people in these burrows looked down on the people in his, that they were more plentiful than his people, and led richer, safer lives—but he still couldn't help feeling sorry for them.

They were nothing but Strangers, after all. He was a member of Mankind.

It wasn't just that Mankind lived in the front burrows, those closest to the Monster larder. This enormous convenience might be counterbalanced, he would readily admit, by the dangers associated with it—although the constant exposure to dangers and death in every form were part of Mankind's greatness. They were great despite their inferior technology. So what if they were primarily a source of raw materials to the more populous but less hardy burrows in the rear? How long would the weaponsmiths, the potters and tanners and artificers of these burrows be able to go on with their buzzing, noisy industries once Mankind ceased to bring them the basic substances—food, cloth, metal—it had so gloriously stolen from fear-filled Monster territory? No, Mankind was the bravest, greatest, most important people in all the burrows, but that still wasn't the point.

The point was that you had nothing more to do with Strangers than was absolutely necessary. They were Strangers: you were Mankind. You stayed proudly aloof from them at all times.

Trading with them—well, you traded with them. Mankind needed spear points and sturdy spear shafts, knapsacks and loin straps, canteens and cooking vessels: you needed these articles and got them in exchange for heavy backloads of shapeless, unprocessed stuff freshly stolen. Mating with them—well, of course you mated with them: one was always on the lookout for extra women who could add to the knowledge and technical abilities of Mankind. But these women became a well-adjusted part of Mankind once they were stolen, just as Mankind's women were complete outsiders and Strangers the moment they had been carried off by a foreign raiding party. And fighting with them, warring with them—next to stealing from the Monsters, that was the sweetest, most exciting part of a warrior's existence.

You traded with Strangers, coldly, suspiciously, always alert for a better bargain; you stole Stranger women whenever you could, gleefully, proudly, because that diminished them and increased the numbers and well-being of Mankind; and you fought Stranger men whenever there was more to be gained that way than by simple trading—and periodically they came upon you as you lay in your burrow unawares and fought you.

But otherwise, for all normal social purposes, they were taboo, almost as taboo and not-to-be-related-to as the Monsters on the other side of Mankind's burrows. When you came upon an individual Stranger wandering apart from his people, you killed him quickly and casually.

You certainly didn't ask him for advice on your Theft.

Eric was still brooding on the unprecedented nature of his uncle's instructions when they came to the end of their journey, a large, blind-alley burrow. There was a line cut deep into the blank wall here, a line that started at the floor, went up almost to the height of a man's head, and then curved down to the floor again.

The door to Monster territory.

Thomas the Trap-Smasher waited for a moment, listening. When his experienced ears had detected no unusual noises in the neighborhood, no hint of danger on the other side, he cupped his hands around his mouth, faced back the way he had come, and softly gave the ululating recognition-call of the band. The four other warriors and the apprentice came up swiftly and grouped themselves about him. Then, at a signal from their leader, all squatted near the door.

They ate first, rapidly and silently, removing from their knapsacks handfuls of food that the women had prepared for them and stuffing their mouths full, the beams from the glow lamps above their eyes darting incessantly back and forth along the arched, empty corridor. This was the place of ultimate, awful danger. This was the place where anything might happen.

Eric ate most sparingly of all, as was correct for an initiate about to emerge upon his Theft. He knew he had to keep his springiness of body and watchfulness of mind at their highest possible pitch. He saw his uncle nodding approvingly as he returned the bulk of his food to the knapsack.

The floor vibrated slightly underfoot; there was a regular, rhythmic gurgling. Eric knew that meant they were in a holy place, directly over a length of Monster plumbing. Two immense pipes ran here side by side. One was the sewer pipe to which Mankind dragged their accumulations of garbage and in which they ceremoniously buried their dead. The other was a prime source of the fresh water without which life came to an end. Upon his return, before the band started homeward, Thomas the Trap-Smasher would make an opening in the plumbing and they would refill their canteens. The water here, close to Monster territory, was always the sweetest and best.

Now his uncle got to his feet and called Roy the Runner to him. While the other warriors watched, tense and still, the two men walked to the curved line and laid their ears against it. Satisfied, finally, they inserted spear points into the door's outline on either side and carefully pried the slab back toward them. They laid it on the floor of the corridor, very gently.

A shimmering blur of pure whiteness appeared where the door had been.

Monster territory. The strange, alien light of Monster territory. Eric had seen many warriors disappear into it to fulfill their manhood tasks. Now it was his turn.

Holding his heavy spear at the ready, Eric's uncle leaned forward into the whiteness. His body twisted as he looked up, down, around, on both sides. He withdrew and came back into the burrow.

"No new traps," he said in a soft voice. "The one I dismantled last expedition is still up there on the wall. It hasn't been repaired. Now Eric. Here you go, boy."

Eric rose and walked with him to the doorway, remembering to keep his eyes on the floor. You, can't look up, he had been told again and again, not right away, not the first time you're in Monster territory. If you do, you freeze, you're lost, you're done for completely.

His uncle checked him carefully and fondly, making certain that his new loin straps were tight, that his knapsack and back sling were both in the right position on his shoulders. He took a heavy spear from Eric's right hand and replaced it with a light one from the back sling. "If you're seen by a Monster," he whispered, "the heavy spear's not worth a damn. You scuttle into the closest hiding place and throw the light spear as far as you can. There's a chance that the Monster can't distinguish between you and the spear. It might follow the spear."

Eric nodded mechanically, although this too had been told many times, this too was a lesson he knew by heart. His mouth was so dry! He wished it weren't unmanly to beg for water at such a moment.

Thomas the Trap-Smasher took his torch from him and slipped a glow lamp about his forehead. Then he pushed him through the doorway. "Go make your Theft, Eric," he whispered. "Come back a man."

Chapter 5

He was on the other side. He was in Monster territory. He was surrounded by the strange Monster light, the incredible Monster world. The burrows, Mankind, everything familiar, lay behind him.

Panic rose from his stomach and into his throat like vomit.

Don't look up. Eyes down, eyes down or you're likely to freeze right where you are. Stay close to the wall, keep your eyes on the wall and move along it. Turn right and move along the wall. Move fast.

Eric turned. He felt the wall brush his right shoulder. He began to run, keeping his eyes down, touching the wall with his shoulder at regular intervals. He ran as fast as he possibly could, urging his muscles fiercely on. As he ran, he counted the steps to himself.

Twenty paces. Where did the light come from? It was everywhere; it glowed so; it was white, white. *Twenty-five paces. Touch the wall with your shoulder. Don't—above everything—don't wander away from the wall. Thirty paces.* In light like this you had no need of the glow lamp. It was almost too bright to see in. *Thirty-five paces.* The floor was not like a burrow floor. It was flat and very hard. So was the wall. Flat and hard and straight. *Forty paces. Run and keep your eyes down. Run. Keep touching the wall with your shoulder. Move fast. But keep your eyes down. Don't look up. Forty-five paces.*

He almost smashed into the structure he had been told about, but his reflexes and the warnings he had received swung him to the left and along it just in time. It was a different color than the wall, he noted, and a different textured material. *Keep your eyes down. Don't look up.*

He came to an entrance, like the beginning of a small burrow.

Don't go in that first entrance, Eric; you pass it by. He began to count again as he ran. Twenty-three paces more, and there was another entrance, a much higher, wider one. He darted inside. *It'll be darker, at first. The walls will soak up light from your glow lamp.*

Eric paused, gasping. He was grateful for the sucking darkness. After that terrible, alien white light, the gloom was friendly, reminiscent of the familiar burrows now so horribly far away.

He could afford to take a breath at this point, he knew. The first, the worst part was over. He wasn't out in the open any more.

He had emerged into Monster territory. He had run fast, following instructions until he was safely under cover again. He was still alive.

The worst was over. Nothing else would ever be as bad as this.

Monster territory. It lay behind him, bathed in its own peculiar light. Now. Why not? Now, when he was in a place of comparative safety. He could take a chance. He *wanted* to take a chance.

He turned, gingerly, fearfully. He raised his eyes. He looked.

The cry that tore from his lips was completely involuntary and frightened him almost as much as what he saw. He shut his eyes and threw himself down and sideways. He lay where he had fallen for a long while, almost paralyzed.

It couldn't be. He hadn't seen it. Nothing was that high, nothing ran on and on for such incredible distances!

After a time, he opened his eyes again, keeping them carefully focused on the dark near him. The gloom in this covered place had diminished somewhat as his eyes had grown more accustomed to it. Yellowish light from his glow lamp was providing illumination now: he could make out the walls, about as far apart from each other as those in a burrow, but—unlike a burrow's walls—oddly straight and at right angles to the floor and ceiling. Far off there was an immense patch of darkness. *The burrow will open out into a great big space, a real big and real dark space.*

What was this place, he wondered? What was it to the Monsters?

He had to take another look behind, into the open. One more quick look. He was going to be Eric the Eye. An Eye should be able to look at anything. He had to take another look.

But guardedly, guardedly.

Eric turned again, opening his eyes a little at a time. He clamped his teeth together so as not to cry out. Even so, he almost did. He shut his eyes quickly, waited, then opened them again. Bit by bit, effort by effort, he found he was able to look into the great open whiteness without losing control of himself. It was upsetting, overpowering, but if he didn't look too long at any one time, he could stand it.

Distance. Enormous, elongated, unbelievable distance. Space upon space upon space—that white light bathing it all. Space far ahead, space on all sides, space going on and on until it seemed to have no end to it at all. But there, fantastically far off, there was an end. There was a wall, a wall made by giants that finally sealed off the tremendous space. It rose hugely from the flat, huge floor and disappeared somewhere far overhead.

And in between—once you could stand to look at it this much—in between, there were objects. Enormous objects, dwarfed only by the greatness of the space which surrounded them, enormous, terribly alien objects. Objects like nothing you had ever imagined.

No, that wasn't quite true. That thing over there. Eric recognized it.

A great, squat thing like a full knapsack without the straps. Since early boyhood, many was the time he had heard it described by warriors back from an expedition into Monster territory.

There was food in that sack and the others like it. Enough food in that one sack to feed the entire population of Mankind for unnumbered auld lang synes. A different kind of food in each sack.

No spear point possessed by Mankind would cut through the fabric of its container, not near the bottom where it was thickest. Warriors had to climb about halfway up the sack, Eric knew, before they could find a place thin enough to carve themselves an entrance. Then the lumps of food would be lowered from man to man all the way down the sack, warriors clinging to precarious handholds every few paces.

Once the pile on the floor was great enough, they would clamber down and fill their specially large, food-expedition knapsacks. Then back to the burrows and to the women who alone possessed the lore of determining whether the food was fit for consumption and of preparing it if it were.

That's where he would be at this moment, on that sack, cutting a hole in it, if he'd chosen a first category Theft like most other youths. He'd be cutting a hole, scooping out a handful of food—any quantity, no matter how small, was acceptable on an initiatory Theft—and be preparing to go home to plaudits from the women and acceptance from the men. He'd be engaged in a normal, socially acceptable endeavor.

Instead of which…

He found that he was able to stare at the Monster room now from under the cover of his hiding place with only a slight feeling of nausea. Well, that in itself was an achievement. After such a relatively short time, here he was, able to look around and estimate the nature of Monster goods like the most experienced warrior. He couldn't look up too high as yet, but what warrior could?

Well and good, but this wasn't getting him anywhere. He didn't have a normal Theft to make. His was third category. Monster souvenirs.

Eric turned and faced the darkness again. He walked rapidly forward into the straight-walled burrow, the glow lamp on his forehead lighting a yellow path. Ahead of him, the great black space grew steadily larger as he pushed toward it.

Everything about his Theft, his initiation into manhood, was extraordinary. Thomas the Trap-Smasher telling the women about his special talents, so that he would be accorded a vision and a name which would fit with them. Visions were supposed to come from the ancestors, through the Ancestor-Science of the Record Machine. Nobody was supposed to have the slightest idea in advance of what the vision would be. That was all up to the ancestors and their mysterious plans for their descendants.

Was it possible, was it conceivable, that all visions and names were prearranged, that the Record Machine was set in advance for every initiation? Where did that leave religion? If that were so, how could you continue to believe in logic, in cause and effect?

And having someone—a Stranger, at that!—help you make your Theft. A Theft was supposed to be purely and simply a test of your male potential; by definition, it was something you did alone.

But if you could accept the concept of prearranged visions, why not prearranged Thefts?

Eric shook his head. He was getting into very dark corridors mentally: his world was turning into sheer confusion.

But one thing he knew. Making an arrangement with a Stranger, as his uncle had done, was definitely an act contrary to all the laws and practices of Mankind. Thomas's uncertain speech had underlined that fact. It was *wrong*.

Yet his uncle was the greatest man in all Mankind, so far as Eric was concerned. Thomas the Trap-Smasher could do no wrong. But Thomas the Trap-Smasher was evidently leaning toward Alien-Science. Alien-Science was wrong. But again, on the other hand, his own parents, according to the Trap-Smasher—his father and his mother had been Alien-Sciencers.

Too much. There was just too much to work out. There was too much he didn't know. He'd better concentrate on his Theft.

The strange burrow had come to an end. The hairs rose on the back of his neck as he walked into the great dark area and sensed enormous black heights above him. He began to hurry, turning every once in a while to make certain that he was staying in a straight line with the light from the entrance. Here, his forehead glow lamp was almost no use at all. He didn't like this place. It felt almost like being out in the open.

What, he wondered again feverishly, was this structure in the world of the Monsters? What function did it have? He was not sure he wanted to know.

Eric was running by the time he came to the end of the open space. He hit the wall so hard that he was knocked over backward.

For a moment, he was badly frightened; then he realized what had happened. He hadn't taken his bearings for a while: he must have moved off at an angle.

Groping along the wall with extended arms, he found the entrance to the low burrow at last. It was quite low—he had to bend his knees and duck his head as he went up it. And it was an unpleasantly narrow little corridor. But then there was an opening on his right—the fork his uncle had told him about—and he turned into it with relief.

He had arrived.

There was a burst of light from a group of glow lamps. And there were Strangers, there were *several* Strangers here. Three of them—no, four—no, five! They squatted in a corner of this large, square burrow, three of them talking earnestly, the other two engaged in some incomprehensible task with materials that were mostly unfamiliar.

All of them leaped to their feet as he trotted in and deployed instantly in a wide semicircle facing him. Eric wished desperately he had been holding two heavy spears instead of the single light one. With two heavy spears you had both a shield and a dangerous offensive weapon. A light spear was good for a single cast, and that was that.

He held it nevertheless in the throwing position above his shoulder and glared fiercely, as a warrior of Mankind should. If he had to throw, he decided, he would spring to one side immediately afterward and try to pluck the two heavy spears from his back sling. But if they rushed him right now—

The tension was broken by a strong-faced, middle-aged man who stepped forward, spear throbbing in an upraised arm, and said cautiously, almost inquiringly: "Safety first?"

Eric began to relax. This was the ancient greeting of peace when warrior met warrior in the dangerous precincts of Monster territory. You said "Safety first!" as recognition of the fact that there were much more fearful creatures than humans about—and as a mutual reminder of what should be uppermost in everyone's mind while they were in this terrible place.

He gave the traditional reply. "Safety above all!" he intoned, announcing his own willingness to observe the truce of Monster territory, to sink any individual belligerence into common alertness and back-to-back protection against the perils that surrounded them.

There was a nod of acceptance from the middle-aged man. "Who are you?" the man said. "What's your name—what's your people?"

"Eric the Only." Then he remembered to add: "I'm destined to be Eric the Eye. My people are Mankind."

"He's expected, one of us," the man told the others, who immediately relaxed, slung their spears and went back to what they had been doing. "Welcome, Eric the Only of Mankind. Put up your spear and sit with us. I am Arthur the Organizer."

Eric gingerly dropped his spear into the back sling. He studied the Stranger.

A man about as old as his uncle and not nearly as hefty, although well-muscled enough for normal warlike purposes. He wore the loin straps of a full warrior, but—as if these were not enough honor for a man—he also wore straps laced about his chest and across his shoulders, though he was carrying no knapsack. This was the fashion of many Strangers, Eric knew, as was the strap at the back of the head that held the hair in a tight tail away from the eyes instead of letting it hang wild and free as the hair of a warrior should. And the straps were decorated with odd, incised designs—another weak and unmanlike Stranger fashion.

Who but Strangers, Eric thought contemptuously, would group up so in an alien place without setting sentries at either end of their burrow? Truly Mankind had good reason to despise them!

But this man was a leader, he realized, a born leader, with an even more self-assured air than Thomas the Trap-Smasher, captain of the best band in all Mankind. He was studying Eric in turn, with eyes that weighed carefully and then, having decided on the measure, made a definite placement, fitting Eric permanently into this plan or that plan. He looked like a man whose head was full of many plans, each one evolving inexorably through action to a predetermined end.

He took Eric's arm companionably and led him to where the others squatted and talked and worked. This was no tribal burrow of any sort: it was quite apparently a temple-in-exile, the field headquarters of a new faith. The men who sat working on the floor would one day be priests of that faith among their various peoples. And Arthur the Organizer would be Supreme Pontiff.

"I met your uncle," he told Eric, "about a dozen auld lang synes ago, when he came to us on a trading expedition—back in our burrows, I mean. A fine man, your uncle, very progressive. He's attending our secret meetings regularly, and there's going to be an important place for him in the great burrows we will dig, in the new world we are making. He reminds me a lot of your father. But so do you, my boy, so do you."

"Did you know my father?"

Arthur the Organizer smiled and nodded. "Very well. He could have been a great man. He gave his life for the Cause. Who among us will ever forget Eric the—the—Eric the Storekeeper or something, wasn't it?"

"The Storeroom-Stormer. His name was Eric the Storeroom-Stormer."

"Yes, of course. Eric the Storeroom-Stormer. An unforgettable name with us, and an unforgettable man. But that's another story; we'll talk about it some other time. You'll have to be getting back to your uncle very soon." He picked up a flat board covered with odd markings and studied it with his glow lamp.

"How do you like that?" one of the men working with the unfamiliar materials muttered to his neighbor. "You ask him his people, and he says, 'Mankind.' *Mankind!*"

The other man chuckled. "A front-burrow tribe. What the hell do you expect—sophistication? Each and every front-burrow tribe calls itself Mankind. As far as these primitives are concerned, the human race stops at their outermost burrow. Your tribe, my tribe—you know what they call us? Strangers. In their eyes, there's not too much difference between us and the Monsters."

"That's what I mean. They're narrow-minded savages—practically Wild Men. Who needs them?"

Arthur the Organizer glanced at Eric's face. He turned sharply to the man who had spoken last.

"I'll tell you who needs them, Walter," he said. "The Cause needs them. If the front-burrow tribes are with us, it means our main lines of supply to Monster territory are kept open. But we need every fighter we can get, no matter how primitive. Every single tribe has to be with us if Alien-Science is to be the dominant religion of the burrows, if we're to avoid the fiasco of the last rising. We need front-burrow men for their hunting, foraging skills and back-burrow men for their civilized skills. We need everybody in this thing, especially now."

The man called Walter put down his work and leaned against the wall. "And I'll tell you who we need most," he said. "Who we need a hell of a lot more than these front-burrow characters. I said they're one step away from being Wild Men, and I'll stick by what I said. But the Aaron People, if the Aaron People were with us..."

The Organizer's face darkened. He seemed to be remembering one major plan that had gone awry. "Those snobs," he muttered. "Those selfish, stuck-up bastards. Damn them. But listen, Walter. If you think there's no difference between a front-burrow tribe and a bunch of Wild Men from the Outside, you go up to the Wild Men next time a mob of them comes through the burrows and try to start a conversation. You know what will happen?"

"He'll be eaten raw," one of the other men called out. "Torn to pieces and eaten raw. A handful of Walter the Weapon-Seeker for anyone who can grab."

There was a grim laugh in which Eric joined after some uncertainty. He'd heard about the Wild Men, hordes who supposedly poured into the burrows at irregular intervals from some strange place called "the Outside," undisciplined, slavering cannibals who used grunts in place of speech—but he'd always understood them to be merely the stuff of legend. If you were an Alien-Sciencer did you have to make believe that Wild Men really existed?

Real or legendary, though, to be compared with Wild Men was an ugly insult.

These arrogant back-burrowers with their ornamented straps and unmilitary manners! Men from different tribes sitting around and talking, when—if they had any sense of propriety at all—they should be killing each other!

And the Aaron People, who or what was this Aaron People, he wondered? A people referred to by these strutting, conceited, dressed-up pseudo-warriors as snobs and stuck-up bastards! He'd never heard of the Aaron People before. He wondered what *they* would be like.

Suddenly, the floor shook under him. He almost fell. He staggered back and forth, trying to grab at the spears in his back sling. He finally got used to it, managed to find a solid footing in the upheaval. The spear he held vibrated in his hand.

From far away came a series of ear-splitting thumps. The floor swung to their rhythm. "What is it?" he cried, turning to Arthur. "What's going on?"

"You've never heard a Monster walking before?" the Organizer asked him unbelievingly. "That's right—this is your Theft, your first time out. It's a Monster, boy: a Monster's moving around in the Monster larder, doing whatever it is that Monsters do. They have a right, you know," he added with a smile. "It's their larder. We're just—visitors."

Eric noticed that none of the others seemed particularly concerned. He drew a deep breath and reslung his spear. How the floor and the walls shook! What a fantastic, enormous creature that must be!

As an apprentice warrior, he had often stood with the rear-guard on the other side of the doorway to Monster territory while the band went in to steal for Mankind. A few times there had been heavy, thumping noises off in the distance, and the walls of the burrow had quivered slightly. But not like this. It had never been remotely as awesome as this.

He raised his eyes to the straight, flat ceiling of the burrow above them. He remembered the dark space further back stretching up limitlessly. "And this," he said aloud. "This structure we're in. What is *this* to them?"

Arthur the Organizer shrugged. "A piece of Monster furniture. Something they use for something or other. We're in one of the open spaces they always leave in the bases of their furniture. Makes the furniture lighter, easier to move around, I guess." He listened for a moment as the thumps drifted farther away and then died out. "Let's get down to business. Eric, this is Walter the Weapon-Seeker. Walter the Weapon-

Seeker of the Maximilian people. Walter, what do you have for Eric's tribe—for, uh, for Mankind?"

"I hate to give anything even halfway good to a front-burrow tribe," the squatting man muttered. "No matter how much you explain it to them, they always use it wrong, they botch it up every single time. Let's see. This should be simple enough."

He rummaged in the pile of strange stuff in front of him and picked up a small, red, jellylike blob. "All you do," he explained, "is tear off a pinch with your fingers. Just a pinch at a time, no more. Then spit on it and throw it. After you spit on it, get it out of your hands fast. Throw it as fast and as far as you can. Do you think you can remember that?"

"Yes." Eric took the red blob from him and stared at it in puzzlement. There was a strange, irritating odor: it made his nose itch slightly. "But what happens? What does it do?"

"That's not your worry, boy," Arthur the Organizer told him. "Your uncle will know when to use it. You have your third category Theft—a Monster souvenir that no one in your tribe has ever seen before. It should make them sit up and take notice. And tell your uncle to bring his band to my burrow three days—three sleep periods—from now. That will be the last time we meet before the rising. Tell him to bring them armed with every last spear they can carry."

Eric nodded weakly. There were so many complex, incomprehensible things going on! The world was a bigger, more active place than he had ever imagined.

He watched Arthur the Organizer add a mark to the flat board on which many symbols were scratched. This was another Stranger practice—made necessary, he knew, by the weak Stranger memory, so inferior to that of Mankind.

The Weapon-Seeker leaped up and stopped him as he was about to put the red blob into his knapsack. "Nothing wet in there?" Walter demanded, opening the bag and rummaging about in Eric's belongings. "No water? Remember, get this stuff wet and you're done for."

"Mankind keeps its water in canteens," Eric explained irritably. "We keep it here," he pointed to the sloshing pouch on his hip, "not splashing around loosely with our provisions." He swung the full knapsack on his back and stepped away with stiff dignity.

Arthur the Organizer accompanied him to the end of the burrow. "Don't mind Walter," he whispered. "He's always afraid that nobody but himself will be able to use the Monster weapons he digs up. He talks that way to everyone. Now, suppose I refresh your memory about the way back. We don't want you to get lost."

"I won't get lost," Eric said coldly. "I have a good memory, and I know enough to perform a simple reversal of the directions on the way here. Besides, I am Eric the Espier, Eric the Eye of Mankind. I won't get lost."

He was rather proud of himself as he trotted away, without turning his head. Let the Strangers know what you think of them. The snobs. The stuck-up bastards.

But still, he felt damaged somehow, made less—as when Roy the Runner had called him a singleton before the entire band. And the last comment he had heard behind him—"These primitives: so damned touchy!"—made it no better.

He crossed the dark open space, still brooding, his eyes fixed on the patch of white light ahead, his mind engaged in a completely unaccustomed examination of values. Mankind's free simplicity against the Stranger multiplicity and intricacy. Mankind's knowledge of basics, the important foraging basics of day-to-day life, against the Stranger knowledge of so many things and techniques he had never even heard about. Surely Mankind's way was infinitely preferable, far superior?

Then why did his uncle want to get mixed up with Stranger politics, he wondered, as he emerged from the structure. He turned left and, passing the small entrance he had ignored before, sped for the wall which separated him from the burrows. And why did all these Strangers, evidently each from a different tribe, agree in the contempt with which they held Mankind?

He had just turned right along the wall, on the last stretch before the doorway, when the floor shook again, jarring him out of his thoughts. He bounced up and down, frozen with fear where he stood.

He was out in the open while a Monster was abroad. A Monster had come into the larder again.

Chapter 6

Far off in the dazzling distance, he caught sight of the tremendously long gray body he had heard about since childhood, higher than a hundred men standing on each other's shoulders, the thick gray legs each wider than two hefty men standing chest to chest. He caught just one wide-eyed, fear-soluble glimpse of the thing before he went into complete panic.

His panic was redeemed by a single inhibition: he didn't spring forward and run away from the wall. But that was only because it would have meant running directly toward the Monster. For one thoroughly insane moment, however, he thought of trying to claw his way through the wall against which his shoulders were pressed.

Then—because it was the direction he had been running in—he remembered the doorway. He must be about thirty, thirty-five paces from it. There lay safety: his uncle, the band. Mankind and the burrows—the blessed, closed-in, narrow burrows!

Eric leaped along the wall for the doorway. He ran as he'd never in his life run before, as he'd never imagined he could run.

But even as he fled madly, almost weeping at the effort he was making, a few sane thoughts—the result of long, tiresome drills as an initiate—organized themselves in his screaming mind. He had been closer to the structure in which the Strangers were hiding, the structure which Arthur the Organizer had explained was a piece of Monster furniture. He should have turned the other way, toward the structure, gotten between it and the wall. There, unless he'd been seen as the Monster entered the larder, he could have rested safely until it was possible to make his escape.

He had gone too far to turn back now. But run silently, he reminded himself: run swiftly but make no noise, make no noise at all. According to the lessons that the warriors taught, at this distance Monster hearing was more to be feared than Monster vision. Run silently. Run for your life.

He reached the door. It had been set back in place!

In disbelief and utter horror he stared at the curved line in the wall that showed where the door had been replaced in its socket. But this was never done! This had never been heard of!

Eric beat frantically on the door with his fists. Would his knuckles make enough noise to penetrate the heavy slab? Or just enough to attract the Monster's attention?

He twisted his head quickly—a look, a deliberately wasted moment, to estimate the closeness of his danger. The Monster's legs moved so slowly: its speed would have been laughable if the very size of those legs didn't serve to push it forward an incredible distance with each step. And there was nothing laughable in that long, narrow neck, almost as long as the rest of the body, and the malevolent, relatively tiny head on the end of the neck. And those horrible pink things, all around the neck, just behind the head—

It was much nearer than it had been just seconds ago, but whether it had noticed him and was coming at him he had no idea. Beat at the door with the shaft of a spear? That should attract attention, that might be heard. Yes, by the Monster too.

There was only one thing to do. He stepped a few paces back from the wall. Then he leaped forward, smashing his shoulder into the door. He felt it give a little. Another try.

The floor-shaking thumps of the Monster's steps were now so close as to be almost deafening. At any moment, a great gray foot might come down and grind out his life. Eric stepped back again, forcing himself not to look up.

Another leap, another bruising collision with the door. It had definitely moved. An indentation showed all around it.

Was he about to be stepped on—to be squashed?

Eric put his hands on the door. He pushed. Slowly, suckingly, it began to leave the place out of which it had been carved long ago.

Where was the Monster? How close? How close?

Suddenly the door fell over into the burrow, and Eric spilled painfully on top of it. He scrambled to his feet and darted down the corridor.

He had no time to feel relief. His mind was repeating its lessons, reminding him what he had to do next in such a situation.

Run a short distance down the burrow. Then stop and wait on the balls of your feet, ready to bolt. Get as much air into your lungs as possible. You may need it. If you hear a hissing, whistling sound, stop breathing and start running. Hold your breath for as long as you can—as long as you possibly can!—then suck another chestful of air and keep running. Keep this up until you are far away. Far, far away.

Eric waited, poised to run, his back to the doorway.

Don't look around—just face the direction you'll have to run. There's only one thing you have to worry about, only one thing you have to listen for. A hissing, whistling sound. When you hear it, hold your breath and run.

He waited, his muscles contracted for instant action.

Time went by. He remembered to count. If you counted up to five hundred, slowly, and nothing happened, you were likely to be all right. You could assume the Monster hadn't noticed you.

So the experienced warriors said, the men who had lived through such an experience.

Five hundred. He reached five hundred and, just to be on the safe side, still tense, still ready to run, counted another five hundred, up to the ultimate number conceived by man, a full thousand.

No hissing, no whistling sounds. No suggestion of danger.

He relaxed, and his muscles—suddenly set free—gave way. He fell to the floor of the burrow, whimpering with the release of tension.

It was over. His Theft was over. He was a man.

He had been in the same place as a Monster, and lived through it. He had met Strangers and dealt with them as a representative of Mankind. Such things as he would have to tell his uncle!

His uncle. Where was his uncle? Where was the band?

Suddenly fully aware of how much was wrong, Eric scrambled to his feet and walked cautiously back to the open doorway. The burrow was empty. They hadn't waited for him.

But that was another incredible thing! A band never gave an initiate up for lost until at least two full days had gone by. In the chief's absence, of course, this was measured by the sleep periods of the band captain. Any band would wait two days before giving up and turning homeward. And, Eric was positive, his uncle would have waited a bit longer than that for *him*. He'd been away for such a short time! Then what had happened?

He crept to the doorway and peeped outside. There was almost no dizziness this time; his eyes adjusted quickly to the different scale of distance. The Monster was busy on the other side of the larder. It had merely been crossing the room, then, not pursuing and attacking. Apparently, it hadn't noticed him at all.

Fantastic. And with all the noise he had made! All that rushing back and forth, that battering down of the door!

The Monster turned abruptly, walked a few gigantic steps and hurled itself at the structure in which Eric had met the Strangers. The walls, the floor, everything, shook mightily in sympathy to the impact of the great organism as it wriggled a bit and became still.

Eric was startled until he realized that the creature had done no more than lie down in the structure. It *was* a piece of Monster furniture, after all.

How had that felt to Arthur the Organizer and Walter the Weapon-Seeker and the others hidden in the base? Eric grinned. Those Strangers must be a little less haughty, a little less sober at this moment.

Meanwhile, he had work to do, things to find out.

He got his fingers under the slab of door and tugged it upright. It was heavy! He pushed against it, slowly, carefully, first one side and then the other, walking it back to the hole in the wall. A final push, and it slid into place tightly, only the thin, curved line suggesting its existence.

Now he could look around.

There had been a fight here—that much was certain. A brief, bitter battle. Examining the area closely, Eric saw unmistakable signs of conflict.

A broken spear shaft. Some blood on the wall. Part of a torn knapsack. No bodies, of course. You were not likely to find bodies after a battle. Any people of the burrows knew that the one unavoidable imperative of victory was to drag the bodies away and dispose of them. No one might ever leave dead enemies to rot where they would foul the corridors.

So there had been a battle. He had been right—his uncle and his uncle's band had not just gone off and left him. There must have been an attack by a superior force: the band had stood its ground for a while, sustained some losses, and then been forced to retreat.

But there were a few things which didn't make sense. First, it was very unusual for a war party of Strangers to come this close to Monster territory. The burrows which were inhabited by Mankind, the natural goal of a war party, were much further back. At this point, you would not expect to find any group larger than a foraging expedition—a Stranger band at most.

His uncle's men, fully armed, operating under battle alert, could easily cope with a single band of weavers, weaponsmiths or traders from the decadent back burrows. They would have driven them off, possibly taking a few prisoners, and continued to wait for him.

That left only two possibilities. The unlikely war party—a two- or three-band attack—and, even more unlikely, a band from another fierce, front-burrow people. But front-burrowers rarely went prowling at random near Monster territory; they would have their own door cut into it and would tend to feel hugely uncertain about one belonging to another people. They too would head for the inhabited burrows if they were on any business other than the important one of stealing for their tribe's needs.

And another thing. Unless his uncle's band had been wiped out to the very last man—a thought Eric rejected as highly improbable—the survivors were honor-bound, by their oath of manhood, after doing whatever the immediate military situation required, from pursuit to retreat, to return as soon as possible to the spot where an initiate was expected back from his Theft. No warrior would dare face the women if he failed to do this.

Possibly the attack had just come. Possibly his uncle's band was a short distance away, still fighting their way from burrow's end to burrow's end; and, once they had gotten clear of the enemy, would make their way back to him.

In that case, he should be able to hear the battle still going on. And the burrows were dreadfully still.

Eric shivered. A warrior was not meant to be abroad without companions. He'd heard of tribeless Strangers—once, as a child, he remembered enjoying the intricate execution of a man who'd been expelled from his own people for some major crime and who had wandered pathetically into the neighborhood of Mankind—but these people were hardly to be considered human: tribes, bands, societies, were the surroundings of human creatures.

It was awful to be alone. It was unthinkable.

Without bothering to eat, though he was quite hungry after his Theft, he began walking rapidly down the corridor. After a while, he broke into a trot. He wanted to get home as soon as possible—to be among his own kind again.

He reached into his back sling and got a spear for each hand.

A nervous business going through the corridors all by yourself. They were so empty and so quiet. They hadn't seemed this quiet when he'd been on expedition with the band. And so fearfully, frighteningly dim. Eric had never before realized how much difference there was between the light you got from one forehead glow lamp and the usual band complement of a half-dozen. He found himself getting more and more wary of the unexpected shadows where the wall curved sharply: he picked up speed as he ran past the black hole of a branching burrow.

At any one of those places, an enemy could be waiting for him, warned by the sound of his approaching footsteps. It could be the same enemy which had attacked his uncle's band, a handful of cruel and murderous Strangers, or a horde of them. It could be something worse: abruptly he remembered legends of unmentionable creatures who lurked in the empty burrows, creatures who fled before the approach of a band of warriors, but who would come noiselessly upon a single man. Big creatures who engulfed you. Tiny creatures who came in their hundreds and nibbled you to pieces. Eric kept jerking his head around to look behind him: at least he could keep his doom from taking him by surprise.

It was *awful* to be alone.

And yet, in the midst of his fears, his mind returned again and again to the problem of his uncle's disappearance. Eric could not believe anything serious had happened to him: Thomas the Trap-Smasher was a veteran of too many bloody adventures, too many battles against unequal odds. Then where had he gone? And where had he taken the band?

And why was there no sound of him anywhere, no sign in all this infinity of gloomy, stretching, menace-filled tunnels?

Fortunately, he was an Eye. He knew the way back and sped desperately along it without the slightest feeling of doubt. The Record Machine was right: he would never be lost. Let him just get safely back to the companionship of Mankind and he would be Eric the Eye.

And there it was again: who had been right, the Record Machine or his uncle? The vision that named him had come from the Record Machine, but his uncle claimed that this was pure political manipulation. The vision had been selected and his name proposed to the women well in advance of the ceremony. And his uncle was an Alien-Sciencer, plotting with Strangers to erect an altar to the new religion in Mankind's burrows, plotting to overthrow the holy prerogatives of Ottilie the Omen-Teller....

So many things had happened in the last two days, Eric felt. So much of his world had shifted. It was as if the walls of the burrows had moved outward and upward until they resembled Monster territory more than human areas.

He was getting close now. These corridors looked friendlier, more familiar. He made himself run faster, although he was almost at the point of exhaustion. He wanted to be home, to be officially Eric the Eye, to inform Mankind of what had happened so that a rescue and searching party could be sent out for his uncle.

That doorway to Monster territory: who had replaced it? If a battle had been fought, and his uncle's band had retreated, still fighting, would the attacker have stopped to put the door neatly back in its socket? No.

Could it be explained by a sudden onslaught and the complete extermination of his uncle's band? Then, before dragging the bodies away, the enemy would have had time to put the door back. A doorway into Monster territory was a valuable human resource, after all, valuable to Mankind and Strangers alike—why jeopardize it by leaving it visible and open?

But who—or what—could have been capable of such a sudden onslaught, such a complete extermination of the best-led band in all Mankind? He'd have to get the answer from one of the other band captains or possibly a wise old crone in the Female Society.

Definitely within the boundaries of Mankind now, Eric forced himself to slow to a walk. He would be coming upon a sentry at any moment, and he had no desire at all to have a spear flung through him. A sentry would react violently to a man dashing out of the darkness.

"Eric the Only," he called out, identifying himself with each step. "This is Eric the Only." Then he remembered his Theft proudly and changed the identification. "Eric the Eye. This is Eric the Eye, the Espier, the further-seeing, less-paying Eye. Eric the Eye coming."

Oddly, there was no returning call of recognition. Eric didn't understand that. Had Mankind itself been attacked and driven away from its burrow? A sentry should respond to a familiar name. Something was very, inexplicably wrong.

Then he came around the last curve and saw the sentry at the other end. Rather, he saw what at first looked like three sentries. They were staring at him, and he recognized them. Stephen the Strong-Armed and two members of Stephen's band. Evidently he had arrived just at the moment when the sentry on duty was about to be relieved. That would account for Stephen and the other man. But why hadn't they replied to his shouts of identification?

They stood there silently as he came up, their spears still at the ready, not going down in welcome. "Eric the Eye," he repeated, puzzled. "I've made my Theft, but something happened to the—"

His voice trailed off, as Stephen came up to him, his face grim, his powerful muscles taut. The band captain shoved a spear point hard against Eric's chest. "Don't move," he warned. "Barney. John. Tie him up."

Chapter 7

His spears taken from him, his arms bound securely behind his back by the thongs of his own knapsack, Eric was pushed and prodded into the great central burrow of Mankind.

The place was almost unrecognizable.

Under the direction of Ottilie, the Chieftain's First Wife, a horde of women—what seemed at first like the entire membership of the Female Society—was setting up a platform in front of the Royal Mound. With the great scarcity of any building materials that Mankind suffered from, a construction of this sort was startling and unusual, yet there was something about it that awoke highly unpleasant memories in Eric's mind. But he was pulled from place to place too fast and there were too many other unprecedented things going on for him to be able to identify the memory properly.

Two women who were accredited members of the Female Society were not working under Ottilie's direction, he noticed. Bound hand and foot, they were lying against the far wall of the great central burrow. They were both covered with blood and showed every sign of having undergone prolonged and most vicious torture. He judged them to be barely this side of death.

As he was jerked past, he recognized them. They were the two wives of Thomas the Trap-Smasher.

Just wait until his uncle got back: someone would really pay for this, he thought, more in absolute amazement than horror. He had the feeling that he must keep the horror away at all costs—once let it in and it would soak through his thoughts right into the memory he was trying to avoid.

The place was full of armed men, running back and forth from their band captains to unknown destinations in the outlying corridors. Between them and around them scuttled the children, fetching and carrying raw materials for the hard-working women. There was a steady buzz of commands in the air— "Go to—," "Bring some more—," "Hurry with the—," —that mingled with the smell of many people whose pores were sweating urgency. And it wasn't just sweat that he smelled, Eric realized as he was dragged before the Royal Mound: it was anger, the anger and fear of all Mankind.

Franklin the Father of Many Thieves stood on the mound, carrying unaccustomed spears in his fat hands, talking rapidly to a group of warriors, band captains and—yes, actually!—*Strangers.* Even now, Eric found he could still be astonished.

Strangers in the very midst of Mankind! Walking around freely and bearing arms!

As the chief caught sight of Eric, his face broke into a loose-skinned smile. He nudged a Stranger beside him and pointed at the prisoner.

"That's him," he said. "That's the nephew. The one that asked for the third category Theft. Now we've got them all."

The Stranger didn't smile. He looked briefly at Eric and turned away. "I'm glad you think so. From our point of view, you've just got one more."

Franklin's smile faded to an uncertain grin. "Well, you know what I mean. And the damned fool came back by himself. It saved us a lot of trouble, I mean, didn't it?" Receiving no answer, he shrugged. He gestured with flabby imperiousness at Eric's guards. "You know where to put him. We'll be ready for them pretty soon."

Again the point of a spear stabbed into Eric's back, and he was forced forward across the central space to a small burrow entrance. Before he could reach it, however, he heard Franklin the Father of Many Thieves call out to Mankind: "There goes Eric, my people. Eric the Only. Now we've got them all."

For a moment, the activity stopped and seemed to focus on him. Eric shivered as a low, drawn-out grunt of viciousness and hatred arose everywhere, but most of all from the women.

Someone ran up to him. Harriet the History-Teller. The girl's face was absolutely contorted. She reached up to the crown of her head and pulled out the long pin held in place by a few knotted scarlet hairs. About her face and neck the hair danced like flames.

"You Alien-Sciencer!" she shrieked, driving the pin straight at his eyes. "You filthy, filthy Alien-Sciencer!"

Eric whipped his head to one side; she was back at him in a moment. His guards leaped at the girl and grappled with her, but she was able to get in one ripping slash that opened up almost all of his right cheek before they drove her away.

"Leave something for the rest of us," one of his guards pleaded the cause of reason as he strolled back to Eric. "After all, he belongs to the whole of Mankind."

"He does not!" she yelled. "He belongs to me most of all. I was going to mate with him when he returned from his Theft, wasn't I, Mother?"

"There wasn't anything official," Eric heard Rita the Record-Keeper admonishing as he tried to stanch the flow of blood by bringing his shoulder up and pressing it against the wound. "There couldn't be anything official about it until he'd achieved manhood. So you'll just have to wait your turn, Harriet darling—you'll have to wait until your elders are finished with him. There'll be plenty left for you."

"There won't be," the girl pouted. "I know what you're like. There won't be hardly anything left."

Eric was shoved at the small burrow entrance again. The moment he was inside it, one of his guards planted a foot in his back, knocking the breath out of him. The kick propelled him forward, staggering wildly for balance, until he smashed into the opposite wall. As he fell, unable to use his arms to cushion himself, he heard laughter behind him in the great central burrow. He rolled on his side dizzily. There was a fresh flow of blood coming down from his cheek.

This wasn't the homecoming he'd imagined after his Theft—not in the slightest! What was going on?

He knew where he was. A tiny, blind-alley burrow off Mankind's major meeting place, a sort of little vault used mostly for storage. Excess food and goods stolen from Monster territory were kept here until there was enough accumulated for a trading expedition to the back burrows. Occasionally, also, a male Stranger, taken prisoner in battle, might be held in this place until Mankind found out if his tribe valued him enough to pay anything substantial for his recovery.

And if they didn't…

Eric remembered the unusual structure that the women had been building near the Royal Mound—and shivered. The memory that he'd suppressed had now come alive in his mind. And it fitted with the way Harriet had acted—and with what her mother, Rita the Record-Keeper, had said.

They couldn't be planning that for him! He was a member of Mankind, almost a full warrior. They didn't even do that to Strangers captured in battle—not normal Strangers. A warrior was always respected as a warrior: at the worst, he deserved a decent execution, quietly done. Except for— Except for—

"*No!*" he screamed. "*No!*"

The single guard who'd been left on duty at the entrance turned around and regarded him humorously.

"Oh, yes," he said. "Oh, definitely yes! We're going to have a lot of fun with both of you as soon as the women say they're ready." He nodded with ominous, emphatic slowness and turned back to miss none of the preparations.

Both of you? For the first time, Eric looked around the little storage burrow. The place was almost empty of goods, but off to one side, in the light of his forehead glow lamp (how proud he had been when it had been bestowed on him at the doorway to Monster territory!) he now saw another man lying against the wall.

His uncle.

Eric brought his knees up and wriggled rapidly over to him. It was a painful business: his belly and sides were not calloused and inured to the rough burrow floor like his feet. But what did a few scratches, more or less, matter any more?

The Trap-Smasher was barely conscious. He had been severely handled, and he looked almost as bad as his wives. There was a thick crust of dried blood on his hair: the haft of a spear, Eric guessed, had all but cracked his head open. And in several places on his body, his right shoulder, just above his left hip, deep in his thigh, were the oozing craters of serious spear wounds.

"Uncle Thomas," Eric urged. "What happened? Who did this to you?"

The wounded man opened his eyes and shuddered. He looked around stupidly as if he had expected to find the walls talking to him. And his powerful arms struggled with the knots that held them firmly behind his back. When he finally located Eric, he smiled.

It was a bad thing to do. Someone had also smashed in most of his front teeth.

"Hello, Eric," he mumbled. "What a fight, eh? How did the rest of the band do—anybody get away?"

"I don't know. That's what I'm asking *you!* I came back from my Theft—you were gone—the band was gone. I got here, and everyone's crazy! There are Strangers out there, walking around with weapons in our burrows. Who are they?"

Thomas the Trap-Smasher's eyes had slowly darkened. They were fully in focus now, and long threads of agony swam in them. "Strangers?" he asked in a low voice.

"Yes, there were Strangers fighting in Stephen the Strong-Armed's band. Fighting against us. That chief of ours—Franklin—he got in touch with Strangers after we left. They compared notes: they must have been working together, been in touch with each other, for a long time. Mankind, Strangers, what difference does it make when their lousy Ancestor-Science is threatened? I should have remembered."

"What?" Eric begged. "What should you have remembered?"

"It's the way they put down Alien-Science in the other rising, long ago. A chief's a chief; he's got more in common with another chief—even a chief of Strangers—than with his own people. You attack Ancestor-Science, and you're attacking their power as chiefs. They'll work together then. They'll give each other men, weapons, information—they'll do everything they can against the common enemy. Against the only people who really want to hit back at the Monsters. I should have remembered! Damn it all," the Trap-Smasher groaned through his ruined mouth, "I saw that the chief and Ottilie were suspicious. I should have realized how they were going to handle it. They were going to call in Strangers, exchange information—and unite against us!"

Eric stared at his uncle, dimly understanding. Just as there was a secret organization of Alien-Sciencers that cut across tribal boundaries, so there was a tacit, rarely used understanding among the chiefs, based on the Ancestor-Science religion that was the main prop of their power. *And* the power of the leaders of the Female Society, come to think of it. All special privileges were derived from their knowledge of Ancestor-Science: take that away from them, and they'd be ordinary women with no more magical abilities than was necessary to tell edible food from Monster poison.

Grunting with pain, Thomas the Trap-Smasher wormed his way up to a sitting position against the wall. He kept shaking his head as if to jar recollection loose.

"They came up to us," he said heavily, "Stephen the Strong-Armed and his band came up to us just after you'd gone into Monster territory. A band from Mankind with a message from the chief—who suspected anything? They might be coming to tell us that the home burrows were under attack by Strangers. Strangers!" he gave a barking laugh, and some blood splashed out of his mouth. "They had Strangers with them, hidden all the way behind in the corridors. Mobs and mobs of Strangers."

Eric began to visualize what had happened.

"Then, when they were among us, when most of us had reslung our spears, they hit us. Eric, they hit us real good. They had us so much by surprise that they didn't even need outside help. I don't think there was much left of us by the time the Strangers came running up. I was down, fighting with my bare hands—and so was the rest of the band. The Strangers did the mopping up. I didn't see most of it—somebody handed me one hell of a wallop—I never expected to wake up alive." His voice got even lower and huskier. "I'd have been lucky not to."

The Trap-Smasher's chest heaved: a strange, long noise came out of it. "They brought me back here. My wives—they were working on my wives. Those bitches from the Female Society—Ottilie, Rita—this part of it is their business—they had my wives pegged out and they worked on them in front of me. I was blanking out and coming to, blanking out and coming to: I was conscious while they—"

He dropped to a bloody mumble again, his head falling forward loosely. His voice became clear for a moment, but not entirely rational. "They were good women," he muttered. "Both of them. Good, good girls. And they loved me. They had their chance to become more important—a dozen times Franklin must have offered to impregnate them, and they turned him down every time. They loved me, they really loved me."

Eric almost sobbed himself. He'd had little to do with them once he'd reached the age of the warrior initiate, but in his childhood, they'd given him all the mother love he ever remembered. They'd cuffed him and caressed him and wiped his nose. They'd told him stories and taught him the catechism of the Ancestor-Science. Neither had sons of his age who had survived the various plagues and the Monster-inflicted calamities that periodically swept through Mankind's burrows. He'd been lucky: he'd received much of the care and affection that their own sons might have enjoyed.

Their fidelity to the Trap-Smasher had been a constant source of astonishment in Mankind. It had cost them more than the large, healthy litters for which the chief had a well-proven capacity: such eccentric, almost nonwomanly behavior had inevitably denied them the high positions in the Female Society they would otherwise have enjoyed.

And now they were dead or dying, and their surviving babies had been apportioned to other women whose importance would thereby be substantially increased.

"Tell me," he asked his uncle. "Why did the Female Society kill them? What did they do that was so awful?"

He saw that Thomas had lifted his head again and was staring at him. With pity. He felt his own body turn completely cold even before the Trap-Smasher spoke.

"You still won't let yourself think about it? I don't blame you, Eric. But it's there. It's being prepared for us outside."

"What?" Eric demanded, although a distant part of him had already worked out the terrible answer and knew what it was.

"We've been declared outlaws, Eric. They say we're guilty of ultimate sacrilege against Ancestor-Science. We don't belong to Mankind anymore—you, me, my family, my band. We're outside Mankind, outside the law, outside religion. And you know what happens to outlaws, Eric, don't you? Anything goes. *Anything.*"

Chapter 8

Ever since early childhood, Eric remembered looking forward to ceremonies of this sort. A Stranger would have been caught by one of the warrior bands, and it would be determined that he was an outlaw. Nine times out of ten, such a man was easy enough to identify—no one but an outlaw, for example, would be wandering the burrows by himself, without a band or at least a single companion to guard his back. The tenth time, when there was the slightest doubt, a request for ransom to his people would make the prisoner's position clear. There would be a story of some unforgivable sacrilege, some particularly monstrous crime that could be punished by nothing but complete anathema and the revocation of all privileges as a human being. The man had escaped the punishment being prepared for him. Do with him as you will, his people would say: he is no longer one of us; he is the same as a Monster; he is something nonhuman so far as we are concerned.

Then a sort of holiday would be declared. Out of the bits and pieces of lumber stolen from Monster territory and set aside by the women for this purpose, the members of the Female Society would erect a structure whose specifications had been handed down from mother to daughter for countless generations—all the way back to the ancestors who had built the Record Machines. It was called a Stage or a Theater, although Eric had also heard it referred to as The Scaffold. In any case, whatever its true name, most of the details concerning it were part of the secret lore of the Female Society and, as such, were no proper concern of males.

One thing about it, however, everyone knew. On it would be enacted a moving religious drama: the ultimate triumph of humanity over the Monsters. For this, the central character had to fulfill two requirements: he had to be an intelligent creature as the Monsters were, so that he could be made to suffer as someday Mankind meant the Monsters to suffer; and he had to be nonhuman as the Monsters were, so that every drop of fear, resentment and hatred distilled by the enormous swaggering aliens could be poured out upon his flesh without any inhibition of compunction or fellow-feeling.

For this purpose, outlaws were absolutely ideal since all agreed that such disgusting creatures had resigned their membership in the human race.

When an outlaw was caught, work stopped in the burrows, and Mankind's warrior bands were called home. It was a great time, a joyous time, a time of festival. Even the children—doing whatever they could to prepare for the glorious event, running errands for the laboring women, fetching refreshment for the stalwart, guarding men—even the children boasted to each other of how they would express their hatred upon this trapped representative of the nonhuman, this bound and shrieking protagonist of the utterly alien.

Everyone had their chance. All, from the chief himself to the youngest child capable of reciting the catechism of Ancestor-Science, all climbed in their turn upon the Stage—or Theater—or Scaffold—that the women had erected. All were thrilled to vent a portion of Mankind's vengeance upon the creature who had been declared alien, as an earnest of what they would someday do collectively to the Monsters who had stolen their world.

Sarah the Sickness-Healer had her turn early in the proceedings; thenceforth, she stood on the structure and carefully supervised the ceremony. It was her job to see that nobody went too far, that everyone had a fair and adequate turn, and that even at the end there was some life left in the victim. Because then, at the end, the structure had to be completely burned—along with its bloody occupant—as a symbol of how the Monsters must eventually be turned into ash and be blown away and vanish.

"And Mankind will come into its own," she would chant, while the charred fragments were kicked out of the burrow contemptuously. *"And the Monsters will be gone. They will be gone forever, and there will be nothing upon all the wide Earth but Mankind."*

Afterward, there was feasting, there was dancing, there was singing. Men and women chased each other into the dimmer side corridors; children whooped and yelled around the great central burrow; the few old folks went to sleep with broad, reminiscent smiles upon their faces. Everyone felt they had somehow struck back at the Monsters. Everyone felt a little like the lords of creation their ancestors had been.

Eric remembered the things he himself had done—the things he had seen others do—on these occasions. A tremendous tic of fear rippled through his body. He had to draw his shoulders up to his neck in a tight hunch and tense the muscles of his arms and legs. Finally, his nerves subsided.

He could think again. Only he didn't want to think.

Those others, those outlaws in previous ceremonies of this sort in auld lang synes long past—was it possible that they had experienced the same sick, bewildered dread while waiting for the structure to be completed? Had they trembled like this, had they also felt wetness running down their backs, had they felt the same pleading squirm in their intestines, the same anticipatory twinges of soft, vulnerable flesh?

The thought had never crossed his mind before. He'd seen them as things completely outside humanity, the compressed symbol of all that was alien. One worried about their feelings no more than about those of the roaches scurrying madly about here in the storage burrow. One squashed them slowly or rapidly—at one's pleasure. What difference did it make: you didn't sympathize with roaches—you didn't identify with them.

But now that he was about to be squashed himself, he realized that it did make a difference. He was human—no matter what Mankind and its leaders now declared him to be—he was human. He felt human fears; he experienced a desperate human desire to live.

Then so had the others been. The outlaws whom he'd helped tear to pieces. Human. Completely human.

They'd sat here, just as he did now, they'd sat and waited....

Only twice in his memory had members of Mankind ever been declared outlaw. Both cases had occurred a long time ago, before he'd even been a warrior-initiate. Eric tried now to remember what they had been like as living people: he wanted to reach out and feel companionship, some sort of companionship, even that of the dead. The dead were better than this beaten, bloody man next to him who had subsided into half-insane mumbles, his battered head on his torn and wound-scribbled chest.

What had they been like? It was no use. In the first case, memory brought back only a picture of a screaming hulk just before the fire was lit. No recollection of a man. No fellow-human in Mankind. And in the second case—

Eric sat bolt upright, straining against his bonds. The second man to be declared an outlaw had escaped! How he had done it Eric had never found out: he remembered only that a guard was severely punished, and that bands of warriors had sniffed for him along far-distant corridors for a long time afterward.

Escape. That was it. He had to escape. Once declared an outlaw, he could have no hope of mercy, no remission of sentence. The religious overtones of the ceremony being prepared were too highly charged to be halted for anything short of the disappearance of its chief protagonist.

Yes, escape. But how? Even if he could get free of the knots which so expertly and so strongly tied his hands behind his back, he had no weapon to hand. The guard at the entrance would transfix him with a spear in a moment. And if he failed, there were others outside, almost the entire warrior strength of the people.

How? *How?* He forced himself to be calm, to go over every possible alternative in his mind. He knew there was not much time. In a little while, the structure would be finished and the leaders of the Female Society would come for him.

Eric began working on the knots behind him. He worked without much hope. If he could get his hands loose, perhaps he might squirm his way carefully to the entrance, leap up suddenly and break into a run. So what if they plunged a spear through him—wouldn't that be better and quicker than the other thing?

But they wouldn't, he realized. Not unless he were very lucky and some warrior forgot to think straight. In cases like this, when it was a matter of keeping, not killing a prisoner, you aimed for the legs. There were at least a dozen men in Mankind with skill great enough to bring him down even at twenty or twenty-five paces. And another dozen who might be able to catch him. He was no Roy the Runner, after all.

Roy! He was dead and sewered by now. He found himself regretting the fight he'd had with Roy.

A Stranger passed by the storage burrow entrance, glancing in with only a slight curiosity. He was followed in a moment by two more Strangers, going the same way. They were leaving, Eric guessed, before the ceremony began. They probably had ceremonies of their own to attend—with their own people.

Walter the Weapon-Seeker, Arthur the Organizer—were they at this moment sitting in similar storage burrows awaiting the same slow death? Eric doubted it. Somehow he couldn't see these men caught as easily as he and his uncle had been. Arthur was too clever, he was certain of that, and Walter, well, Walter would come up with some fantastic weapon that no one had ever seen or heard of....

Like the one he had in his knapsack right now—that red blob the Weapon-Seeker had given him!

Was it a weapon? He didn't know. But even if it wasn't, he had the impression it could create some kind of surprise. "It should make them sit up and take notice," Walter had said back in Monster territory.

Any kind of surprise, any kind of upset and he might have a diversion under cover of which he and his uncle could escape.

But that was the trouble. His uncle. With his hands bound as thoroughly as he could now ascertain they were, he needed his uncle's help to do anything at all. And the Trap-Smasher was obviously too far gone to be at all useful.

He was talking to himself in a steady, monotonous, argumentative mutter, his upper body slumping further and further across his own lap. Every once in a while, the mutters would be broken by a sharp, almost surprised moan as his wounds woke into a clearer consciousness of themselves.

Most other men in his condition, Eric judged, would have been dead by now: only a body as powerful as the Trap-Smasher's could have lasted this long. And—who knew?—if they could escape, it was possible that his uncle's wounds, given care and rest, might heal.

If they could escape.

"Uncle Thomas," he said, leaning toward him and whispering urgently. "I think I know a way out. I think I've figured out a way to escape."

No response. The bloody head continued to talk in a low, toneless voice to the lap. Mutter, mutter, mutter. Moan. Mutter, mutter.

"Your wives," Eric said desperately. "Your wives. Don't you want to get revenge for your wives?"

That seemed to be worth a flicker. "My wives," said the thick voice. "They were good women. Real good women. They never let Franklin near them. They were real good women." Then the flicker was over and the mutters returned.

"Escape!" Eric whispered. "Don't you want to escape?"

A thin, coagulating line of blood dripped out of his uncle's slowly working jaws. There was no other answer.

Eric looked toward the entrance of the storage burrow. The guard posted there was no longer turning from time to time to glance at the prisoners. The structure outside was evidently nearing completion, and his interest in the final preparations had caused him to take a step or two away from the entrance. He was staring off to the left down the great central burrow in absolute fascination.

Well, that was something. It gave them a chance. On the other hand, it also meant that they had scant moments left to their lives. Any time now, the leaders of the Female Society would be coming to drag them to the torture ceremony.

With his eyes on the guard, Eric leaned against the rough burrow wall and began scraping the imprisoning knapsack thongs against the sharpest edges he could find. It wouldn't be fast enough, he realized. If there were only a spear point in this place, something sharp. He looked around feverishly. No, nothing. A few tumbled bags of food over which lazy roaches wandered. Nothing he could use.

His uncle was his only hope. Somehow he had to rouse the man, get through to him. He squirmed up close, his mouth against the Trap-Smasher's ear.

"This is Eric, Eric the Only. Do you remember me, Uncle? I went on the Theft, Uncle Thomas, I went on the Theft with you. Third category. Remember, I asked for a third category Theft, just like you told me to? I did my Theft, I was successful, I made it. I did just what you told me to do. I'm Eric the Eye now, right? Tell me, am I Eric the Eye?"

Mutters, mumbles and moans. The man seemed beyond intelligibility.

"What about Franklin? He can't do this to us, can he, Uncle Thomas? Don't you want to escape? Don't you want revenge on Franklin, on Ottilie, for what they did to your wives? Don't you? *Don't you?*"

He had to cut through his uncle's gathering delirium.

In complete desperation, he lowered his head and sank his teeth into a wounded shoulder.

Nothing. Just the steady flow of argumentative gibberish. And the thin blood dripping from the mouth.

"I saw Arthur the Organizer. He said he'd known you for a long time. When did you meet him, Uncle Thomas? When did you first meet Arthur the Organizer?"

The head drooped lower, the shoulders slumped further forward.

"Tell me about Alien-Science. What is Alien-Science?" Eric was almost gibbering himself now in his frantic efforts to find a key that would unlock his uncle's mind. "Are Arthur the Organizer and Walter the Weapon-Seeker very important among the Alien-Sciencers? Are they the chiefs? What was the name of the structure they were hiding in? What is it to the Monsters? They talked about the Aaron People. Who are the Aaron People? Do you—"

That was it. He had found the key. He had gotten through.

Thomas the Trap-Smasher's head came up waveringly, dimness swirling in his eyes. "The Aaron People. Funny that you should ask about the Aaron People. That you should ask."

"Why? What about them?" Eric fought to hold the key in place, to keep it turning. "Why shouldn't I ask?"

"Your grandmother was from the Aaron People. I remember hearing about it when I was a little boy." Thomas the Trap-Smasher nodded to himself. "Your grandfather's band went on a long journey, the longest they'd ever taken. And they caught your grandmother and brought her back."

"My grandmother?" For the moment, Eric forgot what was being prepared for him outside. He'd known there was some peculiar secret about his grandmother. She had rarely been mentioned in Mankind. Up to now, he'd taken it for granted that this was because she'd had a son who was terribly unlucky—almost the worst thing a person in the burrows could be. The father of a one-child litter, after all, and being killed together with his wife in Monster territory. Very unlucky.

"My grandmother was from the Aaron People? Not from Mankind?" He knew, of course, that several of the women had been captured from other peoples in neighboring burrows and had the good fortune now to be considered full-fledged members of Mankind. Sometimes one of their own women would be lost this way, when she strayed too far down an outlying burrow and stumbled into a band of Stranger warriors. If you stole a woman from another people, after all, you stole a substantial portion of their knowledge. But he'd never imagined—

"Deborah the Dream-Singer." Thomas's head waggled loosely: he dribbled words mixed with red saliva. "Did you know why your grandmother was called the Dream-Singer, Eric? The women used to say that the things she talked about happened only in dreams, and that she couldn't talk straight like other people—she could only sing about her dreams. But she taught your father a lot, and he was like her. Women were a little afraid to mate with him. My sister was the first to take a chance—and everyone said she deserved what she got."

Abruptly, Eric became conscious of a change in the sounds outside the burrow. More quiet. Were they coming for him now?

"Uncle Thomas, listen! I have an idea. Those Strangers—Walter, Arthur the Organizer—they gave me a Monster souvenir. I don't know what it does, but I can't get at it. I'll turn around. You try to reach down into my knapsack with the tips of your fingers and—"

The Trap-Smasher paid no attention to him. "She was an Alien-Sciencer," he rambled on, mostly to himself. "Your grandmother was the first Alien-Sciencer we ever had in Mankind. I guess the Aaron People were all Alien-Sciencers. Imagine—a whole tribe of Alien-Sciencers!"

Eric groaned. This half-alive, delirious man was his only hope of escaping. This bloody wreck who had once been the proudest, most alert band captain of them all.

He turned for another look at the guard. The man was still staring down the length of the great central burrow. There was nothing to be heard now but a terrifying silence, as if dozens of pairs of eyes were glowing in anticipation. And footsteps—weren't those footsteps? He had to find a way to make his uncle cooperate.

"Thomas the Trap-Smasher!" he said sharply, barely managing to keep his voice low. "Listen to me. This is an order! There's something in my knapsack, a blob of sticky stuff. We're going to turn our backs to each other, and you're going to reach in with your hands and tear some off. Do you hear me? That's an order—a warrior's order!"

His uncle nodded, completely docile. "I've been a warrior for over twenty auld lang synes," he mumbled, twisting around. "Six of them a band captain. I've given orders and taken them, given them and taken them. I've never disobeyed an order. What I always say is how can you expect to give orders if you don't—"

"*Now*," Eric told him, bringing their backs together and hunching down so that his knapsack would be just under his uncle's bound arms. "Reach in. Work that mass of sticky stuff out. It's right on top. And hurry!"

Yes. Those were footsteps coming up outside. Several of them. The leaders of the Female Society, the chief, an escort of warriors. And the guard, watching that deadly procession, was liable to remember his duties and turn back to the prisoners.

"*Hurry*," he demanded. "I told you to hurry, dammit! That's an order, too. Get it out fast. Fast!"

And, all this time, as the Trap-Smasher's fumbling fingers wandered about in his knapsack, as he listened with fright and impatience to the sounds of the approaching execution party—all this time, somewhere in his mind, there was astonishment at the orders he was rapping out to an experienced band captain and the incredible authority he had managed to get into his voice.

"Now you're wondering where the Aaron People have their burrow," Thomas began suddenly, reverting to an earlier topic as if they were having a pleasant conversation after a fine, full meal. "Well, I'll tell you."

"Forget it! Get that stuff out. Just get it out!"

"It's hard to describe," the other man's voice wandered on. "A long way off, their burrow is, a long way off. You know the Strangers call us front-burrow people. You know that, don't you? The Strangers are back-burrowers. Well, the Aaron People are the bottommost burrowers of all."

Eric sensed his fingers closing in the knapsack.

The three women who ruled the Female Society came into the storage burrow. Ottilie the Omen-Teller, Sarah the Sickness-Healer and Rita the Record-Keeper. With them were the chief and two band captains, heavily armed.

Chapter 9

Ottilie, the Chieftain's First Wife, was in the lead. She stopped just inside the entrance to the burrow, and the others came to a halt around her.

"Look at them," she jeered. "They're trying to free each other! And what do they plan to do if they get themselves untied?"

Franklin moved to her side and took a long, judicious look at the two men squatting back to back. "They'll try to escape," he explained, continuing his wife's joke. "They'll have their hands free, they figure, and surely Thomas the Trap-Smasher and his nephew are a match, even bare-handed, for the best spearmen in Mankind!"

And then Eric felt the searching hands come up out of the knapsack to which his own arms were tied. Something fell to the floor of the burrow. It made an odd noise, halfway between a splash and a thud. He twisted around for it immediately with his mouth open, flexing his knees in a tight crouch underneath his body.

"You've never seen anything like the burrows of the Aaron People," his uncle was mumbling, as if what his hands had just done was no concern of the rest of him. "And neither have I, though I've listened to the tales. Some of the tales—some of the tales—"

"He won't last long now," Sarah the Sickness-Healer commented. "We'll have to have our fun with the boy."

All you do, Walter the Weapon-Seeker had said, *is tear off a pinch with your fingers. Then spit on it and throw it. Throw it as fast and as far as you can.*

He couldn't use his fingers. But he leaned down to the red fragment and picked it up with his teeth. He brought his tongue against the strange soft substance, lashing saliva into it. And simultaneously he kicked at the burrow floor with curved toes, straightening his legs, jerking his thighs and body upward. Unable to use his arms for balance, he tottered erect and turned, swaying, to face the leaders of his people.

After you spit on it, throw it fast. As fast and as far as you can.

"I don't know what he's doing," someone said, "but I don't like it. Let me through."

Stephen the Strong-Armed stepped ahead of the group and lifted a heavy spear, ready for throwing.

Eric shut his eyes, bent his head far back on his neck and took a deep, deep breath. Then he snapped his head forward, flipping his tongue hard against the object in his mouth. He forced out his breath so abruptly that the exhalation became a wild, barking cough.

The soft little mass flew out of his mouth, and he opened his eyes to watch its course. For a moment, he was unable to find it anywhere; then he located it by the odd expression on Stephen's face and the fearful upward roll of his eyes.

There was a little red splotch in the middle of the band captain's forehead.

What was supposed to happen, he wondered? He had followed directions as well as he could under the circumstances, but he had no idea what the scarlet stain, made loose and moist by his saliva, was supposed to accomplish. He watched it, hoping and waiting.

Then Stephen the Strong-Armed brought his free hand up slowly to wipe the stuff off. Eric stopped hoping. Nothing was going to happen.

Strangers, he had begun to think despairingly, *that's what comes of trusting Strangers—*

The blast of sound was so tremendous that for a moment he thought the roof of the burrow had fallen in. He was slammed backward against the wall and fell as if he'd been walloped with a spear haft. He remembered the cough with which he'd expelled the bit of red blob from his mouth. Had there been a delayed echo to his cough, a gigantic, ear-splitting echo?

He lifted his head from the floor finally, when the reverberations in the little storage burrow had rumbled into a comparative silence. Someone was screaming. Someone was screaming over and over again.

It was Sarah. She was looking at Stephen the Strong-Armed from the rear. She had been standing directly behind him. Now she was staring at him and screaming in sharp steady bursts.

Her mouth was open so wide that it seemed she was about to tear her jaws apart. And with each scream she lifted her arm rigidly and pointed to the back of Stephen's neck. She kept lifting her arm and pointing as if she wanted everyone present to know beyond the least doubt why and how she came to be screaming.

Stephen the Strong-Armed had no head. His body ended at the neck, and flaps of skin fell down to his chest in an irregular wavy pattern. A fountain of blood bubbled and spurted where his head had been. His body still stood upright, feet planted wide apart in a good warrior's stance, one arm holding the spear ready for action and the other congealed in its upward motion to wipe the red blob away. It stood, incredibly straight and tall and alive.

Suddenly, it fell apart.

First the spear slid slowly forward out of the right hand and clattered to the floor. Then the arms began to fall loosely to the sagging knees and the entire great, brawny body slumped as if its bones had left it. It dropped aimlessly to the floor, an arm poking out here, a leg twisting out there, in a pattern as meaningless as if an oddly shaped bag of skin had been flung to one side of the burrow.

It continued to twitch for a moment or two, as the bubbling fountain of blood turned into a sluggishly flowing river. At last it lay still, a motionless heap of limbs and torso. Of the missing head there was no trace anywhere.

Sarah the Sickness-Healer stopped screaming and turned, shaking, to her companions. Their protruding eyes left the body on the floor.

Then they all reacted at once.

They yelled madly, wildly, fearfully, as if they were a chorus and she the conductor. Still bellowing, they made for the narrow entrance behind them. They got through in a pushing, punching scramble that at one point looked like a composite monster with dozens of arms, legs and swinging, naked breasts. They carried the guard outside with them, and with them, too, they carried their panic, screaming it into existence all along the great central burrow.

For a little while, Eric could hear feet pounding into the distant corridors. Then there was quiet. There was quiet everywhere, except for Thomas the Trap-Smasher's interminable mumbling.

Eric forced himself upright again. He was unable to imagine what had happened. That red blob—the Stranger, Walter, had said it was a weapon, but it didn't operate like any weapon he had ever in his life heard of. Except possibly in the times of the ancestors: the ancestors were supposed to have had things which could blow an object apart and leave no trace. But this was an alien artifact, a possession of the Monsters which Walter the Weapon-Seeker had somehow found and appropriated. What was it? How had it exploded the head of Stephen the Strong-Armed?

A lot of it still lay in his knapsack. Meanwhile, he had his chance. It might not last long; he had no idea when the panic might subside and a patrol of warriors be sent back to investigate. He stepped carefully across the red stream flowing from the fallen man's neck. Squatting down in front of the dropped spear, he managed to get a grip on it with his bound hands and rose, holding it awkwardly behind him.

No time to cut his bonds. Not here.

"Uncle Thomas," he called. "We can get away. We have a chance now. Come on, get up!"

The wounded band captain stared up at him without comprehension. "—corridors like you've never seen or imagined," he continued in a low monotone. "Glow lamps that aren't on foreheads. Corridors filled with glow lamps. Corridors and corridors and corridors—"

For a moment, Eric considered. The man would be a heavy liability in fast travel. But he couldn't desert him. This was his last surviving relative, the only person who didn't consider him an outlaw and a thing. And, shattered as he was, also still his captain.

"Get up!" he said again. "Thomas the Trap-Smasher, get up! That's an order, a warrior's order. Get up!"

As he'd hoped, his uncle responded to the old command. He managed to get his legs under his body, and strained against them, but it was no use. He didn't have the energy to rise.

Casting apprehensive looks over his shoulder at the entrance to the storage burrow, Eric ran to the struggling man. Working backward, he managed to get one end of the spear under the crook of his uncle's arm. Then, using his own hip as a fulcrum, he levered hard at the other end.

It was painful, slippery work, since he couldn't bring all of his muscles into play and it was difficult to see what he was doing. In between efforts, he gasped out orders to "Get up, get up, get *up*, damn you!" At last the end of the spear went all the way down. His uncle was on his feet, staggering, but at least on his feet.

Dragging the spear awkwardly, Eric urged and butted him out of the place. The great central burrow was empty of people. Weapons, pots and miscellaneous possessions lay strewn about where they had been dropped. The finished structure of the Stage stood deserted in front of the Royal Mound. And some time before, the bodies of his uncle's wives had evidently been removed.

The chief and the other leaders had bolted to the left once they had clawed their way out of the storage burrow. They had apparently run past the scaffold structure and picked up the rest of Mankind in their panic.

Eric turned right.

His uncle was a problem. Thomas the Trap-Smasher kept coming to a bewildered halt. Again and again he began to tell a story he had heard about the Aaron People by a man who had claimed to have made a journey to the burrows of the strange, distant tribe. Eric had to push against him to keep him moving.

Once they were in the outlying corridors, he felt better. But not until they had made many turns, passed dozens of branches and were well into completely uninhabited burrows, did he feel he could stop and saw himself free of his bonds on the point of the spear. He did the same for his uncle. Then, throwing the Trap-Smasher's left arm across his own shoulders and clutching him tightly about the waist, he started off again. It was slow going; his uncle was a heavy man, but the more distance they could put between themselves and Mankind, the better.

But distance where? Where should they go? He pondered the problem as they tottered together down the silent, branching corridors. One place was as good as another. There was nowhere that they would be welcome. Just keep going.

He may have muttered his questions aloud. To his surprise, Thomas the Trap-Smasher suddenly said in an entirely coherent but very weak voice: "The doorway to Monster territory, Eric. Make for the doorway to Monster territory where you went to make your Theft."

"Why?" Eric asked. "What can we do there?"

There was no answer. His uncle's head fell forward on his chest. He was evidently sliding into a stupor again. And yet, somehow, as long as Eric's encircling arm pulled at his body, the man's legs kept moving forward. There was some residual stamina and a warrior's determination in him yet.

Monster territory. Was there more safety for them there now than among human beings?

Very well then. The doorway to Monster territory. They would have to come around in a wide arc through many corridors to get to it, but Eric knew the way. He was Eric the Eye, after all, he told himself: it was his business always to know the way.

But was it? He had not enjoyed the formal initiation into manhood that was the usual aftermath of a successful Theft. Without that, perhaps he was still Eric the Only, still a boy and an initiate. No, he knew what he was. He was Eric the Outlaw, nothing else.

He was an outlaw, without a home and a people. And, except for the dying man he pulled along, everyone's hand was henceforth against him.

Chapter 10

Thomas the Trap-Smasher had been badly injured in the surprise attack that had wiped out his band. Ordinarily, he would have had his wounds carefully dressed by the cleverness and accumulated experience of Sarah the Sickness-Healer. But Sarah had been anything but a healer to him.

Now, the strain of escape and the forced headlong flight that followed it had emptied his body of its last resources. His eyes were glazed and his strong shoulders hung slack. He was a somnambulist walking jerkily in the direction of death.

When they stopped to rest, Eric—after listening intently for any sounds of pursuit—had washed his uncle's wounds carefully with water from the canteens and had bound the uglier gashes with strips torn from a knapsack. It was all he knew how to do: warrior's first aid. A woman's advanced therapeutic knowledge was needed for anything more complicated.

Not that it would have made very much difference by this time. The Trap-Smasher was too far gone.

Eric felt desperate at the thought of being left alone forever in the dark, uninhabited corridors. He tried to force water and bits of food upon his uncle. The man's head rolled back, nourishment dribbling carelessly down from both sides of his mouth. He was breathing lightly and very rapidly. His body had grown quite warm by the time they stopped.

Eric himself ate ravenously: it was his first meal in a long, long while. He kept staring at his recumbent uncle and trying to work out a line of action that would do some good. In the end, he had thought of nothing better than to hitch the man's arm up over his shoulder again and to keep going in the direction of Monster territory.

Once erect, the Trap-Smasher's feet began walking again, but with a dragging, soggy quality that became more and more pronounced. After a while, Eric had to come to a halt: he had the feeling that he was hauling dead weight.

When he tried to lower his uncle to the floor of the burrow, he found that the body had become almost completely limp. Thomas lay on his back, his eyes staring without curiosity at the rounded ceiling upon which his forehead glow lamp outlined a bright circular patch.

The heartbeat was very, very faint.

"Eric," he heard a weak voice say. He raised his eyes from his uncle's chest and looked at the painfully working mouth.

"Yes, uncle?"

"Listen, Eric. Grow up fast. I mean—I mean, really grow up. It's your only chance. A lad like you—in the burrows, a lad either develops fast, or he's dead. Don't—" the chest arched upward for a sudden coughing spasm, "—don't take anything for granted. Anything—from anybody. Learn, but be—be your own man. And grow up, Eric. Fast."

"I'll try. I'll try as hard as I can."

"I'm sorry—about—what I got you into. I had—no right. Your life—after all—your life. You—my wives—the band. I led—death—everyone. I'm sorry."

Eric fought hard to hold back his tears. "It was for a cause, Uncle Thomas," he said. "It wasn't just you. The cause failed."

There was a hideous cackle from the prone man. For a moment, Eric thought it was a death rattle. Then he realized that it had been a laugh, but such a laugh as he had never heard before.

"A cause?" the Trap-Smasher gasped. "A cause? Do you know—do you—know what—the cause was? I wanted—wanted to be chief. Chief. The only—only way I could—do it—Alien-Science—the Strangers—a cause. Everyone—the killings—I wanted to—to be chief. *Chief!*"

He went rigid as he coughed out the last word. Then slowly, like flesh turning into liquid, he relaxed. He was dead.

Eric stared at the body a long time. It didn't make any difference, he found: the numbness in his mind remained. There was a great paralyzed spot in the center of his brain that was unable to think or to feel.

In the end, he shook himself, bent down and grabbed the body by the shoulders. Walking backward, he dragged it in the direction of Monster territory.

Something he had to do. The duty of anyone who lived in the burrows when death occurred in his neighborhood. Now it filled time and used up energies that he might otherwise have expended in thoughts which were agonizing.

The energies which it demanded were almost more than he was capable of at this point. His uncle had been a heavy, well-built man. Eric found that he had to stop at the end of almost every curving corridor and get his breath back.

He finally arrived at the doorway, grateful for the fact that his uncle had died so relatively close to it. He also felt he understood why this had been suggested as their destination. Thomas the Trap-Smasher had known he had little time left: his nephew would have the responsibility of sewering him. He had tried to make it as easy for Eric as possible by going the greater part of the distance on his own feet.

There was a fresh-water pipe in the wall near the doorway to Monster territory. And wherever there was a fresh-water pipe, the Monsters were likely to have laid a sewer pipe nearby. It was down this, probably, that the men killed in the battle with Stephen the Strong-Armed's band had been disposed of much earlier. And it was down this that Thomas had known his remains must also go—the closest point at which his nephew could sewer him in comparative safety.

This much, at least, he had done for Eric's benefit.

Eric located the fresh-water pipe without much difficulty. There was a constant low rumbling and gurgling underfoot, and—at the spot where it was most pronounced—he found the slab in the floor cut at the cost of infinite labor by some past generation of Mankind. Near it, after the slab was lifted, was another, much wider pipe, large enough to carry several men abreast. As with the other one, the hard stuff of the burrow floor had been scraped away so that a joint lay exposed.

Opening the joint was another matter. Eric had seen it done many times by his elders, but this was his own first attempt. It was a tricky business of tugging a heavy covering plate first right, then left, and getting his fingers under the rim and pulling at just the right moment.

The joint opened at last, and the incredible stink of Monster sewage poured out as the liquid swirled darkly by. Death had always been associated in Eric's mind with this stink, since the pipe carried not only the Monsters' waste matter but also that of Mankind, collected from its burrows every week by the old women who were too feeble for any other work. All that was not alive or useful was carried to the nearest Monster sewer pipe, all that might decay and foul the burrows. And that included, of course, the bodies of the dead.

Eric stripped his uncle's body of all useful gear as he had seen the women do many times. Then he dragged it to the hole in the burrow floor and lowered it carefully, holding on to one arm until the current of the sewage caught it. He repeated as much of the ceremony as he could remember, concluding with the words: *"And therefore, O ancestors, I beg you to receive the body of this member of Mankind, Thomas the Trap-Smasher, a warrior of the first rank, a band captain of renown and the father of nine—four alive and five dead."*

There was usually another line or so—*"Take him to you and keep him with you until the time when the Monsters have been destroyed utterly and the Earth is ours again. Then shall you and he and all human beings who have ever lived rise from the sewers and joyously walk the surface of our world forever."* But this, after all, was a pure Ancestor-Science passage; and his uncle had died fighting Ancestor-Science. What was the Alien-Science equivalent? And was it likely to be any more potent, any less full of false-hood? In the end, Eric omitted those last two lines.

He let go of his uncle's arm. The body shot away and down the pipe. Thomas the Trap-Smasher was gone, he was gone for all time, the way Eric reasoned now. He was dead and sewered, and that was that.

Eric closed the joint, pulled the slab down and stamped it into place.

He was completely alone. An outlaw who could expect nothing from other human beings but death by slow torture. He had no companions, no home, no beliefs of any sort. His uncle's last words still lay, in all their stern ugliness, at the bottom of his mind. *"I wanted to—to be chief."*

It was bad enough to discover that the religion on which he had been raised was a mere prop to the power of the chieftainship, that the mysterious Female Society was completely unable to see into a person's future. But to find out that his uncle's thoughtful antagonism to such nonsense was based on nothing more substantial than simple personal ambition, an ambition murderously unscrupulous and willing to sacrifice anybody who trusted him—well, what was there left to believe in, to base a life upon?

Had his father and mother been any less gullible than the most naive child in the burrows? They had sacrificed themselves—for what? For one superstition as opposed to another, for the secret political maneuvers of this person as opposed to that person.

Not for him. He would be free. He laughed, bitterly and self-consciously. He had to be free. There was no choice: he was an outlaw.

Eric realized he was terribly tired. He'd done his Theft, made the long trip to and from Mankind's burrows and fought what amounted to a full battle—all without any sleep.

He curled back against the wall and napped. It was a warrior's nap, with senses fully alert for the approach of an enemy. His mind submerged only partially into unconsciousness, absorbing rest but preventing full slumber. The part of his mind that remained awake peered restlessly into the future, examining alternatives, making plans.

By the time he arose, stretched, yawned, he had reached a decision.

Eric walked a few steps, putting his hands on the door to Monster territory. To shift it out of its socket was a hard job for one man. He strained and tore his fingers; finally he managed it. The door came away, and he deposited it carefully on the floor of the burrow.

He stared at it for a while, trying to figure out a way of getting it back after he'd passed through the doorway. No, a single man just couldn't do that from the other side. He'd have to leave the doorway open, an incredible social crime.

Well, he couldn't commit a crime any more. He was beyond all rules made by human communities. Ahead lay the glaring white light that he and his kind feared so much. Into this, where there were no illusions to treasure and no help to be expected, into this place he would go.

Behind him lay the dark, safe, intricate burrows. They were tunnels in the walls that surrounded Monster territory. Men lived in these walls, and shivered, and were ignorant, and made fools of each other. He could no longer do these things: he had to face the Monsters.

Could humanity really hit back at the Monsters—in any way at all? Weren't they like a swarm of roaches in the storage burrow who felt they should declare war on a cook busy at preparing the evening meal for Mankind? The cook would roar with laughter at such a thought. Who knew what went on in the mind of a roach—and who cared?

But suppose a roach stopped crawling greedily and aimlessly with his kind? Suppose he hung in a dim crevice and watched his enemy day after day and learned all there was to know about him? Suppose he wiped out of his mind everything that learned fools and ignorant tradition had ever taught him, concentrating exclusively on a totally new way to hit back at his enemy, a totally unexpected quarter from which to mount his attack?

Suppose he operated not from any belief, any preconception at all, but only from a soldier's bitter necessity?

"I'll grow up fast, Uncle," muttered Eric the Only, Eric the Eye, Eric the Outlaw. "I'll grow up fast—I have to."

Then he stepped through the doorway into Monster territory.

PART II: SOLDIERS FOR THEIR VALOR

Chapter 11

The old trap that Thomas the Trap-Smasher had long ago dismantled still hung uselessly on the other side of the wall. And none of the huge creatures was abroad.

That horrifying white, white light again! This insane spaciousness!

Eric turned right and ran along the wall, counting paces. He took the same route as he had on his Theft. Fear made him breathe heavily, but he kept reminding himself that here he ran the same risks, no more and no less, as any other human being. Here, every man was an outlaw, an object of the chase, a thing marked for death. In Monster territory, you enjoyed no special advantages if you still belonged to a people.

Of course, you might have a woman waiting for you back in your burrows, ready to turn into useful articles all the good things with which this place was filled. But she wouldn't be with you at such a moment. Women were the custodians of human life and history and all accumulated knowledge. And the magic rituals they recited were the most precious possession of a people, giving them pride and a fundamental sense of identity. Women were absolutely forbidden to engage in any enterprise for which more readily expendable men might be used. They never entered Monster territory.

And yet, according to his uncle, his mother *had*....

He reached the huge article of Monster furniture and turned left along it. There was just a chance that there would be some Strangers still left where he had met them in the course of his Theft. He could warn them of what was going on in the burrows—they might let him stay with them. Even the companionship of effeminate, talkative, overdressed Strangers would be better than nothing.

As he was about to turn into the dark entrance of the structure, Eric paused. He had been running as he had been taught to run in Monster territory: *don't look up, never look up.* Well, he'd looked up once already, in the course of his Theft—and he'd survived. All that he'd been taught: what was it worth?

Therefore he stopped deliberately well outside the entrance. Making certain again that no Monsters were about, he shoved his hands on his hips belligerently, turned and surveyed the enormous burrow. Yes, it was still a little upsetting at first glance. But you got used to it, you got used to it. Given enough time, no doubt even those incredibly oversize bags and containers, those walls stretching up so high that it hurt one's neck to try to see their upper limits—given enough time, you'd come to notice this place as casually as a narrow storage burrow full of Mankind's odds and ends.

There was nothing he couldn't eventually learn to live with, Eric told himself. As long as he could see clearly what it was.

Eyes open. Look at everything. Judge everything for yourself, with your own vision. He would be Eric the Eye.

He traveled cautiously inside the structure. If there were any Strangers about, they might be expecting attack. They might throw first and examine the spear-pierced body for explanations afterward. Certainly, now at least, if Arthur the Organizer had been alerted to what was going on in the burrows, he would have posted sentries.

And the sentries would be nervous.

He encountered no sentries. He heard voices, however, from the moment he stooped and entered the low tunnel. They grew louder and louder as he turned into the right fork. When he emerged into the large, square burrow he was fully prepared for what he saw: dozens of Strangers, suffering from various degrees of personal damage, talking, gesticulating, arguing. Multitudes of forehead glow lamps created a tremendous flare of illumination.

The scene was like the aftermath of a large-scale raid on an entire people. There were men with slight wounds, the blood having long hardened upon their scratches; there were men with bad wounds, who limped about on a crushed foot or who desperately tried to get aid for the red rip in their chest or side; there were men as mortally hurt as his uncle had been, who—having managed to crawl to this place of comparative safety by themselves or having been helped here by friends—lay now, unnoticed and forgotten along the walls, sliding downward through coma after coma until they smashed into the unyielding surface of death.

And everyone—everyone who was at all conscious—was trying to make himself heard.

Those with relatively minor injuries had clustered about Walter the Weapon-Seeker and Arthur the Organizer at the far corner of the burrow, shrilly trying to tell their own experiences and criticizing the behavior of others. Those whose wounds made it impossible for them to jostle in the main crowd, stood on the outskirts or sat on the floor in groaning groups of two and three, and pointed out to each other the defects in Walter's plans or Arthur's leadership that had brought them to this pass. Even the dying muttered their recent experiences to the friendly floor and suggested, with their last, gasping breath, alternative courses of action that would have developed far better results.

In a sense, Eric thought, his first impression had been correct. It was an entire people after a battle. He was staring at the people of Alien-Science after the other inhabitants of the burrows had crushed them and spat them out.

But, whatever they were, this was his people now. The only one he had. He shrugged and strode into the sharp-angled, noisy place.

Somewhere in the crowd, a man's head swung around and studied him. The face broke into a smile. "Eric," it called out. "Hey, Eric!"

A head that was higher than the others near it. And hair that was loose, not caught by a back strap in the Stranger fashion. A warrior of Mankind.

They elbowed toward each other frantically through the gesticulating debaters, the two beams from their forehead glow lamps making a single line as they kept their eyes locked together.

Long before they met, Eric recognized the man. Tall, thin, nervous-bodied—it could be only one person. The member of his uncle's band who had made his life as an initiate most difficult, the warrior with whom he'd almost fought a duel before setting out on his Theft: Roy the Runner.

Roy seemed to remember none of this as they came together. He threw his bony arms around Eric and embraced him. "A familiar face," he sang out in delight. "Eric the Only, am I glad to see you!"

Eric stiffened and stepped back out of the hug. "Eric the Eye," he said sharply. "I've become Eric the Eye."

The other man held up both hands placatingly. "Eric the Eye. Sure. Eric the Eye. I'm sorry. I'll remember it from now on. Eric the *Eye*. Anything you say, boy. Just be friendly, just talk to me a little. I've been going crazy standing here and listening to these fake warriors, these damn half-women gabble at each other. And trying to figure out what's going on back in Mankind." He grabbed Eric's shoulders and begged: "What *is* going on with our people? How do we stand there?"

"We don't." Eric told him his experiences, beginning with the return from his Theft and the discovery that the door slab had been put back into place. "We're outlaws," he said, when he had finished. "You, I, everyone in the Trap-Smasher's band are outlaws. Who else got away?"

"Nobody, so far as I know. I figured I was the only survivor until I saw you come in. The only reason I got away was because I was on sentry duty all the way at the other end of the corridor when the attack came. I heard the noise and ran back. There was Stephen the Strong-Armed's men slamming it into our band and what looked like a hundred Strangers helping them. They saw me come up and a whole mob of them made for me. I didn't stop to think. I just took off, warrior's oath or no warrior's oath. And believe me, if you ever think you've seen me run, you're mistaken. I picked up each foot and I planted it so far ahead of the other one that I practically split down the middle. And all the time, there were those spears going over my head and past my shoulders and all around me. You never saw so many spears: I bet there was corridor after corridor littered with them."

"And they all missed you? You don't show a scratch."

The Runner shrugged contemptuously. "Strangers. What do you expect? They couldn't hit fat old Franklin himself if he were sitting at their feet. I was lucky none of Stephen's men were in that mob chasing me. Besides, like I told you, I *ran*. I shook most of them off pretty fast: after about a dozen corridors or so, there were only about two or three still following me. Those aren't such good odds for Strangers, not against a full warrior of Mankind, so they gave up too and turned back. I rested, got my breath back—and came here. I used another doorway to Monster territory, though."

"You knew about this place? You'd been here before?"

"Not inside, not in this particular burrow. But you know, we were all Alien-Sciencers pretty much in the band, some a little more, some a little less. Your uncle had been working on us, converting us, for a long time. Lots of times, when we'd be out on an expedition, stealing food and suchlike, he'd make a special trip inside this structure, and he'd leave us on guard outside. He told us how to get in to the square burrow, how to make contact with the Alien-Science headquarters, in case of an emergency. I figured that's what this was—an emergency—and I came here to get help. *Help!*" Roy the Runner looked around and made a face. "From this bunch of yapping, half-female lunatics? More and more of them kept coming in, all banged up and all talking their heads off. That's the one thing Strangers know how to do—talk, talk, talk, talk."

Eric followed his derisive glances and tended to agree with him. There certainly was a lot of talk going on, a lot of unnecessary recapitulation. But what else was there to do?

A major political and religious movement—with adherents all over the burrows—had just been smashed at one stroke, a concerted blow arranged by chiefs who were normally in a state of unvarying war with each other. The survivors had made for their headquarters, which no doubt had been deliberately placed in Monster territory for just such emergencies as this. Arriving here singly and in small groups, they could bind their wounds, rest and discuss alternatives still open to them. In this dangerous, unorthodox hideaway, they could talk and plan in freedom, relatively secure from attack.

But were they? Among this many men, limping and scuttling to doorways to Monster territory, there must have been a few careless enough to have been followed. All this movement in one direction and at one time could well have been noticed in the burrows. And, if they had been followed, if their activity had been observed, then this hideaway might turn out to be a terrible trap—a vast expedition organized by the chiefs might be on its way at this moment to exterminate once and for all the last remnants of the Alien-Science heresy.

No, not very likely, Eric decided upon reflection. With the immediate danger behind them, with their own Alien-Sciencers killed or in flight, the chiefs would have returned to a state of hostility and suspicion of each other. For a while, in fact, there would be even less communication than usual between the various peoples, while defense plans—which had been exposed to temporary allies—were being hurriedly altered. Mankind, for example, would be worrying right now about what the Strangers in their midst had noted: the total strength of fighting effectives, the location of the great central burrow and the specific corridors that led into it—and, possibly, particularly desirable women who might be worth a raid. Xenophobia would be snarling through the burrows once more, and alliances would be out of the question, especially an alliance as enormous and manifold as an expedition of this sort would require. After all, a people—no matter how great their need of food and equipment—rarely sent more than a half-dozen men into the complex dangers of Monster territory at one time. They were unlikely to risk the greater part of their warrior force in such a place.

While the Alien-Sciencers stayed here, then, they were relatively safe from that kind of attack. But still, sentries should have been posted just in case. It was more military, for one thing. And they would need every bit of military cohesiveness if they were to survive.

Roy the Runner agreed with him. "I told that to the leader—what's his name— Arthur the Organizer—as soon as I got here. But these damn Strangers: what can you expect? They don't know how to run an army. He sort of wobbled his head and asked me if there were any contacts, any secret organization of Alien-Sciencers, in the other bands of Mankind. Here we may soon be fighting for our lives, and he's worrying about secret organizations!"

"Well, he can't help it," Eric pointed out. "He's an Organizer. Just like you're a Runner and I'm an Eye. If you lost your legs or if I went blind, how would we feel? Well, he's an Organizer who's lost his organization. It's a terrible thing to happen to a man."

"Um. Maybe. But that's his problem, not mine. Me, I can still outrun any man in the burrows. He also said that if you or your uncle managed to get here, he wants to ask you a couple of questions: I should bring you to him right away. That's what he's doing with all these beaten-up characters around him—filling in the total picture, he calls it."

As they made their way through the crowd, the Runner bent down and muttered into Eric's ear: "Let me tell you, Eric, what we need now—in the spot we're in—is not an Arthur the Organizer. We need a first-rate band captain like your uncle. I've seen him when we won and when we lost, he always knew what to do. There was a man, there was a leader! When to push an attack home, when to retreat, when to regroup and attack from a different, unexpected direction—you could really trust his orders. He knew, he just knew." The tall, thin warrior shook his head. "And now he's riding the sewer! It's hard to believe. Eric—what about my woman? Did they do anything to my woman?"

"I don't think so. The only women I saw catching it were the wives of Thomas the Trap-Smasher."

Roy nodded morosely. "Not my wife. Trust her. I'll bet she's where she always wanted to be—in Franklin's harem. The way she'd repeat his name! Franklin, the Father of Many Thieves, she used to say, of *Many* Thieves. Whenever a woman gave birth who'd lain with the chief, Myra would tell me, 'Five in the litter, Roy. Five! Franklin always fathers at least five.' And her eyes would glitter like a pair of glow lamps. So what if I was the fastest runner in all of Mankind, what if I'd once run the whole length of a larder with two Monsters after me and lived to tell the tale? My family never had more than three to a litter, and Myra knew it damned well."

Eric walked faster, pushing through the noisy, wounded men. Three to a litter! The sour taste of his personal curse filled him again. And it wasn't diluted much by the knowledge that, as things stood, he now had very little chance of having a woman, any woman, to himself. The question of his paternal powers might never come up in this huge, all-male band of outlaws. Any woman they found...

Arthur the Organizer strode out from the clump of vociferous Strangers. He extended his arms in a warm greeting, but his peculiar eyes had nothing to do with warmth. They spun and spun in anxious multiple calculations.

"Welcome, Eric," he said. "Welcome, welcome. I've been hearing a rumor about your uncle. I hope, I sincerely hope, it's not so."

"He's dead. Dead and sewered." Eric fought to control a sudden, murderous anger. His uncle, it was true, had used him, Eric, had used his band and his wives, but, after all, these had been his uncle's own: they had been his to use if he so chose. His uncle had been his uncle, and a great one in Mankind.

This man—this Stranger—with his Stranger ambitions, his Stranger contempt, based on pure ignorance, for whatever was truly majestic and noble—what did he know of Mankind? What did he know of what it had meant to Thomas the Trap-Smasher to be chief of such a people?

He gave the Organizer the same recent history he'd given Roy, skipping much of the personal detail. Partly, he knew the Organizer wouldn't be interested in these minor touches; but partly, his rage at the outsider, standing there, nodding and grunting and checking off points to himself, his rage kept creeping into his voice and could only be controlled by cutting the story as short as possible.

Arthur the Organizer heard nothing but the words. *"Well, now I know what happened to Thomas the Trap-Smasher and Mankind. So much for that,"* his attitude seemed to be. Eric felt as if he had been filling a storage pouch with exactly the right amount for the Organizer, who now thanked him, pulled the draw strings tight and dropped the pouch into his haversack.

"Pretty much like the others," Arthur summed up. "Leader killed, all his known followers exterminated, one, maybe two, manage to get away. The whole business a sudden stroke—chief meshing with chief, tribe with hostile tribe—little or no warning. A beautiful job of organization, I'd say, smooth, smooth as hell. Except, of course, for this inexcusably sloppy business of escapees like yourself and Roy here. But that, I'd lay to the lack of any overall coordinating control—there was no single individual running the whole show who was able to see it all in the round and pick out the weak spots. For a piece of what was essentially committee work, nicely done. Very nicely done."

"I'm glad you can enjoy it. Meanwhile, we—the movement—we're smashed, we're through."

The Organizer smiled and put an arm around his shoulder. "Not at all, boy. Not in the slightest. We merely enter upon a new phase. To quote the Ancestor-Science of our enemies: Action equals reaction. At the moment, reaction is dominant, so action—our action—must build up its strength and search for other paths. All human burrows are closed to us, but the Monster burrows are wide open. How about it—are you up to a little expedition?"

Eric stepped back and away from the friendly arm. "An expedition? To deep Monster territory? Why? For what?"

"To get more Alien-Science to back us up. In other words, to practice what we preach. Here we are Alien-Sciencers, and how much Alien-Science can we exhibit to potential converts? A little of this, a smidgen of that. What we have is tremendous—you yourself have good reason to know that—but it's all bits and pieces, not fully connected, not fully understood. Now, I say this," and here his voice rose, and Eric noticed that they had been slowly surrounded by most of the Strangers who could walk. "I say: if we're going to be Alien-Sciencers, let's be Alien-Sciencers all the way. Let's get the best, the strongest stuff the Monsters have. Let's get something that, when we bring it back to the burrows, will be absolutely irresistible, not merely as a weapon to back us up, but as an irrefutable proof of the validity of our beliefs. Let's get some Alien-Science that will blow Ancestor-Science to hell and gone forever."

Tired faces around them lit up under their glow lamps. "He's got it," someone said enthusiastically.

"He sure has. Arthur's found a way out."

"Good old Arthur. The Organizer. The old Organizer himself."

Even badly wounded men began to sit up and grin with excitement.

"What exactly," Eric asked in a cold, practical voice, "what exactly is it that we get?"

The Organizer turned and lifted one eyebrow at him for a long moment. "Now if we knew that," he chuckled and pointed up to the overhanging darkness, "we'd know as much as they, the Monsters, do, and our worries would be over. We don't know *exactly*. But we know of a place, at least Walter does, where the Monsters keep their strongest, most powerful weapons. Right, Walter?"

A nod from the short, chunky Weapon-Seeker as everyone turned to question him with their eyes. "I've heard of it, and I think I can find it. It's supposed to be the last word in Alien-Science."

"The *last word* in Alien-Science," Arthur repeated as if in awe. "Imagine what that must be like. Just imagine! Well, we go there and that's what we come away with. The *last word!* Then let the chiefs and the Female Society reactionaries stand up to us. Let them try. We'll show them what Alien-Science can do, won't we? We'll show them once and for all."

A man threw his spear up into the air and caught it. He whirled on a blood-dripping leg and shook the spear over his head. "Attaboy, Arthur," he yelled. "Let's show them so they never forget it!"

Eric saw that everyone around him, Roy included, was cheering and waving spears. He shrugged and waved his too. Arthur looked at him; his smile grew bigger, more expansive.

"So they'll never forget it," he repeated. "Now, let's get some sleep, and everyone who's able will hit the trail in the morning. I hereby declare it night."

Roy and Eric went to the edge of the crowd and bedded down together, back to back: they were, after all, the only two warriors of Mankind present. Just before he went to sleep, the Runner said over his shoulder: "What a great idea, isn't it, Eric? Great!"

"Well, at least," Eric muttered, "it keeps us busy and takes our minds off the fact that we're outlaws for the rest of our lives."

Chapter 12

Wandering about next morning, before most of the others were up, Eric observed with contempt that sentries still had not been posted. He had taken it for granted that the leader of a war band would never let his men go through an entire sleep period without setting up a series of guard shifts to watch and give the alarm if enemies approached. True, he had reasoned out last night that, in the present state of resumed hostility in the burrows, they had little to fear from that direction, but that was only a logical hypothesis: one could not be certain. Besides, if a war band was going to function as a war band, function and survive, it had to go through the motions of discipline whether or not they were necessary.

In the face of such sloppy command work, he and Roy had better set up a personal on-off guard system between themselves every night. They wouldn't lose any rest: it was quite apparent that Strangers required much more sleep than the fighting men of Mankind.

Apparently, they also required much more talk. Never had Eric seen an expedition begin with so much discussion. He squatted off to one side, grinning and chuckling. Roy came over and sprawled beside him. He also found the Strangers hilarious.

First, there was the matter of who should go and who should stay. Badly wounded men definitely could not go. But how many should be left behind to take care of them? And what about a sewer detail to dispose of corpses? And should a reserve force be maintained here in their base: first, in case of an unexpected call on them from surviving Alien-Sciencers in the burrows, and second, if the main expeditionary body found that it needed help or supplies of any kind?

Where Thomas the Trap-Smasher would have announced his plans to respectfully nodding followers, Arthur the Organizer asked for suggestions on each point. There were plenty of suggestions.

Everyone had to be heard, complimented if he came up with something good, reasoned with if he didn't. An incredible amount of time was spent persuading one able-bodied man who felt he belonged on the expedition that he would be much more useful staying here among the wounded. Of course, in the end, Eric noticed with a good deal of interest, the arrangements were pretty much those Arthur the Organizer had seemed to want in the first place. And everyone got up with the feeling that it was what he had wanted too, all along.

He could handle men, even if he didn't know the first thing about giving orders.

Nor did he know the first thing about commanding an expedition on the move, Eric decided. Leaving behind them the wounded and the dying, as well as those who would serve as nurses, sewer detail and reserve, they set off in an impossibly long line of twenty-three talkative, gesticulating men, a line that straggled here, straggled there, and that was bunched at various points by especially friendly or argumentative groups.

One such group milled about Arthur, the commander of this overgrown war band, this expedition that was more like a wandering mob. Even in the low tunnel, where the walls were narrow and everyone had to bend over, a steady hum of discussion flowed back toward Eric from Arthur and his closer associates.

"Security, that was why they were able to smash us so suddenly. Our security was never tight enough. There were leaks."

"There are always leaks. The trouble was in our communications. We failed to hear about the leaks fast enough to plug them up."

"I think Walter's right. The trouble lay right there in security. All the chiefs had a spy system of one sort or another and we never really got going on counter-espionage."

"In that case, how do you account for—"

Eric glanced back at Roy, who was staying the regulation distance of fifteen paces behind him. "Hear them?" he asked the Runner. "They're still fighting yesterday's battles. This is how they win. With their mouths."

"Oh, they're Strangers. What do you want? They don't do things our way and we don't do things theirs."

Eric was surprised. He and Roy had evidently reversed positions since yesterday when they had first met. Roy still found Stranger ways very funny, but was forcing himself to be tolerant of them. Why?

As the harsh white light of Monster territory expanded ahead of them, he slowed down and waited for Roy to catch up with him. He was curious about what was going on inside the Runner, the only member of this ridiculous crowd for whom he felt any kind of kinship.

But just as Roy came abreast, all the way up front, the first man in the long line stepped out from the piece of Monster furniture and into whiteness.

There was a rapid, chattering sound. The man screeched once, danced a single, mad, despairing step—and fell over on his face. Everyone froze.

After a while, the man who was next in line edged forward carefully, poked his head out and stared upward. They watched him relax. "Only one," he said in a loud, carrying whisper. "Only one and Dan's sprung it. Nothing else in sight."

Silently now, they crept forward and, one by one, slipped out of the exit. They formed a loose, nervous group around the dead man, eyes whipping from his contorted body to anywhere in the great Monster whiteness from which danger might abruptly materialize and focus on them.

The sprung trap hung from the enormous piece of furniture directly above, its wires hanging slack except for a fitful shudder which occasionally rippled through them like a last lingering memory of the life they had just taken.

Roy moved up to Eric and slung his spear. Then he put his hands on his hips and gestured at the trap with his chin. "We came across one of those about five auld lang synes ago. Your uncle knocked it out. You can't poke a spear in front of it—it won't go for a spear: there has to be living flesh. What you do, you stick your foot out under it and pull back fast. A bit too slow and," he clicked his tongue, "no foot."

Arthur the Organizer had been listening. "You know traps," he said to Roy. "We can use you up front as a scout. From now on, you travel well ahead of the main body."

"I know a bit about traps," Roy told him disgustedly, "but I'm no Trap-Smasher. I'm a Runner. You want a scout, at least use an Eye. Eric, here, is an Eye."

"Both of you then. You'll be our advance party. All right: somebody grab the body and take it back inside to headquarters for sewerage. We'll wait for you." He pointed to the trap and thought carefully for a few moments before speaking. "Now, the way I see it—and either of you feel free to correct me if you think I'm wrong—is that this trap was set in place a relatively short time ago. I base this hypothesis on a single fact: the trap wasn't there last sleep-period, when refugees were still arriving. If this is so— and mind you, I'm only thinking out loud, not coming to anything hard and fast just yet—we can conclude that it was all that coming and going of refugees and messengers, the noise and inevitable clumsiness of the wounded making their way here that attracted the Monsters' attention. They tend to set up traps in places where there are plentiful signs of our activity. All right: does my theory hold together so far?"

"Great, Arthur," said a man who had edged up. "Terrific. You're right on the head. What a mind! What I'm interested in is, where do you take the idea? How do you figure next?"

"What a mind!" Roy whispered bitterly to Eric. "To figure out that the trap was installed between last night and now—that takes an Organizer, that takes brains! Well, what can you expect? Guys don't even know the difference between a Runner and an Eye!"

Arthur, arms folded on his chest, head down, was walking back and forth in front of his anxiously listening followers. "Here's where I take the idea, at least as a preliminary approach. Understand, it's not completely worked out just yet. It seems to me that if the Monsters are aware of our activity in the neighborhood of this particular piece of furniture, if they've seen enough of us swarming in and out of it to justify a trap, and a brand new type of trap, at that, then it's likely that they're on the alert in this entire area. And that, in turn, leads to three conclusions. One, that a scouting party in advance of the main body is doubly necessary, and that the scouts have to be watchful as hell. Two, that until we're a good distance from here, the expedition proceeds in absolute silence, using nothing but hand signals for communication. And three, well, we ought to take a good hard look around before we start out. It's possible we're under observation by the Monsters at this very moment!"

At this, there was a startled look-around by the members of the expedition, all except Eric and Roy, who exchanged disgusted glances. As a matter of course, in the last few minutes, they had each been turning periodically in one direction and another to see if there were any sign of the Monsters in the surrounding whiteness. After a trap had claimed a victim, who but a stupid Stranger would do anything else?

But, a bit later, as they had gone off ahead of the rest along the piece of Monster furniture on their way to the distant wall, Roy's attitude seemed to have changed again.

"After all," he said, as if arguing with himself, "it's a pretty big war band, the size of Mankind's whole damn army roster. Takes a real Organizer to handle a bunch this size. An ordinary band captain—like your uncle, I mean—he wouldn't even know how to hold them together."

Eric laughed. "Holding them together isn't half as important as keeping them alive. I don't think Arthur will be too good at that."

The Runner grunted noncommittally. Eric puzzled over him in silence as they came to the junction of the furniture and wall, turning right in the direction of the doorway that Mankind had used to get back to the burrows. The door lay on the floor: it had still not been set in place since Eric had gone through. The two of them checked the area for new traps; then, without a word, they heaved the door up and worked it back into its socket. When they went on past it, further along the wall into Monster territory, they both grinned at each other happily: they had just acted as respectable warriors of Mankind.

But what was up with the Runner, Eric wondered? What was going on in his head that he should mock Arthur the Organizer one moment and determinedly find some way to praise him the next—even when he showed such obvious ineptitude as a band leader? There was no time to ask questions now: they were moving deeper into territory where only Roy had been before, and Eric's job was to follow quietly, learning the way, keeping his ears alert for the first vibrations that would warn of a Monster's floor-shaking approach.

Three hundred and twelve paces beyond the door was the rendezvous that the Organizer had set with them. Here, a block piece of Monster furniture came close to the wall, a smaller piece than the one they had been in during the night. Eric could see the top of it by twisting his head far back on his neck: it was oddly curved and there were great green knobs sticking out of it. They stopped there, grateful for its cover, and took their first deep breaths. Far off behind them, along the wall, they watched the main body of the expedition trudging a slow single file in their direction. Eric and Roy waved their hands high to indicate that the way was safe.

When the answering waves indicated that the signal had been received, he turned to the Runner and put the question at last. Why this backing and filling, why this talking Arthur up when he was so unequivocally, ridiculously wrong?

Roy thought a moment before answering.

"He's not wrong. I mean he can't be: he's our leader."

"You know better than that, Roy! Not sending scouts ahead from the beginning, letting the men talk and clump up on expedition, not checking the exit overhang for a Monster trap—how far off can he be?"

"He's our leader," the Runner repeated doggedly. "Was your uncle any smarter, with all of his march discipline and trap-smashing? All right, just one mistake—enough to finish him and most of his band. Arthur's alive."

"He's alive because he was safe in Alien-Science Headquarters all through the blowup."

"I'm not interested in why, Eric. He's alive, and he's the only leader we've got. This band's the only people we've got. We've got to make the best of it and kind of, you know, show them we belong to them."

Eric stared past him into the glaring whiteness. Far off, hundreds upon hundreds of paces away, he could make out the dim outlines of the larder sacks in which the Monsters kept their food. Once, the powerful bands of Mankind had come to swarm upon those sacks and bring minute portions of the contents home to their women and their chief. Once, he and Roy had been proud to be reckoned warriors of Mankind. Now were they to start all over again and learn pride at being Strangers? And Strangers on the run, at that. Strangers without even women to guide them, to tell them what was right and what was wrong!

No, he didn't see it, and he said as much. "I'm not running my head into a spear any more for somebody else and his private plans."

"That's you," Roy agreed. "That's the way you've always been: a rebel, a trouble-maker, an outsider. Me, I've always asked only to be allowed to go along with the other guys. Why do you think I became an Alien-Sciencer? Because our band was Alien-Science. If I'd been in an Ancestor-Science band, I'd be backing up the chief right next to Harold the Hurler and Stephen the Strong-Armed and all those reactionary bastards. I'd be carving up people like you and your uncle any time the Female Society told me to. And I'd believe in what I was doing, just as I believed in what I was doing when I followed your uncle and went around saying that Chief Franklin had to go and that the Female Society stood in the way of progress. Being in the center of a bunch of guys that you can trust because you know their thoughts and their thoughts are exactly the same as your thoughts—that's home, that's the only home there is. Everything else is hunger and danger and sleeplessness, with no one to guard your back."

Arthur the Organizer came up at this point, with the rest of the expedition. He gave his scouts orders as to the next advance point they were to reach.

Once more, Eric followed Roy, his senses alert for a sudden change in the environment, his mind busy with personal problems. He couldn't argue with the Runner: the Runner was right for himself. But would Eric the Eye ever find a home, where friends who thought like him could be trusted to guard his back? He didn't want to think like other people—least of all Strangers. Going into great danger to find a weapon which might or might not exist!

The entire expedition camped for the night—once Arthur had officially declared it—in the crevice of a gigantic archway that led out of the Monster larder and into another great white burrow. At least sentries were posted, Eric noticed. They had filled their knapsacks with fresh food from the alien containers in the larder, although Eric's stomach twitched uneasily at the prospect of eating anything that women had not first examined. And they had filled their canteens from an opening in a fresh-water pipe to which Walter the Weapon-Seeker had led them.

"This tribe I used to belong to," Roy the Runner commented to a group of men huddling up for sleep. "Mankind, they called themselves—can you imagine that? *Mankind!*—they had a superstition about only using water from the pipes in the burrows. Once in Monster territory, no eating, no drinking. They could die of thirst—better that than give up the superstition." He guffawed. "They were afraid their dead ancestors would get mad and—"

Eric walked out of earshot. Loneliness crouched on his chest.

Chapter 13

When the expedition started again after the night's rest, Eric found Roy even more unbearable. The Runner had found a small strap somewhere and had bound his hair on the back of his head, Stranger fashion.

And there were three of them now in the scouting party that led the advance through the archway into the next great burrow. Arthur had detailed Walter the Weapon-Seeker to accompany Eric and Roy. The heavy, squat man with the huge, gnarled hands was the only member of the expedition who had penetrated farther into Monster territory than the larder. In search of alien artifacts which could be turned into usable human weapons, he had journeyed many, many times into unbelievably distant Monster burrows.

Roy found this fascinating. He refused to let go of the subject. "This funny little tribe I used to go around with—they'd have called you a back-burrower, they'd have thought you weren't up to them in guts or anything a warrior ought to have. But not one of them had ever gone as far as you, or taken the chances you've taken. The bravest band leader in this tribe, he'd have thought he was really something if once in maybe two or three auld lang synes he'd have gone to the edge of the Monster larder and poked his head into the next burrow."

"We turn right," the Weapon-Seeker said as they came to the end of the archway. "Watch out for traps. There are always a couple at the larder exit."

"I'll bet you've seen traps that his old band leader—" Roy jerked a thumb in Eric's direction, "—never even knew existed. And *he* was supposed to be a Trap-Smasher. Hey, Eric," he inquired solicitously, "doesn't all that hair get in your face? It's not good for an Eye to get hair in his face."

"I manage," Eric said shortly.

"Well, you know. You're an Eye. At least around your people you're an Eye. You're supposed to lead on expeditions, to show the way to the rest. But Walter here, he's only a Weapon-Seeker, he's not an Eye, but he knows the way we're going better than you. That's because Walter and his people, they're the kind of guys who really—"

"Do you want me to move up ahead?" Eric asked the Weapon-Seeker. "How about I act as point?"

"Good idea, young fellow. Your vision's better than mine. We'll just be going along this stretch of wall until the next rest period. If you see anything suspicious, stop right away and signal."

Eric edged around the two of them, the tall, bony Runner and the short, muscular Weapon-Seeker. He moved rapidly off about thirty paces ahead and kept going. At this distance, their low voices were barely audible. He began to feel better immediately.

And he realized how accustomed he had become to the fantastic spaces of Monster territory. It was still difficult to look up and out into the dazzling white illumination—every time he tried it he felt as if his mind were about to wander away and get lost—but he could jog along with the wall brushing his right shoulder, peering all the way ahead and experiencing only the slightest discomfort.

Three times he came to small obstacles which could possibly be traps. Then he signaled to the men behind him, who did the same to the main expedition in the rear. After that, it was a matter of walking cautiously away from the wall in a wide semicircle to avoid the obstacle and continue on his way. He still felt as frantic as ever until he got back to the wall and had to fight hard for self-control. Something about being out in the open in all that spacious whiteness made him want to scream and panic and run madly in absolutely any direction.

He tried hard to analyze the feeling and come to grips with it. He was an Eye, after all: some day it might be necessary for him to lead a group right into the middle of a Monster burrow where there was no wall to provide bearings and a sensation of solidity. But the hysteria seemed to remain in spite of all his efforts; each detour caused by a possible trap was as frightening as the one before it.

After passing the last obstacle, he noticed an odd buzzing sound from the wall. Eric stopped and considered it. A new kind of trap, an invisible one? A warning system that the Monsters used to tell them of the approach of humans? He indicated the sound to Walter and Roy by pointing. The Weapon-Seeker listened too, then shrugged and waved Eric on.

But suddenly the stretch of the wall between Eric and the man behind him developed a fissure. It widened rapidly, as if the fabric of the wall were being rolled back. And then the wall in their immediate neighborhood was no longer there, and they were staring into another great white burrow—and at a Monster who was walking placidly in their direction!

Despite all his warrior training, Eric froze. His arms and legs seemed locked into place. He knew, somewhere in his brain, that he hadn't been noticed, but he stood there, unable to move, while one of the six great legs began to come down immediately over his head. The creature was merely strolling from one Monster burrow to another—it might not even realize it had stepped on a human being.

Walter moved.

He darted away from Roy, who had also become immobilized by terror, and ran around in front of the creature. Then he yelled, waved his arms wildly—and ran straight toward it.

The immense Monster seemed to go into paralysis. It stood rigidly still for a moment as Walter, screaming, waving his arms, his face contorted, kept coming at it. Staring upward, in fear-anguish, Eric could see the flat gray circle that was the underside of its leg—a circle at least twice the thickness of his own body—barely vibrating and poised in the middle of a step as the creature assessed the situation and made up its mind what to do.

Then it reared on its two hind legs, and the entire body, as well as the portion of it that had been about to come down on Eric, went up and up into the dizzying distances overhead. A deafening, low-register, wailing sound came out of it and rolled massive echoes in all directions. It had jumped, Eric realized, and screamed as it jumped. He saw it turn around in mid-air to face the direction from which it had come: the long, long neck with the tiny head at the end strained forward as if to pull the body behind it as far from Walter the Weapon-Seeker as possible. It came down a substantial distance away in the other burrow, and the floor developed incredible solid waves in response to the impact. Eric was flung off his feet and bounced bone-crackingly from wave to wave. When the waves began to dwindle into ripples and then to mere violent vibrations, when the agitated floor was relatively flat again, Eric got his hands on it and lifted his head.

Far off, in the other burrow, the Monster was still running away from them. Its head, held high in the air by the thin and now-rigid neck, was still bellowing mad panic out of an open mouth. Just behind the head, the little pink growths that encircled the neck were standing out stiffly like so many frozen flames. An incredible stink hung in the air. Then the creature rounded a far-distant corner and was lost to sight.

But the fissure that had opened in the wall—through which the Monster had apparently intended to walk—the fissure was closing. And Walter was on the other side of it!

Eric saw the heavy little Weapon-Seeker scrambling frantically toward him. If the wall closed, Walter would be lost to them forever in the unknown depths of Monster territory!

Roy had run up and stood beside Eric. "Move, Walter, *move!*" the Runner breathed. Walter's face was torn with fear as he forced his short legs to their utmost.

The gap in the wall through which they were watching the Weapon-Seeker narrowed smoothly. When he was about a pace and a half away, there was barely enough opening for a man's body to squeeze through.

Without words, both getting the same desperate idea at the same moment, Eric and Roy grabbed the fissure edge at each side and hopelessly tried to keep it from closing further. To their astonishment, no effort was required. The wall stopped coming together the moment their hands were on it: the gap got no narrower.

Walter panted through and flung himself on the floor. Eric and Roy took their hands away. And immediately the wall closed and became solid once more.

Eric poked at it, scratched at it unbelievingly. It was solid enough to break a man's hand if he hit it too hard. And yet it had opened and closed—and temporarily stopped closing when he and the Runner had merely touched it.

And what had been wrong with the Monster? Had it actually been afraid of Walter the Weapon-Seeker, so tiny in comparison with its own fantastic bulk that it could have crushed, squashed, smeared him with one single casual step?

That was exactly what it had been, Walter assured them, once he had gotten back his breath. "Some of the Monsters are scared to death of us, some aren't at all. The ones who are afraid will bolt every time if you run directly at them making a lot of noise. Of course, the trick is to know which will bolt and which won't. The ones who aren't scared will just get a better opportunity to tread on you."

"I've heard of that," Roy said, nodding. "Some of the older warriors sing stories of being trapped outside the burrows by a Monster and seeing the damned big thing turn tail and take off. But there are other warriors who got trapped and didn't come back to sing the tale. You never can tell with a Monster."

"Yes, you can. You know those pink tentacles at the top of the neck, right near the head? They're the things to look for. If they're short and a dark pink, almost red, then the Monster will bolt when a human being runs at it. Those Monsters are as safe to be around as a new-born baby in the burrows. But if the neck tentacles are long and are colored a whitish pink—look out. A Monster with those kind of tentacles isn't afraid of you and will step on you every time."

"Why?" Eric asked. "What's the size and color of the tentacles got to do with it?"

The Weapon-Seeker spread his hands wide. "How should I know? And who cares why? Not even the Aaron People know—with all their piles of records. It's a fact, that's all, a very useful fact."

"Saved your life, that fact did," Roy told Eric. "I'll say it's useful. More useful than most of the facts that your uncle knew—your uncle and the whole people you used to belong to, you know, that bunch you used to call Mankind. *Mankind*, he used to call them," Roy said, turning back to Walter. "As if they were the whole human race!"

"Does anyone have any idea, any theory, why it's so?" Eric kept at the Weapon-Seeker.

Walter glanced back a short distance to where Arthur the Organizer and the rest of the expedition were hurrying up. "What good's a theory? It's only worthwhile if you know something for sure. Something that's usable. Do you remember that other piece of Monster furniture, the first rendezvous back in the larder? Wide and black with green knobs?"

"Yes. I wondered about it."

"So did I. Last auld lang syne, I was leading a band from my tribe on a weapon hunt. The pickings had been poor, we hadn't found anything at all good. So on the way back, I thought: who knows, why not, maybe those green knobs are worth something. I sent one of the younger lads shinnying up the piece of furniture. He got all the way to the top, crawled out near the edge and started working away at one of the green knobs. It turned round and round, and he called down that it was getting looser as he turned it. All of a sudden there was a flash of red from the green knob straight up into the air. The lad comes down in a lump, all black and burned, dead long before he hits the floor. Then, the next thing, all the lights go out. Pitch black in Monster territory, none of that whiteness, nothing. We have to pick our way back to the burrows with our forehead glow lamps. And just before we get to the doorway my people use, the light comes back on, all clear and white, as if nothing had happened. Well, what did happen? I don't know, I don't care. If I could ever figure out a way to turn it into a usable weapon, I might care a lot. Till then, just another Monster doodad."

"Of course, you understand, Eric," said Arthur the Organizer, who had come up and been listening, "you understand that we are interested in the why and wherefore of everything that pertains to the Monsters. As devout Alien-Sciencers, we have to be. It's just that there is, if you follow me, a time and a place for everything. All safe and sound, Walter?"

"Damned well safe and sound," the Weapon-Seeker growled. "It was touchy for at bit, though. Is it all right with you if I keep the kid on point and let him lead us the rest of the way? He is an Eye, a first-class Eye. He heard the buzz of a Monster doorway about to open and warned me. I shrugged it off."

Arthur smiled warningly. "Don't start shrugging at your age. We need you. You know the saying about Monster territory: 'A step in time saves nine in the sewer.'"

Now officially lead-off man for the expedition, Eric received his instructions from Walter the Weapon-Seeker and moved off. He saw Roy scowling. The Runner was to act as liaison between the scout group and the main body: it was evident that he considered it a demotion. Too bad—he just didn't have the blood-line of Eric the Store-room-Stormer, and he should have learned to live with that fact.

The Storeroom-Stormer had been out somewhere deep in Monster territory with his wife, Eric's mother, when he had been killed. That was what his Uncle Thomas had told him. And it had been on a most unusual Theft. Unusual enough to have called for a woman's assistance. What conceivable kind of Theft could that have been?

Eric stared ahead and around into the bright, white distances of the Monster burrow. Here and there, he could see strange, huge objects, not at all like those in the larder. Were they furniture? Weapons? And had his parents once passed this way and seen the same objects, wondered as he was wondering? Or had they possibly known?

But all the time, his mind was on the alert for danger: that was the prime function of an Eye. And all the time, his mind recorded the route, making whatever deductions, whatever generalizations it could for future use: that was the best part of being an Eye.

He knew so little. Walter, uninterested in theory, knew a lot.

Whenever they stopped for a meal, squatting against the wall, he sought Walter out and explored the older man's knowledge, whatever there was of it. Were there human burrows on the other side of this stretch of wall—how could you tell if there were or if there weren't? That pit out there in the floor, in the middle of Monster territory, could it possibly denote a section of plumbing large enough to sewer a Monster corpse? Why, whenever they saw a Monster humping along in the middle of the floor and froze into absolute stillness in response to Eric's signal, was there no likelihood whatever that it would come over and travel along the wall like humans did? Why did humans journey close to walls and Monsters a substantial distance from them?

"You can think up a lot of crazy questions, young fellow," the Weapon-Seeker chuckled. "But that one's easy. Work it out."

Eric thought. "We travel along the wall for cover. We're in a strange place, a dangerous place. We want to keep our visibility down. But to the Monsters this is home. They walk where it's most comfortable, in the middle, just as we would in our own burrows. They have nothing to be afraid of, nothing to hide from. Is that it?"

"I think so. Makes sense, doesn't it? Only thing, don't expect every aspect of the

Monsters to be as logical. They're different from us, they're alien. That's the whole point."

Eric would nod, but immediately come back with another question. Even if the Weapon-Seeker didn't know the answer, he could have a fact which might relate, or which might, upon examination, turn into an important clue—or which might just be important, worth knowing, in and of itself. There was so much to learn, to be worked out. He tore at the Weapon-Seeker's mind as if it were a sack in a Monster larder and he, Eric, were a starving man.

As soon as Arthur declared it night, and they all stopped for sleep, Eric would crawl to where Walter was curled up and begin his questions again. He would ignore a loud remark addressed by Roy to the empty air—"Assistant scouts will go sucking around their chief scout every damn time. Never seen it to fail!"—and ask about any oddity he had observed on the route that day, what he might be expected to see on the next.

Walter had apparently developed a great liking for Eric. He answered the young man's questions with great good humor. "You remind me of a kid in the band I used to lead back with my own people," he said one night. "The kid asks me: 'Our burrows are in the walls of the Monster burrows, right? The Monster burrows are outside and all around us?' 'Right,' I tell him. 'Well, then,' he says, 'what's outside the Monster burrows?' I look at him as if he's crazy. 'What the hell do you mean?' 'I mean,' he says, 'maybe the Monster burrows are in the walls of even bigger burrows. Maybe there are creatures living in those burrows who'd make the Monsters look tiny. Maybe there are such things as Monster Monsters.' Ever hear anything as wild as that?" The Weapon-Seeker lay on his back and roared with delight.

"It's an idea," Eric said, intrigued. "Why is it wild?"

"Oh, kid, please! You know why. You can't have Monsters, and Monster Monsters a hundred times bigger, and Monster-Monster Monsters a hundred times bigger than that. You just can't have it. The whole thing has to stop someplace."

"All right. But suppose—"

"Stop supposing," the Weapon-Seeker admonished. "Stick to facts. They're tough enough and complicated enough. Tomorrow, we'll be heading into the burrow where the Monsters keep the weapon we're after. And don't ask me about that weapon!" he ordered, holding up his hands. "I told you, not a word about it until I see it and we get set to grab it up. I'll know it when I find it—that's my job. But your job is to lead the way, and you're going to need a good night's sleep."

"This burrow we'll be going into—" Eric began.

"And don't ask me about the burrow, either! It's the place where the Monsters keep their best and most powerful weapons. That's all you have to know. Now, for the sweet love of Alien-Science, will you let *me* get some sleep?"

Eric gave up. He lay on his side, as he did part of every sleep period, reviewing and reviewing. The conclusions came just as he began to doze. He was more convinced than ever that there was no specific weapon that Walter was leading them to, merely the hope of one. This burrow they were to enter, on the other hand...

A low, urgent call from the man on guard duty brought him and all the others awake.

When they saw what had startled the guard, they scrambled to their feet, faces turning pale, bodies sweating and shuddering with overwhelming fear.

Two hundred or so paces away, a Monster, one of the largest they'd ever seen, stood staring at them calmly. The great gray legs supporting the enormous gray body were set wide apart, as a man might stand to study carefully an interesting phenomenon. The extended neck waved slightly to and fro, bringing the head with its unblinking eyes first here, then there. The tentacles at the base of the head—they were quite long, Eric noticed, and a very light shade of pink—undulated in sympathy with the neck as if they too had some sort of eyes and were trying to see as well as they could. But there was no suggestion of imminent attack.

On both sides, there was a dead silence. Neither the trembling humans nor the gigantic, watching Monster made a sound. Eric found himself breathing rapidly: he made up his mind that if sudden panic developed, he would try to run in a different direction from the rest.

What did the terrifying creature want? What precisely was it looking at? And what was happening inside its alien mind?

Abruptly, it wheeled and presented its back to them. Then it strode away, off, off into the white distance. Despite its size, the floor shook only slightly as it went. They watched it until it was no longer visible. And the moment it was gone, everyone began to babble, more than a few hysterically.

"Walter," Arthur the Organizer called out. "What do you think? What was going on?"

They all turned to the Weapon-Seeker. He shook his head. "I don't know," he said. "I've never seen one of them do a thing like that before."

Chapter 14

A council of war was held on the incident, to determine whether it should be allowed to affect their plans. There were three men in the council: Arthur the Organizer, who presided, Walter the Weapon-Seeker, since he alone knew anything at all about this area to which they had come, and the oldest member of the expedition, a white-haired and surprisingly spry old fellow by the name of Manny the Manufacturer, selected apparently out of deference to his age and nothing else.

Roy and Eric were asked to participate in a non-voting advisory capacity, it being presumed, Eric decided with a wry, internal giggle, that as scouts and front-burrowers they would know something the others did not about unusual circumstances and extraordinary dangers.

"We can go on or we can go back," Arthur the Organizer pointed out. "If we go back, we've failed and we don't have much. If we go on, we have to take it for granted that we might be—and please notice that I say no more than *might be*—walking straight into disaster."

Walter the Weapon-Seeker drummed on the floor with an impatient foot. "Sure. They'll be expecting us. And they'll be laying for us."

"Possibly. And then again, possibly not." Arthur held up a finger and faced each one of them in turn. "The Monsters don't think as we do: we have no reason to believe that they react as we do, or give alarms as we do. This creature might have been simply curious about us. The way it went on about its business would argue for that point of view. It's one of the things we must consider seriously."

"Consider!" the Weapon-Seeker spat. "Considering is your job, not mine. Doing something is my job. I say we go ahead and do what we started out to do."

"We don't have a choice, anyway," said Manny the Manufacturer. "If we go back without the weapon we came for, we spend the rest of our lives as outlaws. I don't think lives like that are worth a hell of a lot. And neither do most of the men. I say let's take our chances."

Arthur turned to his two front-burrowers. "Eric?"

Eric the Eye tried to give as much formal dignity as possible to his first opinion in a council. "I believe we should go on. As planned."

"Mind telling us your reasons?"

"Well," Eric unbent a bit. "If there's been an alarm, the Monsters know we're here. There's no nearby doorway into the burrows: we can't escape. They could be waiting for us both ways—whether we go on or whether we go back. At least if we go on, we stand a chance of getting something. And I agree with Manny that an outlaw's life is a pretty damn unappetizing prospect."

"Roy?"

The Runner shuffled and made a large, indeterminate gesture with his left hand. "There's this and there's that. There's a lot to consider. It's awfully easy for some people to sound off and say they know for sure what the Monsters are doing—that we should follow our original plans, no matter what. Some people still have hair all over their eyes. The only thing I heard that makes sense is what you said, Arthur—that we should *consider*. It sounds like an intelligent thing to do. I vote to do what you suggested: to consider."

"You don't have a vote," the Weapon-Seeker told him. "All you have a right to give is your opinion. What the kid said," he pointed to Eric with his thumb, "is about it. If they're laying for us, they're laying for us both ways, ahead and behind. Ahead's where we want to go. So let's go."

Arthur summed up. "The sense of this meeting is that at least two of you, Walter and Manny, feel we risk as much by turning back as by going on—and that there are substantial advantages to going on. I'm inclined to go along with that majority view, so long as we proceed with all the caution that these new circumstances make necessary. You see, Roy," he said placatingly, "it's not that we reject your advice, but in a democratic discussion you have to give a little and take a little. You can't always have your own way."

The tall, thin young man looked from Arthur to Eric, then pulled a spear out of his back sling and walked off to the head of the column.

"You give Eric some idea of what to look out for," Arthur suggested to Walter. "I'd like to start moving as soon as possible—before there's much more talk among the men."

"Right!" growled Manny the Manufacturer. "Let's get this expedition off the floor."

There wasn't much that the Weapon-Seeker could tell him, Eric found out. It was now quite clear that Walter had only seen this new Monster burrow from the entrance, and very briefly. He could describe the first piece of Monster furniture in the place—and that was all.

From now on, Eric realized, he would really have to be an Eye.

He went through the archway into the burrow that was the goal of the expedition, Walter some thirty paces behind him. When he saw the succession of tall black rods standing on the floor, crisscrossed horizontally with dozens of other rods, he waved to the Weapon-Seeker, who passed the wave on to the men in his rear. Then the chunky chief scout pointed forward, giving Eric the order to move on.

Now came the hard part, the truly frightening part. At least, there were no Monsters about—none that he could see.

Eric swallowed. He left the archway, and the wall. He crept out into open Monster territory, where there was nothing but the harsh white light and stretching vistas of floor.

His heart began pounding. He found that his regular, cautious breathing was turning into noisy gasps. He felt exposed, terrifyingly vulnerable, completely alone. And lost—he felt as if he would be lost in that whiteness forever.

What was he doing here? He belonged back there, cowering against the blessedly safe wall!

But he put his head down and continued to creep forward. Another step. And another. Now he had to force himself to slow: he'd been about to burst into a mad dash at nowhere.

Easy. Another step. And don't look up—just as when you first came into Monster territory, days ago as an initiate warrior. Another step without looking up, without going wild with panic.

How far away was that rod-supported piece of Monster furniture? Did this floor go on forever? Another step. A great frightened gasp. Another step. And another—

He had arrived. His shoulder touched a rod. He flung his arm around it and hauled his mind back to calmness. He had arrived. He was near cover again. And at last he could look up.

Still no Monsters that he could see anywhere in the place. He held on to the rod with the crook of his elbow and signaled to Walter at the archway. Walter passed the signal on, shuddered, and then left the wall himself.

Eric watched him sympathetically for a moment, then turned back to examine the thing he was standing under. It was composed of these black rods, each as thick as his arm and each rising perpendicularly from the floor straight into the dizzy heights above. Every fifteen or so paces, another rod reared into the air. And at intervals, each many times the height of a man, there were the rods running across at right angles to the others.

Here and there, high among the rods, where a horizontal crossed a vertical, there was a small, semitransparent cube at the junction point. The light was sharply reflected from these cubes, making it difficult to look at them steadily, but some of them had strange shadows flickering inside them. Did the shadows have anything to do with a weapon they might be able to use?

Eric found it was impossible to stare upward very long; he looked back at Walter to see how the chief scout was progressing. Not well: the man's face was almost purple with the overseasoned mixture of effort and fear. His feet were beginning to splay; his knees were folding forward and down. He wouldn't make it.

Taking a deep breath, Eric flung himself away from the relative safety of the rod and leaped across the floor. By the time he reached Walter, the man had almost collapsed. He grabbed Eric's arm with both hands—his eyes were tightly shut by now—and would have pulled him down if fright had not so thoroughly loosened his muscles.

"The wall—" he babbled. "Give it up—let's get back to the wall!"

"Easy," Eric said. "Easy, Walter. We're almost there."

He guided the Weapon-Seeker the last few paces to the rod. Walter held on to the upright post as desperately as Eric had and fought for breath. It was no simple thing for a human being to leave the wall in Monster territory.

Fortunately, there were plenty of upright rods in this structure. They weren't thick, but they were solid: they would give the feeling of cover and at least the semblance of cover to all the men in the expedition. But he and Walter would have to distribute them down the rows of rods—no point in having too many men grouped around any one post. And they'd be dealing with panic-stricken lunatics who would tend to hang on as if for life itself to the first solid things they encountered.

Roy came across next. He had a hard time, but he didn't do nearly as badly as Walter. It was obvious that the younger the man, the more resilient he was psychologically, and the more capable of taking the shattering experience of negotiating open Monster territory. They guided Roy to a rod: he wound himself around it for a dozen tortured breaths before coming to and taking a look up, down, forward, backward.

The rest of the expedition came over in groups of three. They had their hands full with men who slumped to the floor and wound themselves up in tight little balls of refusal, with men whose eyes suddenly rolled up in their heads and who wandered jerkily off in this direction or in that, with men who started to run away and who would bite and kick and gouge when they were caught. But fully half of the men made it across by themselves.

When they had been distributed, one or two men to each upright post climbing above their heads into emptiness, Eric, Roy and Walter discussed the next move with Arthur.

"I think we'll stay here for a while and take a break for a meal," the Organizer decided. "Do you agree? I think we should. We'll wait till everybody calms down and comes back to normal. Meanwhile, do you three feel like going on ahead and taking a look at what we've got coming up? How many more open spaces—you know, problems we might be facing—anything that looks like a weapon—whatever strikes you as a good idea."

Eric and Roy followed Walter to the last row of standing rods. They shaded their eyes and stared across a long empty stretch of floor—to where there was another rod-like structure, very much like the one they were in.

"What do you think those shiny cubes are?" Eric asked, pointing. Here and there, high in the other structure, were semitransparent boxes just like the ones above them. A few contained liquid shadows.

"I don't know," Walter admitted. "But I intend to find out. They're what I noticed when I passed this way before. They look as if they might be useful. Only, how will we get up to them? Think a spry man might climb up one of these rods?"

Eric and Roy considered the height and the lack of handholds. They both shook their heads. The Weapon-Seeker nodded ruefully.

"Then there's only one thing to do. We go on until we find a structure low enough to climb. Monster furniture comes in all kinds of different sizes. We'll find a low one with some shiny boxes close to the floor. And we'll find other stuff, too. In this place, I have a real strong feeling—"

"Hold it!" Eric grabbed his arm. "Listen! Do you hear it?"

The short, heavy man listened anxiously for a moment, then shook his head. "Not a thing. What do you hear?"

But Roy had also tensed at Eric's warning and leaned forward alertly. "Something's coming this way. It's not much of a sound yet, mostly vibration. You can feel it with your feet."

The Weapon-Seeker listened again. This time he nodded rapidly. "Monsters. And more than one." He whirled to face the expedition, strung out at the bases of the rods behind them. Pointing his forefinger straight up in the air, he rotated one hand rapidly over his head. This, the most fearful alarm of all to any band, had to be given silently. It meant: *"Monsters are upon us—up there—look out!"*

No reaction from the others, and the three of them groaned to themselves. The members of the expedition were stuffing food into their mouths, taking swallows out of canteens, chatting together in low, friendly voices. No one was bothering to watch the scouts.

What a bunch, Eric raged hopelessly. *Baby warriors,* his uncle, Thomas the Trap-Smasher, would have called them.

The rumbling noises were getting louder. Walter made up his mind to dispense with expedition security precautions. "You damn fools!" he yelled. *"Monsters!* Don't you hear them?"

That got a reaction. Every man leaped to his feet, knapsacks and canteens rolling away. White faces turned rapidly in their direction, looked off to examine the brilliantly lit spaces above.

Eric slapped the backs of the two scouts on either side of him. "Let's get out of here," he said urgently. This was traditionally an every-man-for-himself situation among the peoples of the burrows. He pointed across the floor to the other rodlike structure. "There! They'll be after the bulk of the men in this one. Let's go!"

Without waiting for a reply, he darted out into the open. From the corners of his eyes, he was conscious as he ran of huge gray Monsters materializing out of the whiteness on all sides. Those things could move fast when they wanted to! And in relative silence, too—the floor was vibrating no more than it had this morning when the creature watching them had walked away.

He ran fast, forcing every bit of speed out of his legs, not at all aware now of the openness of the space he was on. The only thought in his mind concerned the Monsters all about him. Would he be stepped on? When? Would he feel it when it happened—or would it be over too fast?

A moment before he reached the other set of rods, somebody passed him and leaped into hiding among the posts of the structure. Roy the Runner, starting late, had the legs to make up for lost time. Then Eric was there too, cowering behind a rod. He watched Walter the Weapon-Seeker stumble the last couple of paces and fall gasping two rods away from him.

But the rest of the expedition was in trouble. The men scrambled about, mindlessly, shrieking, inside the rod structure they had quit. Five Monsters now stood around it in silence, making any escape to the outside almost impossible.

The Monsters had known where the expedition lay hidden—they had made directly for it. And they were doing something in an organized fashion. What?

Eric strained his eyes to see, but the movements of the gray bodies were unfamiliar and unclear. Suddenly, from each one of them, a long green rope dropped to the floor. The ropes seemed almost alive: as they lay on the floor they quivered and bits of darker color slid up and down their coils.

There was a click from one of the Monsters, then a long, scraping musical note. The ropes began acting even more like live things. They slid into the rodlike structure and among the upright posts. Wherever they touched a man, they turned completely dark and he was carried along with them, apparently stuck to their surface.

"All together, now!" Eric heard Arthur the Organizer yelling. "Stay together and work on these ropes. All we have to do is get each man free—" Then a rope touched him in passing and he became just another shrieking attachment, alternately tugging and pushing at it. In a few brief moments, every man in the other structure was a madly wriggling prisoner.

"They seem to want us alive," Walter whispered to Eric. "And do you notice how these Monsters move around? They're a lot more deliberate than any I've ever seen before."

With their clusters of screaming, arm-waving humanity, the green ropes were picked up one at a time by the Monsters. Eric saw that the long necks came down and the pink tentacles near the head did the grasping. The tentacles, then, were the equivalent of hands—or fingers.

"There goes the entire expedition!" Roy called out hysterically. "What do we do now? What the hell do we do now?"

Walter shot an angry scowl in his direction. "Keep your voice down, you damn fool! If you lose control of yourself, we're all three dead."

As if in corroboration, a long neck twisted down out of the whiteness above, and a Monster's head swung to and fro inquiringly outside the rodlike structure in which they were hiding. It was only a man's height above the floor and Eric, nauseated with fear, felt that the eyes, in each of which a narrow, purple iris swam, were staring directly at him. And that pointed, stinking mouth—at least three men could disappear into it without creating a noticeable bulge!

He forced himself to stand absolutely still, although every muscle in his body yearned to leap off and make a run for it. Those pink tentacles—this close, for the first time, he saw how incredibly long they were—they could probably grab him up with ease.

But the monster, though staring directly in his direction, did not seem to see him. The head poked around among the rods and a corner of it touched Roy where he stood rigidly a short distance away.

The Runner threw his hands up, screamed—and ran. Instantly, the head was pulled up out of sight. Roy flung himself to the other end of the structure.

"Now we're in for it," said Walter the Weapon-Seeker grimly. The two of them saw a rope drop among the rods near Roy. It slid toward him smoothly, caught him—and kept going. It was going for them.

"We scatter," the Weapon-Seeker ordered. "Good luck, kid."

They leaped apart in opposite directions. Eric bent over, trying to keep his body low, for minimum visibility, and sped in a zigzag course among the rods. If he could get to the other side, there might be another structure nearby—

He heard Walter yell, and he spent a precious moment on a look. The Weapon-Seeker was now caught on the green rope only a few paces from the struggling Runner. And the rope was sliding swiftly at Eric, pulling both men along with it.

Eric straightened. Visibility was unimportant now—he might as well be running as fast as he could.

He heard the yells of Walter and Roy coming closer and closer behind him. He could not run any faster. *He just could not run any faster....*

Swift, terrible cold touched his side and he was pulled off his feet. He found himself screaming. He hammered at the green rope, dark black where it was attached to his hip. It was like a part of him—it couldn't be pulled off. He screamed and screamed and screamed.

A Monster head came down and one of the pink tentacles grasped an end of the rope. Up they went, the three of them, screaming, flailing their arms and legs, beating against the rope with their fists, up they went, higher and higher, into the dizzying whiteness, up, up they went to where the floor was no longer visible, to where the Monsters could examine them, the Monsters whose prisoners they were.

Chapter 15

Eric was never able to remember clearly what happened afterward. It was as if a massive hysteria had crashed into his mind and obliterated most of the record. There were isolated, scattered impressions: the rope from which he hung being passed from one neckful of pink tentacles to another, a great purple eye coming intently close, a gust of stinking, suffocating Monster breath—but over all beat the memory of men screaming as they dangled from the heights in clusters all around him, his own will and self-awareness completely lost in that hoarse, unending chorus of the doomed.

The impressions he retained of that moment became coherent only after the rope to which he, Walter and Roy were attached had been dipped by a Monster into a large, transparent box and he suddenly found himself able to walk again on a floor. Near him, the other two scouts were getting to their feet, yells subsiding into painful, sobbing breaths; while over their heads, the rope, of which they were at last gratefully free, was being pulled back into the heights, its color no longer bright but a dirty greenish gray. A large proportion of the expedition was already standing all around him, and the rest arrived in the next few moments as rope after rope was lowered into the transparent box, discharged its prisoners, went limp and was pulled away.

Boxes? Transparent boxes? Eric stared down intently. Through the bottom, he saw layer after layer of intersecting rods under his feet. Every once in a while, at the junction of a set of rods there would be a large box, such as the one he was in. Some of the boxes contained humans; others were empty.

Walter met his eyes when he looked up. "Sure," the Weapon-Seeker said with a grimace. "Those shiny boxes with shadows in them. The shadows were men. The boxes are cages." He cursed. "Walter the Weapon-Seeker, they call me. And this big, new weapon I was going to get from the Monsters turns out to be— We got it all right. We got it good."

The other men had been listening. Manny the Manufacturer came up, holding a forefinger in the air. He looked right past them, his old, wrinkled face heavy with thought. "Cages," he muttered. "There was a legend about these things in the old religion—in the Ancestor-Science we used to believe in. What was it? Something about what happened to people who fooled around with Alien-Science, who had too much to do with the Monsters— Let me remember—"

They waited while he shook the forefinger slowly at his mind. "Cages. Yes. Once, when I was a boy, I heard these things described in terms of Ancestor-Science. The Cages of Sin. That was it—the Cages of Sin! And there was a line about them that went like this: *The Cages of Sin is death.*"

"*Are* death, you mean," someone corrected. "The Cages of Sin *are* death."

"That's not the way the line went," Manny insisted. "Not the way I heard it. It went: *The Cages of Sin is death.* Just like that."

A chilled silence followed. After a while, a man dropped to his knees and began muttering an Ancestor-Science litany used by his own people. Another man from the same tribe knelt beside him and joined in. The chant filled the cage, awoke guilty memories in all of them.

O ancestors, O ancestors, I have failed and I have forgotten. Forgive me. I have failed to hit back at the Monsters in the ways you taught. Forgive me. I have forgotten to follow your ways. Forgive me, forgive me....

Eric shook himself out of the hypnosis of misery the words induced. Give in to this sort of thing and they'd be worth nothing. The whole bunch of them would be so much sewerage.

He still burned with shame when he thought of how the mass panic had swept him up a short while ago. That was no way for an Eye to act—and he was an Eye. An Eye should observe and record, no matter how fearfully unusual the circumstances, even if death seemed imminent. Wherever and however he found himself, an Eye must store impressions for future use: he must act like an Eye.

This cage, now— He walked away from the group surrounding the kneeling men. Roy the Runner and Walter the Weapon-Seeker gave him a startled glance, then fell in behind him. They passed Arthur the Organizer, sitting on the floor, his head in his hands. *"Forgive me,"* Arthur was intoning. *"Forgive me, forgive me...."*

Less than ten paces by twelve paces, those were the dimensions of the cage. Not very much room for so many men—they were pretty crowded. The Monsters would probably make some provision for feeding them: there was no point in taking them alive if they weren't intended to be fed. But there would be the problem of garbage and body waste. Eric studied the floor and saw how it sloped to one corner of the cage where there was a rod junction. A hole in that corner went down into a rod: evidently the rod was hollow. But a very small, single hole for such a large number of men—how did the Monsters propose to keep the cage from becoming foul?

Eric put the problem aside temporarily and walked to one of the four perpendicular walls, Walter and Roy still following him and trying to read the reactions on his face. The wall was transparent and solid: Eric made sure of that by thumping it with his knuckles and trying to scratch it with a spear point. He threw back his head, estimating the distance to the top. About three and a half men high, with a lip that curved in and down for about an arm's length. Still—

"We could get four husky men to stand side by side against it," he suggested to Walter. "Three men standing on their shoulders, two men on theirs. A pyramid. Then a man could scramble up their bodies and pull himself over the lip."

The Weapon-Seeker considered. "He might. But four and three and two—that would leave nine men behind in the cage. Who'd volunteer to be left behind?"

"That's not your problem," said a weak voice behind them. "Your problem is what you do when you get out of here."

They turned. There was an odd-looking man lying on the floor in the midst of the woebegone expedition. He didn't appear to be a Stranger, Eric decided, and he certainly wasn't a member of Mankind. While his hair was tied in the back of his head

Stranger-fashion, he was dressed in some ridiculous garment that was not a loin-cloth and certainly not loin straps—a short leather skirt with pockets all around its circumference. From several pockets, unfamiliar articles protruded.

And he was badly hurt. The upper part of his face and the whole right side of his body showed wide, dark bruises; his right arm and leg were limp and apparently broken.

"Were you already in the cage when they dropped us in?" Eric asked.

"I was. But you people had too many troubles of your own to notice me." He groaned and shut his eyes before going on. "You see, if you get out of here, you've nowhere to go. The walls of the cage are as smooth outside as inside—you'd just drop to the main floor, a full Monster-height below. And even if you made it to one of the rods—what good would that do? No handholds, nothing to grip anywhere along their length. Now, what I've been lying here wondering is this: could you pool your hair straps and your loin straps, braid them into a rope—"

"We could!" Walter broke in excitedly. "I know how, and there are other men here who—"

"But then I dismissed that idea, too. At most, you'd get a rope that only one or two men could use and would have to take with them from rod to rod. You're dealing with fantastic heights, remember. And from what I know of the quality of the leather you people turn out—no, it would just be another way to get killed." He paused, thought a bit. "Although, maybe not a bad way. Not a bad way to get killed at all."

The three of them soaked that in, shuddered. "Speaking of people," the Weapon-Seeker said in a low voice. "What are yours?"

"My tribe, you mean? That's my business. Now—kindly go away. I'm—I'm afraid I'm going to suffer a bit."

Roy the Runner grunted angrily. "We'll go away. Be glad to. Get in touch with us when you learn some manners and friendliness."

He walked off. The Weapon-Seeker scratched his head, looked at Eric, shrugged. He caught up to the Runner.

Eric squatted next to the wounded man. "Can I help you in any way?" he asked. "Could you use some water?"

The man licked his lips. "Water? How would you get water up here when it's not feeding time? Oh, I forgot. You warrior types, you carry canteens around with you. Yes, I'd very much appreciate some water."

Unslinging his canteen, Eric brought it to the man's mouth. The fellow certainly was no warrior—he seemed to know nothing of drinking discipline while on expedition. He would have finished the whole canteen, if Eric, conscious always of what must be set aside for an emergency, had not gently pulled it back and stoppered it.

"Thanks," the man sighed. "I've been taking pills for the pain, but I haven't been able to do anything about thirst. Thank you very much." He looked up. "My name's Jonathan Danielson."

"Mine's Eric. Eric the Eye."

"Hello, Eric. You're from—" a pause, as a twinge of pain arched through the prone body "—from a front-burrow people, aren't you?"

"Yes, my tribe calls itself Mankind. The only one that's left from it, who's still with me, is that tall fellow, Roy the Runner. The one who got mad at you."

"The only one that's left—" the man seemed to be talking to himself. "I'm the only one left. Fourteen of us, and they got every one. Just one kick from a Monster. Broken bodies all over the place. I was lucky: the foot barely touched me. Smashed my ribs—internal hemorrhages—I don't think anyone else got off so lightly."

When his voice trailed off, Eric asked hesitantly: "Is that what we can expect? Is that what the Monsters will do to us?"

Jonathan Danielson jerked his head impatiently, then winced as the movement hurt him. "*Uhh!* No, of course not. All of that happened when I was captured. Anything as crude as a kick—that's the last thing the Monsters are likely to do to you here. You know where you are, don't you?"

"This cage, you mean?"

"This place. This place where all these cages are. It's a Pest Control Center."

"Pest? Control Center?"

The battered face grinned up at him sourly. "You and me. Humans, generally. We're pests as far as the Monsters are concerned. We steal their food, we upset them, we infest their houses. They'd like to get rid of us. This is a place where they do research on ways and means to get rid of us. It's a laboratory where they test all kinds of homicides: sprays, traps, poisoned lures, everything. But they need laboratory animals for the tests. That's what we are, laboratory animals."

Later, Eric made his way back thoughtfully to the center of the cage, where Roy and Walter sat dispiritedly with their arms about their knees.

"People are getting tired, Eric," the Runner said. "They've had a hard day, a real bad day. They'd like to go to sleep. But Arthur just sits there mumbling his prayers. He won't talk to anyone."

Eric nodded. He cupped his hands at his mouth. "Listen, everybody!" he called. "You can go to sleep. I hereby declare it night!"

"Do you hear that?" Roy sang out beside him. "Our leader has declared it night. Everybody go to sleep!"

All over the cage, men began stretching out gratefully on the floor. "Thanks, Eric. Good night. Good night, Eric."

He pointed to Walter and Roy. "You'll be sentries on the first watch. Pick any two men you trust to relieve you. And give orders to wake me if anything out of the ordinary happens."

When they had taken their posts at opposite walls of the cage, he lay down himself and put his arms behind his head. He had a lot to think about, and it was hard to fall asleep.

Pest Control Center...

Laboratory animals...

Where they test all kinds of homicides...

Chapter 16

There was no need to declare it morning. They were awakened by breakfast, quantities of food being dropped into their cage out of a long transparent tube held over the edge by a Monster. Some of the food was familiar to those of them who had seen it freshly stolen from a Monster larder; some of it was new and disquietingly different; but all of it was edible.

After a great pile of the variously colored lumps had rained into their midst, the tube was withdrawn and they saw it inserted in other cages of the rod structure. Shortly after they had finished eating, the Monster brought the tube back and hung it over one corner. Water poured out of it now, so that the men could drink, but it also poured down the sloping floor to the hole in the opposite corner, washing away all leftovers and whatever waste matter had accumulated during the night.

Simple enough, Eric thought. So much for sanitation.

There was a dense crowd pushing and shouldering around the stream of water—he'd have to organize them better the next time. Meanwhile, it would compromise a leader's dignity to join their scramble. He gave his canteen to Roy, telling the Runner to fill it and also see that the wounded man had plenty to drink.

When the Runner looked doubtful, he said simply and definitely: "That's an order, Roy," and turned away. Out of the corner of his eye, he saw the Runner trot off immediately and follow his instructions. Eric felt relieved—after a night's sleep and the general recovery of nerve, he'd been afraid that his position might be questioned.

The important thing, he decided, was to give the men plenty to do. It would keep them from worrying and would at the same time emphasize his new status as leader.

Arthur, his predecessor in command, was a good place to start.

The water from the tube abruptly died to a trickle and the tube itself was pulled away from the lip at the top of the cage. Several of the men who hadn't managed to fill their canteens protested loudly, but the Monster, its pink tentacles holding the dripping tube firmly near its spearpoint-shaped head, walked off about its business.

The Organizer brought his canteen down after a long swallow and wiped his mouth with the back of a hand. Eric crossed to him, conscious that most of the expedition was watching.

"We have a problem in organization here, Arthur," he said. "Something for you to handle. We can't have all the men jostling in a bunch, each man trying to fill his own canteen. That way there'll always be somebody doing without. Think you could work out a better system?"

Arthur was apparently quite content to have given up the function of command decision in favor of the second-level administration planning which he knew so well. He smiled affirmatively. "Yes. I've been thinking about it. I don't see why we couldn't—"

Eric gave him a friendly slap on the shoulder. "Don't tell me. Show me. I'll leave it completely in your hands." He had seen his uncle, Thomas the Trap-Smasher, talk to his men in precisely this way—and he knew it worked.

It worked. Arthur began detailing a group of men to act as guards around any future water supply and another group to practice as a canteen brigade. Eric called Walter the Weapon-Seeker to his side.

"I want you to requisition all spare leather straps that the men are carrying. Braid them into experimental ropes. Try it different ways, two strands, three strands, whatever occurs to you. Let's see how strong a rope we can get."

The Weapon-Seeker shook his head. "Don't expect it to work. We can't do much braiding with the short lengths the men are liable to come up with. I've been turning it over in my mind, and that wounded Stranger was right. The kind of straps we have— they're fine for holding hair in place or even a knapsack, but if you tie them into any kind of length and expect them to support real weight, say three or four men, they'll just snap."

"Try it anyhow," Eric urged. "And use as many men as you can. If they're busy enough, they won't have the time to get scared." He paused. "How come you called the wounded man a Stranger? Isn't that a front-burrow term?"

"Sure. But we back-burrowers use it too. For people like him." Walter gestured with his thumb. "I've seen that kind of skirt before, with pockets all over. You know who wears those skirts? The Aaron People."

Intrigued, Eric stared in the direction that Walter was indicating. The Aaron People again. The legendary people from which his grandmother had come. The people who had refused to join in the Alien-Science revolution, but who also, it seemed, had not particularly opposed it. The man did not look so very different. He was responding to Roy's ministrations feebly, but—except for his clothes—he might just as well have been any one of the men in the expedition who had been wounded.

"Why wouldn't he identify himself? Why keep it a secret?"

"That's the Aaron People for you. They're goddam snobs. They think they're better than the rest of us and that we shouldn't have any idea of what they're up to. They're always like that, the bastards."

Eric was amused to note again that a back-burrower like Walter was as uncertain intellectually relative to the Aaron People as a warrior of Mankind might be when confronted with the superior material culture of almost any Stranger at all.

But he himself was a warrior of Mankind—and most of the expedition was probably aware of it. How long would they follow a front-burrower?

"Get on with those ropes," he said. "We may need them. I'm planning on a mass escape."

"Seriously?" There was a momentary flash of hope in Walter's eyes. "*How?*"

"I'm not too sure, just yet. I'm still working on it. Something we used to do back in my home tribe."

The Weapon-Seeker went off to organize groups of men for rope research. He must have passed on what Eric had said to him: from time to time, a group would whisper excitedly when its young leader walked by.

Eric had seen them sitting around glumly the night before: he knew that men without hope are worse than useless. And he—or somebody else—might come up with a usable idea at any time. The men should be on their toes and ready to move when that happened.

But there was no sense in lying to himself about his primary reason for starting the rumor. He needed it to reinforce his position. Men had to be given reason for believing in their leader—especially when the leader came from a background most of them despised.

He had reached the quiet, flat conviction that he was the best chief they could have, under the circumstances. It was not simply that he'd been the first to recover last night and had taken over because somebody had to. No. He'd seen more than enough of back-burrow methods on expedition: their poor march discipline, their disorganized reactions to the unexpected, their interminable talk when a quick decision was necessary. He was willing to admit now that almost any Stranger knew more facts and could make more things than he, was a better man when it came to large-scale burrow politics or the intricate details of religious discussion—but it took a warrior of Mankind, trained from childhood in the dangerous front burrows, to point the way to survival amid the constantly recurring catastrophes of Monster territory. And he was a warrior of Mankind, the son of one famous band leader and the nephew of another, a proven Eye in his own right. He was the best chief this bunch could have.

Meanwhile, they must be kept occupied and hopeful until a good plan for escape materialized. *If* a good plan for escape materialized.

A Monster's neck writhed out of the harsh white illumination in the direction of their cage. Pink tentacles held a jerking green rope above them for a moment, while the wet purple eyes looked here and there as if making a choice. Then the rope came down near an upward-staring man and fused itself to his back, ripples of darkness pulsating along the part of it that touched him.

When the rope was pulled up, there was a single, startled yelp from the man who went with it. After that, he relaxed and stared curiously about, awaiting developments while he was being carried off. He was evidently not nearly as frightened of this strange method of locomotion as he'd been the day before, the first time he'd experienced it.

Eric strode over to the wounded man whom Roy was tending. "What's going to happen to him?"

Jonathan Danielson had grown worse. His entire body was blotchy and discolored. He gestured toward a corner of the cage with dull, uncaring eyes. "You can see from there. Take a look," he said weakly.

Most of the men followed Eric to the corner. From that point, with a view pretty much unobstructed by rods or other cages, they could see a flat, white surface supported by rods coming up from the floor all around its circumference. At such an enormous distance, it looked rather small, but when the Monster had deposited the captured man on it—carefully fastening down his spread arms and legs with great clips attached to the surface—Eric realized that the entire population of his own tribe, Mankind, could be accommodated there with plenty of room to move about.

At first it was hard to see clearly just what the Monster was doing. A collection of green ropes was assembled near the fastened man. Some of the ropes were short and thick and curled, others were thin and seemed fairly rigid. The Monster would pick up a rope, poke it at the man or touch him with it, then put the rope down and select another one.

The man's body seemed to strain against the fastenings more and more violently. They all leaned forward squinting their eyes. Suddenly, Eric understood what was happening. A long, low groan heaved itself from his chest and tore out of his mouth.

"It's pulling his skin off!" someone behind him said in horrified disbelief.

"It's tearing him to pieces. Look, it's ripping his arms and legs apart!"

"Those bastards! Those bastards! What do they want to do a thing like that for?"

Now, long red lines were radiating from the man's broken body in every direction on the circular white surface. He must have been screeching from the moment the Monster bent to its work, but this far away they could hear nothing.

And still the Monster went on calmly and studiously, this rope, that rope, poking, prodding, slicing, tearing.

All around Eric, the members of the expedition were turning away. Some were throwing up, others were cursing monotonously and hopelessly to themselves. One man kept asking himself in a dazed, pleading voice: "What do they want to do a thing like that for? What do they want to do a thing like that for?"

But Eric forced himself to watch. He was an Eye, and an Eye must see all there is to see. He was also responsible for his men—and anything he could learn about the Monsters might help them.

He saw what was left of the man's body grow still and quiet in its puddle of blood. The Monster's neck bent to one side, came back with a transparent tube. Its pink tentacles unfastened the corpse. Then they held the tube directly over the body. A stream of water shot out, washing the dead man and all the blood that had poured out of him into the center of the white surface, where there was a dark round hole. He disappeared into the hole. The Monster played the stream of water over its collection of green ropes, apparently cleansing them. It put the tube down and walked away from the circular surface, now all white and clean again.

Head bent, his stomach rolling hideously inside him, Eric stumbled back to where Jonathan Danielson lay all alone. The Stranger answered his question before he put it:

"Dissection. They want to find out if you people are like the other humans they've taken apart. I think they dissect one man in every group they capture." He moved his head restlessly back and forth and drew a deep breath. "When they placed me up here, there was another man from my party still alive. Saul Davidson. They kept Saul down there and dissected him."

"And the rest of us," Eric said slowly, "are to be used up in other experiments."

"From what I've seen happening in the cages below—yes." Jonathan Danielson's lips curved in a gray, humorless smile. "Remember my saying that if a rope broke and you fell to the floor of the Monster burrow, it would not be a bad way to die?"

"Those green ropes, the ones the Monsters use—do you know how they work?"

"The basic principle is protoplasm affiliation. The Monsters have been doing a lot with protoplasm affiliation lately. That's why my band was sent out here."

"What kind of affiliation?"

"Protoplasm affiliation," the injured man repeated. "Ever see one of those doorways they set up in walls? They open and close like a curtain; if they're so much as touched, they stop moving."

Eric nodded, remembering the fissure that had suddenly appeared, and which he and Roy had been able miraculously to hold open long enough for Walter the Weapon-Seeker to run back through.

"The doorways reverse the principle. Protoplasm rejection."

"I think I understand you, but what's this word you keep using—this protoplasm?"

Jonathan Danielson swore softly. "Sweet Aaron the Leader!" he said. "I've been carrying on a conversation with a savage who's never even heard of protoplasm!" He turned his face away, sighing hopelessly.

Feeling as inadequate and inferior as when he had first met Arthur the Organizer in the huge piece of Monster furniture, Eric stared down and shifted his weight from one foot to the other.

"Are you from the Aaron People?" he asked at last in an uncertain voice.

No answer.

"My grandmother was from the Aaron People—so they tell me. Deborah the Dream-Singer. Have you heard of her?"

"Oh, go away, go away," Jonathan Danielson murmured. "I'm dying, and I have a right to die with a few civilized thoughts in my head."

Eric tried to bring himself to ask another question and found he couldn't. He wandered away disconsolately, feeling less like a leader than the youngest initiate ever assigned to a war band.

Someone was trying to attract his attention. Walter the Weapon-Seeker. The chunky man was waving a rope made up of many short straps knotted together and then braided. "We're ready to test the first one. Want to watch?"

"Yes. I guess so. Listen, Walter," Eric said with great casualness. "You have all kinds of specialists here from the back-burrow tribes. Do you know anybody who's done work in protoplasm?"

"In *what?*"

"Protoplasm. Protoplasm affiliation or rejection. I don't care which. You know what protoplasm is, don't you?"

"I do not. I never heard of the stuff."

"Well, then, don't bother," Eric told him, feeling immensely better. "I'll take care of it. Let's try the rope."

They set a man at either end of the rope and had him pull against the other. It held. But when the men let the rope go slack and abruptly jerked it taut, it broke in the center.

"So much for the first experiment," Walter said. He placed the palms of his hands together and bowed his head over them. "*Oh, well,*" he said in a low voice, "*back to the drawing boards.*" He looked up shyly at Eric. "I hope you don't mind my using a little Ancestor-Science. That's one of the oldest invocations known to my people."

"Use anything, from any faith. We've had far too much religious narrowness and fanaticism."

The next morning, after they were fed and watered, a Monster appeared again with a searching green rope. But this time, the man selected was removed only after a good deal of uproar. The occupants of the cage stampeded in a tightly packed, roaring mass from one end of it to the other. Eric, fighting for the self-control necessary in a leader, tried to stand aside, but the hysterical mob picked him up and absorbed him in one of its headlong swoops across the cage.

Through it all, the Monster was quite patient, its tentacles twirling the length of green just above the cage until the man it was after was temporarily separated from his fellows. It evidently knew exactly which human being it wanted. Down came the rope, touching the man on the shoulder and pulling him up again. A few of his friends tried to hold on to his legs, but they were forced to let go when they were drawn as high as the upper lip of the wall. Some other men angrily and helplessly threw spears, but these bounced off the Monster's skin. Then they stood weeping in the corner and watched him being carried to the flat white surface.

At least he died quickly. This was no prolonged dissection, but a brief though quite nasty moment of agony in an experimental trap. Again, Eric observed to the end, memorizing the features of the trap for possible use some time in the future.

Again, bloody fragments were washed down a round hole in the middle.

"*Hit back at the Monsters,*" a man near him was praying. "*I don't care how. All I ask is one day to know that I've hit back at them.*"

Eric agreed. The truth in these ancient chants! Alien-Science or Ancestor-Science—whichever would work—anything to hit back—anything!

The stampede had resulted in a casualty. Roy the Runner showed Eric where Jonathan Danielson lay, life trampled out of him by scores of feet. "I saw him try to roll out of the way. He was too weak, poor guy."

They examined the dead man's possessions. Most of the articles in the pockets of his skirt were unfamiliar except for an odd, short spear which someone recognized and called a clasp knife. It looked useful, a bigger version of the shaving tool used by warriors, and Eric appropriated it. Arthur the Organizer removed Jonathan's skirt and spread it over his face.

"If he's one of the Aaron People," Arthur explained, "that's the way he should be sewered. They always cover the faces of their dead."

Sewering was a problem, however, despite the stern injunction of the burrows that it be done immediately. They couldn't get him down the tiny hole in the corner. But they couldn't leave a rotting corpse among them.

Just as Eric had arranged to get the body up the cage wall and have it dropped down the other side, Monster watchfulness and observation took the problem out of his domain. A green rope fell from above and coiled about the body, lifting it into the air with the skirt still held carefully against the face, exactly as Arthur had disposed it.

Did the Monsters understand and respect human religious observances, Eric wondered? No, they probably just took men's bodies as they found them. He saw the corpse carried to the circular dissecting surface and dropped with an unceremonious splash into its central black hole.

Then, astonishingly, the Monster came back to the cage, lowered the green rope once more—and plucked Eric out.

Chapter 17

It all happened so fast, so utterly without warning, that Eric had no time to think of running across the cage or struggling to evade capture. One startled yelp escaped him as he rose high into the air and saw the upturned faces of his companions recede into indistinguishable white dots.

And then he was moving through vastness, dangling from the end of the Monster's rope. There was a cold streak making a diagonal across his back where the rope had welded itself to his flesh. But worse was the cold dampness in his mind, the liquid terror that was congealing into the certainty of imminent and very painful death.

Dissection? No, according to Jonathan Danielson, the Monsters were satisfied with a single sample from each group. More likely another trap to be tried out, something as ugly as the one he'd just seen chew up a man.

…a laboratory where they test all kinds of homicides: sprays, traps, poisoned lures, everything…

Which of these was he to experience? In what Monster test was he to scream out the last tortured shreds of life?

In one respect he was fortunate. He knew roughly what to expect. He would be no docile laboratory animal—that at least. He would fight, as long as he could, in any way that he could. His hand moved to the back sling for a spear, then stopped.

No. Don't waste a spear until there was a chance of a good cast. Wait until he was set down and was close to a vital organ, an eye, say, or a mouth open enough to expose the inside of the throat. A badly thrown spear now would only alert the Monster to his murderous determination. Not that he had too much hope in human weapons: he'd already seen spears bounce harmlessly off that thick gray hide.

What he needed now was one of the unusual implements of warfare that a man like Walter the Weapon-Seeker might come up with. That soft red stuff the chunky man had given him on their first meeting—it had blown the head off Stephen the Strong-Armed—

He still had some of that left! His first Theft—Eric had intended to keep evidence of it until his dying day. But, from the appearance of things, that day had moved into the immediate present.

A weapon Walter had stolen from the Monsters, to be used now against them!

He reached behind him, felt around in the knapsack until he located the stuff. How much should he tear off? A very little bit had done for Stephen quite spectacularly. But the Monster: look at the size of the creature! Better use it all—and make it count.

As he spun from the rope's end, facing first one way, then another, in the soaring white space, Eric weighed the irregular red ball in his right hand and waited for an opportunity. It was going to be complicated: he had to spit on the stuff before he threw it, and, once it was moistened, he had to get rid of it immediately. That meant he had to figure his opening exactly right—if the spin were turning him away from the Monster once he'd spat on the red ball, he'd have to get rid of it anyway; he'd have to throw his only real weapon away into emptiness and waste it.

Obviously, then, as he began to face the Monster, a moment before it was in full range—that was the time to go into action.

Eric began paying careful attention to the duration of each spin, absorbing the rhythm with his mind. There was no fear in him now; instead there was the beginning of an exultation that almost burst from his lips in a song. If he were successful, he knew, it would be the end of him. Once the explosion occurred, once the Monster was killed, he, Eric, would fall—with or without the rope—an enormous distance to the floor. He would be dashed to pieces upon it. But the life of his captor would have been extinguished first. At last a man would have done what so many men had dreamed of for so long—

Hit back at the Monsters!

The members of his own expedition would see it, Roy, Walter the Weapon-Seeker, Arthur the Organizer, they would see it and cheer themselves hoarse. Hit back at the Monsters! Hit back at them, not as a nibbling annoyance, as a thief of food or artifacts, but as a full and deadly antagonist. Hit back at the Monsters—and with their own weapon!

He hoped the expedition could still see him. The Monster had passed the circular table used for dissection and testing and was going on. Where?

It didn't matter. Nor was it important if he were out of sight of his caged friends. Only one thing counted: get the rhythm of the spin right, make a throw at the exactly correct moment—and take a Monster with him into the sewers. What a trophy to exhibit before the ancestors!

Eric was positive he had the timing now. He allowed himself one more spin, however, and went through the whole process in his mind.

Here I spit. Here I throw. Here it hits, just as I begin to turn. Here the explosion. And here, as my back is toward him, the Monster begins to topple!

Yes, he had the rhythm. He started turning toward the Monster again and held the soft mass near his mouth, working up saliva. He began to see the creature out of the corner of one eye.

Now.

Slowly, carefully, he spat on the ball, turning it round and round in his hand. The arm went back and waited while a portion of his mind beat out the pulsations it had learned. Then, when the Monster was almost in front of him, he threw. He threw in a high arc, aiming for the creature's head, which quivered to and fro at the end of that impossibly long neck. It would hit. Holy Ancestors, he had thrown right!

But, as he began the turn away, Eric saw that something had gone wrong. The Monster had noticed the red ball. And its head had moved down to meet it, mouth opened avidly! The Monster was swallowing it! *It was swallowing the weapon!*

The last thing Eric saw on that turn was a ripple that went down the length of the great throat. And in the ugly purple eyes—unmistakable enjoyment.

Then the spin had turned his back to the Monster. He waited despairingly for the sound of an explosion—a cataclysm that would tear the immense creature apart from the inside. He didn't hear it. There was a sound at last behind him, not at all an explosion, but loud and odd nonetheless. Eric allowed himself to hope again. The rope from which he hung jerked back and forth.

He twisted his head and strained his eyes as the spin back began. Where was it? *There!*

Yes, there it was. He could see the Monster again. And his whole body went limp with defeat.

Ripples continued to run down that long stretch of throat, smaller and smaller ripples as the effect, whatever it was, evidently began wearing off. Whenever a ripple came down to the point where the neck joined the body, there was a repetition of the loud, odd sound Eric had heard when his back was to the Monster. Now, facing it and seeing the entire creature, Eric could almost recognize the sound: not quite a sneeze, a little more than a cough, and more than reminiscent of a human moan of pleasure—with the same enjoyment-filled upbeat at the end.

Yes, the effect was definitely wearing off. The odd sounds came at longer and longer intervals; they were less and less loud. At the end of the curving neck, the triangular head probed about restlessly in great arcs, searching, with what seemed to be a delighted hunger, for more red balls. The Monster's eyes were alight with ecstasy.

Apparently, it did not in any way connect its tiny human captive with the pleasures it had experienced.

That was just as well, Eric decided, hanging from the green rope where it adhered to his back. There was enough of a humiliation involved in having the knowledge all to himself.

Eric the Monster-Toppler. Eric the Alien-Killer. That's how he had seen himself in those few fierce moments of anticipation.

"How about Eric the Monster-Tickler?" he asked himself bitterly. "That's a good name."

What had gone wrong with the weapon? Well, to begin with, he realized, it had probably not been a weapon in the first place. Walter the Weapon-Seeker had stolen it from the Monsters and found it could be used as one—against humans. You added your saliva, threw it against a man—and he exploded. But among the Monsters, it could have been something totally different. A food, a condiment of some sort. A drug, perhaps even an aphrodisiac. Or, conceivably, part of some complex game that they played. Mixed with human saliva, its properties had no doubt been altered. But not in the direction of any danger to the Monster. Eric's carefully mounted attack had given the alien no more discomfort than a concentrated, highly individualized orgy.

There was an important lesson here, something that attacked the foundations of Alien-Science with its belief that man could learn important and useful information from the Monsters. What was utterly inimical to humans could be salutary to the Monsters: it might be healthful, it might be merely pleasant, it might be both. And, logically, the proposition should be sometimes true in its reversed form. What nourished or stimulated humans might destroy Monsters—if such a thing could ever be isolated or discovered!

The thought suggested a line of approach to a weapon that men had dreamed of for countless downtrodden centuries—a true Monster-killer.

Eric began to get excited, to run through possibilities for research in his mind. But his captor's abrupt halt brought him back to where he was at the moment: he had no weapons at all except his good right arm and a couple of spears. And if he was going to do any fighting before he was torn to pieces, he'd better get ready.

They had arrived at the Monster's destination. The green rope to which he was attached was being lowered purposefully. He pulled at his back sling and, after a moment's thought, selected a light spear for his right hand and a heavy one for his left.

If he had a chance, if the creature's head came at all close, he would try a cast with the throwing spear. And he would use the heavy one to ward off the various dissecting ropes and implements. Not that he had much hope: the distances were too great for any decent aim, the power and strength which he faced were too far beyond his own.

But he was Eric the Eye, a warrior and a man.

He looked down. Odd, there was no flat white surface below him. Instead, there was—there was another cage! He was merely being transferred!

Eric sighed out his relief gustily. He was about to replace the spears, but just then the rope lowered him into the exact center of the cage and withdrew from his back. He looked about, examining the place.

The spears he held were what saved his life when the naked girl came at him.

Part III: Counselors for Their Wisdom

Chapter 18

As he had dropped into it, still hanging from the rope, the cage had appeared empty. Once on his feet and master of his own motions, he had begun to turn about leisurely. And then that swift, determined patter behind him, a little softer than it should sound when a warrior ran...

Eric whirled, a careful smile on his face, the beginnings of a peaceful greeting on his lips. And he found himself unable to speak.

Because there was a girl charging at him, a stark naked girl with a great mass of light brown hair that spiraled down in one direction to her shoulders and then in the other direction to her hips. And there was a spear in her hands, quite a heavy spear with the longest point Eric had ever seen. The point was aimed at his belly. The girl was coming fast.

Pure reflex. Eric realized that he had parried the spear upward with one of his own spears.

The girl drew back a pace, set herself and lunged again. Again Eric knocked it away but barely: he felt it go past his throat by half a handsbreadth.

Again she came back, again he parried, again and again and again. He felt as if his mind were giving way—this was like a nightmare you had back in the burrows after a full meal and a big celebration. How could a woman be carrying a weapon? How could a woman be attacking a warrior in direct combat?

She was not going to give up. She was absolutely set on killing him, that was certain. Her eyes were narrowed intently and a red bit of her tongue projected thoughtfully from a corner of her mouth. She held the spear tightly, looked him over for a vulnerable, undefended area, then lunged once more. Eric, using his spear as a club, warded off the thrust.

How could he stop her? He couldn't counterattack—there was the danger of hurting or killing the girl. Alien-Science or Ancestor-Science, whatever you believed in, you always accepted as axiomatic that a nubile woman, a woman of child-bearing age, was untouchable with a deadly weapon, was automatically holy. A warrior who killed such a one ceased to be human: even if he were a chief, his tribe would declare him outlaw.

But she was liable to get through his guard sooner or later. And he couldn't try to take the spear away from her. He'd have to let go of his own spears in order to do that, and the moment he stopped parrying her thrusts she'd run him through.

Meanwhile, all he could do was protect himself. And she was so damned determined! They were both breathing heavily to the rhythm of weapon hitting against weapon. Eric jumped as the girl's long spearpoint missed his eyes infinitesimally.

"Almost got me that time," he muttered.

The girl stopped in the middle of a lunge. She teetered a moment, barely holding her balance, staring at him with widened eyes.

"What did you say?" she breathed. "You *said* something."

Eric stared back, wondering if she were insane. Should he take the chance now, while her mind was busy with some unexpected problem, should he drop his spears, leap at her and try to take her weapon away?

"Yes, I said something," he told her, watching the spear in her hands carefully. "So what?"

She lowered the spear and stepped back a few paces, strain going out of her face. "I mean you can talk. You have a language."

"Of course I have a language," Eric said irritably. "What the hell do you think I am—a Wild Man?"

The girl answered by flinging her spear aside and dropping to the floor of the cage. She lowered her head to her knees and rocked herself back and forth.

Eric walked away and retrieved the spear. He slung it, along with his own weapons. When he came back to the girl, she was sobbing. And, puzzled as he was, it was evident to him that the sobs were relief and not pain or sorrow.

He waited. Now that she was disarmed, he could afford to be patient. If she turned out to be crazy after all, he'd have to decide what to do with her. Sharing a cage with nobody but a murderous lunatic was a very disagreeable prospect. On the other hand, even a crazy woman was still sacrosanct....

She stopped crying finally and wiped her eyes with the back of one arm. Then she leaned back, locked her arms behind her head and grinned at him cheerfully. Eric felt more disturbed than ever. This was a real odd one.

"Do you know," she said, "that's exactly what I thought you were. A Wild Man."

Eric was astounded. "Me?"

"You. And I wasn't the only one who thought so."

He looked around the cage. There was nobody else in it. This girl was a lunatic beyond any doubt.

She had followed his glance. She chuckled and nodded. "No, I'm not referring to anyone in the cage. I'm referring to that fellow up there. He thought you were a Wild Man too."

Eric looked up along the line of her pointing thumb. The Monster who had brought him still stared down into the cage, the enormous purple eyes unwinking, the prehensile pink tentacles perfectly still. "Why? Why should he—it—think I'm a Wild Man? Why should you?"

A part of him was deeply outraged. To be mistaken for the mythic, terror-inspiring

Wild Men—that was too much! You frightened naughty children with stories about hordes of semihuman, hairy creatures who had sunk below the level of language, below the level of weapon and artifact, who had lost, long auld lang synes ago, the universal burrow taboo against cannibalism. You hazed gangling young apprentice warriors with tales of vast, ravaging mobs that came out of nowhere and fought your spears with teeth and nails, mobs that fought not for victory, for territory or for women, but for the ripped-off arms and bloody, broken haunches of their antagonists. And when you asked an older warrior how could there really be such a thing as Wild Men, since nobody you knew had ever seen them, he told you that they were a plague peculiar to the back burrows. Wild Men, he would tell you as he himself had been told by the warriors under whom he had studied, Wild Men did not live in Monster territory and they did not live in the burrows. They lived in another place entirely, a place called the Outside. And when you asked him to explain or describe this Outside, he'd shrug and say, "Well, the Outside is a place where the Wild Men live." You'd go away, proud of your maturity for having at last realized that Wild Men were strictly horror-story stuff, as improbable as any of the other burrow legends of lurking creatures: the blood-sucking Draculas, the packs of vicious police dogs, the bug-eyed men from Mars, and, worst of all, the oil-seeking wildcats who drilled for all eternity from one burrow to another.

But Wild Men were not merely the stuff of legend; they were the material of curses and opprobrium. A severely retarded child might be called a Wild Man, as might a warrior who disobeyed his band leader or a woman who was expelled from the Female Society. When someone in the tribe perpetrated a particularly ugly crime and managed to escape to distant burrows before punishment, you said: "May the Wild Men get him. He belongs with them." A Wild Man was anyone who had failed the test of humankind.

But what right did this girl have to pass such a judgment on him? She couldn't possibly know that his own people had declared him outlaw. And she herself—look at her!—a woman in Monster territory where no woman had a legitimate reason to be—she was a fine one to go around insulting people.

"So that's the primary reason I thought you were a Wild Man," the girl was saying. "Because the big fellow did. He's already deposited two Wild Men in here with me. Luckily, he dropped them in one at a time. I was able to kill each of them the moment they landed, before they could collect their faculties and see how pink and edible I was."

"You mean—there really are such things as Wild Men?"

"Really are such things as Wild Men? You've never seen one? Sweet Aaron the Leader, where are you from?"

From Mankind, Eric started to say, with his old, stiff-backed pride. Then he remembered how it sounded to Strangers—he had learned a lot lately. "I'm from a front-burrow tribe," he said. "A rather small one. I don't think you've heard of us."

The girl nodded. "A front-burrow tribe—that would explain your unlaced hair. And anyone with hair hanging loose is somehow related to the Wild Men as far as the

Monsters are concerned. They seem to know enough about me to suspect I'm fe-male—one of the few fully human females they've ever caught, I guess—but because my hair hangs loose they keep hauling Wild Men in here for me to mate with. And it's gotten pretty hectic, let me tell you! The way I feel about myself, a mate for some-one maybe, a dinner no. I'd been conditioned to expect nothing but Wild Men, and the moment I saw you with all that flopping hair, I said to myself, Rachel, here we go again. If I'd had any sense, I'd have paid some attention to the fact that you were car-rying spears and knapsacks and all kinds of fully human equipment."

"Your name is Rachel? Mine's Eric, Eric the Eye."

She scrambled to her feet and held out a small hand warmly. "Hello, Eric. I'm Rachel Esthersdaughter, Rachel for short. It's good to have someone to talk to. A front-burrower," she mused. "Naturally, you've never seen Wild Men. They practically never get to the front burrows—it's too far from the Outside for their comfort. But my people have to be battling them back to their wide open spaces all the time. The Monsters have apparently been picking up a lot of them, though, for experimental purposes; they must have traps all over the Outside. Hey, look."

Eric followed her gaze upwards. The Monster who had brought him was swinging ponderously around and moving off.

Rachel giggled. "Ah-h, how sweet. He feels he's made a match at last. He wants to leave the lovers alone. First time in a long while he hasn't had to remove a corpse from this cage immediately afterward."

Feeling awkward and embarrassed, Eric inquired: "What made him decide that everything is all right?"

"Well, first, the fact that I didn't kill you, of course. Then he sees us shaking hands. I don't think they know any more about us, really, than we know about them. They probably think the act of shaking hands is *it*. You know, Love's Old Sweet Song, one mad moment of passion, my soul shudders and my senses reel."

Eric felt his face turning red. He'd never come across any woman as direct and as casual as this; it was particularly disconcerting in combination with the unbound hair that denoted an unmarried state. He tried to change the subject. "You're from the Aaron People, Rachel, aren't you?"

She had started to walk away from him to a corner of the cage. Now she turned back. "How did you know? Front-burrowers rarely reach our base.... Oh, I remem-ber. I called on Sweet Aaron the Leader."

"That was part of it. And there was your name. In the cage I came from, there was a man of the Aaron People with a name like yours. Jonathan Danielson."

She clutched at his arm. "Jonny? Alive?"

"He died just before I was taken out of the cage. He said that someone called Saul Davidson had also been captured alive, but the Monsters dissected him."

Rachel's eyes shut tight. "Ooh. Saul was my cousin. He was my favorite cousin. We were thinking of asking permission of the Aaron to mate after we came back from this expedition."

Eric patted her hand, which was digging into the muscle of his arm. "Well, the other news I got from Jonathan Danielson is not too good either. He said all fourteen members of the expedition were killed. One blow from a Monster's foot."

Shaking herself, the girl straightened. "Nonsense. I was part of the expedition, and I wasn't harmed. I know of at least three others who were captured and used for experiments. Jonathan Danielson was a bad, bad leader, like all our men in this kind of situation—they're too scholarly, they're not able to handle action and emergencies. He didn't see what happened to the rest of us because he was in a blind panic at the time."

"A band leader who panicked? I never heard of such a thing."

She took a deep breath and the wild, merry grin came back to her lips. "There are more things between the front and back burrows, Eric, my friend, than are dreamt of in your philosophy." She punched at him lightly. "Now, don't get mad—I'm honestly not making fun of you. Your face gets all squooshy when you get upset. Come over here: I want to show you what I mean."

In the corner of the cage, a great expanse of material was laid out. Every few handspreads, there was a pocket from which one or more unfamiliar objects protruded. It was very similar to the skirt worn by Jonathan Danielson and in which his face had been wrapped when he died. Except, Eric realized, this was much, much larger and rather more like a cloak than a skirt: its owner would probably be several times more consequential among the Aaron People than Jonathan Danielson.

"Is this yours?" he asked with cautious respect.

"Mine, all mine. My head goes in that hole and I wear it all around me. It's waterproof."

"Waterproof?"

"Yes. Water runs off it without it getting wet. I've worn it on trips to the Outside where water falls on you from the ceiling. It's also a sort of portable laboratory. You see this intriguing object?" Rachel had pulled a contraption out of one of the pockets. It was a rod folded in sections which she proceeded to open to its full length; at the end of the rod, a few wires attached it to a couple of small cylinders. "Now this device was the whole purpose of the expedition, not so much the device itself as the testing thereof. A group of us in the Female Society developed it and we had the idea it might neutralize the green ropes that the Monsters use. As you probably know, the ropes are based on the principle of protoplasm affiliation."

Eric coughed and nodded gravely. "Like the Monster doorways that reverse the principle. Protoplasm rejection."

Rachel pointed a delighted forefinger at him. "Right! Well, neutralizing protoplasm affiliation is something my people have been trying to do for a long time—and right now it's more important than it ever was. They sent us off, one woman scientist and thirteen men who were supposed to protect her, they sent us off to find out if the thing would really work. And it worked. It worked only too well."

She put the device back in its pocket and stared at it for a moment before going on. "We made it through the burrows all right, and all the way into Monster territory without a casualty. Which is pretty good going for the Aaron People, I'm ashamed to tell you. We encounter a Monster the moment we get here to the lab, and little Rachel steps out to expose herself in the great good cause of scientific research. The Monster lets down a rope to grab me, I apply our neutralizer to it, and it works! The rope turns dark, goes all limp—no adhering capacity, no capturing quality, nothing. Cheers, you know? Applause from the multitude, V for victory, hooray for us and all that sort of thing. As far as I'm concerned, we've accomplished our mission: let's be on our way and bring the glad tidings home. Besides, this Monster territory is not what I'd call cozy. I go stepping off, back to where the expedition is hiding, very happy over the fact that the Monster is all upset and rattled. He's dropped the rope and is examining it with a stupid expression on his silly face. He doesn't connect its failure in any way with Rachel, and, for the moment, he isn't the slightest bit interested in Rachel. Or in her thirteen little protectors. They, unfortunately, have other ideas."

"Jonathan Danielson was a brand-new band leader, and he was itching for glory," Eric suggested. "He saw the chance of bringing a trophy home—a deactivated Monster rope, something that had never been paraded in the burrows before. I don't know if I can blame him."

"I can. Let me tell you, I can. It was a direct violation of our original marching orders, which were to get back as soon as possible with information that was vital to the future of our people. But what's a woman going to do? Once she's completed the heavy thinking, she's got to follow the leadership of the men and obey their instructions in operational matters. Sexual differences are sexual differences, and who am I to put obstructions in a nice straight burrow? So, there I was, halfway back to the safety of the wall when Jonny Danielson gallops past me followed by the rest of the expedition. They all have those heroic masculine looks on their faces. Me—I just stop and watch. They run to the rope that's lying limply on the floor and they're about to pick it up. They're not too worried about the Monster, because we can see it's not carrying another rope—and who ever heard of a Monster picking up humans without a green rope? Those tentacles on the neck are just for fine manipulation. But I'm looking at those neck tentacles, and what I see scares me into absolute fits. Those tentacles are the wrong size and the wrong color."

Eric remembered what Walter the Weapon-Seeker had told him. "You mean they were short and reddish, instead of long and light pink."

"That's exactly what I mean. Hey." Rachel Esthersdaughter twisted her head at him appraisingly. "You know an awful lot for a front-burrower."

"Well—" Eric shrugged. "I've been around and I've kept my ears open. Especially lately. But I thought those short-tentacled Monsters are the least dangerous. They're the ones who run and panic when a man goes directly at them."

"*If* they have a place to run to. This Monster was too close to the wall—not by our standards, but, you know, in terms of the big, big steps that they take. And the men of the expedition were coming at it in a great semicircle. It panicked, all right, but it didn't run. It threw back its head. One tremendous, ear-splitting bellow—you never heard so much quantity of sheer fear packed in a single noise! I saw Jonathan Danielson freeze where he stood. And then *he* went into panic! Instead of realizing what had happened and leading the men back immediately, he threw his spear away and began to run back and forth in a crazy zigzag pattern, yelling his head off. The men looked from him to the Monster, not knowing what to do next. Some followed him, others kept on going for the rope. Suddenly the Monster kicked out. It was a blind, fearful kick, more like a twitch than a kick, but when it was over there were smashed and bleeding men all over the floor. And then other Monsters came hurrying from all directions and grabbed up anyone who was still alive. I was too upset myself—panic again, or just plain shock, I don't know—to think of using my neutralizer on the green rope with which they took me. By the time it occurred to me, I was too high in the air."

"Sure. You'd have been killed if you'd made the green rope let go of you. Then they brought you here."

"Then the Monsters brought me here," the girl agreed. "And now, Eric, they've brought *you* here. To share this cage with me."

Chapter 19

Eric moved a short distance away from the cloak of many pockets. He squatted ceremoniously, placing his hands on the floor and bowing his head. This was the position he'd seen assumed by band leaders high in the councils of Mankind when they wished to consider a matter carefully. And there were many significant details in Rachel's story to turn over in his mind.

First, it was now overwhelmingly clear that Strangers, however superior they might be in knowledge, were not worth a damn as expedition leaders—compared, that is, with the warriors of his own people. They knew so incredibly little of elementary precautions (Arthur the Organizer letting one of his men walk into a trap immediately after leaving the piece of Monster furniture—and remember the execrable march discipline all the way to this place?). And, as commanders, they were downright dangerous when something unexpected happened (Arthur's absolute funk upon arrival in the Cages of Sin, Jonathan Danielson's inexcusable hysteria, a hysteria stimulated by nothing more substantial than noise, but which had cost the lives of almost all his followers). You might make a useful rule out of it: the farther back in the burrows you went, the poorer the quality of the leadership in any emergency situation—when you got to the Aaron People, the *back* back-burrowers, so to speak, you had band leaders capable of committing their men to any imaginable idiocy. The closer you got to Monster territory, possibly because of the unremitting, day-to-day dangers of existence, the more likely you were to find in any given warrior the caution, the alertness and the adaptability that a man had the right to demand of his superior officer. And Strangers seemed to recognize this too: it had been easy for him to take command of the cage away from Arthur. Imagine a Stranger warrior as young as Eric taking over, in a similar position, from his uncle, Thomas the Trap-Smasher!

On the other hand, looked at with a different set of values, the rule reversed itself. The deeper into the burrows you went and the farther from Monster territory, the more complex the technology, the more extensive the knowledge and the more powerful the conceptual daring. Eric had always known that his tribe had traded off its excess food and occasional Monster artifacts to other peoples in the burrows to the rear for the finished spearheads and soft knapsack material which it was incapable of making for itself. Only recently had he learned of the existence of men like Walter the Weapon-Seeker, always on the lookout for strange Monster goods which could be turned to effective human use, and Arthur the Organizer, with his dream of a United Burrows practicing the new religion of Alien-Science. And now the Aaron People, capable of developing equipment which could combat and immobilize the Monsters' own weapons—this was truly carrying the fight to the enemy of Man!

If someone, someday, could ever fuse the two, the battle courage and cleverness of front-burrow tribes with the knowledge and imaginative valor of the back-burrowers, what glories might humanity then accomplish!

He looked up at Rachel. She had been studying him for some time. Her arms were crossed on her chest and her eyes were staring down at him intently.

"Do you know?" she said. "You're not at all bad-looking."

"Thank you, Rachel. This neutralizing device—you say the information about it was vital to the future of your people. In other words, it's part of a plan to hit back at the Monsters?"

"Of course. But so is everything that human beings do these days. Do you have a mate?"

"No, not yet. What kind of a plan? I mean, is it an approach through Alien-Science or Ancestor-Science?"

She fluttered her left hand impatiently. "In the Aaron People we have nothing to do with either of those superstitions. We gave them both up a long time ago. Our Plan to hit back at the Monsters is real and entirely new. It's different from anything you've ever heard of, and it's the only one which will work. How come a healthy, handsome young warrior like you doesn't have a mate?"

"I've only been a full warrior for a short time—I just passed my initiation ceremony. If your plans are neither Alien-Science nor—"

"Is that the only reason for your not having a mate? The fact that you've just celebrated your initiation ceremony?"

Eric rose with dignity. "There are—well, some other reasons. But that's a personal matter. I'd rather not discuss it. What I am interested in is this Plan your people have to hit back at the—"

She smiled and shook her head. "Men and women. Practically two different species. If it weren't for sex, they'd have *nothing* in common. Now I can't tell you any more about my people's strategy with the Monsters—I've talked too much already—but what I do want to canvass with you is the subject of mating. Mating, and nothing but mating, is our agenda, as far as I'm concerned. Mating, the pros and cons, the shades, the nuances, all about mating. What are those other reasons, Eric? I have to know."

He hesitated. "I'm a singleton," he said at last. "An only."

"A *what*? A singleton— Oh. You mean you weren't part of a litter. Your mother had just the one child—you. And the girls back in your tribe were afraid the condition might be hereditary. Well, that's not what I call a problem. Anything else?"

"No, nothing else," he told her angrily. "How can you say it's not a problem? What's worse than having no decent litter potential?"

"Many, many things. But let's not go into them. Among the Aaron People, you may be interested to know, small litters are quite prevalent. Twins are about it for the average woman. For the very largest litters you have to go to the Wild Men, whose women never come up with less than six at a birth. I think it has something to do with the amount of genetic distance from our ancestors. Or, perhaps, the differing infant mortality rates. But me, I'll be quite satisfied with a singleton delivery—especially here, with no midwives from the Aaron People to help me at the confinement."

Eric gaped at her. "Confinement? Here? You mean what you're thinking about— what you're suggesting—"

"My dear barbarian stalwart, I am not thinking and I am not suggesting. I am proposing. I am proposing an alliance betwixt me and thee, from this day forward, to have and to hold, in sickness and in health. Do you accept my proposal, or do you not accept my proposal?"

"But why? You've never seen me before—you don't know anything about me— we come from different peoples. Look, Rachel, it's not that I'm trying to raise objections. But—but, I haven't been in the cage long, and you're moving kind of fast. Too fast for me to understand you. There must be a reason."

"Yes, there is. In fact, there's more than one reason. Let's skip lightly over the fact that I'm not getting any younger and a girl has to think of her future. Let us also merely note in passing that your appearance pleases me and your personality pleases me and that you don't seem to have any vicious characteristics. All well and good, but not crucial. The following, however, is crucial."

She moved closer to him and took his hand. Eric felt excitement begin to build inside his body as he appreciated the girl's nakedness now. All his life he'd been surrounded by girls conventionally naked. But it was different when you realized that very shortly you and she…

"The important reasons," Rachel said softly, "have to do with saving lives. Your life, and probably mine. There were three other boys from the expedition up here with me originally. I saw them taken out, one by one, and I saw them being—each one was—oh, you know. You've seen it."

"I know, all right," Eric told her fiercely. "I saw what they do to us."

"Once they took me out, and I thought it was the end. But after passing me from one green rope to another—four or five Monsters were in a huddle over me—they returned me to the cage. Sammy Josephson—he was the last one left here—Sammy suggested that they might know I was a female and, well, something of a rarity in Monster territory. We talked about it, but before we were sure or had worked out any conclusions, it was Sammy's turn. What they did to him—oh-h! I think that was the worst of them all."

She shook her head heavily from side to side. Eric found himself squeezing her hand. She smiled at him tremulously, nodded, and went on: "And then came the succession of Wild Men, followed by you—all with long, unbound hair, just like mine. It's apparent that the Monsters do know I'm a female, and that they're trying to mate me. Now, Eric, I don't particularly want to cooperate with them in their search for knowledge about human behavior, but on this point and by this time, I'm more than willing to let them have their way. If we don't, they'll take you out of here eventually and tear you apart in an experiment. And they'll probably get tired of waiting and do the same to me. The best I have to hope for, once they remove you, is more and more Wild Men coming in here with their fangs all shiny and that gleam in their eyes which says, 'Food! On two delicious legs, the way it should be!' I'm tired of fighting and killing. That's a man's job. You be my man and do it for me."

Eric adjusted his knapsack straps self-consciously as he absorbed her analysis and her final entreaty. She was right. Given the situation, the only sensible thing was to let the Monsters know they were satisfied with each other and were mating. And he'd fallen into pure luck—Rachel constituted a fantastic prize, far beyond his wildest dreams of a mate. A girl with this much knowledge would outrank anyone in the Female Society of Mankind—probably in most Stranger Female Societies as well. That would automatically mean a tremendous boost to his own rank, if he ever got affiliated with a specific people again.

All well and good. But he was a man and a warrior. And mating was a serious business: it must be conducted with dignity, and according to tradition.

"Turn around," he ordered. "Let me look at you."

Rachel obeyed with complete docility, as he knew she would. Front-burrow or back-burrow, Aaron People or Mankind, there could not be that much difference in the customs of humanity. A man's Right to Examine was everywhere the same.

She stepped away a pace and turned round and round slowly, spreading her hair high behind her with the backs of her hands so that the lines of her body could be completely visible. This also brought her breasts up a bit more prominently: they were by no means the largest breasts he had seen on a girl, Eric noted, but they were pretty enough and would probably do. And while her thighs and hips were a shade too narrow as well, he had to remember that the demands of a singleton birth—the greatest probability here—were much smaller than those of the multiple deliveries a husband usually had to take into consideration.

On the other hand, she had an absolutely lovely, well-shaped rump, which, within the limitations posed by the narrowness of her hips, left nothing to be desired. And her face—he let go of the rump, turned her around again and took hold of her chin with the thumb and forefinger of his right hand—her face was infinitely appealing. Large, glowing brown eyes above a small, impudent nose, a soft mouth full of femininity that held an uncertain smile forever imprisoned at its corners, warm, beautifully curving cheeks, a high, white forehead, and, finally, clouds upon clouds of brown hair that was certainly of decent, adequate length. While her face was the least relevant portion of a woman's attractiveness, Eric had always had certain weaknesses in that respect which he had admitted only to himself. He was glad her face was the best part of her. Add to the face that truly first-class rump, consider that neither her hips, thighs nor breasts were outright failures, throw in the well-stocked mind which provided a magnificent dowry and thus substantial advancement for her man in any conceivable tribe—yes, Eric had to admit that Rachel was a treasure worth shedding blood for.

It would hardly do to tell her so, of course. Members of the Male Society must always maintain a certain essential diplomatic reserve toward members of the Female Society.

He moved back, folding his arms slowly and emphatically on his chest to indicate that the Examination was over.

Rachel relaxed, letting out a huge breath. "Are you satisfied?" she inquired with exactly the proper amount of anxiety. Eric was terribly pleased: he'd been afraid from her jocular manner of speaking that she knew nothing at all of formal behavior.

"I am satisfied," be told her, using the decorous phrases of the courtship formula. "You please me. I want you for my mate."

"Good. I am glad. Now I claim the Right of Invitation. You may not approach me sexually for the first time until I give you leave."

"That is your right," Eric agreed. "I will wait for your call. May it come soon! May it come soon! May it come soon!"

And it was over. They stood apart and grinned at each other self-consciously, observing mutual individuality return as the ritual prototype was sloughed off. Above them, below them, around them, lay the white vastnesses of Monster territory, the transparent cages in which fellow humans awaited fate and the Monsters' pleasure. But here in *this* cage, they were mate and mate, Eric and Rachel, two separate people who would become one, when the girl felt the time was ripe to beckon.

Suddenly Rachel giggled. "I was so nervous! Were you nervous?"

"A little," Eric admitted. "After all, from start to finish, it was a pretty fast mating. One of the fastest I ever heard about."

"I hope we didn't leave anything out, Eric."

"No, we didn't leave anything out. Nothing that was important, anyway. Except," he suddenly remembered with annoyance, "except for a condition I wanted to make. Something I wanted you to agree to do before we went through the ceremony. Then I got so caught up in the ritual responses that I forgot all about it."

"Your tough luck," she sang out and began a mad little dance around him. "Too late, too late! Agreements *before* the mating—never after." At the angry expression on his face, she stopped and took his hands. "I'm only joking, Eric. I have too much of a sense of humor for my own damn good. Among my people, there is a saying: 'Most children are born with a wail. Rachel Esthersdaughter was born with a laugh. And she'll probably die with a laugh.' You tell me what you were going to ask, and I'll do it. Whatever it is. Anything."

"Well." Now that he had come to it, Eric found difficulty in the phrasing. He didn't know if a man had ever asked a woman such a thing before. "I want you to teach me. I want you to teach me everything you know."

"You want me to—you mean, you want an education?"

"That's it, Rachel, that's what I want," he said eagerly. "An education. Knowledge. I don't expect you to tell me the secrets of the Aaron People's Female Society—I'm not asking you to break any oaths. But I want to know what at least the average man in your people knows. About the Monsters, about counting, about the history of our ancestors. How Alien-Science came to be, how Ancestor-Science came to be. How Strangers make the things they do, what the things are used for. How— What— I don't even know what I want to know!" he broke off miserably.

"But I do," she said, gently touching him on the face with an open, caressing palm. "And I'll be very willing to teach you, Eric, very willing indeed, darling. Don't you worry about my Female Society and its secrets: engineering is the last thing we'll get to. Do you want to start now?"

"Yes!" he exclaimed, his eyes shining. "I want to start right this moment!"

"Then sit down." She lowered herself to the floor and took some writing implements from one of the pockets of the nearby cloak. Eric squatted beside her. Now that he'd been able to put it into words, he found himself filled with a hunger such as he'd never known. The hunger for food, the hunger for sex—they were nothing like this. This was a singing hunger that filled your mind and made it want to hear more and more and more of the song.

Rachel looked at him quizzically for a moment. "What a way to begin a mating! With scratcher and repeatable slate. If my friends back in the Aaron People ever heard of this! If *your* friends— But Eric, seriously, I'm very pleased. That was the only thing about mating with you that really bothered me: you being a front-burrow barbarian. In our terms, of course, and who are we to say that our terms are right? But it did bother me. I'll teach you everything I know. Where do you want me to begin?"

Eric leaned towards her, his whole body tense. "Begin with protoplasm. I want to know all there is to know about protoplasm."

Chapter 20

Pursuing knowledge, Eric discovered, was like running through the burrows. The corridor you were traveling kept forking off into two or three others. Most of the time, you could only see a little ways ahead; suddenly, you came around a curve into a confrontation that astonished you.

Astronomy, for example, was such a confrontation. At first, it seemed utterly useless: a body of arcane, almost incomprehensible data, unrelated to anything at all real. You learned astronomy by rote, associating the various strange names with little circles scratched out on the repeatable slate.

First there was Earth, Earth which was to be won back from the Monsters. Earth was some kind of ball which hung, or revolved, or wandered in something that was called space. Earth was a planet, and there were other planets in space; there were also stars and comets and galaxies, dust and gas and radiation, all of them likewise in space, most of them incredible distances from Earth.

Eric kept repeating the names of planets and astronomical objects which meant nothing to him, which simply accumulated in his head like so much fuzz, until one day he stumbled on the trick of analogy. If you thought of Earth like a warm, safe corridor that you were in just before you opened the door to Monster territory, well then, opening the door was like soaring off Earth. Monster territory with its alien environment and incredible dangers would be space, and on the other side of it you might find another doorway leading to a strange new burrow—that would be another planet, or another star.

All right, that helped, it made it a bit more understandable; but certainly no more pertinent or useful.

Then came the confrontation in Eric's mind—and he gasped as he came around the curve. He remembered the conversation with Walter the Weapon-Seeker while they were on expedition to this place. Walter had talked of a boy in his band who had wondered what lay outside of Monster territory itself, what it was that compared to the Monster burrows as the Monster burrows compared to the human ones. Walter had dismissed the idea as too much for the human mind to contemplate. But it wasn't! Here, here in astronomy was the answer. A much larger place, Earth, lay outside and all around Monster territory. And a much, much larger place, interplanetary or interstellar space, lay outside and all around Earth. The Monsters, in terms of what they ultimately inhabited, were as trivial, as insignificant, as infinitesimal as any human beings.

And were human beings truly insignificant? They hadn't always been. Eric thrilled with the pride of belonging to a race that had worked out a system of recorded signals as clever as the alphabet, that could take ordinary numbers and squeeze them into unrecognizable shapes, pulling out a piece here, a piece there....

"No, Eric, no!" Rachel announced definitely, flinging her scratcher down on the cloak near which they were sitting. "There's no point in discussing this any further. You're trying to push me into an explication of Horner's method and synthetic division—and I absolutely refuse. My math isn't that good in the first place, and after all, sweetheart, this is supposed to be a survey course and no more. You're a glutton: you absorb and absorb and absorb. Sometimes you frighten me. You could go without sleep for days, couldn't you?"

Eric nodded. He felt as if he were on a war band foray. Who wanted sleep when you were filled with the excitement of what you might capture if you only kept going? But women, he remembered, were different. They never seemed to feel that particular excitement.

He considered his mate carefully and with tenderness. She did look tired. Well, they had been at their lessons almost from the moment they had opened their eyes. "Do you want to go to sleep, darling?"

"Ooh, I'd love to!" she said, her voice throbbing tragically but her eyes still grinning at him. "I've been thinking of nothing else. But I can't. You're the man and the leader here. You have to declare it night."

"I do," he said. "Night. Let's sack in." He lay back on the hard cage floor and watched her put the writing apparatus away in the proper pocket of her cloak. Eric thought to himself how graceful she was, how very, very desirable. And how much she knew! Much more than she had taught him. This synthetic division, for example, he pondered as she nestled her head into his shoulder—how would you do it? Was it at all like ordinary long division? If it was—

Yes, he thought, while he was opening his eyes and about to declare it day, yes, the pursuit of knowledge was like a trip through an unexplored section of the burrows. Once in a while, you'd say, "That little corridor off there—where does that one lead?" And your teacher would say, just like your band leader had when you'd been an apprentice warrior, "I don't know, and it's not important right now: pay attention to where we're going."

Eric paid attention, and he learned. He learned some chemistry, some physics, some biology. He learned about chlorophyllous plants which he had never been near in his entire life and about one-celled animals which had been around him and about him all through his life but which he had been unable to see any more than the plants.

"And your people really have? Through those microscope things?"

"Not microscope things, Eric—microscope *thing*. We have exactly one set of clumsy, hand-ground lenses. In the time when our ancestors owned the Earth, they had—oh, they must have had *dozens*. But they were an advanced, technologically oriented civilization: it was no trick for them to make two, three, even five microscopes at once. I mean that—don't look dubious—I'm not trying to feed you myths and legends. These were people, remember, who had achieved space travel themselves before the Monsters arrived, not interstellar flight, as the Monsters had, and not colonization as yet of other worlds, but they were making their way from planet to planet of their own system in ships that were almost as wonderful and complicated as those the Monsters suddenly turned up in. Our tragedy was that all the peoples of the Earth had at their disposal no more than about ten spaceships—simple interplanetary exploring craft—when the Monsters came pouring out of the stars with an invasion fleet of thousands. Another century of development, maybe only fifty years, and we'd have had a space navy that wouldn't have been brushed aside by the first Monster patrol to arrive in the solar system."

Eric smiled and stared through the bottom of the cage at other cages suspended in the white vastness where human captives lay sleeping or walked about restlessly. *"The suddenness of the attack..."* he quoted.

"What?"

"Oh, it's part of the catechism I had to learn as a boy—from the Ancestor-Science faith I was brought up in. I remember how shocked I was when my uncle said it was all garbage. I was so upset! But then I learned to live with the idea. You know, that it was garbage, a flock of nonsense imposed on us by our elders to keep us from asking questions and learning the truth about our past. And now, here I am again, learning that the people who have searched out more records concerning our ancestors than anyone else in the burrows—they have no more to say, basically, than that, as to why humanity succumbed. *The suddenness of the attack...* It makes me wonder whether any beliefs are true. Or—I don't know—whether *all* beliefs are true."

"Hey, there." Rachel reached up and grabbed a handful of his hair. She pulled his head back and forth gently. "Just a little education and you feel you're ready for metaphysics."

"Is that metaphysics?" Eric asked, delighted to have rediscovered an ancient human technique all by himself.

The girl elaborately ignored his question. "You have a lot of hard facts to learn yet," she went on, "you old Eric the Eye you, even if you do gulp down information like so much drinking water. Maybe all beliefs are true—in certain ways, for certain people, at certain times. They wouldn't be beliefs if they didn't contain some significant core of reality. Like the stories that have come down to us of a group of our ancestors who believed that man was getting too much above himself, and that the arrival of the Monsters constituted a judgment, a judgment from some supernatural force to obliterate our civilization. They felt that space travel and atomics were just the last straw, and that once we developed those, the supernatural force was compelled to write us off. Well, you know something? They might have been right."

"They were? How?"

Rachel slid the repeatable slate, covered with scientific diagrams, back into a cloak pocket. Then she walked to the wall of the cage near which they had been sitting and leaned against it, rubbing her forehead against the smooth, cold surface. She looked very tired.

"In a couple of ways, Eric. You take your pick. First, religiously. It's always possible that there was—or is—such a supernatural force, capable of coming to just such a judgment. And when you look at how puny, how ridiculously tiny, our species appears today, scuttling about the dwelling places of the Monsters, it does seem that back then, in our last great period, we did get slightly above ourselves. Now, if you ask me why—to use some ancestral phraseology—we should be cast down and the Monsters raised up, I tell you frankly I don't have the least idea. I only say that if you postulate a supernatural force, you are not necessarily postulating a mode of thought understandable by human beings nor necessarily sympathetic to their aspirations."

Eric rose and stood beside her. He leaned against the wall with his back, not taking his eyes off her, completely fascinated by the concepts which her pretty mouth was shaping. "Nor," he suggested, "do we necessarily postulate a mode of thought sympathetic to Monster aspirations."

"Perhaps. But what do we know of Monster aspirations, of the way they live with each other, compared to the ways human beings have always lived with each other? They might be, among themselves, decent and brotherly creatures—and how would we find out? We know as little about them as they know about us. They don't even seem to consider us intelligent, to connect us with the planet-wide civilization they destroyed centuries ago. Well, who knows? In their eyes, maybe it wasn't a real civilization, maybe we look more natural to them in our present state. And us? We don't understand the first thing about them after I don't know how many auld lang synes of observation—what kind of government they have, *if* they have a government, what kind of language they have, *if* they have a language, what kind of sex life they have, *if* they have a sex life."

"What they originally used the explosive red blobs for, why some of them will rush and trample us and others will panic and dash away," Eric added, thinking of the practical problems with which he had been grappling at the times when Rachel had been asleep and he had paced back and forth in the cage by himself. "All that you're saying, though, is that they're different: they're not provably better. Maybe this supernatural force thought so, but then I'd argue with it: I'd question its assumptions. On what other basis did our ancestors—this group of them who believed the coming of the Monsters was a judgment—on what other basis could they have been right?"

Rachel smiled at him, her eyes a tiny distance from his face. "You'd argue with the supernatural force, would you, Eric—you'd tell it that it was wrong? I'll bet you *would*: I can just see you doing it. You're the sum of everything that was ever good and bad about the human male. The second basis is moral; you might say it derived from an abiding and justified sense of guilt."

"Justified? What *kind* of guilt?"

"Certain beliefs, as I said…somewhere, in each, there's a significant core of reality. Man was lord of the Earth for a long time, Eric, and for that long time he was guilt-ridden. All of his religion and all of his literature—the literature that was written by sane men and not madmen—was filled with guilt. If you put the legendary part aside and just look at the things he really did, he had reason to be. He enslaved his fellow men, he tortured and humiliated them. He destroyed his fellow civilizations, he demolished their temples and universities and used the stones to build outhouses. Sometimes men would trample on women and mock their hurt, sometimes women would trample on men and mock *their* hurt. In some places parents would keep children in chains for all of their growing up; in other places children would send useless parents out with orders to die. And this was with his own species, with *homo sapiens.* What did he do with species that were brothers and with whom he grew to maturity? We know what he did with Neanderthal man: how many others lie in the unmarked graves of anthropological history?"

"Man is an animal, Rachel! His duty is to survive."

"Man is more than an animal, Eric. His duty comprehends more than survival. If one animal feeds on another and, in the process, wipes it out, that's biology; if man does the same thing, out of overpowering need or mere caprice, he knows he has committed a crime. Whether he's right or wrong in taking this attitude isn't important: *he knows he has committed a crime.* That is a thoroughly human realization, that it cannot be dismissed with an evolutionary shrug."

He moved away from the wall and strode up and down the cage in front of her, opening and closing his hands uncomfortably, clasping them together and pulling them apart. "All right," he said at last, coming to a stop. "Man murdered his brothers all through history and his brother species all through prehistory. Suppose I don't dismiss it. What then?"

"Then you examine the criminal's record a bit more thoroughly. What about the other species—those you might call his cousins? I've told you of animals he domesticated: the ox, the ass, the horse, the dog, the cat, the pig. Do you know what is covered by the word domestication? Castration, for one thing, hybridization, for another. Taking the mother's milk away from her young. Taking the skin away from the body. Taking the meat away from the bones, as part of a planned economic process, and training one animal to lead others of its kind to slaughter. Taking the form away from the creature so that it becomes a comic caricature of its original self—as was done with dogs. Taking the purpose away from the generative powers so that it becomes a mad, perpetual factory of infertile eggs—as was done with hens. Taking its most basic expression of pride and turning it into drudgery or sport—as was done with horses and bulls.

"Don't laugh, Eric. You're still thinking of man's survival, but I'm still talking of man's very ancient moral sense. You do all those things—to your fellow creatures, your fellow species, your fellow men—you do all those things for millennia upon millennia, while you are examining the question of good and evil, of right and wrong, of decency and cruelty, you do all those things as your father did, and his father before him, and do you mean to tell me that whatever plea is made to justify you—by science, by philosophy, by politics—you are not going to feel forever and omnipresently guilty as you stand shivering and naked in your own awful sight? That you're not going to feel you have accumulated a tremendous debt to the universe in which you live, and that the bill may one day be presented by another species, slightly stronger than yours, slightly smarter, and very different? And that then this new species will do unto you as you have done unto others from the beginning of your life on the planet? And that if what you did when you had the power was justified, then what will be done to you when you no longer have the power is certainly justified, is doubly, triply, quadruply justified?"

Rachel flung her arms out as she finished. Eric looked at her pounding, sweating bosom. Then he followed the direction of her bowed head and stared once more at the transparent cages filled with human beings that dotted the white space beneath them, cages here, cages there, and cages into the furthermost distance.

Chapter 21

Eric learned many things. He learned about love, for example. He learned about the Aaron People.

Love he found very, very sweet. It started with lust and then became much more complicated. Some parts of it—some of the best parts—were downright incomprehensible.

He marveled that Rachel Esthersdaughter, beside whom he was still little more than a bare ignoramus, should defer to his decisions in all matters more and more every day—once she had made the initial decision of giving herself to him. He mar-

veled at the delight she showed in deferring to him, and at the admiration and pleasure she displayed in everything he said and did, he, a brash barbarian who had only
discovered from her recently—and then with open-mouthed astonishment—that
the burrows in which he had spent most of his life were no more than air spaces in the
insulating material with which the Monsters protected their homes from the unpleasant chills of Earth.

He wondered constantly at other changes in her, the way her mad, wild humor
seemed to dissolve in his embrace, the way her flashing grin would be insensibly
replaced by an intense, caressing smile and her customary twinkle by the most searching of looks in suddenly serious brown eyes. Those looks tore at his heart: they seemed
to express a hope that he would treat her well, along with a calm acceptance of the fact
that it was entirely his decision to treat her well or ill—and that whatever his decision, she would cheerfully abide by it.

He was entranced by the differences in her body, not the differences he had always
noted between man and woman so much as the unexpected ones: the smallness of
her fingernails, the otherness of her skin texture, the incredible lightness of her vast
length of brown hair.

"Most of the Aaron People have your kind of coloring, don't they?" he asked, holding her hair in his right hand and winding froths of it round and round upon his
forearm.

Rachel snuggled closer and rubbed the top of her head up and down along his
arm. "Most," she agreed. "We're a bit inbred, I'm afraid. It's been pretty much the
same genetic pool for generations. We don't capture many women from other tribes
and our Male Society rarely initiates an outside warrior."

"But they would take me? I mean, if we ever made it back to them?"

"They would, darling. They'd have to. I have too much knowledge and training for
my people to lose. And they wouldn't get me again without you. 'You take my Eric,' I'd
tell them, 'you take my Eric and make him feel nice and welcome and loved or I'll
get so unhappy that I'll forget everything I ever knew.' That's what I'd say, and there
wouldn't be anything at all to worry about. Especially these days, with their plans
about the Monsters and my very specialized and useful set of facts."

"These plans, Rachel: can't you give me some idea what they are? Hitting back at
the Monsters in a new and different way—it's so exciting, but every time I try to figure
out what they could be—"

She rolled away abruptly and sat up facing him. "Eric," she said, "I can't, and by
now you know better than you ever did before that I can't. Don't keep asking me. It's
a secret that has to do with the future of my people. I've been entrusted with it, and I
can't discuss it with anyone who isn't a member of my people. When you are, you'll
know—and you'll also be a part of the Plan."

Eric held up his hand in the gesture of peace. "All right," he begged, smiling. "Sorry
and never again." He waited for her to come back to his arms, but she continued to sit
a distance away, in thought.

"You were talking about making it back to my people," Rachel said at last, still looking off in the white distance, through the transparent walls of the cage. "Have you thought of how we might do it?"

"Escape, you mean?"

"I mean escape. From this cage."

"No, but I have a couple of ideas. One that I think might be good. It needs a lot of working out."

Her eyes swung back and met his. "Work it out then, darling," she said in a low, steady voice. "Work it out soon. We're liable to be pressed for time."

They sat and stared at each other. Then Rachel rose and Eric did too. She came into his arms.

"I haven't wanted to say anything— I thought— I wasn't certain. I am certain now."

"You're pregnant!"

She nodded, placed her hands on either side of his face and kissed him slowly, softly. "Listen, darling," she whispered, her cheek against his. "Any method of escape is bound to involve a certain amount of gymnastics. And at some time in the not too distant future, little Rachel is going to be a lot less limber than she is now. She's going to be very clumsy about climbing from one place to another—and she's going to be awfully slow if any running has to be done. If we make a move, it has to be well before that."

Eric held her tight against him. "Those damned Monsters!" he swore. "Their damned laboratory! Their damned experiments! They are not going to get my child."

"It could be children," Rachel reminded him. "You may be a singleton, but a real litter is still a definite possibility."

"There'd be no escape, then," he said soberly. "You're right: we've got to get out of here before you give birth. The sooner the better."

Rachel pushed herself away from him and turned aside. "Yes," she whispered, mostly to herself. "It was one thing to save our necks by giving the Monsters what they wanted: a breeding pair. But to give them the results of the breeding—"

"Stop it, Rachel! We're not at that point yet." And Eric moved off to make yet another circuit of the cage, yet another examination of Monster territory as it was visible through the transparent walls and floor. He had to be a warrior again, watching for an advantage, looking for a soft spot at which to aim an attack.

All of the plans for escape he had discussed with Jonathan Danielson and Walter the Weapon-Seeker had been inadequate; but here there was a new factor, something that had been nibbling at his mind for weeks. So far it had been only a nibble, not a bite. He concentrated on it demandingly, impatiently, both outer and inner eyes wide open.

There were no more lessons, at least none where the studies were guided wholly by the girl. Now he sat at her feet and asked her questions, pulling her back and forth in the areas of knowledge that corresponded to the places where he felt the nibbling sensation in his mind.

"Rachel, I must know about every single item in the pockets of your cloak. That small, pointed thing, for example—"

"You told me once what your people think this entire Monster dwelling looks like. Could you draw a picture of it for me—"

"Can you cut up a few small sections of the cloak? Can they be sewn together? You said you had some kind of adhesive, didn't you—"

"Rachel, darling, can you tell me in simple, noncomplicated language what you know of the principles behind the various vehicles our ancestors used? Automobiles, boats, airplanes, spacecraft. Whatever you know about them, whatever you can explain—"

Sometimes he amused her. Sometimes he almost terrified her. Always he ended by exhausting her. "There *is* a difference between men and women," she would mutter as she fell back finally, locking her arms behind her head and closing her eyes. "And now I know what it is. Women have to rest. Men don't."

Truly, Eric seemed to have no need of rest. He would prowl up and down the cage in long, springy, nervous strides, shaking a single fist over and over again, as if he were trying to hammer an idea open in mid-air. Or he would sit in a corner, staring down at a Monster going by—but while he sat and stared, his whole body would vibrate, faster, faster, faster. Or he would get involved in experiments: experiments with the properties of some piece of equipment in the cloak, experiments that could be conducted only when food was being dropped in, or only when the cage was being flooded and washed, or only when one of their immense captors had come by to look them over.

In the beginning, Rachel worked with him and tried to help him—that is, when she could find out what it was that he was investigating: frequently he had no idea of the goal himself. But more and more she tended to leave him to his own researches. She would answer the questions he suddenly snapped at her, giving him relevant data or her carefully considered opinions. Otherwise, she was content to lie and watch him work, smiling at him fondly whenever he turned a look murky with concentration in her direction. And more and more, she spent her time stretched out at full length, dozing.

He understood, even though it was infuriating not to have the full, alert services of her well-stocked mind. First, he was her man: she had put herself and their mutual problem in his hands—and she trusted him. But more important, something was at work that he had seen many times before among the females of Mankind: pregnancy usually created a certain placid euphoria in a woman; it was as if her thoughts were pledged exclusively to the helpless thing growing slowly within her body. With Rachel it was starting early.

Eric understood, but the understanding only made him more frenzied, more restless, more probing and determined. It was up to him and him alone whether his family were ever to wander in the burrows as free creatures—or whether they were to be forever caged and at the mercy of the Monsters' agony-filled investigations. He would escape, he told himself, beginning yet another new line of experimentation. He would. He would.

One day there was an interruption. A Monster came by and dropped Roy the Runner into their cage.

At first, Eric had scrambled for a spear as the strange human, released from the green rope, had struggled to his feet near where Rachel sat, both hands over her mouth and her eyes wide with fear. Then he recognized Roy and called out his name. All three of them relaxed and exhaled prodigiously. They grinned weakly at each other.

The Monster, satisfied after a period of watching that no mayhem was to be committed, rumbled its tremendous bulk away on other business.

Eric had told Rachel about Roy. Now he introduced the Runner to his mate. Roy was enormously impressed. A woman of the Aaron People, willingly, without coercion… His voice, when he began telling the history of the other cage since Eric had left, was low and almost greasily respectful.

"After they took you out, we didn't have a leader for a while—the men had lost the habit of following Arthur the Organizer. He'd lost something also: he wasn't very eager to give orders anymore. So I tried removing my head straps and letting my hair hang free again. You know, to look like you. I figured if I looked like you, maybe the men would take orders from me as if you were giving them. Only it didn't work. Walter the Weapon-Seeker took over for a while, until the—"

"That's it, Eric," Rachel broke in. "The loose hair. That's why they brought him here." She tumbled the hair at her neck with the back of a hand. "The loose hair. You, me, the Wild Men. The Monsters don't know I'm pregnant. They're still trying to get me mated."

Eric nodded, but Roy the Runner looked very puzzled and stared first at one and then at the other of them. "Go on, Roy. I'll explain it all later. How many of the expedition are left?"

"Practically none. About six, besides me. And not all in those Monster experiments, either. A lot of them died in the fighting."

"Fighting? You started fighting among yourselves?"

The tall thin Runner shook his head impatiently. "No—what was there to fight over? Lots of food and no women. What happened was the Monsters put a whole flock of strange men in our cage, men like you've never seen or heard about. I mean not Wild Men even. Little brown men, about half our size, but strong, strong as hell. They didn't use spears. They had clubs and something they called slingshots. It was hard to understand them. They talked—I don't know, they talked funny, not like other human beings at all. None of the Strangers had ever seen men like them before, not Arthur the Organizer, not anybody. They had names like Nicky Five and Harry Twelve and Beelzebub Two. All of them had names like that—it was crazy."

A small noise from Rachel. Eric looked at her. "I know about them," she said. "They're not from this house at all. They're from another house, the one next to ours. Naturally, another house—they're almost a totally different breed of humanity. Men from my people have visited them and brought back some strange, strange tales."

"What does she mean, 'another house'?"

"A Monster house," Eric told Roy. "All of us—Mankind, the Strangers, the Aaron People—we all live in the walls of one particular Monster house. Actually, we all live in just one wing of that one house. In the other wings, there are lots of other peoples, some like us, some different. But people who live in another house entirely have to be very different from us. They've been breeding away from us for centuries, and their language and culture have been changing." At the Runner's bewildered expression, he said: "All right, Roy, I'll explain that later, too. Don't worry about it now. These men came into the cage and started fighting?"

"They did, from the moment they arrived," Roy answered, relieved to get back to a matter that was familiar and somewhat understandable. "They were screaming, just as we were, when the Monsters dropped them into the cage. Then they calmed down: they stopped screaming and they started fighting with us. They didn't like anything we did. They said we didn't even know how to eat: the only right way to eat, according to them, was stretched out at full length on the floor of the cage, face down. And you weren't supposed to touch the food with your hands—you had to eat it off the floor. There were lots of other things: the way we slept, the way we talked, the way we moved our bowels. Everything had to be done their way—they were like lunatics! Day after day we lived in opposite corners of the cage with sentries posted while we slept, and every time we were fed—or watered—or anything—there'd be a full-scale battle in the middle, spears against clubs and slingshots, and three, four corpses for the Monsters to dispose of."

"Finally, though, you beat them?"

"Nobody beat anybody. What happened was the Monsters brought up a big sort of buzzing machine and put it over the cage. From that time on, whenever you felt mad enough to kill someone, you got a terrible pain in the head, and it got worse and worse until you thought you'd go clear out of your mind. The moment you stopped thinking about killing, the pain disappeared. Let me tell you, Eric, we got to be friends, us and those strange little brown men! We got to be friends, no more arguments, no more battles, no more killing—just the Monsters taking a man out every once in a while and tearing him to pieces. You know, good times again?"

Eric and Rachel smiled grimly.

"That's what I expected was going to happen to me when they pulled me out today. Eric, was I glad to see you! I thought you'd been sewered a long, long time ago. They took Arthur the Organizer out only two days ago. He was lucky: they dropped some black powder on him and he was dead fast—just like that. But Manny the Manufacturer—"

Eric held up a hand to stop him. "I'm not interested in that," he said. "Tell me: you said that sometimes there were three or four corpses to dispose of while the fighting was going on. Were they all taken out of the cage together?"

The Runner screwed up his eyes and thought back. "I think so. Yes. Yes, they were all taken out of the cage at the same time. Once a day, whoever was dead, down would come the green ropes and out they'd all go together."

"And whatever they were wearing, whatever spears or clubs might be lying across their bodies—that would go out too?"

"Sure. You saw it. Remember the guy that Walter said was from the Aaron People, the one who died the day after we arrived? They took him out with his skirt wrapped around his face just the way we had placed it. That's the way they dumped him into the black hole—that's the way they do it with everyone who dies in the cage."

"The Monsters do seem to have a thing about death," Rachel mused aloud. "Or at least death as it has to do with human beings. Their interest in us is strictly *in vivo*, as the ancestors would say. But what difference does that make to you, Eric? Once we're dead—"

"Once we're dead, we have a good chance to stay alive," he told her. "And I'm not being funny. Roy, do you want to escape with us?"

After one startled stare, the Runner bobbed his head emphatically. "Do I! Any plan you have, no matter how dangerous it is, count me in. The way I see it, there's no real future here for an ambitious young man."

"The plan I have is very dangerous. An awful lot of things can go wrong, but it's absolutely the only way out of the cage that I can see. All right, let's get started."

Under his instructions, they went into action. He drove them both the way he'd been driving himself, doggedly, unremittingly. And the work went fast.

But once Rachel looked up and asked anxiously: "Aren't you taking a lot for granted, Eric? You have inference piled on inference. We don't know that much for certain about the construction of Monster houses."

"If I'm wrong, we'll be killed. And if we stay here?"

Rachel put her head down, sighed, and went back to her task.

Another time, it was Roy who exploded. He was learning and growing, too—and becoming less deferent. "Look, Eric, you have no reason to believe these things work. Even Rachel—who's from the Aaron People—even she says she's never heard of these things before."

"Yes, she has. She knows them under another name—the Archimedes principle. And I told you, I've experimented with them. I've experimented with them over and over again. They'll work."

When they were almost finished with the construction, they began timing the approach of the Monster who fed them every day. Eric's plan was complicated enough: if the strains upon them were not to be too great, they had to initiate their operation shortly before a feeding time. And it was necessary for them to store food and drinking water. Who knew when they would come close to these essentials again?

Rachel looked at her torn and shredded cloak, the equipment from its pockets scattered about the floor of the cage like so much litter. "The only thing," she said in a low, miserable voice, "that I find really painful, darling, is your destroying my protoplasm neutralizer. The work, the research, that went into that gadget! And it was the whole point of my being sent into Monster territory. To go back to my people without it, after all this—"

"If we get back to your people," Eric told her calmly, working away at a folded section of the rodlike device, "the most important thing you can tell them is that the neutralizer works. Once they know that, they can build others like it. Meanwhile, we have nothing else we can turn into a really strong hook. And without a strong hook—even if everything else works right—we don't have a chance."

The Runner came across the cage and stood beside him. "I've been thinking, Eric. You'd better tie the hook to *my* hands. I'm at least as strong as you. But you're smarter: I think you'll do better with the opening. I promise to hang on with all my might."

Eric finished twisting the rod of the protoplasm neutralizer into a serviceable hook. Then he sat back and thought. He nodded. "All right, Roy," he said. "That's the way we'll do it. But don't let go!" He put the uncurved end of the hook into Roy's hands: the Runner gripped it firmly. Then Eric tied the device to Roy's hands, running more straps from it around his arms, back across his shoulders. The hook had become almost a part of Roy's body.

Now they tied themselves and their equipment to the remains of the cloak. The two men adjusted their forehead glow lamps for the last time. Eric put Rachel between himself and the Runner, lashing her first to Roy's waist and then to his. "Hang on to Roy's shoulders," he advised her, "just in case the straps go. I'll be hanging on to yours."

When he was through, they were three people who formed a bound-together unit, at the furthest end of which was Roy the Runner holding a long hook that was tied to his hands as an extra precaution. They heard the Monster approaching with the food, and they lay down clumsily.

"Here we go, everybody," Eric told them. "Play dead!"

Chapter 22

There was no shower of food into the cage. Instead, there was a long, almost unbearable pause in which they sensed the startled Monster was examining them.

They had agreed to keep their eyes tightly closed—as well as their limbs stiffly extended—until they were out of the cage and well on their way. For all they knew, Monster vision might be acute enough to detect their pupils moving. It also might be able to detect respiration, but here they had to take their chances. "Either we try to hold our breath as long as possible," Eric had pointed out, "and run the risk of a large, noisy gasp just when it's watching us most carefully, or we breathe as softly and as gently as we can. Tell yourself that you're asleep. Try to relax and hope we get away with it."

But it was hard. Moment after dangerous moment, it was hard to lie there perfectly still and not open your eyes for just one fast look at what was happening directly over your head.

At last there was a sensation of movement in the cage: the coldness of the green rope twined about their bodies, fusing itself to their flesh. A jerk, and they rose upward as a unit, their equipment knocking and slapping against them. Now real self-control was necessary; the experience of leaving a solid floor was terrifying enough, but panic began to screech and gibber behind eyes that could not see because they were squeezed shut.

The worst moment of all came when the Monster held them high in the air for a prolonged scrutiny. The ugly stink of alien breath grew overpoweringly strong—apparently the creature's head was very close to them. They had to appear limp and yet maintain control of their diaphragms. Eric hung on to a last inhalation, keeping his chest absolutely motionless. He hoped the others had done the same.

What was being felt by that enormous hulk of flesh? Disappointment over a promising experiment that had gone wrong so abruptly? Was the feeling at all similar to the one which humans knew? And would the disappointment be sharp enough to cause a change in the routine all three of them had observed the Monsters go through on such occasions?

"The Monsters do seem to have a thing about death," Rachel had said. They did: once a human captive appeared lifeless, they were interested only in disposing of him. A vital part of Eric's plan was based on this attitude; suppose curiosity about the causes of death and the changes inside a human body—suppose curiosity became dominant in the creature's mind. Eric fought hard to control a shudder. He failed. Beside him, in the circle of his arms, his mate's warm body shuddered in response.

Apparently having reached a decision, the Monster lowered them a little and set off.

Eric felt he could now venture a careful squint. He opened his eyes slightly, keeping his body, legs and arms as stiff as ever. Visibility was poor—not only were they spinning about at the end of the green rope, but the great bladders tied to each of his shoulders rolled from side to side and intermittently got in front of his face.

It was a long while before he could see for certain that they were being brought to the huge white table surface upon which dissections took place. So far so good. In the middle of the white surface was the dark hole at which his entire scheme had been directed. Would they be torn apart investigatively on the surface, or would they be dropped, casually and immediately, into the disposal hole, as they had hoped and planned they would? At this moment, after weeks of meditation on Monster behavior by himself and after days of reviewing the project with Roy and Rachel, it suddenly seemed too much to expect. He had been an idiot—they would never get away with it! How could he, Eric, have anticipated the thought processes of a Monster!

For that matter, how could the Monster fail to notice the odd equipment with which they were festooned, so unlike that of any other human captives it had ever seen? How could it fail to wonder at the three of them being tied so closely together? Better to untie themselves right now and be prepared to run in different directions as soon as they were deposited on the table top—one of them might survive, might escape. Bound together they'd be completely helpless!

Eric grappled with himself and managed to return to sanity. He must remember that the Monsters ignored all human artifacts. He had seen that proven out dozens of times, and Rachel, from her vaster knowledge, had assured him that no exception to the rule had ever been observed. The Monsters seemed to see no relationship between the equipment men carried about and the possibility of intelligence. It was not just that human artifacts and Monster artifacts were so utterly and essentially different. Men were no more than pests as far as the Monsters were concerned, scuttling, unthinking pests peculiar to this planet, pests who nibbled at Monster food and damaged Monster belongings. The things that men wore on their bodies or conveyed from place to place were the accumulations of vermin, the debris, the litter, of creatures rather low on the evolutionary scale. The Monsters apparently saw no connection between the men who bred inside their walls and the once-proud owners of the planet they had brushed aside centuries ago.

Nor was Monster ignorance on this subject at all remarkable, Eric thought bitterly. When you thought of the cultural abyss between the space-wanderers, the poets and philosophers that Rachel had described in her history lessons—and the blinking, fearful things among whom he had been reared...

No, the plan might work or it might not, but bolting to another one at this point would be bloody suicide. They would find out soon enough.

As he grew relatively calm again, Eric heard the harsh breathing of his companions and realized that pretty much the same thoughts had been going through their minds: they too had been thinking of cutting themselves loose from each other and preparing to make a run for it once they got to the white table surface. He was recalled to his responsibilities as commander.

"Easy, Rachel. Take it slow, take it slow, Roy," he whispered lightly. "Everything's working out fine—couldn't be better. Get ready to go into action."

He didn't dare turn to look at their faces, but the tone of his voice seemed to help. Short, convulsive breaths grew softer, gentler. And he remembered where the words had come from. These were the identical reassurances which his uncle, Thomas the Trap-Smasher, used to chant to the members of his band as they came face to face with battle-danger. Perhaps all military commanders, throughout human history, had used the very same words.

And now they were directly over the great expanse of white table. Eric felt his stomach shift and cower inside him. What was the Monster going to do with them? Was it going to—

The Monster did exactly as he had figured it would. It lowered the green rope to the dark circle of the disposal hole—and released them. If they were dead, they were garbage.

They plummeted down, holding tightly to each other. The hole seemed to widen enormously as they fell toward it.

Just as they dropped beneath its surface, there was a blast of sound. Roy the Runner had screamed. It was not a scream of pain. It was a scream of pure despair, of horror, of overwhelming misery. And, in a flash of sympathetic horror, Eric understood it.

Despite all their preparation and all their discussion, the same mad thought had been pulling against its strap in the back of his own mind, and he had fought hard to keep it from breaking loose. They were going down, if his calculations had been correct, they were going down into the sewers of Monster territory. Only dead people went into the sewers. They were going down to where the dead people were.

What avail were hours or even days of rational, intelligent talk about the use of

Monster plumbing as an escape route—what avail was conscious decision against the dread that had lain buried in one's subconscious since childhood, since one had seen the first corpse ceremoniously sewered? The moist, rotting legions of the dead inhabited the sewers, and the dead were vicious, the dead were nasty. They would allow no one to return who made the same grim journey that they had made.

That was what Roy had remembered at the last moment. Not the sewers as a possible line to freedom which the adult Roy was eager to investigate; but the sewers as a cemetery of time itself from which the child in Roy still shrank back in ultimate loathing. And he had lost control of himself. He had screamed.

It almost cost them everything, that scream.

The green rope whipped down into the hole after them. Craning his neck upward, at the rapidly receding whiteness in which the Monster's pink tentacles were framed, Eric saw the rope come to the end of its length a little more than a man's height above their heads. He saw it grow thin and dwindle in size, still twitching for their flesh, as they continued to fall.

Something hit them a tremendous wallop. It was as if they had smashed into the floor after a drop from a cage high up in Monster territory.

The water, Eric realized, a few moments after impact, as he struggled back to awareness. They had hit the water.

Instinctively, he had held his breath and tightened his grip even further on Rachel. And the straps that lashed them together were holding! Beyond the woman, he could feel her hugging Roy as they plunged down, down, down through the cold wetness. At least they were still together.

This much of his plan had worked. Now it was up to the bladders he had designed. A pair were tied to each of them at shoulder height. They were made of the waterproof material of Rachel's cloak, filled with air that had been blown into them and sealed with an adhesive the Aaron People had developed for mending garments.

"But Eric," Rachel had demurred. "It's never been tested in those conditions— under so much water and pressure for such a long time."

"Then we'll test it," he had told her. "We'll find out how good an adhesive it really is. Our lives will depend on it."

Their lives depended on additional factors as well. On their falling far enough to enter the main sewer pipe, for example. Otherwise, their bladders would take over and pull them back to the surface of the water in the disposal hole, where they would be helpless. The Monster could then pick them out at its pleasure.

They were still falling through the water, but they were falling more and more slowly. When could they breathe again? Down they went and down, and still there was nothing but water all around them. Eric began a slow slide away from consciousness. He dug his fingers deeper into Rachel's arms. His chest was exploding…

Suddenly, the quality of the water changed—and so did their direction. They shot off to one side in the midst of an incredible turbulence, going round and round each other, first this way, then that, up, down, up—and, at last, they stayed up.

They were in the sewer pipes, and they had surfaced.

The bladders kept their heads on top of the swiftly running current. Eric groaned air into his lungs; he heard Rachel and Roy doing the same. Oh, breathing was good, so good! The fetid air of Monster sewage was really *delicious.*

"It worked!" Rachel gasped after a while. "Darling, it worked!"

He forbore to tell her that it had only worked up to now. The third part of his plan was coming up. If that didn't work out right, everything they had achieved would be useless. Where did the Monster sewers empty? Rachel had suggested the ocean or a sewage disposal plant. He'd rather not find out.

"Are you all right, Roy?" Eric called, being careful to lift his chin so that none of the water got into his mouth.

"I'm fine," the Runner yelled back over the booming roar of the current. "And I've got the hook ready. You tell me when."

They were skimming down a pipe whose diameter, Eric estimated, must be about one-half the height of an average burrow. The curving top of the pipe was only a short distance above their heads—a little less than an arm's length.

A difficult command decision was involved here. The only way they could get out was through a pipe joint. Assuming they could open one from the bottom—and though Roy and Rachel had agreed with him that it was possible, they'd both looked as dubious as he felt—the selection of the joint upon which they'd make their attempt had to be a matter of fairly careful timing. It would be useless to try to open one that lay within the boundaries of Monster territory: there would be nothing but hard, immovable flooring above it. Once the pipe had entered the walls and begun running through them, it would be surrounded by the insulating material which human beings knew as the burrows. There, any given pipe joint might well be used for garbage disposal and burial of the dead by a tribe living in its neighborhood—and the tribe would have cut an opening in the burrows floor immediately above the joint.

Uncovering a pipe joint from the bottom would be an incredibly difficult and exhausting piece of work; if, at the end, they found a solid floor above them, they would have to enter the water again very tired and very discouraged. Logically, they should therefore make their attempt later rather than earlier. They should wait until they were certain beyond any doubt that they were back inside the walls.

On the other hand, the water was viciously cold, and being burrows creatures, long removed from the Outside, they were not at all used to cold. Furthermore, they kept passing the mouths of tributary pipes which belched more filth—and more water—into the main channel along which they were hurtling. This had two results: it kept raising the level of the water they were in closer and closer to the curving pipe top overhead—and it kept increasing the speed of the current. The first was frightening enough, but the increased speed might shortly make it impossible for Roy to catch on to a pipe joint with the hook that was tied about his hands and arms. And if Roy failed, they'd never get out.

No, Eric decided, he'd better take the very next pipe joint they passed. The result would be a matter of luck—and he had come to feel he could trust his luck. It was certainly much better than his father's: he had managed to get out of Monster territory, alive and with his mate.

He turned his head and peered down the pipe in front of them, examining its top with the beam from his forehead glow lamp. There, above the wild splashes of water and the somersaulting chunks of offal and rubbish, was that it—a dim patch that seemed to be rushing swiftly in their direction?

Eric narrowed his eyes and strained to see. Yes. It was a joint.

"Roy!" he sang out and brought his arm in a wide motion over his head, pointing with his whole hand. "Do you see it? We'll take that one."

The beam from the Runner's glow lamp crept along his own and focused on the patch in the pipe top, now only a short distance away. "I see it," Roy called. "Get ready. Here we go."

He swung his hook up as they sped under the joint, catching an edge of it. For a moment they paused, swinging from side to side in the noisy, cascading water. Then they were on their way again. The hook had slipped out.

Roy cursed himself bitterly. "I didn't get a grip on it! I almost—damn it, I didn't get a good grip on it! I should be sewered alive."

In spite of their predicament, Eric found himself grinning. That was exactly what was happening to the Runner! But he didn't bother to point it out. "My fault," he told him instead. "I didn't give you enough warning. I'll let you know earlier next time."

But he was worried. The cold from the water had begun to numb his body. The other two were no doubt losing sensation as well: that would make it more difficult for Roy to hold on with his hook. How had the ancestors ever been able to survive low temperatures in the Outside? According to Rachel, some had even thrived on it and taken recreation especially in cold weather. What heroes there must have been in those days!

Well, he was no hero: he found the cold crippling. And it was getting worse every moment. Also, the current was observably much faster than when they had started. If Roy managed to hook the next pipe joint, Eric decided, he couldn't be expected to cling to it for long. They'd have to move very fast indeed.

With this in mind, he reached down to his waist strap and pulled out the knife he'd taken from Jonathan Danielson's body in the first cage a long, long time ago. He cut the thongs that bound him to Rachel. Now, only his arms were holding them together, but he'd be able to do his part of the job much more rapidly.

"How are you, darling?" he asked, suddenly conscious of the fact that she had been silent for some time. This was a pregnant woman, after all. She didn't reply. "How *are* you?" he demanded more urgently.

"I'm cold," she said in a low, dull voice. "Eric, I'm cold and I'm tired. I don't have much left."

Frantically, he turned his head again to scan the top of the pipe. The next chance would be their last. He'd better give Roy plenty of opportunity to prepare. And this time Roy had better—

The moment Eric saw the faint trace of a patch in the distance, he called out and pointed. The Runner located the joint, set himself. "I won't let go—I promise you!" he said between clenched teeth.

As the joint passed overhead, he thrashed wildly with his legs, rising slightly out of the water. He slammed the hook into a crack that ran along an edge of the joint—and twisted it. The curved end of the hook slid and locked inside the joint.

"Up to you, now, Eric," he gasped. "Go ahead!"

Rachel was still tied to Roy, but Eric, depending solely on his grip, was almost torn loose by the suddenness of their stop. It was by one hand only, a hand slipping up her arm to her throat, that he still held himself to her. He threw the other arm around her again and pulled himself close.

Then, reaching past her to Roy, he hauled himself up and over both of them, clambering across their madly jerking bodies until he stood on the Runner's shoulders. These were wet and slippery, but he was able to grab the middle of the hook with his left hand and steady himself. He whipped out his knife and went to work, ferociously, on the joint. Under him, the Runner fought for air, as with Eric's full weight upon him, his face would go slightly below the level of the water, slightly above it, then slightly below again.

Eric knew exactly what he had to do. He had been over this sequence in his mind dozens and dozens of times. He had been reviewing it while in the water, while looking for a joint in the distance, while climbing over Rachel to stand on Roy's shoulders. He had to reverse the process of opening a joint that he had used when standing on the floor of the burrows.

It should work.

On the burrows floor, you first tugged the covering plate to the right. Therefore, operating from underneath and using the knife, Eric pried it to the left. He switched the knife to the other side and pried to the right. Now, at exactly the right moment, while the heavy plate was still sliding, pull down on the knife handle, making the knife into a lever—and pray it doesn't break!

The plate moved upward. Eric let go of the hook with his left hand and grabbed the edge of the plate through the open space he had created. He pushed with all his might. The plate rolled off to one side.

He pulled himself out of the water and through the open joint. Crouched uncomfortably now on top of the pipe, he had flooring directly above him. The question was, what kind of flooring—Monster territory or of the burrows? And if it were burrows flooring, had there been human beings nearby to cut an opening through it?

There had, and he slumped for a moment in abject relief as he saw the familiar outlines of a slab. They could get out! Again he jabbed his knife in the thin space where edge met edge and used it as a lever. Once the slab lifted a bit, he put his shoulders under it, bracing his feet on the pipe—and straightened, pushing up. The slab rose and fell away from the opening, rattling the floor with its weight.

Eric, standing fully upright, could see curved walls and low ceilings all around him. The blessed, blessed burrows!

He scrambled back down and lay on the surface of the pipe, reaching through the joint. The Runner's face was bluish and Rachel's head lolled limply against his back. "Can't help—you much," Roy panted from the water. "You'll have to—all by yourself, if you can. I'm—I'm finished."

Eric got his hands under Roy's armpits and tugged. The Runner and Rachel came up easily about halfway, but there, with no more water to buoy them, they became suddenly far too heavy for him to lift any more. He held on desperately. Then Roy made a last effort. He got his elbows, still tied to the dripping hook, over the top of the pipe and heaved. It was just enough to make a difference. Eric was able to pull them both on to the pipe. They rested for a moment, then Eric and Roy together dragged themselves and Rachel through the opening to the burrows floor.

There they lay, exhausted.

But Eric was a commander—and a husband. He had responsibilities. He forced himself upright and cut Rachel loose from Roy, Roy loose from the hook. Then he addressed himself to his mate.

Her appearance frightened him. She was barely breathing, and her body was cold, very cold. With his own teeth chattering, he began rubbing her body furiously. He massaged her chest, he worked her arms back and forth, he chafed her feet. "Rachel," he called in agony. "Rachel, Rachel darling!"

After all this, to lose her!

Her eyelids fluttered open. "Hello, sweetheart," she said weakly. She took her first deep breath. She took another and managed a smile. "Hello," she said again in a voice a bit more like her own. "We made it!"

"We made it!" Eric joyfully agreed. He hugged her and kissed the paleness from her face. Then he put the joint cover back in place, and returned the slab to its socket in the floor. He was paying respect once more to the human housekeeping habits of the burrows.

"Take my equipment, Roy. Rachel, put your arms around my neck. I'm going to carry you."

"Where?" the Runner asked, picking up Eric's gear and getting heavily to his feet. "Why do we have to move?"

"Because we don't know what kind of tribe may use that particular sewer opening—or how soon they're liable to use it again. We're going to get a distance away and find a safer spot before we begin resting."

Rachel was fairly heavy now, and Eric's weariness hurt all along the calves of his legs and the muscles of his shoulders. But he couldn't ask her to walk so soon after the experience she'd undergone. She went to sleep, nestling her head against his chest.

He didn't go far—just a few burrow turnings, past a couple of intersections. "This is where we'll sleep." he said, putting Rachel down carefully. "I hereby declare it night."

"We made it out of Monster territory," Roy marveled. "Out of the Cages of Sin, out of the sewers themselves. We're alive and safe and warm."

"And we have no idea," Eric reminded him, "where the hell we are."

Chapter 23

Coming awake, Eric paused for a while and thought before announcing the dawn. He caressed his wife as she lay against him, her head on his right shoulder, her mouth nuzzling his chest. Rachel still looked very tired. He decided to stay in this spot and give her another day of rest.

But, once she was up, she wouldn't hear of it. "I know what you're afraid of. You're worrying about a miscarriage. Darling, if it didn't happen yesterday, it's not going to happen. We women of the Aaron People are just as hardy as the females of any front-burrow tribe."

"There's a long journey ahead. Many, many days of travel."

"All the more reason to start immediately, dearest. We don't have food for many, many days. And we can't spare the time for a detour into Monster territory to pick up more. I'll be all right. If I find I'm giving out, I'll start drooping immediately. I promise not to push myself—I'll droop noticeably and emphatically, all over the burrows floor."

Roy, who had come up and squatted near them, said he agreed with Rachel. "It's not only going to be a long journey, Eric. It's liable to be a meandering one, full of false starts and wrong turnings and going back along the way we came. You said last night you didn't know where we are—it's going to be even harder to find out where we want to go. I say let's start now."

Knowing they were right, Eric nevertheless fought to give Rachel a little more time. First, of course, they had to have breakfast. After that, he ordered their equipment checked and inventoried, their food supply examined for possible damage from the lengthly submersion. He sent Roy off to empty their canteens and then refill them with fresh water from the pipes that always ran parallel to the sewer system. And, finally, he asked for the map that Rachel carried and insisted on examining it thoroughly for clues as to the route they might take to their agreed-upon destination—the burrows of the Aaron People.

Roy was very much excited by the map: he'd never seen one before. Having returned with the canteens, he lounged behind Eric and stared respectfully at it, trying to understand how this odd network of lines could be considered a picture of the burrows in which a man traveled with walls on either side of him and fought or avoided enemies. Eric answered his questions patiently and in great detail: every explanation, every digression, meant that much more rest for Rachel. The girl napped on the floor a little distance from them, her face still somewhat haggard and her hands clasped on a belly that was just beginning to look rounder than normal female plumpness.

But as soon as the Runner understood that the place where they were now was not to be found on the map at all, he lost interest. He moved away and began putting his equipment into expedition-readiness, tightening straps, examining his knapsack for any badly frayed area, assembling his spears in front of him and choosing the one he wanted most readily available in the back sling.

"It's like all the other stuff of the Aaron People," Eric heard him grumble. "Just like the rest of these Strangers. They have things that sound great, that are wonderful to look at—only, please, if you don't mind, we can't use it right now. It's not good in this spot, we'll use it tomorrow, we'll use it next week. Damned mouth-warriors and their phony gear. *Maps!*"

Eric was irritated and wanted to remind him of the Aaron People gear that had helped them escape from Monster territory: the waterproof cloak they had used to make bladders, the protoplasm neutralizer that was the only piece of metal among them long enough to be bent into a hook. And how long was it since Roy had been so pathetically imitating Stranger dress and Stranger habits of speech?

But the three of them would have to stay close and depend on each other in the long, difficult journey that lay ahead. A commander, Eric had noted long ago, observing his uncle, did not allow himself to get into arguments, unless they involved a direct challenge to his authority or some other form of danger to the group he led. Besides, Eric suddenly smiled to himself, Roy's griping really meant only one thing: he was back in the burrows and feeling like a warrior of Mankind again.

So did he, he realized. And it was good to be practicing your trade again. Until they reached the Aaron People, at any rate...

He jumped to his feet, then, to get away from the thought that had begun crowding in on him. "All right, everybody," he called, in the ancient band call whose last meaningless phrase was supposed to have come all the way down from the ancestors: "Let's hit the road!"

A few moments later, they were going down the tunnel in single file, Eric in the lead and Rachel in the middle. Since their experience of the day before, he found himself constantly aware of something he had taken for granted all of his life: the warmth of the burrows. It was warmth, he knew now, that the Monsters needed and created for themselves. But it was certainly very comfortable for human beings, too. Man and Monsters, he was beginning to understand, had surprisingly many similar needs.

Where was he leading this tiny band? They were completely lost, in totally unfamiliar and therefore very dangerous territory, yet Eric had an idea. He was an Eye, and an Eye should know the way anywhere he found himself—even if he'd never been there before.

At every branching burrow, he paused and took a good long look, first at the sides and in the distance for any lurking enemies, then at the floor. The floor was most important. Once in a while, he would decide a branch looked promising and turn off into it, the other two following and wondering.

The trouble was, he couldn't expect to see what he was looking for: it was more a matter of *feel*. And for this, this *feel*, his feet were more useful than his eyes. His feet had to find the way. He tried to see with his toes, to watch with his heels, to peer with his soles. He was looking for any information about the floor of the burrow that his feet could give him.

When they stopped finally for sleep and the only big meal of the day, he pulled out the map and studied it. And he was studying it again the next morning, when he awoke Roy and Rachel; he was memorizing this picture of a burrows network far distant from the one they were in. He could see that it didn't make sense to either of them.

"What are you trying to find, darling?" Rachel asked at last, when, after much cogitation, he led them up a branch burrow and, after shaking his head suddenly, turned around and led them back again to the intersection.

"I'm looking for a slope in the floor," he explained. "Any slope, no matter how slight. Your people are known among Strangers and Mankind as the furthest-back burrowers, the bottommost burrowers of all. Whenever Walter the Weapon-Seeker or Arthur the Organizer talked about the Aaron People, they told how they had gone *down* to them. Never *across* to the Aaron People, as when they visited each other's tribes; never *up* to the Aaron People, as when they traded with Mankind; but always *down*. It's the only general direction I have. To get to the bottommost burrow, I have to find and stay on a gradient."

"And if you do," she asked from behind him, falling into step once more, "what then? We may get down to the level of the Aaron People's burrows, but they might be ten or twenty days' march on either side of us. We won't even know *which* side."

"There," Eric shrugged, "I'll be counting on my luck. My luck's been good. And I'll be counting on the map. You see, at that point, the map—"

He froze, flinging up his arms for silence. Rachel and Roy stopped simultaneously in mid-step, staring over his shoulder.

There was a sentry ahead of them. The man was leaning against the burrows wall, facing in their direction, a spear trailing down from his hand to the floor. The light from his forehead glow lamp burned directly at them.

Why didn't he give the alarm? Eric and Roy both now had spears in their hands. Why didn't the sentry try to beat them to the throw?

"He's dead," Rachel breathed. "Don't you see? He's standing there, but he's dead. He's been dead for days. You can smell him."

And they could. Across the intervening space, there drifted the unmistakable odor of a corpse.

The man had died suddenly, while on duty. And he had not been sewered.

Very cautiously, one slow step at a time, they crept up to him. His eyes were open and steadfast, fixed on the tunnel he was supposed to guard, but a gray film had formed over them. His body too was gray: a gray liquid seemed to have oozed out of the pores of his skin and covered the powerful biceps, the alert face, the strong warrior's chest.

Eric looked him over, vaguely puzzled by something he could not quite place. The weapons, the equipment, the clothing—all were slightly alien, and all were, at the same time, tantalizingly familiar.

They went past the guard, walking on the balls of their feet, ready to break and run back at the slightest hint of active danger. After a while, the tunnel broadened into what Eric recognized as a central burrow, a large, high-ceilinged chamber very similar to the central meeting-place of his own people. Here, at last, they could relax and walk about easily, without fear of attack.

The central burrow was filled, from one end to the other, with nothing more hostile than corpses. Long-dead corpses.

Everywhere, men, women and children stood or sat like so many statues that had been carved to exemplify the full range of human activities. An old crone squatted at the magic of food preparation. A warrior lay on his belly watching her, a corner of his mouth twisted in anticipation. A mother had turned a small child over her knee and had her hand raised, high and angry, over his naked rump. A young man, lounging against a wall, was smiling ingratiatingly at a young girl going by, who, while totally oblivious of her admirer, apparently had no way of passing him other than cutting in close enough to brush against his folded arms.

All had succumbed to the same unexpected flash of death. All were covered with the same gray liquid from head to foot.

Seeing them here assembled, Eric understood what had been so familiar about the sentry. This was clearly a front-burrow people. The differences were minor and subtle ones, but he was standing in the midst of a tribe very much like Mankind. A little further along the wall, no doubt, but they were almost exactly as far from Monster territory as his own people. Their artifacts were as simple, their family and social life the same.

And there, sitting comfortably on a mound, surrounded by three women and benignly overseeing his tribe's activities, was an indubitable chieftain, as fat of body and as craftily stupid of expression as Franklin the Father of Many Thieves. Only the face was different.

Somewhere, nearby, there was probably a youngster who had been preparing to go on his first Theft....

Rachel turned from a body she had been scrutinizing closely. "This gray, moist skin," she announced. "I know what causes it. A homicidal spray the Monsters use. But I've only seen individuals who've been caught by that spray. Never a whole people."

"Well, the laboratory we were in, the experiments— The Monsters seem to be a lot more serious than they ever were about getting rid of us," Eric suggested.

The girl nodded grimly. "Very serious, indeed. Eric, we've got to get to my people soon. Not for our sake—for theirs. They have to know what's happened here. It's urgent."

"All right, sweetheart. I'll do my best. Is it safe to use any of the food in this place? I'd like to carry away as much as we can."

"Let me look around. Eric—don't you or Roy touch one of these bodies. That gray liquid can make you very sick. On contact."

Eric watched her opening food containers and sniffing at them gingerly. He was amazed at the strength of the feeling that billowed inside him: a tremendous warmth, a tremendous complacence.

At this moment, he felt for the first time that she was truly his wife. She had taught him a large part of what she knew. She had mated with him, and he had poured love into her body. She had conceived his child and was carrying it now inside her. But until he had stood in a great central burrow and seen her examining food to see that it was fit for him to eat—as all the wives of Mankind had done from his earliest memory—until now there had been something important that was missing. Now there was nothing missing: he knew he was married.

It was like Roy screaming when the Monster dropped them down the disposal hole that led to freedom. The scream hadn't begun then. It had been born long, long before.

A baby's first impressions are the adult's last conclusions—with an adjective or two added from a lifetime of experience.

When they left that great central burrow, the cemetery of a whole people, Roy was uncommunicative for a long time. He didn't even join the discussion by which they decided that to sewer this many human beings was utterly beyond their capacity. Eric thought he knew what was on the Runner's mind. Before they went to sleep, he told him of the similarities he had noticed between this tribe and Mankind.

"I keep thinking of Franklin and Ottilie and Rita the Record-Keeper," Eric told him. "I kept wondering if this spray had been used on them, if they were all standing around at this moment—everybody we knew—gray and wet and stiff and dead."

Roy lay back on the floor. "Mankind's dead," he muttered. "It's dead to me, anyway. I don't give a damn about Franklin and Ottilie and the rest." He turned over on his side.

But the next morning, when Eric awoke, Roy was sitting up, his hands clasped around his knees. He was staring at Rachel. There was a peculiar expression on his face which Eric found hard to analyze.

It was not at all like desire, but it had an uncomfortable intensity. Was the Runner thinking of his own mate, back in Mankind? Had he too observed Rachel selecting food—and had it reminded him of his own wifeless, completely outlaw state?

Eric didn't like it. As he led off after breakfast, he was unpleasantly aware of two situations: Rachel was immediately ahead of Roy where the constant sight of her would likely aggravate whatever was bothering the Runner; and he, Eric, was ahead of Rachel, his back an easy target for a spear cast by an angry, brooding man.

He thought of placing Roy in front of him: as a commander, that was his privilege. But Roy was no Eye, and an Eye was needed to find the way. Damn Roy! Trouble among themselves was the last thing they needed. Eric kept going, alert for any unusual noise behind him.

As a result, he almost led his command directly into destruction. He'd been so intent on what was going on to his rear that he'd failed to be properly aware of the sounds ahead. But as he was crossing an intersection, he heard them clearly. He shot one startled glance off to his left and immediately cupped a hand over his forehead glow lamp to obscure the light. He scrambled backward, shoving Rachel and Roy into the shelter of the branch from which they'd come.

"Wild Men!" he whispered. "A tremendous pack of them coming this way. Get your knapsacks off. We'll have to make a run for it." He wondered how fast Rachel could run. She'd barely been keeping up.

"Let me do it," Roy said, slipping out of his overloaded knapsack swiftly. "You two stay here."

Before they could stop him, he had darted out to the intersection with his forehead light uncovered. He looked off to the left, stiffening as if he couldn't believe what he saw. Then he threw his arms over his head and screamed. He screamed like one gone mad with terror.

The Wild Men heard him and saw him. They bellowed a wall-shaking hunger call in reply.

Roy turned and ran off to the right, screaming as he went. A moment later, the Wild Men roared past the branch in pursuit.

Chapter 24

Eric and Rachel had flattened themselves against the left-hand wall. They clung to each other, afraid to breathe, as the horde thundered past the intersection. If only one of these horrible creatures glanced in their direction, they were done for. They'd never be able to get out of their knapsacks in time, to pick up any speed.

But with live meat visible up ahead, the Wild Men concentrated on that alone. From time to time, they threw their heads back—it seemed in perfect unison—and screeched out a repetition of their hunger call. The rising and falling notes bounced savagely off the walls around Rachel and Eric and made their muscles go rigid with terror spasm. That was the main purpose of the call, Eric realized: to freeze the prey in his tracks. It also served to encourage the slower members of the pack and keep them aware of the hunt's direction.

He'd never seen a Wild Man before, but one look down the corridor had been enough to tell him that the legends had all been true and that Rachel's experiences in the cage had been fully as ugly as she had said. They were as Rachel had described them: a chilling throwback to some original version of the primate horde, and yet with overtones of an all-too-human mob. The mass of hairy bent-over figures, their fingertips dragging along the floor, shambling along in a tight pack shoulder to immense shoulder—somehow even the Monsters weren't as upsetting. These things were foul.

Since there were children among them—tiny bits of shrilling ugliness who bounced past as much on the knuckles of their hands as on their splayed feet—the pack had to consist of both males and females. Yet it was almost impossible to tell one from the other. Perhaps the shorter were female. But short and tall, they all looked alike: they all had vast tangled quantities of head hair—and they all seemed to have beards.

They poured past the intersection in a run that was part roll, part hop and part fast walk, and that had a surprising amount of speed to it. Many of them were holding grisly lanterns: torn-off heads which still had the glow lamps of warriors bound above the eyes. But they carried no weapons, they wore no clothing. They merely pounded on the floor with their fists as they ran and reiterated the slobbering screech of their call. And they exuded an enormous, collective stink that seemed to fill the burrows with its fog.

When the last bellowing straggler had scuttled by, anxiously considering its chance of getting a bite of the distant meal, Eric and Rachel each took an opposite strap of

Roy's knapsack and, heavily loaded themselves, began carrying it back down the tunnel in the direction of the last place they had slept.

There wasn't much chance they'd ever see Roy again, but if he escaped from the Wild Men, this was the only possible place for him to meet them. They got there, unloaded themselves and sank to the floor in each other's arms.

It was time for food, but neither of them even thought of eating. Food reminded them of the Wild Men—and the Wild Men's hunger.

Eric folded his arms and leaned against the wall near which Rachel was sitting. His ears were alert for any sound indicating the approach of Wild Men, but there was a deep, painful puzzle in his mind. "I've never seen anyone do that before," he said. "I've *heard* of such things, but only to save a tribe or a mate and children. And I thought—I was worried about Roy. He was so upset, so angry."

"He was miserable, darling. The closer we were getting to my people, the more he was brooding about his position once we arrived."

"You mean that he'd be nothing but an ignorant, front-burrow savage? I'm facing the same problem. I try not to think about it."

Rachel made a face. She lifted a foot deliberately from where she sat and kicked at his leg—hard. "You're my mate," she pointed out. "The husband of Rachel Esthers-daughter will automatically be a personage among the Aaron People. And you're not an ignorant savage anymore. At least, you're not ignorant," she added with a tiny, warm smile. "But Roy—he felt he had no skills, no knowledge, which would be useful where he was going, nothing to set him off and give him hope of winning a mate. He's had nothing, really, ever since he joined us in the cage. All the planning was yours, all the leading was yours. You pointed the way to every action and did whatever was important. And you were the one with a mate. Roy was feeling that he was just an extra—not at all necessary."

"He was sure as hell necessary in that escape from the Monsters. You'd never have been able to hook the sewer joint, Rachel, and hold on long enough for me to open the thing."

"But you never told him that, darling. Did you? And if Roy thought about it at all, he probably decided that any full-grown man who happened to be along could have done just as well. Roy wasn't *necessary:* nothing about Roy himself was necessary to anything we've done."

She was right, Eric decided. One hell of a commander he'd turned out to be! Leading and directing were only a small part of the command function, his uncle used to say—it was like making love without caresses.

And now there were only two of them again. How long would it be wise to stay here before giving up on Roy? How long would it be safe?

They heard footsteps coming toward them.

Rachel rose and stood behind Eric, who unslung a spear. The footsteps came closer, grew louder. Roy trotted around a curve in the tunnel.

"Roy!" they yelled, and ran at him with open arms. Rachel hugged him, covering his face with kisses. Eric pounded his back, grabbed a fistful of hair and pulled his head back and forth. "You old Runner, you!" he caroled ecstatically. "You crazy old heroic Runner, you!"

When they finally let him go, Roy shook himself and inquired mildly: "Where's the food? I built up a bit of an appetite."

Catching sight of his knapsack, he strode over to it, opened it and squatted to eat. There was a jauntiness in the Runner's bearing that Eric hadn't seen for many a sleep period.

They sat down next to him. "What happened?" they demanded.

"Nothing much," he said with his mouth full. "I led them around and around and around. Then I put on some speed and lost them. Most of the time I've been spending has been to get back here."

"You're wonderful!" Rachel told him. "You're absolutely wonderful! People will make up songs and stories about what you did."

"Oh, I don't know, Rachel. The whole thing wasn't much of a sprint for a Runner. For a real Runner, that is."

"And that's what you are," Eric said earnestly. "The best damn Runner in the whole twisting burrows! Where did you lose them?"

Roy grinned. "Remember that tribe yesterday? The poisoned people?"

They nodded.

"I led them back there. 'You want to eat people?' I said. 'Here you are. Some people. Eat them.' I hope they get a bellyache they'll never forget."

After the meal, it was a while before they started on their way again. They wanted to continue downhill, but it would be stupid to go back to where they had met the Wild Men. Eric had to find a gradient that ran in a slightly different direction.

He'd been turning an idea over in his mind. Now he took a small quantity of food and squeezed it into a ball. He rolled the ball up and down several corridors. When it rolled freely away from them, he picked it up and followed along the slope it had revealed.

In the next five days, they came across two more exterminated tribes. The situation in each was the same as in the first they had encountered, except that, from the greater abundance of material objects and handicrafts generally, Eric knew that in his own section of the burrows he would have labeled them "Strangers." Death had caught these men and women in mid-gesture also; here and there, a laughing child stood poised on one leg, forever immobilized in its play.

But there were individuals who looked frantic, or horrified. And on the further outskirts of these burrows, they found gray statues in running attitudes, whose backs were to their own central burrow. Apparently, there had been some warning—not enough.

They replenished their supplies of food and water at each place. No living thing came across their path, until—a full sleep period past the last of these tribal cemeteries—they saw half a dozen people at the far end of a tunnel. The other group tossed a few spears which fell harmlessly short, and then fled, shrieking.

Refugees from a poisoned burrow, it was obvious, since there were women among them. Refugees fearfully roaming the corridors in a group too small to put up any effective resistance against Wild Men or tribal enemies. Essentially respectable people who had been catapulted into the position of outlaws by the Monsters' pest control program.

"Alien-Science!" Roy commented heavily. "A religion that sets itself up to study the Monsters! Are we supposed to learn how to do things like this?"

"Is Ancestor-Science any better?" Rachel asked him. "You know, Roy, there was a place the ancestors had that they called Hiroshima." She told him about it.

When she had finished, he walked in silence for a few moments. "So they're both filthy. Then what's the answer?"

"The answer lies in a totally different direction. Wait till we get to my people. You'll see. A new kind of answer, a new way of—" She broke off. "Eric, what is it?"

Eric had stopped at an intersection formed by five branching burrows. He walked back slowly, retracing their footsteps to the previous intersection. This one was formed by three branching burrows. He pulled out the map, Rachel and Roy crowding around him.

"Do you see?" he said, pointing to tightly packed and crossing lines at the very edge of the map. "I think this is where we are right now." He smiled at Rachel, flourishing his education. "*Terra cognita,* if you know what I mean."

For a moment, they were all excited. Then Roy said: "There could be lots of places where a five-branch follows a three-branch."

"No, Roy, there aren't very many five-branch intersections in the burrows. You know that. And damned few three-branch ones. Most intersections are a simple cross-through of two tunnels that make four branches. I think we've arrived. We've been on the map for some time."

"Well, if it isn't the Aaron People!" Roy called out, walking up to a section of tunnel wall and holding out his hand in greeting. "How *are* you? and how are all the *little* Aaron People?" He came back to them. "Filthy snobs," he said. "They wouldn't speak to me. They cut me dead." He dodged the mighty punch which Eric swung.

But Eric was right, it became more and more evident. Every tunnel they passed through after this curved the way the map said it should; every intersection now occurred at exactly the right place and forked off in exactly the right manner. Finally, Rachel told Eric to put away the map. She knew the way and could lead them.

They came to an especially long, straight corridor. Three men stood guard at the end of it, two of them armed with long bows and the third with a crossbow. Eric recognized the weapons from Rachel's description of them back in the cage. Such arms could only be used in defense of Aaron People territory. Warriors were forbidden by law to carry them elsewhere; this was partially to prevent their falling into the hands of other tribes who might copy them, and partially to avoid alerting Monsters who might be able to construe these complicated devices as signs of certain human intelligence.

As they came closer, the guards fixed arrows into their bows.

"I'm Rachel Esthersdaughter," the girl called out, stopping a cautious distance away. "Remember me? I went on expedition to Monster territory. Jonathan Danielson was our leader."

The man with the crossbow was evidently the officer in charge. "I recognize you now," he said. "All right—keep coming. But, if you can speak to them, tell those Wild Men behind you to keep their hands high over their heads."

Roy spat angrily. "Wild Men! That's pretty big talk from warriors with such itsy-bitsy spears."

"Take it easy," Eric cautioned him. "Those itsy-bitsy spears can go through you faster and smoother than the longest one you ever saw." Still, it was hard to avoid becoming furious as he raised his hands into the air. Wild Men—it was worse than he had expected. And among these people he would have to live from now on. He was glad that Roy would be with him: someone besides Rachel would consider him human.

As they reached the guard post, Rachel pointed to a contraption that ran along the wall—a string telegraph, Eric realized. "Put me through," she said to the officer. "I want to speak to the Aaron."

"The Aaron? You mean the guard commandant."

"I do not mean the guard commandant," she told him imperiously. "I mean the Aaron. I want to speak to the Aaron direct. And you'll put me through immediately, if you know what's good for you."

The man stared at her. Then he walked to the string telegraph and began to pull on it in a series of rhythmic, staccato jerks. When he had finished and let go, it immediately began to jerk out a reply, tinkling, in the process, a tiny hammer and anvil to which it was attached. Rachel and he nodded when it had stopped, she in triumph, he with eyebrows raised and very respectfully. "All right," he said. "You're connected. Please feel free to use it as long as you like."

Rachel apparently felt free to use it very long indeed. While she worked away at the instrument, pausing every once in a while to hear a question or a response, Eric, still with hands achingly high above his head, took the opportunity to study his guards.

They all wore the skirts he had seen on Jonathan Danielson, short skirts with many, many small pockets. And their hair was tied in the back, Stranger fashion. Besides the bows with which they were armed, and the quivers of arrows, they each carried a single spear in a rather beautifully decorated back sling. But the spear was far too heavy to be used for anything but very close infighting, Eric judged. They looked very much like each other—like Jonathan Danielson—like Rachel. These people were inbred!

He found their warrior discipline highly questionable. Depending on the power and swiftness of their weapons, admittedly unique in the burrows, they were standing far too close to the prisoners. One or the other of them was constantly glancing at Rachel and trying to follow the conversation over the string telegraph. From time to time, all three of them would be looking at the girl. Two fast, tough warriors, like Roy and himself, might be able to take them, even from this position.

The Runner, thinking the same thoughts, nodded at him. Eric grinned.

Rachel called the officer of the guard to listen as the telegraph tinkled out a last response. "You two men," he said to Eric and Roy, in a relatively friendly voice. "You can lower your arms and do whatever you like. The Aaron says you are honored guests of our people, and I'm to serve as your escort. Anything you want, you ask me."

They walked past the guard post, leaving the other two men still on duty. "Well!" Eric said to Rachel. "This is more like it!"

She threw her arms around one of his and squeezed it. "I wanted you to come into our burrows as a free man and a proud one. That was the main reason I asked to speak to the Aaron, darling. But it turns out there are other reasons that make it a very good thing that I did. Our people were hardly hurt at all by the spray, but we know now we have to make our move very soon."

"The Plan, you mean? The Plan to hit back at the Monsters?"

"Yes. It goes into action immediately. There's a ship on the roof."

Eric came to a dead stop while he considered what she had said. "The roof" had to be the roof of the whole enormous Monster dwelling. And "a ship" meant only one thing: a spaceship. Could an entire spaceship—one large enough to transport dozens and dozens of Monsters—could it be accommodated on the roof of a single house? And wouldn't it destroy the house when it took off? He asked Rachel.

She shook her head impatiently. "They don't use rockets as our ancestors did. As far as we know, the ships that take off from the roof are combination lifeboats and ferry launches. We have good reason to believe they rendezvous with a mother ship somewhere near Pluto. They enter the mother ship and travel to the destination with her."

"But then—your Plan—"

Rachel kissed him. "I turn off here. I have to go to the headquarters of the Female Society and help assemble our neutralizers—now that we know they work. Everything has been set to go for a long time: we've been held up for lack of an effective neutralizer. I'll see you later in the Aaron's burrow, darling." She stopped on the verge of darting up a side corridor. "Feel free to ask the Aaron any question you want, Eric. I've made him understand what a dear, wonderful genius you are!"

And she was gone toward a slight glow in the far distance.

A few moments later, they came to a huge slab which completely blocked off the corridor, wall to wall, floor to ceiling. The guard officer jerked out the password on the string telegraph which, at this point, entered a wall. In reply, the slab moved smoothly up into the air, disappearing into a snug socket that was cut out of the ceiling.

Eric heard Roy gasp—and agreed with him. The technology of these people! No wonder the homicidal spray had not wiped them out.

The slab slid down behind them, and they found themselves standing before a series of enormous burrows, each one larger than the great central meeting place of Mankind. Monster territory dwarfed these burrows, it was true, but Monster territory alone.

Hundreds of fat glow lamps hanging from the ceiling lit the place. Crowds of people moved about in these burrows, along the floor and along galleries which ran overhead. Any given crowd was the size of the whole population of Mankind. Eric sensed that there were more of them about than usual, and that they were moving faster than they normally did. There was a feeling of hurry, an urgency in the air. People seemed to be packing goods and assembling in groups, both according to some prearranged plan.

He asked the guard officer if this were so. "Yes," the man said, pulling at his lip and sighing. "We've been drilling at it ever since I was a kid. And today it stops being just a drill. It's like the difference between real battle and a parade. You guys know what I mean."

"I wouldn't like to leave a home as comfortable and as safe as this," Roy told him.

"Well, it's not safe anymore. That's the point. The Monsters have been reaching out for us: they've been getting closer and closer. And the Plan—the Plan is the Plan. You people came back with the last vital piece of information."

It took them a long time to reach the Aaron's burrow, and Eric had learned a great deal before they got there. He had passed rows of cages filled with rats that the Aaron People had managed to preserve for research connected with the Plan. He had never seen rats before. "As pests, they were indestructible," Rachel had told him. "As food, the legends say, they disappeared overnight."

He waited, highly disturbed, while the strong-looking old man, whose cascades of unbound white hair poured down to his shoulders, gave a few last orders to the throng of subordinate officials. "That should be it for a while," the Aaron said. "Don't bother me unless there's a real emergency—Mike Raphaelson will handle everything else. I want to speak to the man who made this day finally possible for us." He gestured at Eric with his outstretched hand, causing the officials to turn in the direction he pointed with startled, but nonetheless warm, smiles. Off to the right, where he was standing with the guard officer, Roy waved proudly and encouragingly.

"Now then, Eric the Eye, Eric the Only," the Aaron half-sung to himself, picking up a document from the large table in front of him and studying it. "Eric, who successfully planned and led the only escape from Monster cages ever achieved by a human being—let me ask you this: are you willing to join our people? Of course you are, of course you are," he went on before Eric had a chance to say a word. "Rachel Esthersdaughter is your mate, and you have no people of your own. You'll be initiated into the Male Society a few days after we're under way. I'll be your sponsor. We don't have a Theft for a test of manhood, as your tribe does—we have an Achievement. Your Achievement, of course, will be the escape. Quite an Achievement. After the ceremony, you'll say a few words. No dance of triumph, or anything like that: just a short speech. It's customary to recite the details of your Achievement—very superficially, you understand—then to thank everybody, then to sit down. Any questions? No, of course not—it's simple enough. Now, once you're officially a member of our people, I don't see why I couldn't— Yes, I think I will."

As he bent over the table, scribbling a note into a corner of the document, Rachel Esthersdaughter, accompanied by several members of the Female Society, came out of a passageway nearby and stood behind him. Rachel, like the women with her, was again wearing an enormous neck-to-ankles cloak whose pockets were filled with equipment. Her dark brown eyes twinkled at Eric.

"The neutralizers all ready to be used?" the Aaron asked, not looking up from the document. "Good. You know your posts—move off. Rachel: you, of course, will stay with me at headquarters, wherever headquarters happens to be. Now, tell me, girl— I'm thinking of making this man of yours a section leader—do you like the idea? I'm sure you do. The leadership of Section 15 was vacant once you told us of Jonathan Danielson's death. Young man, do you think you can handle the lives and destinies of almost two hundred people? There will come a time when you will be alone in that position, when you will be exclusively in charge. Rachel will be your executive assistant, of course. I've put you down for it, and we'll settle the whole matter some time after your initiation. Let me see: we'll need the approval of a Council of the People, as well as the members of Section 15. No problem, there. To move on, however—"

"I don't think I can do it, sir!" Though Rachel had shut her eyes in a wince, he was pleased and astonished to find that he had actually managed to cut in.

The Aaron was even more astonished. He looked up from the document, turned around and studied Eric. Evidently, he was rarely interrupted. His flow of thought was listened to, taken as orders and acted upon.

"Eric, my boy," he said, clearly annoyed. "Please do not waste my time with modest noises. I am grappling with a major transition in the life of an entire people; I cannot be deflected for the purpose of administering first-aid to your ego. You commanded a pretty large group in the cages of the Monsters. You have been educated by Rachel, here, one of the finest minds among us. Anything else you need to know, I'll teach you myself, on the way. And if you're concerned about your front-burrow background, let me tell you this: in terms of our ultimate destination, the final goal of our plan, that background fits perfectly. You are an Eye, which none of us ever—"

"Pardon me, sir!" Eric broke in again. "But that's the reason I don't feel I can do it. It's not my capacity for leadership I'm questioning—it's the Plan. Let me explain," he said hurriedly to the Aaron's terrifying frown. "I didn't have any suspicion as to what the Plan was until I got here. I thought it was some combination of Alien-Science and Ancestor-Science, a new way of hitting back at the Monsters. Then, when I heard about the ship, I had the wild idea that you people were going to take it over, to use their own weapons against the Monsters. All right, it was naive of me—I admit it. But what you're actually planning has nothing to do with hitting back at the Monsters. You're just running away from them."

The frown slowly disappeared from the old man's face. He nodded, as if to say, "Oh, *that* problem." He hitched himself carefully up on a corner of the table and thought for a bit. "Try to understand me, Eric," the Aaron said at last, in a totally different kind of voice. "Try to understand me: put your preconceptions aside for the moment. Alien-Science, Ancestor-Science—we were the first to believe in each of them, here in the Aaron People, and we were the first to discard each of them, many auld lang synes ago. The Plan we have in mind *does* combine both Alien-Science and Ancestor-Science, but that is purely accidental. The Plan, we have come to believe, is the only real and valid way in which man can hit back at the Monsters. We are not running away from them, even though our position here has become more than a little untenable. We are running amongst them—directly amongst them, do you hear?—where we can hit back at them most effectively."

"Hit back at them how? As vermin?" Eric asked bitterly. "As vermin, stealing odds and ends from them for the rest of our existence as a race?"

A gentle, compassionate smile appeared on the Aaron's deeply lined face. "Eric, what do you think *you* are? What do you think you've learned to be best at all through your life in the burrows? Do you think you could change tomorrow and go back to planting crops or tending cattle—as your ancestors did? And if you could, would you want to?"

Eric opened his mouth and shut it again. He did not know what to say. He did not know what to think. Rachel slipped her hand into his and he found himself gripping it desperately.

"That's why we feel our Plan is thoroughly realistic. Our Plan recognizes a fact, Eric: that there are probably more people alive on Earth right now, living in the huge houses of the Monsters, than ever before in human history. And there's something else about human history that our Plan recognizes."

Clasping his arms on his chest, the Aaron shut his eyes and began rocking himself back and forth. His voice changed once more, this time to a kind of chant. "Man shares certain significant characteristics with the rat and cockroach: He will eat almost anything. He is fiercely adaptable to a wide variety of conditions. He can survive as an individual but is at his best in swarms. He prefers to live, whenever possible, on what other creatures store or biologically manufacture. The conclusion is inescapable that he was designed by nature as a most superior sort of vermin—and that only the absence, in his early environment, of a sufficiently wealthy host prevented him from assuming the role of eternal guest and forced him to live hungrily, and more than a little irritably, by his own wits alone."

Chapter 25

Nine days later, Eric stood on a ramp leading up to the Monster spaceship and, by the light of the moon, checked off on a repeatable slate the 192 members of Section 15 as they mounted past him on the way to embarkation.

He would never have believed it was possible to move literally thousands of men, women and children—the entire population of the Aaron People—so rapidly and so smoothly over such a vast distance. They had come from the very bottom burrows, over a route that went around and around in a gently ascending spiral through the layers of insulating material that packed the walls, all the way to a topmost hole that opened on the roof itself. They had lost not a single individual by accident or in battle, though they had passed across the territories of a hundred different tribes. Heavily armed men had seen to that, heavily armed men and experienced diplomatic officials who knew exactly when to negotiate, when to threaten and when to buy. Flying squads of trained emergency workers had swarmed to the scene of anything at all unusual; scholars and scouts had cooperated in selecting, from maps made long ago for this very journey, the best approaches and the most economical shortcuts.

It had been an incredible experience, an amazing performance by a whole society. But it had been in preparation for at least a full generation. Every one of the Aaron People had known exactly what to do.

He would never have believed what the Outside looked like—even after all that Rachel and the others had told him—until he had stood on the roof in the screaming sunlight and seen what it meant to have no ceiling at all, to be unable to observe a wall anywhere. At first, he had fought the terror—rising in his throat like a flood of vomit—simply to preserve his standing in the eyes of his section; but as he heard the whimpers behind him and realized that there were no sturdy explorers among his followers, only homebound artisans and their families, he had forgotten his own panic and gone among them, cheering and chiding and making suggestions. "Then don't look up if it's so upsetting." "Take care of your wife, you—she's fainted." "When you feel you just can't take it anymore, try kneeling and putting your hands on the floor of the roof. It's there, and it's solid."

Still, that first day had been pretty bad. The nights were better: there wasn't nearly as much open space to be seen. They traveled across the roof mostly at night, partly because they found it easier and partly because the Monsters seemed to dislike the night and were rarely abroad in it.

Now, they were embarking at night, climbing wearily up a ramp which led to a hold in which cargo was stacked. They were hurrying too: according to the records kept by the Aaron's planning staff, the ship was due to leave very shortly.

Out of the corner of his eye, as he crossed out the names which their owners announced, he could see his wife, Rachel Esthersdaughter, a dozen or so paces up the ramp from him. She and ten other members of the Female Society were manipulating the unfolded sections of their neutralizers over the writhing orange ropes which lay across the ramp at regular intervals. These orange ropes were the reason that the Monsters felt so secure about leaving their cargo hold open and the ramp down. Unlike the green ropes back in the Cages of Sin, the orange ropes repelled protoplasm violently. It was impossible for a man to approach them in any way without being knocked flat on his back, at the least. Sometimes, they had killed those who got too close. But now the orange ropes wriggled and were harmless.

Eric remembered a comment he had heard at a section leaders' meeting the night before. "The Monsters develop their penetrating spray, and we develop our neutralizer. Everybody makes a breakthrough. Fair's fair."

Roy came up the ramp, waving his hand to indicate that the last of the section had preceded him. Eric checked his list: yes, every name was crossed out, every name but Rachel's. He put the slate under his arm and followed the Runner. Behind him, the leader of Section 16 took his place on the ramp and propped up a slate full of uncrossed names.

As he passed Rachel, Eric lingered for a moment and stroked her arm tenderly.

"You look so tired, darling," he said. "Haven't you done enough on this job? You're pregnant."

Holding her neutralizer in place, she leaned over and kissed him on the cheek. "There are five other pregnant women on this ramp, Eric, or hadn't you noticed? I'm on my last shift. I'll be joining you in the ship very soon."

At the entrance to the hold, where the crowd was still sorting itself out, a young man wearing the brassard of an expeditionary policeman had a message for him. "You're to join the Aaron up ahead. He's with the men assigned to cutting a hole in the wall. I'll take over your section."

Eric gave him his slate. "When my wife comes, please send her directly to me," he asked. Then he signaled Roy to follow and walked along the path indicated by men stationed every thirty or forty paces. Around them, on every side, were great containers piled up to the ceiling. The place was brightly lit, as he now expected Monster territory to be. Monsters left the lights on while they slept.

He arrived at the wall just as the sweating men finally pulled the slab they had cut out away and to one side. A great mob of people had been watching anxiously. It was getting close to dawn, and everyone knew it.

The Aaron was sweating, too. His eyes were red-rimmed. He looked as if he had just about passed the point of complete exhaustion. "Eric," he said, "this is where we need you most. There are no maps from this point on. In there," he pointed at the hole, "only an Eye can lead us."

Eric nodded, adjusted his forehead glow lamp and stepped through the hole.

He looked about him. Yes, the usual tunnels and corridors. It would have been most unpleasant if the Monsters had not employed their basic insulating material in the walls of their spaceships. Here men could live as they were accustomed to live.

Calling back through the hole, he reported the information to the Aaron. A huge sigh of relief went up from the crowd outside. "Good enough," the Aaron said. "Go on ahead—you know what you have to find. We'll be enlarging the hole."

Eric started off. Roy the Runner came through the hole after him, then a series of the youngest, most agile warriors. They formed a single line, constantly enlarging itself from the hole.

He did know what he had to find, but, as he looked for it, past unfamiliar tunnels and completely unknown intersections, he was troubled by an odd factor he had great difficulty in pinning down. Then, as he came around a curve, and into a larger burrow just big enough to provide a temporary though extremely tight meeting place for all of the Aaron People, he understood what was bothering him. The odor—or rather, the absence of one.

These burrows were virgin. Men had never lived and died within them.

"Good enough," he said. "We can camp here until the take-off." And he posted sentries. No need really, but discipline was discipline.

Roy carried the message back swiftly. In a little while, people began to arrive: first expeditionary policemen, who set off areas for each section, then the sections themselves. Rachel came in with Section 15; by that time, the place was getting pretty crowded. The last one in was the Aaron—two husky policemen carried him on their shoulders and had to push hard to make their way through.

They could all hear a distant thumping by then. The Monsters were moving about and working on the machinery.

The Aaron put a megaphone to his lips. "Now hear me, my people!" he called out in a tired, cracked voice. "We have accomplished our Plan. We are all safely inside the burrows of a spaceship which is about to depart for the stars. We have plenty of food and water and can stay out of sight until long after the take-off."

He paused, took a deep breath before going on. "This is a cargo ship, my people. It will make many stops, on many worlds. At each stop, one or more sections will leave the ship and stay in hiding on the planet until their numbers have increased substantially. After all, anywhere that Monsters can live, humans can. Anywhere the Monsters have a settlement, men will thrive. Anything the Monsters provide for themselves, we can probably use. We have learned this on Earth—and we have learned it thoroughly."

The floor began vibrating as the motors went on. They felt the ship shake and start to move.

The Aaron lifted his arms above his head. People everywhere fell to their knees. "The universe!" the Aaron cried ecstatically. "My people, *henceforth the universe is ours!*"

When the ship had stopped accelerating and they could move about freely, Eric and the other section leaders collected their groups and led them to adjoining burrows. Men paced off the areas that their families would occupy. Women began preparing food. And children ran about and played.

It was wonderful the way the children adjusted to the acceleration and the strange, new burrows. Everyone who watched them at their games agreed that they made the place feel like home.

Afterword

Originally, this novel was no more than an outline, one of several requested in the early 1960s by a publisher who had read and liked my short stories and novelettes. The publisher had asked "for a couple of outlines," so I submitted proposals for two novels I very much wanted to write. At the last moment, to give the impression that I was a red-hot, eight-cylinder writer, I added a third, pretty much made up as I typed.

Perhaps inevitably, this was the one, *Of Men and Monsters,* that knocked out the publisher. The other two outlines were dismissed outright as much too complex, and even uninteresting, but *Of Men and Monsters*—wow!, bingo!, "yes, we do *want* that one."

I reacted with dismay, for something much like that had happened to me many times before. Most editors had not been impressed by proposals and outlines for work I badly wanted to do, even though they almost always had purchased the completed pieces—which, of course, I had had to write on spec.

But this time... The rejection of the other two outlines had been so emphatic, and the ardor with which *Of Men and Monsters* was embraced had been so vigorous, that there was no question as to the only book the publisher would now buy.

I responded as I usually did to such crises: I went into block. (I used to tell my writing classes at Penn State that I was convinced that Shakespeare was only the tenth best writer of his time: the other nine were all suffering from writer's block.) The outline was esthetically meaningless to me: It was a tale of Earth conquered by aliens and regained by humanity—it was essentially a dramatization and fulfillment of the cheap "ancestor science" of the later novel.

I pried and poked at the outline and could not get much past a fairly good opening sentence: "Mankind consisted of 128 people." Eventually, in one of my periodic rereadings of Swift, I came across the quotation from the voyage to Brobdingnab that I later used; it gave me enough to name and complete the first part—*Priests for Their Learning*—as well as titles for the other two parts.

Something like the picaresque occurred to me as a possible form, a complicated journey with rogues, or at least with incompetents. And the journey could be a maturing process, too, of course: we watch the boy become a man.

But I still had no novel, at least none with a *point.*

Various things happened. I sold the completed first part to Fred Pohl, the new editor of *Galaxy.* The money from the sale was terribly needed just then, but I still had to go out and get a high-paying job in advertising. Then what was to be the original publisher shrugged out of science fiction and, of course, my unfinished novel. I began writing good nonfiction, and found that I very much enjoyed doing it. I left advertising. I had done well enough to make it to the level of account executive, but I found advertising as well as the man who as my boss personified it far too fantastic to be believable to a mere science-fiction writer. And I tried to go back to the book.

But my phone rang constantly, pulling me from the typewriter (this was before the day of the inexpensive answering machine), and my callers all had bright ideas that took hours to detail or personal crises that were terribly complex and interminable. My wife, Fruma, who was now working as an editor at Harper and Row, pointed out that I picked up friends far too easily, among them cab drivers who had driven me for ten blocks, vacuum-cleaner salesmen who had made me feel guilty because we had no rugs for them to demonstrate on, and female solicitors for good-cause petitions who fell in love with me when I told them I couldn't sign because I was in favor only of very bad things. One evening, when my supper got cold because the phone rang each and every time as soon as I had hung up on the previous caller, she shook her head at me and noted, "You've done it, Phil. You've essentially used up New York City as a place to live."

I denied it. I felt there must be a way for a fellow even as chummy as I to go on writing and living in Manhattan. I decided to get an office, or a writer's equivalent of one.

There was an ad for an unfurnished room—toilet in the hall—above a low-grade men's clothing store on Sixth Avenue that was only three blocks away from the New York Public Library building. The rent (remember please, we're talking about the 1960s) was twenty-eight dollars a month.

For five dollars more a month, they said I could use their phone for local calls. I thanked them, but no. Absolutely no phone.

Fruma and I dragged a cot, a chair and a typewriter table up the stairs and into the room. We learned that the clothing store ended its day at 6:30 PM and put up a metal gate, unlockable only from the outside, in front of the store. There was no back entrance. We both decided that made the place ideal for me.

"All you have to do," Fruma told me, "is to remember to bring up some food at six o'clock before you get locked in. And absolutely not to make friends with any of the clerks in the store or the traffic cop at the corner. And write. And write. And write."

"You can visit me," I reminded her. "The one window in the room looks down into the street. Even after the gate closes, I can yell at you from upstairs."

"You write," she said. "You write that novel."

All well and good, I thought, as I lay on the cot nights, counting the multitudes of yellow plaster cracks in the ceiling. But still, still, what was the point of that novel that I was supposed to be doing nothing but writing? What was it that I cared about saying that the novel would say? Or, to put it another way, what was it about myself or my society that I wanted to investigate, using the novel as an excuse? It had been years since I had tried so hard to pursue affluence by becoming a literary hack, only to discover, as I have noted elsewhere in this volume, that I just did not have the vitally necessary talent of hackhood. I had learned that I couldn't keep writing unless what I wrote had some important meaning, at least for me.

All right, so the boy becomes a man. How? Well, for one thing, he ought to have a substantial and important sexual experience. With whom, with what kind of person? I brooded on that, night after lonely night, until, one afternoon, I broke and went home to Fruma, just—I explained to myself—to have a shower.

And in the shower it was that I first thought of her: Rachel Esthersdaughter. She would speak for me; she would explain the book to me. I hurried back to Sixth Avenue and completed the novel in several all-day and all-night sessions, not doing my duodenal ulcer any particular good.

I showed it to Fruma, who liked it even more than I. And then came the rewriting, making the first two parts mesh with the all-essential third, removing every solecism and cheapness Fruma and I could detect. (I did not remove as many of them from the first part as the second: after all, that was where the immature, half-formed characters had their domain.)

Here, I was interrupted by the most important event of my adult life, after my meeting and marrying Fruma—the move from the Village to State College, Pennsylvania, so that I could start teaching at Penn State. How much I was to find that I loved teaching is, I suppose, neither here nor there in this essay; but for what it's worth, those twenty-three years of teaching completed the construction of the person who's writing this essay.

So—before I go on—I have to say it again: teaching was the only thing I ever did that was as good as writing when the writing was going at its best. And it was wonderful living among colleagues who spent their lives pursuing truth and beauty—however much many of them in the course of this were brutally chasing truth and beauty away.

I had acquired a new agent, Henry Morrison, who sold the novel and several short-story collections, as a package, to Ballantine Books for enough money so that Fruma and I could buy our first house.

We loved that house. Gray Pennsylvania stone. We adored it.

And I was proud of the novel, something not usually true of my attitude when pieces of mine get published. I felt it was a pretty fair book, and the few reviews I got tended to agree with me. Judy Merril, in *Fantasy & Science Fiction,* and George Zebrowski, in *Twentieth Century Science Fiction Writers,* were especially nice about it.

Of Men and Monsters did enjoy a couple of printings, a couple of foreign translations. But it was really not noticed very much.

And it made very little money for the publisher. Or for me.

But, dammit, I've reread the book as it is printed here. And it was worth the writing.

WRITTEN 1965——PUBLISHED 1968

⁂

Afterword to
the Two Volumes

WILLIAM TENN: THE SWIFTEST TORTOISE
George Zebrowski

"The incredible William Tenn," as he has been dubbed by Brian Aldiss, began the whole school of comic and satiric SF in the 1940s. Or, one might say, he restarted a tradition that began with Jonathan Swift.

Usually, we hold Verne and Wells, along with Mary Shelley, to be the great foundations of modern SF. There was "Swiftness" even in them, but in Tenn it ran purer than in any other SF writer of his generation. He quickly seized upon a way of looking at things, at once funny, bitter, and serious, that made him the natural heir to the more softly celebrated tradition of Voltaire and Swift. Eric Frank Russell, Frederik Pohl, Damon Knight, Robert Sheckley, Fredric Brown, Cyril M. Kornbluth, Harlan Ellison, Norman Kagan, R.A. Lafferty, Barry Malzberg, and Douglas Adams, among others, have all echoed Tenn's work one way or another, as his ways influenced them, often through inexplicit ways. I find it humorous when reviewers of Tenn bollix up their timelines and speak of Tenn's stories being influenced by ones that were published later.

Although Tenn is serious humorist, ever alert at catching the reader's understanding before he has a chance to object, Tenn's swift reason has had a double problem. The science-fiction genre has always made it difficult to tell the serious writers from the entertainers, through the manner of publication and because the entertainers often claim to be serious, or have it claimed for them; also, satirists and funny men have rarely risen high in the genre (in terms of awards and sales) purely on the strength of this kind of work. Tenn was a pioneer whose example was imitated by writers who developed in different ways, and who also became known for the angle opened up by Tenn, thus diffusing the effect he might have had if his plumage had not been confused with that of imitators; which is to say that he was a monarch butterfly mistaken for a viceroy (viceroy butterflies taste bitter to birds, monarchs sweet, but you won't know which is which until you bite into one); which is to say again that Tenn was influential, for better and worse.

One can also say that Tenn imitators might have been more acceptable to some editors of the 1950s, because they were milder versions of Tenn—less serious and not so critical of the world and human nature. Tenn's stories are always deceptively disturbing at some level, even when they are breathlessly readable, amusing, or cute.

His conventionality of form is all surface, while his critical radicalism flows deeply, gleefully washing away our preconceptions.

An outgoing but sensitive man, Tenn fell silent by the end of the 1960s, even as his work was gathered and reprinted several times into an impressive, though editorially limited, six-volume set from Ballantine Books (1968). I had the feeling, from conversations with him, that he sometimes imagined his work to be unworthy. He went on to become an award-winning college teacher, leaving behind a body of work sufficient to secure the reputation of any major writer in the field.

He published one notable story in the 1970s, "On Venus, Have We Got a Rabbi," which had long been expected. He had been talking about it since the 1950s. I urged Jack Dann, who was then editing *Wandering Stars* (Harper & Row, 1974), to extract the story from the author. The story was well received, garnering awards nominations and appearing in a best-of-the-year collection.

It should be noted that Tenn contributed to the thinking that is so necessary to accomplished science fiction. *Children of Wonder* (1953) was his pioneering foray into editing a theme anthology. It was notable for its variety of stories and selection of authors from outside the genres, and for its introduction and notes. The anthology was a first-year selection of the Science Fiction Book Club. Two incisive essays, "On the Fiction in Science Fiction" (1955), and "Jazz Then, Musicology Now" (1972) remain required reading for anyone who cares about the ideals of literate science fiction.

Tenn's first two decades include a number of notable stories:

"Brooklyn Project" was called by Fritz Leiber a "marvelously cynical" time-travel story.

"Firewater" is one of the most sophisticated stories ever published by John W. Campbell. It has the distinction of having made Campbell relax his ban on stories in which human beings are bested by aliens, and features the unforgettable lament by Larry for the loss of what he was and what he will never be, as humanity struggles to keep its sanity before the seemingly superior aliens who have taken up residence on earth. This story should have taken all the awards in its year of publication. Read it along with the later "There Were People on Bikini, There Were People on Attu."

"Generation of Noah" is one of the finest atomic threat stories ever written. Along with "Firewater," it was reprinted in best-of-the-year collections.

"It Ends With a Flicker" (originally "Of All Possible Worlds"), "Wednesday's Child" (a fascinating sequel to the often reprinted "Child's Play"), "Time Waits for Winthrop" (also known as "Winthrop Was Stubborn"), "Eastward Ho!", and "The Malted Milk Monster" drew honorable mentions in Judith Merril's best-of-the-year collections; "Bernie The Faust" took pride of place as the first story in the 1964 collection. "Winthrop" shows a remarkable use of exotic ideas, among them fairly advanced biological concepts, another feature of Tenn's stories that makes them unusual for the 1950s.

"The Discovery of Morniel Mathaway" shows an insight into the successful creative process that is too often banally presented. Jacques Sadoul called it "the most beautiful example of a temporal paradox offered by science fiction."

"The Custodian," with its plea for the blending of art and utility, and "Down Among the Dead Men," with its clever use of offstage space opera, both manage to do what few SF stories ever do—move us emotionally and intellectually.

Although the description of "satirist" does fit much of Tenn's work, his stories ("Firewater" and "Brooklyn Project," for example) also feature a level of verisimilitude not usually seen in the "just kidding" school of satire, which in the minds of many dulls the edge of dramatic materials. Tenn is always a master of situations, which at first prod and intrigue us, then provoke a deeper curiosity, make us laugh, then explode into some thoughtful irony or observation. Once you catch on to a Tenn situation, you can't stop reading. The satirical ironies, mockeries, slapstick, and occasional bitterness do wonders for genre materials, because Tenn joins these materials to human experience outside the insular worlds of wish-fulfillment and power fantasy. The science-fictional themes are all there, strong and clear, but just as you are about to accept the story at its face value, Tenn hits you with something close to home and painful. He's a very sly writer, inserting polished, precise narratives into our minds through unexpected channels. Many of his stories blossom into a single line of beauty and recognition; but always the aesthetic fires are banked by irony and wit; above all, eloquent wit, behind which sits the authority of an author who knows what he wants to say, who believes as Oscar Wilde did, that eloquence and wit alone can make the scales fall from human eyes. One spies an author laughing and crying at the same time, writing, exhibiting intellect and dramatic talent within the confines of a marketplace that never knew what to do with his work—so it just left him alone. Fortunately, the tyranny was never perfect, and Tenn's work slipped through into our sight, as did much of science fiction's best.

"A Matter of Frequency," a story satirizing the constant threat of "dumbing down," is just as relevant today as it was in 1951. It's absolutely bone-chilling to realize that this is exactly the way things are, with corporate money hiring "Nuts" to think for them, while dividing the "Nuts" in every field of accomplishment from the "normal" people. Shudder even more while recalling that our constitution recognizes the obligation to educate citizens, because without such an electorate we cannot have a genuine democracy. Our major citizens today are the artificial citizens known as corporations, whose rights exceed that of every other "citizen." To educate everyone would be to give away power and wealth.

Tenn's two long works are the novel *Of Men and Monsters* (1968, *Galaxy* magazine version, 1963), and the short novel *A Lamp for Medusa* (1968; magazine version, 1951). If you are reading this afterword before reading these novels, I recommend the short novel as a place to start. Funny, atmospheric, and wonderfully paced, this neglected work has seen only a shabby paperback appearance. It is not surprising, given Tenn's tendencies, that the story recalls the poise of fantasy fiction from John W. Campbell's *Unknown Worlds* magazine tradition, which was the only sizable market for humorous work of the early 1940s, and Tenn's only antecedent within the genres.

Of Men and Monsters, a story of humanity living in the walls of houses belonging to giant aliens who have occupied the earth, is a vivid, energetically paced story which best embodies one of Tenn's major themes: that humanity is not what it imagines itself to be in its religious and political myths; that implicit in our biological history is a nature not of our making; we may glimpse it, even understand it at times, but it may be a while before we can remake it entire, if ever, because even our heart's desire is not free.

In his awareness of biological and anthropological complexities, Tenn has at the center of his work the most thoroughgoing of science fictional methods: the collision of the possible with the actual, with the actual displaying fantastic staying power. Eric the Eye, the Lilliputian viewpoint character of the novel, learns that his society is not what he thought it was, that its rights of passage are a sham, and finally that human beings have only limited choices to make. Since change on a radical scale seems unlikely, he accepts his newly revealed humanity and joins the plan to make of it something pervasive and powerful. Eric becomes part of the reverse invasion of human vermin as they begin the infestation of the great alien starships, and later the worlds of the alien empire. One thinks of the small mammals, our ancestors, who ate the eggs of the great saurians and survived the great asteroid strike.

I am also reminded of Robert A. Heinlein's "Universe," in which humanity has forgotten that its world is a starship, destined to reach a far star after many generations have lived and died. Both Tenn and Heinlein remind us that we don't know ourselves; that in fact our generations lapse into amnesia, and have to be reminded that we too live on a generation ship parked in orbit around a star; that we have come out of a deep past on our way into a deeper future, and that only knowledge, unblinkered by wishes and myths, has any chance of helping us. Many an unwelcome Galilean and Darwinian revelation waits for us, as developments in cosmology and biology suggest.

Of Men and Monsters is a colorful story. The characters are charming (Eric meets Rachel Esthersdaughter, one of the nicest nice Jewish girls in all science fiction). The death of Eric's uncle is shatteringly presented. There are great wonders and awesome confrontations, sharply realized. Most important, there is anthropological sophistication in the depiction of social systems; the aliens are terrifying, puzzling, and *other*. Tenn's moments of romance, compassion, and hard-bitten sentimentality do not detract from his bitter truth-telling about a pathetic and deluded humanity.

Although he was much imitated (one paperback novel blatantly copied *Of Men and Monsters*), Tenn's new fiction became scarce in the late 1960s and the decades ahead, just when it seemed that the continuous practice of his craft, coupled with his acute and constant rethinking of the nature of fiction and science fiction, would certainly have produced a still mightier development of his skills. To me he still seems poised to start his most mature period. When I recall that Jack Williamson is still writing worthy books in his nineties, I remind myself that Phil is a generation younger than Jack. Tenn can do anything he chooses, when Phil lets him, except hack work ("I have no talent for it," he has said).

Few writers have written so many stories that should have received awards. He belongs to the great generation of Heinlein, Clarke, and Asimov, and is a living reproach to the awards systems. His work is a clear example of SF as a literature that can provoke us to see, feel, and think (SF without thought is not science fiction). Tenn belongs to that unbroken chain of sayers who expose our foibles, our willful blindness and stupidity, and who ultimately stand against death and the amnesia of generations.

To know Philip Klass the man and William Tenn the writer is to become powerless to prevent humorous conceits from falling out of one's head into one's mouth—or from slipping through one's fingers into the words one writes about him. Phil Klass called me just as I was finishing this essay.

"Not now, I'm assaying the work of William Tenn," I said when I heard his voice.

"What do you mean?" he asked, falling neatly into my trap.

"I'm applying the seat of my pants to the chair and writing."

"Oh," he said after a pause, then laughed.

"And so should you," I added, thinking that Robert Silverberg rightly laments (in the introduction to this volume) all the stories and novels that William Tenn did not write. That is, of course, entirely Phil Klass's fault, not Tenn's. To be a good writer requires a certain sensitivity; but you must have a thick skin to survive the warfare of the marketplace. Sadly, that often means survival for the tough-minded, even insensitive. I think Phil was just discouraged and told William Tenn to shut up. Happily, quality more than made up for the quantity of work. Maybe if Tenn had been given a Hugo Award for "Firewater," things might have been different. Tenn is stubborn, and Phil spoils him.

Bob Silverberg calls these two volumes "slender." Try dropping one on your foot, as I did. It hurt. Two volumes would have broken it.

Never fear. There is a Tenn novel, under contract to a publisher, long in the writing. Look for it.

Complain to the author.

I have faith (and I rarely truck with faiths) that I will read this new novel, because, as a competitor once wrote, "Tenn is an artist who won't stop until he's had the last word."

☙

Delmar, New York
June 7, 2001

COLOPHON

This book was set entirely in typefaces from the Adobe Minion font. Minion is a 1990 Adobe Originals font designed by Robert Slimbach, inspired by the classical typefaces of the late Renaissance.

The text was entered and set on a Compaq Presario running Windows NT, using Microsoft Word 7.0 and Adobe PageMaker 6.5. The dust jacket was created on a Macintosh G3 running PageMaker 6.01 and PhotoShop 5.5. The book was printed and bound by Sheridan Books.

The titles of the sections and the order of the stories for both this volume and for *Immodest Proposals* were chosen by Philip Klass.

The New England
Science Fiction Association (NESFA)
and NESFA Press

Recent books from NESFA Press:

The New England Science Fiction Association:

NESFA is an all-volunteer, non-profit organization of science fiction and fantasy fans. Besides publishing, our activities include running Boskone (New England's oldest SF convention) in February each year, producing a semi-monthly newsletter, holding discussion groups relating to the field, and hosting a variety of social events. If you are interested in learning more about us, we'd like to hear from you. Write to our address above!